OCCULT DETECTIVE STORIES

FIGHTERS OF FEAR

EDITED BY MIKE ASHLEY

TALOS

© 2020 by Mike Ashley

See page 611 for an extension of this copyright page.

Talos Press books may be purchased in bulk at special discounts for sales promotion, corporate gifts, fund-raising, or educational purposes. Special editions can also be created to specifications. For details, contact the Special Sales Department, Talos Press, 307 West 36th Street, 11th Floor, New York, NY 10018 or info@skyhorsepublishing.com. Talos Press® is a registered trademark of Skyhorse Publishing, Inc.®, a Delaware corporation.

Visit our website at www.talospress.com.

10 9 8 7 6 5 4 3 2 1

Library of Congress Cataloging-in-Publication Data is available on file.

Hardcover ISBN: 978-1-945863-52-3
Paperback ISBN: 978-1-945863-54-7
Ebook ISBN: 978-1-945863-53-0

Cover illustration by Mélanie Delon
Cover design by Claudia Noble

Printed in the United States of America

CONTENTS

INTRODUCTION

MIKE ASHLEY

THIS ANTHOLOGY BRINGS TOGETHER THIRTY-ONE STORIES FEATURING the investigations of the psychic or occult detective. The detective may not necessarily have any psychic abilities of their own—though some do have a form of second-sight—but usually have a profound knowledge of occult matters, often as a result of years of esoteric studies in remote parts of the world.

The occult detective became a popular theme in weird fiction in the years before and around the First World War, bringing together the two popular genres of the detective story and supernatural fiction. Inevitably the success of Conan Doyle's Sherlock Holmes stories was a prompt to many writers to turn to crime fiction and introduce elements of the strange and outré, even though Holmes himself had no interest in crimes which may have had some occult cause. It provided a format for a detective with astonishing knowledge of the weird and the wonderful to be assisted by a colleague who may not necessarily have the same knowledge or skills, but had abilities of his own which invariably helped resolve the case.

Having said that, stories of psychic detectives go back way earlier than Sherlock Holmes. In this volume I want to follow the growth and development of the psychic detective through the stories and characters ranging from Sheridan Le Fanu's Martin Hesselius from 1869 to Jessica Salmonson's Penelope Pettiweather from 1990, encompassing the classic period from just before the First World War with the Westrel Keen stories by Robert W. Chambers, the Carnacki adventures by William Hope Hodgson, and including such detectives as Moris Klaw by Sax Rohmer, Solange Fontaine by F. Tennyson Jesse, and Francis Chard by A. M. Burrage. I was keen to include many lesser known characters and this volume includes several stories either never previously reprinted, such as those by Allan Upward, L. Adams Beck, Philippa Forest, and Eric Williams, or those otherwise available only in limited edition volumes such as the stories by Jessie Douglas Kerruish, Rose Champion de Crespigny, and Ella Scrymsour. I hope that even though you may have encountered some of these stories before, the majority will be new.

These stories run the full range of weird fiction from the haunted house to afflicted children, possession, crypto-monsters, horrors from the distant past, and a disturbing range of occult powers. Almost all the stories are from connected series and the introductions to each story provide background on the authors and their works so that you can track down further stories featuring these fighters of fear.

The emergence of the occult detective parallels to some degree the growth of interest in spiritualism that emerged following the claims by the New York sisters Kate and Margaret Fox in 1848 that they had made contact with the spirit of a murder victim. The sisters became famous, and even though they eventually confessed that their performances were a hoax, the public had become sufficiently convinced in spiritualist beliefs and the role of a medium that the movement grew. It was through the exploits of certain mediums, such as Daniel Dunglas Home in the 1850s, that the scientific community became interested in spiritualism and hauntings, leading to the emergence of ghost clubs and societies. The first of these, the Ghost Society, was founded by Edward White Benson (the father of writers E. F., A. C., and R. H. Benson) at Cambridge University in 1851 for the serious study of psychic and spiritual phenomena. The Society moved to London in 1862 and was officially relaunched as the Ghost Club, which included Charles Dickens as a member. A leading light amongst these investigators was the philosopher Henry Sidgwick, who became cofounder of the Society for Psychical Research (SPR) in 1882, serving as its first president. The SPR became renowned for its thorough investigations of mediums and psychic phenomena, exposing many hoaxes. Its investigators, which included Frank Podmore, Edmund Gurney, Frederic Myers, and Richard Hodgson, were the real occult detectives.

In fiction, the idea of someone investigating the strange and unusual as a regular part of their work goes back at least as far as 1830. It was then that Samuel Warren began his long running and hugely popular series "Passages from the Diary of a Late Physician" in the Scottish-based *Blackwood's Magazine*. The stories appeared anonymously and many believed they were true, which added to their popularity. Several verged on the macabre and occasionally the supernatural, though Warren's physician explores these as if they were diseases of the mind, way ahead of the theories of psychologists. The best such example is "The Spectre-Smitten" (1831) where a patient is apparently driven crazy by having seen the ghost of a recently deceased neighbour. Warren leaves the final solution open as to whether it was a genuine ghost or a delusion, but the nature of that series was such that it opened the doors to the occult detective and our first author, Joseph Sheridan Le Fanu.

GREEN TEA

JOSEPH SHERIDAN LE FANU

The format used by Samuel Warren in "The Spectre-Smitten" formed the basis of the following story by Sheridan Le Fanu that introduces us to Dr. Martin Hesselius who, although a physician, is drawn to cases of the inexplicable. Le Fanu provides a prologue to the story that includes a number of factors that became common in many later stories. Firstly, it is narrated in the first-person by Dr. Hesselius's private secretary, and it tells us Hesselius has a private fortune, which allows him to pick and choose his cases, and that his knowledge was "immense." He became a dedicated analyst pursuing his cases to the bitter end. He left behind him a significant body of work—two hundred and thirty case files we later learn—which the narrator is organizing. When "Green Tea" was serialized in All the Year Round *in 1869 it was the only story to feature Dr. Hesselius directly, but when Le Fanu included this story in his collection* In a Glass Darkly *in 1872 he brought together four other stories, some of which were revised from their original publication, none of which had featured Hesselius, but which were now presented as being amongst his cases. By so doing Le Fanu established that alluring idea, used so superbly by Arthur Conan Doyle in his Sherlock Holmes stories, of a colleague who has been working through the recorded cases to select those of special interest.*

Sheridan Le Fanu (1814–1873) was an Irish author of Huguenot descent who produced a significant body of work, much of which is in the realms of the supernatural or macabre. His earliest story, "The Ghost and the Bone-Setter" (1838), was later included in the posthumous collection The Purcell Papers

(1880) that also uses the framing device of stories selected from various papers, this time those of the parish priest, Francis Purcell. He collected local stories and oddities, but he did not investigate them, so wasn't a true occult detective. Le Fanu's first collection of weird tales was Ghost Stories and Tales of Mystery *(1851), but during his life he was better known for his novels, notably* The House by the Churchyard *(1863),* Uncle Silas *(1864), and* Wylder's Hand *(1864), which were typical Victorian tales of gothic mystery. It was not until after his death that his ghost stories were rediscovered, such as the volume* Madam Crowl's Ghost *(1923), assembled by M. R. James. Le Fanu is now recognized as one of the pioneers of the modern weird tale, with such classics as "Schalken the Painter" (1839), "Carmilla" (1871), plus the following, which opens the archives of the occult detective.*

PROLOGUE: MARTIN HESSELIUS, THE GERMAN PHYSICIAN

THOUGH CAREFULLY EDUCATED IN MEDICINE AND SURGERY, I HAVE never practised either. The study of each continues, nevertheless, to interest me profoundly. Neither idleness nor caprice caused my secession from the honourable calling which I had just entered. The cause was a very trifling scratch inflicted by a dissecting knife. This trifle cost me the loss of two fingers, amputated promptly, and the more painful loss of my health, for I have never been quite well since, and have seldom been twelve months together in the same place.

In my wanderings I became acquainted with Dr. Martin Hesselius, a wanderer like myself, like me a physician, and like me an enthusiast in his profession. Unlike me in this, that his wanderings were voluntary, and he a man, if not of fortune, as we estimate fortune in England, at least in what our forefathers used to term "easy circumstances." He was an old man when I first saw him; nearly five-and-thirty years my senior.

In Dr. Martin Hesselius, I found my master. His knowledge was immense, his grasp of a case was an intuition. He was the very man to inspire a young enthusiast, like me, with awe and delight. My admiration has stood the test of time and survived the separation of death. I am sure it was well-founded.

For nearly twenty years I acted as his medical secretary. His immense collection of papers he has left in my care, to be arranged, indexed and bound. His treatment of some of these cases is curious. He writes in two distinct characters. He describes what he saw and heard as an intelligent layman might, and when in this style of narrative he had seen the patient either through his own hall-door, to the light of day, or through the gates of darkness to the caverns of the dead, he returns upon the narrative, and in the terms of his art and with all the force and originality of genius, proceeds to the work of analysis, diagnosis and illustration.

Here and there a case strikes me as of a kind to amuse or horrify a lay reader with an interest quite different from the peculiar one which it may possess for an expert. With slight modifications, chiefly of language, and of course a change of names, I copy the following. The narrator is Dr. Martin Hesselius. I find it among the voluminous notes of cases which he made during a tour in England about sixty-four years ago.

It is related in series of letters to his friend Professor Van Loo of Leyden. The professor was not a physician, but a chemist, and a man who read history and metaphysics and medicine, and had, in his day, written a play.

The narrative is therefore, if somewhat less valuable as a medical record, necessarily written in a manner more likely to interest an unlearned reader.

These letters, from a memorandum attached, appear to have been returned on the death of the professor, in 1819, to Dr. Hesselius. They are written, some in English, some in French, but the greater part in German. I am a faithful, though I am conscious, by no means a graceful translator, and although here and there I omit some passages, and shorten others, and disguise names, I have interpolated nothing.

I: DR. HESSELIUS RELATES HOW HE MET THE REV. MR. JENNINGS

THE REV. MR. JENNINGS IS TALL AND THIN. HE IS MIDDLE-AGED AND dresses with a natty, old-fashioned, high-church precision. He is naturally a little stately, but not at all stiff. His features, without being handsome, are well formed, and their expression extremely kind, but also shy.

I met him one evening at Lady Mary Heyduke's. The modesty and benevolence of his countenance are extremely prepossessing.

We were but a small party, and he joined agreeably enough in the conversation. He seems to enjoy listening very much more than contributing to the talk; but what he says is always to the purpose and well said. He is a great favourite of Lady Mary's, who it seems, consults him upon many things, and thinks him the most happy and blessed person on earth. Little knows she about him.

The Rev. Mr. Jennings is a bachelor, and has, they say sixty thousand pounds in the funds. He is a charitable man. He is most anxious to be actively employed in his sacred profession, and yet though always tolerably well elsewhere, when he goes down to his vicarage in Warwickshire, to engage in the actual duties of his sacred calling, his health soon fails him, and in a very strange way. So says Lady Mary.

There is no doubt that Mr. Jennings' health does break down in, generally, a sudden and mysterious way, sometimes in the very act of officiating in his old and pretty church at Kenlis. It may be his heart, it may be his brain. But so it has happened three or four times, or oftener, that after proceeding a certain way in the service, he has on a sudden stopped short, and after a silence, apparently quite unable to resume, he has fallen into solitary, inaudible prayer, his hands and his eyes uplifted, and then pale as death, and in the agitation of a strange shame and horror, descended trembling, and got into the vestry-room, leaving his congregation, without explanation, to themselves. This occurred when his curate was absent. When he goes down to Kenlis now, he always takes care to provide a clergyman to share his duty, and to supply his place on the instant should he become thus suddenly incapacitated.

When Mr. Jennings breaks down quite, and beats a retreat from the vicarage, and returns to London, where, in a dark street off Piccadilly, he inhabits a very narrow house, Lady Mary says that he is always perfectly well. I have my own opinion about that. There are degrees of course. We shall see.

Mr. Jennings is a perfectly gentlemanlike man. People, however, remark something odd. There is an impression a little ambiguous. One thing which certainly contributes to it, people I think don't remember; or, perhaps, distinctly remark. But I did, almost immediately. Mr. Jennings has a way of looking sidelong upon the carpet, as if his eye followed the movements of something there. This, of course, is not always. It occurs now and then. But often enough to give a certain oddity, as I have said, to his manner, and in this glance travelling along the floor there is something both shy and anxious.

A medical philosopher, as you are good enough to call me, elaborating theories by the aid of cases sought out by himself, and by him watched and scrutinised with more time at command, and consequently infinitely more minuteness than the ordinary practitioner can afford, falls insensibly into habits of observation, which accompany him everywhere, and are exercised, as some people would say, impertinently, upon every subject that presents itself with the least likelihood of rewarding inquiry.

There was a promise of this kind in the slight, timid, kindly, but reserved gentleman, whom I met for the first time at this agreeable little evening gathering. I observed, of course, more than I here set down; but I reserve all that borders on the technical for a strictly scientific paper.

I may remark, that when I here speak of medical science, I do so, as I hope some day to see it more generally understood, in a much more comprehensive sense than its generally material treatment would warrant. I believe the entire natural world is but the ultimate expression of that spiritual world from which, and in which alone, it has its life. I believe that the essential man is a spirit, that the spirit is an organised substance, but as different in point of material from what we ordinarily understand by matter, as light or electricity is; that the material body is, in the most literal sense, a vesture, and death consequently no interruption of the living man's existence, but simply his extrication from the natural body—a process which commences at the moment of what we term death, and the completion of which, at furthest a few days later, is the resurrection "in power."

The person who weighs the consequences of these positions will probably see their practical bearing upon medical science. This is, however, by no means the proper place for displaying the proofs and discussing the consequences of this too generally unrecognized state of facts.

In pursuance of my habit, I was covertly observing Mr. Jennings, with all my caution—I think he perceived it—and I saw plainly that he was as cautiously observing me. Lady Mary happening to address me by my name, as Dr. Hesselius, I saw that he glanced at me more sharply, and then became thoughtful for a few minutes.

After this, as I conversed with a gentleman at the other end of the room, I saw him look at me more steadily, and with an interest which I thought I understood. I then saw him take an opportunity of chatting with

Lady Mary, and was, as one always is, perfectly aware of being the subject of a distant inquiry and answer.

This tall clergyman approached me by-and-by; and in a little time we had got into conversation. When two people who like reading, and know books and places, having travelled, wish to discourse, it is very strange if they can't find topics. It was not accident that brought him near me and led him into conversation. He knew German and had read my Essays on Metaphysical Medicine which suggest more than they actually say.

This courteous man, gentle, shy, plainly a man of thought and reading, who moving and talking among us, was not altogether of us, and whom I already suspected of leading a life whose transactions and alarms were carefully concealed, with an impenetrable reserve from, not only the world, but his best beloved friends—was cautiously weighing in his own mind the idea of taking a certain step with regard to me.

I penetrated his thoughts without his being aware of it, and was careful to say nothing which could betray to his sensitive vigilance my suspicions respecting his position, or my surmises about his plans respecting myself.

We chatted upon indifferent subjects for a time but at last he said:

"I was very much interested by some papers of yours, Dr. Hesselius, upon what you term Metaphysical Medicine—I read them in German, ten or twelve years ago—have they been translated?"

"No, I'm sure they have not—I should have heard. They would have asked my leave, I think."

"I asked the publishers here, a few months ago, to get the book for me in the original German; but they tell me it is out of print."

"So it is, and has been for some years; but it flatters me as an author to find that you have not forgotten my little book, although," I added, laughing, "ten or twelve years is a considerable time to have managed without it; but I suppose you have been turning the subject over again in your mind, or something has happened lately to revive your interest in it."

At this remark, accompanied by a glance of inquiry, a sudden embarrassment disturbed Mr. Jennings, analogous to that which makes a young lady blush and look foolish. He dropped his eyes and folded his hands together uneasily and looked oddly, and you would have said, guiltily, for a moment.

I helped him out of his awkwardness in the best way, by appearing not to observe it, and going straight on, I said: "Those revivals of interest in a subject happen to me often; one book suggests another, and often sends me back a wild-goose chase over an interval of twenty years. But if you still care to possess a copy, I shall be only too happy to provide you; I have still got two or three by me—and if you allow me to present one I shall be very much honoured."

"You are very good indeed," he said, quite at his ease again, in a moment: "I almost despaired—I don't know how to thank you."

"Pray don't say a word; the thing is really so little worth that I am only ashamed of having offered it, and if you thank me any more I shall throw it into the fire in a fit of modesty."

Mr. Jennings laughed. He inquired where I was staying in London, and after a little more conversation on a variety of subjects, he took his departure.

II: THE DOCTOR QUESTIONS LADY MARY AND SHE ANSWERS

"I LIKE YOUR VICAR SO MUCH, LADY MARY," SAID I, AS SOON AS HE was gone. "He has read, travelled, and thought, and having also suffered, he ought to be an accomplished companion."

"So he is, and, better still, he is a really good man," said she. "His advice is invaluable about my schools, and all my little undertakings at Dawlbridge, and he's so painstaking, he takes so much trouble—you have no idea—wherever he thinks he can be of use: he's so good-natured and so sensible."

"It is pleasant to hear so good an account of his neighbourly virtues. I can only testify to his being an agreeable and gentle companion, and in addition to what you have told me, I think I can tell you two or three things about him," said I.

"Really!"

"Yes, to begin with, he's unmarried."

"Yes, that's right—go on."

"He has been writing, that is he *was*, but for two or three years perhaps, he has not gone on with his work, and the book was upon some rather abstract subject—perhaps theology."

"Well, he was writing a book, as you say; I'm not quite sure what it was about, but only that it was nothing that I cared for; very likely you are right, and he certainly did stop—yes."

"And although he only drank a little coffee here tonight, he likes tea, at least, did like it extravagantly."

"Yes, that's *quite* true."

"He drank green tea, a good deal, didn't he?" I pursued.

"Well, that's very odd! Green tea was a subject on which we used almost to quarrel."

"But he has quite given that up," said I.

"So he has."

"And, now, one more fact. His mother or his father, did you know them?"

"Yes, both; his father is only ten years dead, and their place is near Dawlbridge. We knew them very well," she answered.

"Well, either his mother or his father—I should rather think his father, saw a ghost," said I.

"Well, you really are a conjurer, Dr. Hesselius."

"Conjurer or no, haven't I said right?" I answered merrily.

"You certainly have, and it *was* his father: he was a silent, whimsical man, and he used to bore my father about his dreams, and at last he told him a story about a ghost he had seen and talked with, and a very odd story it was. I remember it particularly, because I was so afraid of him. This story was long before he died—when I was quite a child—and his ways were so silent and moping, and he used to drop in sometimes, in the dusk, when I was alone in the drawing-room, and I used to fancy there were ghosts about him."

I smiled and nodded.

"And now, having established my character as a conjurer, I think I must say good-night," said I.

"But how *did* you find it out?"

"By the planets, of course, as the gipsies do," I answered, and so, gaily we said good-night.

Next morning I sent the little book he had been inquiring after, and a note to Mr. Jennings, and on returning late that evening, I found that he had called at my lodgings, and left his card. He asked whether I was at home, and asked at what hour he would be most likely to find me.

Does he intend opening his case and consulting me "professionally," as they say? I hope so. I have already conceived a theory about him. It is supported by Lady Mary's answers to my parting questions. I should like much to ascertain from his own lips. But what can I do consistently with good breeding to invite a confession? Nothing. I rather think he meditates one. At all events, my dear Van L., I shan't make myself difficult of access; I mean to return his visit tomorrow. It will be only civil in return for his politeness, to ask to see him. Perhaps something may come of it. Whether much, little, or nothing, my dear Van L., you shall hear.

III: DR. HESSELIUS PICKS UP SOMETHING IN LATIN BOOKS

WELL, I HAVE CALLED AT BLANK STREET.

On inquiring at the door, the servant told me that Mr. Jennings was engaged very particularly with a gentleman, a clergyman from Kenlis, his parish in the country. Intending to reserve my privilege, and to call again, I merely intimated that I should try another time, and had turned to go, when the servant begged my pardon and asked me, looking at me a little more attentively than well-bred persons of his order usually do, whether I was Dr. Hesselius; and, on learning that I was, he said, "Perhaps then, sir, you would allow me to mention it to Mr. Jennings, for I am sure he wishes to see you."

The servant returned in a moment, with a message from Mr. Jennings, asking me to go into his study, which was in effect his back drawing-room, promising to be with me in a very few minutes.

This was really a study—almost a library. The room was lofty, with two tall slender windows and rich dark curtains. It was much larger than I had expected, and stored with books on every side, from the floor to the ceiling. The upper carpet—for to my tread it felt that there were two or three— was a Turkey carpet. My steps fell noiselessly. The bookcases standing out, placed the windows, particularly narrow ones, in deep recesses. The effect of the room was, although extremely comfortable, and even luxurious, decidedly gloomy, and aided by the silence, almost oppressive. Perhaps, however, I ought to have allowed something for association. My mind had connected peculiar ideas with Mr. Jennings. I stepped into this perfectly silent room, of a very silent house, with a peculiar foreboding; and its darkness, and solemn clothing of books, for except where two narrow looking-glasses were set in the wall, they were everywhere, helped this somber feeling.

While awaiting Mr. Jennings' arrival, I amused myself by looking into some of the books with which his shelves were laden. Not among these, but immediately under them, with their backs upward, on the floor, I lighted upon a complete set of Swedenborg's "Arcana Caelestia," in the original Latin, a very fine folio set, bound in the natty livery which theology affects, pure vellum, namely, gold letters and carmine edges. There were paper markers in several of these volumes, I raised and placed them, one after the other, upon the table, and opening where these papers were placed, I read in the solemn Latin phraseology, a series of sentences indicated by a pencilled line at the margin. Of these I copy here a few, translating them into English.

"When man's interior sight is opened, which is that of his spirit, then there appear the things of another life, which cannot possibly be made visible to the bodily sight." . . .

"By the internal sight it has been granted me to see the things that are in the other life, more clearly than I see those that are in the world. From these considerations, it is evident that external vision exists from interior vision, and this from a vision still more interior, and so on." . . .

"There are with every man at least two evil spirits." . . .

"With wicked genii there is also a fluent speech, but harsh and grating. There is also among them a speech which is not fluent, wherein the dissent of the thoughts is perceived as something secretly creeping along within it."

"The evil spirits associated with man are, indeed from the hells, but when with man they are not then in hell, but are taken out thence. The place where they then are, is in the midst between heaven and hell and is called the world of spirits—when the evil spirits who are with man, are in that world, they are not in any infernal torment, but in every thought and affection of man, and so, in all that the man himself enjoys. But when they are remitted into their hell, they return to their former state." . . .

"If evil spirits could perceive that they were associated with man, and yet that they were spirits separate from him, and if they could flow in into the things of his body, they would attempt by a thousand means to destroy him; for they hate man with a deadly hatred." . . .

"Knowing, therefore, that I was a man in the body, they were continually striving to destroy me, not as to the body only, but especially as to the soul; for to destroy any man or spirit is the very delight of the life of all who are in hell; but I have been continually protected by the Lord. Hence it appears how dangerous it is for man to be in a living consort with spirits, unless he be in the good of faith." . . .

"Nothing is more carefully guarded from the knowledge of associate spirits than their being thus conjoint with a man, for if they knew it they would speak to him, with the intention to destroy him." . . .

"The delight of hell is to do evil to man, and to hasten his eternal ruin."

A long note, written with a very sharp and fine pencil, in Mr. Jennings' neat hand, at the foot of the page, caught my eye. Expecting his criticism upon the text, I read a word or two and stopped, for it was something quite different and began with these words, *Deus misereatur mei*—"May God compassionate me." Thus warned of its private nature, I averted my eyes and shut the book, replacing all the volumes as I had found them, except one which interested me, and in which, as men studious and solitary in their habits will do, I grew so absorbed as to take no cognisance of the outer world, nor to remember where I was.

I was reading some pages which refer to "representatives" and "correspondents," in the technical language of Swedenborg, and had arrived at a passage, the substance of which is, that evil spirits, when seen by other eyes than those of their infernal associates, present themselves, by "correspondence," in the shape of the beast (*fera*) which represents their particular lust and life, in aspect direful and atrocious. This is a long passage and particularises a number of those bestial forms.

IV: FOUR EYES WERE READING THE PASSAGE

I WAS RUNNING THE HEAD OF MY PENCIL-CASE ALONG THE LINE AS I read it, and something caused me to raise my eyes.

Directly before me was one of the mirrors I have mentioned, in which I saw reflected the tall shape of my friend Mr. Jennings leaning over my shoulder and reading the page at which I was busy, and with a face so dark and wild that I should hardly have known him.

I turned and rose. He stood erect also, and with an effort laughed a little, saying:

"I came in and asked you how you did, but without succeeding in awaking you from your book; so I could not restrain my curiosity, and very impertinently, I'm afraid, peeped over your shoulder. This is not your first time of looking into those pages. You have looked into Swedenborg, no doubt, long ago?"

"Oh dear, yes! I owe Swedenborg a great deal; you will discover traces of him in the little book on Metaphysical Medicine, which you were so good as to remember."

Although my friend affected a gaiety of manner, there was a slight flush in his face, and I could perceive that he was inwardly much perturbed.

"I'm scarcely yet qualified, I know so little of Swedenborg. I've only had them a fortnight," he answered, "and I think they are rather likely to make a solitary man nervous—that is, judging from the very little I have read—I don't say that they have made me so," he laughed; "and I'm so very much obliged for the book. I hope you got my note?"

I made all proper acknowledgments and modest disclaimers.

"I never read a book that I go with, so entirely, as that of yours," he continued. "I saw at once there is more in it than is quite unfolded. Do you know Dr. Harley?" he asked, rather abruptly.

In passing, the editor remarks that the physician here named was one of the most eminent who had ever practised in England.

I did, having had letters to him, and had experienced from him great courtesy and considerable assistance during my visit to England.

"I think that man one of the very greatest fools I ever met in my life," said Mr. Jennings.

This was the first time I had ever heard him say a sharp thing of anybody, and such a term applied to so high a name a little startled me.

"Really! and in what way?" I asked.

"In his profession," he answered.

I smiled.

"I mean this," he said: "he seems to me, one half, blind—I mean one half of all he looks at is dark—preternaturally bright and vivid all the rest; and the worst of it is, it seems *wilful*. I can't get him—I mean he won't—I've had some experience of him as a physician, but I look on him as, in that sense, no better than a paralytic mind, an intellect half dead. I'll tell you—I know I shall some time—all about it," he said, with a little agitation. "You stay some months longer in England. If I should be out of town during your stay for a little time, would you allow me to trouble you with a letter?"

"I should be only too happy," I assured him.

"Very good of you. I am so utterly dissatisfied with Harley."

"A little leaning to the materialistic school," I said.

"A *mere* materialist," he corrected me; "you can't think how that sort of thing worries one who knows better. You won't tell anyone—any of my friends you know—that I am hippish; now, for instance, no one knows—not even Lady Mary—that I have seen Dr. Harley, or any other doctor. So pray don't mention it; and, if I should have any threatening of an attack, you'll kindly let me write, or, should I be in town, have a little talk with you."

I was full of conjecture, and unconsciously I found I had fixed my eyes gravely on him, for he lowered his for a moment, and he said:

"I see you think I might as well tell you now, or else you are forming a conjecture; but you may as well give it up. If you were guessing all the rest of your life, you will never hit on it."

He shook his head smiling, and over that wintry sunshine a black cloud suddenly came down, and he drew his breath in, through his teeth as men do in pain.

"Sorry, of course, to learn that you apprehend occasion to consult any of us; but, command me when and how you like, and I need not assure you that your confidence is sacred."

He then talked of quite other things, and in a comparatively cheerful way and after a little time, I took my leave.

V: DR. HESSELIUS IS SUMMONED TO RICHMOND

WE PARTED CHEERFULLY, BUT HE WAS NOT CHEERFUL, NOR WAS I. There are certain expressions of that powerful organ of spirit—the human face—which, although I have seen them often, and possess a doctor's nerve, yet disturb me profoundly. One look of Mr. Jennings haunted me. It had seized my imagination with so dismal a power that I changed my plans for the evening and went to the opera, feeling that I wanted a change of ideas.

I heard nothing of or from him for two or three days, when a note in his hand reached me. It was cheerful and full of hope. He said that he had been for some little time so much better—quite well, in fact—that he was going to make a little experiment and run down for a month or so to his parish, to try whether a little work might not quite set him up. There was in it a fervent religious expression of gratitude for his restoration, as he now almost hoped he might call it.

A day or two later I saw Lady Mary, who repeated what his note had announced and told me that he was actually in Warwickshire, having resumed his clerical duties at Kenlis; and she added, "I begin to think that he is really perfectly well, and that there never was anything the matter, more than nerves and fancy; we are all nervous, but I fancy there is nothing like a little hard work for that kind of weakness, and he has made up his mind to try it. I should not be surprised if he did not come back for a year."

Notwithstanding all this confidence, only two days later I had this note, dated from his house off Piccadilly:

Dear sir,—I have returned disappointed. If I should feel at all able to see you, I shall write to ask you kindly to call. At present, I am too low, and, in fact, simply unable to say all I wish to say. Pray don't mention my name to my friends. I can see no one. By-and-by, please God, you shall hear from me. I mean to take a run into Shropshire, where some of my people are. God bless you! May we, on my return, meet more happily than I can now write.

About a week after this I saw Lady Mary at her own house, the last person, she said, left in town, and just on the wing for Brighton, for the London season was quite over. She told me that she had heard from Mr. Jenning's niece, Martha, in Shropshire. There was nothing to be gathered from her letter, more than that he was low and nervous. In those words, of which healthy people think so lightly, what a world of suffering is sometimes hidden!

Nearly five weeks had passed without any further news of Mr. Jennings. At the end of that time I received a note from him. He wrote:

I have been in the country and have had change of air, change of scene, change of faces, change of everything—and in everything—but myself. I have made up my mind, so far as the most irresolute creature on earth can do it, to tell my case fully to you. If your engagements will permit, pray come to me today, tomorrow, or the next day; but, pray defer as little as possible. You know not how much I need help. I have a quiet house at Richmond, where I now am. Perhaps you can manage to come to dinner, or to luncheon, or even to tea. You shall have no trouble in finding me out. The servant at Blank Street, who takes this note, will have a carriage at your door at any hour you please; and I am always to be found. You will say that I ought not to be alone. I have tried everything. Come and see.

I called up the servant and decided on going out the same evening, which accordingly I did.

He would have been much better in a lodging-house, or hotel, I thought, as I drove up through a short double row of sombre elms to a very old-fashioned brick house, darkened by the foliage of these trees, which overtopped and nearly surrounded it. It was a perverse choice, for nothing could be imagined more triste and silent. The house, I found, belonged to him. He had stayed for a day or two in town and, finding it for some cause insupportable, had come out here, probably because being furnished and his own, he was relieved of the thought and delay of selection, by coming here.

The sun had already set, and the red reflected light of the western sky illuminated the scene with the peculiar effect with which we are all familiar. The hall seemed very dark, but, getting to the back drawing-room, whose windows command the west, I was again in the same dusky light.

I sat down, looking out upon the richly-wooded landscape that glowed in the grand and melancholy light which was every moment fading. The corners of the room were already dark; all was growing dim, and the gloom was insensibly toning my mind, already prepared for what was sinister. I was waiting alone for his arrival, which soon took place. The door communicating with the front room opened, and the tall figure of Mr. Jennings, faintly seen in the ruddy twilight, came, with quiet stealthy steps, into the room.

We shook hands, and, taking a chair to the window, where there was still light enough to enable us to see each other's faces, he sat down beside me and, placing his hand upon my arm, with scarcely a word of preface, began his narrative.

VI: HOW MR. JENNINGS MET HIS COMPANION

THE FAINT GLOW OF THE WEST, THE POMP OF THE THEN LONELY woods of Richmond, were before us, behind and about us the darkening room, and on the stony face of the sufferer—for the character of his face, though still gentle and sweet, was changed—rested that dim, odd glow which seems to descend and produce, where it touches, lights, sudden though faint, which are lost, almost without gradation, in darkness. The silence, too, was utter: not a distant wheel, or bark, or whistle from without; and within the depressing stillness of an invalid bachelor's house.

I guessed well the nature, though not even vaguely the particulars of the revelations I was about to receive, from that fixed face of suffering that so oddly flushed stood out, like a portrait of Schalken's, before its background of darkness.

"It began," he said, "on the 15th of October, three years and eleven weeks ago, and two days—I keep very accurate count, for every day is torment. If I leave anywhere a chasm in my narrative tell me.

"About four years ago I began a work, which had cost me very much thought and reading. It was upon the religious metaphysics of the ancients."

"I know," said I, "the actual religion of educated and thinking paganism, quite apart from symbolic worship? A wide and very interesting field."

"Yes, but not good for the mind—the Christian mind, I mean. Paganism is all bound together in essential unity, and, with evil sympathy, their religion involves their art, and both their manners, and the subject is a degrading fascination and the Nemesis sure. God forgive me!

"I wrote a great deal; I wrote late at night. I was always thinking on the subject, walking about, wherever I was, everywhere. It thoroughly infected me. You are to remember that all the material ideas connected with it were more or less of the beautiful, the subject itself delightfully interesting, and I, then, without a care."

He sighed heavily.

"I believe, that every one who sets about writing in earnest does his work, as a friend of mine phrased it, *on* something—tea, or coffee, or tobacco. I suppose there is a material waste that must be hourly supplied in such occupations, or that we should grow too abstracted, and the mind, as it were, pass out of the body, unless it were reminded often enough of the connection by actual sensation. At all events, I felt the want, and I supplied it. Tea was my companion—at first the ordinary black tea, made in the usual way, not too strong: but I drank a good deal, and increased its strength as I went on. I never experienced an uncomfortable symptom from it. I began to take a little green tea. I found the effect pleasanter, it cleared and intensified the power of thought so, I had come to take it frequently, but not stronger than one might take it for pleasure. I wrote a great deal out here, it was so quiet, and in this room. I used to sit up very late, and it became a habit with me to sip my tea—green tea—every now and then as my work proceeded. I had a little kettle on my table, that swung over a lamp, and made tea two or three times between eleven o'clock and two or three in the morning, my hours of going to bed. I used to go into town every day. I was not a monk, and, although I spent an hour or two in a library, hunting up authorities and looking out lights upon my theme, I was in no morbid state as far as I can judge. I met my friends pretty much as usual and enjoyed their society, and, on the whole, existence had never been, I think, so pleasant before.

"I had met with a man who had some odd old books, German editions in mediaeval Latin, and I was only too happy to be permitted access to them. This obliging person's books were in the City, a very out-of-the-way part of it. I had rather out-stayed my intended hour, and, on coming out, seeing no cab near, I was tempted to get into the omnibus which used to drive past this house. It was darker than this by the time the 'bus had reached an old house, you may have remarked, with four poplars at each side of the door, and there the last passenger but myself got out. We drove along rather faster. It was twilight now. I leaned back in my corner next the door ruminating pleasantly.

"The interior of the omnibus was nearly dark. I had observed in the corner opposite to me at the other side, and at the end next the horses, two small circular reflections, as it seemed to me of a reddish light. They were about two inches apart, and about the size of those small brass buttons that yachting men used to put upon their jackets. I began to speculate, as listless men will, upon this trifle, as it seemed. From what centre did that faint but deep red light come, and from what—glass beads, buttons, toy decorations—was it reflected? We were lumbering along gently, having nearly a mile still to go. I had not solved the puzzle, and it became in another minute more odd, for these two luminous points, with a sudden jerk, descended nearer and nearer the floor, keeping still their relative distance and horizontal position, and then, as suddenly, they rose to the level of the seat on which I was sitting and I saw them no more.

"My curiosity was now really excited, and, before I had time to think, I saw again these two dull lamps, again together near the floor; again they disappeared, and again in their old corner I saw them.

"So, keeping my eyes upon them, I edged quietly up my own side, towards the end at which I still saw these tiny discs of red.

"There was very little light in the 'bus. It was nearly dark. I leaned forward to aid my endeavour to discover what these little circles really were. They shifted position a little as I did so. I began now to perceive an outline of something black, and I soon saw, with tolerable distinctness, the outline of a small black monkey, pushing its face forward in mimicry to meet mine; those were its eyes, and I now dimly saw its teeth grinning at me.

"I drew back, not knowing whether it might not meditate a spring. I fancied that one of the passengers had forgot this ugly pet, and wishing to ascertain something of its temper, though not caring to trust my fingers to it, I poked my umbrella softly towards it. It remained immovable—up to it—*through* it. For through it, and back and forward it passed, without the slightest resistance.

"I can't, in the least, convey to you the kind of horror that I felt. When I had ascertained that the thing was an illusion, as I then supposed, there came a misgiving about myself and a terror that fascinated me in impotence to remove my gaze from the eyes of the brute for some moments. As I looked, it made a little skip back, quite into the corner, and I, in a panic, found myself at the door, having put my head out, drawing deep breaths of the outer air, and staring at the lights and tress we were passing, too glad to reassure myself of reality.

"I stopped the 'bus and got out. I perceived the man look oddly at me as I paid him. I dare say there was something unusual in my looks and manner, for I had never felt so strangely before."

VII: THE JOURNEY: FIRST STAGE

"WHEN THE OMNIBUS DROVE ON, AND I WAS ALONE UPON THE ROAD, I looked carefully round to ascertain whether the monkey had followed me. To my indescribable relief I saw it nowhere. I can't describe easily what a shock I had received, and my sense of genuine gratitude on finding myself, as I supposed, quite rid of it.

"I had got out a little before we reached this house, two or three hundred steps. A brick wall runs along the footpath, and inside the wall is a hedge of yew, or some dark evergreen of that kind, and within that again the row of fine trees which you may have remarked as you came.

"This brick wall is about as high as my shoulder, and happening to raise my eyes I saw the monkey, with that stooping gait, on all fours, walking or creeping, close beside me, on top of the wall. I stopped, looking at it with a feeling of loathing and horror. As I stopped so did it. It sat up on the wall with its long hands on its knees looking at me. There was not light enough to see it much more than in outline, nor was it dark enough to bring the peculiar light of its eyes into strong relief. I still saw, however, that red foggy light plainly enough. It did not show its teeth, nor exhibit any sign of irritation, but seemed jaded and sulky, and was observing me steadily.

"I drew back into the middle of the road. It was an unconscious recoil, and there I stood, still looking at it. It did not move.

"With an instinctive determination to try something—anything, I turned about and walked briskly towards town with askance look, all the time, watching the movements of the beast. It crept swiftly along the wall, at exactly my pace.

"Where the wall ends, near the turn of the road, it came down, and with a wiry spring or two brought itself close to my feet, and continued to keep up with me, as I quickened my pace. It was at my left side, so close to my leg that I felt every moment as if I should tread upon it.

"The road was quite deserted and silent, and it was darker every moment. I stopped dismayed and bewildered, turning as I did so, the other way—I mean, towards this house, away from which I had been walking. When I stood still, the monkey drew back to a distance of, I suppose, about five or six yards, and remained stationary, watching me.

"I had been more agitated than I have said. I had read, of course, as everyone has, something about 'spectral illusions,' as you physicians term the phenomena of such cases. I considered my situation and looked my misfortune in the face.

"These affections, I had read, are sometimes transitory and sometimes obstinate. I had read of cases in which the appearance, at first harmless, had, step by step, degenerated into something direful and insupportable, and ended by wearing its victim out. Still as I stood there, but for my bestial companion, quite alone, I tried to comfort myself by repeating again and again the assurance, 'the thing is purely disease, a well-known physical affection, as distinctly as small-pox or neuralgia. Doctors are all agreed on that, philosophy demonstrates it. I must not be a fool. I've been sitting up too late, and I daresay my digestion is quite wrong, and, with God's help, I shall be all right, and this is but a symptom of nervous dyspepsia.' Did I believe all this? Not one word of it, no more than any other miserable being ever did who is once seized and riveted in this satanic captivity. Against my convictions, I might say my knowledge, I was simply bullying myself into a false courage.

"I now walked homeward. I had only a few hundred yards to go. I had forced myself into a sort of resignation, but I had not got over the sickening shock and the flurry of the first certainty of my misfortune.

"I made up my mind to pass the night at home. The brute moved close beside me, and I fancied there was the sort of anxious drawing toward the house, which one sees in tired horses or dogs, sometimes as they come toward home.

"I was afraid to go into town, I was afraid of any one's seeing and recognizing me. I was conscious of an irrepressible agitation in my manner. Also, I was afraid of any violent change in my habits, such as going to a place of amusement, or walking from home in order to fatigue myself. At the hall door it waited till I mounted the steps, and when the door was opened entered with me.

"I drank no tea that night. I got cigars and some brandy and water. My idea was that I should act upon my material system, and by living for a while in sensation apart from thought, send myself forcibly, as it were, into a new groove. I came up here to this drawing-room. I sat just here. The monkey then got upon a small table that then stood *there*. It looked dazed and languid. An irrepressible uneasiness as to its movements kept my eyes always upon it. Its eyes were half closed, but I could see them glow. It was looking steadily at me. In all situations, at all hours, it is awake and looking at me. That never changes.

"I shall not continue in detail my narrative of this particular night. I shall describe, rather, the phenomena of the first year, which never varied, essentially. I shall describe the monkey as it appeared in daylight. In the dark, as you shall presently hear, there are peculiarities. It is a small monkey, perfectly black. It had only one peculiarity—a character of malignity—unfathomable malignity. During the first year it looked sullen and sick. But this character of intense malice and vigilance was always underlying that surly languor. During all that time it acted as if on a plan of giving me as little trouble as was consistent with watching me. Its eyes were never off me. I have never lost sight of it, except in my sleep, light or dark, day or night, since it came here, excepting when it withdraws for some weeks at a time, unaccountably.

"In total dark it is visible as in daylight. I do not mean merely its eyes. It is *all* visible distinctly in a halo that resembles a glow of red embers, and which accompanies it in all its movements.

"When it leaves me for a time, it is always at night, in the dark, and in the same way. It grows at first uneasy, and then furious, and then advances towards me, grinning and shaking, its paws clenched, and, at the same time, there comes the appearance of fire in the grate. I never have any fire. I can't sleep in the room where there is any, and it draws nearer and nearer to the chimney, quivering, it seems, with rage, and when its fury rises to the highest pitch, it springs into the grate and up the chimney, and I see it no more.

"When first this happened, I thought I was released. I was now a new man. A day passed—a night—and no return, and a blessed week—a week—another week. I was always on my knees, Dr. Hesselius, always, thanking God and praying. A whole month passed of liberty, but on a sudden, it was with me again."

VIII: THE SECOND STAGE

"IT WAS WITH ME, AND THE MALICE WHICH BEFORE WAS TORPID under a sullen exterior, was now active. It was perfectly unchanged in every other respect. This new energy was apparent in its activity and its looks, and soon in other ways.

"For a time, you will understand, the change was shown only in an increased vivacity and an air of menace, as if it were always brooding over some atrocious plan. Its eyes, as before, were never off me."

"Is it here now?" I asked.

"No," he replied, "it has been absent exactly a fortnight and a day—fifteen days. It has sometimes been away so long as nearly two months, once for three. Its absence always exceeds a fortnight, although it may be but by a single day. Fifteen days having past since I saw it last, it may return now at any moment."

"Is its return," I asked, "accompanied by any peculiar manifestation?"

"Nothing—no," he said. "It is simply with me again. On lifting my eyes from a book, or turning my head, I see it, as usual, looking at me, and then it remains, as before, for its appointed time. I have never told so much and so minutely before to any one."

I perceived that he was agitated, and looking like death, and he repeatedly applied his handkerchief to his forehead; I suggested that he might be tired, and told him that I would call, with pleasure, in the morning, but he said:

"No, if you don't mind hearing it all now. I have got so far, and I should prefer making one effort of it. When I spoke to Dr. Harley, I had nothing like so much to tell. You are a philosophic physician. You give spirit its proper rank. If this thing is real—"

He paused looking at me with agitated inquiry.

"We can discuss it by-and-by, and very fully. I will give you all I think," I answered, after an interval.

"Well—very well. If it is anything real, I say, it is prevailing, little by little, and drawing me more interiorly into hell. Optic nerves, he talked of. Ah! well—there are other nerves of communication. May God Almighty help me! You shall hear.

"Its power of action, I tell you, had increased. Its malice became, in a way, aggressive. About two years ago, some questions that were pending between me and the bishop having been settled, I went down to my parish in Warwickshire, anxious to find occupation in my profession. I was not prepared for what happened, although I have since thought I might have apprehended something like it. The reason of my saying so is this—"

He was beginning to speak with a great deal more effort and reluctance, and sighed often, and seemed at times nearly overcome. But at this time his manner was not agitated. It was more like that of a sinking patient, who has given himself up.

"Yes, but I will first tell you about Kenlis, my parish.

"It was with me when I left this place for Dawlbridge. It was my silent travelling companion, and it remained with me at the vicarage. When I entered on the discharge of my duties, another change took place. The thing exhibited an atrocious determination to thwart me. It was with me in the church—in the reading-desk—in the pulpit—within the communion rails. At last, it reached this extremity, that while I was reading to the congregation, it would spring upon the book and squat there, so that I was unable to see the page. This happened more than once.

"I left Dawlbridge for a time. I placed myself in Dr. Harley's hands. I did everything he told me. He gave my case a great deal of thought. It interested him, I think. He seemed successful. For nearly three months I was perfectly free from a return. I began to think I was safe. With his full assent I returned to Dawlbridge.

"I travelled in a chaise. I was in good spirits. I was more—I was happy and grateful. I was returning, as I thought, delivered from a dreadful hallucination, to the scene of duties which I longed to enter upon. It was a beautiful sunny evening, everything looked serene and cheerful, and I was delighted. I remember looking out of the window to see the spire of my church at Kenlis among the trees, at the point where one has the earliest view of it. It is exactly where the little stream that bounds the parish passes

23

under the road by a culvert, and where it emerges at the road-side, a stone with an old inscription is placed. As we passed this point, I drew my head in and sat down, and in the corner of the chaise was the monkey.

"For a moment I felt faint, and then quite wild with despair and horror. I called to the driver, and got out and sat down at the road-side, and prayed to God silently for mercy. A despairing resignation supervened. My companion was with me as I re-entered the vicarage. The same persecution followed. After a short struggle I submitted, and soon I left the place.

"I told you," he said, "that the beast has before this become in certain ways aggressive. I will explain a little. It seemed to be actuated by intense and increasing fury, whenever I said my prayers, or even meditated prayer. It amounted at last to a dreadful interruption. You will ask, how could a silent immaterial phantom effect that? It was thus, whenever I meditated praying; it was always before me, and nearer and nearer.

"It used to spring on a table, on the back of a chair, on the chimney-piece, and slowly to swing itself from side to side, looking at me all the time. There is in its motion an indefinable power to dissipate thought, and to contract one's attention to that monotony, till the ideas shrink, as it were, to a point, and at last to nothing—and unless I had started up and shook off the catalepsy I have felt as if my mind were on the point of losing itself. There are other ways," he sighed heavily; "thus, for instance, while I pray with my eyes closed, it comes closer and closer, and I see it. I know it is not to be accounted for physically, but I do actually see it, though my lids are dosed, and so it rocks my mind, as it were, and overpowers me, and I am obliged to rise from my knees. If you had ever yourself known this, you would be acquainted with desperation."

IX: THE THIRD STAGE

"I SEE, DR. HESSELIUS, THAT YOU DON'T LOSE ONE WORD OF MY statement. I need not ask you to listen specially to what I am now going to tell you. They talk of the optic nerves, and of spectral illusions, as if the organ of sight was the only point assailable by the influences that have fastened upon me—I know better. For two years in my direful case that limitation prevailed. But as food is taken in softly at the lips, and then brought under the teeth, as the tip of the little finger caught in a mill crank will draw in the hand and the arm and the whole body, so the miserable mortal who has been once caught firmly by the end of the finest fibre of his nerve, is drawn in and in, by the enormous machinery of hell, until he is as I am. Yes, Doctor, as *I* am, for a while I talk to you and implore relief, I feel that my prayer is for the impossible, and my pleading with the inexorable."

I endeavoured to calm his visibly increasing agitation and told him that he must not despair.

While we talked the night had overtaken us. The filmy moonlight was wide over the scene which the window commanded, and I said:

"Perhaps you would prefer having candles. This light, you know, is odd. I should wish you, as much as possible, under your usual conditions while I make my diagnosis, shall I call it—otherwise I don't care."

"All lights are the same to me," he said; "except when I read or write, I care not if night were perpetual. I am going to tell you what happened about a year ago. The thing began to speak to me."

"Speak! How do you mean—speak as a man does, do you mean?"

"Yes; speak in words and consecutive sentences, with perfect coherence and articulation; but there is a peculiarity. It is not like the tone of a human voice. It is not by my ears it reaches me—it comes like a singing through my head.

"This faculty, the power of speaking to me, will be my undoing. It won't let me pray, it interrupts me with dreadful blasphemies. I dare not go on, I could not. Oh! Doctor, can the skill and thought and prayers of man avail me nothing!"

"You must promise me, my dear sir, not to trouble yourself with unnecessarily exciting thoughts; confine yourself strictly to the narrative of *facts*; and recollect, above all, that even if the thing that infests you be, you seem to suppose a reality with an actual independent life and will, yet it can have no power to hurt you, unless it be given from above: its access to your senses depends mainly upon your physical condition—this is, under God, your comfort and reliance: we are all alike environed. It is only that in your case, the 'paries,' the veil of the flesh, the screen, is a little out of repair, and sights and sounds are transmitted. We must enter on a new course, sir,—be encouraged. I'll give tonight to the careful consideration of the whole case."

"You are very good, sir; you think it worth trying, you don't give me quite up; but, sir, you don't know, it is gaining such an influence over me: it orders me about, it is such a tyrant, and I'm growing so helpless. May God deliver me!"

"It orders you about—of course you mean by speech?"

"Yes, yes; it is always urging me to crimes, to injure others, or myself. You see, Doctor, the situation is urgent, it is indeed. When I was in Shropshire, a few weeks ago" (Mr. Jennings was speaking rapidly and trembling now, holding my arm with one hand and looking in my face), "I went out one day with a party of friends for a walk: my persecutor, I tell you, was with me at the time. I lagged behind the rest: the country near the Dee, you know, is beautiful. Our path happened to lie near a coal mine, and at the verge of the wood is a perpendicular shaft, they say, a hundred and fifty feet deep. My niece had remained behind with me—she knows, of course nothing of the nature of my sufferings. She knew, however, that I had been ill and was low, and she remained to prevent my being quite alone. As we loitered slowly on together, the brute that accompanied me was urging me to throw myself down the shaft. I tell you now—oh, sir, think of it!—the one consideration that saved me from that hideous death was the fear lest the shock of witnessing the occurrence should be too much for the poor girl. I asked her to go on and walk with her friends, saying that I could go no further. She made excuses, and the more I urged her the firmer she became. She looked doubtful and frightened. I suppose there was something in my looks or manner that alarmed her; but she would not go, and that literally saved me. You had no idea, sir, that a living man could be made so abject a slave of Satan," he said, with a ghastly groan and a shudder.

There was a pause here, and I said, "You *were* preserved, nevertheless. It was the act of God. You are in His hands and in the power of no other being: be therefore confident for the future."

X: Home

I MADE HIM HAVE CANDLES LIGHTED, AND SAW THE ROOM LOOKING cheery and inhabited before I left him. I told him that he must regard his illness strictly as one dependent on physical, though *subtle* physical causes.

I told him that he had evidence of God's care and love in the deliverance which he had just described, and that I had perceived with pain that he seemed to regard its peculiar features as indicating that he had been delivered over to spiritual reprobation. Than such a conclusion nothing could be, I insisted, less warranted; and not only so, but more contrary to facts, as disclosed in his mysterious deliverance from that murderous influence during his Shropshire excursion. First, his niece had been retained by his side without his intending to keep her near him; and, secondly, there had been infused into his mind an irresistible repugnance to execute the dreadful suggestion in her presence.

As I reasoned this point with him, Mr. Jennings wept. He seemed comforted. One promise I exacted, which was that should the monkey at any time return, I should be sent for immediately; and, repeating my assurance that I would give neither time nor thought to any other subject until I had thoroughly investigated his case, and that tomorrow he should hear the result, I took my leave.

Before getting into the carriage I told the servant that his master was far from well, and that he should make a point of frequently looking into his room. My own arrangements I made with a view to being quite secure from interruption.

I merely called at my lodgings, and with a travelling-desk and carpet-bag, set off in a hackney carriage for an inn about two miles out of town, called "The Horns," a very quiet and comfortable house, with good thick walls. And there I resolved, without the possibility of intrusion or distraction, to devote some hours of the night, in my comfortable sitting-room, to Mr. Jennings' case, and so much of the morning as it might require.

(There occurs here a careful note of Dr. Hesselius's opinion upon the case, and of the habits, dietary, and medicines which he prescribed. It is curious—some persons would say mystical. But, on the whole, I doubt whether it would sufficiently interest a reader of the kind I am likely to meet with, to warrant its being here reprinted. The whole letter was plainly written at the inn where he had hid himself for the occasion. The next letter is dated from his town lodgings.)

I left town for the inn where I slept last night at half-past nine, and did not arrive at my room in town until one o'clock this afternoon. I found a letter in Mr. Jennings' hand upon my table. It had not come by post, and, on inquiry, I learned that Mr. Jennings' servant had brought it, and on learning that I was not to return until today, and that no one could tell him my address, he seemed very uncomfortable, and said his orders from his master were that that he was not to return without an answer.

I opened the letter and read:

Dear Dr. Hesselius.—It is here. You had not been an hour gone when it returned. It is speaking. It knows all that has happened. It knows every-thing—it knows you, and is frantic and atrocious. It reviles. I send you this. It knows every word I have written—I write. This I promised, and I there-fore write, but I fear very confused, very incoherently. I am so interrupted, disturbed.

Ever yours, sincerely yours,
Robert Lynder Jennings.

"When did this come?" I asked.

"About eleven last night: the man was here again, and has been here three times today. The last time is about an hour since."

Thus answered, and with the notes I had made upon his case in my pocket, I was in a few minutes driving towards Richmond, to see Mr. Jennings.

I by no means, as you perceive, despaired of Mr. Jennings' case. He had himself remembered and applied, though quite in a mistaken way, the principle which I lay down in my Metaphysical Medicine, and which governs all such cases. I was about to apply it in earnest. I was profoundly interested and very anxious to see and examine him while the "enemy" was actually present.

I drove up to the sombre house and ran up the steps and knocked. The door, in a little time, was opened by a tall woman in black silk. She looked ill, and as if she had been crying. She curtseyed and heard my question, but she did not answer. She turned her face away, extending her hand towards two men who were coming downstairs; and thus having, as it were, tacitly made me over to them, she passed through a side-door hastily and shut it.

The man who was nearest the hall, I at once accosted, but being now close to him, I was shocked to see that both his hands were covered with blood.

I drew back a little, and the man, passing downstairs, merely said in a low tone, "Here's the servant, sir."

The servant had stopped on the stairs, confounded and dumb at seeing me. He was rubbing his hands in a handkerchief, and it was steeped in blood.

"Jones, what is it? what has happened?" I asked, while a sickening suspicion overpowered me.

The man asked me to come up to the lobby. I was beside him in a moment, and, frowning and pallid, with contracted eyes, he told me the horror which I already half guessed.

His master had made away with himself.

I went upstairs with him to the room—what I saw there I won't tell you. He had cut his throat with his razor. It was a frightful gash. The two men had laid him on the bed and composed his limbs. It had happened, as the immense pool of blood on the floor declared, at some distance between the bed and the window. There was carpet round his bed and a carpet under his dressing-table, but none on the rest of the floor, for the man said he did not like a carpet on his bedroom. In this sombre and now terrible room, one of the great elms that darkened the house was slowly moving the shadow of one of its great boughs upon this dreadful floor.

I beckoned to the servant, and we went downstairs together. I turned off the hall into an old-fashioned panelled room, and there standing, I heard all the servant had to tell. It was not a great deal.

"I concluded, sir, from your words, and looks, sir, as you left last night, that you thought my master was seriously ill. I thought it might be that you were afraid of a fit, or something. So I attended very close to your directions. He sat up late, till past three o'clock. He was not writing or reading. He was talking a great deal to himself, but that was nothing unusual. At about that hour I assisted him to undress, and left him in his slippers and dressing-gown. I went back softly in about half-an-hour. He was in his bed, quite undressed, and a pair of candles lighted on the table beside his bed. He was leaning on his elbow, and looking out at the other side of the bed when I came in. I asked him if he wanted anything, and he said No.

"I don't know whether it was what you said to me, sir, or something a little unusual about him, but I was uneasy, uncommon uneasy about him last night.

"In another half hour, or it might be a little more, I went up again. I did not hear him talking as before. I opened the door a little. The candles were both out, which was not usual. I had a bedroom candle, and I let the light in, a little bit, looking softly round. I saw him sitting in that chair beside the dressing-table with his clothes on again. He turned round and looked at me. I thought it strange he should get up and dress, and put out the candles to sit in the dark, that way. But I only asked him again if I could do anything for him. He said, No, rather sharp, I thought. I asked him if I might light the candles, and he said, 'Do as you like, Jones.' So I lighted them, and I lingered about the room, and he said, 'Tell me truth, Jones; why did you come again—you did not hear anyone cursing?' 'No, sir,' I said, wondering what he could mean.

"'No,' said he, after me, 'of course, no;' and I said to him, 'Wouldn't it be well, sir, you went to bed? It's just five o'clock;' and he said nothing, but, 'Very likely; good-night, Jones.' So I went, sir, but in less than an hour I came again. The door was fast, and he heard me and called as I thought from the bed to know what I wanted, and he desired me not to disturb him again. I lay down and slept for a little. It must have been between six and seven when I went up again. The door was still fast, and he made no answer, so I did not like to disturb him, and thinking he was asleep, I left him till nine. It was his custom to ring when he wished me to come, and I had no particular hour for calling him. I tapped very gently, and getting no answer, I stayed away a good while, supposing he was getting some rest then. It was not till eleven o'clock I grew really uncomfortable about him—for at the latest he was never, that I could remember, later than half-past ten. I got no answer. I knocked and called, and still no answer. So not being able to force the door, I called Thomas from the stables, and together we forced it and found him in the shocking way you saw."

Jones had no more to tell. Poor Mr. Jennings was very gentle and very kind. All his people were fond of him. I could see that the servant was very much moved.

So, dejected and agitated, I passed from that terrible house and its dark canopy of elms, and I hope I shall never see it more. While I write to you I feel like a man who has but half waked from a frightful and monotonous dream. My memory rejects the picture with incredulity and horror. Yet I know it is true. It is the story of the process of a poison, a poison which excites the reciprocal action of spirit and nerve, and paralyses the tissue that separates those cognate functions of the senses, the external and the interior. Thus we find strange bed-fellows, and the mortal and immortal prematurely make acquaintance.

CONCLUSION: A WORD FOR THOSE WHO SUFFER

MY DEAR VAN L——, YOU HAVE SUFFERED FROM AN AFFECTION similar to that which I have just described. You twice complained of a return of it.

Who, under God, cured you? Your humble servant, Martin Hesselius. Let me rather adopt the more emphasised piety of a certain good old French surgeon of three hundred years ago: "I treated, and God cured you."

Come, my friend, you are not to be hippish. Let me tell you a fact.

I have met with, and treated, as my book shows, fifty-seven cases of this kind of vision, which I term indifferently "sublimated," "precocious," and "interior."

There is another class of affections which are truly termed—though commonly confounded with those which I describe—spectral illusions. These latter I look upon as being no less simply curable than a cold in the head or a trifling dyspepsia.

It is those which rank in the first category that test our promptitude of thought. Fifty-seven such cases have I encountered, neither more nor less. And in how many of these have I failed? In no one single instance.

There is no one affliction of mortality more easily and certainly reducible, with a little patience and a rational confidence in the physician. With these simple conditions, I look upon the cure as absolutely certain.

You are to remember that I had not even commenced to treat Mr. Jennings' case. I have not any doubt that I should have cured him perfectly in eighteen months, or possibly it might have extended to two years. Some cases are very rapidly curable, others extremely tedious. Every intelligent physician who will give thought and diligence to the task, will effect a cure.

You know my tract on "The Cardinal Functions of the Brain." I there, by the evidence of innumerable facts, prove, as I think, the high probability of a circulation arterial and venous in its mechanism, through the nerves. Of this system, thus considered, the brain is the heart. The fluid, which is propagated hence through one class of nerves, returns in an altered state through another, and the nature of that fluid is spiritual, though not immaterial, any more than, as I before remarked, light or electricity are so.

By various abuses, among which the habitual use of such agents as green tea is one, this fluid may be affected as to its quality, but it is more frequently disturbed as to equilibrium. This fluid being that which we have in common with spirits, a congestion found upon the masses of brain or nerve, connected with the interior sense, forms a surface unduly exposed, on which disembodied spirits may operate: communication is thus more or less effectually established. Between this brain circulation and the heart circulation there is an intimate sympathy. The seat, or rather the instrument of exterior vision, is the eye. The seat of interior vision is the nervous tissue and brain, immediately about and above the eyebrow. You remember how effectually I dissipated your pictures by the simple application of iced eau-de-cologne. Few cases, however, can be treated exactly alike with anything like rapid success. Cold acts powerfully as a repellant of the nervous fluid. Long enough continued it will even produce that permanent insensibility which we call numbness, and a little longer, muscular as well as sensational paralysis.

I have not, I repeat, the slightest doubt that I should have first dimmed and ultimately sealed that inner eye which Mr. Jennings had inadvertently opened. The same senses are opened in delirium tremens, and entirely shut up again when the overaction of the cerebral heart, and the prodigious nervous congestions that attend it, are terminated by a decided change in the state of the body. It is by acting steadily upon the body, by a simple process, that this result is produced—and inevitably produced—I have never yet failed.

Poor Mr. Jennings made away with himself. But that catastrophe was the result of a totally different malady, which, as it were, projected itself upon the disease which was established. His case was in the distinctive manner a complication, and the complaint under which he really succumbed, was hereditary suicidal mania. Poor Mr. Jennings I cannot call a patient of mine, for I had not even begun to treat his case, and he had not yet given me, I am convinced, his full and unreserved confidence. If the patient does not array himself on the side of the disease, his cure is certain.

JOHN DYSON IN

THE SHINING PYRAMID
ARTHUR MACHEN

Early in the emergence of the occult detective theme we encounter several investigators who were amateurs and became involved in cases out of curiosity or by involvement with others, but who nevertheless developed a profound understanding of a world beyond. One such hapless soul was John Dyson, a failed artist, a man of letters and a devotee of tobacco who, thanks to a small inheritance, is able to wander London or sit at a fashionable café and observe the world. We first encounter him in "The Inmost Light" (1894) where he and his friend Charles Salisbury become interested in the case of Dr. Black and his dead, possibly murdered, wife. Dyson's true nature comes through in the second story, presented here, where we learn much about Machen's theories of another race of beings, which we usually regard as the fairy-folk, but which are far more dangerous and sinister. Dyson also provides the framing device for the episodic volume The Three Impostors (1895) where he remarks how he likes to "go forth, like a knight-errant in search of adventure," but admits that the adventures usually find him, and that he only need wait, like a spider in its web, "responsive to every move-ment and ever on the alert."

Arthur Machen (1863–1947) was a giant of supernatural fiction, though never fully grasped his true capabilities, spending much of his life as a journalist and, for a while, as an actor. He was not unlike Dyson in that he too enjoyed rambling through the streets of London looking for the awe-some. In his autobiography Far Off Things (1922), he wrote: "the whole matter of imaginative literature depends upon this faculty of seeing the universe, from the aeonian pebble of the wayside to the raw suburban street as something new, unheard of, marvellous, finally, miraculous." His best work was written in the 1890s although not all was collected in book form at the time, so the full impact of his writings became rather diffuse. For a while he was best known for "The Bowmen" (1914) that created the legend of the Angel of Mons, namely that the spirits of Britain's historic longbow men had come to the aid of soldiers in the Great War. Besides the various collections of his work, of which Tales of Horror and the Supernatural *(1948) assembles the best, are his novels* The Hill of Dreams *(1907),* The Great Return *(1915),* The Terror *(1917), and* The Green Round *(1933). The* John Dyson *stories have more recently been reassembled as* The Dyson Chronicles *(2014).*

1. THE ARROW-HEAD CHARACTER

"Haunted, you said?"

"Yes, haunted. Don't you remember, when I saw you three years ago, you told me about your place in the west with the ancient woods hanging all about it, and the wild, domed hills, and the ragged land? It has always remained a sort of enchanted picture in my mind as I sit at my desk and hear the traffic rattling in the Street in the midst of whirling London. But when did you come up?"

"The fact is, Dyson, I have only just got out of the train. I drove to the station early this morning and caught the 10.45."

"Well, I am very glad you looked in on me. How have you been getting on since we last met? There is no Mrs. Vaughan, I suppose?"

"No," said Vaughan, "I am still a hermit, like yourself. I have done nothing but loaf about."

Vaughn had lit his pipe and sat in the elbow chair, fidgeting and glancing about him in a somewhat dazed and restless manner. Dyson had wheeled round his chair when his visitor entered and sat with one arm fondly reclining on the desk of his bureau, and touching the litter of manuscript.

"And you are still engaged in the old task?" said Vaughan, pointing to the pile of papers and the teeming pigeon-holes.

"Yes, the vain pursuit of literature, as idle as alchemy, and as entrancing. But you have come to town for some time I suppose; what shall we do tonight?"

"Well, I rather wanted you to try a few days with me down in the west. It would do you a lot of good. I'm sure."

"You are very kind, Vaughan, but London in September is hard to leave. Doré could not have designed anything more wonderful and mystic than Oxford Street as I saw it the other evening; the sunset flaming, the blue haze transmuting the plain street into a road 'far in the spiritual city.'"

"I should like you to come down though. You would enjoy roaming over our hills. Does this racket go on all day and night? It quite bewilders me; I wonder how you can work through it. I am sure you would revel in the great peace of my old home among the woods."

Vaughan lit his pipe again, and looked anxiously at Dyson to see if his inducements had had any effect, but the man of letters shook his head, smiling, and vowed in his heart a firm allegiance to the streets.

"You cannot tempt me," he said.

'Well, you may be right. Perhaps, after all, I was wrong to speak of the peace of the country. There, when a tragedy does occur, it is like a stone thrown into a pond; the circles of disturbance keep on widening, and it seems as if the water would never be still again."

"Have you ever any tragedies where you are?"

"I can hardly say that. But I was a good deal disturbed about a month ago by something that happened; it may or may not have been a tragedy in the usual sense of the word."

"What was the occurrence?"

"Well, the fact is a girl disappeared in a way which seems highly mysterious. Her parents, people of the name of Trevor, are well-to-do farmers, and their eldest daughter Annie was a sort of village beauty; she was really remarkably handsome. One afternoon she thought she would go and see her aunt, a widow who farms her own land, and as the two houses are only about five or six miles apart, she started off, telling her parents she would take the short cut over the hills. She never got to her aunt's, and she never was seen again. That's putting it in a few words."

"What an extraordinary thing! I suppose there are no disused mines, are there, on the hills? I don't think you quite run to anything so formidable as a precipice?"

"No; the path the girl must have taken had no pitfalls of any description; it is just a track over wild, bare hillside, far, even from a byroad. One may walk for miles without meeting a soul, but it is perfectly safe."

"And what do people say about it?"

"Oh, they talk nonsense—among themselves. You have no notion as to how superstitious English cottagers are in out-of-the-way parts like mine. They are as bad as the Irish, every whit, and even more secretive."

"But what do they say?"

"Oh, the poor girl is supposed to have 'gone with the fairies,' or to have been 'taken by the fairies.' Such stuff!" he went on, "one would laugh if it were not for the real tragedy of the case."

Dyson looked somewhat interested.

"Yes," he said, "'fairies' certainly strike a little curiously on the ear in these days. But what do the police say? I presume they do not accept the fairy-tale hypothesis?"

"No; but they seem quite at fault. What I am afraid of is that Annie Trevor must have fallen in with some scoundrels on her way. Castletown is a large seaport, you know, and some of the worst of the foreign sailors occasionally desert their ships and go on the tramp up and down the country. Not many years ago a Spanish sailor named Garcia murdered a whole family for the sake of plunder that was not worth sixpence. They are hardly human, some of these fellows, and I am dreadfully afraid the poor girl must have come to an awful end."

"But no foreign sailor was seen by anyone about the country?"

"No; there is certainly that; and of course country people are quick to notice anyone whose appearance and dress are a little out of the common. Still it seems as if my theory were the only possible explanation."

"There are no data to go upon," said Dyson, thoughtfully. "There was no question of a love affair, or anything of the kind, I suppose?"

"Oh, no, not a hint of such a thing. I am sure if Annie were alive she would have contrived to let her mother know of her safety."

"No doubt, no doubt. Still it is barely possible that she is alive and yet unable to communicate with her friends. But all this must have disturbed you a good deal."

"Yes, it did; I hate a mystery, and especially a mystery which is probably the veil of horror. But frankly, Dyson, I want to make a clean breast of it; I did not come here to tell you all this."

"Of course not," said Dyson, a little surprised at Vaughan's uneasy manner. "You came to have a chat on more cheerful topics."

"No, I did not. What I have been telling you about happened a month ago, but something which seems likely to affect me more personally has taken place within the last few days, and to be quite plain, I came up to town with the idea that you might be able to help me. You recollect that curious case you spoke to me about on our last meeting; something about a spectacle-maker."

"Oh, yes, I remember that. I know I was quite proud of my acumen at the time; even to this day the police have no idea why those peculiar yellow spectacles were wanted. But, Vaughan, you really look quite put out; I hope there is nothing serious?"

"No, I think I have been exaggerating, and I want you to reassure me. But what has happened is very odd."

"And what has happened?"

"I am sure that you will laugh at me, but this is the story. You must know there is a path, a right of way, that goes through my land, and to be precise, close to the wall of the kitchen garden. It is not used by many people; a woodman now and again finds it useful, and five or six children who go to school in the village pass twice a day. Well, a few days ago I was taking a walk about the place before breakfast, and I happened to stop to fill my pipe just by the large doors in the garden wall. The wood, I must tell you, comes to within a few feet of the wall, and the track I spoke of runs right in the shadow of the trees. I thought the shelter from a brisk wind that was blowing rather pleasant, and I stood there smoking with my eyes on the ground. Then something caught my attention. Just under the wall, on the short grass; a number of small flints were arranged in a pattern; something like this": and Mr. Vaughan caught at a pencil and piece of paper, and dotted down a few strokes.

"You see," he went on, "there were, I should think, twelve little stones neatly arranged in lines, and spaced at equal distances, as I have shown it on the paper. They were pointed stones, and the points were very carefully directed one way."

"Yes," said Dyson, without much interest, "no doubt the children you have mentioned had been playing there on their way from school. Children, as you know, are very fond of making such devices with oyster shells or flints or flowers, or with whatever comes in their way."

"So I thought; I just noticed these flints were arranged in a sort of pattern and then went on. But the next morning I was taking the same round, which, as a matter of fact, is habitual with me, and again I saw at the same spot a device in flints. This time it was really a curious pattern; something like the spokes of a wheel, all meeting at a common centre, and this centre formed by a device which looked like a bowl; all, you understand done in flints."

"You are right," said Dyson, "that seems odd enough. Still it is reasonable that your half-a-dozen school children are responsible for these fantasies in stone."

"Well, I thought I would set the matter at rest. The children pass the gate every evening at half-past five, and I walked by at six and found the device just as I had left it in the morning. The next day I was up and about at a quarter to seven, and I found the whole thing had been changed. There was a pyramid outlined in flints upon the grass. The children I saw going by an hour and a half later, and they ran past the spot without glancing to right or left. In the evening I watched them going home, and this morning when I got to the gate at six o'clock there was a thing like a half moon waiting for me."

"So then the series runs thus: firstly ordered lines, then, the device of the spokes and the bowl, then the pyramid, and finally, this morning, the half moon. That is the order, isn't it?"

"Yes; that is right. But do you know it has made me feel very uneasy? I suppose it seems absurd, but I can't help thinking that some kind of signalling is going on under my nose, and that sort of thing is disquieting."

"But what have you to dread? You have no enemies?"

"No; but I have some very valuable old plate."

"You are thinking of burglars then?" said Dyson, with an accent of considerable interest, "but you must know your neighbours. Are there any suspicious characters about?"

"Not that I am aware of. But you remember what I told you of the sailors."

"Can you trust your servants?"

"Oh, perfectly. The plate is preserved in a strong room; the butler, an old family servant, alone knows where the key is kept. There is nothing wrong there. Still, everybody is aware that I have a lot of old silver, and all country folks are given to gossip. In that way information may have got abroad in very undesirable quarters."

"Yes, but I confess there seems something a little unsatisfactory in the burglar theory. Who is signalling to whom? I cannot see my way to accepting such an explanation. What put the plate into your head in connection with these flints signs, or whatever one may call them?"

"It was the figure of the Bowl," said Vaughan. "I happen to possess a very large and very valuable Charles II punch-bowl. The chasing is really exquisite, and the thing is worth a lot of money. The sign I described to you was exactly the same shape as my punch-bowl."

"A queer coincidence certainly. But the other figures or devices: you have nothing shaped like a pyramid?"

"Ah, you will think that queerer. As it happens, this punch-bowl of mine, together with a set of rare old ladles, is kept in a mahogany chest of a pyramidal shape. The four sides slope upwards, the narrow towards the top."

"I confess all this interests me a good deal," said Dyson. "Let us go on then. What about the other figures; how about the Army, as we may call the first sign, and the Crescent or Half moon?"

"Ah, there is no reference that I can make out of these two. Still, you see I have some excuse for curiosity at all events. I should be very vexed to lose any of the old plate; nearly all the pieces have been in the family for generations. And I cannot get it out of my head that some scoundrels mean to rob me, and are communicating with one another every night."

"Frankly," said Dyson, "I can make nothing of it; I am as much in the dark as yourself. Your theory seems certainly the only possible explanation, and yet the difficulties are immense."

He leaned back in his chair, and the two men faced each other, frowning, and perplexed by so bizarre a problem.

"By the way," said Dyson, after a long pause, "what is your geological formation down there?"

Mr. Vaughan looked up, a good deal surprised by the question.

"Old red sandstone and limestone, I believe," he said. "We are just beyond the coal measures, you know."

"But surely there are no flints either in the sandstone or the limestone?"

"No, I never see any flints in the fields. I confess that did strike me as a little curious."

"I should think so! It is very important. By the way, what size were the flints used in making these devices?"

"I happen to have brought one with me; I took it this morning."

"From the Half moon?"

"Exactly. Here it is."

He handed over a small flint, tapering to a point and about three inches in length.

Dyson's face blazed up with excitement as he took the thing from Vaughan.

"Certainly," he said, after a moment's pause, "you have some curious neighbours in your country. I hardly think they can harbour any designs on your punch-bowl. Do you know this is a flint arrowhead of vast antiquity, and not only that, but an arrow-head of a unique kind? I have seen specimens from all parts of the world, but there are features about this thing that are quite peculiar." He laid down his pipe and took out a book from a drawer.

"We shall just have time to catch the 5.45 to Castletown," he said.

2. THE EYES ON THE WALL

MR. DYSON DREW IN A LONG BREATH OF THE AIR OF THE HILLS AND felt all the enchantment of the scene about him. It was very early morning, and he stood on the terrace in the front of the house.

Vaughan's ancestor had built on the lower slope of a great hill, in the shelter of a deep and ancient wood that gathered on three sides about the house, and on the fourth side, the southwest, the land fell gently away and sank to the valley, where a brook wound in and out in mystic esses, and the dark and gleaming alders tracked the stream's course to the eye. On the terrace in the sheltered place no wind blew, and far beyond, the trees were still. Only one sound broke in upon the silence, and Dyson heard the noise of the brook singing far below, the song of clear and shining water rippling over the stones, whispering and murmuring as it sank to dark deep pools.

Across the stream, just below the house, rose a grey stone bridge, vaulted and buttressed, a fragment of the Middle Ages, and then beyond the bridge the hills rose again, vast and rounded like bastions, covered here and there with dark woods and thickets of undergrowth, but the heights were all bare of trees, showing only grey turf and patches of bracken, touched here and there with the gold of fading fronds; Dyson looked to the north and south, and still he saw the wall of the hills and the ancient woods and the stream drawn in and out between them; all grey and dim with morning mist beneath a grey sky in a hushed and haunted air.

Mr. Vaughan's voice broke in upon the silence.

"I thought you would be too tired to be about so early," he said. "I see you are admiring the view. It is very pretty, isn't it, though I suppose old Meyrick Vaughan didn't think much about the scenery when he built the house. A queer grey, old place, isn't it?"

"Yes, and how it fits into the surroundings; it seems of a piece with the grey hills and the grey bridge below."

"I am afraid I have brought you down on false pretences, Dyson," said Vaughan, as they began to walk up and down the terrace. "I have been to the place, and there is not a sign of anything this morning."

"Ah, indeed. Well, suppose we go round together."

They walked across the lawn and went by a path through the ilex shrubbery to the back of the house. There Vaughan pointed out the track leading down to the valley and up to the heights above the wood, and presently they stood beneath the garden wall, by the door.

"Here, you see, it was," said Vaughan, pointing to a spot on the turf. "I was standing just where you are now that morning I first saw the flints."

"Yes, quite so. That morning it was the Army, as I call it; then the Bowl, then the Pyramid, and, yesterday, the Half moon. What a queer old stone that is," he went on, pointing to a block of limestone rising out of the turf just beneath the wall. "It looks like a sort of dwarf pillar, but I suppose it is natural."

"Oh, yes, I think so. I imagine it was brought here, though, as we stand on the red sandstone. No doubt it was used as a foundation stone for some older building."

"Very likely," Dyson was peering about him attentively, looking from the ground to the wall, and from the wall to the deep wood that hung almost over the garden and made the place dark even in the morning.

"Look here," said Dyson at length, "it is certainly a case of children this time. Look at that." He was bending down and staring at the dull red surface of the mellowed bricks of the wall.

Vaughan came up and looked hard where Dyson's finger was pointing, and could scarcely distinguish a faint mark in deeper red.

"What is it?" he said. "I can make nothing of it."

"Look a little more closely. Don't you see it is an attempt to draw the human eye?"

"Ah, now I see what you mean. My sight is not very sharp. Yes, so it is, it is meant for an eye, no doubt, as you say. I thought the children learnt drawing at school."

"Well, it is an odd eye enough. Do you notice the peculiar almond shape; almost like the eye of a Chinaman?"

Dyson looked meditatively at the work of the undeveloped artist, and scanned the wall again, going down on his knees in the minuteness of his inquisition.

"I should like very much," he said at length, "to know how a child in this out of the way place could have any idea of the shape of the Mongolian eye. You see the average child has a very distinct impression of the subject; he draws a circle, or something like a circle, and put a dot in the centre. I don't think any child imagines that the eye is really made like that; it's just a convention of infantile art. But this almond-shaped thing puzzles me extremely. Perhaps it may be derived from a gilt Chinaman on a tea-canister in the grocer's shop. Still that's hardly likely."

"But why are you so sure it was done by a child?"

"Why! Look at the height. These old-fashioned bricks are little more than two inches thick; there are twenty courses from the ground to the sketch if we call it so; that gives a height of three and a half feet. Now, just imagine you are going to draw something on this wall. Exactly; your pencil, if you had one, would touch the wall somewhere on the level with

43

your eyes, that is, more than five feet from the ground. It seems, therefore, a very simple deduction to conclude that this eye on the wall was drawn by a child about ten years old."

"Yes, I had not thought of that. Of course one of the children must have done it."

"I suppose so; and yet as I said, there is something singularly unchild-like about those two lines, and the eyeball itself, you see, is almost an oval. To my mind, the thing has an odd, ancient air; and a touch that is not alto-gether pleasant. I cannot help fancying that if we could see a whole face from the same hand it would not be altogether agreeable. However, that is nonsense, after all, and we are not getting farther in our investigations. It is odd that the flint series has come to such an abrupt end."

The two men walked away towards the house, and as they went in at the porch there was a break in the grey sky, and a gleam of sunshine on the grey hill before them.

All the day Dyson prowled meditatively about the fields and woods surrounding the house. He was thoroughly and completely puzzled by the trivial circumstances he proposed to elucidate, and now he again took the flint arrow-head from his pocket, turning it over and examining it with deep attention. There was something about the thing that was altogether different from the specimens he had seen at the museums and private col-lections; the shape was of a distinct type, and around the edge there was a line of little punctured dots, apparently a suggestion of ornament. Who, thought Dyson, could possess such things in so remote a place; and who, possessing the flints, could have put them to the fantastic use of designing meaningless figures under Vaughan's garden wall? The rank absurdity of the whole affair offended him unutterably; and as one theory after another rose in his mind only to be rejected, he felt strongly tempted to take the next train back to town. He had seen the silver plate which Vaughan treasured, and had inspected the punch-bowl, the gem of the collection, with close attention; and what he saw and his interview with the butler convinced him that a plot to rob the strong box was out of the limits of enquiry. The chest in which the bowl was kept, a heavy piece of mahogany, evidently dating from the beginning of the century, was certainly strongly suggestive of a pyramid, and Dyson was at first inclined to the inept manoeuvres of the detective, but a little sober thought convinced him of the impossibility of the burglary hypothesis, and he cast wildly about for something more satisfying. He asked Vaughan if there were any gipsies in the neighbourhood, and heard that the Romany had not been seen for years. This dashed him a good deal, as he knew the gipsy habit of leaving queer hieroglyphics on the line of march, and had been much elated when the thought occurred to him. He was facing Vaughan by the old-fashioned hearth when he put the question, and leaned back in his chair in disgust at the destruction of his theory.

"It is odd," said Vaughan, "but the gipsies never trouble us here. Now and then the farmers find traces of fires in the wildest part of the hills, but nobody seems to know who the fire-lighters are."

"Surely that looks like gipsies?"

"No, not in such places as those. Tinkers and gipsies and wanderers of all sorts stick to the roads and don't go very far from the farmhouses."

"Well, I can make nothing of it. I saw the children going by this afternoon, and, as you say, they ran straight on. So we shall have no more eyes on the wall at all events."

"No, I must waylay them one of these days and find out who is the artist."

The next morning when Vaughan strolled in his usual course from the lawn to the back of the house he found Dyson already awaiting him by the garden door, and evidently in a state of high excitement, for he beckoned furiously with his hand and gesticulated violently.

"What is it?" asked Vaughan. "The flints again?"

"No; but look here, look at the wall. There; don't you see it?"

"There's another of those eyes!"

"Exactly. Drawn, you see, at a little distance from the first, almost on the same level, but slightly lower."

"What on earth is one to make of it? It couldn't have been done by the children; it wasn't there last night, and they won't pass for another hour. What can it mean?"

"I think the very devil is at the bottom of all this," said Dyson. "Of course, one cannot resist the conclusion that these infernal almond eyes are to be set down to the same agency as the devices in the arrow-heads; and where that conclusion is to lead us is more than I can tell. For my part, I have to put a strong check on my imagination, or it would run wild."

"Vaughan," he said, as they turned away from the wall, "has it struck you that there is one point—a very curious point—in common between the figures done in flints and the eyes drawn on the wall?"

"What is that?" asked Vaughan, on whose face there had fallen a certain shadow of indefinite dread.

"It is this. We know that the signs of the Army, the Bowl, the Pyramid, and the Half moon must have been done at night. Presumably they were meant to be seen at night. Well, precisely the same reasoning applies to those eyes on the wall."

"I do not quite see your point."

"Oh, surely. The nights are dark just now, and have been very cloudy, I know, since I came down. Moreover, those overhanging trees would throw that wall into deep shadow even on a clear night."

"Well?"

"What struck me was this. What very peculiarly sharp eyesight, they, whoever 'they' are, must have to be able to arrange arrow-heads in intricate order in the blackest shadow of the wood, and then draw the eyes on the wall without a trace of bungling, or a false line."

"I have read of persons confined in dungeons for many years who have been able to see quite well in the dark," said Vaughan.

"Yes," said Dyson, "there was the abbé in Monte Cristo. But it is a singular point."

3. THE SEARCH FOR THE BOWL

"WHO WAS THAT OLD MAN THAT TOUCHED HIS HAT TO YOU JUST now?" said Dyson, as they came to the bend of the lane near the house.

"Oh, that was old Trevor. He looks very broken, poor old fellow."

"Who is Trevor?"

"Don't you remember? I told you the story that afternoon I came to your rooms—about a girl named Annie Trevor, who disappeared in the most inexplicable manner about five weeks ago. That was her father."

"Yes, yes, I recollect now. To tell the truth I had forgotten all about it. And nothing has been heard of the girl?"

"Nothing whatever. The police are quite at fault."

"I am afraid I did not pay very much attention to the details you gave me. Which way did the girl go?"

"Her path would take her right across those wild hills above the house: the nearest point in the track must be about two miles from here."

"Is it near that little hamlet I saw yesterday?"

"You mean Croesyceiliog, where the children came from? No; it goes more to the north."

"Ah, I have never been that way."

They went into the house, and Dyson shut himself up in his room, sunk deep in doubtful thought, but yet with the shadow of a suspicion growing within him that for a while haunted his brain, all vague and fantastic, refusing to take definite form. He was sitting by the open window and looking out on the valley and saw, as if in a picture, the intricate winding of the brook, the grey bridge, and the vast hills rising beyond; all still and without a breath of wind to stir the mystic hanging woods, and the evening sunshine glowed warm on the bracken, and down below a faint mist, pure white, began to rise from the stream. Dyson sat by the window as the day darkened and the huge bastioned hills loomed vast and vague, and the woods became dim and more shadowy: and the fancy that had seized him no longer appeared altogether impossible. He passed the rest of the evening in a reverie, hardly hearing what Vaughan said; and when he took his candle in the hall, he paused a moment before bidding his friend good-night.

"I want a good rest," he said. "I have got some work to do tomorrow."

"Some writing, you mean?"

"No. I am going to look for the Bowl."

"The Bowl! If you mean my punch-bowl, that is safe in the chest."

"I don't mean the punch-bowl. You may take my word for it that your plate has never been threatened. No; I will not bother you with any suppositions. We shall in all probability have something much stronger than suppositions before long. Good-night, Vaughan."

The next morning Dyson set off after breakfast. He took the path by the garden wall, and noted that there were now eight of the weird almond eyes dimly outlined on the brick.

"Six days more," he said to himself, but as he thought over the theory he had formed, he shrank, in spite of strong conviction, from such a wildly incredible fancy. He struck up through the dense shadows of the wood, and at length came out on the bare hillside and climbed higher and higher over the slippery turf, keeping well to the north, and following the indications given him by Vaughan. As he went on, he seemed to mount ever higher above the world of human life and customary things; to his right he looked at a fringe of orchard and saw a faint blue smoke rising like a pillar; there was the hamlet from which the children came to school, and there the only sign of life, for the woods embowered and concealed Vaughan's old grey house. As he reached what seemed the summit of the hill, he realized for the first time the desolate loneliness and strangeness of the land; there was nothing but grey sky and grey hill, a high, vast plain that seemed to stretch on for ever and ever, and a faint glimpse of a blue-peaked mountain far away and to the north. At length he came to the path, a slight track scarcely noticeable, and from its position and by what Vaughan had told him he knew that it was the way the lost girl, Annie Trevor, must have taken. He followed the path on the bare hill-top, noticing the great limestone rocks that cropped out of the turf, grim and hideous, and of an aspect as forbidding as an idol of the South Seas; and suddenly he halted, astonished, although he had found what he searched for.

Almost without warning the ground shelved suddenly away on all sides, and Dyson looked down into a circular depression, which might well have been a Roman amphitheatre, and the ugly crags of limestone rimmed it round as if with a broken wall. Dyson walked round the hollow and noted the position of the stones, and then turned on his way home.

"This," he thought to himself, "is more than curious. The Bowl is discovered, but where is the Pyramid?"

"My dear Vaughan," he said, when he got back, "I may tell you that I have found the Bowl, and that is all I shall tell you for the present. We have six days of absolute inaction before us; there is really nothing to be done."

4. THE SECRET OF THE PYRAMID

"I HAVE JUST BEEN ROUND THE GARDEN," SAID VAUGHAN ONE MORNing. "I have been counting those infernal eyes, and I find there are fourteen of them. For heaven's sake, Dyson, tell me what the meaning of it all is."

"I should be very sorry to attempt to do so. I may have guessed this or that, but I always make it a principle to keep my guesses to myself. Besides, it is really not worth while anticipating events; you will remember my telling you that we had six days of inaction before us? Well, this is the sixth day, and the last of idleness. Tonight, I propose we take a stroll."

"A stroll! Is that all the action you mean to take?"

"Well, it may show you some very curious things. To be plain, I want you to start with me at nine o'clock this evening for the hills. We may have to be out all night, so you had better wrap up well, and bring some of that brandy."

"Is it a joke?" asked Vaughan, who was bewildered with strange events and strange surmises.

"No, I don't think there is much joke in it. Unless I am much mistaken we shall find a very serious explanation of the puzzle. You will come with me, I am sure?"

"Very good. Which way do you want to go?"

"By the path you told me of; the path Annie Trevor is supposed to have taken."

Vaughan looked white at the mention of the girl's name.

"I did not think you were on that track," he said. "I thought it was the affair of those devices in flint and of the eyes on the wall that you were engaged on. It's no good saying any more, but I will go with you."

At a quarter to nine that evening the two men set out, taking the path through the wood and up the hill-side. It was a dark and heavy night, the sky was thick with clouds, and the valley full of mist, and all the way they seemed to walk in a world of shadow and gloom, hardly speaking, and afraid to break the haunted silence. They came out at last on the steep hill-side, and instead of the oppression of the wood there was the long, dim sweep of the turf, and higher, the fantastic limestone rocks hinted horror through the darkness, and the wind sighed as it passed across the mountain to the sea, and in its passage beat chill about their hearts. They seemed to walk on and on for hours, and the dim outline of the hill still stretched before them, and the haggard rocks still loomed through the darkness, when suddenly Dyson whispered, drawing his breath quickly, and coming close to his companion:

"Here," he said, "we will lie down. I do not think there is anything yet."

"I know the place," said Vaughan, after a moment. "I have often been by in the daytime. The country people are afraid to come here, I believe; it is supposed to be a fairies' castle, or something of the kind. But why on earth have we come here?"

"Speak a little lower," said Dyson. "It might not do us any good if we are overheard."

"Overheard here! There is not a soul within three miles of us."

"Possibly not; indeed, I should say certainly not. But there might be a body somewhat nearer."

"I don't understand you in the least," said Vaughan, whispering to humour Dyson, "but why have we come here?"

"Well, you see this hollow before us is the Bowl. I think we had better not talk even in whispers."

They lay full length upon the turf; the rock between their faces and the Bowl, and now and again, Dyson, slouching his dark, soft hat over his forehead, put out the glint of an eye, and in a moment drew back, not daring to take a prolonged view. Again he laid an ear to the ground and listened, and the hours went by, and the darkness seemed to blacken, and the faint sigh of the wind was the only sound.

Vaughan grew impatient with this heaviness of silence, this watching for indefinite terror; for to him there was no shape or form of apprehension, and he began to think the whole vigil a dreary farce.

"How much longer is this to last?" he whispered to Dyson, and Dyson who had been holding his breath in the agony of attention put his mouth to Vaughan's ear and said:

"Will you listen?" with pauses between each syllable, and in the voice with which the priest pronounces the awful words.

Vaughan caught the ground with his hands and stretched forward, wondering what he was to hear. At first there was nothing, and then a low and gentle noise came very softly from the Bowl, a faint sound, almost indescribable, but as if one held the tongue against the roof of the mouth and expelled the breath. He listened eagerly and presently the noise grew louder, and became a strident and horrible hissing as if the pit beneath boiled with fervent heat, and Vaughan, unable to remain in suspense any longer, drew his cap half over his face in imitation of Dyson, and looked down to the hollow below.

It did, in truth, stir and seethe like an infernal caldron. The whole of the sides and bottom tossed and writhed with vague and restless forms that passed to and fro without the sound of feet, and gathered thick here and there and seemed to speak to one another in those tones of horrible sibilance, like the hissing of snakes, that he had heard. It was as if the sweet turf and the cleanly earth had suddenly become quickened with some foul writhing growth. Vaughan could not draw back his face, though he felt Dyson's finger touch him, but he peered into the quaking mass and saw faintly that there were things like faces and human limbs, and yet he felt his inmost soul chill with the sure belief that no fellow soul or human thing stirred in all that tossing and hissing host. He looked aghast, choking back sobs of horror, and at length the loathsome forms gathered thickest about some vague object in the middle of the hollow, and the hissing of their speech grew more venomous, and he saw in the uncertain light the abominable limbs, vague and yet too plainly seen, writhe and intertwine, and he thought he heard, very faint, a low human moan striking through the noise of speech that was not of man. At his heart something seemed to whisper ever "the worm of corruption, the worm that dieth not," and grotesquely the image was pictured to his imagination of a piece of putrid offal stirring through and through with bloated and horrible creeping things. The writhing of the dusky limbs continued, they seemed clustered round the dark form in the middle of the hollow, and the sweat dripped and poured off Vaughan's forehead, and fell cold on his hand beneath his face.

Then, it seemed done in an instant, the loathsome mass melted and fell away to the sides of the Bowl, and for a moment Vaughan saw in the middle of the hollow the tossing of human arms.

But a spark gleamed beneath, a fire kindled, and as the voice of a woman cried out loud in a shrill scream of utter anguish and terror, a great pyramid of flame spired up like a bursting of a pent fountain, and threw a blaze of light upon the whole mountain. In that instant Vaughan saw the myriads beneath; the things made in the form of men but stunted like children hideously deformed, the faces with the almond eyes burning with evil and unspeakable lusts; the ghastly yellow of the mass of naked flesh and then as if by magic the place was empty, while the fire roared and crackled, and the flames shone abroad.

"You have seen the Pyramid," said Dyson in his ear, "the Pyramid of Fire."

5. THE LITTLE PEOPLE

"Then you recognize the thing?"

"Certainly. It is a brooch that Annie Trevor used to wear on Sundays; I remember the pattern. But where did you find it? You don't mean to say that you have discovered the girl?"

"My dear Vaughan, I wonder you have not guessed where I found the brooch. You have not forgotten last night already?"

"Dyson," said the other, speaking very seriously, "I have been turning it over in my mind this morning while you have been out. I have thought about what I saw, or perhaps I should say about what I thought I saw, and the only conclusion I can come to is this, that the thing won't bear recollection. As men live, I have lived soberly and honestly, in the fear of God, all my days, and all I can do is believe that I suffered from some monstrous delusion, from some phantasmagoria of the bewildered senses. You know we went home together in silence, not a word passed between us as to what I fancied I saw; had we not better agree to keep silence on the subject? When I took my walk in the peaceful morning sunshine, I thought all the earth seemed full of praise, and passing by that wall I noticed there were no more signs recorded, and I blotted out those that remained. The mystery is over, and we can live quietly again. I think some poison has been working for the last few weeks; I have trod on the verge of madness, but I am sane now."

Mr. Vaughan had spoken earnestly, and bent forward in his chair and glanced at Dyson with something of entreaty.

"My dear Vaughan," said the other, after a pause, "what's the use of this? It is much too late to take that tone; we have gone too deep. Besides you know as well as I that there is no delusion in the case; I wish there were with all my heart. No, in justice to myself I must tell you the whole story, so far as I know it."

"Very good," said Vaughan with a sigh, "if you must, you must."

"Then," said Dyson, "we will begin with the end if you please. I found this brooch you have just identified in the place we have called the Bowl. There was a heap of grey ashes, as if a fire had been burning, indeed, the embers were still hot, and this brooch was lying on the ground, just outside the range of the flame. It must have dropped accidentally from the dress of the person who was wearing it. No, don't interrupt me; we can pass now to the beginning, as we have had the end. Let us go back to that day you came to see me in my rooms in London. So far as I can remember, soon after you came in you mentioned, in a somewhat casual manner, that an unfortunate and mysterious incident had occurred in your part of the country; a girl named Annie Trevor had gone to see a relative and had disappeared. I confess freely that what you said did not greatly interest me; there are so many reasons which may make it extremely convenient for a man and more especially a woman to vanish from the circle of their relations and friends. I suppose, if we were to consult the police, one would find that in London somebody disappears mysteriously every other week, and the officers would, no doubt, shrug their shoulders and tell you that by the law of averages it could not be otherwise. So I was very culpably careless to your story, and besides, here is another reason for my lack of interest; your tale was inexplicable. You could only suggest a blackguard sailor on the tramp, but I discarded the explanation immediately.

"For many reasons, but chiefly because the occasional criminal, the amateur in brutal crime, is always found out, especially if he selects the country as the scene of his operations. You will remember the case of that Garcia you mentioned; he strolled into a railway station the day after the murder, his trousers covered with blood, and the works of the Dutch clock, his loot, tied in a neat parcel. So rejecting this, your only suggestion, the whole tale became, as I say, inexplicable, and, therefore, profoundly uninteresting. Yes, therefore, it is a perfectly valid conclusion. Do you ever trouble your head about problems which you know to be insoluble? Did you ever bestow much thought on the old puzzle of Achilles and the tortoise? Of course not, because you knew it was a hopeless quest, and so when you told me the story of a country girl who had disappeared I simply placed the whole thing down in the category of the insoluble, and thought no more about the matter. I was mistaken, so it has turned out; but if you remember, you immediately passed on to an affair which interested you more intensely, because personally, I need not go over the very singular narrative of the flint signs, at first I thought it all trivial, probably some children's game, and if not that a hoax of some sort; but your showing me the arrow-head awoke my acute interest. Here, I saw, there was something widely removed from the commonplace, and matter of real curiosity; and as soon as I came here I set to work to find the solution, repeating to myself again and again the signs you had described. First came the sign we have agreed to call the Army; a number of serried lines of flints, all pointing in the same way. Then the lines, like the spokes of a wheel, all converging towards the figure of a Bowl, then the triangle or Pyramid, and last of all the Half moon. I confess that I exhausted conjecture in my efforts to unveil this mystery, and as you will understand it was a duplex or rather triplex problem. For I had not merely to ask myself: what do these figures mean? but also, who can possibly be responsible for the designing of them? And again, who can possibly possess such valuable things, and knowing their value thus throw them down by the wayside? This line of thought led me to suppose that the person or persons in question did not know the value of unique flint arrow-heads, and yet this did not lead me far, for a well-educated man might easily be ignorant on such a subject. Then came the complication of the eye on the wall, and you remember that we could not avoid the conclusion that in the two cases the same agency was at work. The peculiar position of these eyes on the wall made me inquire if there was such a thing as a dwarf anywhere in the neighbourhood, but I found that there was not, and I knew that the children who pass by every day had nothing to do with the matter. Yet I felt convinced that whoever drew the eyes must be from three and a half to four feet high, since, as I pointed out at the time, anyone who draws on a perpendicular surface chooses by instinct a spot about level with his face. Then again, there was the question of the peculiar shape of the eyes; that marked Mongolian character of which the English countryman could have no conception, and for a final cause of confusion the obvious fact that the designer or designers must be able practically to see in the dark. As you remarked, a man who has been confined for many years in an extremely dark cell or dungeon might acquire that power; but since the days of Edmond Dantès, where would such a prison be found in Europe? A sailor, who had been immured for a considerable period in some horrible Chinese oubliette, seemed the individual I was in search of, and though it looked improbable, it was not absolutely impossible that a sailor or, let us say, a man employed on shipboard, should be a dwarf. But how to account for my imaginary sailor being in possession of prehistoric arrow-heads? And the possession granted, what was the meaning and object of these mysterious signs of flint, and the almond-shaped eyes? Your theory of a contemplated burglary I saw, nearly from the first, to be quite untenable, and I confess I was utterly at a loss for a working hypothesis. It was a mere accident which put me on the track; we passed poor old Trevor, and your mention of his name and of the disappearance of his daughter, recalled the story which I had forgotten, or which remained unheeded. Here, then, I said to myself, is another problem, uninteresting, it is true, by itself; but what if it prove to be in relation with all these enigmas which torture me? I shut myself in my room and endeavoured to dismiss all prejudice from my mind, and I went over everything de novo, assuming for theory's sake that the disappearance of Annie Trevor had some connection with the flint signs and the eyes on the wall. This assumption did not lead me very far, and I was on the point of giving the whole problem up in despair, when a possible significance of the Bowl struck me. As you know there is a 'Devil's Punchbowl' in Surrey, and I saw that the symbol might refer to some feature in the country. Putting the two extremes together, I determined to look for the Bowl near the path which the lost girl had taken, and you know how I found it. I interpreted the sign by what I knew, and read the first, the Army, thus:

'there is to be a gathering or assembly at the Bowl in a fortnight (that is the Half moon) to see the Pyramid, or to build the Pyramid.'

"The eyes, drawn one by one, day by day, evidently checked off the days, and I knew that there would be fourteen and no more. Thus far the way seemed pretty plain; I would not trouble myself to inquire as to the nature of the assembly, or as to who was to assemble in the loneliest and most dreaded place among these lonely hills. In Ireland or China or the

West of America the question would have been easily answered; a muster of the disaffected, the meeting of a secret society; vigilantes summoned to report: the thing would be simplicity itself; but in this quiet corner of England, inhabited by quiet folk, no such suppositions were possible for a moment. But I knew that I should have an opportunity of seeing and watching the assembly, and I did not care to perplex myself with hopeless research; and in place of reasoning a wild fancy entered into judgment: I remembered what people had said about Annie Trevor's disappearance, that she had been 'taken by the fairies.' I tell you, Vaughan, I am a sane man as you are, my brain is not, I trust, mere vacant space to let to any wild improbability, and I tried my best to thrust the fantasy away. And the hint came of the old name of fairies, 'the little people,' and the very probable belief that they represent a tradition of the prehistoric Turanian inhabitants of the country, who were cave dwellers: and then I realized with a shock that I was looking for a being under four feet in height, accustomed to live in darkness, possessing stone instruments, and familiar with the Mongolian cast of features! I say this, Vaughan, that I should be ashamed to hint at such visionary stuff to you, if it were not for that which you saw with your very eyes last night, and I say that I might doubt the evidence of my senses, if they were not confirmed by yours. But you and I cannot look each other in the face and pretend delusion; as you lay on the turf beside me I felt your flesh shrink and quiver, and I saw your eyes in the light of the flame. And so I tell you without any shame what was in my mind last night as we went through the wood and climbed the hill, and lay hidden beneath the rock.

"There was one thing that should have been most evident that puzzled me to the very last. I told you how I read the sign of the Pyramid; the assembly was to see a pyramid, and the true meaning of the symbol escaped me to the last moment. The old derivation from 'up, fire,' though false, should have set me on the track, but it never occurred to me.

"I think I need say very little more. You know we were quite helpless, even if we had foreseen what was to come. Ah, the particular place where these signs were displayed? Yes, that is a curious question. But this house is, so far as I can judge, in a pretty central situation amongst the hills; and possibly, who can say yes or no, that queer, old limestone pillar by your garden wall was a place of meeting before the Celt set foot in Britain. But there is one thing I must add: I don't regret our inability to rescue the wretched girl. You saw the appearance of those things that gathered thick and writhed in the Bowl; you may be sure that what lay bound in the midst of them was no longer fit for earth."

"So?" said Vaughan.

"So she passed in the Pyramid of Fire," said Dyson, "and they passed again to the underworld, to the places beneath the hills."

THE HAUNTED CHILD

ARABELLA KENEALY

Lord Syfret isn't a professional occult investigator—he's more of a busy-body who, because of his wealth and achievements, has become bored with his own life while developing an insatiable curiosity for the lives of others. As a result, he intrudes upon events, the more bizarre the better. He finds himself drawn to such cases by some inner feeling, suggesting that he might have an innate psychic ability, though he does not use it. The series ran in The Ludgate *magazine from June 1896 to April 1897, but only seven of the eleven stories were collected in* Belinda's Beaux, *published in 1897. For some reason the following story, which was the first in the series, appeared last in the book as "An Expiation." Several of the stories are macabre but only one other, "A Beautiful Vampire," verges on the fantastic.*

Arabella Kenealy (1859–1938) was a writer and physician. She was the daughter of the celebrated, some say notorious, Irish barrister Edward Vaughan Kenealy who was dismissed from the bar because of his conduct in court. She exhibited some of her father's inflexibility, such as her intractable view of the decline and degradation of the human race. She was an advocate of the now discredited theory of eugenics and her novel The Whips of Time *(1908) explores the idea of whether one's station in life is a result of nature or nurture. Kenealy may have had some psychic abilities herself, as recorded in her eccentric book* The Human Gyroscope *(1934) where she believed that, in certain conditions, she became telepathic and could sense others' strong emotions. Just like Lord Syfret.*

AT FORTY I HAD EXHAUSTED ALL THE RESOURCES OF CIVILISED LIFE. I had health, wealth, and position, yet I knew that unless I could devise some new expedient for passing time suicide would be my last sensation. As to whether suicide were justifiable or not I did not concern myself. I was bored and I did not purpose to continue being bored. Exploring my mental reserves I lighted upon a vein which, suitably worked, might profit me. I set about working it. So far I have done so successfully. Once more life is tolerable, occasionally exhilarating.

The vein is an insatiable and absorbing interest—curiosity—call it what you will—in other people's lives. Fiction has no charm for me. I am always conscious that its personages are but printer's ink. And I like my pages of story wet with the ink of life. I meet a man or a woman whose appearance or conditions stir me. By the expenditure of a little ingenuity, some trouble, and more or less hard cash, that person's story lies in my hand. Aided by a staff of well-drilled agents, whose duty I have made it to shadow in one capacity or another the fortunes of such persons as roused my curiosity—I am enabled to read their stories like a book. And, I tell you, few romances approach in interest some of the realities I have thus been able to trace. My right to peer into my fellows' lives may be denied. I myself have never considered the question. To do so amuses me. That is sanction enough for my morality.

It has occurred to me to record a few of the stories I have chanced upon. That thus set down they will interest others as they interested me who watched them as they were wrought in the forge of life I do not pretend. Yet they may serve for entertainment. As already stated my concern is purely psychological, or, if you prefer a simpler term, impertinent curiosity. With the right or wrong of things I do not meddle. Only in exceptional cases do I even trouble to put the law on the track of murder, though, in the course of their activities on my behalf, my agents should witness the commission of such a crime. For my part I prefer the delinquent to escape, that I may find, as I do, penalty closing in on him as an indirect consequence of his action, rather than that it shall take the clumsy form we dignify by the title of justice. Far crueller, subtler, and a hundredfold more fitting to a particular crime are the methods whereby time, character and circumstance enmesh the criminal. Expedient it may be to rid ourselves of the confessedly vicious. But the Powers which are moulding us to ends our finite minds have so far failed to grasp are neither assisted in their ultimate objects nor appeased in their far-reaching wrath—so to put it—by our crude expedients. The long arm of development which encompasses the human family and places effect in the unerring train of cause will find the murderer, many years it may be after we have done with him, but find him it will as inevitably as the impulse given to pool by pebble laps the shore.

How can it reach him after death? you ask. Death is but change of identity. Entities in the school of evolution pass through myriad lives in training for eternity, and the ill acts of one existence may not find expiation until a later one. A theory, you say. A theory, I admit. But I ask you for another that shall equally explain the inexplicabilities of human life. I have a story illustrative of my theory. Read into it any other interpretation that you will, and judge if it apply as mine does.

In a cottage on one of my estates a gamekeeper lived, some ten years since, with his young and pretty wife. He was middle-aged and morose, considering, as does many another, that the one cardinal virtue he practised—in his case that of honesty—absolved him from the obligation of practising any of the minor amenities and amiabilities of life. Nobody could imagine by what sorcery or fortuitous concomitance of accidents he had persuaded pretty Polly Penrose to mate with him. He had saved a certain sum of money, for to other unlovable qualities he added that of screw. Polly had swains better circumstanced than he, however, so that this offered no solution of the problem. The village wondered, chattered, and finally decided that "you could nivver calculate on what gells do, for they're chock full o' whimsies"; and so they let the matter drop. Cooper was but one of Polly's "whimsies."

It is probable I should never have concerned myself with Polly's affairs had I not one day come upon her crying her eyes out in a wood. On seeing me, she blushed and stole away. Matters just then were dull with me. I had no other case on hand; and, without anticipating much result, idly determined to trace the cause of Polly's tears. I had, among my agents, a girl of about her age and temperament; and, putting her to lodge in the village, she soon made Polly's acquaintance. It came out then that

Polly had married for pique. There was a certain stalwart sweetheart of hers—another of my keepers—of whom she was fond, but he rousing her jealousy by attention to a rival, in a fit of temper she accepted Cooper. To make a long story short—for this is but a preface—Polly and her lover made it up again too late, for Polly was then Mrs. Cooper.

Polly was a good girl, and I do not believe Cooper had any substantial reason for complaint, as she saw Dell but rarely. But she grew pallid and depressed. Occasionally she was seen with Dell. The circumstances reaching Cooper's ears, with doubtless some embellishment, there was trouble in the cottage. Cooper even went so far as to strike her. In her fear and agitation—the poor girl was soon to be a mother—she fled to Dell.

Cooper, following, found her in a shed near the latter's cottage. From words the men passed to blows, and eventually Dell struck Cooper over the head with the butt-end of his gun. Whether he meant murder or not, who can say? but a long acquaintance with the poor fellow makes me confident the impulse was momentary and uncontrollable. But murder it turned out. Cooper's skull was fractured and he died in a few hours.

Dell made no effort to escape. His one fear seems to have been for Polly. He remained with her in the cottage, soothing and re-assuring her till he was handcuffed and taken to gaol. I did all I could on his behalf. I even had the gaol-lock tampered with. I had an instinct of what would happen should his case come to trial, and hanging was the last death for the fine young fellow he was.

I was a magistrate and could easily have contrived his escape. But the blockhead would not take his liberty. He could not now marry Polly he said, and he did not care for life.

A thick-skulled jury, directed by a judge who on the Bench was as keen a stickler for the proprieties as off the Bench he was obtuse about them, put the worst—and, I believe, the false—construction on Dell's and Polly's fondness. He was convicted of murder and sentenced to death. Under the circumstances, it was a monstrous sentence. There had been assuredly no premeditation, and his provocation was great. We petitioned the Home Secretary; we petitioned Parliament. We might have spared our signatures and ink. When Dell's time came he was hanged. And now comes the gist of my story.

I filled up the places left vacant by Dell and his victim, putting in two keepers from a distance. There was a strong local feeling against the occupation of either of the cottages. Presently it was rumoured that the shed wherein the murder had occurred was haunted. But the new keepers, unaffected by the tragedy which to them was merely hearsay, pooh-poohed the rumour.

Curiously enough, the wife of one turned out to be a distant cousin of Dell's. She was a buxom person, strong-nerved and braced with common sense. She scoffed at ghost-talk.

"Depend on it, your lordship," she said once to me, "there's a deal more to be afeart on in the livin' than the dead; and as long as it's noboddy comin' to meddle wi' Johnson's belongins, why, let the poor things, if things there be, come an' go as it pleases 'em."

I mention this to free my story from an implication to which it may presently seem open. Mrs. Johnson was as unimpressionable a woman as could be and was as little affected by the talk of ghosts as she would have been by their apparition.

Now the ghost which was said to walk and to have been seen by more than one person, was not, as I have gathered is the way of ghosts, the shade of the murdered man, but that of his murderer. All who had caught the fleeting glimpse—which is as much as the ghost-seer generally permits himself—agreed that the apparition haunting the wood-shed was Dell's. Round and round in a restricted circle, skirting the space whereon a ghastly form had stretched, the ghost was seen to pass. Its head was bent, its face leaned down. Its eyes stared, frozen with horror. Moans and sighs of the direst distress were heard to issue from the shed. But the man from whom I had a description, a tramp who, unwitting of its reputation, had stolen there one rainy evening for the purpose of a night's lodging, described the thing he saw as mute and noiseless, making a dumb and ceaseless circuit of the floor. To him the circuit taken by the apparition was but a stretch of dusty boards, but the stark horror in the shadow's eyes told of some ghastly visibility.

The man was green with fright. He had lain there staring nearly all the night, afraid to move, afraid almost to breathe, lest he should turn the horror of the eyes upon himself. He painted in the vivid speech of panic the curious effect of morning: how as the light grew, it left less and still less of the apparition visible, how from being something luminous against the darkness it passed into a thin translucent shade against the light, how the outlines slowly faded and the form was lost, yet he could see it whirling like a grey smoke round and round six feet of floor. When the sun came up it slipped away as mist slips into air. In the morning when the man was brought to me he was piebald. The hair and beard of one side had gone white in the night.

A time came when the ghost was seen no more. The sighs and moanings ceased. Still the shed lost no whit of its evil reputation.

A year after the Johnsons' advent to the cottage, a child was born to them. They had already several children—buxom, cherry-cheeked youngsters, after the type of their mother. This child was different. The difference did not show at first. The infant was as other infants—a mere homogeneous mass of red-pink flesh, with the slate-grey eyes of its kind; eyes that deluded mothers call dark or light according to their fancy, for the rest of the world perceives that not until long after seeing the light do babies' eyes take on the shade they eventually keep. But this infant, though like enough to others, differed from them in one particular—it had a large blood-red spot in the palm of its right hand. The doctor pronounced the spot merely accidental and ephemeral; it would disappear before the week was out. Subsequently he modified his opinion. It was a variety of naevus, but he considered that it did not call for operation. The child would outgrow it. But the doctor was wrong. As the palm grew the blood-spot grew, and its colour did not wane. Presently, when the child assumed with age the waxen whiteness that afterwards characterised it, the spot had a curious effect of focussing all the blood in its body. As the baby slowly evolved an individuality out of its pink homogeneousness, it was seen to differ singularly from the rest of the Johnson children. In the place of their fair chubbiness, it was pallid and dark. Its brows were strongly and sombrely marked, and its eyes gathered slowly a look of weird horror. It cried rarely or never. Nor did it smile. It sat staring before it with a fixed expression and a blood-red palm upturned.

A child is born with its hands knotted into fists, fists which for months are opened with difficulty. It is an instinctive action of grasping the life before it. A man or woman dies with the palms extended. The life has been

63

wrought and is rendered up. The Johnson baby never curled its fists as normal babies do. It held its palms limply open with the blood-red spot for all to see. The villagers talked as villagers always talk of something out of the common. They drew conclusions—the short-sighted conclusions of their kind. They pronounced the child's uncanniness a judgment on the mother for her scoffing.

"It don't do to make light o' they things," they croaked. They predicted the baby's early death. The child attracted my attention from the first. I got a curious impression about it. Its face had a familiar look. The horror in its eyes reminded me of something. It was not until later that I knew of what.

I had a vacant cottage near. In it I installed an elderly woman of observant faculty. She made friends with the mother, and having leisure took the infant frequently off her hands. By her means I am able to relate what happened. So soon as it showed signs of intelligence—signs such as those used to children interpret, while to others they are still meaningless—the Johnson baby developed interest in the haunted shed—now, it must be remembered, no longer haunted.

The moment it was taken out of doors its eyes turned in the direction of the building, that stood but a short distance from the cottage. It was restless and wayward out of sight of it, and would weary and fret with inarticulate demands until carried whence it could see it. So soon as it was able, it would drag itself along the floor and out at the door to sit there with hands on tiny knees, staring with fascinated looks.

Before it was ten months old, it was found, having crept across the patch of ground between the house and shed, tired with its efforts, lying extended on the grass, its waxen face turned solemnly upon the building, its eyes fixed. Later it managed to escape attention long enough to reach the shed, shuffling along as infants do on hands and legs. It was discovered crouching at the open door, its head dropt till its chin rested almost in its lap, its pupils wide upon some portion of the floor. An illness followed, and for some weeks the child's life was in danger. It had taken a chill, the doctor said. Even then, though weakened with fever, the poor little creature left for a moment, would struggle feebly to the foot of the bed, whence through the window a corner of the shed was visible. There it would be found staring with grave, frightened eyes.

When strong enough to be up again it made always for the window, to stand there with its face pressed close against the glass. The doctor diagnosed the child as weak-minded, but I cannot say the term at all described the terrible intelligence that looked out of its eyes. The women shook their heads.

"It knows too much, poor little dear," they said. "There isn't nothing that's said it don't know. If anybody could find out what it's always askin' in its eyes per'aps it ud be able to die quiet, for anybody can see it ain't long for this world."

Mrs. Johnson paid but little heed to all the talk.

"I don't see anything much different in the child from other children," she said impatiently, "only it don't thrive. I expect it'll be stronger on its legs when it's got its teeth and can take a bit o' meat wi' the rest of us."

But the child grew no stronger on its legs, nor did it grow the least bit less unlike the chubby-cheeked Johnson brood. It seemed to have no wish to walk. It was a patient little thing, and when planted by a chair would stand there; but so soon as attention was drawn from it, it would drop to its hands and knees again, and creep to the door.

Johnson made a little fence, to keep it from straying; but it developed a weird sagacity for evading this, wriggling through or clambering over, or escaping by a back door. Then, if not intercepted, it would work its way across the patch of ground till it reached the doorway of the shed. There it would sit for hours together, straining its eyes upon some portion of the floor—always the same portion. Rain, snow, or wind it minded not. Frequently it was found squatted there in the entrance, wet to the skin, with a heavy rain beating on it, to all appearance unconscious of its wet and chilled condition—its gaze and powers magnetised. It took but little food and was a puny, miserable morsel. Such food as it took, it took mechanically and in obedience to its mother. It never seemed hungry, or interested, as babies are interested, in the sweet and edible.

It did not play, nor did it seem to have a notion of the use of toys. A doll or painted ball it would turn seriously over in its fingers, then lay aside with a quaint solemnity as though it had weightier matters on hand. Its only comfort was its thumb, which it sucked gravely, and with a thoughtful sobriety as of an old man smoking a pipe. It had no fear of darkness. It was found in the shed at dead of night, having scrambled stealthily from its cot, down the cottage stairs and out at the door. Sometimes it sat at a distance gazing spell-bound. Generally it spent its time shuffling round and round a certain area of floor dragging itself laboriously on hands and knees as one doing penance.

The villagers grew scared at it, and whispered that it had the evil eye. They would turn back to avoid passing it in the road. I have had boys thrashed for stoning it. Even its matter-of-fact mother came to have a horror of it, with its weird ways and terrible eyes. Yet it was patient and gave no trouble, so long as it were permitted to be in the shed. Its limbs, they told me, were raw and red, from the continuous rub of the boards against its baby skin. And the nails of toes and fingers were worn to the quick with its ceaseless clambering.

That the child suffered mentally, I cannot say. Possibly not. It seemed to gather satisfaction from its treadmill labours, though there was always that horror in its eyes.

"Perhaps your lordship would be pleased to come and see it," my agent suggested one day, when I chanced to pass the Johnson cottage. "Mrs. Johnson has gone into the village. The baby was shut in, but it has got out somehow and crept to the shed."

I followed her. We went quietly; but I doubt if the child would have heard in any case, so absorbed was it. We watched it through the window. Its frock and feet were stained with the soil over which it had dragged itself. The day was damp, and mud clung about its hands. But it minded nothing. In the half-sitting, half-kneeling posture of creeping children it dragged itself sideways round and round a circle encompassing some six feet of floor—six feet in length and from three to four in breadth. Dust lay thick on the boards, so that the circuit made by it was clearly traced. It went always over the same ground, marking a curious zigzagged shape. Round and round, now up, now down, tracing the same inexplicable course it plodded, a thick dust rising on either side to the infantile flop of its skirts.

Its face was bent towards the centre of the trail it followed, its eyes rivetted. Sweat stood moist on its skin, and in the moisture dust clung, giving it a dark, unearthly look. It sighed and panted at its task. Every now and again it would cease from utter weariness and, sitting up, would lift its dusty frock and wipe its lips. After a minute it resumed its treadmill round. I went in. It lifted its awed and grimy countenance and looked at me with that terrible intelligence. Then it resumed its dusty way.

I took it up and sat it on a pile of wood. It whined and fretted, stretching its arms to the shape on the floor. I left it where it was and, crossing the shed, stood looking down upon the figure it had traced. I could make nothing of it. It was an irregular oblong of indefinite form, wider to one end, narrowing to the other. A grim thought struck me that it resembled a coffin. I was interested. What was the meaning of it all? What, if anything, did those weird eyes see? I bade the woman bring some cake or sweets. She came back with an orange.

"He'll do anything for an orange," she said.

I made her take the child and set him on the floor to one side of the figure. I placed myself on the other. The oblong was between us at its widest part. I held the orange up and beckoned him.

"Go get it!" the woman urged.

He gazed at me questioningly, as though probing my intention. His eyes rested on the orange; then something that in another child would have been a smile floated over his face. He set out, creeping toward me. I watched him intently. Would he cross that circle? He came on, shuffling slowly, raising a cloud of dust. But when he reached the further limit of the oblong, he stopped short. He turned his face down and bent his looks on something that he seemed to see within the circle—something about the level of his eyes.

I stamped my foot and called to him. He looked up curiously but did not move. I held the orange toward him. He stretched his hand out, raising it carefully as though to prevent it coming into contact with the something that was there.

"Come," I said.

His eyes again levelled. They travelled slowly over that I could not see. Then he looked up at me, dully reproachful.

"Come," I called again, tossing the orange.

He shook his head with a grave, old-man solemnity. I stamped my foot once more.

"Come," I insisted.

His lips quivered feebly. Tears came into his eyes. Suddenly his features quickened with a new sagacity. He swerved aside and came creeping to me round the outer edge of the figure he had traced, bending his looks with an awed avoidance upon that he saw there. I tried a dozen times. But he would not cross the line. He scanned me plaintively. Why did I so torment him?

I took him in my arms. I carried him toward the charmed circle. Looking back I can see that the act was a brutal one, such a brutal one as the curiosity we dignify by the terms intellectual or scientific is frequently guilty of. But the woman stopped me. She caught him out of my arms.

"For heaven's sake, don't, my lord," she gasped, "I did it once. I thought he would have died."

Thank goodness she was in time! I looked down into his face. Poor little wretch! There was all the dumb agony of a ripe intelligence frozen on it. He clung to me strenuously, turning his rigid looks from that over which we stood. I gave him to her.

"Take him away. Get the poor little wretch out into the air. Give him the orange. Give him anything—only drive that look from his face." She took him out. He turned a shuddering head over her shoulder seeking that spot. It was the spot where Cooper had lain. I knew it now. He had lain there stretched full length, and over him Dell had stood with stricken eyes. Heavens! Why had the child those eyes? And why had it been cursed with this terrible vision? Had re-birth come so soon? Were the retributive forces of murder thus expiating in a little child?

I stood looking down at the figure traced in dust. I thrust my stick into it. Did I really feel a dull resistance? I lowered my hand to within some inches of the floor. Was the air really chill? Pshaw! The babe had infected me. It was but a draught from the door. As I stood my stick slipped from my hold, and sliding stopped between the curves composing the lower end of the oblong. A tree-branch, stirred by the wind, shot its shadow through the doorway immediately across the tracery. In a moment, as a few strokes put to outlines which had had no meaning gather the lines into life, so now the unmeaning tracery took shape. The stick formed a line of demarcation between extended legs, a limb of the shadow-tree lay like an outstretched arm and hand. Even for a moment convulsing features were given to a curve that might have been a face, as a flicker of twigs and fluttering leaves hurried like vanishing pencil marks across the outline. In that moment the murdered body of Cooper was reproduced as I had seen it. I am sufficiently strong-nerved. Yet I admit I turned sick. I picked up my stick and went out.

I knew now that what had been momentarily visible to me was ever before the doomed baby, that to its eyes the murdered man was always there. I felt my hair lift as though an ice-wind swept under my hat.

I had the shed pulled down. I had the ground it covered sown with flowers. But the spot kept its old fascination for the poor little creature. He could not now drag round it, the way being barred. But he sat for hours tracing with waxen fingers something that for him lay there, something that to us was but space between flower-stalks.

I sent him to the sea, a hundred miles away. In three days his life was despaired of. His impulse in living was gone. He fell into a state of stupor. He revived when brought back. He dragged himself out to the flower-bed and sat there crooning with a kind of plaintive content, tracing that outline with his pallid hands.

One morning they found him dead there. He had crept from his cot at some time during the night and had scrambled in the darkness—he never learned to walk—to the old spot. Rain was falling, and he lay on his back with face upturned and wet, his fair hair limp about him. His brows were unbent and tranquil, through his half-unclosed lids at last peace looked. The flowers stood round him like gentle sentinels, their flower-cups full of rain as eyes with tears. For the first time in his life the smile of a child lay over his lips. And the blood-spot in his palm was white as wool.

THE MYSTERY OF THE FELWYN TUNNEL

L. T. MEADE & ROBERT EUSTACE

With John Bell we reach our first true psychic investigator. He tells of his own origins in A Master of Mysteries *(1898) in which these stories were collected after being serialized in* Cassell's Magazine, *during 1897. "From my earliest youth the weird, the mysterious had an irresistible fascination for me. Having private means, I resolved to follow my unique inclinations, and I am now well known to all my friends as a professional exposer of ghosts, and one who can clear away the mysteries of most haunted houses." His use of the word "professional" is key here. This is no amateur seeker of the curious, or a doctor who occasionally encounters the bizarre, but a true explorer of the unexplained. Although Meade makes no specific reference to the Society for Psychical Research, Bell is clearly modeled on those who worked for the Society, such as Frank Podmore or Edmund Gurney. Like them, Bell looks for a natural solution to the mystery.*

Elizabeth Thomasina Meade (1844–1914), usually known as Lillie, was a prolific Irish-born writer, producing some 280 books in her near forty-year career. She wrote for all ages and became highly collectible for her books for girls, being voted the top writer of girls' school stories. She edited the magazine for adolescent girls, Atalanta, *from 1887 to 1893, but once freed from the shackles of editorial duties her output rocketed. She became a regular contributor to the newly emerging popular illustrated magazines of the day such as* The Strand *and* Cassell's *producing a breathtaking number of series. To help her in her research she relied on a couple of doctor friends who became pseudonymous collaborators, firstly Clifford Halifax, who was really Edgar Beaumont (1860–1921), and then Robert Eustace, who was Eustace Robert Barton (1868–1943). The series included* Stories from the Diary of a Doctor *(1894, with a second series, 1896),* The Brotherhood of the Seven Kings *(1899), and* The Sorceress of the Strand *(1903). One short series that ran in* Pearson's Magazine *in 1902 introduced Diana Marburg who, while not an occult detective, nevertheless solved normal crimes through the reading of palms.*

Meade became something of a figurehead for the suffragette movement as an example of a woman who could earn her own way in the world. She was a leading figure in the Pioneer Club for progressive women. She married the solicitor Alfred Toulmin-Smith with whom she had a son and two daughters.

I WAS MAKING EXPERIMENTS OF SOME INTEREST AT SOUTH Kensington, and hoped that I had perfected a small but not unimportant discovery, when, on returning home one evening in late October in the year 1893, I found a visiting card on my table. On it were inscribed the words, "Mr. Geoffrey Bainbridge." This name was quite unknown to me, so I rang the bell and inquired of my servant who the visitor had been. He described him as a gentleman who wished to see me on most urgent business, and said further that Mr. Bainbridge intended to call again later in the evening. It was with both curiosity and vexation that I awaited the return of the stranger. Urgent business with me generally meant a hurried rush to one part of the country or the other. I did not want to leave London just then; and when at half-past nine Mr. Geoffrey Bainbridge was ushered into my room, I received him with a certain coldness which he could not fail to perceive. He was a tall, well-dressed, elderly man. He immediately plunged into the object of his visit.

"I hope you do not consider my unexpected presence an intrusion, Mr. Bell," he said. "But I have heard of you from our mutual friends, the Greys of Uplands. You may remember once doing that family a great service."

"I remember perfectly well," I answered more cordially. "Pray tell me what you want; I shall listen with attention."

"I believe you are the one man in London who can help me," he continued. "I refer to a matter especially relating to your own particular study. I need hardly say that whatever you do will not be unrewarded."

"That is neither here nor there," I said; "but before you go any further, allow me to ask one question. Do you want me to leave London at present?"

He raised his eyebrows in dismay.

"I certainly do," he answered.

"Very well; pray proceed with your story."

He looked at me with anxiety.

"In the first place," he began, "I must tell you that I am chairman of the Lytton Vale Railway Company in Wales, and that it is on an important matter connected with our line that I have come to consult you. When I explain to you the nature of the mystery, you will not wonder, I think, at my soliciting your aid."

"I will give you my closest attention," I answered; and then I added, impelled to say the latter words by a certain expression on his face, "if I can see my way to assisting you I shall be ready to do so."

"Pray accept my cordial thanks," he replied. "I have come up from my place at Felwyn today on purpose to consult you. It is in that neighbourhood that the affair has occurred. As it is essential that you should be in possession of the facts of the whole matter, I will go over things just as they happened."

I bent forward and listened attentively.

"This day fortnight," continued Mr. Bainbridge, "our quiet little village was horrified by the news that the signalman on duty at the mouth of the Felwyn Tunnel had been found dead under the most mysterious circumstances. The tunnel is at the end of a long cutting between Llanlys and Felwyn stations. It is about a mile long, and the signal-box is on the Felwyn side. The place is extremely lonely, being six miles from the village across the mountains. The name of the poor fellow who met his death in this mysterious fashion was David Pritchard. I have known him from a boy, and he was quite one of the steadiest and most trustworthy men on the line. On Tuesday evening he went on duty at six o'clock; on Wednesday morning the day-man who had come to relieve him was surprised not to find him in the box. It was just getting daylight, and the 6.30 local was coming down, so he pulled the signals and let her through. Then he went out, and, looking up the line towards the tunnel, saw Pritchard lying beside the line close to the mouth of the tunnel. Roberts, the day-man, ran up to him and found, to his horror, that he was quite dead. At first Roberts naturally supposed that he had been cut down by a train, as there was a wound at the back of the head; but he was not lying on the metals. Roberts ran back to the box and telegraphed through to Felwyn Station. The message was sent on to the village, and at half-past seven o'clock the police inspector came up to my house with the news. He and I, with the local doctor, went off at once to the tunnel. We found the dead man lying beside the metals a few yards away from the mouth of the tunnel, and the doctor immediately gave him a careful examination. There was a depressed fracture at the back of the skull, which must have caused his death; but how he came by it was not so clear. On examining the whole place most carefully, we saw, further, that there were marks on the rocks at the steep side of the embankment as if some one had tried to scramble up them. Why the poor fellow had attempted such a climb, God only knows. In doing so he must have slipped and fallen back on to the line, thus causing the fracture of the skull. In no case could he have gone up more than eight or ten feet, as the banks of the cutting run sheer up, almost perpendicularly, beyond that point for more than a hundred and fifty feet. There are some sharp boulders beside the line, and it was possible that he might have fallen on one of these and so sustained the injury. The affair must have occurred some time between 11.45 p.m. and 6 a.m., as the engine-driver of the express at 11.45 p.m. states that the line was signalled clear, and he also caught sight of Pritchard in his box as he passed."

"This is deeply interesting," I said; "pray proceed."

Bainbridge looked at me earnestly; he then continued—"The whole thing is shrouded in mystery. Why should Pritchard have left his box and gone down to the tunnel? Why, having done so, should he have made a wild attempt to scale the side of the cutting, an impossible feat at any time? Had danger threatened, the ordinary course of things would have been to run up the line towards the signal-box. These points are quite unexplained.

Another curious fact is that death appears to have taken place just before the day-man came on duty, as the light at the mouth of the tunnel had been put out, and it was one of the night signalman's duties to do this as soon as daylight appeared; it is possible, therefore, that Pritchard went down to the tunnel for that purpose. Against this theory, however, and an objection that seems to nullify it, is the evidence of Dr. Williams, who states that when he examined the body his opinion was that death had taken place some hours before. An inquest was held on the following day, but before it took place there was a new and most important development. I now come to what I consider the crucial point in the whole story.

"For a long time there had been a feud between Pritchard and another man of the name of Wynne, a platelayer on the line. The object of their quarrel was the blacksmith's daughter in the neighbouring village—a remarkably pretty girl and an arrant flirt. Both men were madly in love with her, and she played them off one against the other. The night but one before his death Pritchard and Wynne had met at the village inn, had quarrelled in the bar—Lucy, of course, being the subject of their difference. Wynne was heard to say (he was a man of powerful build and subject to fits of ungovernable rage) that he would have Pritchard's life. Pritchard swore a great oath that he would get Lucy on the following day to promise to marry him. This oath, it appears, he kept, and on his way to the signal-box on Tuesday evening met Wynne, and triumphantly told him that Lucy had promised to be his wife. The men had a hand-to-hand fight on the spot, several people from the village being witnesses of it. They were separated with difficulty, each vowing vengeance on the other. Pritchard went off to his duty at the signal-box and Wynne returned to the village to drown his sorrows at the public-house.

"Very late that same night Wynne was seen by a villager going in the direction of the tunnel. The man stopped him and questioned him. He explained that he had left some of his tools on the line and was on his way to fetch them. The villager noticed that he looked queer and excited, but not wishing to pick a quarrel thought it best not to question him further. It has been proved that Wynne never returned home that night but came back at an early hour on the following morning, looking dazed and stupid. He was arrested on suspicion, and at the inquest the verdict was against him."

"Has he given any explanation of his own movements?" I asked.

"Yes; but nothing that can clear him. As a matter of fact, his tools were nowhere to be seen on the line, nor did he bring them home with him. His own story is that being considerably the worse for drink, he had fallen down in one of the fields and slept there till morning."

"Things look black against him," I said.

"They do; but listen, I have something more to add. Here comes a very queer feature in the affair. Lucy Ray, the girl who had caused the feud between Pritchard and Wynne, after hearing the news of Pritchard's death, completely lost her head and ran frantically about the village declaring that Wynne was the man she really loved, and that she had only accepted Pritchard in a fit of rage with Wynne for not himself bringing matters to the point. The case looks very bad against Wynne, and yesterday the magistrate committed him for trial at the coming assizes. The unhappy Lucy Ray and the young man's parents are in a state bordering on distraction."

"What is your own opinion with regard to Wynne's guilt?" I asked.

"Before God, Mr. Bell, I believe the poor fellow is innocent, but the evidence against him is very strong. One of the favourite theories is that he went down to the tunnel and extinguished the light, knowing that this would bring Pritchard out of his box to see what was the matter, and that he then attacked him, striking the blow which fractured the skull."

"Has any weapon been found about, with which he could have given such a blow?"

"No; nor has anything of the kind been discovered on Wynne's person; that fact is decidedly in his favour."

"But what about the marks on the rocks?" I asked.

"It is possible that Wynne may have made them in order to divert suspicion by making people think that Pritchard must have fallen, and so killed himself. The holders of this theory base their belief on the absolute want of cause for Pritchard's trying to scale the rock. The whole thing is the most absolute enigma. Some of the country folk have declared that the tunnel is haunted (and there certainly has been such a rumour current among them for years). That Pritchard saw some apparition, and in wild terror sought to escape from it by climbing the rocks, is another theory, but only the most imaginative hold it."

"Well, it is a most extraordinary case," I replied.

"Yes, Mr. Bell, and I should like to get your opinion of it. Do you see your way to elucidate the mystery?"

"Not at present; but I shall be happy to investigate the matter to my utmost ability."

"But you do not wish to leave London at present?"

"That is so; but a matter of such importance cannot be set aside. It appears, from what you say, that Wynne's life hangs more or less on my being able to clear away the mystery?"

"That is indeed the case. There ought not to be a single stone left unturned to get at the truth, for the sake of Wynne. Well, Mr. Bell, what do you propose to do?"

"To see the place without delay," I answered.

"That is right; when can you come?"

"Whenever you please."

"Will you come down to Felwyn with me tomorrow? I shall leave Paddington by the 7.10 and, if you will be my guest, I shall be only too pleased to put you up."

"That arrangement will suit me admirably," I replied. "I will meet you by the train you mention, and the affair shall have my best attention."

"Thank you," he said, rising. He shook hands with me and took his leave.

The next day I met Bainbridge at Paddington Station, and we were soon flying westward in the luxurious private compartment that had been reserved for him. I could see by his abstracted manner and his long lapses of silence that the mysterious affair at Felwyn Tunnel was occupying all his thoughts.

It was two o'clock in the afternoon when the train slowed down at the little station of Felwyn. The station-master was at the door in an instant to receive us.

"I have some terribly bad news for you, sir," he said, turning to Bainbridge as we alighted; "and yet in one sense it is a relief, for it seems to clear Wynne."

"What do you mean?" cried Bainbridge. "Bad news? Speak out at once!"

"Well, sir, it is this: there has been another death at Felwyn signal-box. John Davidson, who was on duty last night, was found dead at an early hour this morning in the very same place where we found poor Pritchard."

"Good God!" cried Bainbridge, starting back, "what an awful thing! What, in the name of Heaven, does it mean, Mr. Bell? This is too fearful. Thank goodness you have come down with us."

"It is as black a business as I ever heard of, sir," echoed the station-master; "and what we are to do I don't know. Poor Davidson was found dead this morning, and there was neither mark nor sign of what killed him— that is the extraordinary part of it. There's a perfect panic abroad, and not a signalman on the line will take duty tonight. I was quite in despair and was afraid at one time that the line would have to be closed, but at last it occurred to me to wire to Lytton Vale, and they are sending down an inspector. I expect him by a special every moment. I believe this is he coming now," added the station-master, looking up the line.

There was the sound of a whistle down the valley, and in a few moments a single engine shot into the station, and an official in uniform stepped on to the platform.

"Good-evening, sir," he said, touching his cap to Bainbridge; "I have just been sent down to inquire into this affair at the Felwyn Tunnel, and though it seems more of a matter for a Scotland Yard detective than one of ourselves, there was nothing for it but to come. All the same, Mr. Bainbridge, I cannot say that I look forward to spending tonight alone at the place."

"You wish for the services of a detective, but you shall have someone better," said Bainbridge, turning towards me. "This gentleman, Mr. John Bell, is the man of all others for our business. I have just brought him down from London for the purpose."

An expression of relief flitted across the inspector's face.

"I am very glad to see you, sir," he said to me, "and I hope you will be able to spend the night with me in the signal-box. I must say I don't much relish the idea of tackling the thing single-handed; but with your help, sir, I think we ought to get to the bottom of it somehow. I am afraid there is not a man on the line who will take duty until we do. So, it is most important that the thing should be cleared, and without delay."

I readily assented to the inspector's proposition, and Bainbridge and I arranged that we should call for him at four o'clock at the village inn and drive him to the tunnel.

We then stepped into the wagonette which was waiting for us and drove to Bainbridge's house.

Mrs. Bainbridge came out to meet us and was full of the tragedy. Two pretty girls also ran to greet their father, and to glance inquisitively at me. I could see that the entire family was in a state of much excitement.

"Lucy Ray has just left, father," said the elder of the girls. "We had much trouble to soothe her; she is in a frantic state."

"You have heard, Mr. Bell, all about this dreadful mystery?" said Mrs. Bainbridge as she led me towards the dining-room.

"Yes," I answered; "your husband has been good enough to give me every particular."

"And you have really come here to help us?"

"I hope I may be able to discover the cause," I answered.

"It certainly seems most extraordinary," continued Mrs. Bainbridge. "My dear," she continued, turning to her husband, "you can easily imagine the state we were all in this morning when the news of the second death was brought to us."

"For my part," said Ella Bainbridge, "I am sure that Felwyn Tunnel is haunted. The villagers have thought so for a long time, and this second death seems to prove it, does it not?" Here she looked anxiously at me.

"I can offer no opinion," I replied, "until I have sifted the matter thoroughly."

"Come, Ella, don't worry Mr. Bell," said her father; "if he is as hungry as I am, he must want his lunch."

We then seated ourselves at the table and commenced the meal. Bainbridge, although he professed to be hungry, was in such a state of excitement that he could scarcely eat. Immediately after lunch he left me to the care of his family and went into the village.

"It is just like him," said Mrs. Bainbridge; "he takes these sort of things to heart dreadfully. He is terribly upset about Lucy Ray, and also about the poor fellow Wynne. It is certainly a fearful tragedy from first to last."

"Well, at any rate," I said, "this fresh death will upset the evidence against Wynne."

"I hope so, and there is some satisfaction in the fact. Well, Mr. Bell, I see you have finished lunch; will you come into the drawing-room?"

I followed her into a pleasant room overlooking the valley of the Lytton.

By-and-by Bainbridge returned, and soon afterwards the dog-cart came to the door. My host and I mounted, Bainbridge took the reins, and we started off at a brisk pace.

"Matters get worse and worse," he said the moment we were alone. "If you don't clear things up tonight, Bell, I say frankly that I cannot imagine what will happen."

We entered the village, and as we rattled down the ill-paved streets I was greeted with curious glances on all sides. The people were standing about in groups, evidently talking about the tragedy and nothing else. Suddenly, as our trap bumped noisily over the paving-stones, a girl darted out of one of the houses and made frantic motions to Bainbridge to stop the horse. He pulled the mare nearly up on her haunches, and the girl came up to the side of the dog-cart.

"You have heard it?" she said, speaking eagerly and in a gasping voice. "The death which occurred this morning will clear Stephen Wynne, won't it, Mr. Bainbridge?—it will, you are sure, are you not?"

"It looks like it, Lucy, my poor girl," he answered. "But there, the whole thing is so terrible that I scarcely know what to think."

She was a pretty girl with dark eyes, and under ordinary circumstances must have had the vivacious expression of face and the brilliant complexion which so many of her countrywomen possess. But now her eyes were swollen with weeping and her complexion more or less disfigured by the agony she had gone through. She looked piteously at Bainbridge, her lips trembling. The next moment she burst into tears.

"Come away, Lucy," said a woman who had followed her out of the cottage; "Fie—for shame! don't trouble the gentlemen; come back and stay quiet."

"I can't, mother, I can't," said the unfortunate girl. "If they hang him, I'll go clean off my head. Oh, Mr. Bainbridge, do say that the second death has cleared him!"

"I have every hope that it will do so, Lucy," said Bainbridge, "but now don't keep us, there's a good girl; go back into the house. This gentleman has come down from London on purpose to look into the whole matter. I may have good news for you in the morning."

The girl raised her eyes to my face with a look of intense pleading. "Oh, I have been cruel and a fool, and I deserve everything," she gasped; "but, sir, for the love of Heaven, try to clear him."

I promised to do my best.

Bainbridge touched up the mare, she bounded forward, and Lucy disappeared into the cottage with her mother.

The next moment we drew up at the inn where the Inspector was waiting, and soon afterwards were bowling along between the high banks of the country lanes to the tunnel. It was a cold, still afternoon; the air was wonderfully keen, for a sharp frost had held the countryside in its grip for the last two days. The sun was just tipping the hills to westward when the trap pulled up at the top of the cutting. We hastily alighted, and the Inspector and I bade Bainbridge good-bye. He said that he only wished that he could stay with us for the night, assured us that little sleep would visit him, and that he would be back at the cutting at an early hour on the following morning; then the noise of his horse's feet was heard fainter and fainter as he drove back over the frost-bound roads. The Inspector and I ran along the little path to the wicket-gate in the fence, stamping our feet on the hard ground to restore circulation after our cold drive. The next moment we were looking down upon the scene of the mysterious deaths, and a weird and lonely place it looked. The tunnel was at one end of the rock cutting, the sides of which ran sheer down to the line for over a hundred and fifty feet. Above the tunnel's mouth the hills rose one upon the other. A more dreary place it would have been difficult to imagine. From a little clump of pines a delicate film of blue smoke rose straight up on the still air. This came from the chimney of the signal-box.

As we started to descend the precipitous path the Inspector sang out a cheery "Hullo!" The man on duty in the box immediately answered. His voice echoed and reverberated down the cutting, and the next moment he appeared at the door of the box. He told us that he would be with us immediately; but we called back to him to stay where he was, and the next instant the Inspector and I entered the box.

"The first thing to do," said Henderson the Inspector, "is to send a message down the line to announce our arrival."

This he did, and in a few moments a crawling goods train came panting up the cutting. After signalling her through we descended the wooden flight of steps which led from the box down to the line and walked along the metals towards the tunnel till we stood on the spot where poor Davidson had been found dead that morning. I examined the ground and all around it most carefully. Everything tallied exactly with the description I had received. There could be no possible way of approaching the spot except by going along the line, as the rocky sides of the cutting were inaccessible.

"It is a most extraordinary thing, sir," said the signalman whom we had come to relieve. "Davidson had neither mark nor sign on him—there he lay stone dead and cold, and not a bruise nowhere; but Pritchard had an awful wound at the back of the head. They said he got it by climbing the rocks—here, you can see the marks for yourself, sir. But now, is it likely that Pritchard would try to climb rocks like these, so steep as they are?"

"Certainly not," I replied.

"Then how do you account for the wound, sir?" asked the man with an anxious face.

"I cannot tell you at present," I answered.

"And you and Inspector Henderson are going to spend the night in the signal-box?"

"Yes."

A horrified expression crept over the signalman's face.

"God preserve you both," he said; "I wouldn't do it—not for fifty pounds. It's not the first time I have heard tell that Felwyn Tunnel is haunted. But, there, I won't say any more about that. It's a black business, and has given trouble enough. There's poor Wynne, the same thing as convicted of the murder of Pritchard; but now they say that Davidson's death will clear him. Davidson was as good a fellow as you would come across this side of the country; but for the matter of that, so was Pritchard. The whole thing is terrible—it upsets one, that it do, sir."

"I don't wonder at your feelings," I answered; "but now, see here, I want to make a most careful examination of everything. One of the theories is that Wynne crept down this rocky side and fractured Pritchard's skull. I believe such a feat to be impossible. On examining these rocks I see that a man might climb up the side of the tunnel as far as from eight to ten feet, utilising the sharp projections of rock for the purpose; but it would be out of the question for any man to come down the cutting. No; the only way Wynne could have approached Pritchard was by the line itself. But, after all, the real thing to discover is this," I continued: "what killed Davidson? Whatever caused his death is, beyond doubt, equally responsible for Pritchard's. I am now going into the tunnel."

Inspector Henderson went in with me. The place struck damp and chill. The walls were covered with green, evil-smelling fungi, and through the brickwork the moisture was oozing and had trickled down in long lines to the ground. Before us was nothing but dense darkness.

When we re-appeared the signalman was lighting the red lamp on the post, which stood about five feet from the ground just above the entrance to the tunnel.

"Is there plenty of oil?" asked the Inspector.

"Yes, sir, plenty," replied the man. "Is there anything more I can do for either of you gentlemen?" he asked, pausing, and evidently dying to be off.

"Nothing," answered Henderson; "I will wish you good-evening."

"Good-evening to you both," said the man. He made his way quickly up the path and was soon lost to sight.

Henderson and I then returned to the signal-box.

By this time it was nearly dark.

"How many trains pass in the night?" I asked of the Inspector.

"There's the 10.20 down express," he said, "it will pass here at about 10.40; then there's the 11.45 up, and then not another train till the 6.30 local tomorrow morning. We shan't have a very lively time," he added.

I approached the fire and bent over it, holding out my hands to try and get some warmth into them.

"It will take a good deal to persuade me to go down to the tunnel, whatever I may see there," said the man. "I don't think, Mr. Bell, I am a coward in any sense of the word, but there's something very uncanny about this place, right away from the rest of the world. I don't wonder one often hears of signalmen going mad in some of these lonely boxes. Have you any theory to account for these deaths, sir?"

"None at present," I replied.

"This second death puts the idea of Pritchard being murdered quite out of court," he continued.

"I am sure of it," I answered.

"And so am I, and that's one comfort," continued Henderson. "That poor girl, Lucy Ray, although she was to be blamed for her conduct, is much to be pitied now; and as to poor Wynne himself, he protests his innocence through thick and thin. He was a wild fellow, but not the sort to take the life of a fellow-creature. I saw the doctor this afternoon while I was waiting for you at the inn, Mr. Bell, and also the police sergeant. They both say they do not know what Davidson died of. There was not the least sign of violence on the body."

"Well, I am as puzzled as the rest of you," I said. "I have one or two theories in my mind, but none of them will quite fit the situation."

The night was piercingly cold, and, although there was not a breath of wind, the keen and frosty air penetrated into the lonely signal-box. We spoke little, and both of us were doubtless absorbed by our own thoughts and speculations. As to Henderson, he looked distinctly uncomfortable, and I cannot say that my own feelings were too pleasant. Never had I been given a tougher problem to solve, and never had I been so utterly at my wits' end for a solution.

Now and then the Inspector got up and went to the telegraph instrument, which intermittently clicked away in its box. As he did so he made some casual remark and then sat down again. After the 10.40 had gone through, there followed a period of silence which seemed almost oppressive. All at once the stillness was broken by the whirr of the electric bell, which sounded so sharply in our ears that we both started. Henderson rose.

"That's the 11.45 coming," he said, and, going over to the three long levers, he pulled two of them down with a loud clang. The next moment, with a rush and a scream, the express tore down the cutting, the carriage lights streamed past in a rapid flash, the ground trembled, a few sparks from the engine whirled up into the darkness, and the train plunged into the tunnel.

"And now," said Henderson, as he pushed back the levers, "not another train till daylight. My word, it is cold!"

It was intensely so. I piled some more wood on the fire and, turning up the collar of my heavy ulster, sat down at one end of the bench and leant my back against the wall. Henderson did likewise; we were neither of us inclined to speak. As a rule, whenever I have any night work to do, I am never troubled with sleepiness, but on this occasion I felt unaccountably drowsy. I soon perceived that Henderson was in the same condition.

"Are you sleepy?" I asked of him.

"Dead with it, sir," was his answer; "but there's no fear, I won't drop off."

I got up and went to the window of the box. I felt certain that if I sat still any longer I should be in a sound sleep. This would never do. Already it was becoming a matter of torture to keep my eyes open. I began to pace up and down; I opened the door of the box and went out on the little platform.

"What's the matter, sir?" inquired Henderson, jumping up with a start.

"I cannot keep awake," I said.

"Nor can I," he answered, "and yet I have spent nights and nights of my life in signal-boxes and never was the least bit drowsy; perhaps it's the cold."

"Perhaps it is," I said; "but I have been out on as freezing nights before, and—"

The man did not reply; he had sat down again; his head was nodding.

I was just about to go up to him and shake him, when it suddenly occurred to me that I might as well let him have his sleep out. I soon heard him snoring, and he presently fell forward in a heap on the floor. By dint of walking up and down, I managed to keep from dropping off myself, and in torture which I shall never be able to describe, the night wore itself away. At last, towards morning, I awoke Henderson.

"You have had a good nap," I said; "but never mind, I have been on guard and nothing has occurred."

"Good God! have I been asleep?" cried the man.

"Sound," I answered.

"Well, I never felt anything like it," he replied. "Don't you find the air very close, sir?"

"No," I said; "it is as fresh as possible; it must be the cold."

"I'll just go and have a look at the light at the tunnel," said the man; "it will rouse me."

He went on to the little platform, whilst I bent over the fire and began to build it up. Presently he returned with a scared look on his face. I could see by the light of the oil lamp which hung on the wall that he was trembling.

"Mr. Bell," he said, "I believe there is somebody or something down at the mouth of the tunnel now." As he spoke he clutched me by the arm. "Go and look," he said; "whoever it is, it has put out the light."

"Put out the light?" I cried. "Why, what's the time?"

Henderson pulled out his watch.

"Thank goodness, most of the night is gone," he said; "I didn't know it was so late, it is half-past five."

"Then the local is not due for an hour yet?" I said.

"No; but who should put out the light?" cried Henderson.

I went to the door, flung it open, and looked out. The dim outline of the tunnel was just visible looming through the darkness, but the red light was out.

"What the dickens does it mean, sir?" gasped the Inspector. "I know the lamp had plenty of oil in it. Can there be any one standing in front of it, do you think?"

We waited and watched for a few moments, but nothing stirred.

"Come along," I said, "let us go down together and see what it is."

"I don't believe I can do it, sir; I really don't!"

"Nonsense," I cried. "I shall go down alone if you won't accompany me. Just hand me my stick, will you?"

"For God's sake, be careful, Mr. Bell. Don't go down, whatever you do. I expect this is what happened before, and the poor fellows went down to see what it was and died there. There's some devilry at work, that's my belief."

"That is as it may be," I answered shortly; "but we certainly shall not find out by stopping here. My business is to get to the bottom of this, and I am going to do it. That there is danger of some sort, I have very little doubt; but danger or not, I am going down."

"If you'll be warned by me, sir, you'll just stay quietly here."

"I must go down and see the matter out," was my answer. "Now listen to me, Henderson. I see that you are alarmed, and I don't wonder. Just stay quietly where you are and watch, but if I call come at once. Don't delay a single instant. Remember I am putting my life into your hands. If I call 'Come,' just come to me as quick as you can, for I may want help. Give me that lantern."

He unhitched it from the wall, and taking it from him, I walked cautiously down the steps on to the line. I still felt curiously, unaccountably drowsy and heavy. I wondered at this, for the moment was such a critical one as to make almost any man wide awake. Holding the lamp high above my head, I walked rapidly along the line. I hardly knew what I expected to find. Cautiously along the metals I made my way, peering right and left until I was close to the fatal spot where the bodies had been found. An uncontrollable shudder passed over me. The next moment, to my horror, without the slightest warning, the light I was carrying went out, leaving me in total darkness. I started back, and stumbling against one of the loose boulders reeled against the wall and nearly fell. What was the matter with me? I could hardly stand. I felt giddy and faint, and a horrible sensation of great tightness seized me across the chest. A loud ringing noise sounded in my ears. Struggling madly for breath, and with the fear of impending death upon me, I turned and tried to run from a danger I could neither understand nor grapple with. But before I had taken two steps my legs gave way from under me, and uttering a loud cry I fell insensible to the ground.

Out of an oblivion which, for all I knew, might have lasted for moments or centuries, a dawning consciousness came to me. I knew that I was lying on hard ground; that I was absolutely incapable of realising, nor had I the slightest inclination to discover, where I was. All I wanted was to lie quite still and undisturbed. Presently I opened my eyes.

Some one was bending over me and looking into my face.

"Thank God, he is not dead," I heard in whispered tones. Then, with a flash, memory returned to me.

"What has happened?" I asked.

"You may well ask that, sir," said the Inspector gravely. "It has been touch and go with you for the last quarter of an hour; and a near thing for me too."

I sat up and looked around me. Daylight was just beginning to break, and I saw that we were at the bottom of the steps that led up to the signal-box. My teeth were chattering with the cold and I was shivering like a man with ague.

"I am better now," I said; "just give me your hand."

I took his arm, and holding the rail with the other hand staggered up into the box and sat down on the bench.

"Yes, it has been a near shave," I said; "and a big price to pay for solving a mystery."

"Do you mean to say you know what it is?" asked Henderson eagerly.

"Yes," I answered, "I think I know now; but first tell me how long was I unconscious?"

"A good bit over half an hour, sir, I should think. As soon as I heard you call out I ran down as you told me, but before I got to you I nearly fainted. I never had such a horrible sensation in my life. I felt as weak as a baby, but I just managed to seize you by the arms and drag you along the line to the steps, and that was about all I could do."

"Well, I owe you my life," I said; "just hand me that brandy flask, I shall be the better for some of its contents."

I took a long pull. Just as I was laying the flask down Henderson started from my side.

"There," he cried, "the 6.30 is coming." The electric bell at the instrument suddenly began to ring. "Ought I to let her go through, sir?" he inquired.

"Certainly," I answered. "That is exactly what we want. Oh, she will be all right."

"No danger to her, sir?"

"None, none; let her go through."

He pulled the lever and the next moment the train tore through the cutting.

"Now I think it will be safe to go down again," I said. "I believe I shall be able to get to the bottom of this business."

Henderson stared at me aghast.

"Do you mean that you are going down again to the tunnel?" he gasped.

"Yes," I said; "give me those matches. You had better come too. I don't think there will be much danger now; and there is daylight, so we can see what we are about."

The man was very loth to obey me, but at last I managed to persuade him. We went down the line, walking slowly, and at this moment we both felt our courage revived by a broad and cheerful ray of sunshine.

"We must advance cautiously," I said, "and be ready to run back at a moment's notice."

"God knows, sir, I think we are running a great risk," panted poor Henderson; "and if that devil or whatever else it is should happen to be about—why, daylight or no daylight—"

"Nonsense! man," I interrupted; "if we are careful, no harm will happen to us now. Ah! and here we are!" We had reached the spot where I had fallen. "Just give me a match, Henderson."

He did so, and I immediately lit the lamp. Opening the glass of the lamp, I held it close to the ground and passed it to and fro. Suddenly the flame went out.

"Don't you understand now?" I said, looking up at the Inspector.

"No, I don't, sir," he replied with a bewildered expression.

Suddenly, before I could make an explanation, we both heard shouts from the top of the cutting, and looking up I saw Bainbridge hurrying down the path. He had come in the dog-cart to fetch us.

"Here's the mystery," I cried as he rushed up to us, "and a deadlier scheme of Dame Nature's to frighten and murder poor humanity I have never seen."

As I spoke, I lit the lamp again and held it just above a tiny fissure in the rock. It was at once extinguished.

"What is it?" said Bainbridge, panting with excitement.

"Something that nearly finished *me*," I replied. "Why, this is a natural escape of choke damp. Carbonic acid gas—the deadliest gas imaginable, because it gives no warning of its presence, and it has no smell. It must have collected here during the hours of the night when no train was passing, and gradually rising put out the signal light. The constant rushing of the trains through the cutting all day would temporarily disperse it."

As I made this explanation Bainbridge stood like one electrified, while a curious expression of mingled relief and horror swept over Henderson's face.

"An escape of carbonic acid gas is not an uncommon phenomenon in volcanic districts," I continued, "as I take this to be; but it is odd what should have started it. It has sometimes been known to follow earthquake shocks, when there is a profound disturbance of the deep strata."

"It is strange that you should have said that," said Bainbridge, when he could find his voice.

"What do you mean?"

"Why, that about the earthquake. Don't you remember, Henderson," he added, turning to the Inspector, "we had felt a slight shock all over South Wales about three weeks back?"

"Then that, I think, explains it," I said. "It is evident that Pritchard really did climb the rocks in a frantic attempt to escape from the gas and fell back on to these boulders. The other man was cut down at once, before he had time to fly."

"But what is to happen now?" asked Bainbridge. "Will it go on for ever? How are we to stop it?"

"The fissure ought to be drenched with lime water, and then filled up; but all really depends on what is the size of the supply and also the depth. It is an extremely heavy gas, and would lie at the bottom of a cutting like water. I think there is more here just now than is good for us," I added.

"But how," continued Bainbridge, as we moved a few steps from the fatal spot, "do you account for the interval between the first death and the second?"

"The escape must have been intermittent. If wind blew down the cutting, as probably was the case before this frost set in, it would keep the gas so diluted that its effects would not be noticed. There was enough down here this morning, before that train came through, to poison an army. Indeed, if it had not been for Henderson's promptitude, there would have been another inquest—on myself."

I then related my own experience.

"Well, this clears Wynne, without doubt," said Bainbridge; "but alas! for the two poor fellows who were victims. Bell, the Lytton Vale Railway Company owe you unlimited thanks; you have doubtless saved many lives, and also the Company, for the line must have been closed if you had not made your valuable discovery. But now come home with me to breakfast. We can discuss all those matters later on."

THE STORY OF YAND MANOR HOUSE

E. & H. HERON

Most studies of the occult detective start with Flaxman Low, with some good reason, because here we have an individual who specializes in the study of strange phenomena from which he has developed a profound knowledge of the supernatural which, unlike the cases of John Bell, are at the core of his investigations. When we are introduced to him in "The Story of the Spaniards, Hammersmith," we are told that the name Flaxman Low is a "thin disguise" masking the identity of a psychologist and one of the leading scientists of his day. What's more he occasionally wrote up his cases for the Society for Psychical Research. This added to the general belief that the stories were true. When the first series appeared in Pearson's Magazine from January to June 1898 it ran under the heading "Real Ghost Stories" together with a picture of a haunted house. The series was so popular that a second ran from January to June 1899, all twelve then being issued in the now very rare volume, Ghosts (1899).

The byline E. and H. Heron hid the identities of a mother-and-son writing partnership Kate (1851–1935) and Hesketh (1876–1922) Prichard. They had most success with their series about the Spanish outlaw Don Q., which ran through several series and books starting in 1903. Kate was born in India in a military family and later married into another military family, also in India. Her husband died of typhoid just before young Hesketh was born and she returned to England to raise the boy, who was always known as Hex, on her own. He had a fine education and trained as a lawyer but never practised preferring to travel, play sport and, with his mother's help, write. Among his many skills he was a champion shot, and during the First World War he helped train soldiers as snipers. Unfortunately, his health failed, chiefly as a result of malaria, and he died of what we now call sepsis at the age of only forty-five. His mother survived him by thirteen years but did not return to writing.

By looking through the notes of Mr. Flaxman Low, one sometimes catches through the steel-blue hardness of facts, the pink flush of romance, or more often the black corner of a horror unnameable. The following story may serve as an instance of the latter. Mr. Low not only unravelled the mystery at Yand, but at the same time justified his life-work to M. Thierry, the well-known French critic and philosopher.

At the end of a long conversation, M. Thierry, arguing from his own standpoint as a materialist, had said:

"The factor in the human economy which you call 'soul' cannot be placed."

"I admit that," replied Low. "Yet, when a man dies, is there not one factor unaccounted for in the change that comes upon him? Yes! For though his body still exists, it rapidly falls to pieces, which proves that that has gone which held it together."

The Frenchman laughed and shifted his ground.

"Well, for my part, I don't believe in ghosts! Spirit manifestations, occult phenomena—is not this the ashbin into which a certain clique shoot everything they cannot understand, or for which they fail to account?"

"Then what should you say to me, Monsieur, if I told you that I have passed a good portion of my life in investigating this particular ashbin and have been lucky enough to sort a small part of its contents with tolerable success?" replied Flaxman Low.

"The subject is doubtless interesting—but I should like to have some personal experience in the matter," said Thierry dubiously.

"I am at present investigating a most singular case," said Low. "Have you a day or two to spare?"

Thierry thought for a minute or more.

"I am grateful," he replied. "But, forgive me, is it a convincing ghost?"

"Come with me to Yand and see. I have been there once already and came away for the purpose of procuring information from MSS. to which I have the privilege of access, for I confess that the phenomena at Yand lie altogether outside any former experience of mine."

Low sank back into his chair with his hands clasped behind his head—a favourite position of his—and the smoke of his long pipe curled up lazily into the golden face of an Isis, which stood behind him on a bracket. Thierry, glancing across, was struck by the strange likeness between the faces of the Egyptian goddess and this scientist of the nineteenth century. On both rested the calm, mysterious abstraction of some unfathomable thought. As he looked, he decided.

"I have three days to place at your disposal."

"I thank you heartily," replied Low. "To be associated with so brilliant a logician as yourself in an inquiry of this nature is more than I could have hoped for! The material with which I have to deal is so elusive, the whole subject is wrapped in such obscurity and hampered by so much prejudice, that I can find few really qualified persons who care to approach these investigations seriously. I go down to Yand this evening, and hope not to leave without clearing up the mystery."

"You will accompany me?"

"Most certainly. Meanwhile pray tell me something of the affair."

"Briefly the story is as follows. Some weeks ago I went to Yand Manor House at the request of the owner, Sir George Blackburton, to see what I could make of the events which took place there. All they complain of is the impossibility of remaining in one room—the dining-room."

"What then is he like, this M. le Spook?" asked the Frenchman, laughing.

"No one has ever seen him, or for that matter heard him."

"Then how—"

"You can't see him, nor hear him, nor smell him," went on Low, "but you can feel him and—taste him!"

"Mon Dieu! But this is singular! Is he then of so bad a flavour?"

"You shall taste for yourself," answered Flaxman Low smiling. "After a certain hour no one can remain in the room, they are simply crowded out."

"But who crowds them out?" asked Thierry.

"That is just what I hope we may discover tonight or tomorrow."

The last train that night dropped Mr. Flaxman Low and his companion at a little station near Yand. It was late, but a trap in waiting soon carried them to the Manor House. The big bulk of the building stood up in absolute blackness before them.

"Blackburton was to have met us, but I suppose he has not yet arrived," said Low. "Hullo! the door is open," he added as he stepped into the hall.

Beyond a dividing curtain they now perceived a light. Passing behind this curtain they found themselves at the end of the long hall, the wide staircase opening up in front of them.

"But who is this?" exclaimed Thierry.

Swaying and stumbling at every step, there tottered slowly down the stairs the figure of a man.

He looked as if he had been drinking, his face was livid, and his eyes sunk into his head.

"Thank Heaven you've come! I heard you outside," he said in a weak voice.

"It's Sir George Blackburton," said Low, as the man lurched forward and pitched into his arms.

They laid him down on the rugs and tried to restore consciousness.

"He has the air of being drunk, but it is not so," remarked Thierry. "Monsieur has had a bad shock of the nerves. See the pulses drumming in his throat."

In a few minutes Blackburton opened his eyes and staggered to his feet.

"Come. I could not remain there alone. Come quickly."

They went rapidly across the hall, Blackburton leading the way down a wide passage to a double-leaved door, which, after a perceptible pause, he threw open, and they all entered together.

On the great table in the centre stood an extinguished lamp, some scattered food, and a big, lighted candle. But the eyes of all three men passed at once to a dark recess beside the heavy, carved chimneypiece, where a rigid shape sat perched on the back of a huge, oak chair.

Flaxman Low snatched up the candle and crossed the room towards it.

On the top of the chair, with his feet upon the arms, sat a powerful-ly-built young man huddled up. His mouth was open, and his eyes twisted upwards. Nothing further could be seen from below but the ghastly pallor of cheek and throat.

"Who is this?" cried Low. Then he laid his hand gently on the man's knee.

At the touch the figure collapsed in a heap upon the floor, the gaping, set, terrified face turned up to theirs.

"He's dead!" said Low after a hasty examination. "I should say he's been dead some hours."

"Oh, Lord! Poor Batty!" groaned Sir George, who was entirely unnerved. "I'm glad you've come."

"Who is he?" said Thierry, "and what was he doing here?"

"He's a gamekeeper of mine. He was always anxious to try conclusions with the ghost, and last night he begged me to lock him in here with food for twenty-four hours. I refused at first, but then I thought if anything happened while he was in here alone, it would interest you. Who could imagine it would end like this?"

"When did you find him?" asked Low.

"I only got here from my mother's half an hour ago. I turned on the light in the hall and came in here with a candle. As I entered the room, the candle went out, and—and—I think I must be going mad."

"Tell us everything you saw," urged Low.

"You will think I am beside myself; but as the light went out and I sank almost paralysed into an armchair, I saw two barred eyes looking at me!"

"Barred eyes? What do you mean?"

"Eyes that looked at me through thin vertical bars, like the bars of a cage. What's that?"

With a smothered yell Sir George sprang back. He had approached the dead man and declared something had brushed his face.

"You were standing on this spot under the overmantel. I will remain here. Meantime, my dear Thierry, I feel sure you will help Sir George to carry this poor fellow to some more suitable place," said Flaxman Low.

When the dead body of the young gamekeeper had been carried out, Low passed slowly round and about the room. At length he stood under the old carved overmantel, which reached to the ceiling and projected bodily forward in quaint heads of satyrs and animals. One of these on the side nearest the recess represented a griffin with a flanged mouth. Sir George had been standing directly below this at the moment when he felt the touch on his face. Now alone in the dim, wide room, Flaxman Low stood on the same spot and waited. The candle threw its dull yellow rays on the shadows which seemed to gather closer and wait also. Presently a distant door banged, and Low, leaning forward to listen, distinctly felt something on the back of his neck!

He swung round. There was nothing! He searched carefully on all sides, then put his hand up to the griffin's head. Again came the same soft touch, this time upon his hand, as if something had floated past on the air.

This was definite. The griffin's head located it. Taking the candle to examine more closely, Low found four long black hairs depending from the jagged fangs. He was detaching them when Thierry reappeared.

"We must get Sir George away as soon as possible," he said.

"Yes, we must take him away, I fear," agreed Low. "Our investigation must be put off till tomorrow."

On the following day they returned to Yand. It was a large country-house, pretty and old-fashioned, with lattice windows and deep gables, that looked out between tall shrubs and across lawns set with beaupots, where peacocks sunned themselves on the velvet turf. The church spire peered over the trees on one side; and an old wall covered with ivy and creeping plants, and pierced at intervals with arches, alone separated the gardens from the churchyard.

The haunted room lay at the back of the house. It was square and handsome, and furnished in the style of the last century. The oak overmantel reached to the ceiling, and a wide window, which almost filled one side of the room, gave a view of the west door of the church.

Low stood for a moment at the open window looking out at the level sunlight which flooded the lawns and parterres.

"See that door sunk in the church wall to the left?" said Sir George's voice at his elbow. "That is the door of the family vault. Cheerful outlook, isn't it?"

"I should like to walk across there presently," remarked Low.

"What! Into the vault?" asked Sir George, with a harsh laugh. "I'll take you if you like. Anything else I can show you or tell you?"

"Yes. Last night I found this hanging from the griffin's head," said Low, producing the thin wisp of black hair. "It must have touched your cheek as you stood below. Do you know to whom it can belong?"

"It's a woman's hair! No, the only woman who has been in this room to my knowledge for months is an old servant with grey hair, who cleans it," returned Blackburton. "I'm sure it was not here when I locked Batty in."

"It is human hair, exceedingly coarse and long uncut," said Low; "but it is not necessarily a woman's."

"It is not mine at any rate, for I'm sandy; and poor Batty was fair. Goodnight; I'll come round for you in the morning."

Presently, when the night closed in, Thierry and Low settled down in the haunted room to await developments. They smoked and talked deep into the night. A big lamp burned brightly on the table, and the surroundings looked homely and desirable.

Thierry made a remark to that effect, adding that perhaps the ghost might see fit to omit his usual visit.

"Experience goes to prove that ghosts have a cunning habit of choosing persons either credulous or excitable to experiment upon," he added.

To M. Thierry's surprise, Flaxman Low agreed with him.

"They certainly choose suitable persons," he said, "that is, not credulous persons, but those whose senses are sufficiently keen to detect the presence of a spirit. In my own investigations, I try to eliminate what you would call the supernatural element. I deal with these mysterious affairs as far as possible on material lines."

"Then what do you say of Batty's death? He died of fright—simply."

"I hardly think so. The manner of his death agrees in a peculiar manner with what we know of the terrible history of this room. He died of fright and pressure combined. Did you hear the doctor's remark? It was significant. He said: 'The indications are precisely those I have observed in persons who have been crushed and killed in a crowd!'"

"That is sufficiently curious, I allow. I see that it is already past two o'clock. I am thirsty; I will have a little seltzer." Thierry rose from his chair, and, going to the side-board, drew a tumblerful from the syphon. "Pah! What an abominable taste!"

"What? The seltzer?"

"Not at all?" returned the Frenchman irritably. "I have not touched it yet. Some horrible fly has flown into my mouth, I suppose. Pah! Disgusting!"

"What is it like?" asked Flaxman Low, who was at the moment wiping his own mouth with his handkerchief.

"Like? As if some repulsive fungus had burst in the mouth."

"Exactly. I perceive it also. I hope you are about to be convinced."

"What?" exclaimed Thierry, turning his big figure round and staring at Low. "You don't mean—" As he spoke the lamp suddenly went out.

"Why, then, have you put the lamp out at such a moment?" cried Thierry, "I have not put it out. Light the candle beside you on the table." Low heard the Frenchman's grunt of satisfaction as he found the candle, then the scratch of a match. It sputtered and went out. Another match and another behaved in the same manner, while Thierry swore freely under his breath.

"Let me have your matches, Monsieur Flaxman; mine are, no doubt damp," he said at last.

Low rose to feel his way across the room. The darkness was dense.

"It is the darkness of Egypt—it may be felt. Where then are you, my dear friend?" he heard Thierry saying, but the voice seemed a long way off.

"I am coming," he answered, "but it's so hard to get along." After Low had spoken the words, their meaning struck him.

He paused and tried to realise in what part of the room he was. The silence was profound, and the growing sense of oppression seemed like a nightmare. Thierry's voice sounded again, faint and receding.

"I am suffocating, Monsieur Flaxman, where are you? I am near the door. Ach!"

A strangling bellow of pain and fear followed, that scarcely reached Low through the thickening atmosphere.

"Thierry, what is the matter with you?" he shouted. "Open the door."

But there was no answer. What had become of Thierry in that hideous, clogging gloom! Was he also dead, crushed in some ghastly fashion against the wall? What was this? The air had become palpable to the touch, heavy, repulsive, with the sensation of cold humid flesh!

Low pushed out his hands with a mad longing to touch a table, a chair, anything but this clammy, swelling softness that thrust itself upon him from every side, baffling him and filling his grasp.

He knew now that he was absolutely alone—struggling against what? His feet were slipping in his wild efforts to feel the floor—the dank flesh was creeping upon his neck, his cheek—his breath came short and labouring as the pressure swung him gently to and fro, helpless, nauseated!

The clammy flesh crowded upon him like the bulk of some fat, horrible creature; then came a stinging pain on the cheek. Low clutched at something—there was a crash and a rush of air—the next sensation of which Mr. Flaxman Low was conscious was one of deathly sickness. He was lying on wet grass, the wind blowing over him, and all the clean, wholesome smells of the open air in his nostrils.

He sat up and looked about him. Dawn was breaking windily in the east, and by its light he saw that he was on the lawn of Yand Manor House. The latticed window of the haunted room above him was open. He tried to remember what had happened. He took stock of himself, in fact, and slowly felt that he still held something clutched in his right hand—something dark-coloured, slender, and twisted. It might have been a long shred of bark or the cast skin of an adder—it was impossible to see in the dim light.

After an interval the recollection of Thierry recurred to him. Scrambling to his feet, he raised himself to the window-sill and looked in. Contrary to his expectation, there was no upsetting of furniture; everything remained in position as when the lamp went out. His own chair and the one Thierry had occupied were just as when they had arisen from them. But there was no sign of Thierry.

Low jumped in by the window. There was the tumbler full of seltzer, and the litter of matches about it. He took up Thierry's box of matches and struck a light. It flared, and he lit the candle with ease. In fact, everything about the room was perfectly normal; all the horrible conditions prevailing but a couple of hours ago had disappeared.

But where was Thierry? Carrying the lighted candle, he passed out of the door and searched in the adjoining rooms. In one of them, to his relief, he found the Frenchman sleeping profoundly in an armchair.

Low touched his arm. Thierry leapt to his feet, fending off an imaginary blow with his arm.

Then he turned his scared face on Low.

"What! You, Monsieur Flaxman! How have you escaped?"

"I should rather ask you how you escaped," said Low, smiling at the havoc the night's experiences had worked on his friend's looks and spirits.

"I was crowded out of the room against the door. That infernal thing—what was it?—with its damp, swelling flesh, inclosed me!" A shudder of disgust stopped him. "I was a fly in an aspic. I could not move. I sank into the stifling pulp. The air grew thick. I called to you, but your answers became inaudible. Then I was suddenly thrust against the door by a huge hand—it felt like one, at least. I had a struggle for my life, I was all but crushed, and then, I do not know how, I found myself outside the door. I shouted to you in vain. Therefore, as I could not help you, I came here, and—I will confess it, my dear friend—I locked and bolted the door. After some time, I went again into the hall and listened; but, as I heard nothing, I resolved to wait until daylight and the return of Sir George."

"That's all right," said Low. "It was an experience worth having."

"But, no! Not for me! I do not envy you your researches into mysteries of this abominable description. I now comprehend perfectly that Sir George has lost his nerve if he has had to do with this horror. Besides, it is entirely impossible to explain these things."

At this moment they heard Sir George's arrival and went out to meet him.

"I could not sleep all night for thinking of you!" exclaimed Blackburton on seeing them; "and I came along as soon as it was light. Something has happened."

"But certainly something has happened," cried M. Thierry shaking his head solemnly; "something of the most bizarre, of the most horrible! Monsieur Flaxman, you shall tell Sir George this story. You have been in that accursed room all night and remain alive to tell the tale!"

As Low came to the conclusion of the story Sir George suddenly exclaimed:

"You have met with some injury to your face, Mr. Low."

Low turned to the mirror. In the now strong light three parallel weals from eye to mouth could be seen.

"I remember a stinging pain like a lash on my cheek. What would you say these marks were caused by, Thierry?" asked Low.

Thierry looked at them and shook his head.

"No one in their senses would venture to offer any explanation of the occurrences of last night," he replied.

"Something of this sort, do you think?" asked Low again, putting down the object he held in his hand on the table.

Thierry took it up and described it aloud.

"A long and thin object of a brown and yellow colour and twisted like a sabre-bladed corkscrew," then he started slightly and glanced at Low.

"It's a human nail, I imagine," suggested Low.

"But no human being has talons of this kind—except, perhaps, a Chinaman of high rank."

"There are no Chinamen about here, nor ever have been, to my knowledge," said Blackburton shortly. "I'm very much afraid that, in spite of all you have so bravely faced, we are no nearer to any rational explanation."

"On the contrary, I fancy I begin to see my way. I believe, after all, that I may be able to convert you, Thierry," said Flaxman Low.

"Convert me?"

"To a belief in the definite aim of my work. But you shall judge for yourself. What do you make of it so far? I claim that you know as much of the matter as I do."

"My dear good friend, I make nothing of it," returned Thierry, shrugging his shoulders and spreading out his hands. "Here we have a tissue of unprecedented incidents that can be explained on no theory whatever."

"But this is definite," and Flaxman Low held up the blackened nail.

"And how do you propose to connect that nail with the black hairs—with the eyes that looked through the bars of a cage—the fate of Batty, with its symptoms of death by pressure and suffocation—our experience of swelling flesh, that something which filled and filled the room to the exclusion of all else? How are you going to account for these things by any kind of connected hypothesis?" asked Thierry, with a shade of irony.

"I mean to try," replied Low.

At lunch time Thierry inquired how the theory was getting on.

"It progresses," answered Low. "By the way, Sir George, who lived in this house for some time prior to, say, 1840? He was a man—it may have been a woman, but, from the nature of his studies, I am inclined to think it was a man—who was deeply read in ancient necromancy, Eastern magic, mesmerism, and subjects of a kindred nature. And was he not buried in the vault you pointed out?"

"Do you know anything more about him?" asked Sir George in surprise.

"He was I imagine," went on Flaxman Low reflectively, "hirsute and swarthy, probably a recluse, and suffered from a morbid and extravagant fear of death."

"How do you know all this?"

"I only asked about it. Am I right?"

"You have described my cousin, Sir Gilbert Blackburton, in every particular. I can show you his portrait in another room."

As they stood looking at the painting of Sir Gilbert Blackburton, with his long, melancholy, olive face and thick, black beard, Sir George went on. "My grandfather succeeded him at Yand. I have often heard my father speak of Sir Gilbert, and his strange studies and extraordinary fear of death. Oddly enough, in the end he died rather suddenly, while he was still hale and strong. He predicted his own approaching death and had a doctor in attendance for a week or two before he died. He was placed in a coffin he had had made on some plan of his own and buried in the vault. His death occurred in 1842 or 1843. If you care to see them I can show you some of his papers, which may interest you."

Mr. Flaxman Low spent the afternoon over the papers. When evening came, he rose from his work with a sigh of content, stretched himself, and joined Thierry and Sir George in the garden.

They dined at Lady Blackburton's, and it was late before Sir George found himself alone with Mr. Flaxman Low and his friend.

"Have you formed any opinion about the thing which haunts the Manor House?" he asked anxiously.

Thierry elaborated a cigarette, crossed his legs, and added: "If you have in truth come to any definite conclusion, pray let us hear it, my dear Monsieur Flaxman."

"I have reached a very definite and satisfactory conclusion," replied Low. "The Manor House is haunted by Sir Gilbert Blackburton, who died, or, rather, who seemed to die, on the 15th of August, 1842."

"Nonsense! The nail fifteen inches long at the least—how do you connect it with Sir Gilbert?" asked Blackburton testily.

"I am convinced that it belonged to Sir Gilbert," Low answered.

"But the long black hair like a woman's?"

"Dissolution in the case of Sir Gilbert was not complete—not consummated, so to speak—as I hope to show you later. Even in the case of dead persons the hair and nails have been known to grow. By a rough calculation as to the growth of nails in such cases, I was enabled to indicate approximately the date of Sir Gilbert's death. The hair too grew on his head."

"But the barred eyes? I saw them myself!" exclaimed the young man.

"The eyelashes grow also. You follow me?"

"You have, I presume, some theory in connection with this?" observed Thierry. "It must be a very curious one."

"Sir Gilbert in his fear of death appears to have mastered and elaborated a strange and ancient formula by which the grosser factors of the body being eliminated, the more ethereal portions continue to retain the spirit, and the body is thus preserved from absolute disintegration. In this manner true death may be indefinitely deferred. Secure from the ordinary chances and changes of existence, this spiritualised body could retain a modified life practically for ever."

"This is a most extraordinary idea, my dear fellow," remarked Thierry.

"But why should Sir Gilbert haunt the Manor House, and one special room?"

"The tendency of spirits to return to the old haunts of bodily life is almost universal. We cannot yet explain the reason of this attraction of environment."

"But the expansion—the crowding substance which we ourselves felt? You cannot meet that difficulty," said Thierry persistently.

"Not as fully as I could wish, perhaps. But the power of expanding and contracting to a degree far beyond our comprehension is a well-known attribute of spiritualised matter."

"Wait one little moment, my dear Monsieur Flaxman," broke in Thierry's voice after an interval; "this is very clever and ingenious indeed. As a theory I give it my sincere admiration. But proof—proof is what we now demand."

Flaxman Low looked steadily at the two incredulous faces.

"This," he said slowly, "is the hair of Sir Gilbert Blackburton, and this nail is from the little finger of his left hand. You can prove my assertion by opening the coffin."

Sir George, who was pacing up and down the room impatiently, drew up.

"I don't like it at all, Mr. Low, I tell you frankly. I don't like it at all. I see no object in violating the coffin. I am not concerned to verify this unpleasant theory of yours. I have only one desire; I want to get rid of this haunting presence, whatever it is."

"If I am right," replied Low, "the opening of the coffin and exposure of the remains to strong sunshine for a short time will free you for ever from this presence."

In the early morning, when the summer sun struck warmly on the lawns of Yand, the three men carried the coffin from the vault to a quiet spot among the shrubs where, secure from observation, they raised the lid.

Within the coffin lay the semblance of Gilbert Blackburton, maned to the ears with long and coarse black hair. Matted eyelashes swept the fallen cheeks, and beside the body stretched the bony hands, each with its dependent sheaf of switch-like nails. Low bent over and raised the left hand gingerly.

The little finger was without a nail!

Two hours later they came back and looked again. The sun had in the meantime done its work; nothing remained but a fleshless skeleton and a few half-rotten shreds of clothing.

The ghost of Yand Manor House has never since been heard of.

When Thierry bade Flaxman Low good-bye, he said:

"In time, my dear Monsieur Flaxman, you will add another to our sciences. You establish your facts too well for my peace of mind."

THE TAPPING ON
THE WAINSCOT

ALLEN UPWARD

Following the success of the Flaxman Low series, the publisher C. Arthur Pearson sought to repeat the experiment, running Allen Upward's "The Ghost Hunters" series in The Royal Magazine *in 1905 and Jessie Adelaide Middleton's rather more factual "True Ghost Stories" in* Pearson's Magazine *in 1907. Upward's series is significant for including a woman investigator, Miss Sargent, who is the secretary to the firm of estate agents Mortimer & Hargreaves, but also has talents as a medium. Although Jack Hargreaves, who buys and sells haunted houses, initially has some concerns, he soon realizes how useful Alwyne Sargent's talents are and thereafter they form a team. The first story in the series, "The Story of the Green House, Wallington," is a fairly mundane episode but Upward found the right mood with this next story.*

A barrister by training but with a yearning to be a politician, George Allen Upward (1863–1926) led a rather diverse, one might almost say impulsive, career. Besides his literary works as poet, novelist, and essayist, he fought as a volunteer in the invasion of Turkey by the Greeks in 1897, he was in charge of a mission to Macedonia in 1907, and at the start of the First World War he travelled to Belgium dressed in his scoutmaster's uniform. He enjoyed exploring secret histories and was perhaps best known for the series "Secrets of the Courts of Europe" that ran in Pearson's Magazine *during 1896. He also wrote two series of "Historic Mysteries" during 1900 and 1901; and "Behind the Scenes of Europe" in 1917. His death was itself something of a mystery. He was found dead of a gunshot wound at his cottage but his adopted son, Richard, who was in bed upstairs, heard no shot, and both he and Upward's sister did not believe that Upward was depressed. A verdict of suicide while of unsound mind was recorded, but was it an accident or something more sinister?*

Amongst his books was The Discovery of the Dead *(1910) where a scientist discovers a way of communicating with the dead, or "necromorphs," which is the next stage of spiritual existence after death.*

THE MYSTERIOUS INCIDENT WHICH I AM GOING TO NARRATE IS ONE which seems to have a particular interest for those who study occult phenomena.

According to some who have discussed it with me, it throws an important light on the conditions which prevail in the world of spirits, and the limitations to their action.

However, I do not care to say anything on the subject myself. My object is simply to set down facts, and leave others to draw their own conclusions.

It was about a year after the affair of the Green House, Wallington, already related, when our firm received instructions from the solicitors of Sir Henry Weetman to dispose by auction of his family mansion, Hailesbury Manor, Sussex.

I was told that Sir Henry was a distant relation, who had recently come into the title and estate on the death of the last baronet, and preferred to live abroad. The furniture and effects had been sold already by a firm of auctioneers, well known for their sales of that kind, and the house and estate were to follow.

I went down with a clerk to view the place and found it to be a very handsome old Jacobean mansion, with valuable oak wainscot in all the principal rooms.

The caretaker who showed us over it was a dear old lady who had been housekeeper to the last baronet, and was evidently heartbroken at the prospect of the old family seat passing into the possession of strangers.

"Sir Christopher—that's my late master—would turn in his grave if he knew what was being done with the old place," she lamented. "And I shouldn't wonder if he did know."

I was busy directing the clerk in taking measurements of the more important rooms and did not pay much heed to this obscure intimation.

In due course we reached the first floor, and the housekeeper conducted us into a great, square room with a huge fireplace and two windows commanding a view over the park.

I was surprised to find that this room had not been stripped so completely as the ones downstairs. It still contained a magnificently carved oak bedstead, a four-poster, equal in size to the bedroom of a modern flat.

"This is the room Sir Christopher died in," the old lady said impressively. "He died in that bed King Charles I once slept in it."

"And why hasn't it been removed like the rest of the furniture?" I naturally asked.

"It is fixed to the floor, for one thing," was the answer. "And Sir Henry thought; it would fetch more by leaving it where it is. But I believe he would have it taken away now if he knew what I know."

Mrs. Musgrave, as the old housekeeper was named, nodded her head and pursed up her lips, after the manner of old ladies when they have a secret which they are longing to tell, but which they think it due to their dignity only to part with under pressure.

"Why, what is it you know?" I asked, with an interest by no means feigned.

"Perhaps I ought not to speak of it," the housekeeper returned, with a glance at my clerk.

I sent the young man into the other room and repeated my question.

"Well, sir, it may be that I ought not to be the first to mention it, but it's being talked of in the village, and if you didn't hear of it from me you'd hear of it from somebody else, most likely." Mrs. Musgrave lowered her voice: "This house is haunted, sir."

Remembering my late grisly experience, I did not reply as lightly as I might have done once to such a statement.

"Haunted? How? In what way?"

"You may believe me, or you may not, sir," Mrs. Musgrave said with deliberation, evidently in no hurry to come to the point. "There are some who can hear it, and some who can't. Some say it's only fancy, and others that it's the spirit of Sir Christopher. But all I can say is, I wouldn't pass a night in this room again, not if you were to offer me fifty pounds."

This was not very pleasant hearing. If a report of this kind were current in the village, it would be pretty sure to reach the ears of any intending purchaser, and perhaps choke him off.

An old family ghost, or the tradition of one, is sometimes considered an attraction to a venerable country seat. But any really unpleasant phenomena, particularly if of quite recent date, would be a very decided drawback in most people's eyes.

"Can you tell me exactly what you did hear?" I asked.

"It is a tapping, sir, a tapping on the wainscot just over there," she pointed to the wall opposite the foot of the bed. "I was lying asleep in the bed, sir,—for when the house was stripped, and Sir Henry went away, I thought there would be no harm in my sleeping here, and I wanted to say I had slept in the same bed as King Charles. But it's my belief that Sir Henry must have heard the tapping himself, and seen something as well, that frightened him; and that's why he was so anxious to clear everything out of the house and leave it."

I listened, hardly knowing what question to put next. At last I inquired:

"Do you suggest—is there any reason to suppose—that there was anything wrong about Sir Christopher Weetman's death?"

The question took Mrs. Musgrave by surprise.

"Wrong, sir? What should there be wrong? I'm sure the poor gentleman couldn't have died more peacefully. Miss Alice and I were with him the whole time."

"Who was Miss Alice?"

"His daughter—at least, his adopted daughter. She had lived with him since she was a baby, and he made no difference between her and his own flesh and blood." Mrs. Musgrave's voice changed again, as she added: "And in my belief it's on her account that Sir Christopher walks."

"Why?"

"Because when Sir Henry came down he turned her out of the house with nothing but the clothes she stood in. Sir Christopher hadn't made a will, and he came into everything as the heir. Miss Alice had to go to London and take a situation as a waitress."

I mused in silence, Could there be anything in that strange suggestion? Was it not more likely that the old housekeeper's indignation at her new master's conduct had made her fancy that the ordinary noises of an old mansion by night were a protest on the part of the dead?

"And have you heard the tapping since?" I asked.

"*I hear it every night!*" was the startling answer. "I have shifted my bed to half the rooms in the house, but it makes no difference. Wherever I am, the taps come; and then they move along the wall and by the staircases and the corridors till they reach this room and stop there!"

"Have you followed them?" I exclaimed, astonished.

"I did the first time—now I daren't," the housekeeper answered. "But I got Jim Bateman from the lodge to come up one night, and he heard them, and followed them, and they led him to the same place. And now he would no more cross the threshold of the house after dark than he would fly."

It was clear to me by this time that, whether fact or fancy, the story called for investigation.

I am not naturally nervous, and in spite of the disagreeable memories of the last haunted house I had spent a night in, I determined to face whatever there was to face in Hailesbury Manor.

Accordingly, I arranged with Mrs. Musgrave to make up a bed for me the next night but one. Not in the haunted room itself, that I did not feel disposed to risk, but so as to enable me to be at hand when the mysterious tapping began.

I was careful to say nothing in the office meanwhile, and, above all, to keep the matter from the ears of my lady secretary. Miss Sargent had solved the mystery of the Green House for me, but she had done so at the cost of an experience to which I could not think of exposing her a second time.

On the appointed evening I returned to Hailesbury with a small dressing-bag, prepared to stay the night.

The housekeeper had prepared a bedroom for me on one of the upper floors, not far from her own. But as she told me that the ghostly tapping usually began about midnight, I decided to sit up for it and persuaded her to do the same.

We had supper together in a room downstairs, the old lady getting it ready herself. Not a girl in the village, it appeared, could be induced to remain in the house after sunset.

After supper Mrs. Musgrave nodded off to sleep in a rocking-chair before the fire, while I lit a cigar and waited in some excitement for what was to come.

The room in which we sat was wainscotted, like all those on the ground floor. Every time a coal dropped from the fire, or a window-frame rattled, I fancied the mysterious summons had come and started nervously in my chair.

I believe it is not merely fancy which causes us to hear so many more small noises in a house at night than in the day time, but that there is some scientific reason for it. Be that as it may, everyone must admit that the sense of hearing is more acute in the darkness than in the light.

As twelve o'clock approached I deliberately turned the lamp out, keeping a candle and some matches by my side.

Hardly had I done this when I received a shock which nearly made me jump out of my chair. It was a tap—loud, sharp, and imperative—on the door of the room.

In my agitation the habitual phrase, "Come in," rose to my lips, and I uttered it. At the same moment my companion woke with a start, and stared about her wildly in the dim firelight.

"Did you hear It?" she asked in an awestruck whisper.

"Yes. Did you?"

As she nodded in answer, the tap sounded a second time, seeming fainter and further off.

I rose to my feet and lit the candle.

"Are you going to follow It?" the old woman breathed.

"Yes; will you come?"

She shook her head.

"I dare not. Give me the matches! Don't go till I have lit the lamp, for my sake!"

I lingered, my own nerves becoming affected in sympathy with hers, while the frightened woman clutched the box from my hand and struck a match, which she applied to the wick of the lamp.

At the same moment I heard the Tap for the third time, low, and fading away in the distance.

I strode to the door of the room, opened it, and passed out into the passage, leaving the door ajar.

The ghostly Tap sounded again far away in front of me, at the foot of the great staircase.

I strode after It, with quickening steps and throbbing pulses, carefully screening the candle flame with one hand. It moved on up the stairs, seeming to fly before me, and I almost raced to catch up that beckoning sound.

Along the main corridor overhead I was drawn, straight to the door of the death-chamber.

As I crossed the threshold, and the huge four-poster loomed up in the shadow, the character of the ghostly sound underwent a change.

Instead of a single tap, travelling with the speed of a terrified man fleeing from pursuit, it became a hurried knocking, moving round the room behind the wainscot as if in search of something. I could have sworn that Someone or Something was *feeling its way along.*

The daunting sounds arrived at the middle of the wall opposite the foot of the great bed, and became stationary.

Once—twice—thrice—that awful Tap broke the silence, louder and more menacing each time.

And then all at once the flame of the candle turned blue and went out, leaving me in the stillness and the darkness, with the feeling that I was *not alone.*

How I got downstairs again I can hardly remember, but I am not ashamed to say that never was sight more welcome than the lamplight streaming through the open door on to the passage as I rushed towards it.

Mrs. Musgrave gave me a glance, and screamed:

"You have seen It?"

"No, no," I said, "but the light went out, and I had no matches."

I related my experience in a few words, and then made a confession.

"I cannot sleep in this house tonight, Mrs. Musgrave. I must go down to the village and try to get into the inn."

To my relief she offered no opposition. I fancy I was not the first person who had left her at the same hour for the same reason.

Not even in the morning did I feel inclined to return to the haunted house. I went up to London by the first train, and, going straight to the office, asked Miss Sargent to come into my room, and told her everything.

She listened with intense interest, not interrupting by so much as a movement till I had come to the end.

Then she said with grave decision:

"You must let me go down and spend a night in that room, Mr. Hargreaves."

"Don't think of such a thing!" I exclaimed. "I should never permit you to run the risk of such a shock as I had last night."

"It is a matter of necessity," Miss Sargent replied firmly. "It is a matter of duty. I cannot doubt that the tapping on the wainscot has a meaning. It is a message from the dead."

"A message! I don't understand."

"I don't profess to understand it myself at present. But I do not believe that it is an ordinary case of what is called haunting, where a spirit appears to be bound in some way to a particular spot. Neither do I believe that the object of this manifestation has been to drive the new owner of the house away, or to render it uninhabitable."

"Then what do you suggest?"

"I feel sure there is a reason for the taps always coming back to one particular place on the wall of that one room."

A light seemed to break on her mind as she spoke, and she added quickly:

"I should not wonder if there were something hidden behind the wainscot, perhaps a will or a paper of some kind."

I recalled what the housekeeper had told me about the adopted child of the dead man, turned adrift so heartlessly by the heir to his wealth.

"Pray Heaven you are right!" I ejaculated fervently. "I will go down again and have the wainscot removed. But, mind, this must be kept a strict secret. If Sir Henry Weetman or his solicitors heard what I was doing, I might get into serious trouble."

Out of gratitude for Miss Sargent's suggestion, I invited her to be present at the opening of the wainscot. I had confided my hopes and intentions to Mrs. Musgrave, who was intensely excited at the prospect of justice being done to her beloved young mistress.

"To think that I should never have guessed what it meant!" she cried. "And I thought I understood it better than anyone else, too."

"Did you think there was any reason for the tapping on that particular spot, then?" Miss Sargent asked.

"To be sure I did. That is just where Miss Alice's picture used to hang, so that Sir Christopher could see it every morning when he woke. Sir Henry had the picture sold with all the others, and I thought that was why Sir Christopher couldn't rest in his grave."

I saw a look of disappointment steal over Miss Sargent's face.

"It may be that Mrs. Musgrave is right," she said thoughtfully. "Very often the spirits seem to have very little motive—or what seems very little to us—for what they do."

"Well, we shall see," I responded, not willing to give up my hope on the poor orphan's behalf.

I had brought down an expert cabinetmaker from London, and he went to work quickly and neatly. A great space of the wall was stripped of its wainscot, and we searched anxiously for any sign of a hiding-place behind.

We searched vainly. To the bitter disappointment of all three of us there was not even a vestige, not so much as a scratch on the wall, to indicate that anything had ever been concealed there.

To complete our discomfiture the cabinetmaker gave it as his opinion that the wainscot had never been disturbed since it was put up in the reign of James I.

"I was right, you see, Miss," said good Mrs. Musgrave sorrowfully. "It's the thought of Miss Alice's picture that keeps Sir Christopher out of his grave."

She spoke as though the deceased baronet were an invalid suffering from sleeplessness at night.

Miss Sargent shook her head, but said nothing. She seemed to be reflecting deeply.

We left the cabinetmaker with strict instructions to replace the wainscot, so as to leave no trace of his operations, and went downstairs.

Half-an-hour later, as we were sitting at lunch, Miss Sargent suddenly spoke.

"You must let me sleep in that bed, Mr. Hargreaves. I am a clairvoyant in sleep, as you know, and I may see something which will explain the mystery."

We both returned to town in the afternoon to make our arrangements. The following day we came down again, prepared to spend the night.

None of us intended to go to bed. The four-poster in the haunted room had been furnished with blankets and pillows to serve as a bed for the clairvoyant. Mrs. Musgrave was to instal herself on a sofa before the fireplace, in which a fire had been lit, and I was to sit up in the next room, ready to come at the first call.

Miss Sargent, who fortunately possessed the power of falling asleep at will, retired to her strange couch a little before eleven, accompanied by the housekeeper, whose excitement promised to keep her awake.

As for myself, I cherished no wish to sleep. I had provided myself with lights, cigars, and a book to read, but I am bound to confess that I found it impossible to get interested in it.

An hour later I heard a low tapping on the door of my own room.

Not a little startled, I sprang up, only to find that the sound this time was free from any element of mystery.

The old housekeeper had come to summon me.

"Will you come and see the young lady?" she said. "I think something is the matter."

I felt myself turning cold.

"What do you mean? Has the tapping begun?"

The answer surprised me.

"No, that is what frightens me. This is the first night I have not heard it for four months. But I think Miss Sargent sees something."

I led the way into the haunted room. There was not a sound to be heard, and the lights had been put out by the clairvoyant's desire. But she was sitting half up in bed, her eyes fast closed, and yet appearing to stare with the most deadly fear at the opposite wall.

Suddenly a sharp cry broke from her, followed immediately by the same frantic rush of half-articulated syllables which had so alarmed me on that night in the Green House.

"Leave—it—alone—leave—it—alone—leave—it—alone—put—it—back—put—it—back—put—it—back——*Ah, he's taken it!*"

With these last words, uttered loudly in distinct tones, the sleeper's eyes suddenly opened, and she gave a fearful shudder.

Tap! tap! tap!

If ever I have heard any sounds in my life I heard those knocks by an unseen hand on the wainscot at which we all gazed, unable to stir till the knocks ceased.

It was too much for the nerves of any of us to bear. I caught the half-fainting girl in my arms as she threw herself from the great four-poster, and the three of us did not breathe again till we were safe in the housekeeper's little sitting-room downstairs.

There, after she had rested and taken a soothing draught prescribed by the housekeeper, Miss Sargent related her vision.

"I saw a picture hanging on the wall, the picture of a young girl, about seventeen, with blue eyes and very light golden hair."

"Miss Alice!" the old lady interrupted.

"Two men came into the room, and moved about. I could not see what they were doing. Presently, one of them, who was in his shirt-sleeves, and looked like a workman, approached the picture, and raised his hands to take it down."

"One of the auctioneer's men, my dear," was Mrs. Musgrave's murmured comment.

"At that instant I saw suddenly, appearing from nowhere, in front of the picture, a corpse."

"A corpse!" we both ejaculated in horror.

"Yes, a dead man, in a winding sheet, with his head swathed in white bandages. The corpse seemed to try to thrust back the living man. He went on without noticing it, and took down the picture, I can hardly describe how, but just as though the corpse were not there. The dead man seemed to try to detain him, but he walked off with it. Then I awoke."

A cry burst from the poor old housekeeper.

"It was my poor master," she moaned, "trying to save Miss Alice's nice picture."

The other said nothing, but bent her brows as though profoundly dissatisfied with this seemingly puerile interpretation of the mystery.

I watched her with expectation. I had come to look on Alwyne Sargent as a woman of more than ordinary powers of mind, apart altogether from her extraordinary occult faculty, and I confidently anticipated that she would not let the matter rest there.

"The picture must be replaced," she said, after a long interval of meditation. "We cannot leave things as they are. At all costs the picture must be found, and hung up there again, if it is only for one night."

"I should think that could be managed," I said, though I did not much relish the idea.

I saw that Miss Sargent wanted to make fresh trial of her clairvoyant powers, with the picture in its place, and I dreaded the injury which these agitating experiences seemed likely to do her.

However, I shared her feeling that the mystery must be probed to the bottom. The very next day I called on the auctioneers who had charge of the sale at Hailesbury Manor, and asked them to let me go through their books. I told them nothing except that I had been asked to recover a family portrait included in the sale by oversight.

They were very obliging, and with their assistance I found that a picture catalogued as "Portrait of a Girl" had been sold for £12 to a gentleman living at Sydenham.

I went out there the same evening, and saw the purchaser, who was a Common Councilman of the City of London, and evidently given to speculating in pictures, with which the house was crowded.

He saw his advantage, and drove a rather hard bargain with me, but in the end he agreed to let me have the picture to show to the client whom I pretended to have in the background, on my paying a deposit.

Then he led me upstairs to a small smoking-room, where I saw the picture hanging in an obscure corner.

With hands trembling with excitement, I took hold of the frame to lift it off the nail. As I did so, the nail itself gave way, and the precious portrait crashed to the ground, the frame coming in pieces.

I fell on my knees with a cry of dismay, when I was astonished to see, among the broken portions of the frame, a blue foolscap envelope indorsed in shaky handwriting—"*Will of Sir C. Weetman, Bart.*" The will gave the whole of his property to his adopted daughter, Alice Weetman.

Human nature is a curious thing. As soon as I had made out the contents of the document thus miraculously discovered, and he knew that the picture was that of a young lady who had come into a great fortune, the owner insisted on my accepting it as a free gift for the fortunate heiress.

It now hangs, in its carefully restored frame, in its old place at the foot of the historic bed; and the tapping on the wainscot in Hailesbury Manor has been heard no more.

SAMARIS

ROBERT W. CHAMBERS

Robert W. Chambers (1865–1933) was a bestselling writer of romantic fiction and society novels, none of which is remembered today. What he is remembered for is an idiosyncratic little book, The King in Yellow *(1895). This collection, a cornerstone of weird fiction, tells of events associated with a play called* The King in Yellow, *which has unsettling effects upon those who read it and hints at a real supernatural King in Yellow. Chambers studied as an artist and initially worked for many leading American magazines such as* Life *at the start of the 1890s, sharing a studio with Charles Dana Gibson. But he soon turned to writing. He wrote a few other volumes of weird fiction, including* The Maker of Moons *(1896),* The Mystery of Choice *(1897), and* In Search of the Unknown *(1904). Often overlooked amongst his many books is* The Tracer of Lost Persons *(1906). This book introduced Westrel Keen who runs an agency that claims to be able to trace anybody, living or dead. The series is a mixture of detective and weird tales, and it seems evident that Keen, with his immense fortune and network of contacts, does have some psychic abilities. Unfortunately, the book has some gratuitous racist passages, but the following story, thankfully, had to be edited for just one word. Westrel Keen was given a new lease of life when the book was adapted as* Mr. Keen, Tracer of Lost Persons *for a long-running radio series that ran from 1937 to 1955. Its theme music was titled, "Someday, I'll Find You."*

ON THE THIRTEENTH DAY OF MARCH, 1906, KERNS RECEIVED THE following cable from an old friend:

Is there anybody in New York who can find two criminals for me? I don't want to call in the police.

J.T. BURKE.

To which Kerns replied promptly:

Wire Keen, Tracer of Lost Persons, N.Y.

And a day or two later, being on his honeymoon, he forgot all about his old friend Jack Burke.

On the fifteenth day of March, 1906, Mr. Keen, Tracer of Lost Persons, received the following cablegram from Alexandria, Egypt:

Keen, Tracer, New York:—*Locate Joram Smiles, forty, stout, lame, red hair, ragged red mustache, cast in left eye, pallid skin; carries one crutch; supposed to have arrived in America per S. S.* Scythian Queen, *with man known as Emanuel Gandon, swarthy, short, fat, light bluish eyes, Eurasian type.*

I will call on you at your office as soon as my steamer, Empress of Babylon, *arrives. If you discover my men, keep them under surveillance, but on no account call in police. Spare no expense. Dundas, Gray & Co. are my bankers and reference.*

JOHN TEMPLETON BURKE.

On Monday, April 2nd, a few minutes after eight o'clock in the morning, the card of Mr. John Templeton Burke was brought to Mr. Keen, Tracer of Lost Persons, and a moment later a well-built, wiry, sun-scorched young man was ushered into Mr. Keen's private office by a stenographer prepared to take minutes of the interview.

The first thing that the Tracer of Lost Persons noted in his visitor was his mouth; the next his eyes. Both were unmistakably good—the eyes which his Creator had given him looked people squarely in the face at every word;

the mouth, which a man's own character fashions agreeably or mars, was pleasant, but firm when the trace of the smile lurking in the corners died out.

There were dozens of other external characteristics which Mr. Keen always looked for in his clients; and now the rapid exchange of preliminary glances appeared to satisfy both men, for they advanced toward each other and exchanged a formal hand clasp.

"Have you any news for me?" asked Burke.

"I have," said the Tracer. "There are cigars on the table beside you—matches in that silver case. No, I never smoke; but I like the aroma—and I like to watch men smoke. Do you know, Mr. Burke, that no two men smoke in the same fashion? There is as much character in the manner of holding a cigar as there is difference in the technique of artists."

Burke nodded, amused, but, catching sight of the busy stenographer, his bronzed features became serious, and he looked at Mr. Keen inquiringly.

"It is my custom," said the Tracer. "Do you object to my stenographer?"

Burke looked at the slim young girl in her black gown and white collar and cuffs. Then, very simply, he asked her pardon for objecting to her presence, but said that he could not discuss his case if she remained. So she rose, with a humorous glance at Mr. Keen; and the two men stood up until she had vanished, then reseated themselves *vis-a-vis*. Mr. Keen calmly dropped his elbow on the concealed button which prepared a hidden phonograph for the reception of every word that passed between them.

"What news have you for me, Mr. Keen?" asked the younger man with that same directness which the Tracer had already been prepared for, and which only corroborated the frankness of eyes and voice.

"My news is brief," he said. "I have both your men under observation."

"Already?" exclaimed Burke, plainly unprepared. "Do you actually mean that I can see these men whenever I desire to do so? Are these scoundrels in this town—within pistol shot?"

His youthful face hardened as he snapped out his last word, like the crack of a whip.

"I don't know how far your pistol carries," said Mr. Keen. "Do you wish to swear out a warrant?"

"No, I do not. I merely wish their addresses. You have not used the police in this matter, have you, Mr. Keen?"

"No. Your cable was explicit," said the Tracer. "Had you permitted me to use the police it would have been much less expensive for you."

"I can't help that," said the young man. "Besides, in a matter of this sort, a man cannot decently consider expense."

"A matter of what sort?" asked the Tracer blandly.

"Of *this* sort."

"Oh! Yet even now I do not understand. You must remember, Mr. Burke, that you have not told me anything concerning the reasons for your quest of these two men, Joram Smiles and Emanuel Gandon. Besides, this is the first time you have mentioned pistol range."

Burke, smoking steadily, looked at the Tracer through the blue fog of his cigar.

"No," he said, "I have not told you anything about them."

Mr. Keen waited a moment; then, smiling quietly to himself, he wrote down the present addresses of Joram Smiles and Emanuel Gandon, and, tearing off the leaf, handed it to the younger man, saying: "I omit the pistol range, Mr. Burke."

"I am very grateful to you," said Burke. "The efficiency of your system is too famous for me to venture to praise it. All I can say is 'Thank you'; all I can do in gratitude is to write my check—if you will be kind enough to suggest the figures."

"Are you sure that my services are ended?"

"Thank you, quite sure."

So the Tracer of Lost Persons named the figures, and his client produced a check book and filled in a check for the amount. This was presented and received with pleasant formality. Burke rose, prepared to take his leave, but the Tracer was apparently busy with the combination lock of a safe, and the young man lingered a moment to make his adieus.

As he stood waiting for the Tracer to turn around he studied the writing on the sheet of paper which he held toward the light:

Joram Smiles, no profession, 613 West 24th Street.
Emanuel Gandon, no profession, same address.
Very dangerous men.

It occurred to him that these three lines of pencil-writing had cost him a thousand dollars—and at the same instant he flushed with shame at the idea of measuring the money value of anything in such a quest as this.

And yet—and yet he had already spent a great deal of money in his brief quest, and—*was* he any nearer the goal—even with the penciled addresses of these two men in his possession? Even with these men almost within pistol shot!

Pondering there, immersed in frowning retrospection, the room, the Tracer, the city seemed to fade from his view. He saw the red sand blowing in the desert; he heard the sickly squealing of camels at the El Teb Wells; he saw the sun strike fire from the rippling waters of Saïs; he saw the plain, and the ruins high above it; and the odor of the Long Bazaar smote him like a blow, and he heard the far call to prayer from the minarets of Sa-el-Hagar, once Saïs, the mysterious—Saïs of the million lanterns, Saïs of that splendid festival where the Great Triad's worship swayed dynasty after dynasty, and where, through the hot centuries, Isis, veiled, impassive, looked out upon the hundredth king of kings, Meris, the Builder of Gardens, dragged dead at the chariot of Upper and Lower Egypt.

Slowly the visions faded; into his remote eyes crept the consciousness of the twentieth century again; he heard the river whistles blowing, and the far dissonance of the streets—that iron undertone vibrating through the metropolis of the West from river to river and from the Palisades to the sea.

His gaze wandered about the room, from telephone desk to bookcase, from the table to the huge steel safe, door ajar, swung outward like the polished breech of a twelve-inch gun.

Then his vacant eyes met the eyes of the Tracer of Lost Persons, almost helplessly. And for the first time the full significance of this quest he had undertaken came over him like despair—this strange, hopeless, fantastic quest, blindly, savagely pursued from the sand wastes of Saïs to the wastes of this vast arid city of iron and masonry, ringing to the sky with the menacing clamor of its five monstrous boroughs.

Curiously weary of a sudden, he sat down, resting his head on one hand. The Tracer watched him, bent partly over his desk. From moment to moment he tore minute pieces from the blotter, or drew imaginary circles and arabesques on his pad with an inkless pen.

"Perhaps I could help you, after all—if you'd let me try," he said quietly.

"Do you mean—*me?*" asked Burke, without raising his head.

"If you like—yes, you—or any man in trouble—in perplexity—in the uncertain deductions which arise from an attempt at self-analysis."

"It is true; I am trying to analyze myself. I believe that I don't know how. All has been mere impulse—so far. No, I don't know how to analyze it all."

"I do," said the Tracer.

Burke raised his level, unbelieving eyes.

"You are in love," said the Tracer.

After a long time Burke looked up again. "Do you think so?"

"Yes. Can I help you?" asked the Tracer pleasantly.

The young man sat silent, frowning into space; then:

"I tell you plainly enough that I have come here to argue with two men at the end of a pistol; and—you tell me I'm in love. By what logic—"

"It is written in your face, Mr. Burke—in your eyes, in every feature, every muscle's contraction, every modulation of your voice. My tables, containing six hundred classified superficial phenomena peculiar to all human emotions, have been compiled and scientifically arranged according to Bertillon's system. It is an absolutely accurate key to every phase of human emotion, from hate, through all its amazingly paradoxical phenomena, to love, with all its genera under the suborder—all its species, subspecies, and varieties."

He leaned back, surveying the young man with kindly amusement.

"You talk of pistol range, but you are thinking of something more fatal than bullets, Mr. Burke. You are thinking of love—of the first, great, absorbing, unreasoning passion that has ever shaken you, blinded you, seized you and dragged you out of the ordered path of life, to push you violently into the strange and unexplored! That is what stares out on the world through those haunted eyes of yours, when the smile dies out and you are off your guard; that is what is hardening those flat, clean bands of muscle in jaw and cheek; that is what those hints of shadow mean beneath the eye, that new and delicate pinch to the nostril, that refining, almost to sharpness, of the nose, that sensitive edging to the lips, and the lean delicacy of the chin."

He bent slightly forward in his chair.

"There is all that there, Mr. Burke, and something else—the glimmering dawn of desperation."

"Yes," said the other, "that is there. I am desperate."

"*Exactly*. Also you wear two revolvers in a light, leather harness strapped up under your armpits," said the Tracer, laughing. "Take them off, Mr. Burke. There is nothing to be gained in shooting up Mr. Smiles or converting Mr. Gandon into nitrates."

"If it is a matter where one man can help another," the Tracer added simply, "it would give me pleasure to place my resources at your command—without recompense—"

"Mr. Keen!" said Burke, astonished.

"Yes?"

"You are very amiable; I had not wished—had not expected anything except professional interest from you."

"Why not? I like you, Mr. Burke."

The utter disarming candor of this quiet, elderly gentleman silenced the younger man with a suddenness born of emotions long crushed, long relentlessly mastered, and which now, in revolt, shook him fiercely in every fiber. All at once he felt very young, very helpless in the world— that same world through which, until within a few weeks, he had roved so confidently, so arrogantly, challenging man and the gods themselves in the pride of his strength and youth.

But now, halting, bewildered, lost amid the strange maze of byways whither impulse had lured and abandoned him, he looked out into a world of wilderness and unfamiliar stars and shadow shapes undreamed of, and he knew not which way to turn—not even how to return along the ways his impetuous feet had trodden in this strange and hopeless quest of his.

"How can you help me?" he said bluntly, while the quivering undertone rang in spite of him. "Yes, I am in love; but how can any living man help me?"

"Are you in love with the dead?" asked the Tracer gravely. "For that only is hopeless. Are you in love with one who is not living?"

123

"Yes."

"You love one whom you know to be dead?"

"Yes; dead."

"How do you know that she is dead?"

"That is not the question. I knew that when I fell in love with her. It is not that which appals me; I ask nothing more than to live my life out loving the dead. I—I ask very little."

He passed his unsteady hand across his dry lips, across his eyes and forehead, then laid his clinched fist on the table.

"Some men remain constant to a memory; some to a picture—sane, wholesome, normal men. Some men, with a fixed ideal, never encounter its facsimile, and so never love. There is nothing strange, after all, in this; nothing abnormal, nothing unwholesome. Grünwald loved the marble head and shoulders of the lovely Amazon in the Munich Museum; he died unmarried, leaving the charities and good deeds of a blameless life to justify him. Sir Henry Guest, the great surgeon who worked among the poor without recompense, loved Gainsborough's 'Lady Wilton.' The portrait hangs above his tomb in St. Clement's Hundreds. D'Epernay loved Mlle. Jeanne Vacaresco, who died before he was born. And I—I love in my own fashion."

His low voice rang with the repressed undertone of excitement; he opened and closed his clinched hand as though controlling the lever of his emotions.

"What can you do for a man who loves the shadow of Life?" he asked.

"If you love the shadow because the substance has passed away—if you love the soul because the dust has returned to the earth as it was—"

"It has *not*!" said the younger man.

The Tracer said very gravely: "It is written that whenever 'the Silver Cord' is loosed, 'then shall the dust return unto the earth as it was, and the spirit shall return unto Him who gave it.'"

"The spirit—yes; *that* has taken its splendid flight—"

His voice choked up, died out; he strove to speak again, but could not. The Tracer let him alone, and bent again over his desk, drawing imaginary circles on the stained blotter, while moment after moment passed under the tension of that fiercest of all struggles, when a man sits throttling his own soul into silence.

And, after a long time, Burke lifted a haggard face from the cradle of his crossed arms and shook his shoulders, drawing a deep, steady breath.

"Listen to *me*!" he said in an altered voice.

And the Tracer of Lost Persons nodded.

"WHEN I LEFT THE POINT I WAS ASSIGNED TO THE COLORED CAV-alry. They are good men; we went up Kettle Hill together. Then came the Philippine troubles, then that Chinese affair. Then I did staff duty, and could not stand the inactivity and resigned. They had no use for me in Manchuria; I tired of waiting, and went to Venezuela. The prospects for service there were absurd; I heard of the Moorish troubles and went to Morocco. Others of my sort swarmed there; matters dragged and dragged, and the Kaiser never meant business, anyway.

"Being independent, and my means permitting me, I got some shoot-ing in the back country. This all degenerated into the merest nomadic wandering—nothing but sand, camels, ruins, tents, white walls, and blue skies. And at last I came to the town of Sa-el-Hagar."

His voice died out; his restless, haunted eyes became fixed.

"Sa-el-Hagar, once ancient Saïs," repeated the Tracer quietly; and the young man looked at him.

"You know *that*?"

"Yes," said the Tracer.

For a while Burke remained silent, preoccupied, then, resting his chin on his hand and speaking in a curiously monotonous voice, as though repeating to himself by rote, he went on:

"The town is on the heights—have you a pencil? Thank you. Here is the town of Sa-el-Hagar, here are the ruins, here is the wall, and some-where hereabouts should be the buried temple of Neith, which nobody has found." He shifted his pencil. "Here is the lake of Saïs; here, standing all alone on the plain, are those great monolithic pillars stretching away into perspective—four hundred of them in all—a hundred and nine still upright. There were one hundred and ten when I arrived at El Teb Wells."

He looked across at the Tracer, repeating: "One hundred and ten—when I arrived. One fell the first night—a distant pillar far away on the horizon. Four thousand years had it stood there. And it fell—the first night of my arrival. I heard it; the nights are cold at El Teb Wells, and I was lying awake, all a-shiver, counting the stars to make me sleep. And very, very far away in the desert I heard and felt the shock of its fall—the fall of forty centuries under the Egyptian stars."

His eyes grew dreamy; a slight glow had stained his face.

"Did you ever halt suddenly in the Northern forests, listening, as though a distant voice had hailed you? Then you understand why that far, dull sound from the dark horizon brought me to my feet, bewildered, listening, as though my own name had been spoken.

"I heard the wind in the tents and the stir of camels; I heard the reeds whispering on Saïs Lake and the yap-yap of a shivering jackal; and always, always, the hushed echo in my ears of my own name called across the starlit waste.

"At dawn I had forgotten. An Arab told me that a pillar had fallen; it was all the same to me, to him, to the others, too. The sun came out hot. I like heat. My men sprawled in the tents; some watered, some went up to the town to gossip in the bazaar. I mounted and cast bridle on neck—you see how much I cared where I went! In two hours we had completed a circle—like a ruddy hawk above El Teb. And my horse halted beside the fallen pillar."

As he spoke his language had become very simple, very direct, almost without accent, and he spoke slowly, picking his way with that lack of inflection, of emotion characteristic of a child reading a new reader.

"The column had fallen from its base, eastward, and with its base it had upheaved another buried base, laying bare a sort of cellar and a flight of stone steps descending into darkness.

"Into this excavation the sand was still running in tiny rivulets. Listening, I could hear it pattering far, far down into the shadows.

"Sitting there in the saddle, the thing explained itself as I looked. The fallen pillar had been built upon older ruins; all Egypt is that way, ruin founded on the ruin of ruins—like human hopes.

"The stone steps, descending into the shadow of remote ages, invited me. I dismounted, walked to the edge of the excavation, and, kneeling, peered downward. And I saw a wall and the lotus-carved rim of a vast stone-framed pool; and as I looked I heard the tinkle of water. For the pillar, falling, had unbottled the ancient spring, and now the stone-framed lagoon was slowly filling after its drought of centuries.

"There was light enough to see by, but, not knowing how far I might penetrate, I returned to my horse, pocketed matches and candles from the saddlebags, and, returning, started straight down the steps of stone.

"Fountain, wall, lagoon, steps, terraces half buried—all showed what the place had been: a water garden of ancient Egypt—probably royal— because, although I am not able to decipher hieroglyphics, I have heard somewhere that these picture inscriptions, when inclosed in a cartouch like this"—he drew rapidly—

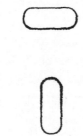

"or this

... indicate that the subject of the inscription was once a king.

"And on every wall, every column, I saw the insignia of ancient royalty, and I saw strange hawk-headed figures bearing symbols engraved on stone—beasts, birds, fishes, unknown signs and symbols; and everywhere the lotus carved in stone—the bud, the blossom half-inclosed, the perfect flower."

His dreamy eyes met the gaze of the Tracer, unseeing; he rested his sunburned face between both palms, speaking in the same vague monotone:

"Everywhere dust, ashes, decay, the death of life, the utter annihilation of the living—save only the sparkle of reborn waters slowly covering the baked bed of the stone-edged pool—strange, luminous water, lacking the vital sky tint, enameled with a film of dust, yet, for all that, quickening with imprisoned brilliancy like an opal.

"The slow filling of the pool fascinated me; I stood I know not how long watching the thin film of water spreading away into the dimness beyond. At last I turned and passed curiously along the wall where, at its base, mounds of dust marked what may have been trees. Into these I probed with my riding crop, but discovered nothing except the depths of the dust.

"When I had penetrated the ghost of this ancient garden for a thousand yards the light from the opening was no longer of any service. I lighted a candle; and its yellow rays fell upon a square portal into which led another flight of steps. And I went down.

"There were eighteen steps descending into a square stone room. Strange gleams and glimmers from wall and ceiling flashed dimly in my eyes under the wavering flame of the candle. Then the flame grew still— still as death—and Death lay at my feet—there on the stone floor—a man, square shouldered, hairless, the cobwebs of his tunic mantling him, lying face downward, arms outflung.

"After a moment I stooped and touched him, and the entire prostrate figure dissolved into dust where it lay, leaving at my feet a shadow shape in thin silhouette against the pavement—merely a gray layer of finest dust shaped like a man, a tracery of impalpable powder on the stones.

"Upward and around me I passed the burning candle; vast figures in blue and red and gold grew out of the darkness; the painted walls sparkled; the shadows that had slept through all those centuries trembled and shrank away into distant corners.

"And then—and then I saw the gold edges of her sandals sparkle in the darkness, and the clasped girdle of virgin gold around her slender waist glimmered like purest flame!"

Burke, leaning far across the table, interlocked hands tightening, stared and stared into space. A smile edged his mouth; his voice grew wonderfully gentle:

"Why, she was scarcely eighteen—this child—there so motionless, so lifelike, with the sandals edging her little upturned feet, and the small hands of her folded between the breasts. It was as though she had just stretched herself out there—scarcely sound asleep as yet, and her thick, silky hair—cut as they cut children's hair in these days, you know—cradled her head and cheeks.

"So marvelous the mimicry of life, so absolute the deception of breathing sleep, that I scarce dared move, fearing to awaken her.

"When I did move I forgot the dusty shape of the dead at my feet, and left, full across his neck, the imprint of a spurred riding boot. It gave me my first shudder; I turned, feeling beneath my foot the soft, yielding powder, and stood aghast. Then—it is absurd!—but I felt as a man feels who has trodden inadvertently upon another's foot—and in an impulse of reparation I stooped hastily and attempted to smooth out the mortal dust which bore the imprint of my heel. But the fine powder flaked my glove, and, looking about for something to compose the ashes with, I picked up a papyrus scroll. Perhaps he himself had written on it; nobody can ever know, and I used it as a sort of hoe to scrape him together and smooth him out on the stones."

The young man drew a yellowish roll of paper-like substance from his pocket and laid it on the table.

"This is the same papyrus," he said. "I had forgotten that I carried it away with me until I found it in my shooting coat while packing to sail for New York."

The Tracer of Lost Persons reached over and picked up the scroll. It was flexible still, but brittle; he opened it with great care, considered the strange figures upon it for a while, then turned almost sharply on his visitor.

"Go on," he said.

And Burke went on:

"The candle was burning low; I lighted two more, placing them at her head and feet on the edges of the stone couch. Then, lighting a third candle, I stood beside the couch and looked down at the dead girl under her veil-like robe, set with golden stars."

He passed his hand wearily over his hair and forehead.

"I do not know what the accepted meaning of beauty may be if it was not there under my eyes. Flawless as palest amber ivory and rose, the smooth-flowing contours melted into exquisite symmetry; lashes like darkest velvet rested on the pure curve of the cheeks; the closed lids, the mouth still faintly stained with color, the delicate nose, the full, childish lips, sensitive, sweet, resting softly upon each other—if these were not all parts of but one lovely miracle, then there is no beauty save in a dream of Paradise. . . .

"A gold band of linked scarabs bound her short, thick hair straight across the forehead; thin scales of gold fell from a necklace, clothing her breasts in brilliant discolored metal, through which ivory-tinted skin showed. A belt of pure, soft gold clasped her body at the waist; gold-edged sandals clung to her little feet.

"At first, when the stunned surprise had subsided, I thought that I was looking upon some miracle of ancient embalming, hitherto unknown. Yet, in the smooth skin there was no slit to prove it, no opening in any vein or artery, no mutilation of this sculptured masterpiece of the Most High, no cerements, no bandages, no gilded carven case with painted face to stare open eyed through the wailing cycles.

"This was the image of sleep—of life unconscious—not of death. Yet is was death—death that had come upon her centuries and centuries ago; for the gold had turned iridescent and magnificently discolored; the sandal straps fell into dust as I bent above them, leaving the sandals clinging to her feet only by the wired silver core of the thongs. And, as I touched it fearfully, the veil-like garment covering her, vanished into thin air, its metal stars twinkling in a shower around her on the stone floor."

The Tracer, motionless, intent, scarcely breathed; the younger man moved restlessly in his chair, the dazed light in his eyes clearing to sullen consciousness.

"What more is there to tell?" he said. "And to what purpose? All this is time wasted. I have my work cut out for me. What more is there to tell?"

"What you have left untold," said the Tracer, with the slightest ring of authority in his quiet voice.

And, as though he had added "Obey!" the younger man sank back in his chair, his hands contracting nervously.

"I went back to El Teb," he said; "I walked like a dreaming man. My sleep was haunted by her beauty; night after night, when at last I fell asleep, instantly I saw her face, and her dark eyes opening into mine in childish bewilderment; day after day I rode out to the fallen pillar and descended to that dark chamber where she lay alone. Then there came a time when I could not endure the thought of her lying there alone. I had never dared to touch her. Horror of what might happen had held me aloof lest she crumble at my touch to that awful powder which I had trodden on.

"I did not know what to do; my Arabs had begun to whisper among themselves, suspicious of my absences, impatient to break camp, perhaps, and roam on once more. Perhaps they believed I had discovered treasure somewhere; I am not sure. At any rate, dread of their following me, determination to take my dead away with me, drove me into action; and that day when I reached her silent chamber I lighted my candle, and, leaning above her for one last look, I touched her shoulder with my finger tip.

"It was a strange sensation. Prepared for a dreadful dissolution, utterly unprepared for cool, yielding flesh, I almost dropped where I stood. For her body was neither cold nor warm, neither dust-dry nor moist; neither the skin of the living nor the dead. It was firm, almost stiff, yet not absolutely without a certain hint of flexibility.

"The appalling wonder of it consumed me; fear, incredulity, terror, apathy succeeded each other; then slowly a fierce shrinking happiness swept me in every fiber.

"This marvelous death, this triumph of beauty over death, was mine. Never again should she lie here alone through the solitudes of night and day; never again should the dignity of Death lack the tribute demanded of Life. Here was the appointed watcher—I, who had found her alone in the wastes of the world—all alone on the outermost edges of the world—a child, dead and unguarded. And standing there beside her I knew that I should never love again."

He straightened up, stretching out his arm: "I did not intend to carry her away to what is known as Christian burial. How could I consign her to darkness again, with all its dreadful mockery of marble, all its awful emblems?

"This lovely stranger was to be my guest forever. The living should be near her while she slept so sweetly her slumber through the centuries; she should have warmth, and soft hangings and sunlight and flowers; and her unconscious ears should be filled with the pleasant stir of living things. ... I have a house in the country, a very old house among meadows and young woodlands. And I—I had dreamed of giving this child a home—"

His voice broke; he buried his head in his hands a moment; but when he lifted it again his features were hard as steel.

"There was already talk in the bazaar about me. I was probably followed, but I did not know it. Then one of my men disappeared. For a week I hesitated to trust my Arabs; but there was no other way. I told them there was a mummy which I desired to carry to some port and smuggle out of the country without consulting the Government. I knew perfectly well that the Government would never forego its claim to such a relic of Egyptian antiquity. I offered my men too much, perhaps. I don't know. They hesitated for a week, trying by every artifice to see the treasure, but I never let them out of my sight.

"Then one day two white men came into camp; and with them came a government escort to arrest me for looting an Egyptian tomb. The white men were Joram Smiles and that Eurasian, Emanuel Gandon, who was partly white, I suppose. I didn't comprehend what they were up to at first. They escorted me forty miles to confront the official at Shen-Bak. When, after a stormy week, I was permitted to return to Saïs, my Arabs and the white men were gone. And the stone chamber under the water garden wall was empty as the hand I hold out to you!"

He opened his palm and rose, his narrowing eyes clear and dangerous.

"At the bazaar I learned enough to know what had been done. I traced the white men to the coast. They sailed on the *Scythian Queen*, taking with them all that I care for on earth or in heaven! And you ask me why I measure their distance from me by a bullet's flight!"

The Tracer also rose, pale and grave.

"Wait!" he said. "There are other things to be done before you prepare to face a jury for double murder."

"It is for them to choose," said Burke. "They shall have the choice of returning to me my dead, or of going to hell full of lead."

"*Exactly*, my dear sir. That part is not difficult," said the Tracer quietly. "There will be no occasion for violence, I assure you. Kindly leave such details to me. I know what is to be done. You are outwardly very calm, Mr. Burke—even dangerously placid; but though you maintain an admirable command over yourself superficially, you are laboring under terrible excitement. Therefore it is my duty to say to you at once that there is no cause for your excitement, no cause for your apprehension as to results. I feel exceedingly confident that you will, in due time, regain possession of all that you care for most—quietly, quietly, my dear sir! You are not yet ready to meet these men, nor am I ready to go with you. I beg you to continue your habit of self-command for a little while. There is no haste— that is to say, there is every reason to make haste slowly. And the quickest method is to seat yourself. Thank you. And I shall sit here beside you and spread out this papyrus scroll for your inspection."

Burke stared at the Tracer, then at the scroll.

"What has that inscription to do with the matter in hand?" he demanded impatiently.

"I leave you to judge," said the Tracer. A dull tint of excitement flushed his lean cheeks; he twisted his gray mustache and bent over the unrolled scroll which was now held flat by weights at the four corners.

"Can you understand any of these symbols, Mr. Burke?" he asked.

"No."

"Curious," mused the Tracer. "Do you know it was fortunate that you put this bit of papyrus in the pocket of your shooting coat—so fortunate that, in a way, it approaches the miraculous?"

"What do you mean? Is there anything in that scroll bearing on this matter?"

"Yes."

"And you can read it? Are you versed in such learning, Mr. Keen?"

"I am an Egyptologist—among other details," said the Tracer calmly.

The young man gazed at him, astonished. The Tracer of Lost Persons picked up a pencil, laid a sheet of paper on the table beside the papyrus, and slowly began to copy the first symbol:

"The ancient Egyptian word for the personal pronoun 'I' was *anuk*," said the Tracer placidly. "The phonetic for *a* was the hieroglyph

a reed; for *n* the water symbol

for *u* the symbols

for *k*

Therefore this hieroglyphic inscription begins with the personal pronoun

or *I*. That is very easy, of course.

"Now, the most ancient of Egyptian inscriptions read vertically in columns; there are only two columns in this papyrus, so we'll try it vertically and pass downward to the next symbol, which is inclosed in a sort of frame or cartouch. That immediately signifies that royalty is mentioned; therefore, we have already translated as much as 'I, the king (or queen).' Do you see?"

"Yes," said Burke, staring.

"Very well. Now this symbol, number two,

spells out the word '*Meris*,' in this way: M (pronounced *me*) is phonetically symbolized by the characters

r by

(a mouth) and the comma

and the hieroglyph

i by two reeds

and two oblique strokes,

and *s* by

This gives us Meris, the name of that deposed and fugitive king of Egypt who, after a last raid on the summer palace of Mer-Shen, usurping ruler of Egypt, was followed and tracked to Saïs, where, with an arrow through his back, he crawled to El Teb and finally died there of his wound. All this Egyptologists are perfectly familiar with in the translations of the boastful tablets and inscriptions erected near Saïs by Mer-Shen, the three hundred and twelfth sovereign after Queen Nitocris."

He looked up at Burke, smiling. "Therefore," he said, "this papyrus scroll was written by Meris, ex-king, a speculative thousands of years before Christ. And it begins: 'I, Meris the King.'"

"How does all this bear upon what concerns me?" demanded Burke.

"Wait!"

Something in the quiet significance of the Tracer's brief command sent a curious thrill through the younger man. He leaned stiffly forward, studying the scroll, every faculty concentrated on the symbol which the Tracer had now touched with the carefully sharpened point of his pencil:

"That," said Mr. Keen, "is the ancient Egyptian word for 'little,' 'Ket.' The next, below, written in two lines, is 'Samaris,' a proper name—the name of a woman. Under that, again, is the symbol for the number 18; the decimal sign,

and eight vertical strokes,

Under that, again, is a hieroglyph of another sort, an ideograph representing a girl with a harp; and, beneath that, the symbol which always represented a dancing girl and also the royal symbol inclosed in a cartouch,

which means literally 'the Ruler of Upper and Lower Egypt.' Under that is the significant symbol

representing an arm and a hand holding a stick. This always means *force*— to take forcibly or to use violence. Therefore, so far, we have the following literal translation: 'I, Meris the King, little Samaris, eighteen, a harpist, dancing girl, the Ruler of Upper and Lower Egypt, to take by violence—'"

"What does that make?" broke in Burke impatiently.

"*Wait!* Wait until we have translated everything literally. And, Mr. Burke, it might make it easier for us both if you would remember that I have had the pleasure of deciphering many hundreds of papyri before you had ever heard that there were such things."

"I beg your pardon," said the young man in a low voice.

"I beg yours for my impatience," said the Tracer pleasantly. "This deciphering always did affect my nerves and shorten my temper. And, no doubt, it is quite as hard on you. Shall we go on, Mr. Burke?"

"If you please, Mr. Keen."

So the Tracer laid his pencil point on the next symbol

"That is the symbol for night," he said; "and that

is the water symbol again, as you know; and that

is the ideograph, meaning a ship. The five reversed crescents

record the number of days voyage; the sign

means a house, and is also the letter H in the Egyptian alphabet.

"Under it, again, we have a repetition of the first symbol meaning *I*, and a repetition of the second symbol, meaning 'Meris, the King.' Then, below that cartouch, comes a new symbol,

which is the feminine personal pronoun, *sentus*, meaning '*she*'; and the first column is completed with the symbol for the ancient Egyptian verb, *nehes*, 'to awake,'

"And now we take the second column, which begins with the jackal ideograph expressing slyness or cleverness. Under it is the hieroglyph meaning 'to run away,' 'to escape.' And under that, Mr. Burke, is one of the rarest of all Egyptian symbols; a symbol seldom seen on stone or papyrus,

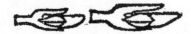

except in rare references to the mysteries of Isis. The meaning of it, so long in dispute, has finally been practically determined through a new discovery in the cuneiform inscriptions. It is the symbol of two hands holding two *closed* eyes; and it signifies power."

"You mean that those ancients understood hypnotism?" asked Burke, astonished.

"Evidently their priests did; evidently hypnotism was understood and employed in certain mysteries. And there is the symbol of it; and under it the hieroglyphs

meaning 'a day and a night,' with the symbol

as usual present to signify force or strength employed. Under that, again, is a human figure stretched upon a typical Egyptian couch. And now, Mr. Burke, *note carefully* three modifying signs: first, that it is a *couch* or *bed* on which the figure is stretched, not the funeral couch, not the embalming slab; second, there is no mummy mask covering the face, and no mummy case covering the body; third, that under the recumbent figure is pictured an *open* mouth, not a *closed* one.

"All these modify the ideograph, apparently representing death. But the sleep symbol is not present. Therefore it is a sound inference that all this simply confirms the symbol of hypnotism."

Burke, intensely absorbed, stared steadily at the scroll.

"Now," continued Mr. Keen, "we note the symbol of force again, always present; and, continuing horizontally, a cartouch quite empty except for the midday sun. That is simply translated; the midday sun illuminates nothing. Meris, deposed, is king only in name; and the sun no longer shines on him as 'Ruler of Upper and Lower Egypt.' Under that despairing symbol, 'King of Nothing,' we have

the phonetics which spell *sha*, the word for garden. And, just beyond this, horizontally, the modifying ideograph meaning 'a *water* garden';

a design of lotus and tree alternating on a terrace. Under that is the symbol for the word '*aneb,*'

a 'wall.' Beyond that, horizontally, is the symbol for 'house.' It should be placed under the wall symbol, but the Egyptians were very apt to fill up spaces instead of continuing their vertical columns. Now, beneath, we find the imperative command

'arise!' And the Egyptian personal pronoun '*entuten,*'

which means 'you' or 'thou.'

"Under that is the symbol

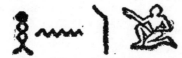

which means 'priest,' or, literally, 'priest man.' Then comes the imperative 'awake to life!'

After that, our first symbol again, meaning '*I*,' followed horizontally by the symbol

signifying 'to go.'

"Then comes a very important drawing—you see?—the picture of a man with a jackal's head, not a dog's head. It is not accompanied by the phonetic in a cartouch, as it should be. Probably the writer was in desperate haste at the end. But, nevertheless, it is easy to translate that symbol of the man with a jackal's head. It is a picture of the Egyptian god, Anubis, who was supposed to linger at the side of the dying to conduct their souls. Anubis, the jackal-headed, is the courier, the personal escort of departing souls. And this is he.

"And now the screed ends with the cry 'Pray for me!'

the last symbol on this strange scroll—this missive written by a deposed, wounded, and dying king to an unnamed priest. Here is the literal translation in columns:

I	*cunning*
Meris the King	*escape*
little	*hypnotize*
Samaris	*King of Nothing*
eighteen	*place forcibly*
a harpist	*garden*
a dancing girl—Ruler of	*water garden*
Upper and Lower	*wall*
Egypt	*house*
took forcibly—night	*Arise. Do*
by water	*Thou*
five days	*Priest Man*
ship	*Awake*
house	*To life*
I	*I go*
Meris the King	*Anubis*
she	*Pray*

awake

"And this is what that letter, thousands of years old, means in this language of ours, hundreds of years young: 'I, Meris the King, seized little Samaris, a harpist and a dancing girl, eighteen years of age, belonging to the King of Upper and Lower Egypt, and carried her away at night on shipboard—a voyage of five days—to my house. I, Meris the King, lest she lie awake watching cunningly for a chance to escape, hypnotized her (or had her hypnotized) so that she lay like one dead or asleep, but breathing, and I, King no longer of Upper and Lower Egypt, took her and placed her in my house under the wall of the water garden. Arise! therefore, O thou priest; (go) and awaken her to life. I am dying (I go with Anubis!). Pray for me!'"

FOR A FULL MINUTE THE TWO MEN SAT THERE WITHOUT MOVING OR speaking. Then the Tracer laid aside his pencil.

"To sum up," he said, opening the palm of his left hand and placing the forefinger of his right across it, "the excavation made by the falling pillar raised in triumph above the water garden of the deposed king, Meris, by his rival, was the subterranean house of Meris. The prostrate figure which crumbled to powder at your touch may have been the very priest to whom this letter or papyrus was written. Perhaps the bearer of the scroll was a traitor and stabbed the priest as he was reading the missive. Who can tell how that priest died? He either died or betrayed his trust, for he never aroused the little Samaris from her suspended animation. And the water garden fell into ruins and she slept; and the Ruler of Upper and Lower Egypt raised his columns, lotus crowned, above the ruins; and she slept on. Then—*you* came."

Burke stared like one stupefied.

"I do not know," said the Tracer gravely, "what balm there may be in a suspension of sensation, perhaps of vitality, to protect the human body from corruption after death. I do not know how soon suspended animation or the state of hypnotic coma, undisturbed, changes into death—whether it comes gradually, imperceptibly freeing the soul; whether the soul hides there, asleep, until suddenly the flame of vitality is extinguished. I do not know how long she lay there with life in her."

He leaned back and touched an electric bell, then, turning to Burke:

"Speaking of pistol range," he said, "unstrap those weapons and pass them over, if you please."

And the young man obeyed as in a trance.

"Thank you. There are four men coming into this room. You will keep your seat, if you please, Mr. Burke."

After a moment the door opened noiselessly. Two men handcuffed together entered the room; two men, hands in their pockets, sauntered carelessly behind the prisoners and leaned back against the closed door.

"That short, red-haired, lame man with the cast in his eye—do you recognize him?" asked the Tracer quietly.

Burke, grasping the arms of his chair, had started to rise, fury fairly blazing from his eyes; but, at the sound of the Tracer's calm, even voice, he sank back into his chair.

"That is Joram Smiles? You recognize him?" continued Mr. Keen.

Burke nodded.

"*Exactly*—alias Limpy, alias Red Jo, alias Big Stick Joram, alias Pinky; swindler, international confidence man, fence, burglar, gambler; convicted in 1887, and sent to Sing Sing for forgery; convicted in 1898, and sent to Auburn for swindling; arrested by my men on board the S. S. *Scythian Queen*, at the cabled request of John T. Burke, Esquire, and held to explain the nature of his luggage, which consisted of the contents of an Egyptian vault or underground ruin, declared at the customhouse as a mummy, and passed as such."

The quiet, monotonous voice of the Tracer halted, then, as he glanced at the second prisoner, grew harder:

"Emanuel Gandon, general international criminal, with over half a hundred aliases, arrested in company with Smiles and held until Mr. Burke's arrival."

Turning to Burke, the Tracer continued: "Fortunately, the *Scythian Queen* broke down off Brindisi. It gave us time to act on your cable; we found these men aboard when she was signaled off the Hook. I went out with the pilot myself, Mr. Burke."

Smiles shot a wicked look at Burke; Gandon scowled at the floor.

"Now," said the Tracer pleasantly, meeting the venomous glare of Smiles, "I'll get you that warrant you have been demanding to have exhibited to you. Here it is—charging you and your amiable friend Gandon with breaking into and robbing the Metropolitan Museum of ancient Egyptian gold ornaments, in March, 1903, and taking them to France, where they were sold to collectors. It seems that you found the business good enough to go prowling about Egypt on a hunt for something to sell here. A great mistake, my friends—a very great mistake, because, after the Museum has finished with you, the Egyptian Government desires to extradite you. And I rather suspect you'll have to go."

He nodded to the two quiet men leaning against the door.

"Come, Joram," said one of them pleasantly.

But Smiles turned furiously on the Tracer. "You lie, you old gray rat!" he cried. "That ain't no mummy; that's a plain dead girl! And there ain't no extrydition for body snatchin', so I guess them blacks at Cairo won't get us, after all!"

"Perhaps," said the Tracer, looking at Burke, who had risen, pale and astounded. "Sit down, Mr. Burke! There is no need to question these men; no need to demand what they robbed you of. For," he added slowly, "what they took from the garden grotto of Saïs, and from you, I have under my own protection."

The Tracer rose, locked the door through which the prisoners and their escorts had departed; then, turning gravely on Burke, he continued:

"That panel, there, is a door. There is a room beyond—a room facing to the south, bright with sunshine, flowers, soft rugs, and draperies of the East. *She* is there—like a child asleep!"

Burke reeled, steadying himself against the wall; the Tracer stared at space, speaking very slowly:

"Such death I have never before heard of. From the moment she came under my protection I have dared to doubt—many things. And an hour ago you brought me a papyrus scroll confirming my doubts. I doubt still— Heaven knows what! Who can say how long the flame of life may flicker within suspended animation? A week? A month? A year? Longer than that? Yes; the Hindoos have proved it. How long? The span of a normal life? Or longer? Can the life flame burn indefinitely when the functions are absolutely suspended—generation after generation, century after century?"

Burke, ghastly white, straightened up, quivering in every limb; the Tracer, as pale as he, laid his hand on the secret panel.

"If—if you dare say it—the phrase is this: '*O Ket Samaris, Nehes!*'—'O Little Samaris, awake!'"

"I—dare. In Heaven's name, open that door!"

Then, averting his head, the Tracer of Lost Persons swung open the panel.

A flood of sunshine flashed on Burke's face; he entered; and the paneled door closed behind him without a sound.

Minute after minute passed; the Tracer stood as though turned to stone, gray head bent.

Then he heard Burke's voice ring out unsteadily:

"O Ket Samaris—Samaris! O Ket Samaris—*Nehes!*"

And again: "Samaris! Samaris! O beloved, awake!"

And once more: "*Nehes!* O Samaris!"

Silence, broken by a strange, sweet, drowsy plaint—like a child awakened at midnight by a dazzling light.

"Samaris!"

Then, through the stillness, a little laugh, and a softly tremulous voice:

"*Ari un āhā, O Entuk sen!*"

THE WHISTLING ROOM
WILLIAM HOPE HODGSON

In 1908 the publisher Eveleigh Nash had considerable success with Algernon Blackwood's collection, John Silence, Physician Extraordinary which introduced the occult detective to a wide audience. Reviewers proclaimed Silence "the occult Sherlock Holmes." Blackwood had originally written the stories as a series of occult studies, and it was at the publisher's request that they were brought together as the investigations of one experienced specialist. Nash was keen to publish a second volume but Blackwood's thoughts were "elsewhere and otherwise," as he liked to term it, and so Nash cast around for another writer. He latched on to William Hope Hodgson (1877–1918) a former merchant seaman and keep-fit specialist who had turned to writing fiction in 1904. He had already published three novels, The Boats of the 'Glen Carrig' (1907), The House on the Borderland (1908), and The Ghost Pirates (1909), all of which had more critical than financial success, but his reputation was growing through his many short supernatural stories, most with nautical settings. What would prove to be his best known and most reprinted story, "The Voice in the Night," had already been published in the United States in 1907 and now found a British publication in Nash's new Nash's Magazine for January 1910. At the same time Hodgson had started his series of stories featuring Carnacki, the Ghost-Finder in The Idler magazine. The Idler was in financial difficulties, and ceased publication in March 1911. It ran only five of the Carnacki series, a sixth, "The Thing

Invisible" appearing in The New Magazine *in January 1912. Nash saw the potential in the series and published these six stories as* Carnacki, the Ghost-Finder *in March 1913.*

Carnacki (we are not told his first name in the stories and it only surfaced when Hodgson copyrighted the stories in the United States) is a modern psychic sleuth using his Electric Pentacle but also such ancient texts as the Sigsand Manuscript, the Saaamaaa Ritual, and Harzam's Monograph. There is little doubt that after the early years of the occult specialist, with Carnacki we enter the realms of the sensationalist.

Hodgson had completed three further Carnacki stories but these were not published until after his death—he was killed in the Great War—and were eventually assembled in a new edition of Carnacki, the Ghost-Finder *in 1947. Since then others have continued to chronicle his adventures including A. F. Kidd and Rick Kennett in* No. 472 Cheyne Walk *(2002),* William Meikle in *Carnacki: Heaven and Hell* (2011) and *The Edinburgh Townhouse *(2017), and two anthologies edited by Sam Gafford,* Carnacki: The New Adventures *(2013) and* Carnacki: The Lost Cases *(2016).*

CARNACKI SHOOK A FRIENDLY FIST AT ME AS I ENTERED, LATE. THEN he opened the door into the dining room, and ushered the four of us—Jessop, Arkright, Taylor and myself—in to dinner.

We dined well, as usual, and, equally as usual, Carnacki was pretty silent during the meal. At the end, we took our wine and cigars to our usual positions, and Carnacki—having got himself comfortable in his big chair—began without any preliminary:—

"I have just got back from Ireland, again," he said. "And I thought you chaps would be interested to hear my news. Besides, I fancy I shall see the thing clearer, after I have told it all out straight. I must tell you this, though, at the beginning—up to the present moment, I have been utterly and completely 'stumped.' I have tumbled upon one of the most peculiar cases of 'haunting'—or devilment of some sort—that I have come against. Now listen.

"I have been spending the last few weeks at Iastrae Castle, about twenty miles northeast of Galway. I got a letter about a month ago from a

Mr. Sid K. Tassoc, who it seemed had bought the place lately, and moved in, only to find that he had bought a very peculiar piece of property.

"When I got there, he met me at the station, driving a jaunting car, and drove me up to the castle, which, by the way, he called a 'house shanty.' I found that he was 'pigging it' there with his boy brother and another American, who seemed to be half-servant and half-companion. It seems that all the servants had left the place, in a body, as you might say, and now they were managing among themselves, assisted by some day-help.

"The three of them got together a scratch feed, and Tassoc told me all about the trouble whilst we were at table. It is most extraordinary, and different from anything that I have had to do with; though that Buzzing Case was very queer, too.

"Tassoc began right in the middle of his story. 'We've got a room in this shanty,' he said, 'which has got a most infernal whistling in it; sort of haunting it. The thing starts any time; you never know when, and it goes on until it frightens you. All the servants have gone, as you know. It's not ordinary whistling, and it isn't the wind. Wait till you hear it.'

"'We're all carrying guns,' said the boy; and slapped his coat pocket.

"'As bad as that?' I said; and the older boy nodded. 'It may be soft,' he replied; 'but wait till you've heard it. Sometimes I think it's some infernal thing, and the next moment, I'm just as sure that someone's playing a trick on me.'

"'Why?' I asked. 'What is to be gained?'

"'You mean,' he said, 'that people usually have some good reason for playing tricks as elaborate as this. Well, I'll tell you. There's a lady in this province, by the name of Miss Donnehue, who's going to be my wife, this day two months. She's more beautiful than they make them, and so far as I can see, I've just stuck my head into an Irish hornet's nest. There's about a score of hot young Irishmen been courting her these two years gone, and now that I'm come along and cut them out, they feel raw against me. Do you begin to understand the possibilities?'

"'Yes,' I said. 'Perhaps I do in a vague sort of way; but I don't see how all this affects the room?'

"'Like this,' he said. 'When I'd fixed it up with Miss Donnehue, I looked out for a place, and bought this little house shanty. Afterward, I told her—one evening during dinner, that I'd decided to tie up here. And then she asked me whether I wasn't afraid of the whistling room. I told her it must have been thrown in gratis, as I'd heard nothing about it. There were some of her men friends present, and I saw a smile go 'round. I found out, after a bit of questioning, that several people have bought this place during the last twenty-odd years. And it was always on the market again, after a trial.

"'Well, the chaps started to bait me a bit, and offered to take bets after dinner that I'd not stay six months in the place. I looked once or twice to Miss Donnehue, so as to be sure I was "getting the note" of the talkee-talkee; but I could see that she didn't take it as a joke, at all. Partly, I think, because there was a bit of a sneer in the way the men were tackling me, and partly because she really believes there is something in this yarn of the Whistling Room.

"'However, after dinner, I did what I could to even things up with the others. I nailed all their bets, and screwed them down hard and safe. I guess some of them are going to be hard hit, unless I lose; which I don't mean to. Well, there you have practically the whole yarn.'

"'Not quite,' I told him. 'All that I know, is that you have bought a castle with a room in it that is in some way "queer," and that you've been doing some betting. Also, I know that your servants have got frightened and run away. Tell me something about the whistling?'

"'Oh, that!' said Tassoc; 'that started the second night we were in. I'd had a good look 'round the room, in the daytime, as you can understand; for the talk up at Arlestrae—Miss Donnehue's place—had made me wonder a bit. But it seems just as usual as some of the other rooms in the old wing, only perhaps a bit more lonesome. But that may be only because of the talk about it, you know.

"'The whistling started about ten o'clock, on the second night, as I said. Tom and I were in the library, when we heard an awfully queer whistling, coming along the East Corridor—The room is in the East Wing, you know.

"'That's that blessed ghost!' I said to Tom, and we collared the lamps off the table, and went up to have a look. I tell you, even as we dug along the corridor, it took me a bit in the throat, it was so beastly queer. It was a sort of tune, in a way; but more as if a devil or some rotten thing were laughing at you, and going to get 'round at your back. That's how it makes you feel.

"'When we got to the door, we didn't wait; but rushed it open; and then I tell you the sound of the thing fairly hit me in the face. Tom said he got it the same way—sort of felt stunned and bewildered. We looked all 'round, and soon got so nervous, we just cleared out, and I locked the door.

"'We came down here and had a stiff peg each. Then we got fit again and began to think we'd been nicely had. So we took sticks, and went out into the grounds, thinking after all it must be some of these confounded Irishmen working the ghost-trick on us. But there was not a leg stirring.

"'We went back into the house, and walked over it, and then paid another visit to the room. But we simply couldn't stand it. We fairly ran out and locked the door again. I don't know how to put it into words; but I had a feeling of being up against something that was rottenly dangerous. You know! We've carried our guns ever since.

"'Of course, we had a real turn out of the room next day, and the whole house place; and we even hunted 'round the grounds; but there was nothing queer. And now I don't know what to think; except that the sensible part of me tells me that it's some plan of these Wild Irishmen to try to take a rise out of me.'

"'Done anything since?' I asked him.

"'Yes,' he said—'watched outside of the door of the room at nights, and chased 'round the grounds, and sounded the walls and floor of the room. We've done everything we could think of; and it's beginning to get on our nerves; so we sent for you.'

"By this, we had finished eating. As we rose from the table, Tassoc suddenly called out:—'Ssh! Hark!'

"We were instantly silent, listening. Then I heard it, an extraordinary hooning whistle, monstrous and inhuman, coming from far away through corridors to my right.

"'By G— d!' said Tassoc; 'and it's scarcely dark yet! Collar those candles, both of you, and come along.'

"In a few moments, we were all out of the door and racing up the stairs. Tassoc turned into a long corridor, and we followed, shielding our candles as we ran. The sound seemed to fill all the passage as we drew near, until I had the feeling that the whole air throbbed under the power of some wanton Immense Force—a sense of an actual taint, as you might say, of monstrosity all about us.

"Tassoc unlocked the door; then, giving it a push with his foot, jumped back, and drew his revolver. As the door flew open, the sound beat out at us, with an effect impossible to explain to one who has not heard it—with a certain, horrible personal note in it; as if in there in the darkness you could picture the room rocking and creaking in a mad, vile glee to its own filthy piping and whistling and hooning. To stand there and listen, was to be stunned by Realization. It was as if someone showed you the mouth of a vast pit suddenly, and said:—That's Hell. And you knew that they had spoken the truth. Do you get it, even a little bit?

"I stepped back a pace into the room, and held the candle over my head, and looked quickly 'round. Tassoc and his brother joined me, and the man came up at the back, and we all held our candles high. I was deafened with the shrill, piping hoon of the whistling; and then, clear in my ear, something seemed to be saying to me:—'Get out of here—quick! Quick! Quick!'

"As you chaps know, I never neglect that sort of thing. Sometimes it may be nothing but nerves; but as you will remember, it was just such a warning that saved me in the 'Grey Dog' Case, and in the 'Yellow Finger' Experiments; as well as other times. Well, I turned sharp 'round to the others: 'Out!' I said. 'For God's sake, *out* quick.' And in an instant I had them into the passage.

"There came an extraordinary yelling scream into the hideous whistling, and then, like a clap of thunder, an utter silence. I slammed the door and locked it. Then, taking the key, I looked 'round at the others. They were pretty white, and I imagine I must have looked that way too. And there we stood a moment, silent.

"'Come down out of this, and have some whisky,' said Tassoc, at last, in a voice he tried to make ordinary; and he led the way. I was the back man, and I know we all kept looking over our shoulders. When we got downstairs, Tassoc passed the bottle 'round. He took a drink, himself, and slapped his glass down on to the table. Then sat down with a thud.

"'That's a lovely thing to have in the house with you, isn't it!' he said. And directly afterward:—'What on earth made you hustle us all out like that, Carnacki?'

"'Something seemed to be telling me to get out, quick,' I said. 'Sounds a bit silly, superstitious, I know; but when you are meddling with this sort of thing, you've got to take notice of queer fancies, and risk being laughed at.'

"I told him then about the 'Grey Dog' business, and he nodded a lot to that. 'Of course,' I said, 'this may be nothing more than those would-be rivals of yours playing some funny game; but, personally, though I'm going to keep an open mind, I feel that there is something beastly and dangerous about this thing.'

"We talked for a while longer, and then Tassoc suggested billiards, which we played in a pretty half-hearted fashion, and all the time cocking an ear to the door, as you might say, for sounds; but none came, and later, after coffee, he suggested early bed, and a thorough overhaul of the room on the morrow.

"My bedroom was in the newer part of the castle, and the door opened into the picture gallery. At the East end of the gallery was the entrance to the corridor of the East Wing; this was shut off from the gallery by two old and heavy oak doors, which looked rather odd and quaint beside the more modern doors of the various rooms.

"When I reached my room, I did not go to bed; but began to unpack my instrument trunk, of which I had retained the key. I intended to take one or two preliminary steps at once, in my investigation of the extraordinary whistling.

"Presently, when the castle had settled into quietness, I slipped out of my room, and across to the entrance of the great corridor. I opened one of the low, squat doors, and threw the beam of my pocket searchlight down the passage. It was empty, and I went through the doorway, and pushed-to the oak behind me. Then along the great passageway, throwing my light before and behind, and keeping my revolver handy.

"I had hung a 'protection belt' of garlic 'round my neck, and the smell of it seemed to fill the corridor and give me assurance; for, as you all know, it is a wonderful 'protection' against the more usual Aeiirii forms of semi-materialization, by which I supposed the whistling might be produced; though, at that period of my investigation, I was quite prepared to find it due to some perfectly natural cause; for it is astonishing the enormous number of cases that prove to have nothing abnormal in them.

"In addition to wearing the necklet, I had plugged my ears loosely with garlic, and as I did not intend to stay more than a few minutes in the room, I hoped to be safe.

"When I reached the door, and put my hand into my pocket for the key, I had a sudden feeling of sickening funk. But I was not going to back out, if I could help it. I unlocked the door and turned the handle. Then I gave the door a sharp push with my foot, as Tassoc had done, and drew my revolver, though I did not expect to have any use for it, really.

"I shone the searchlight all 'round the room, and then stepped inside, with a disgustingly horrible feeling of walking slap into a waiting Danger. I stood a few seconds, waiting, and nothing happened, and the empty room showed bare from corner to corner. And then, you know, I realized that the room was full of an abominable silence; can you understand that? A sort of purposeful silence, just as sickening as any of the filthy noises the Things have power to make. Do you remember what I told you about that 'Silent Garden' business? Well, this room had just that same *malevolent* silence—the beastly quietness of a thing that is looking at you and not seeable itself and thinks that it has got you. Oh, I recognized it instantly, and I whipped the top off my lantern, so as to have light over the *whole* room.

"Then I set-to, working like fury, and keeping my glance all about me. I sealed the two windows with lengths of human hair, right across, and sealed them at every frame. As I worked, a queer, scarcely perceptible tenseness stole into the air of the place, and the silence seemed, if you can understand me, to grow more solid. I knew then that I had no business there without 'full protection'; for I was practically certain that this was no mere Aeiirii development; but one of the worst forms, as the Saiitii; like that 'Grunting Man' case—you know.

"I finished the window and hurried over to the great fireplace. This is a huge affair, and has a queer gallows-iron, I think they are called, projecting from the back of the arch. I sealed the opening with seven human hairs— the seventh crossing the six others.

"Then, just as I was making an end, a low, mocking whistle grew in the room. A cold, nervous pricking went up my spine, and 'round my forehead from the back. The hideous sound filled all the room with an extraordinary, grotesque parody of human whistling, too gigantic to be human—as if something gargantuan and monstrous made the sounds softly. As I stood there a last moment, pressing down the final seal, I had no doubt but that I had come across one of those rare and horrible cases of the *Inanimate* reproducing the functions of the *Animate*, I made a grab for my lamp, and went quickly to the door, looking over my shoulder, and listening for the thing that I expected. It came, just as I got my hand upon the handle—a squeal of incredible, malevolent anger, piercing through the low hooning of the whistling. I dashed out, slamming the door and locking it. I leant a little against the opposite wall of the corridor, feeling rather funny; for it had been a narrow squeak. . . . 'Theyr be noe sayfetie to be gained bye gayrds of holieness when the monyster hath pow'r to speak throe woode and stoene.' So runs the passage in the Sigsand MS., and I proved it in that 'Nodding Door' business. There is no protection against this particular form of monster, except, possibly, for a fractional period of time; for it can reproduce itself in, or take to its purpose, the very protective material which you may use, and has the power to 'formewythine the pentycle'; though not immediately. There is, of course, the possibility of the Unknown Last Line of the Saaamaaa Ritual being uttered; but it is too uncertain to count upon, and the danger is too hideous; and even then it has no power to protect for more than 'maybee fyve beats of the harte,' as the Sigsand has it.

"Inside of the room, there was now a constant, meditative, hooning whistling; but presently this ceased, and the silence seemed worse; for there is such a sense of hidden mischief in a silence.

"After a little, I sealed the door with crossed hairs, and then cleared off down the great passage, and so to bed.

"For a long time I lay awake; but managed eventually to get some sleep. Yet, about two o'clock I was waked by the hooning whistling of the room coming to me, even through the closed doors. The sound was tremendous and seemed to beat through the whole house with a presiding sense of terror. As if (I remember thinking) some monstrous giant had been holding mad carnival with itself at the end of that great passage.

"I got up and sat on the edge of the bed, wondering whether to go along and have a look at the seal; and suddenly there came a thump on my door, and Tassoc walked in, with his dressing gown over his pajamas.

"'I thought it would have waked you, so I came along to have a talk,' he said. '*I* can't sleep. Beautiful! Isn't it!'

"'Extraordinary!' I said, and tossed him my case.

"He lit a cigarette, and we sat and talked for about an hour; and all the time that noise went on, down at the end of the big corridor.

"Suddenly, Tassoc stood up:—

"'Let's take our guns, and go and examine the brute,' he said, and turned toward the door.

"'No!' I said. 'By Jove—*no*! I can't say anything definite, yet; but I believe that room is about as dangerous as it well can be.'

"'Haunted—*really* haunted?' he asked, keenly and without any of his frequent banter.

"I told him, of course, that I could not say a definite *yes* or *no* to such a question; but that I hoped to be able to make a statement, soon. Then I gave him a little lecture on the False Re–Materialization of the Animate–Force through the Inanimate–Inert. He began then to see the particular way in the room might be dangerous, if it were really the subject of a manifestation.

"About an hour later, the whistling ceased quite suddenly, and Tassoc went off again to bed. I went back to mine, also, and eventually got another spell of sleep.

"In the morning, I went along to the room. I found the seals on the door intact. Then I went in. The window seals and the hair were all right; but the seventh hair across the great fireplace was broken. This set me thinking. I knew that it might, very possibly, have snapped, through my having tensioned it too highly; but then, again, it might have been broken by something else. Yet, it was scarcely possible that a man, for instance, could have passed between the six unbroken hairs; for no one would ever have noticed them, entering the room that way, you see; but just walked through them, ignorant of their very existence.

"I removed the other hairs, and the seals. Then I looked up the chimney. It went up straight, and I could see blue sky at the top. It was a big, open flue, and free from any suggestion of hiding places, or corners. Yet, of course, I did not trust to any such casual examination, and after breakfast, I put on my overalls, and climbed to the very top, sounding all the way; but I found nothing.

"Then I came down and went over the whole of the room—floor, ceiling, and walls, mapping them out in six-inch squares, and sounding with both hammer and probe. But there was nothing abnormal.

"Afterward, I made a three-weeks search of the whole castle, in the same thorough way; but found nothing. I went even further, then; for at night, when the whistling commenced, I made a microphone test. You see, if the whistling were mechanically produced, this test would have made evident to me the working of the machinery, if there were any such concealed within the walls. It certainly was an up-to-date method of examination, as you must allow.

"Of course, I did not think that any of Tassoc's rivals had fixed up any mechanical contrivance; but I thought it just possible that there had been some such thing for producing the whistling, made away back in the years, perhaps with the intention of giving the room a reputation that would ensure its being free of inquisitive folk. You see what I mean? Well, of course, it was just possible, if this were the case, that someone knew the secret of the machinery, and was utilizing the knowledge to play this devil of a prank on Tassoc. The microphone test of the walls would certainly have made this known to me, as I have said; but there was nothing of the sort in the castle; so that I had practically no doubt at all now, but that it was a genuine case of what is popularly termed 'haunting.'

"All this time, every night, and sometimes most of each night, the hooning whistling of the Room was intolerable. It was as if an intelligence there knew that steps were being taken against it, and piped and hooned in a sort of mad, mocking contempt. I tell you, it was as extraordinary as it was horrible. Time after time, I went along—tiptoeing noiselessly on stockinged feet—to the sealed door (for I always kept the Room sealed). I went at all hours of the night, and often the whistling, inside, would seem to change to a brutally malignant note, as though the half-animate monster saw me plainly through the shut door. And all the time the shrieking, hooning whistling would fill the whole corridor, so that I used to feel a precious lonely chap, messing about there with one of Hell's mysteries.

"And every morning, I would enter the room, and examine the different hairs and seals. You see, after the first week, I had stretched parallel hairs all along the walls of the room, and along the ceiling; but over the floor, which was of polished stone, I had set out little, colorless wafers, tacky-side uppermost. Each wafer was numbered, and they were arranged after a definite plan, so that I should be able to trace the exact movements of any living thing that went across the floor.

"You will see that no material being or creature could possibly have entered that room, without leaving many signs to tell me about it. But nothing was ever disturbed, and I began to think that I should have to risk an attempt to stay the night in the room, in the Electric Pentacle. Yet, mind you, I knew that it would be a crazy thing to do; but I was getting stumped, and ready to do anything.

"Once, about midnight, I did break the seal on the door, and have a quick look in; but, I tell you, the whole Room gave one mad yell, and seemed to come toward me in a great belly of shadows, as if the walls had bellied in toward me. Of course, that must have been fancy. Anyway, the yell was sufficient, and I slammed the door, and locked it, feeling a bit weak down my spine. You know the feeling.

"And then, when I had got to that state of readiness for anything, I made something of a discovery. It was about one in the morning, and I was walking slowly 'round the castle, keeping in the soft grass. I had come under the shadow of the East Front, and far above me, I could hear the vile, hooning whistle of the Room, up in the darkness of the unlit wing. Then, suddenly, a little in front of me, I heard a man's voice, speaking low, but evidently in glee:—

"'By George! You Chaps; but I wouldn't care to bring a wife home in that!' it said, in the tone of the cultured Irish.

"Someone started to reply; but there came a sharp exclamation, and then a rush, and I heard footsteps running in all directions. Evidently, the men had spotted me.

"For a few seconds, I stood there, feeling an awful ass. After all, *they* were at the bottom of the haunting! Do you see what a big fool it made me seem? I had no doubt but that they were some of Tassoc's rivals; and here I had been feeling in every bone that I had hit a real, bad, genuine Case! And then, you know, there came the memory of hundreds of details, that made me just as much in doubt again. Anyway, whether it was natural, or ab-natural, there was a great deal yet to be cleared up.

"I told Tassoc, next morning, what I had discovered, and through the whole of every night, for five nights, we kept a close watch 'round the East Wing; but there was never a sign of anyone prowling about; and all the time, almost from evening to dawn, that grotesque whistling would hoon incredibly, far above us in the darkness.

"On the morning after the fifth night, I received a wire from here, which brought me home by the next boat. I explained to Tassoc that I was simply bound to come away for a few days; but told him to keep up the watch 'round the castle. One thing I was very careful to do, and that was to make him absolutely promise never to go into the Room, between sunset and sunrise. I made it clear to him that we knew nothing definite yet, one way or the other; and if the room were what I had first thought it to be, it might be a lot better for him to die first, than enter it after dark.

"When I got here, and had finished my business, I thought you chaps would be interested; and also I wanted to get it all spread out clear in my mind; so I rung you up. I am going over again tomorrow, and when I get back, I ought to have something pretty extraordinary to tell you. By the way, there is a curious thing I forgot to tell you. I tried to get a phonographic record of the whistling; but it simply produced no impression on the wax at all. That is one of the things that has made me feel queer, I can tell you. Another extraordinary thing is that the microphone will not magnify the sound—will not even transmit it; seems to take no account of it, and acts as if it were nonexistent. I am absolutely and utterly stumped, up to the present. I am a wee bit curious to see whether any of your dear clever heads can make daylight of it. *I* cannot—not yet."

He rose to his feet.

"Good night, all," he said, and began to usher us out abruptly, but without offence, into the night.

A fortnight later, he dropped each of us a card, and you can imagine that I was not late this time. When we arrived, Carnacki took us straight into dinner, and when we had finished, and all made ourselves comfortable, he began again, where he had left off:—

"Now just listen quietly; for I have got something pretty queer to tell you. I got back late at night, and I had to walk up to the castle, as I had not warned them that I was coming. It was bright moonlight; so that the walk was rather a pleasure, than otherwise. When I got there, the whole place was in darkness, and I thought I would take a walk 'round outside, to see whether Tassoc or his brother was keeping watch. But I could not find them anywhere, and concluded that they had got tired of it, and gone off to bed.

"As I returned across the front of the East Wing, I caught the hooning whistling of the Room, coming down strangely through the stillness of the night. It had a queer note in it, I remember—low and constant, queerly meditative. I looked up at the window, bright in the moonlight, and got a sudden thought to bring a ladder from the stable yard, and try to get a look into the Room, through the window.

"With this notion, I hunted 'round at the back of the castle, among the straggle of offices, and presently found a long, fairly light ladder; though it was heavy enough for one, goodness knows! And I thought at first that I should never get it reared. I managed at last, and let the ends rest very quietly against the wall, a little below the sill of the larger window. Then, going silently, I went up the ladder. Presently, I had my face above the sill and was looking in alone with the moonlight.

"Of course, the queer whistling sounded louder up there; but it still conveyed that peculiar sense of something whistling quietly to itself—can you understand? Though, for all the meditative lowness of the note, the horrible, gargantuan quality was distinct—a mighty parody of the human, as if I stood there and listened to the whistling from the lips of a monster with a man's soul.

"And then, you know, I saw something. The floor in the middle of the huge, empty room, was puckered upward in the center into a strange soft-looking mound, parted at the top into an ever-changing hole, that pulsated to that great, gentle hooning. At times, as I watched, I saw the heaving of the indented mound, gap across with a queer, inward suction, as with the drawing of an enormous breath; then the thing would dilate and pout once more to the incredible melody. And suddenly, as I stared, dumb, it came to me that the thing was living. I was looking at two enormous, blackened lips, blistered and brutal, there in the pale moonlight. . . .

"Abruptly, they bulged out to a vast, pouting mound of force and sound, stiffened and swollen, and hugely massive and clean-cut in the moon-beams. And a great sweat lay heavy on the vast upper-lip. In the same moment of time, the whistling had burst into a mad screaming note, that seemed to stun me, even where I stood, outside of the window. And then, the following moment, I was staring blankly at the solid, undisturbed floor of the room—smooth, polished stone flooring, from wall to wall; and there was an absolute silence.

"You can picture me staring into the quiet Room and, knowing what I knew, I felt like a sick, frightened kid, and wanted to slide *quietly* down the ladder, and run away. But in that very instant, I heard Tassoc's voice calling to me from within the Room, for help, *help*. My God! but I got such an awful dazed feeling; and I had a vague, bewildered notion that, after all, it was the Irishmen who had got him in there, and were taking it out of him. And then the call came again, and I burst the window, and jumped in to help him. I had a confused idea that the call had come from within the shadow of the great fireplace, and I raced across to it; but there was no one there.

"'Tassoc!' I shouted, and my voice went empty-sounding 'round the great apartment; and then, in a flash, *I knew that Tassoc had never called*. I whirled 'round, sick with fear, toward the window, and as I did so, a frightful, exultant whistling scream burst through the Room. On my left, the end wall had bellied-in toward me, in a pair of gargantuan lips, black and utterly monstrous, to within a yard of my face. I fumbled for a mad instant at my revolver; not for *it*, but myself; for the danger was a thousand times worse than death. And then, suddenly, the Unknown Last Line of the Saaamaaa Ritual was whispered quite audibly in the room. Instantly, the thing happened that I have known once before. There came a sense as of dust falling continually and monotonously, and I knew that my life hung uncertain and suspended for a flash, in a brief, reeling vertigo of unseeable things. Then *that* ended, and I knew that I might live. My soul and body blended again, and life and power came to me. I dashed furiously at the window, and hurled myself out head-foremost; for I can tell you that I had stopped being afraid of death. I crashed down on to the ladder, and slithered, grabbing and grabbing; and so came some way or other alive to the bottom. And there I sat in the soft, wet grass, with the moonlight all about me; and far above, through the broken window of the Room, there was a low whistling.

"That is the chief of it. I was not hurt, and I went 'round to the front, and knocked Tassoc up. When they let me in, we had a long yarn, over some good whisky—for I was shaken to pieces—and I explained things as much as I could, I told Tassoc that the room would have to come down, and every fragment of it burned in a blast-furnace, erected within a pentacle. He nodded. There was nothing to say. Then I went to bed.

"We turned a small army on to the work, and within ten days, that lovely thing had gone up in smoke, and what was left was calcined, and clean.

"It was when the workmen were stripping the paneling, that I got hold of a sound notion of the beginnings of that beastly development. Over the great fireplace, after the great oak panels had been torn down, I found that there was let into the masonry a scrollwork of stone, with on it an old inscription, in ancient Celtic, that here in this room was burned Dian Tiansay, Jester of King Alzof, who made the Song of Foolishness upon King Ernore of the Seventh Castle.

"When I got the translation clear, I gave it to Tassoc. He was tremendously excited; for he knew the old tale, and took me down to the library to look at an old parchment that gave the story in detail. Afterward, I found that the incident was well-known about the countryside; but always regarded more as a legend than as history. And no one seemed ever to have dreamt that the old East Wing of Iastrae Castle was the remains of the ancient Seventh Castle.

"From the old parchment, I gathered that there had been a pretty dirty job done, away back in the years. It seems that King Alzof and King Ernore had been enemies by birthright, as you might say truly; but that nothing more than a little raiding had occurred on either side for years, until Dian Tiansay made the Song of Foolishness upon King Ernore, and sang it before King Alzof; and so greatly was it appreciated that King Alzof gave the jester one of his ladies, to wife.

"Presently, all the people of the land had come to know the song, and so it came at last to King Ernore, who was so angered that he made war upon his old enemy, and took and burned him and his castle; but Dian Tiansay, the jester, he brought with him to his own place, and having torn his tongue out because of the song which he had made and sung, he imprisoned him in the Room in the East Wing (which was evidently used for unpleasant purposes), and the jester's wife, he kept for himself, having a fancy for her prettiness.

"But one night, Dian Tiansay's wife was not to be found, and in the morning they discovered her lying dead in her husband's arms, and he sitting, whistling the Song of Foolishness, for he had no longer the power to sing it.

"Then they roasted Dian Tiansay, in the great fireplace—probably from that selfsame 'galley-iron' which I have already mentioned. And until he died, Dian Tiansay ceased not to whistle the Song of Foolishness, which he could no longer sing. But afterward, 'in that room' there was often heard at night the sound of something whistling; and there 'grew a power in that room,' so that none dared to sleep in it. And presently, it would seem, the King went to another castle; for the whistling troubled him.

"There you have it all. Of course, that is only a rough rendering of the translation of the parchment. But it sounds extraordinarily quaint. Don't you think so?"

"Yes," I said, answering for the lot. "But how did the thing grow to such a tremendous manifestation?"

"One of those cases of continuity of thought producing a positive action upon the immediate surrounding material," replied Carnacki. "The development must have been going forward through centuries, to have produced such a monstrosity. It was a true instance of Saiitii manifestation, which I can best explain by likening it to a living spiritual fungus, which involves the very structure of the aether-fiber itself, and, of course, in so doing, acquires an essential control over the 'material substance' involved in it. It is impossible to make it plainer in a few words."

"What broke the seventh hair?" asked Taylor.

But Carnacki did not know. He thought it was probably nothing but being too severely tensioned. He also explained that they found out that the men who had run away, had not been up to mischief; but had come over secretly, merely to hear the whistling, which, indeed, had suddenly become the talk of the whole countryside.

"One other thing," said Arkright, "have you any idea what governs the use of the Unknown Last Line of the Saaamaaa Ritual? I know, of course, that it was used by the Ab-human Priests in the Incantation of Raaaee; but what used it on your behalf, and what made it?"

"You had better read Harzan's Monograph, and my Addenda to it, on Astral and Astral Co-ordination and Interference," said Carnacki. "It is an extraordinary subject, and I can only say here that the human vibration may not be insulated from the astral (as is always believed to be the case, in interferences by the Ab-human), without immediate action being taken by those Forces which govern the spinning of the outer circle. In other words, it is being proved, time after time, that there is some inscrutable Protective Force constantly intervening between the human soul (not the body, mind you,) and the Outer Monstrosities. Am I clear?"

"Yes, I think so," I replied. "And you believe that the Room had become the material expression of the ancient Jester—that his soul, rotten with hatred, had bred into a monster—eh?" I asked.

"Yes," said Carnacki, nodding, "I think you've put my thought rather neatly. It is a queer coincidence that Miss Donnehue is supposed to be descended (so I have heard since) from the same King Ernore. It makes one think some curious thoughts, doesn't it? The marriage coming on, and the Room waking to fresh life. If she had gone into that room, ever . . . eh? IT had waited a long time. Sins of the fathers. Yes, I've thought of that. They're to be married next week, and I am to be best man, which is a thing I hate. And he won his bets, rather! Just think, *if* ever she had gone into that room. Pretty horrible, eh?"

He nodded his head, grimly, and we four nodded back. Then he rose and took us collectively to the door, and presently thrust us forth in friendly fashion on the Embankment and into the fresh night air.

"Good night," we all called back, and went to our various homes. If she had, eh? If she had? That is what I kept thinking.

THE WOMAN WITH THE CROOKED NOSE

VICTOR ROUSSEAU

Few of the earlier occult detective stories had appeared in the United States. The stories by L. T. Meade and E. & H. Heron were reprinted in the American editions of the British magazines, and Algernon Blackwood's John Silence *was published in Boston in 1909, but there would not be an occult investigator created by an American-born writer until John U. Giesy and Junius B. Smith began their long-running series of novels and novellas featuring Prince Abdul Omar, known as Semi Dual, with "The Occult Detector," serialized in* The Cavalier *in early 1912. But there was an original series created by a British writer and first published in the United States in the Ivan Brodsky stories by Victor Rousseau.*

Born of a Jewish father and French mother young Avigdor Rousseau Emanuel (1879–1960) seems to have lived a rather regimented life. He was well educated and was steered by his father who hoped the lad would follow in his footsteps, and those of his elder brother, and become a lawyer. Victor—he adopted that version of his name in his teens—rebelled. At the first opportunity, when he was twenty-one, went to South Africa and joined the infantry to fight in the Boer War. This inspired his first book, Derwent's Horse *(1901). Soon after he returned to England he set sail for the United States where he became a reporter on the New York World. He began writing material for other magazines, including* Harper's Weekly, *in*

1905. It seems he also became a spiritualist, if the references in "Discovery of the Soul" (1909) mean anything. He adapted these thoughts for a series of stories about Ivan Brodsky, a professor of nervous diseases who initially worked in a hospital attached to a penitentiary before setting himself up as a consultant. The series was syndicated through newspapers during 1909 and 1910 under the alias H. M. Egbert, but were thereafter to all intents forgotten. It was not until Rousseau resold several of the series to Weird Tales *in 1926 that Brodsky was rediscovered. Even then, the stories were not published in book form until 2006 as* The Surgeon of Souls.

Rousseau became a prolific contributor to the pulp magazines, and he is remembered today chiefly for his science fiction that included The Messiah of the Cylinder *(1917), Rousseau's answer to H. G. Wells's* When the Sleeper Awakes. *He wrote a further series of occult detective stories featuring Dr. Martinus for* Ghost Stories *in 1926-7, which remains to be collected in book form, and the remarkable exploits of Dr. Phileas Immanuel, who explores people's souls in* The Tracer of Egos, *a series that was first published in 1913 and that only appeared in book form in 2007.*

THERE EXISTS A SMALL GENERAL PUBLIC THAT IS ALWAYS ACQUAINTED in advance with current affairs, is abreast of modern investigation and discovery, and lives, as it were, fifteen or twenty years in advance of its contemporaries. It was among such people that Dr. Brodsky's reputation had spread after the remarkable cure he had effected in the case of the jailer's daughter who was possessed by the soul of the Slav murderer. Thenceforward, while wholly unknown to that portion of the public that gleans its information through the medium of the press, he began to be besieged by requests for his assistance in many instances. He was asked to cure obsessions, to clean out haunted houses, to act as intermediary between the living and the dead by persons who misunderstood his powers.

Dr. Brodsky was in no sense a medium; he could not even produce the very ordinary phenomenon of making a table spin, and was, if anything, more lacking than most persons in psychic development. He was the first to disclaim any gift in this direction. His skill as a hypnotist, he always insisted, was no more than that attainable by anyone who devoted himself to the study of this acquirement. It was, therefore, embarrassing in the extreme to him when the ignorant mistook his abilities for those of the thaumaturgist, and for a long time he endeavored to escape the notoriety and persecution that pursued him.

Finally, however, principally at my own instigation, he determined to give up his medical practice—which by now had netted him a comfortable competency—and to devote his services, gratuitously, to the science of physics.

"I can neither evoke ghosts nor lay them through any magic art," he explained to me in his self-deprecatory way. "All I can do is to apply my knowledge of physics to the production of results which could be brought about just as efficiently by the most ignorant person gifted with those mediumistic powers that I lack. Nor is my knowledge of these matters in any way one which originated with me. The knowledge of physical phenomena has always existed, whether we consider the oracle of the Greeks, the Roman Sibyl, the Indian Shahman, or the witch of Endor who raised up the spirit of Samuel. But mostly it has been confined hitherto to the domains of faith and religion instead of being accepted boldly by science.

"Would you care to accompany me to a country house tomorrow to investigate a remarkable problem?" he continued, changing the subject in that sudden manner of his.

I was eager to accept, and the next morning I met him by appointment at the depot. While we were being whirled in the train through rural New England he recounted to me the particulars of the case—the first which he had consented to investigate since the matter of the jailer's daughter.

He had been called upon for aid, it appeared, by a former patient of his, a certain Miss Suydam, whom he had once cured of a long nervous ailment. She was in great distress. A maiden lady of mature age, descended from one of the oldest families in America, she had lived since childhood with her younger sister in the old family mansion which they inherited. Possessed of a meager income, alone in the world, they had existed simply but not penuriously, expecting to pass the remainder of their lives in the solitude of the little village where they had been born. But some months previously the sister, who was of unusual beauty except for a slight facial irregularity, had suddenly become engaged to, and married, a young artist of much unrecognized talent, and the three had made their home happily together within a period of a few weeks, when the sister fell sick of a mysterious, wasting malady. Her husband appeared devoted to her and unremitting in his attention; nevertheless the disease continued to progress. Day by day the patient became more attenuated and despondent, until at last the local physicians gave up the case in despair, saying that there appeared to be neither means of making a diagnosis nor hopes for recovery.

And then (said Brodsky) something had occurred which struck terror into the maiden sister's heart. There was an old family legend in the effect that each death—especially when caused by violence or foul play—was presaged by the appearance of a ghost that glided silently along the passages of the old mansion by night and took, in each instance, the aspect of the person, male or female, who was about to pass over. On three successive nights the sister had seen this phantom move along the corridors, and, almost paralyzed with fear, saw it vanish through the closed door of her sister's room. When, on the last occasion, she gathered fortitude to enter, nothing was visible and her sister was peacefully sleeping. The phantom was the double of the sister, but etherealized beyond almost possible conception of beauty, and Miss Suydam had particularly observed that the slight facial irregularity mentioned was not apparent.

Then she thought of Dr. Brodsky, and begged him, if he could not save her sister's life, at least to endeavor to banish this awful messenger from the world beyond. So distraught was she, that she had even dared to suspect that the sister was being slowly poisoned by the artist, though for such a crime no motive existed.

We were to go down in the guise of two physicians—as indeed we were—and to make the fullest investigations.

"What inference do you draw, Dr. Brodsky?" I asked him.

"It is as yet impossible to say," the doctor answered. "We must see what sort of a man this artist is. The theory of poison would, on the face of it, appear very probable. It may be that this is one of those rare cases, yet recorded among old families, in which the dead form, as it were, a guardianship over the lives of the living, and, at the appointed time, send one of their number to summon them into the world beyond. The fact that the spirit bears the family type of feature would bear out this supposition. However, we shall see."

We descended from the train at a little wayside hamlet, where we found a carriage waiting for us. The driver was a young man of great natural refinement, who introduced himself to us as the sister's husband—Walter Fotheringham.

He shook hands with us cordially. We stepped into the carriage, and the horse of his own accord took us up a steep hill that led to the mansion, which we could now see, looking very forlorn and dilapidated, perched upon the summit in the center of a desolate and extensive garden. We were shown into a large parlor, furnished in the style of the last generation, and more or less gloomy in aspect, though comfortable. Our host offered us wine and seated himself beside us.

"And now, gentleman," he said. "I believe in frankness. Let us come to an understanding immediately therefore. Let me say that I know your entire purpose in coming here, and shall assist you with all my ability."

It was impossible not to be impressed with the young fellow's sincerity.

"A painful scene occurred this morning between myself and my sister-in-law, Miss Suydam," he continued. "She has, I fancy, always been a little jealous of her sister's love for me. From words which she let fall during the heat of passion, I infer that she actually suspects me of administering some slow poison to my wife with object of securing her death—I need hardly say that I should have no object to gain thereby."

"And this apparition?" queried the doctor.

"Dr. Brodsky, I have seen it," said Fotheringham. "I would hesitate to admit so to another man, but I have seen it on four occasions, and it is the exact reproduction of my wife."

"One thing is clear," said Brodsky slowly. "Events of grave importance are pending in the spiritual world. There is no physical change that does not in some way betoken a spiritual one, and your wife is in grave danger. You are fond of one another?"

"We are devoted," said the artist, sadly. "Doctor, if you can only save her—"

He choked with his emotion. I, looking at him, could not longer suspect him, nor I am sure, did the doctor.

"Your relations are absolutely ideal, then?" queried Brodsky. "There is nothing about your wife that you could cavil at, nothing which has caused mental perturbation?"

Fotheringham started and shot a keen glance at his questioner.

"Why, the fact is, there is one small matter, but it is so ridiculous that I am heartily ashamed to confess it."

"Nothing upon earth is ridiculous," said Brodsky.

"It is a preposterous matter, and the fact that I am obliged to keep it to myself adds to the little rankle. You may know, doctor, that some of us unfortunate persons are cursed with what is vulgarly termed the artistic temperament and are destined to go through life always seeking perfection, and never attaining it?"

There was a wealth of enigma in the doctor's smile.

"I thought that in my wife I had discovered a sublimation of every virtue of soul and body," said the young man. "But there is one slightest flaw in her appearance. I am ashamed to say it, but her nose is not entirely straight—a trifling flaw such as would pass unnoticed in one of less beauty, but in her is the most evident because of her singularly perfect features otherwise. Of late the perception of this has become an obsession with me.

"But this is a scruple," he continued, angrily. "I don't know why I should have bothered you with a foolish detail. Certainly it in no measure affects my love for her."

"One question," said Brodsky. "This phantom—is the nose also crooked?"

"No, absolutely straight," said Fotheringham, "but in all other respects it is a duplication of my dear wife."

At this moment Miss Suydam entered and greeted us cordially. It was evident, however, that relations between herself and the young artist were considerably strained. She took us up the stairs and along a winding passage to the room in which the sick woman lay propped up by pillows. She was wasted greatly and of an extreme pallor; there did not seem to be enough blood in the body to support life. She opened her eyes, looked at us with indifference, and closed them.

At once I perceived the slight facial deformity, which was visible the more by contrast with the delicate perfection of the rest of her face.

The room in which the patient lay was one of those large old-fashioned apartments with small panes of glass let into enormous window frames and low ceilings, built out irregularly so that they form an irregular space bounded by eight or ten walls. At the far end the room tapered in toward the window seat, which had been fitted up as a couch on which Miss Suydam rested in the intervals of watching by her sister's side. It was arranged that Dr. Brodsky and I should watch here during the following night. The space was so screened off from the corner in which the patient lay as to form, to all intents, a separate apartment, while enabling us to be on hand should anything occur.

"It will not be necessary for us to watch all night," said Dr. Brodsky. "At what time have you seen the apparition?"

"Between three and four in the morning," Miss Suydam answered.

Dr. Brodsky was evidently pleased. "The period of the lowest vitality," he said. "We are getting upon our trail," he added to me. I would have questioned him, but knew from experience that it would procure me no information. Brodsky liked to work out his theories alone. I could see that he had already formed one.

"You say you saw this apparition in the corridor?" he said next to Miss Suydam. "How did you happen to go into the corridor at four in the morning."

Miss Suydam appeared embarrassed. "The fact is," she explained, "on each occasion I have had the most peculiar illusion that my sister had gone out of the room. I find it so difficult to keep awake about that hour, and invariably the same experience comes to me. I dream that my sister has left her bed, and awake to find myself upon my feet in the passage, watching this horrible, trailing figure disappear in the distance. Then I come back to find my sister asleep."

"You doze off immediately when you return," said Dr. Brodsky.

Miss Suydam looked guilty.

"I don't know how you know it, doctor," she said, "but I find it impossible to keep my eyes open. And in the morning my dear sister is always at lower ebb than before. I blame and reproach myself—"

"Never mind, never mind," said Brodsky, patting her hand. "You are certain that you did not dream all this?"

"I sprinkled flour beside my door last night and found my footsteps in it this morning. Besides, Mr. Fotheringham claims to have seen it. But how can I believe him, when I am tortured by such doubts?"

"Hush!" said the doctor. "You have grievously wronged him. Of that I am sure."

Miss Suydam's eyes lightened. "You are sure?" she cried. "I am so glad."

"I am sure," said the doctor. "Now I want three yards of fine steel wire and a couple of stout staples," he added in his sudden manner. "Can you procure these before nightfall?"

"I can get them at the village, I suppose," said Miss Suydam.

"Get them before night, please," said the doctor.

They arrived shortly before supper. The doctor put the wire in his pocket and then drove in the staples outside the frame of the bedroom door, one on either side, some four feet above the ground. At Brodsky's suggestion I retired to bed immediately after I had eaten. He himself promised to call me at two for the beginning of our watch. After hours of restless tossing and turning I slept, but it was only a moment, it seemed, before I heard Brodsky calling me. I awoke to find him standing, fully dressed, at my bedside, a candle in his hand.

"It's two o'clock," he said, softly. "Dress yourself quietly and come."

He waited at my side until I had thrust on my clothes; then grasped me by the arm very earnestly and said:

"The watch will not be long, but you must not fall asleep. It is a matter of life and death for that poor bed-ridden woman, and evil things will be stirring abroad tonight. Unless we both keep awake the issue will be fatal for her."

"Then—this apparition really exists?" I stammered.

"My dear boy," said the doctor, earnestly, "nothing is more real. And it is of incarnate evil. But come."

In our stocking feet we crept into the patient's room. Miss Suydam rose up to welcome us. "I am going to try to keep awake tonight," she said. By the light of the candle I could see that the patient was slumbering soundly. She looked less pale and emaciated than during the day.

"She always looks better just before—it happens," said Miss Suydam.

"And in the morning—Oh, it is terrible. What is it?" she cried, hysterically. "For heaven's sake, what does it mean?"

"Tonight will be the end," said the doctor, kindly. "Now sit beside her and watch. We will wait behind the screen."

We took our seats in silence. Dr. Brodsky blew out the candle, and the room was thinly illuminated by the half moon that shone crookedly through the little window panes. From our position, unknown to Miss Suydam, we could see her and the patient, clearly outlined against the wall. We waited, waited—

"Remember, at all hazard, do not sleep," were the doctor's last instructions. Then silence descended upon us. I heard the ticking of my watch, the distant night noises; everything seemed to blend into a monotonous and assuaging harmony. . . .

Somebody was shaking me. The doctor was shaking me. My eyelids seemed to have glued themselves down upon my eyes. With the utmost difficulty I forced them apart. The moon had risen, flooding the room with light, and Brodsky was standing by me.

"Wake, for God's sake," he whispered. Something was trickling down the sleeve of his coat. I learned afterward that he had stabbed himself with his pen-knife to fight off that overmastering drowsiness. Then, with a desperate effort, I shook it off, threw back that enchantment of slumber, and followed the direction of the doctor's gaze.

Beside the bed Miss Suydam sat, sunk into her chair, her eyes closed, her head bowed forward upon her breast. And from the bed, where the sick woman moaned and tossed restlessly, a filmy vapor seemed to detach itself, issuing, apparently, from her side. It rose and floated over her, gradually assuming the form of her own self, but even more entrancingly beautiful. It gathered shape and grew, suspended in the air face downward, chin to chin and lip to lip. Then, when it had become of the same consistency, it gradually assumed an upright posture, floated down to the ground, and seemed to pass bodily through the door. At the same instant I looked at the sleeping patient. She had ceased to moan and lay profoundly still, but shrunken up among the pillows like a seven-year-old child. Then, with a start, Miss Suydam sprang to her feet and wrenched at the door handle.

But the doctor had anticipated her. He sprang from where he was standing, I following, tossed Miss Suydam back into the room as lightly as a feather, and dashed out into the passage. There he stood, his back to the door, pressing it close.

My blood curdled and grew cold. Moving away, moving along the corridor without sound of any footsteps that awful phantom glided. A thing of devilish beauty. And I felt that at all hazard I must follow it, though it led me into hell. I must have started forward, for suddenly I was called to myself by feeling the little doctor's strong arms around me.

"Ah, thank God!" he whispered, seeing, I suppose, sanity return to me. "If you had followed, boy, God help your soul. Can you resist?"

Far away, farther and farther it moved, until it reached the bend in the passage and disappeared around it. It was moving in the direction of Fotheringham's room.

"Yes," I muttered, reeling unsteadily. "But it is going to him. Save him, save him."

The doctor reassured me. "It can not harm him so long as his wife lives," he said. "They are united by a more subtle bond. This is the last night; another and it would have sucked the last of her vitality from her and achieved its ends. We shall save two lives tonight. But we have work to do before it returns."

"It is coming back?" I stammered.

"It must come back," he cried, and, whipping out the coil of wire from his coat, he fastened one end tightly to the staple and began to draw it across the door. And instantly, to my horror, I saw the thing reappear, begin to return upon its horrible passage.

Every evil impulse that I had ever known seemed to leap into activity as I gazed at it. It was the exact replica of Mrs. Fotheringham, but of hellish beauty, a caricature of beauty, as I might call it. And I felt my heart hammer within my breast, my hands fall to my sides nervelessly. But Dr. Brodsky had drawn the wire across the door, so that it ran taut and true, a steel barrier, across the wood of the panels. Then, as the thing drew near he turned and confronted it. And suddenly the moon went out and everything was plunged into profound darkness.

I felt an icy air breathe upon me: I heard a cry. I felt, rather than saw, that the little doctor had hooked his arms around the phantom thing and struggled with it. I heard him gasp, choke as a strangled man. I heard his heels hammering upon the floor. And all at once I fainted.

When I recovered consciousness it was broad daylight. The sun was streaming into the room, full upon the couch on which I lay. Beside me sat the doctor, with his usual cheery aspect. But there was something strange about his throat. I looked more closely; it was discolored by five small, livid spots, like fingerprints.

"It's all right, boy," he said, cheerily. "We've scotched the demon and our patient's going to get well. Miss Suydam and Mr. Fotheringham will be here in a moment and then explanations will be in order. Lie still and don't attempt to move. You've had a bad shock, but you'll be all right in a day or two."

Soon afterward Miss Suydam appeared upon the arm of her brother-in-law. Peace had evidently been restored between these two, judging from their behavior.

"We found you insensible upon the floor," the young artist explained, "and Dr. Brodsky in a hardly better condition. He looked like a man who had been putting up a stiff fight with a burglar. He must have been unconscious too, for it was early morning."

"He locked me in my room," said Miss Suydam, "so that I could not go to his assistance. But tell us the explanation."

"We are all going to be frank," said the doctor, "and so we will go back to the beginning. Miss Suydam, you suspected Mr. Fotheringham here of the most hideous crime that is conceivable."

"I wronged him greatly, and he has forgiven me," said Miss Suydam, smiling at her brother-in-law.

"You wronged him, but your suspicions were to a certain extent justified," said the doctor. "Unconsciously, Mr. Fotheringham nearly murdered his wife."

"What?" we all exclaimed in astonishment.

"Ah, when will you people learn that thoughts are more potent than things?" said Brodsky. "It is the easiest thing in the world to create a thought; it is almost impossible to undo it. In a sense we are all creators, and, if we only knew it, to every man is open the possibility of becoming as a god, by fashioning a universe. Mr. Fotheringham, you created this apparition."

"I—created it?" stammered the artist.

"You had married the best wife in the world, but you were not content with her. You desired perfection, that perfection which is unattainable. And you began to brood. Would to heaven that one slight blemish were removed from her features! This intensity of thought, acting upon the ether, actually formed a shadow after your own imaginings. You made a spirit, and it wanted a body. Vampire-like, it preyed upon the body of your wife. Night after night it drew away her vitality.

"At first a shadowy wraith, it became stronger and stronger. It became a substantial thing, composed of all the essential elements of flesh. It grew in wickedness, every created thing must that does not come from God, the source of all goodness. And, had it succeeded in destroying her, it would have turned upon you and destroyed you body and soul.

"It was at the very threshold of the consummation of this achievement when I was sent for. I had my suspicions from the first, when you made your confession to me. Such cases are on record, notably in the records of Japan, in which country they usually assume the form of cats or foxes. From my cross-examinations of Miss Suydam I ascertained that this evil thing, working in the atmosphere of artificially induced slumber, fed upon the life-blood of your wife during her sleep, grew strong thereby, and went through the passage seeking you. Had it been strong enough it would have destroyed you. But, though it grew and grew like some horrible cancer, it could not conquer you so long as Mrs. Fotheringham lived. So it had to return.

"You must have read that, in the making of Solomon's temple, no tool of iron was allowed to come upon the stones. Iron was also banned from the Vestals' house at Rome. The reason for these ordinances was that evil spirits can never cross it, nor good ones, either. It is the most earthly of all elements. No temple could bring down the favor of the protecting spirits were iron used in its construction.

"Accordingly, I barred the door with a wire of fine steel, which made it impossible for the vampire to return. Wood it could pass through, but that fine barrier was more effective than a thousand tons of oak. Well, the rest you know. Leave on the wire for a few nights, though its powers are broken, and it is not likely to trouble you again. It will soon pass back into that elemental source from which you, wretched man, fashioned it.

"So go back to your wife and be satisfied with her," the doctor concluded. "And take a word of advice: The next time you brood over things put a wire across your door and wear a steel waistcoat."

THE SORCERER
OF ARJUZANX

MAX RITTENBERG

*Dr. Xavier Wycherley is a consultant psychologist and proclaims defiantly
in his stories that he is not a detective. Even so, in some stories, such as the
following, he has to use his exceptional power and knowledge to investigate the nature of mental afflictions and often to combat evil. His creator,
Max Rittenberg (1880–1963), was born in Australia of Jewish parents
who returned to Europe, settling in England when Max was aged seven or
eight. Max had a good education and a creative mind. He became fascinated by puzzles, later setting crossword puzzles for Punch. He was also a
good player of bridge and chess. This creative imagination worked well both
for his series featuring Dr. Wycherley and for a series featuring Magnum,
the Scientific Detective. Only a few of the Wycherley stories were serialized
in England while the full run appeared in the United States during 1913 to
1915. Rittenberg revised several of the stories as The Mind-Reader, published in the United States in 1913, but the full series in its original form
has never been reprinted.*

SHE WAS CLIMBING PAINFULLY ON HER KNEES THE LONG FLIGHT OF
stone steps that leads from the Grotto of the Vision of Bernadette up to
the great double Basilique of Lourdes. With her, helping and encouraging,
was her parish priest, Père Bonivet.

"Courage, my child, and faith!" he was whispering. "Have faith, and all will be well. Only faith in Our Lady can cure you."

Out of the crowd of the sick and the dying that had come to Lourdes—the lame, the blind, the palsied, the epileptic, the tuberculous, the cancerous—this peasant girl had above all attracted the attention of Dr. Wycherley. He was there in pursuit of his life-study, psychological research, for at Lourdes there gather a great multitude of those who are sick in mind. Apart from his study of the cures that earnest faith brings to pass at the Shrine of Notre Dame de Lourdes, many of his previous cases had been garnered there—cases where faith had been powerless to heal the injured mind.

This young peasant girl—scarcely more than a child—now on her knees on the long flight of stone steps, had attracted Dr. Wycherley's attention above all the rest. There was that in her face that lifted her out of the ruck of peasants. Not the beauty of her features, nor her soft, liquid eyes, nor her raven-black hair was it that first caught the attention of the observer, but the spiritual light in her soul that shone through her face as a light shines through wax.

She might have posed as a model for a Joan of Arc when the call first came to her at Domrémy.

Dr. Wycherley watched the girl and the priest on their painful climb to the Basilique, as he had watched them on many days previously; he waited outside the church until they came from their long devotions. In Père Bonivet's face was a look of deep disappointment; in the eyes of the girl was a hardened look, a glitter that had not been there before. The light on her soul no longer shone clear—it was as though a marsh mist had dimmed it with a clammy film.

As the priest was hurrying her to their temporary home in the town, Dr. Wycherley raised his hat and addressed him.

"Mon père," he said, "I ask your pardon for this intrusion if it is unwelcome. But I, like yourself, do my humble best to help the weak and the suffering, and I see clearly that your pilgrimage to Lourdes has not brought the benefit you hoped for mademoiselle."

"We must be patient. In God's good time He will vouchsafe His mercies," returned the priest. "But I thank you—I see that you have the good heart."

"If you should need me . . ." said Dr. Wycherley, and wrote the name of his hotel on his card. Père Bonivet took the card and thanked him courteously.

On the evening of the next day the priest called on Dr. Wycherley in anxious distress of mind.

"I have come," he said, "because I fear that this case is beyond my powers. It may be that I am unworthy—that my soul is too stained with the cares and pettinesses of this world to take my prayers before the Most High. Tonight I can do nothing with Jeanne. She has blasphemed against the Holy Name—she will not listen to me! It is terrible, pitiable! And"—he lowered his voice to an impressive whisper—"the mark of the beast is coming upon her!" He shuddered at his own words.

Dr. Wycherley drew a chair forward for Père Bonivet. "Will you not sit down and tell me the trouble of mademoiselle? I have studied many cases of diseased mind, and it may be my knowledge can help. She is *hystérique*, is it not so?"

"So the doctor has told us, but in the Landes, where Jeanne Dorthez lives and where I go about the work of my Master, the peasants give it another name—a very terrible name. They say that she is possessed—bewitched!

"Myself I believe nothing of that," added the priest hastily. "I am of the modern school, and such things belong to the superstitions of the Middle Ages. So I laid the case of Jeanne Dorthez before Monseigneur the Bishop, and he advised me to take her on a pilgrimage to Lourdes. Out of his own purse our good bishop gave the money that was necessary for us, for Jeanne is but a poor peasant girl, the daughter of a woodcutter of the Landes, and myself I have little to spare."

"If they say she is bewitched, then they must have in mind some man or woman on whom they place suspicion of sorcery."

"You are right, monsieur. They say that Osper Camargo has bewitched her. They whisper many terrible things of Osper Camargo, that he is in league with the Evil One—but you and I, should we put belief in the superstitious chatter of peasants?"

The mental healer did not answer this. "Jeanne is a good girl," he said;

"it is plain for all to read. When her attacks come upon her, she changes in mind, is it not so?"

"She changes terribly. Tonight she blasphemed against the Holy Name. I greatly fear that she may lose her reason."

"What other signs?"

"Of course, monsieur, it is nonsense what I have now to tell you. But one day the women of the village forced her to be examined, and they whisper that upon her they found places where the prick of a pin was not felt!"

"Those places were of a definite and regular shape?"

"How did monsieur guess? Yes. The shape of the pentacle—that is what they whisper. The doctor at Mont de Marsan could find nothing, and myself I did not believe it. But tonight I have *seen* the mark of the beast upon her! Red upon her breast!" Again he shuddered, and crossed himself hastily.

Dr. Wycherley looked very thoughtful. "Let us go to see Jeanne," he suggested, and from a travelling medicine-chest slipped a few phials into his pocket.

The girl was lodging near at hand, and in a few minutes they had arrived at the house, a humble dwelling in a little back street of the town. When they were a few yards from the door the figure of a man slipped out quickly from the threshold and into the darkness of an alleyway.

The priest started back. "For a moment I thought that was Osper Camargo! But the light is tricky in this narrow ruelle."

"He has a scrawny beard and a pair of evil-looking eyes?" asked Dr. Wycherley.

"Camargo has that and a nose crushed by the fall of a pine-tree upon his face. It was at the time of the accident—many years ago now—that he ceased to attend Mass, and after that he gradually became feared by the villagers. But of course it could not be Camargo, for he is far from here in the salt-marshes of the Landes—there would be no reason why he should come to Lourdes."

The woman who opened the door to them put her finger to her lips. "S'sh, *mon père*, she is at last asleep! It was with difficulty that we could quiet her."

They moved softly upstairs to the room, and at Dr. Wycherley's request the woman turned back the bedclothes and opened the girl's nightgown.

Above and between her breasts, distinct and unmistakable, was an angry reddish patch of the shape of a pentacle.

"Last night I saw it for the first time!" whispered the woman, with horror in her voice. "Tonight it is much redder! Monsieur le Curé, Monsieur le Docteur, what can it mean?"

Jeanne stirred in her sleep, and in her sleep murmured: "I will come. Oh, cease to torment me, for I will come!"

Dr. Wycherley stayed the night through in the girl's room—watching and studying her. Outside the window the Gave de Pau roared unceasingly down its torrential bed. There was menace in its voice.

Jeanne awoke in the morning with a curious dull glaze in her eyes. She expressed a strong desire to return home to her hamlet of Aureilhac, in spite of the counsels of Père Bonivet still to have patience and faith.

He appealed to Dr. Wycherley, but the latter drew him aside and suggested earnestly: "Let Jeanne have her way, *mon père*. I think it will be for the best. . . . It is upon your lips to tell me that if she will only have faith enough, she will be cured. Yes, but she has not the faith—she has lost heart. . . . Now you are about to ask me what can be hoped for if the pilgrimage to Lourdes has failed."

"You read my thoughts, monsieur!" said the priest in surprise.

"And you, *mon père*, read mine, for you see that I wish for Jeanne only what will be for her good."

"Yes, yes. But if she goes back to the Landes with her faith broken, who can save her from madness? I, alas, am not worthy to do this work for my Master—that I bow my head in sorrow to acknowledge."

"We must work together—I will return with you."

"But her father, Pierre Dorthez, is only a poor woodcutter. In the Landes we are all poor. How could we pay you, monsieur? No doubt you would need many francs—perhaps many hundred francs." To his simple mind the sum loomed vast.

"*Mon père*, you and I have both learnt that the true money lies in the grateful hearts of men and women."

The priest raised his hand in benediction. "I know not if you are of our faith, monsieur, but may the blessing of God be upon you!"

They travelled by slow, cross-country trains to the village of Labouheyre in the middle of the Landes district. It was a hot and sultry day, and the hundred-mile train journey seemed interminable.

Beyond Dax they had come into the true Landes country—great silent pine-forests alternating with wide stretches of sedgy marshland. At Labouheyre their arrival was unexpected, but one of the villagers at once offered to drive them in his ox-cart to Aureilhac. It was an honour to do a service for Père Bonivet.

But Dr. Wycherley noted that the villager took care that Jeanne should not touch him even with her garment.

The two oxen drew them along the great silent highway that runs, level and straight, northwards to Bordeaux, stone-paved like the streets of a town to bear the weight of the lumbering timber-waggons. The oxen plodded along with the slow patience which is theirs.

The silence of the great forest fell upon them. Even in the full light of the afternoon the sombre forest carried something of the grim and awesome. No wonder that for the simple peasants there were still spirits of evil that lurked in its shadows and on Midsummer Eve gathered together for unholy revels out in the marsh of Arjuzanx.

From time to time they would pass a solitary goatherd lying down on his rough skin coat and dully guarding his little flock of long-haired goats. Once they caught sight of the local postman making his round on the stilts of the Landes to the outlying huts and farms, separated by stretches of marshland impassable on foot.

The ox-cart turned off the highway into a forest track deep-rutted from its winter traffic of heavy timber-waggons. The forest took them to its sombre heart. A grey film began to spread across the sky, shutting out the sunlight. But still it was hot and oppressive.

Late in the afternoon they reached the hamlet of Aureilhac—a few low-roofed wooden houses in a clearing where lean hens scratched for food. Pierre Dorthez, returning from his day's work in the forest, raised his hat to Père Bonivet and greeted them dully. He said little, either of comment or question, but ordered Jeanne to make ready a dinner for the visitors. Himself he would kill a fowl and gather vegetables for the soup.

As the girl set about her work, Dr. Wycherley watched her keenly from his seat in the kitchen that served also as living-room. She was intent on her duties by the *pot-au-feu,* but there was a suppressed excitement underlying her that showed in the twitchings of her hands and the pallor of her face. It was no longer translucent in its whiteness, but of a dull and clammy pallor like the colour of a marsh mist. And in her eyes there was once more the hard glitter. Now and again she would secretly put her hand to her bosom as though to satisfy herself that something of value hidden beneath her dress was still there.

When the simple dinner was over, Dr. Wycherley drew Père Bonivet aside.

"Where does this Osper Camargo live?" he asked. "I wish to see him."

"But surely you do not believe in these superstitions of the ignorant peasants, monsieur?"

"In my studies I have met many strange things, and I try to keep the open mind. I would see this man for myself."

"He lives in a solitary hut out on the marshes—on the marsh of Arjuzanx. But do not go tonight, for the way is treacherous!"

"I must go tonight, *mon père*—or it may be too late. Can one of the villagers show me the path?"

"At night-time they would not dare to."

"Can I find it for myself?"

"On the stilts there are many paths, but on foot only one that is safe. If you are determined to go, I must lead you there myself."

"Thank you—I accept your help willingly. But I shall ask you to return without me and keep guard over Jeanne while I am away."

The last gleams of the setting sun shone from between an angry bank of clouds as they came out of the forest on to the marshland. The pools, stagnant with slime, turned to blood, then grew dark and chill.

"It may be a bad night, monsieur," said the priest warningly. "See how the clouds have massed in the west, over the Bay of Biscay!"

"If necessary, I will spend the night with Osper Camargo," answered Dr. Wycherley quietly.

A tortuous path amongst the firmer parts of the marshland brought them within sight of a low hut. It was surrounded by a few stunted trees on ground a little above the general level. Around them again were the dark sedges, whispering amongst themselves, and the chill, dank pools of slime. A marsh bird called to its mate with a strange, eerie cry.

"Is the way straight from here onwards?" asked Dr. Wycherley at length.

"Yes, you have but to follow the path. Only be careful that you sound around you with your stick should the foot tread on ground that gives."

"Then I would ask you to return at once to guard Jeanne. If necessary, give her bromide from the tablets in this phial. See to it that she does not leave the house tonight. *Au revoir, mon père.*"

The hut was silent and lightless. After knocking at the door fruitlessly, Dr. Wycherley lifted the latch and entered.

It was empty save for a lean grey cat that arched her back and spat at him. The bigger of the two rooms, serving as kitchen and bedroom, showed by small signs that it had been unoccupied for days. There was nothing to be done but to wait for the return of the owner, for no one at Aureilhac had been able to tell of his movements.

It was a lonesome, weary vigil. The cat, refusing overtures of friendship, had stalked out into the night. The clock over the fireplace was silent, for it had run down during the owner's absence. Around the room were tokens that this Osper Camargo worked on the superstitions of his neighbours, for conspicuous on the walls were a human skull, dead bats nailed up with outspread wings, snakes and blindworms preserved in spirit, and other devices common to the sorcerers of all ages. A heavy locked chest doubtless contained more of his paraphernalia.

But to Dr. Wycherley the most significant object in the room was hung above the bed where the peasant of the Landes would place his crucifix.

It was a small pentacle in hammered iron.

For many hours the doctor waited patiently in the lightless hut. For times such as this he had trained himself to a habit of deep thought that lost count of place and time, but yet was alert to the least unusual sign. He had made his brain his servant to an extent far beyond the usual with men.

His thoughts ran on the records in hieroglyphic that have come down to us of the sorcerers of ancient Egypt, the men who claimed that they could use the gods to work their will. He had spent many interesting hours with Professor Clovis Marnier, the great Egyptologist, listening to his demonstration of the meaning of the hieroglyphs.

There was a sound out of the darkness—a plash in a distant pool.

At the instant his watchful senses had flashed the message to his brain, and he was awake and alert. But he kept still in his chair.

The sounds came nearer. The door opened, and a man entered with a lantern, under his arm a pair of stilts slimy from the marsh pools. Placing the lantern on a table, he began to lay sticks on the dead ashes of the hearth, the grey cat rubbing affectionately round his legs. He had a ragged, scrawny beard and moustache, and his nose was crushed in the way Père Bonivet had described. A face with evil lines—an evil mind behind it.

He had not seen Dr. Wycherley. When at length he caught sight of him, sitting quietly in the chair in a corner of the room, he started violently and called out in the harsh, twanging dialect of the Landes: "*Sangrediable,* get on your knees!"

The doctor made no reply, but sat still.

"Who are you?" cried Camargo, flashing the lantern upon him.

"Peace, brother!" answered Dr. Wycherley. "Peace to you in the names of Khabbakhel and Knouriphariza, our masters."

"But I don't know you! What are you doing here?"

"We have met in the plane of the spirit," answered Dr. Wycherley courteously. "Though I live afar off, I have long wished to visit you and learn of your wisdom."

The man was clearly puzzled. Suspicion lay behind his narrow eyes. And yet his vanity was touched. Dr. Wycherley had allowed no trace of irony or ridicule to appear in his words—they had a tone of grave deference in them. Osper Camargo twisted his hands uneasily. Finally he hit on a satisfactory answer: "You want to buy wisdom from me—hein?"

"Come!" remonstrated the doctor. "Payment between brothers of the craft?"

"If you want to learn, you pay!"

"Very well," answered the doctor, with assumed reluctance, and drew out a gold piece from his pocket.

The man's eyes glittered cunningly.

"Not enough!"

"This I will give you beforehand, and again a louis when you have shown me what I do not know already."

He showed a second gold piece.

"Do you know the incantation that brings the sickness upon the oxen? Or the incantation that drives the goats to madness? With them one can make money."

"Those," answered Dr. Wycherley, "are elementary. I had hoped to see bigger proof of your powers. Even in my land they speak of the spells you can lay on man or woman."

Osper Camargo's pride was awakened.

"They speak well, for I have those powers, and I use them. But"—a cunning glitter came again into his eyes—"I work within the law. Whatever I do, it is such that the law cannot touch me. Oh, I am careful!"

"We have all to be prudent. A friend of mine, the great sorcerer, Smith—doubtless you have heard of him?—desired greatly a young girl of his neighbourhood, but she was of tender years, and the law of his country would not permit that he cast spells to bring her to his side. So he waited."

"As I have waited!" cried Camargo fiercely. "As I have waited these long years! If the mother would have none of me, the child shall—and willingly! It is my right! Everything is prepared!"

With a dramatic gesture he drew out a key from his pocket and opened the heavy oaken chest. The upper part of it was filled with dresses and dress material. There was silk and good cambric in the heap. He plunged his hands into it, fondling the garments, letting them rustle through his fingers.

"A fine trousseau for the bride," commented Dr. Wycherley. "She should be well pleased."

"A bride? Maybe yes or maybe no. Of one girl one may get tired. Why tie oneself up with the law?" He shut the lid of the chest and turned the key. "But that is not the only reason why I desire her. No, no. There is another reason, a stronger reason—a reason that *you* of the craft should well know!"

Now it was Dr. Wycherley's turn to be puzzled. He thought he had gauged the man's mainspring of action. His motive was surely horrible enough—what worse could lie behind? And yet it must be something within the law, for the man was plainly stating truth as to his devilish prudence.

To gain time, Dr. Wycherley asked: "What is her name?"

"Ask at Aureilhac," answered Camargo. "They will tell you quickly enough!"

There was a note of triumph in his tone that expressed the near fulfilment of his desire. From the law he had nothing to fear, for the law takes no cognisance of wizardry as such, and it was plain that he had no fear of man's intervention. Perhaps they could keep the girl away from his hut for a week, two weeks, a month even—but what of that? He had waited many long years—he could wait a little longer if necessary. Small wonder that Osper Camargo boasted openly of his desires.

"You do not know my second motive!" mocked the sorcerer.

Dr. Wycherley replied deferentially:

"No, I am but a learner at the craft, and you are a master. I have come from afar to drink of your wisdom."

"This much will I show you. Today I procured it, and it completes the preparations that are necessary."

He flashed a small corked glass tube from his pocket, and quickly returned it to its shelter. In the fitful light from the lantern Dr. Wycherley could only gather the impression that it contained the dried ear of some cereal—barley or perhaps rye. It puzzled him still further. The thought of poison passed across his mind, but this he at once put aside—Osper Camargo was a coward at heart and would never risk the vengeance of the law in that way. But if not poison, what could it mean? A dried ear of barley—or perhaps rye.

"You speak of your powers," said Dr. Wycherley, "but you give me no proof. It may be that this girl is in love with you and will come willingly at your call."

"Ask at Aureilhac!" returned the sorcerer again, licking his lips. "Ask if she has been willing to come. But now I have her in my hands. When I crook my little finger, she will come."

From the west a flash of lightning filled the hut with light, shoeing with startling distinctness the fire of evil passion in the face of Osper Camargo.

"Shall I give you proof of my power?" he asked fiercely.

"For that I have journeyed from afar, and for that I will pay the further louis," returned the doctor.

The sorcerer set about his preparations quickly, while outside the storm gathered and the distant lightning flashed. First he lit a fire on the hearth and into it threw some powder that gave out a strong odour of balsam. Next he took down the small iron pentacle from its nail over the bed, and hung it by a string round the neck of the grey cat. Then he scattered sand on the floor, and on the sand traced a magical enclosure fringed with mystic signs. In the enclosure he placed a small iron vessel containing a slow-burning pastille with a pungent odour, and next to it a rough wax doll, which bore a certain resemblance to Jeanne Dorthez.

His preparations completed, the sorcerer began to recite strange incantations, swaying himself backwards and forwards in time to the words, beginning low and quietly and gradually working himself up to a pitch of hysterical frenzy. Finally he reached the stage where automatism of the lower centres holds sway in the brain. Writhing and foaming at the mouth, he fell in a fit upon the bed. After a little the jerking muscles quieted down—the sorcerer was in a trance.

Dr. Wycherley had watched with intense interest every detail of the fantastic operation, endeavouring to disentangle the essential and the significant from the gibberish of abracadabra and the puerilities of the wax doll. From the first there had been no doubt in his mind that this Osper Camargo was a dangerous man. The problem in hand was: how far did his powers in the realm of the supernormal extend?

The anaesthetic patches on the body of Jeanne Dorthez which had seemed of such horrible significance to the goodwives of the neighbourhood—these were a not unusual symptom of a patient suffering from hysteria. The shape of the patches was probably the result of a post-hypnotic suggestion; the red mark on the breast of the girl could be produced by the same means. At the Salpêtrière Hospital in Paris many such experiments have been carried out. Dr. Wycherley had no doubt whatever that this Osper Camargo had gained influence over her mind and had been working to bend it to his own will—the appearance on her body of the symbolic pentacle would react on her mind and convince her that she belonged to him, body and soul.

But how would Camargo bring her over the marshes that night? How far did his telepathic powers extend, if he possessed them at all?

Dr. Wycherley searched the room for some indication that might have escaped him, and suddenly he found it. It was a negative indication—during the rigmarole of the incantations and the rhythmic swayings the grey cat had slipped out of the room.

At once a vivid mental picture came before his eyes of the cat padding swiftly over the dark path through the marshes—through the forest to the hamlet of Aureilhac—reaching the low wooden house of the Dorthez—scratching at the bedroom window of the girl—Jeanne opening the window at the call and seeing the pentacle around its neck, the sign of her master—dressing swiftly and slipping out of the window—following it back to the marsh of Arjuzanx and the hut of the sorcerer.

How could he wrest the girl from the power of Osper Camargo? It would be difficult in the extreme. With her mind so under the power of the sorcerer, counter-suggestions might be of very little effect. Was there no way in which the law could step in, so that this man's power of working evil would be fettered?

Perhaps there might be some hope of this if he could discover the ulterior purpose at which Camargo had hinted. His eye turned to the oaken chest, and at once he went over to it. In his excitement, Camargo had forgotten to take away the key.

Dr. Wycherley swiftly opened it and turned over the pile of garments, seeking for something hidden in the box which might give him a clue to the great ulterior motive. His hand brushed against parchment, and he drew it out and took it over to the light—a parchment yellow with age and written in faded ink with words of French many centuries old. But it was possible to get its general purport, even if single words here and there conveyed no meaning:

The Potion.
Of Which Whosoever Shall Drink Shall Become Immortal.

It was a lengthy recipe full of such ingredients as the eyes of bats, the powdered forehand of a toad, broth of blindworms, and others nauseating in the extreme, but the culmination of the recipe sent a chill of horror coursing down the doctor's spine. Though he had watched by the bedside of raving madmen, he had never had to listen to imaginings so devilish as this. His eye ran over it hurriedly before he thrust it into his pocket to bring if necessary before a court of law:

"... *a maiden undefiled, a first-born ... when she is with, child ... an infusion of the spotted rye ... the left eye and the right ear ... see to it that you both drink, the potion together ..."*

Dr. Wycherley realised as never before the feelings of our ancestors when, centuries ago, they had had to deal with the sorcerers of their age. Small wonder that they had lynched at the stake men who put into practice what had been written on this old parchment. Small wonder that in their zeal to stamp out such devilish imaginings they had persecuted the innocent as well as the guilty.

Outside, the lightning flashed and the thunder tore across the swishing rain, but through the noise Dr. Wycherley sensed a footstep. He moved towards the door, but at the same moment the man on the bed stirred and rose up. He too had sensed the presence outside, the presence for which he in his trance was feverishly waiting.

Osper Camargo thrust back the doctor and strode to fling open the door. And as he did so, as he stepped out of the threshold to lay hand on the girl who had come at the call of the grey cat, a blinding flash of lightning, followed on the instant by the roar of thunder from directly overhead, struck upon him.

The sorcerer staggered back, his hands to his eyes, moaning horribly.

Groping, he blundered about the room, and a torrent of blasphemies poured from his lips as he realised what had come upon him. Then, little by little, the stream of imprecations died down, and as the girl moved to his side, shivering in her sodden clothes, Osper Camargo cried out pitifully, in a voice so changed from his previous tone that Dr. Wycherley started at it: "Keep away from me, for I am accursed! The judgment of God is upon me—He has struck me blind for my sins!"

He fell on his knees, and as from a little child there came from him the prayer of the Paternoster. One of those strange instantaneous conversions, the rationale of which is so veiled from us, had been witnessed. For a long hour, until exhaustion set in, the sorcerer laid bare his soul before his Maker and prayed for forgiveness. Let it be granted to him that he should work out his salvation in the cell of a monk, sworn to perpetual silence, and he would be content.

When the morning broke through the grey mists of the marshes, Dr. Wycherley and Jeanne Dorthez were leading by the hand over the marsh-path a blind man who murmured continuously the prayers he had learnt in his youth.

Behind them smoke curled up from the hut of the sorcerer that was. Dr. Wycherley had set fire to it so that the ghastly tokens and records it contained might never fall into the hands of any human being.

THE IVORY STATUE

SAX ROHMER

The name of Sax Rohmer, the writing persona of Arthur Sarsfield Ward (1883–1959), will forever be associated with the character of the Oriental supervillain Fu Manchu, whose stories first appeared in 1912 and continued through to Rohmer's death. The success of the books plus the many film, radio, and television adaptations made the name of Fu Manchu famous, almost a synonym for all Oriental villains, but in so doing they overshadowed much of Rohmer's other work. This includes the character of Moris Klaw, the "dream detective," whose stories first appeared in 1913, soon after the first Fu Manchu adventures. Klaw is an odd individual, usually almost entirely draped in a black cape, with skin showing that he is of a great age, yet he has a young, beautiful, and seemingly ageless daughter, Isis. Klaw runs a curio shop full of ancient relics that form just part of his knowledge of and connection with the past. Klaw believes that everything has a personality, a vibration, and by sleeping at the location of any crime or disturbance, he is able to connect with events which come to him in a dream. Hence his soubriquet and the title of the collection, The Dream Detective, which appeared in 1920. The stories tend to be impossible crimes rather than true supernatural cases, but it is Klaw and his paraphernalia that make this series so effective.

I

WHERE A CASE DID NOT TOUCH HIS PECULIAR INTEREST, APPEALS to Moris Klaw fell upon deaf ears. However dastardly a crime, if its details were of the sordid sort, he shrank within his Wapping curio-shop as closely as any tortoise within its shell.

"Of what use," he said to me on one occasion, "are my acute psychic sensibilities to detect who it is with a chopper that has brained some unhappy washerwoman? Shall I bring to bear those delicate perceptions which it has taken me so many years to acquire in order that some ugly old fool shall learn what has become of his pretty young wife? I think not—no!"

Sometimes, however, when Inspector Grimsby of Scotland Yard was at a loss, he would induce me to intercede with the eccentric old dealer, and sometimes Moris Klaw would throw out a hint.

Beyond doubt the cases that really interested him were those that afforded scope for the exploiting of his pet theories; the Cycle of Crime, the criminal history of all valuable relics, the indestructibility of thought. Such a case came under my personal notice on one occasion, and my friend Coram was instrumental in enlisting the services of Moris Klaw. It was, I think, one of the most mysterious affairs with which I ever came in contact, and the better to understand it you must permit me to explain how Roger Paxton, the sculptor, came to have such a valuable thing in his studio as that which we all assumed had inspired the strange business.

It was Sir Melville Fennel, then, who commissioned Paxton to execute a chryselephantine statue. Sir Melville's museum of works of art, ancient and modern, is admittedly the second finest private collection of the kind in the world. The late Mr. Pierpont Morgan's alone took precedence.

The commission came as something of a surprise. The art of chryselephantine sculpture, save for one attempt at revival, in Belgium, has been dead for untold generations. By many modern critics, indeed, it is condemned, as being not art but a parody of art.

Given carte-blanche in the matter of cost, Paxton produced a piece of work which induced the critics to talk about a modern Phidias. Based upon designs furnished by the eccentric but wealthy baronet, the statue represented a slim and graceful girl reclining as in exhaustion upon an ebony throne. The ivory face, with its wearily closed eyes, was a veritable triumph, and was surmounted by a head-dress of gold intertwined among a mass of dishevelled hair. One ivory arm hung down so that the fingers almost touched the pedestal; the left hand was pressed to the breast as though against a throbbing heart. Gold bracelets and anklets, furnished by Sir Melville, were introduced into the composition; and, despite the artist's protest, a heavy girdle, encrusted with gems and found in the tomb of some favourite of a long-dead Pharaoh, encircled the waist. When complete, the thing was, from a merely intrinsic point of view, worth several thousand pounds.

As the baronet had agreed to the exhibition of the statue prior to its removal to Fennel Hall, Paxton's star was seemingly in the ascendant, when the singular event occurred that threatened to bring about his ruin.

The sculptor gave one of the pleasant little dinners for which he had gained a reputation. His task was practically completed, and his friends had all been enjoined to come early, so that the statue could be viewed before the light failed. We were quite a bachelor party, and I shall always remember the circle of admiring faces surrounding the figure of the reclining dancer—warmed in the soft light to an almost uncanny semblance of fair flesh and blood.

"You see," explained Paxton, "this composite work although it has latterly fallen into disrepute, affords magnificent scope for decorative purposes; such a richness of colour can be obtained. The ornaments are genuine antiques and of great value—a fad of my patron's."

For some minutes we stood silently admiring the beautiful workmanship; then Harman inquired: "Of what is the hair composed?"

Paxton smiled. "A little secret I borrowed from the Greeks!" he replied, with condonable vanity "Polyclitus and his contemporaries excelled at the work."

"That jewelled girdle looks detachable," I said.

"It is firmly fastened to the waist of the figure," answered the sculptor. "I defy any one to detach it inside an hour."

"From a modern point of view the thing is an innovation," remarked one of the others, thoughtfully.

Coram, curator of the Menzies Museum, who up to the present had stood in silent contemplation of the figure, now spoke for the first time. "The cost of materials is too great for this style of work ever to become popular," he averred. "That girdle, by the way, represents a small fortune, and together with the anklets, armlets and head-dress, might well tempt any burglar. What precautions do you take, Paxton?"

"Sleep out here every night," was the reply; "and there is always some one here in the daytime. Incidentally, a curious thing occurred last week. I had just fixed the girdle, which, I may explain, was once the property of Nicris, a favourite of Ramses III., and my model was alone here for a few minutes. As I was returning from the house I heard her cry out, and when I came to look for her she was crouching in a corner trembling. What do you suppose had frightened her?"

"Give it up," said Harman.

"She swore that Nicris—for the statue is supposed to represent her—had moved!"

"Imagination," replied Coram; "but easily to be understood. I could believe it, myself, if I were here alone long enough."

"I fancy," continued Paxton, "that she must have heard some of the tales that have been circulated concerning the girdle. The thing has a rather peculiar history. It was discovered in the tomb of the dancer by whom it had once been worn; and it is said that an inscription was unearthed at the same time containing an account of Nicris's death under particularly horrible circumstances. Seton—you fellows know Seton—who was present at the opening of the sarcophagus, tells me that the Arabs, on catching sight of the girdle, all prostrated themselves and then took to their heels. Sir Melville Fennel's agent sent it on to England, however, and Sir Melville conceived the idea of this statue."

"Luckily for you," added Coram.

"Quite so," laughed the sculptor; and, carefully locking the studio door, he led the way up the short path to the house.

We were a very merry party, and the night was far advanced ere the gathering broke up. Coram and I were the last to depart; and having listened to the voices of Harman and the others dying away as they neared the end of the street, we also prepared to take our leave.

"Just come with me as far as the studio," said Paxton, "and having seen that all's well I'll let you out by the garden door."

Accordingly, we donned our coats and hats, and followed our host to the end of the garden, where his studio was situated. The door unlocked, we all three stepped inside the place and gazed upon the figure of Nicris—the pallid face and arms seeming almost unearthly in the cold moonlight, wherein each jewel of the girdle and head-dress glittered strangely.

"Of course," muttered Coram, "the thing's altogether irregular—a fact which the critics will not fail to impress upon you; but it is unquestionably very fine, Paxton. How uncannily human it is! I don't entirely envy you your bedchamber, old man!"

"Oh, I sleep well enough," laughed Paxton. "No luxury, though; just this corner curtained off and a camp bedstead."

"A truly Spartan couch!" I said. "Well, goodnight, Paxton. We shall probably see you tomorrow—I mean later today!"

With that we parted, leaving the sculptor to his lonely vigil at the shrine of Nicris, and as my rooms were no great distance away, some half-hour later I was in bed and asleep.

I little suspected that I had actually witnessed the commencement of one of the most amazing mysteries which ever cried out for the presence of Moris Klaw.

II

SOME FEW MINUTES SUBSEQUENT TO RETIRING—OR SO IT SEEMED to me; a longer time actually had elapsed—I was aroused by the ringing of my telephone bell. I scrambled sleepily out of bed and ran to the instrument.

Coram was the caller. And, now fully awake, I listened with an ever-growing wonder to his account of that which had prompted him to ring me up. Briefly, it amounted to this: some mysterious incident, particulars of which he omitted, had aroused Paxton from his sleep. Seeking the cause of the disturbance, the artist had unlocked the studio door and gone out into the garden. He was absent but a moment and never out of earshot of the door; yet, upon his return, *the statue of Nicris had vanished!*

"I have not hesitated to 'phone through to Wapping," concluded Coram, "and get a special messenger sent to Moris Klaw. You see, the matter is urgent. If the statue cannot be recovered, its loss may spell ruin for Paxton. He had heard me speak of Moris Klaw, and of the wonders he worked in the Greek Room mysteries and accordingly called me up. I knew, if Klaw came, you would be anxious to be present."

"Certainly," I replied, "I wouldn't miss one of his inquiries for anything. Shall I meet you at Paxton's?"

"Yes."

I lost little time in dressing. From Coram's brief account, the mystery appeared to be truly a dark one. Would Moris Klaw respond to this midnight appeal? There was little chance of a big fee; for Paxton was not a rich man; but in justice to the remarkable person whom it is my privilege to present to you in these papers, I must add that monetary considerations seemingly found no place in Klaw's philosophy. He acted, I believe, from sheer love of the work; and this affair, with its bizarre details—the ancient girdle of the dancing girl—the fear of the model, who had declared that the statue moved—was such, I thought, as must appeal to him.

Ten minutes later I was at Paxton's house. He and Coram were in the hall, and Coram admitted me.

"Do you mean," he asked of Paxton, pursuing a conversation which my advent had interrupted, "that the statue melted into the empty air?"

"The double doors opening on to the street were securely locked and barred; that of the garden was also locked; I was in the garden, and not ten yards from the studio," was Paxton's reply. "Nevertheless, Nicris had vanished, leaving no trace behind!"

Incredible though the story appeared, its confirmation was to be found in the speaker's face. I was horrified to see how haggard he looked.

"It will ruin me!" he said, and reiterated the statement again and again.

"But, my dear fellow," I cried, "surely you have not given up hope of recovering the statue? After all, such a robbery as this can scarcely have been perpetrated without leaving some clue behind."

"Robbery!" repeated Paxton, looking at me strangely: "you would be less confident that it is a case of robbery, Searles, if you had heard what I heard!"

I glanced at Coram, but he merely shrugged his shoulders.

"What do you mean?" I said.

"Then Coram has not told you?"

"He has told me that something aroused you in the night and that you left the studio to investigate the matter."

"Correct, so far. Something did arouse me; and the thing was a voice!"

"A voice?"

"It would be, I suppose, about two hours after you had gone, and I was soundly asleep in the studio, when I suddenly awoke and sat up to listen—for it seemed to me that I heard a cry immediately outside the door."

"What kind of cry?"

"Of that I was not, at first, by any means certain; but after a brief interval the cry was repeated. It sounded more like the voice of a boy than that of a man and it uttered but one word: 'Nicris!'"

"And then?"

"I sprang on to the floor, and stood for a moment in doubt—the thing seemed so uncanny. The electric light is not, as you know, installed in the studio, or I should have certainly switched it on. For possibly a minute I hesitated, and then, as I pulled the curtains aside and stood by the door to listen, for the third occasion the cry was repeated, this time coming indisputably from immediately outside."

"You refer to the door that opens on to the garden?"

"Exactly—close to which stands my bed. This, then, decided me. Taking up the small revolver which I have always kept handy since Nicris was completed, I unlocked the door and stepped out into the garden—"

A vehicle, cab or car, was heard to draw up outside the house. Came the sound of a rumbling voice. Coram sprang to the door.

"Moris Klaw!" I cried.

"Good-morning, Mr. Coram!" said the strange voice, from the darkness outside. "Good-morning, Mr. Searles!"

Moris Klaw entered.

He wore his flat-topped, brown bowler of effete pattern; he wore his long, shabby, caped coat; and from beneath it gleamed the pointed, glossy toe-caps of his continental boots. Through his gold-rimmed glasses he peered into the shadows of the hall. His scanty, colourless beard appeared less adequate than ever to clothe the massive chin. The dim light rendered his face more cadaverous and more yellow even than usual.

"And this," he proceeded, as the anxious sculptor came forward, "is Mr. Paxton, who has lost his statue? Good-morning, Mr. Paxton!"

He bowed, removing the bowler and revealing his great, high brow. Coram was about to reclose the door.

"Ah, no!" Moris Klaw checked him. "My daughter is to come yet with my cushion!"

Paxton stared, not comprehending, but stared yet harder when Isis Klaw appeared, carrying a huge red cushion. She was wrapped in a cloak which effectually concealed her lithe figure, and from the raised hood her darkly beautiful face looked out with bewitching effect. She divided between Coram and myself one of her dazzling smiles.

"It is Mr. Paxton," said her father, indicating the sculptor. Then, indicating the girl: "It is my daughter, Isis. Isis will help us to look for Nicris. Why am I here, an old fool who ought to be asleep? Because of this girdle your statue wore. I so well remember when it was dug up. I cannot know its history; but be sure it is evil. From the beginning, please, Mr. Paxton!"

"I am awfully indebted to you! Won't you come in and sit down?" said Paxton, glancing at the girl in bewilderment.

"No, no!" replied Klaw, "let us stand. It is good to stand, and stand upright; for it is because he can do this that man is superior to the other animals!"

Coram and I knew Klaw's mannerisms, but I could see that Paxton thought him to be a unique kind of lunatic. Nevertheless he narrated something of the foregoing up to the point reached at Moris Klaw's arrival.

"Proceed slowly, now," said Klaw. "You left the door open behind you?"

"Yes; but I was never more than ten yards from it. It would have been physically impossible for any one to remove the statue unknown to me. You must remember that it was no light weight."

"One moment," I interrupted. "Are you sure that the statue was in its place before you came out?"

"Certain! There was a bright moon, and the figure was the first thing my eyes fell upon when I pulled the curtain aside."

"Did you *touch* it?" rumbled Moris Klaw.

"No. There was no occasion to do so."

"How much to be regretted, Mr. Paxton! The sense of touch is so exquisite a thing!"

We all wondered at his words.

"Stepping just outside the door," Paxton resumed, "I looked to right and left. There was no one in sight. Then I walked to the wall—a matter of some ten yards—and, pulling myself up by my hands, looked over into the street. It was deserted, save for a constable on the opposite corner. I know him, slightly, and his presence convinced me that no one could either have come into or gone out of the garden by way of the wall. I did not call him, but immediately returned to the studio door."

"In all, you were absent from the studio about how long?" asked Moris Klaw.

"Not a second over half a minute!"

"And on returning once more to the door?"

"A single glance showed me that the statue had gone!"

"Good Heavens!" I said; "it sounds impossible. Was the constable on point duty?"

"He was; there is always an officer there. He stood in sight of the double doors opening on to the street during the whole time, so that 'Nicris' unquestionably came out by way of the garden or melted into thin air. Since the only exit from the garden also opens on to the street, how, but by magic, can the statue have been removed from the premises?"

"Ah, my friend," said Moris Klaw, "you talk of magic as one talks of onions! How little you know"—he swept wide his arms, looking upward—"of the phenomena of the two atmospheres! Proceed!"

"The throne," continued Paxton, who was becoming impressed as was evident by the uncanny sense of power which emanated in some way from Moris Klaw—"remains."

"And the statue—it was attached to it?"

"As to the figure being attached, I may say that it was only partially so. Materials for completing the work were to have arrived today."

"How long would it have taken to detach it?" growled Klaw.

"Granting some knowledge of the nature of the work, not long—for, as I have said, in this respect it was incomplete. Half an hour or so, I should have believed!"

"Then," I said, "the matter, in brief, stands thus: In the course of thirty seconds, during which time a constable was in view of one entrance and you were ten yards from the other, some one detached the statue from the throne—an operation involving half an hour's skilled labour—and unseen by yourself or the officer, removed it from the premises."

"Oh, the thing is impossible!" groaned Paxton. "There is something unearthly in the affair. I wish I had never set eyes upon that accursed girdle!"

"Curse not the girdle," rumbled Moris Klaw. "Curse instead its wearer, and inform us on finding Nicris to be missing, what did you do?"

"I hastily searched the studio. A brief investigation convinced me that neither statue nor thief was concealed there. I then came out, locked the door, and having examined the garden, hailed the constable. He had been on duty for four hours at that point and had observed absolutely nothing of an unusual nature. He saw you fellows come out by the garden entrance, and from that time until I hailed him, nothing, he declared, had come in or gone out!"

"He heard no cry?"

"No; it was not loud enough to be audible from the corner."

"Lastly," said Klaw, "have you informed Scotland Yard?"

"No," answered the sculptor; "nor will the constable lodge information; moreover, I withheld from him the object of my inquiries. If this business gets into the papers I shall be a ruined man!"

"I have hopes," Klaw assured him, "that it will get in no papers. Let us proceed now to the scene of these wonderful happenings. It is my custom, Mr. Paxton, to lay my old head down upon the scene of a mystery, and from the air I can sometimes recover the key to the labyrinth!"

"So I have heard," said Paxton.

"You have heard so, yes? You shall see! Lead on, Mr. Paxton! No time must be wasted. I am another like Napoleon, and can sleep on an instant. I do not know insomnia! Lead on. Isis, my child, be careful that it brushes against no object in passing—my odically sterilised cushion!"

We proceeded to the studio.

"I feel that I am responsible for dragging you here at this unearthly hour," said Paxton to Isis Klaw.

She turned her fine eyes upon him.

"My father is indebted for the opportunity," she replied; "and since he has need of me, I am here. I, too, am indebted."

Her supreme self-possession and tone of finality silenced the artist. So far as I could see, everything in the studio was exactly as before, save that

Nicris's throne was vacant. The top of the studio was partially glazed, and Moris Klaw peered up at it earnestly.

"From above," he rumbled, "I should wish to look down into below. How do I reach it?"

"The only step-ladder is that in the studio," answered Paxton. "I will bring it out."

He did so. The grey light of dawn was creeping into the sky and against that sombre background we watched Moris Klaw crawling about the roof like some giant spider.

"Did you find anything?" asked Paxton, anxiously, as the investigator descended.

"I find what I look for," was the reply; "and no man is entitled to find more. Isis, my child, place that cushion in the ebony chair."

The girl stepped on to the dais, and disposed the red cushion as directed.

"You see," explained Moris Klaw, "whoever has robbed you, Mr. Paxton, runs some one great danger, however clever his plans. There is, in every criminal scheme, one little point that only Fate can decide— either to hitch or to smooth out—to bring success and riches or whistling policemen and Brixton Gaol! Upon that so critical point his or her mind will concentrate at the critical moment. The critical moment, here, was that of getting Nicris out of your studio.

"I sleep upon that throne where she reclined—the ivory dancer. This sensitive plate—" he tapped his brow—"will reproduce a negative of that critical moment as it seemed in the mind of the one we look for. Isis, return in the cab that waits and be here again at six o'clock."

He placed his quaint bowler upon a table and laid beside it his black cloak. Then, a ramshackle figure in shabby tweed, reclined upon the big ebony chair, his head against the cushion.

"Place my cloak about me, Isis."

The girl did so.

"Good-morning, my child! Good-morning, Mr. Searles! Goodmorning, Mr. Coram and Mr. Paxton!"

He closed his eyes.

"Excuse me," began Paxton.

Isis placed her finger to her lips, and signed to us to withdraw silently. "Ssh!" she whispered. "He is asleep!"

III

AT FIVE MINUTES TO SIX SOUNDED ISIS KLAW'S RING UPON THE door bell. Paxton, Coram, and I had spent the interval in discussing the apparently supernatural happening which threatened to wreak the artist's ruin. Again and again he had asked us: "Should I call in the Scotland Yard people? If Moris Klaw fails, consider the priceless time lost!"

"If Moris Klaw fails," Coram assured him, "no one else will succeed!"

We admitted Isis, who wore now a smart tweed costume and a fashionable hat. Beyond doubt, Isis Klaw was strikingly beautiful.

At the door of the studio stood her father, staring straight up to the morning sky, as though by astrological arts he hoped to solve the mystery.

"What times does your model come?" he asked, ere Paxton could question him.

"Half-past ten. But, Mr. Klaw—" began our anxious friend.

"Where does it lead to," Klaw rumbled on, "that lane behind the studio?"

"Tradesmen's entrance to the next house."

"Whose house?"

"Dr. Gleeson."

"M.D.?"

"Yes. But tell me, Mr. Klaw—tell me, have you any clue?"

"My mind, Mr. Paxton, records for me that Nicris was not stolen away, but *walked!* Plainly, I feel her go tip-toe, tip-toe, so silent and cautious! She is concerned, this barbaric dancing-girl who escapes from your studio, with two things. One is some very big man. She thinks, as she tip-toes, of one very tall; six feet and three inches at least! So it is not of you she thinks, Mr. Paxton. We shall see of whom it is. Tell me the name of your acquaintance, the point-policeman."

We were all staring at Moris Klaw, spellbound with astonishment. But Paxton managed to mumble—

"James—Constable James."

"We shall seek him, this James, at the section-house of the police depot," rumbled Klaw. "Be silent, Mr. Paxton; let no one know of your loss. And hope."

"I can see no ground for hope!"

"No? But I? I recognise the clue, Mr. Paxton! What a great science is that of mental photography!"

What did he mean? None of us could surmise, and I could see that poor Paxton reposed no faith whatever in the eccentric methods of the investigator. He would have voiced his doubts, I think, but he met a glance from the dark eyes of Isis Klaw which silenced him.

"My child," said Klaw to his daughter, "take the cushion and return. My negative is a clear one. You understand?"

"Perfectly," replied Isis with composure.

"Breakfast—" began Paxton, tentatively.

But Moris Klaw waved his hands, and enveloped himself in the big cloak.

"There is no time for such gross matters!" he said. "We are busy."

From the brown bowler he took out a scent-spray, and bedewed his high, bald forehead with verbena.

"It is exhausting, that odic photography!" he explained.

Shortly afterwards he and I walked around to the local police depot. Something occurred to me, *en route*.

"By the way," I said, "what was the other thing of which you spoke? The thing that you declared Nicris to be thinking of, though I don't understand in the least how one can refer to the 'thoughts' of an ivory statue!"

"Ah," rumbled my companion, "it is something I shall explain later— that other fear of the missing one."

Arriving at the police depot, "Shall I ask for Constable James?" I said.

"Ah, no," replied Klaw. "It is for the constable that he relieved at twelve o'clock I am looking."

Inquiry showed that the latter officer—his name was Freeman—had just entered the section-house. Moris Klaw's questions elicited the following story—although its bearing upon the matter in hand was not evident to me.

Towards twelve o'clock, that is, shortly before Freeman was relieved, a man, supporting a woman, came down the street and entered the gate of Dr. Gleeson's house. The woman was enveloped in a huge fur cloak which entirely concealed her face and figure, but from her feeble step the constable judged her to be very ill. Considering the lateness of the hour, also, he concluded that the case must be a serious one; he further supposed the sick woman to be resident in the neighbourhood, since she came on foot.

He had begun to wonder at the length of the consultation, when, nearly an hour later, the man appeared again from the shadows of the drive, still supporting the woman. Pausing at the gate he waves his hand to the policeman.

Constable Freeman ran across the road immediately.

"Fetch me a taxicab, officer!" said the stranger, supporting his companion and exhibiting much solicitude.

Freeman promptly ran to the corner of Beira Road, and returned with a cab from the all-night rank.

"Open the door!" directed the man, who was a person of imposing height—some six-feet-three, Freeman averred.

"Ha, ha!" growled Moris Klaw, "six-feet-three! What a wondrous science!"

He seemed triumphant; but I was merely growing more nonplussed.

With that, carefully wrapping the cloak about the woman's figure, the big man took her up in his arms and placed her inside the cab—the only glimpse of her which the constable obtained being that of a small foot clad in a silk stocking. She had apparently dropped her shoe.

Tenderly assisting her to a corner of the vehicle, the man, having bent and whispered some word of encouragement in her ear, directed the cabman to drive to the Savoy.

"Did you give him your assistance?" asked Moris Klaw.

"No. He did not seem to require it."

"And the number of the cabman?"

Freeman fetched his notebook and supplied the required information.

"Thank you, Constable Freeman," said Klaw. "You are a very alert constable. Good-morning, Constable Freeman!"

Again satisfaction beamed from behind my companion's glasses. But to my eyes the darkness grew momentarily less penetrable. For these inquiries bore upon matters which had occurred prior to twelve o'clock; and, Coram, myself, and Paxton had seen the statue in its usual place considerably after midnight! My brain was in a turmoil.

Said Moris Klaw: "That cab was from the big garage at Brixton. We shall ring up the Brixton garage and learn where the man may be found. Perhaps, if Providence is with us—and Providence is with the right—he has not yet again left home."

From a public call-office we rang up the garage, and learned that the man we wanted was not due to report for duty until ten o'clock. We experienced some difficulty in obtaining his private address, but finally it was given to us. Thither we hastened, and aroused the man from his bed.

"A big gentleman and a sick lady," said Moris Klaw, "they hired your cab from Dr. Gleeson's, near Beira Road, at about twelve o'clock last night, and you drove them to the Savoy Hotel."

"No, sir. He changed the address afterwards. I've been wondering why. I drove him to Number 6A, Rectory Grove, Old Town, Clapham."

"Was the lady by then recovered—no? Yes?"

"Partly, sir. I heard him talking to her. But he carried her into the house."

"Ah," said Moris Klaw, "there is much genius wasted; but what a great science is the science of the mind!"

IV

MANY TIMES MORIS KLAW KNOCKED UPON THE DOOR OF THE HOUSE in Clapham Old Town, a small one standing well back from the roadway. Within we could hear some one coughing.

Then the door was suddenly thrown open, and a man appeared who must have stood some six feet three inches. He had finely chiselled features, was clean-shaven and wore pince-nez.

Klaw said a thing that had a surprising effect.

"What!" he rumbled, "has Nina caught cold?"

The other glared, with a sudden savagery coming into his eyes, fell back a step, and clenched his great fists.

"Enough, Jean Colette!" said Moris Klaw, "you do not know me, but I know you. Attempt no tricks, or it is the police and not a meddlesome, harmless old fool who will come. Enter, Jean! We follow."

For a moment longer the big man hesitated, and I saw the shadows of alternate resolves passing across his fine features. Then clearly he saw that surrender was inevitable, shrugged his shoulders, and stared hard at my companion.

"Enter, messieurs," he said, with a marked French accent.

He said no more, but led the way into a long, bare room at the rear of the house. To term the apartment a laboratory would be correct but not inclusive; for it was, in addition, a studio and a workshop. Glancing rapidly around him, Moris Klaw asked: "Where is it?"

The man's face was a study as he stood before us, looking from one to the other. Then a peculiar smile, indescribably winning, played around his lips. "You are very clever, and I know when I am beaten," he remarked; "but had you come four hours later it would have been one hour too late."

He strode up the room to where a tall screen stood, and, seizing it by the top, hurled it to the ground.

Behind, on a model's dais, reclined the statue of Nicris, in a low chair!

"You have already removed the girdle and one of the anklets," rumbled Klaw.

This was true. Indeed, it now became evident that the man had been interrupted in his task by our arrival. Opening a leather case that stood upon the floor by the dais, he produced the missing ornaments.

"What action is to be taken, messieurs?" he asked, quietly.

"No action, Jean," replied Moris Klaw. "It is impossible, you see. But why did you delay so long?"

The other's reply was unexpected.

"It is a task demanding much time and care, if the statue is not to be ruined; otherwise I should have performed it in Mr. Paxton's studio instead of going to the trouble of removing the figure—and—Nina's condition has caused me grave anxiety throughout the night." He stared hard at Moris Klaw. We could hear the sound of coughing from some room hard by. "Who are you, m'sieur?" he asked pointedly.

"An old fool who knew Nina when she posed at Julien's, Jean," was the reply, "and who knew you, also, in Paris."

V

Paxton, Coram, myself, and Moris Klaw sat in the studio, and all of us gazed reflectively at the recovered statue.

"It was so evident," explained Klaw, "that since you were absent from here but thirty seconds, for any one to have removed the statue during that time was out of the question."

"But some one did—"

"Not during that time," rumbled Moris Klaw. "Nicris was removed whilst you all made merry within the house!"

"But, my dear Mr. Klaw, Searles, Coram and I saw the statue long after that—some time about one o'clock!"

"Wrong, my friend! You saw the *model!*"

"What! Nina?"

"Madame Colette, whom you knew in Paris as Nina—yes! Listen— when I drop off to sleep here and dream that I am afraid for what may happen to some very large man, I dream, also, that I fear to be *touched!* I look down at myself, and I am beautiful! I am ivory of limb and decked with gold! I creep, so cautiously, out of the studio (in my dream; *you* would call it a dream) and I know, when I wake, that I must have been Nicris! Ah, you wonder! Listen.

"At about midnight, whilst your party is amiable together, comes one, Jean Colette, a clever scamp from that metropolis of such perverted genius—Paris. Into Dr. Gleeson's he goes, supporting Madame—your model. This is seen by Constable Freeman. When the trees hide them they climb over the fence into the lane and over the wall into your garden. Nina has a cast of the studio key. How easy for her to get it!

"Jean, a clever rogue with his hands, and a man who promised to be, once, a great artist, detaches the figure from the throne and arrays it as Madame—in Madam's outer garb! Beneath her cloak, Madame is Nicris—with copies of the jewels and all complete. He is clever, this Jean! He is, too, a man of vast strength—a modern Crotonian Milo. Not only does he carry that great piece of ivory from the studio, he lifts it over the wall—did Madame assist?—and into Dr. Gleeson's drive. He bears it to the gate, wrapped in Nina's furs. He calls a policeman! Ah, genius is here! He gives the wrong address. He is as cool as an orange!

"Do they escape now? Not so! He sees that you, finding Nicris missing, will apply to the point-policeman and get hold upon a thread. He says, 'I will make it to appear that the robbery took place at a later time. I will thus gain hours! Another policeman will be on duty when the discovery is made; he will know nothing. He leaves Nina to pretend to be Nicris!

"Ah! she has courage, but her fears are many. Most of all she dreads that you will *touch* her! You do not. And Jean, the ivory statue safe at Clapham, returns for Nina. He comes into the doctor's drive by the further gate—where the point-policeman cannot see him. He wears rubber shoes. He mounts to the studio roof. He lies flat upon the ledge above the door. His voice is falsetto. He calls 'Nicris!'

"Presently, you come out. You peep over the wall. Ah! out, also, is Madame! She stretches up her white arms—so like the real ivory!—he stretches down his steel hands. He raises her beside him! Name of a dog, he is strong!

"Why to the roof and not over the wall? The path is of gravel and her feet are bare. On the roof, to prove me correct, upon the grime are marks of small, bare feet; are marks of men's rubber shoes; are, half-way along, marks of smaller rubber shoes—which he had brought for Nina. He has forethought. They retire by the further gate of your neighbour's drive.

"No doubt he bring her furs as well—no doubt. But she contracts a chill, no wonder! Ah! he is cool, he is daring, he is a great man—"

A maid entered the studio.

"A gentleman to see you, sir."

"Ask him to come along here."

A short interval—and Jean Colette entered, hat in hand!

"These two wedges, m'sieur—" he bowed to Paxton—"which help to attach the girdle. I forgot to return them. Adieu!"

He placed the wedges on a table, and amid a dramatic silence withdrew.

Moris Klaw took out the cylindrical scent-spray from the lining of the brown bowler.

"A true touch of Paris!" he rumbled. "Did I not say he was a great man?"

THE STRANGER

CLAUDE & ALICE ASKEW

By the time we reach Aylmer Vance, called the Ghost-Seer, the role of the occult detective and ghost hunter had become well established in British short fiction. Vance, like his rivals, had had many experiences, had uncovered frauds, but had also on occasion been utterly baffled. He is befriended by a level-headed barrister, Dexter, to whom Vance tells his stories with the initial hook that he must some day tell him the story of Lady Green-Sleeves, which keeps Dexter hanging on. Before the story of the Lady is revealed, Vance launches into the following strange case of the afflicted Daphne Darrell.

Both Claude Askew (1865–1917) and his wife Alice (1874–1917), born Alice Jane de Courcy Leake, had dabbled with writing before they married in 1900, but once settled in the matrimonial home they wrote prodigiously, producing hundreds of stories and close on a hundred books. Unfortunately their output and their lives were cruelly ended during the Great War when they were helping Serbian refugees in the Balkans and their hospital ship was torpedoed. Alice's body was washed up on the shores of Corfu, where she was buried, but Claude's was never recovered.

The duo had an early success with The Shulamite (1904) a story of love, passion, and rivalry in South Africa. But only occasionally did they turn to the supernatural, first with the novel The Devil and the Crusader (1909), in which London faces the horrors after a man summons Satan, and then with the Aylmer Vance series. The stories appeared in the penny

Weekly Tale-Teller, which was ably edited by Isabel Thorne, who had helped Edgar Wallace reestablish himself financially after the costs incurred with The Four Just Men. *Thorne enjoyed stories of the bizarre and unusual including not just the following story by the Askews but the story that comes after it in this anthology ("The Swaying Vision" by Jessie Douglas Kerruish).*

I REMINDED AYLMER VANCE OF HIS PROMISE TO TELL ME ABOUT THE little ghost whom he called Lady Green-Sleeves next evening, for, needless to state, I had stayed on at the Magpie Inn for another day's pike fishing; in fact, I had determined to spend a week in Surrey, for I had found out from Vance that he would not be taking his departure before the end of the week, and I wanted to remain as long as he did—to see as much of my new friend as possible.

I had been thinking of the strange story Aylmer Vance had told me the previous evening—the tale of the Sinclair tragedy. The horror of it had got hold of me—haunted me all day long—and now, as we sat in the little parlour of the quaint, old-fashioned inn, I wondered what other weird experiences Vance had gone through.

It was a wet night; no moon lit up the skies this evening, and heavy rain was falling—drenching rain. The weather had suddenly turned much colder—so damp and chilly that our worthy landlady had lit a fire, and I confess that the sight of that crackling fire pleased me. Besides, the parlour smelt rather musty; a fire in the room would do all the good in the world.

Vance drew up a big armchair to the hearth when we entered the parlour after dinner. He held out his hands to the cheerful blaze, a slow smile playing about his thin lips.

"I call this very comfortable," he exclaimed. "Very comfortable indeed. We will send for a bottle of port presently. We will drink old wine and we will crack old jokes. We will forget that it is raining and that the wind is howling outside."

"And you will tell me all about Lady Green-Sleeves?" I interrupted. "We will drink a toast to her—a toast to her sweet memory—for I am sure that she was gentle and young and fair."

"Lady Green-Sleeves was small and dark, a little, eager, twinkling flame; but I am not going to tell you about her tonight. We will leave that for another evening—a warm, star-lit evening. I think I will tell you Daphne Darrell's story—Daphne Darrell's."

He moved his chair closer to mine—he gazed right into the heart of the glowing fire. His very voice had changed—it was charged with a regretful tenderness.

"Yes, I will tell you Daphne Darrell's story tonight, and if it is a fine evening tomorrow, you shall hear all about little Lady Green-Sleeves—the dainty ghost I met face to face. I don't mind telling you my tales, Dexter, for you've a spark of romance in your heart. You're a dreamer as well as a shrewd barrister; but I wonder what you will make of Daphne Darrell's story? Anyway, the poetry of it will appeal to you—it must."

He bent forward. The firelight flickered over his pale, thin face; he laughed softly to himself.

"The great elemental forces, Dexter—why do we no longer believe in them—the old gods and goddesses—the lost faiths? Either we are much wiser than our forefathers, or our forefathers were much wiser than us. But that's a question for the gods to decide—they who know."

Vance paused—one of those long pauses to which I was getting accustomed—then he suddenly started and looked up at me.

"I was going to tell you about Daphne Darrell. I happened to be her guardian. She was the posthumous child of a cousin of mine, a young fellow who met his death under very tragic circumstances about six months after his marriage. He and his wife were pioneers of the open-air movement. They were immensely rich folk, but they liked to jog about the country in a big caravan during the summer, and live a sort of gipsy life.

"It was whilst they were on one of these caravan expeditions that the great tragedy happened. Robert Darrell, bathing in the Thames one morning, was suddenly seized with cramp and drowned before his wife's eyes. Poor Lucy Darrell was prostrate with grief at first, for she was absolutely devoted to her husband, but she kept up as bravely as she could for the sake of her unborn child. Nothing would induce her to go back to Darrell Court, however—my cousins had a fine place in Hampshire, I must tell you. She continued her nomad life all that summer, and the baby was actually born in the caravan, the caravan pitched for the night in Savernake Forest.

"Poor Lucy died within a few days of her child's birth, and perhaps it was just as well, for she was a heart-broken woman; but it seemed a little rough on Daphne—for the child, I must explain, was christened Daphne at her mother's request—to have lost both her parents in her infancy. However, an old aunt came forward—one of those dear, sweet, maiden ladies who are always ready to step into the breach in moments of difficulty, and Miss Jane Darrell volunteered to look after her little niece and make her home at Darrell Court. It was a bit of a sacrifice, I can tell you, for the old lady had a charming house in London and a big circle of friends.

"She was a delightful old gentle-woman was Miss Jane, and it was a great pleasure to me to run down to Darrell Court whenever I found myself in England. It interested me greatly to watch my little ward in the various stages of her evolution. She was a very interesting child, strikingly original in her thoughts and ways, but she was the terror of her nurse and governess, for Daphne would never take the least trouble to learn her lessons, and it made her ill to be kept indoors. She would have liked to spend all her time in the woods and the stately park that fenced Darrell Court from the world. She hated indoor life, and Miss Jane gave way to Daphne in everything. She spoilt her niece shamefully; the consequence was that Daphne grew up lovely, but quite uneducated—a wild, woodland creature."

"Was she very lovely?" I leaned back in my chair as I spoke. It was pleasant to sit in this warm, cosy little parlour and listen to the rain pelting outside, and the melancholy howling of the wind—interesting to watch Aylmer Vance as he talked, very interesting.

"Lovely—was Daphne Darrell lovely?" Vance laughed. "Why, at eighteen she was the most beautiful creature that ever trod the earth! She was tall and slim as a young pine tree, with the most wonderful dark blue eyes and any amount of fair hair. Her face was pure Greek; she had a forehead—a brow—that Clytie herself might have envied. She was flawless—perfect; she reminded one of a nymph, so there was some reason for the pride Miss Jane took in her niece. There was no one like Daphne in her eyes, and I can assure you that Miss Jane's opinion was shared by a good many people; for what did it matter if Daphne had never learnt her dates, if her spelling was atrocious, her knowledge of history nil, her French accent hopeless? She made other women in a room look dim when she walked in; she was the living incarnation of youth and strength. She had a clear, beautiful voice, that was not unlike the sound of rippling waters, and her laugh—why, woodland nymphs must have laughed like that when the world was young; our girls have lost the trick of it nowadays.

"She was very fond of me; a curious rapport prevailed between us—a strange comradeship; in fact, years ago—when Daphne was a child of eight or nine—she confided a great secret to me—a secret she had shrunk from telling anyone else, even Miss Jane. She whispered it into my ear one afternoon as we walked up and down the long green terrace walk—the terrace that stretched out in front of Darrell Court. She explained that she was in the habit of meeting someone in the woods—a tall youth, as far as I could make out—and playing with him.

"'I hide behind the bushes, and he runs after me,' Daphne explained; 'but he never catches me—I never let him. He is so tall and graceful, and so strong.'

"'You mustn't play with strangers, Daphne,' I remarked; 'with strange young men. Is this youth a village boy?'

"Daphne shook her head. To this day I can remember the curious smile that played about her lips—the wise smile.

"'A village boy—oh, no!' she answered. 'And yet he is not a stranger; I have known him—'

"She paused, and did not finish the sentence. A strange look came into her deep blue eyes—a look that puzzled and vaguely alarmed me.

"She would never tell me any more about the youth, except once, when I had taken her up to London to see the Academy. I remember her standing entranced in front of a statue by one of our rising young artists—a statue of the god Apollo.

"'Do you like this statue, Daphne?' I queried.

"The child—for Daphne was little more than a child—turned to me with shining eyes and flaming cheeks.

"'Like it?' she cried. 'Why of course I do; it's so like him.' She paused and laughed—shy, rather conscious laughter. 'I mean like the stranger I meet in the woods sometimes—the stranger I play hide-and-seek with.'

"'You mustn't be so fanciful, Daphne,' I remember saying. 'Of course, this is only a game of make-believe; you don't really meet anyone in the woods.'

"'No, I suppose not,' Daphne admitted. She spoke with a singular reluctance, and we did not refer to the subject again; but three years later, on Daphne's seventeenth birthday, she bought a small marble copy of the famous Apollo Belvedere statue, and put it on a small table in her bed-room, and there was always a vase standing in front of the statue; and the curious thing was that Daphne never put flowers in this vase, but only grass—the freshest, greenest, and juiciest grass she could find.

"By the time Daphne was nineteen there was hardly a young man in Hampshire who was not in love with her, but her choice finally fell on Anthony Halbert. Anthony's father and mother, Sir George and Lady Melton, were devoted to Daphne. She had known the family all her life, for the two estates joined; also Miss Jane was very much in favour of the marriage, for she was an old friend of Tony's mother.

"Besides, Miss Jane felt—at least, so she confided to me afterwards that it would be a very good thing if Daphne had a husband to look after her, for she was getting just a little out of hand. She did unconventional things that worried Miss Jane—worried her exceedingly. She would go off to the woods for whole days at a time, quite oblivious of the social engagements which her aunt had made for her—the garden-parties and tennis-parties which would have appealed to most young girls—the local race meetings.

"Daphne also insisted, during the spring and summer months, on sleeping out of doors. She had a hammock slung between the boughs of two high cedars on the lawn, and nothing would content her but she must sleep in this hammock. Notwithstanding all Miss Jane's entreaties, she absolutely refused to wear corsets—not that that mattered in the very least—her firm young figure needed no artificial support. Also, she had a marked aversion to wearing hats—it was difficult to persuade her ever to put one on; and she loved to take off her shoes and stockings and wade through long wet grass. She would throw herself down with a cry of the purest physical enjoyment amongst bracken; she loved to lie for hours on the lawn in the sunshine, hardly moving a finger—just sleeking her body in the hot sun-rays.

"Of course, these traits in Daphne's character were partly hereditary, but, all the same, Miss Jane was uncommonly glad when young Tony Halbert got Daphne's promise to marry him. She felt as if a great load had been taken off her shoulders—as if she had been relieved from an immense responsibility, for to look after Daphne the child was quite a different matter to looking after Daphne the woman; and the poor old lady realised this—realised it keenly."

Vance paused and drew a deep breath, then he stroked his chin meditatively with his left hand. His eyes looked very dreamy and reflectful.

"Daphne wrote to me herself to announce her engagement. I had just returned to England from Egypt; I had been spending a fine time in Egypt, exploring some old temples, and I remember being profoundly struck by Daphne's letter, and dismayed.

'I am engaged to be married to Tony Halbert, dear guardian'—so the note began, as well as I can remember—'and I am sure you will approve of my choice. Tony is absolutely devoted to me, and so are his people, and I am very, very fond of him; also, I think in many ways it would be a good thing for me to marry and settle down, as Aunt Jane puts it.

'Come and stay with us as soon as you can, guardy dear; and please give me away at my wedding. We are going to be married quite soon—in about six weeks' time.

DAPHNE.

'P.S.—You are a dreadfully clever man, guardy, and you investigate, don't you, for the Ghost Circle? So will you please tell me what people ought to do when they see visions—visions in broad daylight? Ought they to regard themselves as mentally afflicted, or believe that their eyes, for some purpose, have been opened? Do you think this world only belongs to the living, or do you believe that the past still has some hold on it—some claim? And have we lived before, or are we just ourselves?'

"I answered Daphne's letter in person. I do not mind confessing to you, Dexter, that it worried me—that I felt distinctly uneasy, but when I arrived at Darrell Court I was quite reassured.

"Daphne was playing tennis with her fiancé, and she looked splendidly healthy, exceedingly happy, not at all the sort of girl to indulge in delusions. She threw down her racquet directly she caught sight of me, and ran across the lawn to meet me, Tony following her. She seemed in wonderful spirits, and she could talk of nothing else but her forthcoming wedding. She told me, all in a breath, where she and Tony were going for their honeymoon—what beautiful presents friends were sending them—how there was to be a presentation from the tenantry in a day or two's time, and Daphne was especially eloquent about the dance that was to be given at Darrell Court the night before the wedding.

"'I am having the dance the night before,' she exclaimed, 'because I think it's such a silly thing to have the dance after the wedding, when the bride and bridegroom have gone. Besides, Tony and I both love dancing. There's to be a big ballroom built out on the lawn, and we are having the Blue Hungarian Band, and it's sure to be a lovely midsummer night. I hope you will enjoy the dance, guardy—I think we must open it together.'

"I laughed and shook my head.

"'No, Daphne,' I answered. 'I think it will be Tony's place to lead you out. Now, if that young man of yours can spare you to me for a few minutes, I think we will take a turn together, for your old guardian has all sorts of questions to ask you.'

"Tony surrendered Daphne to me at once. He was a tall, good-looking young fellow, with an honest face and a pair of good, brown eyes. He was close on six feet in height, a very muscular young Englishman—a sweetheart to be proud of.

"I led Daphne into the rose garden. It was a quaint, old-fashioned little garden, sheltered by high yew hedges, and roses bloomed there in great masses—the air was heavy with their fragrance. There was a marble seat in one corner of the rose garden, and Daphne and I sat down. She was all in white, I remember, and, as usual, she wore no hat; her hair shone in the sunlight gold. Her beautiful throat was bare, and she wore no rings on her hands; she had refused—so I learnt afterwards—to wear an engagement ring.

"'You are quite happy, Daphne, are you not?' I began. 'I don't think you could possibly be engaged to a nicer young fellow. I have always liked Tony Halbert, and I have never heard anything but good of him; in fact, your guardian highly approves of the match you are making—he considers it a most suitable one.'

"Daphne looked at me queerly.

"'That's how I feel myself, guardy—that I am doing a very sensible thing in marrying Tony, for I could never marry anyone who was nicer—in fact, half so nice; but—' She paused. Colour suddenly flooded her face, warm colour. She turned to me nervously, a little shyly. 'Did you think me mad when I wrote that postscript to my letter, guardy—quite mad?'

"I shook my head.

"'No, Daphne,' I answered, 'but I felt a little puzzled by that postscript. What does it mean, my dear, tell me frankly, what does it mean?'

"'I don't know myself.' She shook her head. 'Except that I fancy I must suffer from hallucinations at times—ridiculous hallucinations. Do you remember when I was quite a little girl, guardy, how I told you one day about the beautiful stranger whom I said I used to meet in the woods and play hide and seek with behind the trees and bushes? Well, I expect you thought I was romancing, telling stories, but I wasn't. I really used to meet that stranger, and—and I meet him still.'

"'My dear Daphne!' I looked at my ward sternly. 'You really mustn't say such things to me—such absurd things.'

"'But it's the truth, guardy. I do meet someone in the woods. I have never spoken to him, nor has he spoken to me; I have never even touched his hand, and I always call him the stranger to myself, except when I call him the—the god.'

"She lowered her voice to a faint whisper. An extraordinary look had come into her eyes—a look that frightened me.

"'He's glorious—so glorious that I cannot believe him to be mortal man. He frightens me a little now, though he never frightened me when I was a child. He is as bright as a flame is bright; his shining flesh gleams like marble through the green bushes. His eyes draw me—compel me, and yet they are fierce eyes—very fierce.'

"She checked herself abruptly.

"'Tell me that it is all nonsense, guardy—that it is only an hallucination of mine. That I shall forget all about my stranger—my god—once Tony has got me in his own safe keeping.'

"'Of course it is all nonsense, Daphne,' I replied. 'You fancied that you met this—this stranger when you were a child, and you have kept up the fancy all your life, and it's become a sort of delusion with you—an unhealthy delusion. But, as you truly say, once you are married to Tony you will put all this nonsense out of your head; you will have to.'

"'Yes, I shall have to.' She gave a quiet little nod, then she crept closer to me on the seat. 'Guardy, I must tell you something else. I had better confess straight out that though I am awfully fond of Tony I am not the least bit in love with him. It's the stranger I love; why, I should die with sheer delight if he kissed me, I think, but he is only a dream, I suppose, a dream.'

"I took Daphne by one of her cold hands. I looked straight into her eyes.

"'Child, madness lies in such dreams,' I cried. 'Do you realise that?—madness. You must forget all about this stranger—you must put him out of your life, out of your thoughts; but with Tony to help you, my dear, you will soon succeed in conquering this hallucination. Thank God you are going to be married, Daphne, and that the wedding is fixed to take place soon.'"

Aylmer Vance rose from his chair, and began to walk up and down the room. His long arms hung down by his side, his face looked thinner and paler than ever.

"Just listen to the rain, how it beats against the windows. Does my story interest you, Dexter?"

"Distinctly. Please go on—don't stop at such an exciting moment. What did Miss Darrell say in answer to your speech?"

"Very little, nor did she appear at all disposed to continue the conversation. She merely gave me a faint, shadowy smile; and Tony turned up a few minutes later and carried her back to the tennis court to finish the game I had interrupted. They ran off together, laughing like two children, but I thought Daphne looked very distrait during dinner. She hardly ate or drank anything, and she kept staring vaguely through the open window—gazing in the direction of the wise green woods. She wanted to go out for a walk after dinner, to roam with Tony in the grounds, but Miss Jane asked her to sing to us instead—I must hear how wonderfully Daphne's voice had improved, the old lady said. But Daphne wouldn't sing, and she grew more and more restless as the evening wore on. She even seemed in a hurry to get rid of Tony; certainly she did not press him to stay when he finally rose to depart, nor were their *adieux* very prolonged.

"'You are not going to sleep out of doors again this evening, are you, darling?' Miss Jane asked, rather anxiously, as she kissed Daphne good night a few minutes later. 'I can hardly bear to think of you in the darkness—your hammock swinging from those big cedar trees.'

"'Why, it's lovely out of doors, Aunt Jane,' Daphne answered. 'I couldn't sleep indoors—I really couldn't—on such a hot night as this, and I'm not a bit frightened. Why should I be frightened? Do you think someone will steal out of the woods and carry me away—some stranger?'

"She laughed and left the room laughing. Miss Jane and I looked at each other anxiously.

"'Isn't she a queer girl?' Miss Jane exclaimed. 'Oh, I shall be thankful, Mr. Vance, when Daphne is safely married to dear Tony.'

"'And I shall be thankful too,' I answered, and I meant what I said."

Vance walked back to his chair again. The fire was beginning to burn down; he put some more coals on, and I noticed that his hands were shaking a little.

"Well, you want to hear the rest of my yarn, I supposed, Dexter? I left Darrell Court next morning. I had only been able to arrange to come down for the night—I had a lot of business to attend to, you see, having so recently returned to England. But I promised Daphne that I would come back the day before the wedding in order to be present at her dance, and I gave her a word of warning as we said goodbye.

"'Don't think any more of that dream of yours, Daphne—that silly delusion. Forget it, my dear—keep your thoughts fixed on Tony.'

"Daphne smiled and nodded her head.

"'That's all right, guardy,' she answered. 'You can trust me to be quite sensible in the future.'

"She waved her hand to me gaily enough as I drove away, and how was I to guess that even then her thoughts were turning to the stranger in the forest—that she was deceiving all of us, and perhaps herself?

"I returned to Darrell Court for the dance, as I had arranged to do.

"I found the house packed with young people; four of the bridesmaids were staying there and several of the groomsmen. The sound of wedding bells was in the air, a happy excitement prevailed, and Daphne herself seemed the gayest of the gay, not that I saw much of her; she seemed to be always surrounded by a bevy of girls—pretty girls, who chattered at the top of their voices.

"She sought me out of her own free will just before dinner, however. I had dressed early, and had gone down to the study, feeling a little out of things, for the young people were having it all their own way in the drawing-room; they were dancing there already.

"'Guardy, I want to speak to you.' Daphne spoke in low, rather hesitating tones, then she shut the study door behind her and walked up to me. She looked more beautiful than I had ever seen her. She was dressed all in white, as became tomorrow's bride, and her gown clung tightly to her glorious young figure. She wore no jewels beyond a fillet of pearls in her hair; but the expression in her face troubled me—there was such a yearning look in her eyes—such a strange look.

"'What's the matter, Daphne?' I asked. 'My dear, you are not unhappy, are you?'

"'I am very unhappy, guardy.' She bowed her head; two big tears rolled down her cheeks. 'I don't love Tony, I shall never love Tony, and I am going to marry him tomorrow; and he will take me away from all that I care for most—from my freedom, my solitude, my woods. I shall never be able to spend long days by myself in the future, alone with the wild things. I shall have to become domesticated; I shall be a wife—perhaps later on a mother.'

"She paused, then added, speaking very quickly and nervously:

"'I ought never to have become engaged, I see that now. I ought always to have belonged to myself. I oughtn't to have been afraid of my dreams, my fancies, and anxious to have them dispelled, for what can Tony give me in exchange—what can he give me?' She threw back her head—she gazed at me defiantly.

"'Tony can give you love,' I answered steadily. 'He can give you reality.'

"'I want neither.' She laughed, queer broken laughter. 'I want, guardy, what I shall never find—what I never can find now.'

"She swayed from foot to foot, such a slim young figure, then she suddenly sank on her knees and raised her white arms high above her head.

"'Oh, my dreams—my beautiful dreams,' she moaned, 'my lost dreams! Have I got to say goodbye to them forever tonight, and goodbye to the stranger, goodbye to the lover who has never kissed me, who never will kiss me, but whose kisses I desire above all things, whose love I crave for?'

"She trembled violently. I remember putting my hand upon her shoulder and feeling how her flesh quivered. I also recollect that I shook Daphne—shook her fiercely.

"'Child, don't talk so madly,' I cried. 'You forget yourself; you don't know what you are saying. You are overtired, you are hysterical tonight— you must be hysterical.'

"Daphne swayed slowly to her feet, then a film seemed to gather over her eyes. She laughed, soft, broken laughter.

"'Yes, that's what's the matter with me, guardy,' she murmured. 'I am hysterical—overwrought. I have been trying on clothes all this last week without ceasing, and there's been so much to see to with regard to the wedding. I must pull myself together now. I shall be all right for the dance tonight, and quite all right tomorrow; and of course I don't want to fail Tony at the last minute I wouldn't do that for anything. Think how Tony loves me, and what a dear he is!'

"She ran out of the room before I could say another word, and joined her guests in the drawing-room, and I got no opportunity of talking to her during dinner.

"Directly after dinner the entire house-party made their way in gay procession to the huge marquee that had been built out on the lawn and turned into a temporary ballroom. The band struck up a waltz as we entered. Tony caught Daphne round her waist and spun her into the middle of the floor, and in a few minutes the whole house-party was danc- ing, and Daphne's laugh rang out gaily as Tony waltzed her round. It was hard to believe that I had seen her on her knees in the study only an hour before, indulging in passionate invocation.

"Guests began to arrive. Miss Jane insisted on introducing me to vari- ous ladies, with whom I was in duty bound to dance, but at last I managed to sneak off by myself to enjoy a quiet cigarette on the terrace. It was a stiflingly hot evening, and I had rather a bad headache. I fancied there was a storm about; once or twice I thought I heard the distant rumble of

223

thunder, but I hoped the storm would not come on before morning. Still there were not so many stars out as there had been an hour ago.

"I lit my cigarette, and proceeded to stroll up and down the terrace. Suddenly I caught sight of Daphne's figure in the distance, stealing out of the ballroom, and she was alone, much to my amazement; she had evidently deserted her partner. She ran like a hare across the lawn—ran straight in the direction of the woods that slope to the right of Darrell Court; I determined to follow at a safe distance, and see for myself what would happen in those woods—and I did see."

A curious change came over Aylmer Vance's voice as he said the last words. His whole body appeared to stiffen as he sat in his chair. A strange thrill ran through me; I sat up erect in my chair, too.

"Daphne gained the wood without noticing that I was following her. She ran at a breathless pace, as if she was in the greatest hurry, and when we entered that dark wood, Dexter, I was distinctly conscious of the sound of music—the music of the flute. I told myself at once—for I hope I am a sensible man—that of course it was merely the echo of the dance music that I was listening to, and I suppose that's what it was."

Vance hesitated, and bit his lips.

"I hardly know how to describe to you what happened next. I don't want you to think me a lunatic, but it seemed to me as though the wood was full of people, and yet I could see no one actually; but every now and then I caught glimpses of the white arms of girls. I could hear what sounded like soft girlish laughter, and once a long tress of hair seemed to be blown right across my face; I could have sworn to this at the time, but perhaps it was only my fancy. Maybe it was merely some dark bough I brushed against—some soft, sweet-scented bough, for everything was so vague, Dexter, so hopelessly indefinite, and yet, if I can make you under-stand, so real."

Vance half-closed his eyes. He was talking in very, slow, measured tones; I strained my ears to catch every word.

"Daphne ran on right into the heart of the wood. It was getting very dark overhead. I was certain that the storm would break quite soon, the thunderstorm I had been anticipating. The angry rumbles of distant thun-der had grown much louder lately, but the strange thing was I never once thought of calling to Daphne to come back with me to the house, or of warning her that a storm was approaching. Perhaps I was no more myself that night than she was—maybe we were both fay, but I was conscious as I followed her through the wood that there were strange powers abroad that evening—strange forces. I felt curiously excited—oddly stirred. A longing to say goodbye to civilisation and to conventionality came over me. I yearned for greater freedom than I had ever known—for a more intimate knowledge of nature. I felt it would be delightful to cast my clothes from me and bathe in the dew-moistened grass. I forgot that I was a staid and respectable man of forty; all the feelings of youth came back—the sublime intoxication of youth."

Vance's head dropped forward on his breast. His eyes were completely closed.

"Well, Dexter, I must make an end of my story, or I shall weary you to death. Daphne suddenly fell down on her knees, just as she had done in the study, and she held up her white arms and seemed to cry to someone to come to her—a long, passionate, half-inarticulate cry, and it was the cry of a woman calling to her beloved, summoning him to her, and as I am a living man, Dexter, something—someone—came in answer to Daphne's cry. He—for it was a man—seemed to shoot down from the branches of a high fir tree, and he was white and shining and nude. A fierce brightness seemed to diffuse from him, and he carried a bow in his hand—he was the archer."

Vance raised his head as he said the last words, opened his eyes, and stared me in the face.

"I am not asking you to believe me, Dexter—I know that my tale sounds too incredible but I tell you when I saw this flash of light descending, as it were, upon Daphne, I covered my face with my hands, and fell to the ground myself, for what right had I, a mere man, to spy upon this meeting of a maid and an immortal? Yes, I crouched abashed to the ground, and as I did so a great thunder clap seemed to shake the earth to its foundations—such a thunder clap."

Vance bent forward in his chair and put a hand upon my arm.

"There's very little more to tell you now," he whispered. "There was no wedding at Darrell Court the next day, for the tragic reason that the bride had been struck by lightning the night before. We don't believe, you and I, being wise, sensible, practical men, that it was a lover's kiss that killed her—a lover's burning kiss; and yet the lightning had hardly scarred her sweet body, though it had struck her dead."

"What a horrible—what a ghastly tragedy!" I interrupted. A cold shiver ran through my spine as I spoke, but Aylmer Vance shook his head.

"You're making a mistake, my dear friend. There was nothing really tragic about Daphne Darrell's death. It was the fate she would have chosen, I have no doubt, if she had been given her choice, for remember if we are to believe her own story—she was not the least in love with Tony Halbert; and think what a loveless marriage would have meant to a girl of Daphne's temperament! She met her dream and her death at the same time. Besides, have you forgotten, Dexter, that 'those whom the gods love die young?'"

I made no answer, but as I watched Aylmer Vance kneel down in front of the fire to warm his hands, I ventured to ask him a question.

"Do you believe that the old gods are dead, Vance?—do you really believe that?"

Vance smiled—a strange inscrutable smile.

"They are dead to some," he answered, "but they are alive to others."

THE SWAYING VISION

JESSIE DOUGLAS KERRUISH

Jessie Douglas Kerruish (1884–1949), who came from an ancient Manx family, ensured her immortality, at least amongst devotees of weird fiction, with The Undying Monster *(1922), a tale of lycanthropy and a family curse that also included one of the few female occult detectives of the period, Luna Bartendale. Little of her other stories are known, though she was a frequent contributor to* The Weekly Tale-Teller. *Her series of Arabian tales,* Babylonian Nights' Entertainment, *ran there in 1915 and eventually appeared in book form in 1934. Kerruish was fortunate in winning the first prize of £750 in a competition in 1917 for her adventure novel set in Mesopotamia,* Miss Haroun al-Raschid. *The sum of £750 in 1917 is equal to around £50,000 ($66,000) today. She followed this with* A Girl from Kurdistan *(1918), this time set in Persia (modern Iran), and is every bit as contemporary in its study of the conflict between Christianity and Islam.* The Hull of Coins *(1928) is a treasure-hunt adventure for a sunken vessel off the English coast. These later novels are long forgotten, but Kerruish's name was kept alive by* The Undying Monster, *which was filmed in 1942 though, alas, the sex of the occult investigator was changed. Little else of her works have survived but, tucked away in the pages of* The Weekly Tale-Teller *in January 1915 is the following, which introduces us to an earlier investigator, Lester Stukeley.*

CHADWICK BOUGHT THE DESIRABLE SEMI-DETACHED RESIDENCES, Nos. 75 and 77, Herald Crescent, Willingborough, to fulfil the ideal of middle-class retirement; a house to live in and another to pay rates and taxes and the coal bill. He was not a man to buy a pig in a poke, or a house in a strange town in a hurry; he held strict inquest on the birth and death rates of the locality, and on the drains of his prospective purchase, its damp courses, and the character of the immediate neighbourhood. He welcomed a two days' downpour that triumphantly vindicated the water-tightness of the buildings, and he found that the pair were the only ones to let in the Crescent.

What else, within the limits of the normal Three Dimensions, could a man have done further?

On March 25 he, with his family consisting of Mrs. Chadwick and their two daughters, moved into No. 75. On the 26th he consorted with his next-door neighbour and learnt the worst.

"It was really nobody's affair," the next-door neighbour protested. "How could anybody warn you? Of course you might," he added, as the aggrieved Chadwick breathed threats relating to the ex-landlord of his new demesne and the house agent. "Still, I must remind you it's a penal offence to kill people, even if they have landed you with one of the most notorious haunted houses in England."

It was bad enough, the worst. No. 77—under an alias for the law of libel's sake—had figured five times in the pages of a certain psychic review, and times innumerable in magazines of a sensational tendency. It had been let twelve times in eight years; no tenant stayed out his term. The first one paid up to avoid trouble, and reimbursed himself by spreading information concerning his experiences. He stayed a month. The second, at the end of a week, wanted to horsewhip the landlord for letting in his wife for nervous breakdown. So the tale went on, the last occupants had left at the half-quarter before Chadwick acquired the treasure; they had refused to pay for the remainder of the year they had agreed on, and had dared the landlord to sue them and embellish the reputation the place already owned. So there had been nothing left for the landlord to do but to sell to some stranger while he removed to a far city.

Local house-agents, consulted, confirmed the tale. They said they would try to get a tenant, but mentioned, pessimistically, that No. 79 was let at thirty per cent below the regular rent in the road because only the detaching tradesmen's entrances divided from No. 77. Yes, the Psychic Society had investigated, they had even taken up the flooring in the noted front room. And they had found no explanation.

Chadwick was no coward; he spent that evening in the front room of No. 77. At 3 a.m. he stumbled into his own parlour in the throes of panic. Next day he repaired to London to seek aid from Lester Stukeley.

Stukeley and Chadwick were old schoolfellows. Chadwick at fifty was a retired merchant, with gardening for his hobby; Stukeley, at near the same age, still adorned the Civil Service, and had taken to psychic investigation.

"It was utterly beastly, Stukeley," said Chadwick, mopping his ample bald brow at the recollection.

"We will go into it systematically," said his friend. "To begin, the house is of modern construction!"

"Built twenty years ago."

"Of new materials, if you know?"

"I know. Yes. Why, Stukeley?"

"Because I've known things happen in modern houses built out of the debris of old ones. You say twelve tenants have lived there in eight years, that leaves twelve since the building of the place to be accounted for."

"It was in the hands of two tenants; neither complained of any disturbance; the first stayed his full term of five years, the second, by renewals, stayed for seven in all."

"So it was after the departure of this second tenant that the trouble began? That looks suspicious."

"I know his address. He is an old Frenchman, and by the house-agents' accounts most harmless and above-board. He declared, when questioned, that he never noticed anything wrong, nor did his family."

"There's always the possibility that they were merely of a solid and unsusceptible nature. Still, I'll remember this Frenchman. It is somewhat unusual to encounter occult manifestations in a house of such recent construction with no sinister tale attached to it. Has anyone died in it?"

"It happens no death has so far taken place in it."

"This increases the mystery. Now, if you know, Chadwick, what was the site like before the building took place?"

"My communicative neighbour remembers it; it was a meadow."

229

"Were there any knolls that had to be levelled for the building—if you know?"

"My informant describes it as perfectly flat."

"I must congratulate you, Chadwick, on your foresight in procuring such exhaustive information. I confess I thought a burial barrow might have been disturbed for the builders' benefit. You watched last night?"

Chadwick got scarlet, then blurted out, "I watched for a while. Then— then I bolted. It was just what all the other people described—the unutterably abominable smell—faugh!—and I knew I'd be compelled to turn out the light in a minute—I just hurled myself through the doorway."

"To turn out the light?" repeated Stukeley inquiringly.

"Yes," Chadwick answered explosively. "Everybody agreed about that. It can't be seen in the dark distinctly, and it can't be seen at all in full light, a faint light is what suits it. You feel it's there, and you smell it—heavens, that's the horrible part of it! Not strong, you'll understand, but beastly— viscid—and—and—a sort of pale yellow-green, sticky stench."

"I understand. A strongly developed colour sense is useful in description. And what is seen?"

"I didn't see. I knew it would give me the horrors. But the people who saw it because they hadn't gumption to run away all agreed. 'Pon my word, Stukeley, it sounds absurd, but I thought the description of the first feeling absurd, too, before I'd experienced it, and now I've experienced that, and know how utterly loathsome it is, I can believe the rest is as bad."

"One moment," said Stukeley, with the air of one struck by a sudden thought. "Do not tell me what is said about the ocular manifestation. Let me try with an open mind, and see if what I see agrees with the other accounts. Will you watch with me?"

"Will you draw the protective thing, the what d'ye call it?" Chadwick hesitated.

"The pentacle? Most certainly I will erect it. With no reason for occult manifestations to be found there is always room for hoaxing, but it is well to take precautions."

"I'll watch then—inside the pentacle. I don't believe it is hoaxing, Stukeley, but as nobody has received bodily harm, beyond shock, so far, I feared you would not trouble with the pentacle."

"I know, Chadwick, that one can never tell when occult manifestations may become dangerous to life. Tomorrow night, then, I hope it will prove a hoax.

"Tomorrow night," Chadwick repeated. "We'll have the house to ourselves. Mary and the girls got hold of the tale soon enough. The servants we brought left this morning, they'd heard it, too, and we are staying at the nearest hotel while I decide what is to be done. They all drew the line at even being next door to the thing."

When Stukeley unloaded his bag from the cab next evening and took a look up and down Herald Crescent, nothing could have presented a more reassuring appearance. The place shouted of respectability, leisure, and fish-and-soup-course-dinners. The kind of place where occult manifestations were the very last things that might be expected to happen. Two rows of three-storey, semi-detached residences sloped before his gaze to a quiet twilight sky, every house a replica of its fellows, white-curtained, brass-plated, trim and commonplace.

No. 77 was only singled out from its neighbours because it was the only one to let, and was plus a brace of notice boards and minus plate and curtains.

In the dining-room of No. 75 the table awaited the dinner for two which a near-by restaurant was to furnish in an hour, the brave charwoman who had agreed to stop till sunset and return at sunrise to see to the wants of the two men was in attendance, and Chadwick was ready for a preliminary daylight inspection of the scene of forthcoming vigil.

Under Chadwick's key the front door of No. 77 swung open with a reassuring squeak.

Stukeley and his aide went through to the back and inspected the garden. Then they locked and sealed the back door, and set out on an exhaustive tour of the house, leaving the front room to the last, and making a species of drive down to it from the garret.

As each room was overhauled the door was shut, locked, and sealed behind them until of all the apartments in the house only the front one was open. The windows even were closed and sealed, and narrow strips of paper sealed in a network across the register of every chimney.

Chadwick stood nervously by the open door as Stukeley went round the front room.

The occultist raised the blinds, flooding the place with harsh reflected sunset light from the windows opposite.

The apartment was the largest in the house, measuring some twenty feet by thirty, the ceiling was high, the walls painted dull olive-green, the floor oak-stained and polished. Stukeley went round several times, tapping walls and floor questingly, peered up the chimney, then nodded gravely.

"Once we have locked ourselves in this bare room, nothing outside of the Fourth Dimension could get us without our knowledge," he commented.

"Lock ourselves in?" Chadwick repeated, without relish.

"Within the pentacle, old chap. Now what is the spot at which the manifestations begin?"

"Between the chimney and the west wall," Chadwick answered.

The room was bounded at one side by the entry-lobby, the wall opposite was conterminous with the passage of the tradesmen's entrance outside, the east wall contained the large bay window, the west one separated it from the next room.

Stukeley stamped and tapped the flooring at the indicated spot, but elicited no more signs of hollowness than the ventilation space beneath would justify. They then returned to No. 75, locking the front door of No. 77 carefully behind them.

Dinner put more heart into Chadwick. At eleven, the charwoman having long departed, they locked No. 75 up and adjourned to No. 77 again.

Gas was laid on. Stukeley went all over again, ascertaining that the seals were unbroken before opening each door. Satisfying himself that nobody had been in, he lit the gas all over the place, and repeated the drive of the earlier hour, leaving the light on full cock in each room and the doors open, and seeing that the chimneys and windows were well sealed.

With the blaze of light Chadwick's courage was augmented. The front room was furnished with an incandescent burner in a hanging chandelier set in the centre of the ceiling. When it was lit the whole apartment was plain and bare to the view. Chadwick shuddered a little as the door was closed. Stukeley laid his bag in the middle of the floor together with a pair of camp stools.

"Now, we will stay here while I make my arrangements," he said, and Chadwick felt emboldened as he watched the said arrangements.

Producing a little bundle of twigs from the bag, the occultist swept the floor in a circle, extending nearly to the walls, keeping himself within the limit of it. Then, in the same way he drew a pentacle with charcoal within the bounds of the swept space.

"It's charred rowan wood," he explained over his shoulder, as he traced with a continuous line the five-pointed figure. "Now just remember, Chadwick, that if either of us should step outside the line, or even touch it sufficiently to break the continuity of it, the pentacle will lose its protective power. Should danger threaten safety lies within this line. But if even a match should fall across it linking the space within to the space without, the virtue of the pentacle is gone."

In the five points of the star he placed five crusts, each wrapped in a slip of linen, and between, in the five angles, five pinches of white powder.

"Bread and salt, with charcoal, are great protective influences," he said, standing up. "I'll guarantee that within this we will be safe from all molestation."

They established themselves on the camp stools, full in the light of the gas, and waited. Chadwick's courage oozed. Herald Crescent is a quiet thoroughfare, and before midnight traffic in it practically ceased.

Silence settled down; with it Chadwick knew that darkness—wholesome, respectable darkness—also came to the other houses, with drawn blinds and extinguished lights. Now and then a chance cab rattled past, clattering eerily over the wood-paving between the hushes that followed and preceded its progress.

A couple of strayed revellers fared homewards, none too steadily, their footsteps ringing irregularly; the policeman, who had been apprised of the reason for the lights in No. 77, passed by with a slow tramp of ample boots.

An hour passed. Stukeley sat quiet. Chadwick copied him outwardly, and inwardly quaked. His imagination shudderingly played with the fancy that they were sitting in an island of light in the dark street; it felt as though everybody else in the world were dead; there was no help to be had if help were needed.

A rogue horror, a muddle-headed sense of the bounds of matter, began to grip him. He tried to reassure himself by thoughts of the nearness of his kind. It was a failure.

Looking before him at the brightly illuminated wall, he told himself that beyond the wall was a narrow passage, an open passage full of the blessed free air of heaven, then another wall, and beyond that the merry family of children who, with a jolly father and cheery mother, lived in No. 79.

The thought was of no use, the family would not be in the room beyond the dividing passage now, but upstairs, ever so many walls away, and that boundary passage full of open air—it was a terrible place, with no bound between it and the stars, and the void beyond the stars. It was a continuation of space, it was an immeasurable sundering gap between himself in the haunted room and his kind, as represented by the jolly family in the next house.

Chadwick shuddered and tried another tack. His back was to the door, but if he slewed round there would be nothing but the room wall, the width of the passage, and another wall to divide him from the refuge of No. 75.

Nothing but two walls and the passage—a thousand miles would be no more barrier—he could not leap through solid walls if the need for refuge came when the lights had to be lowered. He must open the door of the room, traverse the passage, open the front door—heavens! It was a tremendous way to go if need pressed and something was after him.

New Zealand came into his mind. It seemed within nearer reach, for all the hours of train journeying and half a world of sea between, than his own home next door, with but the six-foot width of passage and two walls between.

He came to himself with a little cry and sat bristling. By his side Stukeley fumed with a little cool nod.

"Do you feel it?" Chadwick gasped.

Stukeley nodded again, holding up a hand for silence. Chadwick braced himself and steadied his quivering under-jaw.

"My God, don't you taste it?" he cried suddenly.

Stukeley made no answer. A faint, thin viscid flavour in the air was but too perceptible to him. He sat with his eyes turned to the front of him. Chadwick followed his gaze to the floor, and sat tense with expectation.

The burner high above and somewhat behind the men cast the shadows before them. The shadows were clear-cut, reflected light from the walls lit them to a dark transparency. In them the lines where the floorboards met were defined blackly. Stukeley's extended the farthest, nearly to the wall by the fireplace, it went over that side of the pentacle, a sharp cut patch of clear dark.

Within the span of this cast shadow one of the angles and half a point of the pentacle were included, the intersecting charcoal lines clear black, the little heap of salt in the angle dusky grey, half the wrapped crust in the point in shadow, a dirty, white little mass, the other half dazzling white against the lit boards beyond the shadow edge.

Chadwick looked at these details until his gaze swam, then his senses woke and his scalp drew together, chilled and twitching. He had become aware of another bit of darkness on the floor, a flood of black that was creeping steadily forward towards them across Stukeley's shadow.

It began, clear cut, as the edge of the shadow, and was spreading in a little stream, about a hand-breadth in width, progressing with the lazy, rolling deliberation of spilt ink. For several moments the men sat immovable. Stukeley speculated, clear-brained, as to its origin. Where could it come from, starting, as it apparently did, at the edge of his shadow?

As they watched it languidly split into two irregular branches and so continued on its way.

"It will touch our feet!" Chadwick screamed, springing up and retreating a pace.

Stukeley got up more quietly to join him. The move brought them immediately beneath the gas, and their shadows were concentrated under their feet. The floor around was all in light, no sign of the creeping shadow stream was visible.

Chadwick trembled violently.

"Do you hear it?" he quavered.

Stukeley's eyes searched the floor. "A little hissing and bubbling near the fireplace," he said gravely.

"And the—the stench?" gulped his companion. "Blood—and—corruption—"

"No, new blood," said Stukeley. "It is like the scent of the drain pit in a Dakhma I examined near Bombay."

"A Dakhma?"

"Tower of Silence. A Parsee, corpse-exposing building."

The occultist stepped forward; his shadow ran over the floor to its old place. The creeping stain appeared as before, farther advanced to them.

"It is only visible in the dark," he commented.

"Come before it touches us," Chadwick mouthed.

"Stay in the pentacle," Stukeley commanded sternly. "It is our safety— see!"

Chadwick, half-frantic with horror, glanced along his indicating finger. The stream touched the point of the pentacle, turned as though it had encountered a wall, and ran along outside against the charcoal mark. In its flow it met the pile of salt and laved it without penetrating the absorbent stuff. It continued to spread itself along against the charcoal line. Chadwick understood, and felt less dread: it could not penetrate the pentacle.

Stukeley stepped forward, keeping his shadow crosswise over the mystic one, and advancing parallel to it. As he advanced the edge of his shadow still remained the edge of the other. At last the shadow of his head was low on the wall by the fireplace and that of his shoulders on the floor beneath.

And right in the middle of the shadowed left shoulder was the beginning of the dark stream—a rectangular spot that hissed softly and gave forth bubbles of shadow which rose from it and broke sibilantly.

He moved his shadow away, and the bubbling stream was gone; he moved the shadow back and it reappeared. Behind him Chadwick suddenly cried out in a shrill tone, "Stukeley, there's something over the stream! It will be on us! I can't stand it—invisible! I must see it!"

He snatched upwards and turned the gas low. From both men came a gasp. Over the bubbling stream, now clearly defined in the gloom, lay a figure.

It was stretched apparently on the floor, some ten feet from them; they saw it clearly; it was solid to view, yet they could not exactly define details. To each it appeared as though he was wearing spectacles unsuited to his eyes. The figure, naked and flaccid, was half-corpse, half-skeleton. In parts the bones protruded, but the head was untouched; a handsome young head, a face young behind its ashiness, hollow-cheeked and unshaven. As they looked it slowly rose in the air almost as high as the ceiling, then swept down again to the floor.

Again it rose, canted at a different angle, and descended at another tilt, so that for several seconds it seemed to stand upright before them, the jaw dropping with a jerk. Then it went up and turned so that it appeared to stand head down with its back to them.

A dozen times these gyrations were repeated, and at each repetition the form was displayed at a slightly varying angle; the movements were accomplished with a horrible lazy deliberation, then with a jar the figure stopped in mid-air, level with their eyes, and was jerked double, so that it appeared to be sitting up bent forward from the hips, the head almost butting on its knees.

"It will fall on us!" screamed Chadwick. He turned for the door, but Stukeley caught him.

"Stay in the pentacle!" he shouted.

Chadwick looked over his shoulder. The figure had risen and was almost over them and almost flat against the ceiling, face up. He gave a little whimpering cry, and fainted.

Chadwick issued from his swoon all sore and cramped.

He was lying full-length within the limits of the pentacle; Stukeley's folded coat was under his head, and his friend was sitting on a stool beside him, chin on palm and eyes full of thought. Daylight was striking in through the chinks of the blinds; the room was bare and empty of anything outside the five-pointed star.

He sat up and stared, terrified, towards the fireplace. Walls, floor, and ceiling were plain and prosaic. Meeting his eyes, Stukeley stepped out of the pentacle and stamped questingly on the very boards whence the horror had issued.

"I'd advise you to have this up, Chadwick," he advised.

His masterful tone was a tonic. Chadwick scrambled up, shuddering.

"Let's get out of this," he shivered.

As he opened the front door Stukeley pointed to the unbroken seals. The rose and amber sunrise was billowing over the houses opposite; Chadwick stood by the gate basking in the clean morning air while Stukeley went over the house, putting out the lights.

"No seal disturbed," reported the occultist.

"I can't stand four walls at present," Chadwick groaned.

They passed into the back garden of 75 and paced up and down between the laurels.

"That's just what all the tenants said," Chadwick burst out suddenly. "A decayed corpse that sprang up and down, and threatened to topple over on you—ugh!"

"It was not decayed, and it did not spring up and down," Stukeley corrected.

"Eh?"

"I watched it until at the first streak of daylight the bubbling ceased and it vanished. It was not decayed at all."

"Eh? The scent—"

"Scent of death, but of new death."

"The bones—"

"The flesh had been purposely removed."

"Mangled by beasts or birds?"

"No. Cut off neatly. Partly dissected, in a word."

"What do you make of it, then?"

"I'm nonplussed."

"Well, it jumped up and down," Chadwick said ruminatively. "No. It swayed and dipped with the exact motion a ship in a heaving sea would display."

"By George—"

"It was just as though the thing was lying on the deck of a vessel, invisible to us, that swayed and jerked it about."

"But, Stukeley, what connection could that house have with a ship?"

"I don't know. What I say is—have the floor up."

They had the workmen in that very morning, but with no more result than the Psychic Society had achieved before them. At two or three places by the walls, including the spot where the bubbling rose, the planking had been repaired; mouse-holes beneath explained that, however. Below was the innocuous ventilation space, and below they found virgin earth that revealed nothing though they dug it up for some depth.

"Chadwick, one thing struck me," said Stukeley, as they sat at lunch. "Did you notice any connection between the bubbling and the figure?"

"No. Truth is I was too frightened to notice much."

"You are not used to these investigations, as I am," the occultist replied charitably. "Wherever the figure moved a band of something like vapour rose, fanlike, from the bubbling, and always touched it. There *should* have been something under the floor." He seemed quite annoyed at the lack. "I wonder where the second tenant, the Frenchman, lives?"

"My neighbour, who knew him well, might know."

The neighbour, questioned, had lost touch with Monsieur Duhamel, but knew that he was an occasional contributor to *The One Weekly*.

That same afternoon saw Stukeley, fresh from a brief interview with the editor of *The One Weekly,* en route for Balham and the modest abode of M. Auguste Duhamel.

M. Duhamel was reassuring; a fat, genial old gentleman, prosy and cheery.

"Indeed, I regret the distress of the good M. Chadwick," he asseverated. "Ourselves, we never used the front room, so saw nothing."

"If I am not trenching on the impertinent, M. Duhamel, it seems strange that you did not use the large front room."

"I will explain. My late respected father was a collector of curiosities, and all of them he left to me. They were of value, but ugly; African witch-masks, mummy cases—*Le bon Dieu* alone knows what! There was no inducement to live with them; the front room was the only one large enough to hold all, therefore we put them there. You understand, *monsieur?* We put them there in order that our friends might come to see them sometimes, but—*tiens!*—they are ugly, ugly as *le diable*—our friends preferred to glance at them by day, and our servant washed and dusted them by day likewise."

"Curios?" And Stukeley pricked up his ears.

"*Oui, monsieur.* Curiosities. My father loved them. I do not. This year I have sold all to a museum. I was nursing them for years while prices went up. That was all the good of them in my eyes." M. Duhamel made a gesture of large scorn. "However, I kept the room in good repair, the landlord repaired the outside, the tenant the inside; that is the rule. When the mice ate holes in the flooring I mended it; I myself mended it. I am a great amateur carpenter."

"You mended the place by the fire? And you found nothing when you worked?" asked Stukeley eagerly.

M. Duhamel shook his head decisively, and Stukeley added, "It was from there the apparition rose."

"*En passant,* M. Stukeley, I have heard much about this apparition, but never have I had a good description of it. May I ask?"

Stukeley gave a sketch of his experience of the previous night. He came out of absorption in his own recital to find the Frenchman gaping with dawning enlightenment in his eyes.

"*Monsieur,*" said Duhamel, "I myself am a man of rational cast of mind, but you who believe in the spirit world, you hold that the blood is the very vehicle of life and the soul, is it not? And that with blood many marvellous feats can be performed? I have read even that from the emanations of fresh blood spirit forms can be conjured."

"Some belief of the kind is current with certain people. And what, *monsieur*—"

"Mr. Stukeley, is it possible that old blood may have strange properties? Power, for instance, to show to living eyes what it once was?"

Stukeley answered affirmatively. The Frenchman slapped his thigh.

"Then, *m'sieur,* I will tell you. In my father's collection were many things whose bone fides it would be difficult to prove. Pieces of wood or stone from famous or infamous erections, for instance. As I care nothing for curios, and knew that it would be impossible to sell things of this species, I did not scruple to make practical use of them. It is said, *monsieur,* that in the famed Chicago pork-canning factories nothing of the pig is wasted but the squeak. I am more economical than that; I would make use of the squeak by calling in all the neighbours' little ones to enjoy the sound—"

He paused to laugh. Stukeley quivered, all impatience.

"Ah, M. Stukeley, the stone that forms so good a foundation for the little rockery in the back garden of our friend No. 77 is from the old Bastille. But who could have proved it? Who would have bought? The same with pieces of wood. When the mice ate holes in the floor I mended it, and I said to myself, 'I will make that certain piece of wood in the cabinet of use.' That piece cut down to a suitable size to fit the place by the fire, the chips from it went into our stove that same day. Now in the piece of wood a stain was deeply sunk, and my father held that it was blood—"

"Where from? What from?" demanded the Englishman, as the narrator paused.

"In a moment, *monsieur.* I mended it well. I am a good amateur carpenter. Undoubtedly it is the piece from whence your mysterious bubbling came."

"Where was that piece of wood from?" demanded Stukeley hoarsely.

"From the raft of the *Medusa,* monsieur."

That evening, directly he had returned from the metropolis to Willingborough, Stukeley took Chadwick into the dismembered room and hunted amidst the scattered planks. It was easy to identify the piece that had mended the part by the fireplace; it was small, thick, and was of a different colour to the larger planks. From the oak stain on top through half its thickness was a deeper tint than that of the lower half.

"It's my opinion that the thing remained quiescent until it was insulted by being put to a practical use," said Stukeley. "When I've destroyed it—reverently—Chadwick, I've every hope your house will become marketable property again."

In the back garden he kindled a fire, feeding it to a good heat with shavings, and planted the piece of wood on it. He further scratched a pentacle round the blaze. The wood burnt slowly; Chadwick thought he detected a curious acrid odour in the smoke from it.

"'*Requiescat in pace,*'" muttered Stukeley. "So a collector of ghastly relics is to be blamed for it all! By Jove, one certainly never knows what the final reflex of one's actions may be!"

Chadwick looked puzzled.

"But Stukeley, I do not understand. What was the *Medusa?* And the raft? I seem to recollect the name vaguely, but nothing about it."

"You might recollect it through Géricault's famous picture of it—a monument of ill-taste. The *Medusa,* Chadwick, was a French vessel, and she happened to be wrecked, decades and decades ago. The survivors made a raft, and on it knocked about the open sea until—it's a horrible tale, Chadwick, need I tell it all? Can't you piece it together? They were starving—think of the wood with the indelible stain on it—and the man with a lot of flesh hacked off him that's what a relic of the *Medusa's* raft meant!"

THE SANATORIUM

F. TENNYSON JESSE

Wynifried Tennyson Jesse (1889–1958), who switched her first name round to Fryniwyd, and was usually called Fryn, was the granddaughter of the sister of the poet, Alfred, Lord Tennyson. She is another British writer who is remembered now chiefly for one novel, A Pin to See the Peepshow (1934), a tragedy based on a real life case. Jesse was an expert on legal history, contributing several essays to the series Notable British Trials in the 1920s. During her lifetime she was best known for The Lacquer Lady (1928), a fictionalized account of how an Englishwoman was involved in the fall of the Burmese royal family. Jesse's interest in criminology inspired her to write a series featuring a young woman, Solange Fontaine, who while not a psychic detective in the usual sense, clearly had psychic abilities as she could sense evil, and this led her to explore further. The first series appeared in England in The Premier Magazine in 1919. Some ten years later Jesse returned to the series. This second series was published as The Solange Stories in 1931. The first series meanwhile languished in the lost pages of The Premier until rescued by bookdealer George Locke and published in a very limited edition as The Adventures of Solange Fontaine in 1995. These earlier stories show Fontaine's psychic abilities at their most acute, but they also emphasise her fear of pursuing them because of inadvertent consequences.

ONE DAY SOLANGE FONTAINE AND HER GREATEST FRIEND, Raymond Ker, the American writer, sat together in the garden of a villa on the sea-coast of the Riviera. It was a languorous day in April; already the burning sea was beginning to refract the heat unpleasantly to any whose senses were not steeled to the sun by much experience of tropic days, but Solange lay basking, her pale face unflushed and her tranquil eyes fixed on the sparkling blue of the little waves in utter contentment with her surroundings. And if Raymond's content were more with his companion than with circumstances, then at least he was only now beginning to be aware of it, while as for her—she was as yet only aware of his awareness, not of any satisfaction there might be to herself in his presence.

For, though friendship ripens strongly with the impersonal of mind, yet its almost imperceptible transition to that stage when it may turn to something warmer and less reasonable is but slowly suspected by them, and to Solange the fact that her increasing intimacy with the man who had stood by her in so much danger might be transmuted into that more hazardous state known as "being in love" had not yet occurred. For habit of mind plays a great part in lulling the danger instinct to sleep, and though Solange could tell at the meeting of the eyes, at the touch of a palm, the presence of something evil, she could not detect by precisely the same mediums the presence of a danger to herself. For danger "falling in love" meant, or would mean to her, and she had always known it. She had always recognised that her nicely balanced instincts would not only be upset, but probably destroyed by the intrusion of "falling in love."

Just as a woman who is an artist is bound to lose her artistry—for all but the art of living—as long as the madness lasts, even if her art of creation be enriched afterwards, so Solange would lose that instinct for being aware of evil, together with the science with which it was allied, as soon as she allowed herself to be swept away by the common lot of women. It was a question, as is so much in life, of relative values.

No thought of that danger was in her mind now as she turned her head, pale under the shade of her white parasol, upon its green cushion—pale as the head of a mermaid, and as barely human, with its greenish eyes and faintly tinted mouth; as barely human, in all save its tenderness of curves—towards Raymond in answer to what he had been saying. His argument had been that criminals were men even as the rest of us, but subjected to overwhelming temptation, and Solange had roused herself for her pet topic.

"Raymond, how badly I must have trained you! Don't you know that you are ignoring the only vital division in criminology, that which marks off the instinctive criminal from the occasional criminal? Of course, everyone had his breaking-point, but in the instinctive criminal the breaking-point is set very low. It is the low breaking-point that marks out the great malefactors of the world."

"The people who can't help it, eh? Doesn't that make them blameless?"

"Blame?" She made a little movement of contempt. "What does blame amount to, anyway? It's only a word, like forgiveness, it doesn't really stand for anything. Nevertheless it's only the sins that we can't help which matter at all."

"That sounds very unfair."

"Unfair to the sinner, you mean. And what if it is? It is the community that matters, every time. The occasional criminal can be cured, and, better still, prevented, but for the born killer there is no remedy; he has to work out his own damnation. It's nature's doing, not law."

"Then the born killers can't help themselves?"

"Oh, I don't say that. Irresponsibility is quite a different thing from congenital tendency. Nine times out of ten the born killers know perfectly well what they are doing, but they choose, though aware of their abnormal tendencies, deliberately to turn them to account. Think of the notorious examples of Jegado, Van der Leyden, Zwanziger, to cite three criminal women—why did they poison in the wholesale manner that they did? Not merely for gain sometimes there was none attached. Not merely for revenge, though to people of such colossal vanity as the congenital criminal any slight is cause for revenge—but sometimes merely to feel their own power of life and death. To be omnipotent. Also, of course, they have a supreme disregard for the value of human life, which, when not carried to such excess, is no bad thing. To be as squeamish about it as we moderns are is a weakness, because it makes us rate our own too highly! One should not, of course, carry disregard to the same extent as the Brinvilliers—who thought so little of it that she poisoned poor people in the hospitals wholesale, simply to test her art—a far more unforgivable proceeding than the subsequent removal of the whole of her family, though in those undemocratic times it wasn't made so much of."

"The Brinvilliers always knew why she poisoned, right enough," objected Raymond; "there was no weak indulgence in pleasure about her. Hard cash was at the root of it."

"Mostly; but don't forget she tried to poison her daughter because she was growing too tall! The only really human motive that tigress ever displayed!"

"Solange, you're very flippant today."

"It's the heat. I love it so it makes the cords of my mind and my morals relax. Also, I think I am half-consciously gathering myself together for what may be rather a trying time."

Raymond questioned, but no more could he get out of her.

That afternoon a caller came to the Fontaines' villa. It was a man of whom Raymond had occasionally heard, a doctor who had started a sanatorium for consumptives, up in the mountains behind the sea-board. He had heard nothing but good of the man, who bore shining testimonials, and yet he found himself disliking him, though for no cause he could assign, beyond the unreasonable one that he seemed to admire Solange more than he, Raymond, found fitting. Also he was too handsome; it really wasn't decent, the lantern-jawed American found himself deciding—no man ought to have that straight profile, those handsome grey eyes that looked out so finely, even with a touch of arrogance, from their well-modelled brows, above all, no man ought to have hair that showed a tendency to curl. And yet he could not suggest, even to himself, that Dr. Fulgence Galtie was effeminate—his frame was too powerful, his jaw too heavy, his whole aspect too masculine for that charge to be brought against him. Yet there was something strange about the doctor Raymond had only to watch Solange to be aware. He knew her so well by now, knew the varying expressions that she could not hide from him, because he knew what signs to look out for, though no stranger would have guessed that the young doctor roused any feelings but those of friendliness in her. It was only because by now Raymond felt himself so one with her that he knew that she was in the grip of some strong spiritual distaste.

The odd thing was that it was evident Dr. Galtie was a more or less unwilling visitor. Solange chaffed him about the difficulty she had had in getting him to fix a day to come and see her, and even now that he was sitting in their pleasant drawing-room, he seemed, for all his charming, easy manners, to be rather plainly making the visit as formal as possible. It was with all the more surprise that Raymond heard Solange say, as she leant back on her *chaise-longue*, as though the effort of pouring out tea had taxed her strength:

"Papa has set his heart on my trying a month at your sanatorium, Dr. Galtie. The symptoms refuse to yield to treatment down here. Please say you will consent to put up with me, after all. There can't really be any objection, you know, and I shall feel you have taken a dislike to me personally, or that you think I will make a bad patient, if you refuse. Or, worse still, that you despair of curing me, and that would be too depressing."

There was a little silence, and then Galtie said, putting down his cup and looking straight at Solange:

"I have already told you, mademoiselle, that not only can I find no trace of organic disease in you, but not even the danger of it which you and your father seem to fear. My sanatorium is for consumptives."

"Not for hypochondriacs, he means," said Solange, laughing; "but I'm really not that, M. Galtie. It's papa's fault. You see he fusses over me absurdly, and when you have a thing like that in the family, and your only child loses strength and languishes, you naturally get alarmed. I know his panic must seem inexcusable in a man of science, but you must remember he is a parent as well, and parents are notoriously unreasonable."

Dr. Galtie's face still looked unyielding, but at that moment the maid announced another visitor, and at the name of "Madame Sorel," Solange got to her feet and went to meet the little lady who advanced into the room.

Madame Sorel, though only a couple of years older than Solange, who was thirty-one, looked nearly forty, for life had dealt hardly with her. Raymond, looking at her sensitive, eager little face, began to remember various things Solange had let fall about the little lady from time to time. She had been at the same convent school as Solange, and had married almost at once on leaving. He remembered Solange and her father discussing the marriage one day, saying how badly it had turned out, how Monsieur Sorel, a man much older than herself, had played ducks and drakes with her, and finally died, leaving her and her two little girls very ill-provided for.

She and Solange greeted each other affectionately, while the two men stood waiting, and then Valerie Sorel caught sight of Dr. Galtie. A wave of deep red flowed up over her small face as she put out her hand.

"M. Galtie; I did not know you knew my dear Mademoiselle Fontaine. What a pleasant surprise to find you here."

"And I, madame," returned Galtie, "was not aware you had any friends in Nice—except myself, if I may dare to call myself your friend."

"Who should if not you?" said Valerie artlessly; and turning to Solange, she went on: "You can't think how good Dr. Galtie is being to me. Fancy, he is having the children up at his place for the summer. You may imagine the weight it is off my mind. Nice gets so dreadfully hot, and little Fernande has such a horrid cough."

"Ninette has it, too, I fear," said Galtie; "but," as she turned startled eyes on him, "don't worry. They will soon be all right. Leave them in my hands, and you will see how strong and fat they will grow and what roses they will bring back to Nice for the winter."

The next twenty minutes were rather painful. It was so obvious that the faded little Madame Sorel was in love with the handsome doctor who was befriending her. When she got up to go she practically asked him if he were not leaving also, and Raymond—much as he disliked the man—felt almost sorry for him as he gallantly, if reluctantly, offered to drive her home in his car. Farewells were said, and the two went through to the hall, but in a moment Galtie was back, his hat in his hand.

"Mademoiselle Fontaine," he said, speaking quickly, "I have been thinking it over, and, after all, I see no reason why you should not try my sanatorium. You are undoubtedly very run down, and the air would do you good. You need not mix with the patients, so there would be no fear of infection."

"I'm not in the least afraid, anyway," said Solange. "But thank you so much. I'll write and arrange the date of my arrival. It is *au revoir* then, M. Galtie."

"It is *au revoir*, mademoiselle."

The two looked at each other for a moment, then the doctor bowed politely, and went out to rejoin Madame Sorel again. Solange met Raymond's amazed eyes with a laugh.

"Well, what do you know about that?" murmured Raymond.

"Not much yet," said Solange, "but I think I'm going to know a good deal. Raymond,"—and getting to her feet she went over to him and laid a hand on his shoulder—"I shall want you to help. I think we're going to find ourselves in a very tight corner."

"Solange, you aren't really ill?"

"No, of course not. That's all put on to get to the sanatorium. Raymond, that doctor, with his splendid looks and his charming manners and his goodness—oh, yes, he does innumerable good actions, and the poor of Nice worship him—fills me with fear. He's evil, he's horribly evil, and he's planning something, but what I don't know. I only feel it's something to do with my little friend Valerie or her children."

"My dear, how can it be? I hated the man myself, but be reasonable. She hasn't a penny, nor have her children; what designs could he have on them, even if he has an evil heart?"

"I don't know," repeated Solange—"I don't know. But I do know that he was afraid to have me at his sanatorium, and that now he sees I know Madame Sorel he is willing to have me out of the way of what he may do in Nice. It makes me wonder whether I am on the right track, whether I ought not to stay here and guard her. And yet when I think of those children—"

"Solange, I wish you wouldn't go. I'm not thinking of Madame Sorel or her children, I'm thinking of you. You know you've never made a mistake when you've felt that warning sense of evil. If you go up there, you yourself may not be safe."

"That's what I meant by the tight corner. If he's what I think, if the propensities I feel in him are really developed and not merely latent, then he may not be content with merely having me out of the way temporarily. However, it's no good worrying, especially when one can hardly see a step of the way ahead, the only thing to do is to proceed very cautiously."

"Your father must be mad. Why on earth does he let you risk yourself? Surely his daughter is more to him than a little dressmaker he hardly knows?"

"His daughter is, yes; but there's something that to him ranks above everything—as it does, I hope, to me."

"And that is?"

"Truth. When you see your job you can't neglect it, no matter what the risks. That's the only morality worth anything. I risk myself, papa would go one higher, he would risk me. But, as a matter of fact, he knows nothing about this. I bluffed when I talked about him to Galtie. He's in Paris for the next few weeks, attending a scientist's conference. So you must be ready to help me, because I'm sure I shall need you badly."

And what could Raymond do but promise his help, deeply as the egoism of a would-be lover disapproved the enterprise?

Solange sat on the wide verandah of the sanatorium. At her feet lay mile upon mile of undulating country stretching away to the glittering blue of the Mediterranean; country blurred with olive-trees as with silvery puffs of smoke, and touched here and there with the vivid, tender green of young larches, country whose rugged outlines only showed occasionally in an outcrop of grey boulders, or fields of hardened lava, where even the juniper and myrtle could not encroach. The air was filled with the delicate scent of many flowers, for in that district the blossoms that go to the scent factories of Grasse are grown, and here and there against the sky the mimosa hung out its tassels of vivid yellow.

It was a good world, and, as far as the eye could see, the sanatorium of Dr. Fulgence Galtie went to make it better. The long white building, with its wing-wide emerald green shutters, its deeply fluted roof, its spacious verandah where the shadow lay coolly banded as in a soft blue ribbon amidst all the sun-dazzled whiteness, and where the patients sat or lay about in cushioned chairs, dozing from one meal to the next—all this surely was pleasant not only to the eye but to the mind.

Solange was isolated from the rest of the patients by a woven grass wind-screen that hung across the verandah. The only people near here were two little girls, who were playing with a doll on a rug beside her chair, and talking together in low voices over its blonde tousled head. They were Ninette and Fernande, the children of Valerie Sorel. They wore their black hair cropped square about their transparent, waxen ears, their little faces were pale, and their big brown eyes dark-rimmed; but their business, that exquisite, idle business of children, which stirs a queer pity in the heart, was untouched by any gravity other than the seriousness of intense childhood. Solange watched them gravely, then her eyes wandered to the misty blue of the horizon, where the blatant sea deigned to lose its sparkle at last in a hint of mystery.

Solange had been at the sanatorium three weeks, three long, idle weeks, during which the oppression that the handsome young doctor bore for her slackened somewhat, contrary to her expectations. She had found out nothing.

Madame Sorel, radiant with a glow that seemed miraculously to wipe ten of her hard years from her vivid, eager, dark little face, had motored up once in the doctor's car and had dropped hints to Solange—hints of a great prosperity to come, of a happiness that might follow in its train. But, oddly enough, these hints, which Valerie evidently thought would rejoice her friend, did nothing of the sort—so much was evident, and Madame Sorel saw it with resentment.

Solange was aware of the resentment, yet was unable to rid herself entirely of the thought that Galtie had a scheme which would not bear the light of day; although not yet had she managed to obtain the smallest scrap of evidence that would show him up unfavourably. The children seemed to grow weaker rather than stronger, that was the only thing, and yet the only credible suspicion—that Galtie might have got the unsuspecting mother to insure them while he was slowly loosening their frail tenure on life—did not seem likely. No company would have insured the two delicate little girls heavily enough to make such a course of action seem worth while. That difficulty was not insuperable there have been many murders planned for quite inadequate insurance money, though perhaps not by the dashing Dr. Galties of the criminal world, but there was a stronger reason why Solange still half-believed, against all proof, that the immediate danger, if any, threatened not the children but their mother, and that was the fact that when he discovered she, Solange, knew Madame Sorel, he had been anxious to have her up at the sanatorium after all.

That could only mean that she would be more in the way in Nice than under his own eye—and yet Solange could not make up her mind to leave the sanatorium. For she realised that, though Dr. Fulgence Galtie might recognise her as a danger, having heard of her as a criminologist of note, yet he was not aware that she was convinced of his evil propensities. He might well think—doubtless did think, knowing she could not really know anything about him—that he had only to keep any suspicious circumstances from her gaze and he would be safe. As far as Solange knew, he did not suspect her of suspicions, there was no reason why he should. Her known skill as a specialist in the detection of criminals was enough to make him nervous if he had anything culpable in his mind, and would make him unwilling to have her in any position where she would have to see him every day. Thus it was easy to see why, in the first place, he was anxious to keep her away from his house, and yet, when he had discovered she was a friend of Madame Sorel's, it should seem to him expedient to alter his mind and invite her up into the hills. And in his ignorance lay her chance, for in her daily study of the doctor, piecing little thing to little thing in a way only possible when living under the same roof, she might suddenly see the solution to the puzzle more clearly than with all the ordinary detective "stunts" of observing incomings and outgoings that she might have achieved in Nice. There she could have watched his movements—here, she felt, unless she were very dull and dense, she could watch his soul.

But—had she grown dense? That was what was perplexing and torturing her. Had the fine balance of her soul, that exquisite sixth sense by which she had always been able to distinguish evil as an animal smells water, grown blunted, and, if so, why?

Her own heart fearfully prompted the answer. She was thinking of Raymond too much. It had become a species of almost voluptuous rest with her to let her mind stray from the problem before her and dwell upon Raymond, not only on what he looked like, on things he said, on the quick turns of the head or the characteristic attitudes both of mind and body which always occupy the thoughts of a woman prepared to fall in love, but also on imaginary scenes that the future might hold if she only would. What he would say, what she could answer—what "it" would all be like, all the delicious comedy played by every man and woman since the beginning of the world, the comedy that seems at the time of playing so intense, so serious, and that to old age is a memory as sharply sweet as the smell of the autumn earth after rain. Might it not be for her also, this playing with life that made life so much keener a thing? Why not? And even as, in her weakness—that charmed new weakness of soul that enwrapped her—she took the thought out day after day and juggled with it, even in those moments there knocked at her heart the deadly fear that already she was losing keenness of vision. For, so she was fearful, her gift had lain in her impersonality, as any great gift must, and there is nothing so selfishly, ragingly, personal as the period called "being in love."

Was it the very thought of it, the mere admitting of it as a possibility, that was dulling her fine senses, giving her this distressing sensation of groping in a fog, this fear that unless she found out something soon she might be too late? She tortured herself with the question as she lay on the warm verandah, and her eyes rested on the sleek, dark heads of the two intent children.

The answer to everything was to come to her more suddenly than she, who felt hopelessly "stuck," could have thought possible. It was to come in the next twenty-four hours, the answer to her own problem, to that of Valerie Sorel, to that of the whole little group—ardent, intelligent, but simple-souled Raymond, pitiful Valerie, helpless children, and daring, anxious, frantic Fulgence Galtie.

It was nearly two weeks since Valerie had come up to the sanatorium, and Solange was wondering uneasily about her. She herself had been down to Nice, but had not succeeded in seeing her friend, for the little house where Valerie lived alone was dumb and blind, and after much knocking Solange had had to conclude she was out. As Solange lay in the verandah, she decided she must go down to Nice again soon, even if it meant breaking all the rules of the establishment and led to her expulsion from it. She was wondering when she had better go, when Raymond Ker was announced.

Raymond looked very unlike himself, one glance at him was sufficient to show her that it was not the urgency of the lover which prompted his visit, and all her thoughts of self fell away from her, over-borne by the older passion, the passion for helping in the dark places.

"Something has happened to Valerie," she said, running towards him.

He gave one glance at the children, a thoughtfulness for which, even in that moment, she loved him, as he answered:

"I can't tell you here. Come into the garden."

They went together past the hideous, formal beds, where palm-trees raised mournful heads above stiff carpet-plants, into the tangle of wild orchard beyond, followed by scandalised glances from patients who would never walk with the heart of youth beneath flowering trees again, before Raymond told her. Then he said:

"Valerie Sorel is very ill. She may be dying."

"Raymond, I knew it. And I up here, useless—"

"No, you mustn't think that. Even you couldn't have watched more carefully than I have. Believe me, the only thing to do now is to entrap him. But let me tell you, it's so difficult to arrange."

Raymond paused a minute, and then began again.

"She has been well, perfectly well, all the time you have been here, till ten days ago. Then she fell downstairs at her lodging. Apparently, she only jarred herself, but she took to her bed, and sent for the doctor— not Galtie, but a stranger, a Dr. Charlot, who lived in the next street. He treated her for shock, but, after a few days, came to the conclusion she was hysterical, and told her to get up. She doesn't seem to have had any confidence in him, as he caught her pouring his medicine down the sink, which he has never forgiven."

"Wait a moment," said Solange. "What day was it exactly when she fell downstairs?"

"Last Friday week."

"Dr. Galtie was here all that day and all the evening. Well?"

"Well, she's been in bed ever since."

"But I've been to see her since then."

"It seems she had said she did not wish to admit anyone but Dr. Charlot and Dr. Galtie. Galtie was there to lunch with her when I hired a car and came up to you."

"But, Raymond, you, the least suspicious of men! Something more than all this must have happened. What is it?"

"Don't think I am giving way to imagination if I tell you. It's this. I got in to see her this morning, I met Charlot leaving, and he let me up. I had a few words with him, and he was evidently in a bad temper. Then I went on up to see Valerie. She was out of bed, looking ghastly, in a rose-coloured kimono, with her face made up as I have never seen it. You know how, usually, she looks a little, pale, rabbity thing. She was rouged and pencilled and done up to the last degree, and somehow it only made her look more dreadful. Lunch for two was laid on the table, with a bottle of wine and a lot of flowers. And I knew, as surely as though she had told me—which she didn't—that she was expecting the unspeakable Fulgence to lunch with her. But she was full of hints—it was as though she were so bubbling with something that she couldn't altogether repress it. She simply showered hints. That there-was nothing to worry over, that she wasn't really at all ill, that it was all a sort of huge practical joke, and that I was to tell you so—you particularly. You would understand some day, and she knew you wouldn't be hard on her when you did.

"Then she began to want to push me off; she kept looking towards the door, and then she let fall that 'he' mustn't find me there. Of course I knew, as you know, there is only one 'he' to Madame Sorel, I came away with I don't know what foreboding. For Solange, the little annoyed doctor I met on the step told me that the fall was mere hysteria, that she hadn't been hurt, but that she was undoubtedly ill now, and he had warned her he thought it was a slight touch of cholera, which might become serious. There is a lot of cholera in the poorer parts of Nice just now. And she—she obviously had paid no heed to him. She seemed to have an inner knowledge that told her she was not stricken with cholera, something that made her feel perfectly confident, and even amused; and yet—she looked so ill, she obviously felt so ill, that the wonder is she was on her feet. It all seemed so sinister—the table for two, which she had evidently begun to lay as soon as the doctor's back was turned—for she was still at it when I came in—her gaiety, her queer, concealed joy, and the dreadful physical discomfort she was unmistakably suffering from, and that yet didn't seem to frighten her."

"We must go down at once," said Solange.

She threw on a motor-bonnet and veil and a wrap, and in a very few minutes she and Raymond were speeding down the steep mountain road that wound and wound its way down to Nice. Neither she nor he spoke on the whole of that nightmare journey down, except to say a few meaningless little things, that neither paid any attention to, when the strain of the two hours in the swift car became too much to be borne in total silence. Half way down they passed a closed car, similar to Fulgence Galtie's, on its way up.

The street was hot and white when they drew up outside the house where Valerie Sorel lodged, and on every glaring house-front the shutters were folded like tired eyelids across the windows; only at the room which was Valerie's they were flung wide, as though to admit even the hot air of the afternoon as something better than none. And as they waited for a moment, listening for they knew not what, after the engine had been stopped, they heard a faint noise, as of an animal in pain, that rose and fell with a horrible persistency in the still street. Solange rang and rang, and then Raymond smashed the glass panel with a blow of his gloved fist, put in his hand, and unlatched the door, and they entered. They ran up the narrow stairs— though the moans were lower now they held no quality as though the pain were abated, but sounded rather as though the increasing weakness of the sufferer muffled them—and when Solange and Raymond ran into the bed-room, it was a livid face that Valerie Sorel turned on them from the tumbled pillows. She was in bed, with the pretty rose-coloured kimono still about her writhing shoulders, and paste pins flashing in her disordered hair.

Solange ran towards her and took her hand.

"Have you sent for your doctor, the one who has been attending you, Valerie?" she asked; and the sick woman, with a twisted smile, gasped out:

"No, no, there's no need. He's already told me it's a touch of cholera. I shall be all right."

"He must come at once," said Solange. "Raymond—"

But Valerie raised herself in bed by a supreme effort.

"Solange! Stop, stop!" she cried. "You'll spoil everything!"

"What do you mean? Come, Valerie, you must tell me everything, or I shall send for him at once. What do you mean? What shall I spoil?"

Valerie, her lips dry with her pain, began to gasp out her story, desperate to keep Solange from doing anything to spoil the splendid scheme; the scheme that Fulgence Galtie had concocted, which they had been building up with such care all the past weeks.

She was poor, deadly poor, Solange knew it, with two children to support; children who had lately shown terrible signs of delicacy. And Galtie had fallen in love with her, but he was a young man with his way to make, and it was not possible for him to take on the burden of a wife and two growing children, that was obvious, was it not? So they had devised—or, rather, Fulgence had devised, for he was so clever—a plan by which they could make a good enough income on which to marry. It was perhaps not quite honest, but it only meant cheating an insurance company, and that wasn't like cheating a person, was it? Insurance companies had no feelings, after all.

"Yes? Tell me, what was it, this scheme?" asked Solange.

Well, it appeared the plan was to insure Valerie's life for a large sum—a very large sum—two and a half hundred thousand francs—ten thousand pounds. It had startled her when Fulgence had first suggested it; it had seemed to bring death so close to her, who was just beginning to feel young for the first time, but he soon explained what he meant.

She was in perfect health, and the insurance companies would certainly accept her, and he would pay the premiums, which would amount to about four hundred pounds a year. It could be told the insurance people that her idea was to provide for the children, of whom she could say he was the father. For even at this slur on her whole past life Valerie, in her infatuation, had not hesitated. And then she could pretend to have an illness, an accident, and the insurance companies, alarmed, would compound with her to pay her an annuity in lieu of paying a huge sum to the children in case of her death.

It would probably be quite a comfortable little annuity, not less than two or three thousand francs, and then she could gradually get better and enjoy it for the rest of her life.

As to the illness, that would have to be real to impress the doctor she called in, and she would have to set her teeth and put up with a good deal of pain and discomfort, and feel as though she were dying, or wanted to, for several days; but after that she and he could be happy for the rest of their lives. He would give her a medicine containing a drug that produced the illness in her, and, though she would suffer, she would not for a single moment be in any danger.

"And we have done it all beautifully!" gasped Valerie. "The doctor is sure it is cholera, and the insurance people are to be told tomorrow. But you mustn't send for him now because he has already seen me today, and is satisfied what is the matter, and now that I am feeling so much worse, as Fulgence said I should be bound to, he might guess. Doctors are so clever. But by tomorrow I shall be feeling all right, only very weak, and then everything will be arranged. It is six months since we fixed it up and paid the first *premiums, and they will suspect nothing. I shall get my* annuity, recover, and Fulgence and I will be able to get married, and the children will grow strong and well with proper food."

Valerie fell back on her pillows, exhausted, and Solange whispered to Raymond to fetch Dr. Charlot; but by the time he arrived, fussy, out of temper at what he considered the vagaries of a capricious woman—he had never forgiven her for having poured away his medicine—Valerie Sorel was unconscious, and in a few more hours she was dead.

Solange had a fight with Raymond to get him to allow her to return to the sanatorium that night. He was fearful that Galtie, prompted by his knowledge of guilt, would guess where she had gone, and that her life might not be safe. But, as Solange pointed out, it was the only possible course of action. Proof had to be found against Galtie, and at once, for it was this night that he would try to destroy all the proof possible. At last he consented to her returning on one condition, that, while pretending to leave her there, he kept the car at the bend in the road, and himself stayed within call just outside the house.

They parted at the front door, talking cheerfully in loud voices, and Galtie stood at the top of the steps to greet her with a few scolding words for her wrong behaviour in going motoring without the permission of her doctor. She confessed to an afternoon spent in the rooms at the Casino at Monte Carlo, and waved a laughing farewell to Raymond as the car slid down the drive.

Then, at nearly midnight, standing there in the dimly lit hall with the pale-faced, smiling doctor, Solange felt her nerve slipping for the first time in her life. She felt utterly helpless, utterly alone, and Raymond, stationed outside the sanatorium, seemed immensely far away. She was suddenly aware of acute and immediate danger.

She smiled at the doctor, and made as though to go to her own room. For one second it seemed as though he would bar the way, then he fell back and let her pass. She did not undress, merely taking off her motor-bonnet, slipping a dressing-gown over her frock, and letting down her hair, so that she should look as though preparing for bed if surprised.

She waited half an hour in her room before she very gently opened her door, having turned out her light. In the long corridor all was still, and the one electric light bulb only served to intensify its dimness. Nevertheless, Solange softly turned off the switch as she passed it on her way to the room where Dr. Galtie often sat up half the night working.

What she hoped to find out she could not have told, probably at the back of her mind was the hope of being able to search the room for hidden poisons, not kept tabulated and ranged duly as in his laboratory. She knew that even he would not be sitting up working on the night after Valerie Sorel had died at his hands; even for his iron nerves there must be reaction.

To get to the workroom she had to pass the bedroom where the two little Sorels slept, and when she reached their door she paused, thinking of their unconscious slumber and of what they would have to be told on the morrow. In the stillness she heard a faint sound from within—a sound of metal chinking against glass. In an instant fear, a monstrous fear, rushed over her in a wave. It was as though she could feel the very hair on her head prickling with it; the hot blood rushed to her face and ebbed away, and she stood trembling in the knowledge that something terrible was going forward behind that closed door.

She fled on noiseless feet down the corridor. Next door to the room of the Sorels was an empty room. She went in, passed through to the long window, opened it, and went swiftly up the balcony to their window. Contrary to all rules of the establishment, it was closed.

Solange always thought afterwards that that was the most horrible moment of her life, while she hesitated whether to creep away and find Raymond or boldly to break the glass and startle the criminal within. If she decided on the former course, she might be too late, if on the latter, she might only precipitate a catastrophe without power to prevent it.

A little cry, a child's cry, decided her. Wrapping the folds of her dressing-gown round her hand, she drove in the pane with one blow, and herself followed as she burst the leaves of the window apart.

Fernande Sorel lay in bed, sleeping heavily, her usually pale little face flushed a dark red, while Ninette, drowsy but conscious enough to mirror acute fear in her half-shut eyes, was lying propped up by pillows in a chair, her bare arm, pathetically thin, stretched across Galtie's knees. He held it firmly in one hand, while his other still held poised, as he sat stricken with alarm, a hypodermic syringe.

What happened after was a swift but violent nightmare. He closed with Solange as she began to call for help at the top of her power, and they were still struggling backwards and forwards, she rapidly getting the worst of it, when Raymond burst into the room. Even then, such was the fury with which Galtie fought, he might have got away, had not the noise aroused a male patient, who came rushing in, and luckily, seeing a woman attacked, sided against his doctor with true French gallantry. The patient was glad enough himself in the days that followed, when little by little Galtie's plans were unfolded by the merciless inquisition of French justice, which is so much harder on the guilty and so much kinder to the community than is the British.

That Galtie had caused the infatuated Valerie to poison herself by taking his medicine in her blind trust was soon evident. Enormous quantities of digitaline were found in her body, and the evidence of Solange and Raymond would have been enough without the large sums of the insurances, which, though not made out as payable to Galtie, she had left to him in her will as the guardian of her children. Those children, so that they should not long incommode him, he had drugged with veronal, preparatory to inoculating them with typhoid germs, which was what he had been about to do when Solange stopped him. The broken bacilli tube was found beside the charged syringe.

But Galtie was a great murderer; he was of the true breed of born killers. One little dressmaker and her children were a mere morsel by the way for him. The trays for the early morning tea of the patients were always set over-night with biscuits and milk, so that only the tea had to be added to them next day, and in the milk on Solange's tray there was digitaline. If Raymond had not been so prompt in answer to her frantic cries, he probably would never have found her alive. The born killer was uppermost in Galtie when he was pinioned—the thwarted killer, who is the most dangerous of all the phenomena of human society. He had already prepared her death, ready to be taken to her by an unsuspecting maid, and caught at his work on the children he would not have hesitated, in his blind rage, at putting that death forward, whatever the consequences to himself.

He managed to open a vein in prison, and so cheated the guillotine, but of all his intended victims at the sanatorium—and there was a rich spinster, who had nearly decided to make her will in his favour, a spinster who seemed to have grown worse rather than better—all recovered and survived him. The little Sorels got over their delicacy with proper treatment, and it was their mother only who paid for Galtie's greed with her life.

Yet, on looking at the whole affair, Solange could not be sorry she had acted as she had. If she had stayed in Nice she might have saved the life of the mother, but the more valuable lives of the children would have been sacrificed. Her regrets in the whole ghastly affair were for herself—for the self that had been killed, as surely as her physical self would have been killed had she taken Galtie's poison, by that night of horror.

For she saw, with that clarity of hers, that there was no evading even by herself that her growing sentiment for Raymond had indeed clouded both her vision and her judgment, that it had caused her to lie steeped in langour at the critical time, so that it was thanks to him and not to her that she had been able to save the children's lives and bring Galtie to book. Her instinct, that had never failed her in the smallest way before, had only worked partially in the case of Fulgence Galtie. It had warned her along every nerve when she first met him, but it had not kept up the warnings since, or never could she have lain day after day at the sanatorium and dreamt of her own affairs till she had almost grown to wonder if her feeling against Galtie were not imagination after all.

She had seen him day after day with the rich spinster, and detected nothing sinister in his attitude towards her—and she had never failed in so clear a case before. She had not even been sure in which direction the danger most clearly threatened. She had hesitated between Valerie and the children, the children and Valerie. That she had been enabled at the end to do the most useful thing did not make the matter any better. The fact remained that even the approach of personal emotion had tarnished the fine surface of her gift, which was put out of order by it as a compass is deflected from the truth by the presence of magnetic iron.

She had to choose whether her work or Raymond meant most to her, and the trouble was that that meant—did herself or humanity mean most?

It was not for several months that she could be strong enough to be glad that she had chosen her work. Raymond, she knew only too surely, would "get over it," for by temperament he was younger far than she, though their years were the same, and he would come to be glad of her as a friend, while probably showing her with pride the photograph of some fluffy-haired little girl from America who was the "one girl in the world." But for her, slight as some people might have thought it, it was her only love affair, because he was the only man for whom she had felt that tentative and delicious softening.

Her first real consolation came about six months after the *affaire* Galtie, in a manner which her sense of humour could not but appreciate. She sat next to a murderer in a train, felt the old spiritual distress, and was proved right by his subsequent trial.

It was not without humour that it should be a murderer who consoled her for the loss of Raymond, but she knew that there was more to it than that. She had lost Raymond and personal joy, but she had also lost bondage and the failure of her powers. She had found not only the ability to work again, but also the freedom which is only attained when no other human being can enslave the imagination, though the whole world can delight it without harm.

THE VILLA ON THE BORDERIVE ROAD

ROSE CHAMPION DE CRESPIGNY

Rose Champion de Crespigny (1859–1935), wife of Philip Augustus Champion de Crespigny, whose brother, Claude, was the 4th Baronet, hardly sounds like someone who might churn out historical romances, detective stories, and the occasional supernatural story. Born Annie Rose Key, daughter of Sir Astley Cooper Key, Admiral and First Sea Lord, she had married at the tender age of eighteen and bore her husband four children, two of whom became future baronets before the line died out. But her husband, who was himself a lieutenant in the Royal Navy, died in 1912, and thereafter she turned increasingly to spiritualism. She had been writing stories and poems since the mid-1890s, moving to fiction after several years researching the Huguenots in England, the Highland clans, and the folklore of the New Forest. She was also a passable artist, especially of ships and seascapes. Her first book, From Behind the Arras, *appeared in 1901. She was not a prolific writer but produced regular competent material as the muse dictated. Her growing interest in spiritualism turned her more toward the occult and the series about Norton Vyse. It ran in* The Premier Magazine *during 1919. Vyse is portrayed as a psychic and clairvoyant with an ability as a psychometrist, not unlike Moris Klaw. He is portrayed as being calm, able to induce peace, but at the same time his eyes have a "hint of hidden things carefully guarded." Again, we have that suggestion that the occult*

detective knows far more than he ever reveals. Mrs. Champion de Crespigny
had planned a second series of Vyse stories but it never materialized and the
stories remained uncollected until the publication of Norton Vyse: Psychic
in 1999. In her later years Mrs. Champion de Crespigny was actively
involved in psychic research and was vice-chairman of the British College
of Psychic Science. At her funeral, after her sudden death from pneumonia
in February 1935, there was a huge crowd, not only of representatives of
society, but also among spiritualists.

NORTON VYSE LAID THE LETTER DOWN ON THE TABLE AND FROWNED.
The frown—a gentle drawing together of the brows—was of perplexity rather than annoyance; his eyes, grey and unusually transparent, stared
into vacancy, blind for the moment to the lawn, across which the cloud
shadows drifted in alternating light and shade; blind even to the peacock
trailing, with evident desire to attract attention, its preposterously gorgeous tail in the sunshine.

In the letter lay the cause of his perplexity, and his indifference to the
antics of that incarnation of vanity, arriving as it had on the eve of the holiday and change he so much needed.

The postmark was that of a small town in France; the address at the top
of the notepaper, Villa Adelaide, Borderive; the signature a strange one,
although the surname had been familiar to him in Oxbridge days.

It was to ask for help, or at least advice, the usual appeal in letters to
him from strangers or friends. How best to give it had drawn the lines on
his forehead, and sent the clear, grey eyes searching into space.

After absently fingering one or two objects lying on the writing-table,
he turned to the window—a big bay, designed to catch all the sunshine
obtainable from a none too generous climate—and seating himself on the
low sill, his back to the lawn, he spread out the letter and read it over again.

"Dear Mr. Vyse," (it ran) "will you forgive me if in my distress and perplexity I turn to you, a perfect stranger, for help? You are so well-known
to me by name, and I have heard so much of your wonderful powers and
knowledge about things which, I suppose, would be called psychic, that
I feel if you cannot help me no one can, and I must just live out my present trouble—of a most extraordinary nature—by myself. If, however, you

will take pity on a rather lonely girl, and let me state my case, I will send details of the astonishing events of which I seem to be the centre. Or, better still, if anything should by chance be bringing you to the South of France, you would find waiting for you as my guest more than a hearty welcome. Hoping in any case you will forgive me for troubling you.— Yours sincerely, AVERY WHITBURN."

Vyse shook his head. Nothing was by any sort of chance going to take him to the South of France at that moment. On the morrow he was to start for Wales, on a long-arranged holiday with an old college friend, who, although not endowed with Vyse's gifts and supersensitiveness, was in sympathy with his aims and an admirer of his perfect control of the physical body and the powers acquired thereby.

Now, at the eleventh hour, he could not possibly throw Michael Swinnerton over, but to any advice communicable by letter Avery Whitburn was welcome. It was all he could do for her at the moment.

He turned to the writing-table, wrote a short note to this effect, addressed it, and the frown vanished; the clear, grey eyes returned from "nowhere," and he stepped over the door-sill on to the grass, conscious at last of the insistent bird, who, finding all other methods unavailing, had spread his tail, and now strutted in front of his lord and master with an overweening conceit of himself.

Whitburn? He remembered the name. There had been a Whitburn at Oxbridge in the old days when he and Swinnerton were there; an unpleasant sort of chap, and clever as the devil. Since then he had heard of him once or twice as dabbling in a certain form of occultism—Vyse disliked the word, but there seemed nothing else to call it—and always in the unpleasant side of it. For years now he had lost sight of him; had never wished, in fact, to see him again. Odd if this girl Avery should turn out to be connected with Oliver Whitburn.

He would have preferred personal contact with the applicant in the case, but advice by post might be sufficient. His knowledge and help were always at the disposal of any who required assistance, and "a lonely girl" was not likely to appeal in vain. In this instance there might be nothing personal about it; Miss Whitburn might want advice about some outside happening, something detached, aloof, in which case correspondence on the subject might do as well as anything else. Among the rugged Welsh highlands Vyse always felt himself at his best. The clear air, the absence of contact with the rest of humanity, the great silences, the opportunities for meditation alone with Nature, all conspired to bring him into closer touch with that other world that lies around us, interpenetrating our own, accessible only to those who have eyes to see, ears to hear.

For hours he loved to sit on the lonely mountain side, close to the music of the trickling stream, and losing all sense of the material world around him, become aware of that other, hidden by so thin a veil that the marvel is it should prove so impervious to ordinary senses.

"You come in from the mountains with the peace of all the world in your eyes," his friend said one evening, as after the hotel dinner they sat together on a balcony overlooking a long valley with a high rocky peak standing guard at the far end.

"I find it," he answered, smiling, "in the valleys of Wales, and on the hill-tops. It is not that it is there more particularly than anywhere else if you know how to look for it, but it is easier come by."

Swinnerton looked at him earnestly.

"If the study of the hidden side of things, the spiritual, psychic, whatever you like to call it, had the effect on all its votaries that it has on you, it would need no further arguments in its favour," he observed.

"The spiritual and the psychic are not at all the same thing; you shouldn't bracket them like that," Vyse urged. "The psychic has to do mainly with the plane next our own, a state of matter vibrating just a little more rapidly than the physical. The spiritual is in touch with things far higher and nearer the essence of all things. Physical phenomena come under the former head."

"You mean table-turning, banging tambourines, and so on?"

"Don't throw contempt on what are merely the readiest means of communication," the other laughed. "You remind me of Naaman, in the Bible, and his chagrin when told to cure his leprosy by bathing in the Jordan when he expected some highly dramatic ceremonial. You don't ask to be assisted by pomp and ritual when speaking on the telephone. If you take the trouble to train for clairvoyance and clairaudience, you will be independent of such instruments."

"It would have saved a lot of trouble if we had been shown how to establish this communication, instead of having to worry it out for ourselves," Swinnerton grumbled, lighting his pipe.

"It would have saved a lot of trouble if Adam had been shown how to make aeroplanes," Vyse laughed; "but he wasn't. If we had not had to worry everything out for ourselves the evolution of man's brain would have remained at a standstill; and perfect communication with the plane next to ours is about the toughest proposition we have been up against; but, mark me, Swinnerton, it will be done. Got a letter from France today," he went on, drawing an envelope from his pocket, "about that case I told you of—there is nothing confidential about it. It seems likely to be interesting."

"Your 'cases' always interest me, although I know so little about it all. Go ahead, let's have the letter."

Vyse gazed thoughtfully into the dusk, already purpling in the shadow of the great hills; then turning the letter to the fading light, he read:

"Dear Mr. Vyse,—I can't say how good I think it of you to have given me such kind encouragement. As you ask me to be frank, I will begin at the beginning; a few family details may be of service before giving your advice.

"Firstly: Yes, I have an uncle whose name is Oliver, and who was at Oxbridge at about the date you mention. He was my father's younger brother, but they quarrelled and I neither saw nor heard anything of him until quite lately. The family considered him odd, more than eccentric, wrapped up in his books, and dreadfully fond of money. My father said the accumulation of it pleased him more than the spending. I can't see the sense in having money if you don't spend it. But since my father's death he has been quite nice to me, writing friendly letters, and even supplying me with a French companion, whose family he knew about, and who seems quite a pleasant sort of woman.

"I must first describe the house—I warn you this is going to be a very long letter, but you said no details were to be considered too trifling to mention—this Villa Adelaide, where I am living with Mlle. Gourget. If you understand the ins and outs you will be the better able to understand what follows. It's long and low, two-storied, and stands back from the high road to Borderive in a wood of fir-trees. For years my father and I spent our summers here, in spite of a report the place was haunted by something unpleasant. In all the years we were there we neither heard nor saw anything unusual, and in the beauty and peace of the surroundings forgot the old rumours of uncanny visitors.

"I must tell you there was one exception, but we were never quite clear about the truth of it. My father and I were in England at the time, and the caretaker called in a temporary maid to do some scrubbing. Something happened that scared the caretaker out of his life, but I believe it was put down to tricks played by the maid, as the hauntings never took place unless she was in the house. She was summarily dismissed, and from that day to the time of my father's death nothing abnormal ever disturbed the peace of the villa."

Vyse paused.

"I wonder how much longer the world is to continue perpetrating injustices through ignorance—colossal ignorance!" he murmured.

"What makes you say that?" Swinnerton asked, refilling his pipe, and looking out over the darkened valley with a sigh of content.

Instead of answering, Vyse continued to read.

"Just round the house the trees have been cleared away, and a garden full of flowering shrubs stretches to the south; on the north runs a wild belt of firs, the sough of which in breezy weather might be mistaken for a hundred thousand ghosts. We are one kilometre from the nearest village, and five from Borderive. The house is built of rough stone, and the rooms communicate—drawing-room, dining-room, and library, all opening into one another, and overlooking the garden. A wide corridor runs the whole length of the building, into which the rooms also open. Since my father's death the drawing-room has been shut up; Mlle. Gourget and I occupy the dining-room and library.

"My father was not altogether easy to live with, and he and my grandfather had a life-long feud; I need not go into the cause of it. At the latter's death it was found he had left every penny he possessed to Oliver, the younger son, my father's portion being this villa. We lived in it on a very small income, and on his death he left it to me, with the proviso that I was to live in it for six months of every year. If I failed in these conditions the villa was to pass to my uncle Oliver. He was fond of the place, and I suppose wished to ensure its proper upkeep.

"Is that enough of past history to enable you to understand the situation?" Vyse broke off and looked up.

"Why do the dead interfere in the affairs of the living?" he exclaimed. "Half the trouble in the world is the result of post-mortem interference!"

Swinnerton laughed.

"A mania for having a finger in the pie as long as possible. They can't believe the pie will get on as well without them."

"Now I am coming to exactly why I asked you to help me," Vyse resumed. "The villa is very lonely, and I could never have contemplated living alone with the solitary maid who has been with us since my childhood, so I advertised for a companion. It was that advertisement that brought me the letter from my uncle Oliver. On his strong recommendation, I engaged Mlle. Gourget, who is nothing very pronounced in any respect, but I get on with her quite well. As I have spent six months of this year in England, I must live here for the remaining six if I wish to fulfil the conditions which make the Villa Adelaide mine. At one time these conditions presented no difficulties, but lately I have begun to wonder if I shall ever have the courage to carry them out.

"The beginning of the trouble was about a month after I had settled in with the new companion. I was passing from the library, where we had been sitting together, into the dining-room in the dusk, when on the threshold of the door connecting the two rooms, a hand gripped me by the shoulder. It is quite impossible to describe my sensations—not fear in that first moment so much as a sort of staggering surprise. It gripped and held me. I felt the fingers close on my flesh. Before I could speak or cry out, it was gone, leaving a tingling imprint where the fingers had rested. I turned sharply, resenting the liberty, but there was no one close behind me. Mlle. Gourget was on the point of resuming her seat by the table, having apparently risen while I was crossing the room. Naturally I suspected her.

"'Did you put your hand on my shoulder?' I asked quickly. She appeared surprised.

"'*Mais non!*' she replied, looking at me quite frankly. 'I have not moved, except to pick up my scissors from the floor.'

"'I could have sworn someone gripped my shoulder,' I protested.

"She smiled, rather oddly I thought, but that may have been imagination, and shook her head. '*Ce n'est pas moi*. A contraction of the muscles perhaps—'

"But I interrupted impatiently. 'I am not an imbecile,' for I *knew* someone had caught hold of my shoulder; it was useless to discuss it.

"The old tales ran through my mind; after all the years of immunity I had forgotten them, they had made so little impression. Perhaps even after that astonishing moment in the doorway I should have forgotten them again, had not the same thing happened two days later. I was going up to bed, candlestick in hand—lighting arrangements at the villa are still primitive—and had placed a foot on the first stair, when a hand again seized me, this time by the elbow, gripping it so tightly that I cried out, and dropped the candlestick on the floor.

"'It *was* you that time!' I exclaimed with some heat to my companion close behind. But again she denied it emphatically, and when she tried to make out I was suffering from nerves, it was too much. With the pain and fright in addition, I lost my temper, and, pulling up the sleeve, felt a natural satisfaction in showing a faintly red mark above the elbow that might well have been inflicted by the pressure of a thumb. Mademoiselle was, however, hard to convince, and we parted for the night with some coldness."

Vyse paused, staring into the darkness lost in thought. He could no longer see to read. The outlines of the great peaks surrounding them were only faintly visible against the sky; there was no moon, but stars shone softly in the clear vault of indigo. His mind was evidently working—had strayed probably to the Villa Adelaide, trying to unravel tangled problems, and Swinnerton refilled his pipe without breaking the silence.

After a moment or two Vyse spoke.

"What do you make of it?" he asked abruptly.

"I should like to know something more about Mlle. Gourget," Swinnerton replied. "I don't altogether trust her."

Vyse rose, entered the room behind him by the window, and returned with an oil lamp the maid had deposited on the table. It was as still outside as a scene on the stage; not a breath to rouse the flame into a flicker, and placing it between them on the seat, he held the letter to the light.

"It is impossible," he said before continuing to read, "to come to any sort of decision yet. But I think you are right and I think you are wrong."

With which enigmatical reply Swinnerton for the moment had to be content.

"During the next few days," Vyse read on, "I felt that horrid hand three or four times. It began to shake my nerve. It was always at dusk or in the dark, always when mademoiselle was in the room, and always absolutely unmistakable. It was ridiculous to try and persuade me, as she did, that it was a freak of my own imagination. On one occasion it left a bruise on my left wrist that has not yet faded. She said I must have knocked it against something without knowing it.

"Then one evening I saw it.

"I had walked into Borderive to do some shopping alone—mademoiselle is not fond of walking. I felt rather tired; it had been hot, and the road dusty. As dusk fell, I was sitting by the window, hands folded idly in my lap, thinking of nothing in particular. Mademoiselle also seemed disinclined to do anything, rather drowsy, sitting by the table in the centre of the room, and we talked, with intervals of silence, lazily, when I felt the grip I had learnt to dread on my folded hands.

"I looked down, and there, quite visible in the fading light, lay a third hand, coarse with gnarled knuckles, clenched on mine, a great scar spreading across the two first fingers, and fading away into a sort of thick mist at the wrist. The grip was so strong, so compelling it pulled me to my feet, and I flung the loathsome fingers off with a scream.

"'The hand!' I cried. 'The horrid hand! I saw it; I felt its clammy fingers!' But, to my surprise, mademoiselle was asleep in her chair—asleep, and almost snoring. Running across to her side I had quite a difficulty in waking her up. I had to shake her more than once, and she seemed half dazed as her eyes opened.

"That is what is troubling me, Mr. Vyse—she seemed so very sound asleep, and yet only a moment before she had been talking! She was almost unnaturally difficult to wake, and I cannot help having my suspicions. It is hard to see how it could be a trick, to do it seems almost impossible—and the reason? Can you help me to be free of this nightmare! What is your opinion? No one can help me if you cannot, I am sure of that—but if this goes on, I must leave the villa, and forfeit it under my father's will. My nerves are already on edge; the hand will draw me some day, and I shall follow—I feel it—follow those most repulsive, crooked fingers—and go mad! I am going to marry the dearest, most—but I won't trouble you with that—and I don't want to go to him quite empty-handed. Tell me what to do—how to stop this horrible visitation that for all these years past has never troubled us at all. Why should it do so now? I am trying to be brave, I want to stay and face it, but some day it will be too much for me. Is Mlle. Gourget playing tricks? She seems so pleasant and friendly it is hard to believe—or were the old tales true? I know you will help me if you can.—Yours sincerely, AVERY WHITBURN."

"It would seem Miss Whitburn agrees with your suspicions of the companion," Vyse remarked, putting the letter into his pocket. "As for me—I have my opinion, but for the present it can wait."

Three days later he produced a telegram.

"As you are evidently interested in the case, Swinnerton, you may as well know how it progresses. I wired to Miss Whitburn after receiving her letter, urging her to do nothing definite until she heard further from me, and asking for details of what she calls 'the old tales' immediately."

The message ran, "Will obey directions, posting details asked for," and the following morning Vyse received the letter.

He slipped it into his pocket unopened, and after finishing breakfast caught up his hat and walked off towards the mountainside without a word, leaving Swinnerton, whose interest in further developments was now thoroughly aroused, to make what conjectures he saw fit.

At twelve-thirty he returned.

"We will have lunch and then walk to the post-office, if you feel inclined," he replied to the other's unspoken question, "the poor girl is getting pretty desperate. I want Oliver Whitburn's address, and as we walk I will tell you the past history of the Villa Adelaide."

As they set out along a narrow lane towards the primitive hamlet, tucked into a fold of high hills, where lay the nearest post-office, Vyse began:

"This, according to Miss Whitburn's letter, is the story. Fifty years ago it belonged to a Frenchman called Chamies, who lived there alone with his step-daughter. By all accounts he led her an awful life; screams were heard late at night from the cottage as it was then, and three times she tried to escape. She ran away, but each time he caught her and brought her back. On the last occasion she attacked him with a carving knife, inflicting a terrible gash across his fingers—you may remember the scar Miss Whitburn mentioned having noticed on the hand? Finally, she disappeared; no one knew what became of her, and apparently no one made it their business to find out. The old man died, having led the life of a hermit, soon after. The next occupants were a man and his family of two or three boys, but after living in the place for a week or two, they complained of hair-raising experiences and left hurriedly. It then remained empty for some years, until Avery Whitburn's grandfather bought it, built on to it, made it habitable and attractive, and lived there for a good part of every year. He would never believe a word against it, and 'didn't believe in ghosts,' flattering himself doubtless he knew everything in Heaven and earth there is to be known! From that time till now, with the exception of the occasion when the caretaker called in the assistance of the scrubbing-maid, there have never been any complaints. The general opinion seems to be that the maid played the tricks to frighten the caretaker. I think they were wrong," Vyse remarked with decision, "but that is the history of the Villa Adelaide, or all of it Miss Whitburn seems likely to get."

"What do you make of it?" Swinnerton asked, "the clutching hand— the hand that brought the poor girl back each time she tried to get away? There seems a connection between present experiences and that story?"

"The step-daughter, you mean? He probably murdered her," Vyse replied abstractedly, "but I don't think we need trouble ourselves further about the past. It is the present—but here we are," he finished, stopping short at what appeared to be a universal emporium in miniature, with a rustic porch overshadowed by a tangle of wild clematis. "We shall know more in a day or two. I don't want to cross to France just now, if the matter can be settled on this side."

Two days later Vyse sauntered into the small parlour with a telegram in his hand.

273

"Do you feel inclined to do a little journey with me?" he asked his friend. "I may be glad of you as a witness, and anyway the expedition won't take more than a few hours."

The offer was accepted without hesitation.

"Had an answer to the wire?"

Vyse nodded.

"I have also had another letter in reply to certain questions. The poor girl is growing desperate. Twice since writing the 'hand' has not only grasped her, but each time shown itself in the act. She can neither eat nor sleep, so she says, starts at every sound, and lives in constant terror of feeling the horror on her shoulder. There is no time to be lost if we are to be of practical assistance."

"May I ask if you have learnt anything more of value?"

"I have learnt that Mlle. Gourget is always present when these manifestations take place; that she is normal in appearance and behaviour; and that she certainly does not give the impression of a woman likely to play practical jokes. Miss Whitburn is now rather indignant at the hint of suspicion"—Vyse smiled gently—"and writes she is sure it is mere accident that her companion happens to be always present"; and, somewhat to Swinnerton's surprise, he added, "and I think so, too—in a way. Miss Whitburn adds that she has generally been quite out of reach of contact in any form whatever, and has actually been asleep in her chair more than once."

"Well," Swinnerton remarked sapiently, "I would put my money on the companion all the same! It's easy enough to pretend to be asleep, and as for the form of trickery"—he hesitated—"if one were present oneself—"

"Your superior intelligence would easily detect fraud where other intelligences have failed," Vyse laughed. "The attitude is familiar to me."

And Swinnerton, after an instant's pause, laughed too.

"I expect that is what I mean! Human nature coming out. But do you really think the companion innocent?"

"I do—and I don't," was the reply. "I shall know more about it after today's journey. If there is any delay, Miss Avery will either go off her head or the Villa Adelaide will revert to Oliver Whitburn—which would annoy me very much."

"You mean you don't think she will 'stick it' much longer?"

"I mean just that, and if you will be ready at ten-thirty, we'll walk to the station and catch the eleven-five to Little Mongrove."

When, a few hours later, they were ushered into the library where Oliver Whitburn sat writing, Swinnerton received something of a shock. He hardly knew what he had expected, but he saw a small, wizened, weasel-faced man, with little eyes looking hither and thither with uneasy restlessness, as though anxious to avoid the direct glance of other eyes, and a perfunctory smile, more a distortion of the lips than an expression of either welcome or amusement. Vyse's vague memory of the man of early college days had hardly prepared him for this unimpressive, freakish specimen of his sex, who spoke with a whine in his voice and looked straight-forwardly at no man.

The approach to the house had borne eloquent testimony to its owner's character. The drive was wild and unkempt, the building itself in bad repair. The hall-door cried for a fresh coat of paint, the library for a new carpet. A general air of neglect and economy, amounting to parsimony in a man of Whitburn's means, told Vyse an illuminating tale. A maid, slipshod and not too clean, announced them, and Vyse, following close on her heels, intercepted a frown and muttered anathema from her master. But the coolness of the welcome only confirmed his intention to see the matter through.

Their host glanced at the card handed to him by the maid, and rose with an obvious change of manner.

"Mr. Vyse, I see," he said, looking at anything rather than the man he addressed, but speaking with an evident desire to placate. Vyse hated him for a manner that was almost servile. "I know you by name. I am interested in the subjects you have made your special study, but—?"

He ended on an interrogative note. As he made no reference to college days, his visitor felt no inclination to remind him of them.

"But you don't know what business I have here," Vyse rejoined cheerfully, summing up his man at a glance, and accepting the chair pushed towards him. "None in the world, Mr. Whitburn, unless it is everybody's business to help a fellow creature in distress. I may as well come to the point at once, and waste neither my own time nor yours." He had never believed in circuitous methods. "Did you ever hear that the Villa Adelaide was—haunted?" he finished, looking at him sharply.

Whitburn started, gripped the arms of the chair, let them go again, and frowned. Then the frown changed to a deprecatory smile.

"I have heard a good bit of nonsense in my day, and—"

"You who have studied these things know as well as I do that stories of hauntings are not all nonsense, but, on the contrary, can be very serious. Is the villa haunted?" Vyse repeated steadily.

The other rubbed his hands together and laughed smoothly.

"Are you thinking of renting it?" he asked facetiously.

"I don't fancy it is in the market," Vyse replied pleasantly. "Your niece, Miss Avery, intends to stay there. That is, in fact, what I have come to talk about. I suggest, Mr. Whitburn"—he leaned forward, speaking seriously—"that you telegraph to your—protege, Mlle. Gourget, to leave the villa at once—at once!" he insisted. "It can be easily done"—he rose as he spoke—"and I mean to see that it is done."

"Well"—Whitburn began, in an attempt at bluster—"of all the impertinent—"

"Never mind about that," Vyse interrupted. "It can be done without any scandal, or in any way injuring Mlle. Gourget, who I think myself is more or less an innocent instrument. You doubtless discovered her peculiar gifts—that she was a powerful—"

"That will do," the other rejoined querulously. "You can't prove a thing. What court of law would listen?" He laughed unpleasantly. "I can see the faces of the jury—"

"We needn't discuss the jury," Vyse observed drily. "It won't come to that. Heavens, man," he cried, laying a hand on the other's shoulder, "do you understand you are driving a poor girl mad?"

"There is an alternative," Whitburn retorted.

"To your advantage," Vyse snapped. "You have got to do it, Whitburn, or—"

He broke off so suddenly that Swinnerton, from the other side of the table, glanced at him quickly. There was a moment's pause, then:

"I'll tell you a story," Vyse said slowly; and Swinnerton noticed he looked curiously tense—wound up—"of a house. It is a square house, built of stone, with honeysuckle hanging over the porch. A woman lives in it—a woman dressed in black." He paused, and the man on whose shoulder his hand still rested sat quite still, as though half paralysed. "Her husband is dead—died for his country—for you and me, Whitburn. Two children cling to her, and she is crying—bitterly—hopelessly. There is a letter in her hand—a legal-looking thing—"

Whitburn seemed suddenly to regain control of himself; he rose, shaking Vyse's hand from his shoulder.

"Where the devil—" he began.

"Shall I finish the story?" Vyse broke in blandly. "Or would it be better for Mlle. Gourget to leave the villa? Come, Swinnerton," he went on, picking up hat and stick, "I feel sure we may leave it in Mr. Whitburn's hands now. The world would, of course, be very interested in the end of that story—an unfinished tale is always unsatisfying. There is a certain newspaper I am in touch with—but I fancy, somehow, it will not be necessary to publish the story at all. I am sure Mr. Whitburn will think so on reflection"; and with a glance of contempt at the ignoble specimen of humanity huddled at the table in a paroxysm of indecision, he preceded Swinnerton into the open air.

"What a cur!" he exclaimed, walking down the untidy approach. "And like all such cattle, he will cave in!"

"I would like to know the end of that story," Swinnerton observed curiously. But Vyse, vouchsafing nothing, only laughed.

He was unexpectedly recalled to London the following morning, and it was three weeks or more before Swinnerton heard the sequel to that day's expedition.

"Oh, yes," Vyse replied, in answer to a leading question, "the French companion was sent away right enough, and, as I foresaw, Miss Avery has not been troubled since. The 'hand' has vanished. I heard from her only yesterday, overflowing with gratitude, and happily settled with an English woman of her own choosing."

Swinnerton hesitated before asking the question on his lips; Vyse was not always tolerant of questions.

"And yet you said you thought she was innocent—Mlle. Gourget, I mean?"

They were sitting on the lawn; it was late autumn, and dusk was already throwing its veil over the glories of a radiant sunset.

"Yes," he replied after a pause, "the French companion was a more or less innocent instrument, in my opinion, though she probably had her suspicions. I made some inquiries through a friend in the neighbourhood."

"I never saw guilt more clearly depicted on a face than when you threatened to tell the end of that story," Swinnerton remarked; "but I am still in the dark as to the true explanation of the apparition at the villa."

"Mlle. Gourget was a medium," Vyse said abruptly. Swinnerton laughed.

"I have no doubt that ought to be very enlightening, but I am not sure I know what a medium really is. I have always associated the word with fraud and credulity."

"Most people do," Vyse replied, "who have never taken the trouble to try and understand. A medium is—a medium—literally, between physical matter and the more subtle, less tangible matter of the next plane. He—or she, as the case may be—has a superfluity of etheric substance in their composition. This etheric matter vibrates—and, as you doubtless know, all differentiation of matter is merely a question of the rate of its vibration—at a rate to which our five senses can barely respond, and forms the link with vibrations to which our physical senses cannot respond at all; without that link no physical phenomena can take place; they on that next plane are as hopelessly cut off from physical matter as the physical is from them. Without the presence of the medium the 'hand' could neither have made itself felt nor seen. You have heard of cases," Vyse went on, pushing an open box of cigarettes towards his guest, "of haunted houses in which a family may live for years and nothing of a disturbing nature appears; another family takes it, and the 'ghost' shows itself at once, worries them out of the house, and gives it a character hard to live down."

"And the explanation?" Swinnerton asked, taking a cigarette and striking a match.

"That in the first case there is no medium present in the family, and that in the second there is; possibly one of the servants, not even aware of it. There you have the truth of the scrubbing-maid incident at the Villa Adelaide. She was, unconsciously, a medium, and unless she was present, of course, no phenomena occurred. Roughly speaking, you can divide manifestations into two forms—astral, and apparent only to the *inner* senses; and physical, when everyone is conscious of them through the *physical* senses. There are other explanations of a few exceptional cases not necessary to go into now. What I mean is that when some only can perceive, you may take it as clairvoyance on the part of the percipient; where everyone can see or hear, you may conclude it to be a case of materialisation, and a medium for physical phenomena must necessarily be present. That may all sound great nonsense," Vyse finished with a laugh, "it depends on your point of view, but I assure you it is the result of long years of study by those who are capable of investigating the subject."

"I am always interested in the 'whys' of things," Swinnerton rejoined, "also I begin to get light on the Villa Adelaide case. I conclude it was through Mlle. Gourget's mediumship the defunct owner of other days was able to make his unpleasant presence felt?"

"Just so. I guessed the truth when Miss Whitburn wrote that the French woman was always present on these occasions. Also, that she was often found afterwards to be asleep. Some mediums go into trance when the etheric matter is drawn from them; some have so much to spare that loss of consciousness does not intervene; they remain perfectly normal during the manifestation."

Swinnerton seemed puzzled.

"But the absence of the medium does not actually drive the 'ghost' away, I presume?"

"Certainly not; but if it has no means of materialising no one is aware of its presence—a case of where ignorance is bliss!" Vyse replied.

"According to that every house may be haunted?"

"More than likely, but if no one is aware of it—what matter?"

Swinnerton did not appear to consider this as consoling as it might be.

"I am not keen on 'ghosts' as constant companions," he protested. "And you think Oliver Whitburn knew all this when he sent Mlle. Gourget to his niece?"

"Certainly. That is proved by his removal of her under my threat."

"Of finishing the story?"

Vyse nodded, and the other went on:

"I had meant to ask you about that. You had a lucky hold of him there. How," he asked with some curiosity, "did you get hold of the story?"

"I saw it," Vyse said slowly, "quite suddenly, in the polished top of the table as I put my hand on his shoulder. Clairvoyance, of course—the whole picture—the house, the woman in black, crying—the children. That man is a scoundrel, if ever there was one!"

"It put the screw on all right—and what *was* the end of the story?" Swinnerton looked at him with interest; Vyse was staring into the gathering darkness.

"I haven't the least idea," he said calmly, rising as he spoke. "The whole scene vanished when the man jerked my hand off his shoulder."

And he disappeared into the room behind them. Swinnerton watched him go in silence. Then he laughed gently to himself.

SHIELA CRERAR IN

THE ROOM OF FEAR

ELLA SCRYMSOUR

Until now, the occult detectives we have encountered have all been experts, or at least knowledgeable enthusiasts, in their field, and the stories show them as masters of their art. The stories about Shiela Crerar, though, which began with "The Eyes of Doom" in The Blue Magazine in May 1920, tell her story from the start. An orphan, raised by her uncle in the Scottish islands, Sheila finds she must make her own way in the world when her uncle suddenly dies. Her one talent is that she is psychic. She travels to London, places an advert in The Times, and work starts to trickle in. We watch her learn through her experiences so that by the time of the following story, the third in the series, she is growing in confidence.

Ella Scrymsour (1888–1962), born Ella Campbell Robertson, was born in London of Scottish parents and, like her character, was left fatherless when only seven and her mother sent her to Scotland to be cared for by an aunt and uncle. She took to the stage and through the theatre met her future husband, Charles Scrymsour Nichol, who acted under the name Nicholas Thorpe Mayne. After their marriage in 1916 she adopted his name as her stage name, performing as Joan Thorpe-Mayne. Her husband's mother, Catherine Scrymsour Nichol, had written a lost-race novel, The Mystery of the North Pole (1908) in which a utopia, founded by the ancient Israelites, is discovered in the Arctic. This may have inspired Ella because she worked on a book, The Perfect World, published in 1922. Some of this work may well have been written earlier.

The first half, which tells of the discovery of a race of troglodytes, descend-
ants of one of the Lost Tribes of Israel, takes place in a world deep under
the Earth's surface. The book is really in two halves: The first half is set
before the Great War, and the second half is set after the war, when our
intrepid explorers blast off into space and discover a perfect world on
Jupiter. Ella went on to write another nine books, but the Sheila Crerar
stories were among her first stories. They remained uncollected until 2006
when they were published as Shiela Crerar, Psychic Investigator.

MENZIES CASTLE WAS A HOUSE OF MOURNING! SIR JOHN BAVERIE—
delightful guest and most companionable of friends—was dead. Mollie,
Lady Menzies, the youthful chatelaine of the historic house was red-eyed
with weeping, as she flung herself into her husband's arms.

"Archie, I shall go mad if we stay here another day. It's too awful!"

Lord Menzies smoothed his wife's hair and fondled her tenderly. He
was a gaunt man of forty-odd years, and his young wife was the apple of
his eye.

"Little one, don't worry," he said quietly. "It's just a coincidence. You
heard what the doctors said. Sir John died of heart failure and—"

"Yes," she broke in, "but so did Tom Estcourt. Tom—who was never
ill in his life. And then Rosa Mullindon. No one could deny that Rosa was
healthy enough—yet she died. And now dear old Sir John. I'm sure the
Tower Room is haunted!"

"My dear Mollie, you really must not give way to such fancies. We live
in the twentieth century, and rooms and places aren't haunted now. The
Tower Room is perfectly safe, and it is only an extraordinary coincidence
that on the three occasions it has been used as a bedchamber, its occupants have died of heart failure."

But little Mollie Menzies shook her head. She still believed in the
uncanny.

"Look here," he said at last. "I'll sleep there myself, one day soon. You
see, I shall be quite all right."

"No, no," cried his wife. "You mustn't—I'm so afraid, Archie, I—"

A bell clanged through the great hall. A second later the butler
announced "Miss Shiela Crerar."

Lord Menzies smiled.

"All right, little girl. See your psychic investigator. She has evidently agreed to take your case up for you."

Shiela came forward quickly.

"I was so sorry to hear of your trouble, Lady Menzies, and I do hope I shall be able to help you."

"You don't know how thankful I was to hear you were still staying with Lady Morven, Miss Crerar. She told me how wonderful you were over that peculiar affair at Duroch Lodge, and so I telephoned through on chance."

"And as it was only a matter of fifteen miles I motored here at once," finished Shiela with a smile.

"My husband, Miss Crerar. Now you must go, Archie, I can't possibly talk in front of you. You don't know how horribly material he is, Miss Crerar."

As soon as the two women were alone Lady Menzies began.

"There isn't a great deal to tell," she said thoughtfully. "I will show you over the Castle later on. The Tower Room is the oldest part of it, and dates from the tenth century. There were originally four stories to it, now nothing is left but the Tower Room itself, which is built on a higher level than the rest of the Castle. Underneath it are cellars, which were originally used as kitchens, I believe. The room was closed up in my husband's grandfather's time—it was supposed to be damp. About two years ago, the Earl had the door re-opened, and the room furnished as a studio for me. The light is excellent there for painting. That is my great hobby, you know."

"Well?" said Shiela interestedly.

"Well, there is no more to tell. I used the room constantly with no ill effect. A year ago this very month we had the entire west wing redecorated. There was a small house party here at the time, and I was rather pushed for room. I—I had the Tower Room fitted up as a bedroom for a distant cousin of mine." Her voice broke slightly. "I had known Tom Estcourt all my life. He was a sailor—a jolly, lighthearted fellow that nothing could upset. He slept in that room for three nights. He never complained about anything, on the fourth he was found dead in bed. It was 'just heart failure' the doctor said. A few weeks later Rosa Mullindon came to stay with me. She had been engaged to Tom, and expressed a desire to occupy the same room in which he died. We tried to dissuade her, but she urged us to give in to her wishes; she was broken-hearted over his death. I went in to her at eleven—she was quite happy, reading a book of his that had never been removed. Next morning she was dead. Everyone thought it was just a coincidence, and when the ceiling fell down in Sir John's bedroom, he it was who suggested sleeping in the Tower Room. He knew of the deaths of Tom and Rosa, and always laughed at me when I said that some uncanny influence must be at work. I told him there was plenty of room, and there was not the slightest necessity to use that horrible room, but he insisted. That was last night. He was as merry as could be, and made arrangements to be called earlier this morning, as he had arranged to play nine holes of golf with the minister before breakfast. When his man went in to call him, he was dead, had been dead for some hours. Dr. Brown was sent for at once, and certified, as before, heart failure. He seemed dissatisfied with his own diagnosis, however, and phoned to Taynuilt for Dr. Andrew, and to Oban for Professor Weymiss. They arrived an hour ago, and corroborated his verdict. Just heart failure, with no complications. But I am not satisfied, Miss Crerar."

"But it seems a very straightforward story," said Shiela. "So far it is strange that three deaths should have taken place there, but you say you used the room constantly as a studio with no ill effects?"

Lady Menzies held out her hands pathetically.

"That's the story," she said. "Sir John's relatives are very anxious that his body should be taken to England to his home there. It will leave by the night express tomorrow, so you can commence your investigations the day after. Meanwhile, the house is too sad to offer much entertainment. Sir John was very popular, you know."

"Please don't bother about me," said Shiela. "If you will let me go to my room I shall be quite happy with a book."

"Most of my guests left considerately this morning," went on Mollie, "and by lunch tomorrow the last one will have gone, so there will be a quiet house in which you can work. I'll take you to your room. We dine at seven."

When Shiela was alone she sat at her open window and drank in the balmy air. Her life was altered by the merest chance. So far she had been successful. Would she continue so?

On the following evening the minister held a brief service in the darkened death-chamber, and then the coffin was carried on stalwart shoulders to the ferry, where it was taken across the Loch to the nearest station—Taynuilt.

The castle was empty at last—Shiela its only guest. It was with mixed feelings she entered the Tower Room. In her heart she hoped that if some sinister influence was at work she would be able to discover it. But, on the whole, she felt rather sceptical, and thought Lady Menzies was distressing herself over nothing.

There was certainly nothing ghostly about the Tower Room. It was a long apartment, with a circular alcove at one end, lighted as well by large windows on either side. In the alcove was a glass door, which led down a short flight of steps to the garden and the cellars below. A huge stone hearth, with massive brass dogs, was built cornerwise across the room, which added considerably to its picturesque appearance.

There was neither cupboard nor recess, and nowhere where anyone could hide. Lady Menzies led the way down to the cellars. There was nothing even gloomy about these. They were lit by electricity, and the sandy floor was dry and clean. Both the Tower Room and the vaults seemed above reproach.

"I'll stay here all night," announced Shiela, when once they were in the Tower Room.

"No, no," gasped Lady Menzies. "I am sure it's not safe. I couldn't allow it—"

"Nonsense," smiled Shiela. "If I am to investigate, I must stay here. Now please don't worry. I promise you I shall be quite all right. Oh, there is a bell. Is it in working order?" and she pulled at an old-fashioned bell cord.

Immediately there clanged out a cracked and plaintive call, and a maid came scared into the room.

"It's all right, Sanders," said Lady Menzies. "Miss Crerar was trying the bell."

"Now," said Shiela, "if anything happens I'll peal the bell, and you can send someone in to me."

It was not without misgivings that Lady Menzies left her in the ill-fated room that night. But Shiela was very cheerful. The lights were full on and a fire burnt merrily, and as Lady Menzies shut the door after her, Shiela heard the muffled tones of the big grandfather clock outside strike eleven. She had really no preparations to make. She had no plan of campaign, for she didn't know what she was waiting for—what she expected even. However, she drew a chair close to the blazing fire and began to read.

The book was rather dull, and she dozed over it; the fire burned low, and suddenly she awoke with a start. The grandfather clock outside chimed the three-quarters. It must be a quarter to one! She had been asleep nearly an hour. She stretched her arms in delicious contentment, her mouth was wide open in a yawn, but even as the last silvery notes died away in the silence she became conscious of fear, fear of something intangible, and she realised she was shivering from head to foot. With an effort she relaxed her muscles, and her arms fell to her sides, but the effort left her weak and trembling. Her mouth was stiff with horror, and she closed it with a jerk.

She looked round the room—there was nothing to be seen—the lights shone steadily, and a faint glow came from the fast-dying embers. Suddenly her knees gave way under her, and she sank exhausted to the floor. The grandfather clock chimed again and in a mellow tone proclaimed the hour of one.

For fifteen minutes she had lain upon the floor in an uncontrollable fit of fear. She tried to reason with herself, but could scarcely command her thoughts. She was only conscious of one thing, one sensation—terror, a blind terror that was all the more hideous as its source was nameless.

There was no unreal quiet about the room—no ghostly calm. There was no strange light to be seen or unaccustomed cry to be heard. Everything was quite natural—there was absolutely nothing to account for her nervous state.

She managed to raise herself on one elbow, and was shocked to find the sweat pouring off her forehead, while her heart pumped painfully. She dragged herself to her chair and fell back exhausted into it. As the minutes passed so her terror increased until she felt suffocated. The grandfather clock chimed with monotonous regularity, and presently struck two. An hour and a quarter had passed! Shiela felt powerless to move—the minutes were the most awful in her life. The fire burnt lower still until the embers of wood became white and lifeless. Again and again the silvery chimes rent the air, but the girl was as if under a spell, and remained motionless, her eyes glazed with terror, her face white and drawn, and her limbs quaking.

Three o'clock—four! Already the grey dawn was creeping in through the curtained windows and the birds had commenced their morning song.

As the last stroke of four died away the nauseating pall that had hung over Shiela like an unwholesome garment lifted. She became aware of a sense of relief. Her limbs ceased trembling. She was weak, it was true, but she was clothed once more in her right mind. Tired and worn out with her vigil of terror, she flung herself on the bed and drew the eiderdown about her cold shoulders.

At eight tea was brought her by a frightened maid, who feared what she might find in that room of tragedy. But Shiela was sleeping peacefully, and there was no hint of mystery or horror.

She awoke lazily, and drank her tea greedily. She was tired and very thirsty. She looked round the room, and gradually the night's events unfolded themselves to her sleepy brain. She remembered the unholy terror she had suffered. From a quarter to one until four she had been within its awful grasp. She had suffered the tortures of the damned, yet there was nothing to account for it. She dressed slowly, and thought deeply. Yes, there must be something wrong with the room! She knew now that the doctor's verdict of heart failure was correct. The inmates had died of heart failure brought on by fear. But fear of what?

She tapped the walls; they were all solid stone, and gave out no hollow sound. She looked up the chimney; it was a very old-fashioned one, and she could see the glimmer of light beyond the gloom. It was a very puzzled Shiela that appeared at breakfast. Lady Menzies looked at her anxiously.

"How did you sleep?" she asked.

"When I got to bed—very well indeed. But I sat up rather late. I feel tired this morning."

"You saw nothing—heard nothing?"

"Nothing."

Her hostess seemed relieved, and spent the day with Shiela in the open air. They had a round of golf, and in the afternoon explored the glens and woods.

The second night she sat up as before. Again the room had no perceptible change, but as the last sound of the clock chiming the quarter to one broke the stillness, the same terror came over her. This time the fear was more intense. She experienced her old childish fears of the dark, but they were intensified a thousandfold. She was horribly frightened, she crouched down in a corner of the room as if waiting for some terrible doom. Her heart beat painfully—her throat was parched—her lips cracked. She tried to remonstrate with herself for her stupidity, but the ever present feeling of terror overwhelmed her. Her head was bent as if waiting for a blow—she anticipated the hideousness of pain.

Her wonderful will power was hardly strong enough to help her in her fears, and as she involuntarily gave way to them, her sufferings were more acute than before.

She made one more effort to reach the door, but her limbs refused to work, and she sank down, muttering incoherent gibberings. Time passed—she had lost the sense of where she was. Dimly she heard four silvery notes. Four o'clock! And as if by magic, the fear left her.

This time she felt weaker than on the previous night, and when the maid called her in the morning she was flushed and feverish, and said she would have her breakfast in bed.

Lady Menzies came in to see her, and realised at once that something had happened. Shiela, however, refused to tell her anything, and only announced that she intended going on with her investigations.

Three more nights passed, but the strain was growing too much for the girl. She grew to dread the days, because they would lead to the nights. She dreaded the nights, and longed for day to dawn. Every night, as regularly as clockwork, as soon as the clock chimed the quarter to one, the feeling of terror claimed her, and for hours she was in its cold embrace.

She was very reticent about her discovery, but Lady Menzies felt alarmed as she saw the roses fading from her cheeks, and the deep shadows under her eyes growing darker day by day.

The mystery remained unsolved. Try as she might, she could discover no reason for the paroxysms that oppressed her.

One day she asked Lord Menzies to send for Robert Moffat, a well-known chemical analyst of Glasgow. Carefully he examined the room, but could find not the slightest sign of poison or noxious gas concealed in the wallpapers or furniture. After a long examination he announced that there was absolutely nothing the matter with the room at all!

Then they brought an architect in to see if he could discover any secret chamber leading from the Tower Room, but his examinations only proved that the walls were quite solid.

A fortnight passed, and Shiela had become very nervy and restless. The nightly torment she went through was beginning to undermine her constitution. Each night left her weaker than the previous one; she began to suffer from palpitations of the heart, and experienced great pain when she breathed.

"I won't give in," she said to herself, between tightly clenched teeth. I *will* master this stupid terror."

Although the fear was still intangible, it had become more real. She suffered actual physical pain at times. It varied in intensity, but, always sensitive to the slightest scratch, her sufferings at times were almost unbearable. Then came the night when her whole body felt as if it was on the rack. Her joints cracked—her muscles swelled, and when she woke in the morning, her arms were inflamed and sore.

She felt the time had come to speak of the terror she was going through. Lord Menzies looked grave.

"If there is anything supernatural at work, don't you think it would be wiser if I had the door blocked up again? The room needn't be used, and I think it would be wiser for you to give up this search."

"No," said Shiela, defiantly; "I am determined to get to the bottom of this mystery. I wonder if you would have the room entirely re-decorated?"

"Why, certainly, if you think it will make any difference."

"And the chimney swept?"

"Certainly."

The orders were given, and for a week Shiela slept in peace, and to some extent recovered her nerve.

When the room was finished, Shiela again insisted on sleeping there, but the horror was worse, if anything, than it was before. She felt the cold sweat running down her body; her hands were clammy and cold, and as the clock outside struck three, she realised she could no longer stand the strain. She dragged herself across the floor to the bell-pull—unconsciously her lips moved. "Stavordale! Stavordale! help me," she cried. A harsh bell clanged through the oaken corridors with startling suddenness. Lady Menzies stirred uneasily, and then woke to life.

"Archie—It's Miss Crerar; she's in danger," she cried.

"Quickly—quickly."

But the servants were before her, and when she reached the Tower Room, Shiela was being carried out. She was quite stiff; her eyes were closed, and her breath came in short convulsive gasps. Tenderly she was placed on a settee, and brandy was forced between her tightly clenched teeth. She moaned slightly, and opened her eyes, and then fell into a rather restless sleep.

Lady Menzies watched by her side through the rest of the night, and in the morning, although she was much better, a doctor was sent for.

"Heart trouble," he said, quickly, when he first glanced at her, but after examination—"Very strange. She shows every sign of having a badly strained heart. Yet it is working quite normally now. I should say she has had some great shock. Plenty of rest and quiet, a light diet, and she will be quite all right in a couple of days."

About ten, Stavordale Hartland came over in a great state of excitement.

"Shiela—Miss Crerar?" he asked. "Is she ill?"

"Why, how did you know?" asked Lady Menzies in some surprise. "She is certainly not very well. She fainted last night, but there is not the slightest cause for alarm."

Stavordale's face whitened.

"It's damnable," he cried. "I beg your pardon, Lady Menzies, but it really is. It's perfectly mad of a child like Shiela to meddle with the unknown. When may I see her?" he added eagerly.

"Tomorrow. She will be quite herself, I hope."

Next morning Stavordale arrived with an armful of flowers for Shiela. She smiled shyly as she took them.

"How did you know I was ill?" she asked.

"You told me yourself," he said, grimly.

"I did?" she replied in some astonishment.

"Yes. I awoke and heard you calling me. 'Stavordale, Stavordale, help me,' you seemed to say. Oh, so distinctly that I thought for the moment you were still with us in the house. The horror in your voice nearly maddened me—I knew something was wrong. Little girl," he went on hoarsely, "if you called for me in distress, surely it proves you think of me sometimes? Won't you give all this up and be my wife?"

"Oh, I can't," she cried tremulously. "I—I can't. I have a mission to fulfil I can't explain. If you will only be patient—"

"Will you send for me if you ever want any help?" he pleaded. "I promise you I will be patient. I won't worry you any more—"

"If I ever need any help I will send for you," she said sweetly, and he had to be content with that.

"I am going to stay in the cellars under the Tower Room," announced Shiela a few days later. In vain they threatened—forbade—commanded.

"Won't you let someone watch with you?" pleaded Lady Menzies, but she refused all help.

At eleven she went down and turned the lights on full. It was rather chilly, and she buttoned up her coat and drew a rug round her shoulders. The hours passed slowly. One—two—three—four. At seven she went to her own room, and slept peacefully until late in the morning. The next night found her in the cellars again, but nothing disturbed her tranquillity. The cellars were obviously immune from the phenomena that haunted the upper chamber.

In desperation she fulfilled her promise to Stavordale and sent for him.

"I can't fathom this at all," she said. "I wonder if you and Lord Menzies would sit up with me tonight in the Tower Room? I want to see if the same fear will affect you both."

That night there were three watchers. It was very still, and there was a pleasant smell of cigar smoke in the room. They talked on all subjects but one—psychology was taboo. Lord Menzies was in the midst of a funny story when the clock chimed the quarter to one. He stopped in the middle of a word, his face whitened, and he stared at Shiela out of glassy eyes. Stavordale moved restlessly. Shiela had lost consciousness, fear the omnipotent held her within its thrall.

Lord Menzies staggered to his feet, and gasped in unnatural tones, "I'm stifling. Let's get out of this accursed place."

It took the united efforts of the three to force themselves out of the room. They staggered, supported each other, staggered again, and eventually reached the door. The sweat was running down the two men's faces, and it was with a sigh of relief that they closed the door behind them. But as they reached the passage the terror left them.

"This is the end," said Lord Menzies dryly. "You don't sleep there again, young lady. Tomorrow I have the door bricked up. Why, it's worse than uncanny—it's unholy."

Next day Shiela went to the Tower Room. She was very disappointed. All the suffering she had gone through had been for nought. She had not discovered the sinister secret of the room. Already the furniture was gone, and the carpet had been taken away. The sunlight streamed in and its beams strayed into the passage beyond. Almost without thinking, she noticed the difference in the flooring. Out in the passage it was black and shining, slightly rough and uneven in places. In the Tower Room itself the floor was more even—newer, smoother.

"I wonder," she said to herself, and went in search of the earl.

"Before the door is bricked up," she said abruptly, "I wonder if you would try and prise up some of the flooring in the Tower Room?"

"Why?" he asked.

"I was looking at it just now, and the floor looks altogether newer than that outside. Surely if the Tower is the oldest part of the castle, and the original flooring is in the passage, the Tower Room ought to have still older boards?"

"Start at the door," she directed. "One of the boards looks quite loose there."

With great difficulty he succeeded in raising one of the narrow boards. Eagerly they peered underneath. A wooden step, black with age, worm-eaten, and uneven, met their astonished gaze. He prised open a second and a third board, and three more steps were laid bare before them.

"This room was on a lower level at one time," said Shiela in excitement. "Oh, have the floor all taken up, Lord Menzies."

With the help of some of the outdoor servants, the whole of the flooring was removed, and the original floor was open to view, some three and a half feet below; three stairs led down to it from the other portion of the house.

Shiela gazed at it uncomprehendingly. It was a very rough, uneven floor, great knots were in the wood, and in parts it was very frail. Here and there iron rings and rusty bolts were fixed to the ground. In one corner an iron slab was raised perhaps a foot from the ground. On the slab itself were fastened metal sockets in the shape of a boot. Shiela gazed at them curiously, and slipped her little feet into them.

"Whatever are they for?" she asked, and suddenly gave a cry of pain. "Oh, help me, Lord Menzies. I can't get out. Something is hurting me."

The earl bent over her. A rusty catch on one side still worked, and he opened the boot-shaped metal. Inside were sharp iron spikes that fell into position when the foot was slipped into the "boot"; but they were so cunningly fixed that they would not allow the feet to come out again, and the slightest movement gave the most excruciating pain.

Shiela was scared. "What is it?" she asked.

"Torture," he breathed.

He picked up an old and rusty pair of thumbscrews. "A torture chamber," he repeated, "and I should say one of the most horrible of its kind, yet I have never heard of it. Who used it—whether it was civil or religious—I don't know. It must have been complete in its terrors."

Blood stains on the floor had turned brown and rusty, but they were ominous reminders of the horrors of bygone days. In one corner lay a spiked iron club, rusted with blood. There was a rack fixed to the floor itself. Chains, clubs, iron masks with bloody spikes inside—the room was completely equipped for its dreadful purpose.

"It's horrible," said Shiela, shuddering. "I wonder I didn't think of the solution myself. This was a torture chamber, and probably always used at the dead of night.

"From about a quarter to one until four o'clock," put in Lord Menzies.

"Yes. It would be the most unlikely time for discovery. It was no doubt entirely secret. That is the reason you have no records of its existence. You see," she went on excitedly, "the hideous fear of the unhappy victims communicated itself to the very room. The walls, the wood, the bricks, were impregnated with wave upon wave of terror from the suffering ones. They retained it throughout the ages, and each night the terror that was once inflicted here, is let loose again at the hour it used to take place."

"But is such a thing possible?" asked the earl.

Shiela smiled. "It seems like it, doesn't it? What other explanation can you give? At any rate, may I suggest that you have the old floor taken away altogether?"

"Well?"

"Have the cavity between the old and new floors filled in, and destroy"—pointing with a shudder—"these."

"And you think that the room will be all right then?"

"I don't know. It seems possible."

"You will stay till it is all complete," urged Lady Menzies.

"With pleasure."

The work was set in motion at once, and in the course of excavations the workmen discovered a charred skeleton. The fingers were gone, and the way the bones were twisted proved only too plainly the pain that the unhappy creature must have suffered.

"May it rest in peace," said Lord Menzies, and he gave orders for its burial.

The hideous belts and torture instruments the earl caused to be thrown into the loch. He never found any records of the terrible place. He searched his own family histories, but never a sign or clue was given to point to its existence.

Shiela, Lord Menzies, and Stavordale Hartland stayed in the room the first night that the floor had been relaid. At a quarter to one they all became nervous, but the night passed with no ill effects. Clearly the Room of Fear no longer justified its name. The intangible horrors of the past had gone.

The sounds of agony, the horror and terror, the awe inspiring spectacles that had been absorbed into the very room itself, and that were nightly exuded from it, had gone never to return. The Torture Chamber was no more.

It was early September when Shiela once more boarded a train en route for Edinburgh.

Stavordale Hartland saw her off from Benderloch. She had stayed a couple of nights at Duroch Lodge after leaving Menzies Castle. As the guard waved his flag, Stavordale drew towards her, and instinctively their lips met. The whistle blew, and Shiela, blushing rosy red, slipped back into her corner seat, trembling with happiness.

Stavordale Hartland watched the train fade away in the distance. What mattered it that no smiling face leant out of the window and waved him a farewell? He pictured the rosy face in the corner, the tremulous lips, the downcast eyes. He was well content.

THE SEVEN FIRES

PHILIPPA FOREST

Philippa Forest was the writing alias of journalist and suffragette Marion Holmes (1867–1943). She was even imprisoned for her beliefs in 1907 for taking part in a protest march at the House of Commons. But she was also convinced she was psychic, because in her childhood she had had a vision when playing in an old shed of something swinging above her. A week later a man hanged himself there. She wrote just four stories about Peter Carwell and his "Watson," an artist called Wilton. Carwell is a successful business-man who trades in Oriental fare but has developed a detailed knowledge of esoteric matters. The stories were published in Pearson's Magazine *from March to June 1920, of which this is the first.*

I MET HIM FIRST IN THE WAY OF BUSINESS. QUILTER, AN OLD SCHOOL friend, introduced him. Quilter, who was one of the biggest duffers at school I remember, now brokers, tea, or palm oil, or something of the kind, in the City with extraordinary success. He drops into my studio occasionally "to have a talk over old times," he says, but the talk generally resolves itself into a series of explosive diatribes against the latest Budget, though what he has to complain of I never can understand, for he is mak-ing money hand over fist.

I was putting the last touch to a picture one afternoon some years ago when he entered. He came and looked over my shoulder, and the next minute I heard a gasp of horror.

"Good Lord, man!" he said, "where did you get the idea for that—that nightmare? Why, it's a murderer—not a wolf. What a brute!"

I drew back and looked at it. A big grey wolf was slinking away from a huddled heap in the snowy foreground—a heap suggestive of riven clothes and limbs. There was a pine wood in the background and a pale, frosty moon riding low down in the sky. The wolf was looking back over its shoulder at the mangled heap it had just left.

Well, that was all right; it was the scene I had meant to paint. But now, for the first time I saw that the brute's furtive eyes were uncannily human. There were hate and fear and malicious triumph—all the emotions of a degraded human soul lurking there.

"Well, I've never noticed it before, I give you my word," I gasped. "You're right, it's a murderer—not a wolf. How on earth did that look get there, I wonder?"

"Isn't it beastly? It gives me cold shivers all down my back. But d'ye mean to tell me you didn't do it on purpose? Don't be an ass!"

It was perfectly true, though. Of course, every painter experiences this kind of thing occasionally. Both beautiful and sinister details will spring to life under his brush quite unintentionally. Indeed, he often doesn't notice them until the picture is finished, and then, alter as he will, he can't get rid of them.

I didn't try to explain this to Quilter, however. He's not the kind—or at least he wasn't *then*—to appreciate a psychological riddle.

We both stood staring at it for a few minutes in silence, then I moved to take it down from the easel.

"No, don't," he begged, "let's have another look. I know what it is, but the name escapes me for the minute. . . . Ah! I've got it now!" triumphantly, "it's a werwolf! Carwell was talking about them only the other night—but lor'! I thought it was just one of his hair raising yarns. Wilton, you must let him see this. He positively levels in uncanniness; makes a hobby of it in fact."

"Can he afford to buy it?" I asked with unashamed sordidness, as I wiped my brushes.

"Ra-ther! He's the head of one of the best-known firms in the City—Chinese silks, carvings, porcelain, and such-like. A tip-top business man too—keeps his crankiness for private consumption only. You'd never guess there was anything at all out of the way about him, except that he has a trick of suddenly turning his eyes on you when he's interested or roused, and then you see there's—oh, well! sort of something behind 'em you know," finished Quilter feebly. Description was never his strong point.

Mr. Peter Carwell called two days afterwards. He looked like a prosperous solicitor or an unusually well-groomed scientist, I thought, he was so tall and slender and dressed with such meticulous care. His lean, clean-shaven face appeared to be dominated by a long, high-bridged nose, but this was a false impression I discovered afterwards. It was the eyes, small and deep-set though they were, that really stamped the face with its look of strength and power. When his interest was roused the grey irises turned a peculiar golden red, almost as if a flame were lit behind them.

I went forward to meet him with the gracious smile that—like other impecunious members of my profession—I keep on tap for prospective patrons. Half an hour afterwards I had sold him "The Werwolf" for twenty guineas, and, to be quite candid, would have counted myself well rid of it for half the sum.

Our friendship was a matter of gradual growth. When I first met him I neither knew nor cared about so-called "occult" subjects, but I defy anyone to come into close contact with Peter Carwell without developing an interest in them sooner or later.

His knowledge was unique and prodigious. When I visited his place at Hampstead I found a room lined from floor to ceiling with books bearing on the subject, and another had been turned into a veritable museum of charms, amulets, mascots, and other adjuncts of the magical arts.

Mrs. Carwell, a plump, fair little woman with merry blue eyes and a rosy complexion, threw up her hands in mock dismay when she heard that I was the painter of "The Werwolf."

"If only you played golf or grew chrysanthemums, or did something equally commonplace, how much better pleased I should be to see you!" she said, giving me a very gracious handshake nevertheless. "Peter takes far too much interest in these uncomfortable subjects. You won't encourage him, will you?"

"It's a good thing my wife has common-sense enough for both of us, isn't it?" he asked, giving her an affectionate pat on the shoulder.

I couldn't help thinking what a comical contrast they made, and yet how happy and contented they looked, as they stood there smiling indulgently and affectionately at each other.

I had known him some time before I had my first experience of the practical use to which he occasionally put his knowledge.

We were walking up to Hampstead Heath one evening in July, when the quiet of the side street up which we were strolling was suddenly broken by the distant clanging of a bell.

Carwell stopped in the middle of a discourse on Michael Scot, the famous wizard of the thirteenth century, and his delvings into Arabian magic.

"That's the fire-engine," he said. "I wonder—"

His wonder was abruptly cut short by an agitated voice. It came from a man who shot from a large iron gate on our right with dramatic suddenness. He was short, stout, and elderly, and his sparse grey hair was standing almost upright with excitement.

"Have you heard or seen anything of the fire-engine—why, *Carwell!*"

"Masterman!" responded Carwell with equal surprise. "I'd no idea you lived in this neighbourhood!"

"I shan't much longer! I shan't live *anywhere* if this goes on! I'm being burnt out of house and home. Seven outbreaks in four days—my nerves won't stand it! Nobody's would. Ah, here they are at last!" as a sound of shouting mingled with incessant clanging came from the end of the street.

The engine, followed by the usual train of errand-boys, nursemaids, and shrieking children, drew up opposite us, and the firemen were in the road and hauling out serpentine lengths of tubing in less time than it took Carwell to introduce me to his agitated friend.

"Don't go away. I'm at my wits' end, and should be glad to know what you think of it, Carwell," he said, as he turned to a tall man—evidently the Chief—who was gloomily regarding him from the edge of the pavement. "It's no use glaring at me like that, Henderson! You seem to think I'm indulging in a silly practical joke—"

"Well, if you are, it's one that'll cost you pretty dear, sir—that's all I got to say," Henderson curtly observed. "Seven calls in four days! Where's it broke out *this* time?"

"I should think it was pretty evident," said Masterman, pointing to a window on the ground floor of the house to our right, from which smoke was issuing in a thin cloud.

"Cost me pretty dear!" he went on in an angry aside to us. "It will ruin me if there's much more of it. Those are gold damask curtains from Cairo, for which I paid the Lord knows what a pair, that are being reduced to charred rags now! These fool officials seem to think I'm burning my place piecemeal simply for the satisfaction of seeing how smartly they can turn out! Come in, both of you, won't you? We can't talk in front of these gaping idiots!"—with a furious glance at the shrilly ejaculating crowd.

We followed the angrily snorting figure through the gate and up the path of an untidy garden. The flower-beds had been trampled into heaps of tangled stalks and leaves, and the lawn showed marks of ruthless feet in all directions.

Before we reached the door two of the firemen jumped through the window on to the grass and flung down a smouldering mass of material, on which the hose at once began to play.

"Why the deuce didn't the silly old josser pull 'em down hisself?" I heard one growl to the other as I passed. "There ain't been no real body in any o' these last attacks. I hope the Chief'll give him a bit of 'is mind this time—keeping us on the 'op like this!"

"Go in; I'll be with you in a minute," said Masterman, opening the door. "I must just see the extent of the damage and have another word with Henderson. Go into the dining-room at the end there—last door on the left," he called over his shoulder as he bustled down the steps again.

I gave a gasp of surprise as we entered the room. The level rays of the setting sun filled it with a glow that brought into glittering prominence a wealth of treasures that would have graced a royal palace or—more fitly—a national museum. Busts, statuary, an exquisite Adams bookcase, a Chippendale sideboard, a Queen Anne "day-bed," Jacobean chairs, were all crowded together in hopeless and incongruous confusion. A priceless "pilgrim" table heaped with books and papers ran down one side of the room. A French ormolu clock ticked on the mantelpiece cheek by jowl with some vases that made my mouth water, they were such exquisite specimens of their kind. And over everything lay a thick veil of dust.

"Masterman is a bachelor, I believe," said Carwell—superfluously in the presence of that dust!—as he removed a length of gold-encrusted embroidery from a big claw-fooled chair before he sat down. "He is a tea merchant—I met him first in that capacity—but business, though he's keen and capable enough at it, is not his ruling passion. In his 'off' hours he is an enthusiastic student of Grecian and Roman art, an antiquarian of sorts, and an insatiable collector of old furniture."

"It's a pity his taste in arrangement isn't equal to his taste in acquirement," I said testily. "Everything in this room shouts crude abuse at everything else. Look at those vases next that clock! They are by Teucer himself, I really believe—according to Pliny, the most famous authority of his day. They are so exquisite and rare that they ought to be under glass in a museum—not at the mercy of a careless housemaid."

"What are they?"

"Specimens of the best period of toreutic art—perfect—priceless! We have never been able to touch the Greeks as repoussé workers," I said, reverently wiping them with my handkerchief. "Come and look at this; it's Hercules at work in his forge. See the loving finish of every detail! Each nail stands out as if you could pick it up."

"I like this better," answered Carwell, stooping and looking intently at something on the hearth.

I also bent to examine a brass tripod that stood about three feet high. Figures of Vestal virgins linked hands in a ceremonial dance on the outside of the deep, bell-shaped bowl that rested on three beautifully curved and decorated supports. The inside of the bowl was scarred and rough, but all the rest was without blemish.

"Isn't it gorgeous? It's one of the earlier Roman vessels sacred to Vesta, isn't it? I wonder how many domestic sacrificial fires that has held?" Carwell mused. "Ah, here you are, Masterman!" as the door opened stormily. "Now tell us what all this about 'seven outbreaks in four days' means. It sounds mysterious—unless you've upset one of your servants and she's taking this spiteful way of paying you out."

"No servant has had a hand in this unless she's in league with the devil!" answered Masterman emphatically. "It's too clever for any mere female brain to hatch out. Why, yesterday it broke out in my bedroom when no one but myself was upstairs."

"Let's have the narrative in orderly fashion," interrupted Carwell. "Take your time and don't miss anything out. We'd light up if you don't mind. A pipe will keep Wilton here from bursting out into irrelevant raptures over your toreutic treasures."

"Ah, you understand them, do you?" he turned to me with a look of gratification. "That tripod is my latest acquisition—gorgeous isn't it? Oh! all right, Carwell; don't get impatient. One so seldom meets a kindred spirit. Now to begin at the beginning, as you say. Well, it was on Tuesday last—just four days ago—that a small fire broke out in this room. Alice, the housemaid, came in during the afternoon and found a rug in front of tint sideboard smouldering. Instead of gathering it together and beating it out she ran in to the kitchen for water, and when she came back the flames had burst out and were flickering up the legs of the sideboard. She and the cook lost their heads and screamed, but the boy who helps in the kitchen had the sense to ring up the fire station. It was out, however, before the men came—the women say they smothered it with their wet cloths—but I'll let the boy put 'em up to it, or did it himself if the truth were known. Unfortunately it had had time to do some damage—look at the polish on that cupboard door! It will take heaven knows how long to get it right again."

He sighed heavily and mopped his hot face with a handkerchief that looked like a cushion cover." Funny how a man with such immaculate taste in artistic masterpieces could go so wrong in little details like that, I reflected. But it often is so.

"The next outbreak was in the kitchen," he resumed. "A heap of clothes ready for the laundry broke spontaneously into flames. The servants were upstairs at the time, and when they came down the clothes and a wooden chair were blazing fiercely. The room opposite this was the scene of the next holocaust—another rug, but luckily not a particularly valuable one. Of course I suspected the women—how could I help it? They are infernally careless with their cleaning utensils—paraffin rags and oil and all sorts of inflammable stuff. Indeed, I've forbidden them to do any more cleaning than is absolutely necessary."

"Of course you're insured?" I broke in. "It would be madness—"

"It certainly would, and though I'm a good many things I shouldn't be, I'm not mad. But what insurance company would cover the worth of these?" He waved his hand expressively round the room. "I've been meaning to have a special fool-proof, fire-proof, damp-proof place built for them for years, but somehow I can't make a start. As you know, if you know anything about such things, some of them are absolutely priceless. That cylix there—it beats the one in Berlin that the German collectors brag so insufferably about into a cocked hat! And those vases by Teucer— they're unique—irreplaceable! Lord knows I have drilled it into those fool women often enough, and they have learnt to keep their dusters, at least, off 'em. . . . Where was I? Oh. I know! It was the fourth outbreak that convinced me that the fires were not due to carelessness, for that happened yesterday morning when I was dressing and both the servants were downstairs. While I was shaving the head-curtains of my bed suddenly flared up, and before I could get any water the whole contraption was on fire. Luckily there was nothing that mattered much up there to spoil, but if there had been it would have been ruined, for the firemen drenched everything. They were furious because I had dared them to bring the hose into the house unless it was absolutely necessary. Of all the pig-headed—"

Carwell raised a protesting hand.

"If you let yourself go on that subject we shall be here till midnight!"

"All right—but if you knew what I've been through you'd sympathise. Well, to get on with it. Another fire broke out in the kitchen last night— another on the first floor landing at six o'clock this morning—and the last you have just witnessed. I discovered it half an hour ago. No one had been in the room since ten this morning, so Alice assures me. Now, do you wonder that I say the devil must be at the bottom of it? Certainly nothing human can be, and as I know you specialise in ghosts and elementals and suchlike mysterious things, I felt when you turned up so auspiciously just now that it was like an answer to prayer!"

He lay back in his chair and fanned himself vigorously with the appalling handkerchief.

Carwell laughed, then sent his eyes questing slowly round the room. "It began in here, you say?"

"With a smouldering rug," affirmed Masterman.

"Are the attacks increasing, or decreasing, in intensity do you think?"

"Decreasing, I should say. The one in my room was undoubtedly the worst. Henderson told me pretty plainly just now that if I'd 'just scrunched them curtains up in my 'ands' when I first noticed the smoke I could have put it out quite easily. 'There was nobody in it,' he declared contemptuously. I've no doubt I could—and should—have done if it had been a solitary instance, but these repeated shocks have so shaken my nerves that I hardly know what I'm doing half the time."

The Borderland Expert did not appear to be listening; his glance had fastened on the tripod, and the golden-red flame of absorbed interest had suddenly kindled behind the grey of his eyes.

"When did you say you got that?"

"Last month. I picked it up outside Rome in a peasant's cottage. Gave five pounds for it."

"Five pounds!" I ejaculated enviously. "You could get five hundred any day."

"If I wanted to sell it, but I don't! What of it, Carwell? What has it got to do with—what *are* you doing?"

He was scraping an inquisitive finger nail on the inside of the bowl.

"Can we have Alice in?" he asked, after a short scrutiny of the result.

"You'll get nothing out of Alice!" said Alice's master decidedly. "She's scared into hysterics, and the cook's nearly as bad. However, you can try"—ringing the bell.

"If you leave her entirely in my hands I may; but," warningly, "if you explode in your usual fashion you'll frighten her into hysterics again, or—what will be worse—stubborn silence. Promise not to interrupt whatever the provocation."

Alice entered as he spoke. She was a little dark-haired, pale-faced girl of about twenty-five, with a shrinking, timid manner.

"I want you to answer a few questions if you will be so good, Alice," said Carwell with pleasant courtesy. "We want to clear up the mystery of these fires, and if we succeed it will be a relief to your and cook's minds, as well as Mr. Masterman's, won't it?"

"Yes, indeed, sir," answered the girl fervently. "I'm sure them firemen think we done it on purpose. As if anybody 'ud be so silly—not to say wicked!"

"Quite so; and we will prove them wrong if you will answer my questions frankly. Now, please tell me, when did you burn something in this tripod?"

He took it from the hearth as he spoke and placed it in the middle of the rug. Alice flushed and began a stammering "I—I never—"

"It was an accident I feel sure," interrupted Carwell. "Tell me exactly what happened, please."

The girl gave him a quick, intent look, then turned her back on Masterman and faced her questioner. I liked the look of her. Timid and inefficient she might be, but she was fundamentally truthful and honest, and Carwell's courtesy and trust in her was bringing these qualities out.

"Very well, I will, sir. It was Tuesday mornin' about eight o'clock. I'd come in here to take up the pieces an' lay the master's breakfast. I'd have dusted, too, but he won't 'ear of it, though the place is a disgrace"—with a defiant glance over her shoulder at the silently fuming culprit. "Cook an' me know that well enough, but it isn't our fault really, sir."

"No, I'm sure it isn't"—soothingly. "Well?"

"I'd taken up the pieces—an' a nice lot there was, too—heaps of torn papers in the 'earth, an' was rubbing up the fender—"

"With a beastly paraffin rag, I'll bet!" interjected Masterman indignantly.

"When I suddenly thought it would be a good plan to put all the rubbish in the grate an' burn it up. I did it to save myself trouble, I know; there was such a lot it would have meant several journeys through the kitchen to the dustbin outside—"

"Quite a sensible idea," commented Carwell. "And then?"

"So I stacked it in the grate an' set a light to it. I'd put that tripod thing, as you call it, on the rug beside me, with my cloths an' things in it, to save 'em from messing the rug, an'—an' I must have put the lighted match on 'em. I thought I'd blown it out, but it was one of them wax ones, an' you know how they keep on burnin'. Anyway, the next thing I knew, a sudden flare shot up beside me. It scared me nearly into a fit. There was no water in the room, an' I daren't leave it, an' I daren't take anything to smother it with, as all the curtains an' such-like in 'ere are worth their weight in gold so the master says, so I took some of the fruit from the sideboard there— grapes an' oranges an' things—an' squashed 'em down on the flames with my hands, but it seemed to burn fiercer for a minute or two, so I put a chunk of bread on it, an'—an' poured some wine out of the decanter . . . An' at last it died down."

"It struck you as being more difficult to put out thin an ordinary flare!"

"Yes, sir. It seemed," she hesitated and drew a little nearer to him, "You'd think me silly, perhaps, but it really did seem as if there was some- thing, or—or someone there, tryin to keep it goin', or tryin' their best to prevent me puttin' it out, an' I felt as if I oughtn't to; as if I should make somebody dreadful angry if I did. I really thought—it seemed—" her voice sank lower and her lips trembled—"as if a whip was goin' to be laid across my shoulders every minute. But, of course, I knew that was silly!" she ended with a gulp.

"Darn silly!" growled Masterman, but no one took any notice of him.

"This room faces west, doesn't it? Did you move about at all—round the tripod, I mean—when you were trying to put the fire out? Can you remember?"

"Yes, I walked round and round it."

"Start from the sideboard there and show me, will you? Be sure and go the exact way you did before."

Alice approached the tripod with evident trepidation. She spread her little work-worn hands above it and circled round slowly, beating the air with outspread fingers. Carwell watched her keenly.

"That will do," he said presently, "that is all I want to know, thank you, Alice."

"Well, if you've gained any information about the mystery from the story of that girl's infernal carelessness you're a marvel!" said Masterman as the door closed behind her. "It seems to me the most irrelevant non- sense—with all due respect to your superior knowledge, old man."

"Her carelessness was the starting point," answered the expert confidently, "but there were unusual accompanying factors at work as well … By the way, what is the date today?"

"The twelfth," I answered.

"Ah!"—with an air of triumph—"then she lit the sacrificial fire on the ninth. Does that convey nothing to you, Wilton?"

"Nothing in the world. It wasn't even rent-day!"

He treated my frivolity with the contempt it deserved, and turned to Masterman.

"Now you're going to find my explanation difficult to believe," he said warningly. "But you have admitted, yourself, that the fires were not, in your opinion, due to any human agency, haven't you?"

"They weren't; they couldn't have been; my bed broke out into flames when only I was present."

"Just so. The presiding deities of an ancient Greek or Roman household were manifesting their wrath in their own characteristic fashion on the person who had provoked it! They showed their resentment at the removal of their shrine from the land—probably from the very hearthstone, for anything you know—to which it had been attached for centuries, along the line of least resistance—that of fire! If you study the records of any tribal deities, Biblical or otherwise, you will find they always 'brought down fire from heaven' on those who had displeased them."

Masterman gasped as the meaning of this amazing statement gradually dawned on him.

"But—but—household deities—do you mean the Lares and Penates? They are myths—fables—pagan gods that never had any existence," he stammered feebly.

"How do you know they hadn't?" countered Carwell. "For hundreds of years they lived in the daily thoughts of thousands, and if you knew anything about occult law you would know that thought is the greatest creative force in the world. What man thinks, he not only becomes, but he *makes*. A strong, clearly defined thought produces a corresponding image in the plastic medium that interpenetrates the denser stuff we call 'matter.' That is a fact that has been scientifically demonstrated, remember.

Thought forms have been photographed under test conditions by men of the highest repute. You can understand, then, that the devotional thought of generations must result in the creation of something—we needn't pin ourselves down to too precise a definition—an entity—an astral image—a tribal deity—that will manifest itself in various ways."

"Bless my soul!" said Masterman in an awed voice. "It sounds like one of those mediaeval tales of black magic or witchcraft—things we all stopped believing in when steam engines came!"

"Black magic, which is only a name for the evil use of occult power, is just as prevalent today as it was before Stephenson was born—indeed, more so, I should say. Enormous bodies of people are being encouraged sedulously to cultivate hate, suspicion, greed of power and other ignoble sentiments. And this output of emotion is being stored up in the plane where thought takes form, and will filter down into the material world some day in an outburst of evil such as we have never seen ... But we're rather getting away from our original subject, aren't we? That tripod was the focus of the stream of thought and devotion that gave vitality to the man-created gods of the ancient days. It has held many fires lit with ceremonial observances of considerable power. Offerings of fruit and flowers and bread have been placed in it, and oblations of wine poured out upon it. It's not unreasonable to suppose, then, that the revival of some of these practices has roused into a semblance of life the astral images that were created round it long ago. That, at any rate, is what I feel sure has happened.

"All the same," he continued thoughtfully, "I doubt if Alice's action by itself would have been enough to produce so prompt and strong a result. As I intimated just now, an unusual combination of factors has been at work, and acting together they proved dynamic in their force. You noticed that I got her to show me how she had walked round the tripod. It was as I suspected. She walked 'widder-shins'—from west to east."

"And what under heaven is that?" our host demanded.

"It is to walk round an object in a direction opposed to the sun's course, and is an occult way of rendering active any force that may be lurking at hand."

"What had the date to do with it?" I asked, when I had digested this amazing bit of information.

"Oh, yes, the date. I'd forgotten that for the moment, but it was really one of the most important of the subsidiary details, if I may call them so. It was the ninth of July on Tuesday, and that—as *you* ought to know, Wilton, being an artist and presumably interested in Grecian history—was the date of the Vestalia, the feast of the vestal virgins in whose charge the sacred fires were. The household fires were specially lit by brands from the temple flames on that day, and exceptional offerings were made on every hearth. Add to all of these Alice's psychic 'make-up'—"

"I was just going to ask about that," I broke in eagerly. "Her feeling that there was someone there, that she was going to be lashed by a whip—why, that is what happened to the vestals if they let the fire out!" I added, with a sudden flash of illumination.

"*Don't* tell me that my simple—indeed, rather silly—little servant girl is a reincarnation of a vestal virgin!" implored Masterman pathetically. "I really can't take in any more!"

"I'm not going to," laughed Carwell. "I should never make such a positive statement as that on such slight evidence. The girl is undoubtedly mediumistic, and probably caught some impressions from the astral memories and entities she unconsciously evoked. That among them there might be the fear and apprehension of a long dead guardian of the flame is by no means impossible."

"And what's going to happen now? Am I likely to get any more of it?" asked Masterman, as we rose to go.

"I hardly think so, but if you do it will be a very feeble manifestation. The attacks have been decreasing in intensity, you say, and the force is probably exhausted by now, but as a precautionary measure I should shut this room up for a few days. The impetus that Alice gave was only just a flash in the pan, and the astral images will slowly dissolve again into quiescent etherial particles. No life-giving current of thought has been going out to them for centuries. Their worship is a thing of the past, and gods, like men, die when they are forgotten."

"Well, that's a comfort," said Masterman heartily, giving Carwell's hand a grateful grip. "I'm no end obliged to you, you know, old man, and I daresay when I've thought it over a bit I shall see that your explanation is the right one. But—Lares and Penates—in Hampstead—in these days of motors and aeroplanes—it does seem a bit staggering, what? To a plain business man—"

"Ah!" said the Expert with a sudden change of manner, "talking of business, what do you think of—?"

I had a gorgeous gloat over Masterman's treasures while they discussed the latest fluctuations in the price of something they called "green Souchong."

THE SUBLETTING OF THE MANSION

DION FORTUNE

So far the authors in this volume have been mostly writers by profession with little, if any, psychic abilities. But with Dion Fortune, real name Violet Mary Firth (1890–1946), we have a genuine ritual magician. Early in her childhood she believed she could tap into inherited memories, possibly from Atlantis, and she became fascinated with the operations of the mind, studying psychology and, at the start of the Great War, working as a counselor and psychotherapist. It was while working at the clinic that she met the Irish occultist Theodore Moriarty (1873–1923) who introduced her to the tenets of theosophy and freemasonry and helped prepare her for her initiation into the London Temple of Alpha and Omega, an offshoot of the original Hermetic Order of the Golden Dawn in 1919. She soon transferred to the Stella Matutina Lodge of the Golden Dawn and developed her skills as a medium. She subsequently founded her own Community of the Inner Light (now the Society of the Inner Light) in 1924. She wrote many books on occultism and psychic power starting with The Machinery of the Mind *(1922) as well as several occult novels, including* The Demon Lover *(1927),* The Winged Bull *(1935), and* The Goat-Foot God *(1936). But her earliest foray into writing fiction was her series featuring Dr. John Taverner, which was serialized in* The Royal Magazine *in 1922 before appearing in book form as* The

Secrets of Dr. Taverner *in 1926. At the start of the series Taverner runs, in addition to his own clinic, a nursing home specializing in nervous disorders and diseases of the mind, not too far from the original interests of both Samuel Warren and Martin Hesselius. With Taverner, though, his investigations take him far deeper.*

"Build thou more stately mansions, O my soul"

THE POST BAG OF THE NURSING HOME WAS ALWAYS SENT TO THE village when the gardeners departed at six, so if any belated letter-writer desired to communicate with the outer world at a later hour, he had to walk to the pillar box at the cross roads with his own missives. As I had little time for my private letter-writing during the day, the dusk usually saw me with a cigar and a handful of letters taking my after-dinner stroll in that direction.

It was not my custom to encourage the patients to accompany me on these strolls, for I felt that I did my duty towards them during working hours, and so was entitled to my leisure, but Winnington was not quite in the position of an ordinary patient, for he was a personal friend of Taverner's, and also, I gathered, a member of one of the lesser degrees of that great fraternity of whose work I had had some curious glimpses; and so the fascination which this fraternity always had for me, although I have never aspired to its membership, together with the amusing and bizarre personality of the man, made me meet halfway his attempt to turn our professional relationship into a personal one.

Therefore it was that he fell into step with me down the long path that ran through the shrubbery to the little gate, at the far end of the nursing home garden, which gave upon the cross roads where the pillar box stood.

Having posted our letters, we were lounging back across the road when the sound of a motor horn made us start aside, for a car swung round the corner almost on top of us. Within it I caught a glimpse of a man and a woman, and on top was a considerable quantity of luggage.

The car turned in at the gates of a large house whose front drive ran out at the cross roads, and I remarked to my companion that I supposed Mr. Hirschmann, the owner of the house, had got over his internment and come back to live there again, for the house had stood empty, though furnished, since a trustful country had decided that its confidence might be abused, and that the wily Teuton would bear watching.

Meeting Taverner on the terrace as we returned to the house, I told him that Hirschmann was back again, but he shook his head.

"That was not the Hirschmanns you saw," he said, "but the people they have let the house to. Bellamy, I think their name is, they have taken the place furnished; either one or other of them is an invalid, I believe."

A week later I was again strolling down to the pillar box when Taverner joined me, and smoking vigorously to discourage the midges, we wandered down to the cross roads together. As we reached the pillar box a faint creak attracted our attention, and looking round, we saw that the large iron gates barring the entrance to Hirschmann's drive had been pushed ajar and a woman was slipping softly through the narrow opening they afforded. She was obviously coming to the post, but, seeing us, hesitated; we stood back, making way for her, and she slipped across the intervening gravel on tip-toe, posted her letter, half bowed to us in acknowledgement of our courtesy, and vanished as silently as she had come.

"There is a tragedy being worked out in that house," remarked Taverner.

I was all interest, as I always am, at any manifestation of my chief's psychic powers, but he merely laughed.

"Not clairvoyance this time, Rhodes, but merely common sense. If a woman's face is younger than her figure, then she is happily married; if the reverse, then she is working out a tragedy."

"I did not see her face," I said, "but her figure was that of a young woman."

"I saw her face," said Taverner, "and it was that of an old one."

His strictures upon her were not entirely justified, however, for a few nights later Winnington and I saw her go to the post again, and although her face was heavily lined and colourless, it was a very striking one, and the mass of auburn hair that surrounded it seemed all the richer for its pallor. I am afraid I stared at her somewhat hard, trying to see the signs from which Taverner had deduced her history. She slipped out through the scarcely opened gate, moving swiftly but stealthily, as one accustomed to need concealment, gave us a sidelong glance under long dark lashes, and retreated as she had come.

It was the complete immobility of the man at my side which drew my attention to him. He stood rooted to the ground, staring up the shadowed drive where she had disappeared as if he would send his very soul to illuminate the darkness. I touched his arm. He turned to speak, but caught his breath, and the words were lost in the bubbling cough that means haemorrhage. He threw one arm round my shoulders to support himself, for he was a taller man than I, and I held him while he coughed up the scarlet arterial blood which told its own story.

I got him back to the house and put him to bed, for he was very shaky after his attack, and reported what had happened to Taverner.

"I don't think he is going to last long," I said.

My colleague looked surprised. "There is a lot of life in him," he said.

"There is not much left of his lungs," I answered, "and you cannot run a car without an engine."

Winnington was not laid up long, however, and the first day we let him out of bed he proposed to go to the post with me. I demurred, for it was some little distance there and back, but he took me by the arm and said: "Look here, Rhodes, I've *got* to go."

I asked the reason for so much urgency. He hesitated, and then he burst out, "I want to see that woman again."

"That's Mrs. Bellamy," I said. "You had better let her alone; she is not good for you. There are plenty of nice girls on the premises you can flirt with it you want to. Let the married women alone, the husbands only come round and kick up a row, and it is bad for the nursing home's reputation."

But Winnington was not to be headed off.

"I don't care whose wife she is; she's the woman I—I—never thought I should see," he finished lamely. "Hang it all, man, I am not going to speak to her or make an ass of myself, I only want to have a look at her. Any way, I don't count, I have pretty nearly finished with this sinful flesh, what's left of it."

He swayed before me in the dusk; tall, gaunt as a skeleton, with colour in his cheeks we should have rejoiced to see in any other patient's, but which was a danger signal in his.

I knew he would go, whether I consented or not, so I judged it best we should go together; and thereafter it became an established thing that we should walk to the cross roads at post time whether there were letters or not. Sometimes we saw Mrs. Bellamy slip silently out to the post, and sometimes we did not. If we missed her for more than two days, Winnington was in a fever, and when for five consecutive days she did not appear, he excited himself into another haemorrhage and we put him to bed, too weak to protest.

It was while telling Taverner of this latest development that the telephone bell rang. I, being nearest the instrument, picked it up and took the message.

"Is that Dr. Taverner?" said a woman's voice.

"This is Dr. Taverner's nursing home," I replied.

"It is Mrs. Bellamy of Headington House who is speaking. I should be very grateful if Dr. Taverner would come and see my husband, he has been taken suddenly ill."

I turned to give the message to Taverner, but he had left the room. A sudden impulse seized me.

"Dr. Taverner is not here at the moment," I said; "but I will come over if you like. I am his assistant; my name is Rhodes, Dr. Rhodes."

"I should be very grateful," replied the voice. "Can you come soon? I am anxious!"

I picked up my cap and went down the path I had so often followed with Winnington. Poor chap, he would not stroll with me again for some time, if ever. At the cross roads I paused for a moment, marvelling that the invisible barrier of convention was at last lowered and that I was free to go up the drive and speak with the woman I had so often watched in Winnington's company. I pushed the heavy gates ajar just as she had done, walked up the deeply shaded avenue, and rang the bell.

I was shown into a sort of morning-room where Mrs. Bellamy came to me almost immediately.

"I want to explain matters to you before you see my husband," she said. "The housekeeper is helping me with him, and I do not want her to know; you see the trouble—I am afraid—is drugs."

So Taverner had been right as usual, she was working out a tragedy.

"He has been in a stupor all day, and I am afraid he has taken an overdose; he has done so before, and I know the symptoms. I felt that I could not get through the night without sending for someone."

She took me to see the patient and I examined him. His pulse was feeble, breathing difficult, and colour bad, but a man who is as inured to the drug as he seemed to be is very hard to kill, more's the pity.

I told her what measures to take; said I did not anticipate any danger, but she could phone me again if a change took place.

As she wished me goodbye she smiled, and said: "I know you quite well by sight, Dr. Rhodes; I have often seen you at the pillar box."

"It is my usual evening walk," I replied. "I always take the letters that have missed the post bag."

I was in two minds about telling Winnington of my interview, wondering whether the excitement into which it would throw him or his continued suspense would be the lesser of the two evils, and finally decided in favour of the former. I went up to his room when I got back, and plunged into the matter without preamble.

"Winnington," I said, "I have seen your divinity."

He was all agog in a minute, and I told him of my interview, suppressing only the nature of the illness, which I was in honour bound not to reveal. This, however, was the point he particularly wished to know, although he knew that I naturally could not tell him. Finding me obdurate, he suddenly raised himself in bed, seized my hand, and laid it to his forehead.

"No, you don't!" I cried, snatching it away, for I had by now seen enough of Taverner's methods to know how thought-reading was done, but I had not been quick enough, and Winnington sank back on the pillowless bed chuckling.

"Drugs!" he said, and breathless from his effort, could say no more; but the triumph in his eyes told me that he had learnt something which he considered of vital importance.

I went round next morning to see Bellamy again. He was conscious, regarded me with sulky suspicion, and would have none of me, and I saw that my acquaintance with his household was likely to end as it had begun, at the pillar box.

An evening or two later Mrs. Bellamy and I met again at the cross roads. She answered my greeting with a smile, evidently well enough pleased to have some one to speak to beside her boorish husband, for they seemed to know no one in the district.

316

She commented on my solitary state. "What has become of the tall man who used to come with you to the post?" she enquired.

I told her of poor Winnington's condition.

Then she said a curious thing for one who was a comparative stranger to me, and a complete stranger to Winnington.

"Is he likely to die?" she asked, looking me straight in the face with a peculiar expression in her eyes.

Surprised by her question, I blurted out the truth.

"I thought so," she said. "I am Scotch, and we have second sight in our family, and last night I saw his wraith."

"You saw his wraith?" I exclaimed, mystified.

She nodded her auburn head. "Just as clearly as I see you," she replied. "In fact he was so distinct that I thought he must have been another doctor from the nursing home whom you had sent over in your stead to see how my husband was getting on.

"I was sitting beside the bed with the lamp turned low, when a movement caught my notice, and I looked up to see your friend standing between me and the light. I was about to speak to him when I noticed the extraordinary expression of his face, so extraordinary that I stared at him and could find no word to say, for he seemed to be absolutely gloating over me—or my husband—I could not tell which.

"He was standing up straight, not his usual stoop." ("So you have been watching him too!" I thought.) "And his face wore a look of absolute triumph, as if he had at last won something for which he had waited and worked for a very long time, and he said to me quite slowly and distinctly: 'It will be my turn next.' I was just about to answer him and ask what he meant by his extraordinary behaviour, when I suddenly found that I could see the lamp *through* him, and before I had recovered from my surprise he had vanished. I took it to mean that my husband would live, but that he himself was dying."

I told her that from my knowledge of the two cases her interpretation was likely to prove a true one, and we stood for some minutes telling ghost stories before she returned through the iron gates.

Winnington was slowly pulling round from his attack, though as yet unable to leave his bed. His attitude concerning Mrs. Bellamy had undergone a curious change; he still asked me each day if I had seen her at the pillar box and what she had had to say for herself, but he showed no regret that he was not well enough to accompany me thither and make her acquaintance; instead, his attitude seemed to convey that he and she were partners in some secret in which I had no share.

Although he was over the worst, his last attack had so pulled him down that his disease had got the upper hand, and I saw that it was unlikely that he would ever get out of bed again, so I indulged his foible in regard to Mrs. Bellamy, feeling sure that no harm could come of it. Her visits to the pillar box, what she said, and what I said were duly reported for the benefit of the sick man, whose eyes twinkled with a secret amusement while I talked. As far as I could make out, for he did not give me his confidence, he was biding his time till Bellamy took another overdose, and I should have felt considerable anxiety as to what he intended to do then had I not known that he was physically incapable of crossing the room without assistance. Little harm could come, therefore, from letting him daydream, so I did not seek to fling cold water on his fantasies.

One night I was roused by a tap at my door and found the night nurse standing there. She asked me to come with her to Winnington's room, for she had found him unconscious, and his condition gave her anxiety. I went with her, and as she had said, he was in a state of coma, pulse imperceptible, breathing almost non-existent; for a moment I was puzzled at the turn his illness had taken, but as I stood looking down at him, I heard the faint click in the throat followed by the long sibilant sigh that I had so often heard when Taverner was leaving his body for one of those strange psychic expeditions of his, and I guessed that Winnington was at the same game, for I knew that he had belonged to Taverner's fraternity and had doubtless learnt many of its arts.

I sent the nurse away and settled myself to wait beside our patient as I had often waited beside Taverner; not a little anxious, for my colleague was away on his holiday, and I had the responsibility of the nursing home on my shoulders; not that that would have troubled me in the ordinary way, but occult matters are beyond my ken, and I knew that Taverner always considered that these psychic expeditions were not altogether unaccompanied by risk.

I had not a long vigil, however; after about twenty minutes I saw the trance condition pass into natural sleep, and having made sure that the heart had taken up its beat again and that all was well, I left my patient without rousing him and went back to bed.

Next morning, as Winnington did not refer to the incident, I did not either, but his ill-concealed elation showed that something had transpired upon that midnight journey which had pleased him mightily.

That evening when I went to the pillar box I found Mrs. Bellamy there waiting for me. She began without preamble:

"Dr. Rhodes, did your tall friend die during the night?"

"No," I said, looking at her sharply. "In fact he is much better this morning."

"I am glad of that," she said, "for I saw his wraith again last night, and wondered if anything had happened to him."

"What time did you see him?" I enquired, a sudden suspicion coming into my mind.

"I don't know," she replied; "I did not look at the clock, but it was some time after midnight; I was wakened by something touching my cheek very softly, and thought the cat must have got into the room and jumped on the bed; I roused myself, intending to put it out of the room, when I saw something shadowy between me and the window; it moved to the foot of the bed, and I felt a slight weight on my feet, more than that of a cat, about what one would expect from a good-sized terrier, and then I distinctly saw your friend sitting on the foot of the bed, watching me. As I looked at him, he faded and disappeared, and I could not be sure that I had not imagined him out of the folds of the eiderdown, which was thrown back over the footboard, so I thought I would ask you whether there was—anything to account for what I saw."

"Winnington is not dead," I said. And not wishing to be questioned any further in the matter, wished her good night somewhat abruptly and was turning away when she called me back.

"Dr. Rhodes," she said, "my husband has been in that heavy stupor all day; do you think that anything ought to be done?"

"I will come and have a look at him if you like," I answered. She thanked me, but said she did not want to call me in unless it were essential, for her husband so bitterly resented any interference.

"Have you got a butler or valet in the house, or is your husband alone with you and the women servants?" I enquired, for it seemed to me that a man who took drugs to the extent that Bellamy did was not the safest, let alone the pleasantest company for three or four women.

Mrs. Bellamy divined my thought and smiled sadly. "I am used to it," she said. "I have always coped with him single-handed."

"How long has he been taking drugs?" I asked.

"Ever since our marriage," she replied. "But how long before that I cannot tell you."

I did not like to press her any further, for her face told me of the tragedy of that existence, so I contented myself with saying:

"I hope you will let me know if you need help at any time. Dr. Taverner and I do not practise in this district, but we would gladly do what we could in an emergency."

As I went down the shrubbery path I thought over what she had told me. Taking into consideration that Winnington had been in a trance condition between two and two-thirty, I felt certain that what she had seen was no fantasy of her imagination. I was much puzzled how to act. It seemed to me that Winnington was playing a dangerous game, dangerous to himself, and to the unsuspecting woman on whom he was practising, yet if I spoke to him on the matter, he would either laugh at me or tell me to mind my own business, and if I warned her, she would regard me as a lunatic. By refusing to admit their existence, the world gives a very long start to those who practise the occult arts.

I decided to leave matters alone until Taverner came back, and therefore avoided deep waters when I paid my evening visit to Winnington. As usual he enquired for news of Mrs. Bellamy, and I told him that I had seen her, and casually mentioned that her husband was bad again. In an instant I saw that I had made a mistake and given Winnington information that he ought not to have had, but I could not unsay my words, and took my leave of him with an uneasy feeling that he was up to something that I could not fathom. Very greatly did I wish for Taverner's experience to take the responsibility off my shoulders, but he was away in Scotland, and I had no reasonable grounds for disturbing his well-earned holiday.

About an hour later, as I had finished my rounds and was thinking of bed, the telephone bell rang. I answered, and heard Mrs. Bellamy's voice at the end of the line.

"I wish you would come round, Dr. Rhodes," she said. "I am very uneasy."

In a few minutes I was with her, and we stood together looking at the unconscious man on the bed. He was a powerfully built fellow of some thirty-five years of age, and before the drug had undermined him, must have been a fine-looking man. His condition appeared to be the same as before, and I asked Mrs. Bellamy what it was that had rendered her so anxious, for I had gathered from the tone of her voice over the phone that she was frightened.

She beat about the bush for a minute or two, and then the truth came out.

"I am afraid my nerve is going," she said. "But there seems to be something or somebody in the room, and it was more than I could stand alone; I simply had to send for you. Will you forgive me for being so foolish and troubling you at this hour of the night?"

I quite understood her feelings, for the strain of coping with a drug maniac in that lonely place with no friends to help her a strain which I gathered, had gone on for years—was enough to wear down anyone's courage.

"Don't think about that," I said. "I'm only too glad to be able to give you any help I can; I quite understand your difficulties."

So, although her husband's condition gave no cause for anxiety, I settled down to watch with her for a little while, and do what I could to ease the strain of that intolerable burden.

We had not been sitting quietly in the dim light for very long before I was aware of a curious feeling. Just as she had said, we were not alone in the room. She saw my glance questing into the corners, and smiled.

"You feel it too?" she said. "Do you see anything?"

"No," I answered, "I am not psychic, I wish I were; but I tell you who will see it, if there is anything to be seen, and that is my dog; he followed me here, and is curled up in the porch if he has not gone home. With your permission I will fetch him up and see what he makes of it."

I ran downstairs and found the big Airedale, whose task it was to guard the nursing home, patiently waiting on the mat. Taking him into the bedroom, I introduced him to Mrs. Bellamy, whom he received with favour, and then, leaving him to his own devices, sat quietly watching what he would do. First he went over to the bed and sniffed at the unconscious man, then he wandered round the room as a dog will in a strange place, and finally he settled down at our feet in front of the fire. Whatever it was that had disturbed our equanimity he regarded as unworthy of notice.

He slept peacefully till Mrs. Bellamy, who had brewed tea, produced a box of biscuits, and then he woke up and demanded his share; first he came to me, and received a contribution, and then he walked quietly up to an empty armchair and stood gazing at it in anxious expectancy. We stared at him in amazement. The dog, serenely confident of his reception, pawed the chair to attract its attention. Mrs. Bellamy and I looked at each other.

"I had always heard," she said, "that it was only cats who liked ghosts, and that dogs were afraid of them."

"So had I," I answered. "But Jack seems to be on friendly terms with this one."

And then the explanation flashed into my mind. If the invisible presence were Winnington, whom Mrs. Bellamy had already seen twice in that very room, then the dog's behaviour was accounted for, for Winnington and he were close friends, and the presence which to us was so uncanny, would, to him, be friendly and familiar.

I rose to my feet. "If you don't mind," I said, "I will just go round to the nursing home and attend to one or two things, and then we will see this affair through together."

I raced back through the shrubberies to the nursing home, mounted the stairs three at a time, and burst into Winnington's bedroom. As I expected, he was in deep trance.

"Oh you devil!" I said to the unconscious form on the bed, "what games are you up to now? I wish to Heaven that Taverner were back to deal with you."

I hastened back to Mrs. Bellamy, and to my surprise, as I re-entered her room I heard voices, and there was Bellamy, fully conscious, and sitting up in bed and drinking tea. He looked dazed, and was shivering with cold, but had apparently thrown off all effects of his drug. I was nonplussed, for I had counted on slipping away before he had recovered consciousness, for I had in mind his last reception of me which had been anything but cordial, but it was impossible to draw back.

"I am glad to see you are better, Mr. Bellamy," I said. "We have been rather anxious about you."

"Don't you worry about me, Rhodes," was the reply. "Go back to bed, old chap; I'll be as right as a trivet as soon as I get warm."

I withdrew; for there was no further excuse for my presence, and back I went to the nursing home again to have another look at Winnington. He was still in a state of coma, so I settled down to watch beside him, but hour after hour went by while I dozed in my chair, and finally the grey light of dawn came and found his condition still unchanged. I had never known Taverner to be out of his body for such a length of time, and Winnington's condition worried me considerably. He might be all right, on the other hand, he might not; I did not know enough about these trances to be sure, and I could not fetch Taverner back from his holiday on a wild goose chase.

The day wore itself away, and when night found Winnington still in the same state I decided that the time had come for some action to be taken, and went to the dispensary to get the strychnine, intending to give him an injection of that and see if it would do any good.

The minute I opened the dispensary door I knew there was someone there, but when I switched on the light the room stood empty before me. All the same, a presence positively jostled my elbow as I searched among the shelves for what I required, and I felt its breath on my neck as I bent over the instrument drawer for the hypodermic syringe.

"Oh Lord!" I said aloud. "I wish Taverner would come back and look after his own spooks. Here, you, whoever you are, go on, clear out, go home; we don't want you here!" And hastily gathering up my impedimenta, I beat a retreat and left it in possession of the dispensary.

My evil genius prompted me to look over my shoulder as I went down the passage, and there, behind me, was a spindle-shaped drift of grey mist some seven feet high. I am ashamed to admit it, but I ran. I am not easily scared by anything I can see, but these half-seen things that drift to us out of another existence, whose presence one can detect but not locate, fill me with cold horror.

I slammed and locked Winnington's door behind me and paused to recover my breath; but even as I did so, I saw a pool of mist gathering on the floor, and there was the creature, oozing through the crack under the door and re-forming itself in the shadow of the wardrobe.

What would I not have given for Taverner's presence as I stood there, helplessly watching it, syringe in hand, sweating like a frightened horse. Then illumination suddenly burst upon me; what a fool I was, of course it was Winnington coming back to his body!

"Oh Lord!" I said. "What a fright you gave me! For goodness' sake get back into your body and stop there, and we'll let bygones by bygones."

But it did not heed my adjuration; it seemed as if it were the hypodermic syringe that attracted it, and instead of returning to its physical vehicle, it hung round me.

"Oh," I said. "So it is the strychnine you are after? Well then, get back into your body and you shall have some. Look, I am going to give your body an injection. Get back inside it if you want any strychnine."

The grey wraith hung for a moment over the unconscious form on the bed, and then, to my unspeakable relief, slowly merged into it, and I felt the heart take up its beat and breathing recommence.

I went to my room dead beat, for I had had no sleep and much anxiety during the past forty-eight hours, so I left a note on my mat to say that I was not to be disturbed in the morning; I felt I had fairly earned my rest, I had pulled two tricky cases through, and put my small knowledge of occultism to a satisfactory test.

But in spite of my instructions I was not left undisturbed. At seven o'clock the matron routed me out.

"I wish you would come and look at Mr. Winnington, Doctor; I think he has gone out of his mind."

I wearily put on my clothes and dipped my heavy head in the basin and went to inspect Winnington. Instead of his usual cheery smile, he greeted me with a malign scowl.

"I should be very glad," he said, "if you would kindly tell me where I am."

"You are in your own room, old chap," I said. "You have had a bad turn, but are all right again now."

"Indeed," he said. "This is the first I have heard of it. And who may you be?"

"I'm Rhodes," I replied. "Don't you know me?"

"I know you right enough. You are Dr. Taverner's understrapper at that nursing home place. I suppose my kind friends have put me here to get me out of the way. Well, I can tell you this, they can't make me stop here. Where are my clothes? I want to get up."

"Your clothes are wherever you put them," I replied. "We have not taken them away; but as for getting up, you are not fit to do so. We have no wish to keep you here against your will, and if you want to be moved we will arrange it for you, but you will have to have an ambulance, you have been pretty bad you know." It was my intention to play for time till this sick mood should have passed, but he saw through my manoeuvre.

"Ambulance be damned," he said. "I will go on my own feet." And forthwith he sat up in bed and swung his legs over the edge. But even this effort was too much for him, and he would have slid to the floor if I had not caught him. I called the nurse, and we put him to bed, incapable of giving any further trouble for the moment.

I was rather surprised at this ebullition as coming from Winnington, who had always shown himself a very sweet-tempered, gentle personality, though liable to fits of depression, which, however, were hardly to be wondered at in his condition. He had not much to make him cheerful, poor chap, and but for Taverner's intervention he would probably have ended his days in an infirmary.

When I went down to the pillar box that evening, there was Mrs. Bellamy, and to my surprise, her husband was with her. She greeted me with some constraint, watching her husband to see how he would take it, but his greeting lacked nothing in the way of cordiality: one would have thought that I was an old friend of the family. He thanked me for my care of him, and for my kindness to his wife, whom, he said, he was afraid had been going through rather a bad time lately.

"I am going to take her away for a change, however, a second honeymoon, you know; but when we get back I want to see something of you, and also of Dr. Taverner. I am very anxious to keep in touch with Taverner."

I thanked him, marvelling at his change of mood, and only hoping for his wife's sake that it would last; but drug takers are broken reeds to lean upon and I feared that she would have to drain her cup to the dregs.

When I got back to the nursing home I was amazed to find Taverner there.

"Why, what in the world has brought you back from your holiday?" I demanded.

"You did," he replied. "You kept on telepathing SOS messages, so thought I had better come and see what was the matter."

"I am most awfully sorry," I said. "We had a little difficulty, but got over it all right."

"What happened?" he enquired, watching me closely, and I felt myself getting red like a guilty schoolboy, for I did not particularly want to tell him of Mrs. Bellamy and Winnington's infatuation for her.

"I fancy that Winnington tried your stunt of going subconscious," I said at length. "He went very deep, and was away a long time, and I got rather worried. You see, I don't understand these things properly. And then, as he was coming back, I saw him, and took him for a ghost, and got the wind up."

"You *saw* him?" exclaimed Taverner. "How did you manage to do that? You are not clairvoyant."

"I saw a grey, spindle-shaped drift of mist, the same as we saw the time Black, the airman, nearly died."

"You saw that?" said Taverner in surprise. "Do you mean to say that Winnington took the etheric double out? How long was he subconscious?"

"About twenty-four hours."

"Good God!" cried Taverner. "The man's probably dead!"

"He's nothing of the sort," I replied. "He is alive and kicking. Kicking vigorously, in fact," I added, remembering the scene of the morning.

"I cannot conceive," said Taverner, "how the etheric double, the vehicle of the life forces, could be withdrawn for so long a time without the disintegration of the physical form commencing. Where was he, and what was he up to? Perhaps, however, he was immediately over the bed, and merely withdrew from his physical body to escape its discomfort."

"He was in the dispensary when I first saw him," I answered, devoutly hoping that Taverner would not need any further information as to Winnington's whereabouts. "He followed me back to his room and I coaxed him into his body."

Taverner gave me a queer look. "I suppose you took the preliminary precaution of making sure that it *was* Winnington you had got hold of?"

"Good Lord, Taverner, is there a possibility—?"

"Come upstairs and let us have a look at him, I can soon tell you."

Winnington was lying in a room lit only by a night-light, and though he turned his head at our entrance, did not speak. Taverner went over to the bed and switched on the reading lamp standing on the bedside table. Winnington flinched at the sudden brightness, and growled something, but Taverner threw the light full into his eyes, watching them closely, and to my surprise, the pupils did not contract.

"I was afraid so," said Taverner.

"Is anything wrong?" I enquired anxiously. "He seems all right."

"Everything is wrong, my dear boy," answered Taverner. "I am sure you did the best you knew, but you did not know enough. Unless you thoroughly understand these things it is best to leave them to nature."

"But—but—he is alive," I exclaimed, bewildered.

"*It* is alive," corrected Taverner. "That is not Winnington you know."

"Then who in the world is it? It looks like it to me."

"That we must try and find out. Who are you?" he continued, raising his voice and addressing the man on the bed.

"You know damn well," came the husky whisper.

"I am afraid I don't," answered Taverner. "I must ask you to tell me."

"Why, W—" I began, but Taverner clapped his hand over my mouth.

"Be quiet, you fool, you have done enough damage, never let it know the real name."

Then, turning back to the sick man again, he repeated his question.

"John Bellamy," came the sulky answer.

Taverner nodded and drew me out of the room.

"Bellamy?" he asked. "That is the name of the man who took the Hirschmann's house. Has Winnington had anything to do with him?"

"Look here, Taverner," I said, "I will tell you something I had not meant to let you know. Winnington has got a fixation on Bellamy's wife, and apparently he has brooded over it, and fantasised over it, till in his unconscious imagination he has substituted himself for Bellamy."

"That may quite well be, it may be an ordinary case of mental trouble, we will investigate that end of the stick by and by; but, for the present, why has Bellamy substituted himself for Winnington?"

"A wish-fulfilment," I replied. "Winnington is in love with Bellamy's wife; he wishes he were Bellamy in order to possess her, therefore his delirium expresses the subconscious wish as an actuality, the usual Freudian mechanism, you know—the dream as the wish-fulfilment."

"I dare say," answered Taverner. "The Freudians explain a lot of things they don't understand. But what about Bellamy, is he in a trance condition?"

"He is apparently quite all right, or he was, about half an hour ago. I saw him when he came down to the post with his wife. He was quite all right, and uncommon civil, in fact."

"I dare say," said Taverner dryly. "You and Winnington always were chums. Now look here, Rhodes, you are not being frank with me, I must get to the bottom of this business. Now tell me all about it."

So I told him. Narrated in cold blood, it sounded the flimsiest fantasy. When I had finished, Taverner laughed.

"You have done it this time, Rhodes," he said. "And you who are so straight-laced, of all people!" and he laughed again.

"What is your explanation of the matter?" I enquired, somewhat nettled by his laughter. "I can quite understand Winnington's soul, or whatever may be the technical name for it, getting out of its body and turning up in Mrs. Bellamy's room, we have had several cases of that sort of thing; and I can quite understand Winnington's Freudian wish-fulfillment, it is the most understandable thing of the whole business; the only thing that is not clear to me is the change in character of the two men; Bellamy is certainly improved, for the moment, at any rate; and Winnington is in a very bad temper and slightly delirious."

"And therein lies the crux of the whole problem. What do you suppose has happened to those two men?"

"I haven't a notion," I answered.

"But I have," said Taverner. "Narcotics, if you take enough of them, have the effect of putting you out of your body, but the margin is a narrow one between enough and too much, and if you take the latter, you go out and don't come back. Winnington found out, through you, Bellamy's weakness, and, being able to leave his body at will as a trained Initiate can, watched his chance when Bellamy was out of his body in a pipe dream, and then slipped in, obsessed him, in fact, leaving Bellamy to wander houseless. Bellamy, craving for his drug, and cut off from the physical means of gratification, scents from afar the stock we have in the dispensary, and goes there; and when he sees you with a hypodermic syringe—for an ensouled etheric can see quite well—he instinctively follows you, and you, meddling in matters of which you know nothing, put him into Winnington's body."

As Taverner was speaking I realised that we had the true explanation of the phenomena; point by point it fitted in with all I had witnessed.

"Is there anything that can be done to put matters right?" I asked, now thoroughly chastened.

"There are several things that can be done, but it is a question as to what you would consider to be right."

"Surely there can be no doubt upon that point?—get the men sorted back into their proper bodies."

"You think that would be right?" said Taverner. "I am not so certain. In that case you would have three unhappy people; in the present case, you have two who are very happy, and one who is very angry, the world on the whole, being the richer."

"But how about Mrs. Bellamy?" I said. "She is living with a man she is not married to?"

"The law would consider her to be married to him," answered Taverner. "Our marriage laws only separate for sins of the body, they do not recognise adultery of the soul; so long as the body has been faithful, they would think no evil. A change of disposition for the worse, whether under the influence of drugs, drink, or insanity, does not constitute grounds for a divorce under our exalted code, therefore a change of personality for the better under a psychic influence does not constitute one either. The mandarins cannot have it both ways."

"Anyway," I replied, "it does not seem to me moral."

"How do you define morality?" said Taverner.

"The law of the land—" I began.

"In that case a man's admission to Heaven would be decided by Act of Parliament. If you go through a form of marriage with a woman a day before a new marriage law takes effect, you will go to prison, and subsequently to hell, for bigamy; whereas, if you go through the same ceremony with the same woman the day after, you will live in the odour of sanctity and finally go to heaven. No, Rhodes, we will have to seek deeper than that for our standards."

"Then," said I, "how would you define immorality?"

"As that," said Taverner, "which retards the evolution of the group soul of the society to which one belongs. There are times when law-breaking is the highest ethical act; we can all think of such occasions in history, the many acts of conformity, both Catholic and Protestant, for example. Martyrs are law-breakers, and most of them were legally convicted at the time of their execution; it has remained for subsequent ages to canonise them."

"But to return to practical politics, Taverner, what are you going to do with Winnington?"

"Certify him," said Taverner, "and ship him off to the county asylum as soon as we can get the ambulance."

"You must do as you see fit," I replied, "but I am damned if I will put my name on that certificate."

"You lack the courage of your convictions, but may I take it that you do not protest?"

"How the hell can I? I should only get certified myself."

"You must expect your good to be evil spoken of in this wicked world," rejoined my partner, and the discussion was likely to have developed into the first quarrel we had ever had when the door suddenly opened and the nurse stood there.

"Doctor," she said, "Mr. Winnington has passed away."

"Thank God!" said I.

"Good Lord!" said Taverner.

We went upstairs and stood beside that which lay upon the bed. Never before had I so clearly realised that the physical form is not the man. Here was a house that had been tenanted by two distinct entities, that had stood vacant for thirty-six hours, and that now was permanently empty. Soon the

330

walls would crumble and the roof fall in. How could I ever have thought that this was my friend? A quarter of a mile away the soul that had built this habitation was laughing in its sleeve, and somewhere, probably in the dispensary, a furious entity that had recently been imprisoned behind its bars, was raging impotently, nosing at the stoppers of the poison bottles for the stimulants it no longer had the stomach to hold. My knees gave under me, and I dropped into a chair, nearer fainting than I have ever been since my first operation.

"Well, that is settled, any way," I said in a voice that sounded strange in my own ears.

"You think so? Now I consider the trouble is just beginning," said Taverner. "Has it struck you that so long as Bellamy was imprisoned in a body we knew where he was, and could keep him under control; but now he is loose in the unseen world, and will take a considerable amount of catching."

"Then you think he will try to interfere with his wife and—and her husband?"

"What would you do if you were in his shoes?" said Taverner.

"And yet you don't consider the transaction is immoral?"

"I do not. It has done no harm to the group spirit, or the social morale, if you prefer the term. On the other hand, Winnington is running an enormous risk. Can he keep Bellamy at bay now he is out of the body? and if he cannot, what will happen? Remember Bellamy's time to die had not come, and therefore he will hang about, an earth-bound ghost, like that of a suicide; and if tuberculosis is a disease of the vital forces, as I believe it to be, how long will it be before the infected life that now ensouls it will cause the old trouble to break out in Bellamy's body? And when Bellamy the second is out on the astral plane—dead, as you call it—what will Bellamy the first have to say to him? And what will they do to Mrs. Bellamy between them, making her neighbourhood their battleground?

"No, Rhodes, there is no special hell for those who dabble in forbidden things, it would be superfluous."

THE JEST OF
WARBURG TANTAVUL

SEABURY QUINN

Although Victor Rousseau's stories about Ivan Brodsky had been syndicated through major city newspapers in 1909–10, and the stories about Semi Dual by John U. Giesy and Junius B. Smith had been appearing in the Munsey pulps since 1912, there had been no series about an occult detective in the specialist pulp magazines in the United States until Seabury Quinn introduced Jules de Grandin and his chronicler and co-adventurer Dr. Trowbridge in "The Horror on the Links" in the October 1925 issue of Weird Tales. *There were also the Simon Iff stories by occultist Aleister Crowley, which ran in* The Internationalist *during 1917, and the Godfrey Usher stories by Herman Landon in* Detective Story Magazine *during 1918, but these are minor pieces, which scarcely qualify as genuine psychic sleuths. Iff is a magician, but the only skills he uses to resolve a mystery (which he tends to do as an armchair detective enjoying outdoing his colleagues at the Club) is from his psychoanalytical abilities. Godfrey Usher solves mundane crime by using intuition. But with Jules de Grandin we are thrown to the wolves, literally, as he and Trowbridge use all their medical and occult knowledge to battle every conceivable enemy from werewolves and vampires, human or beast, dead or alive, or any combination thereof. What's more, whereas previous writers had produced maybe a half-dozen or so stories about their investigator, Quinn kept on writing them for over twenty-five years, resulting in ninety-three stories including one complete novel. It still stands as the longest-running occult detective series. Jules de Grandin bears some comparison with Agatha Christie's Hercule Poirot, although he is French rather than Belgian. Both he and Trowbridge are physicians, but de Grandin had also served with the French Sûreté and had spent years studying the occult in Asia and Africa. With a series so long, Quinn was able to experiment with a variety of subjects and ideas, as the following story shows.*

By profession Seabury Quinn (1889–1969) was a lawyer specializing in medical jurisprudence, and he edited several trade journals including the magazine for morticians, Casket & Sunnyside, *from 1926 to 1937. Yet he was a prolific writer and amongst his others works, not involving de Grandin, are the novella* Roads *(1948—originally in* Weird Tales *in 1938), the erotic Egyptian fantasy* Alien Flesh *(1977), and the collections* Is the Devil a Gentleman? *(1970),* Night Creatures *(2003), and* Demons of the Night *(2009). A selection of the de Grandin stories was first collected as* The Phantom Fighter *in 1966, but the definitive edition runs to five volumes,* The Horror on the Links, The Devil's Rosary, The Dark Angel, A Rival from the Grave, *and* Black Moon *(2017–19).*

WARBURG TANTAVUL WAS DYING. LITTLE MORE THAN SKIN AND bones, he lay propped up with pillows in the big sleigh bed and smiled as though he found the thought of dissolution faintly amusing.

Even in comparatively good health the man was never prepossessing. Now, wasted with disease, that smile of self-sufficient satisfaction on his wrinkled face, he was nothing less than hideous. The eyes, which nature had given him, were small, deep-set and ruthless. The mouth, which his own thoughts had fashioned through the years, was wide and thin-lipped, almost colorless, and even in repose was tightly drawn against his small and curiously perfect teeth. Now, as he smiled, a flickering light, lambent as the quick reflection of an unseen flame, flared in his yellowish eyes, and a hard white line of teeth showed on his lower lip, as if he bit it to hold back a chuckle.

"You're still determined that you'll marry Arabella?" he asked his son, fixing his sardonic, mocking smile on the young man.

"Yes, Father, but—"

"No buts, my boy"—this time the chuckle came, low and muted, but at the same time glassy-hard—"no buts. I've told you I'm against it, and you'll rue it to your dying day if you should marry her; but"—he paused, and breath rasped in his wizened throat—"but go ahead and marry her, if your heart's set on it. I've said my say and warned you—heh, boy, never say your poor old father didn't warn you!"

He lay back on his piled-up pillows for a moment, swallowing convulsively, as if to force the fleeting life-breath back, then, abruptly: "Get out," he ordered. "Get out and stay out, you poor fool; but remember what I've said."

"Father," young Tantavul began, stepping toward the bed, but the look of sudden concentrated fury in the old man's tawny eyes halted him in midstride.

"Get—out—I—said," his father snarled, then, as the door closed softly on his son:

"Nurse—hand—me—that—picture." His breath was coming slowly, now, in shallow labored gasps, but his withered fingers writhed in a gesture of command, pointing to the silver-framed photograph of a woman which stood upon a little table in the bedroom window-bay.

He clutched the portrait as if it were some precious relic, and for a minute let his eyes rove over it. "Lucy," he whispered hoarsely, and now his words were thick and indistinct, "Lucy, they'll be married, spite of all that I have said. They'll be married, Lucy, d'ye hear?" Thin and high-pitched as a child's, his voice rose to a piping treble as he grasped the picture's silver frame and held it level with his face. "They'll be married, Lucy dear, and they'll have—"

Abruptly as a penny whistle's note is stilled when no more air is blown in it, old Tantavul's cry was hushed. The picture, still grasped in his hands, fell to the tufted coverlet, the man's lean jaw relaxed and he slumped back on his pillows with a shadow of the mocking smile still in his glazing eyes.

Etiquette requires that the nurse await the doctor's confirmation at such times, so, obedient to professional dictates, Miss Williamson stood by the bed until I felt the dead man's pulse and nodded; then with the

334

skill of years of practice she began her offices, bandaging the wrists and jaws and ankles that the body might be ready when the representative of Martin's Funeral Home came for it.

My friend de Grandin was annoyed. Arms akimbo, knuckles on his hips, his black-silk kimono draped round him like a mourning garment, he voiced his complaint in no uncertain terms. In fifteen little so small minutes he must leave for the theatre, and that son and grandson of a filthy swine who was the florist had not delivered his gardenia. And was it not a fact that he could not go forth without a fresh gardenia for his lapel? But certainly. Why did that *sale chameau* procrastinate? Why did he delay delivering that unmentionable flower till this unspeakable time of night? He was Jules de Grandin, he, and not to be oppressed by any species of a goat who called himself a florist. But no. It must not be. It should not be, by blue! He would—

"Axin' yer pardon, sir," Nora McGinnis broke in from the study door, "there's a Miss an' Mr. Tantavul to see ye, an'—"

"Bid them be gone, *ma charmeuse*. Request that they jump in the bay— *Grand Dieu*"—he cut his oratory short—"*les enfants dans le bois!*"

Truly, there was something reminiscent of the Babes in the Wood in the couple who had followed Nora to the study door. Dennis Tantavul looked even younger and more boyish than I remembered him, and the girl beside him was so childish in appearance that I felt a quick, instinctive pity for her. Plainly they were frightened, too, for they clung hand to hand like frightened children going past a graveyard, and in their eyes was that look of sick terror I had seen so often when the X-ray and blood test confirmed preliminary diagnosis of carcinoma.

"*Monsieur, Mademoiselle!*" The little Frenchman gathered his kimono and his dignity about him in a single sweeping gesture as he struck his heels together and bowed stiffly from the hips. "I apologize for my unseemly words. Were it not that I have been subjected to a terrible, calamitous misfortune, I should not so far have forgotten myself—"

The girl's quick smile cut through his apology. "We understand," she reassured. "We've been through trouble, too, and have come to Dr. Trowbridge—"

"Ah, then I have permission to withdraw?" he bowed again and turned upon his heel, but I called him back.

"Perhaps you can assist us," I remarked as I introduced the callers.

"The honor is entirely mine, *Mademoiselle*," he told her as he raised her fingers to his lips. "You and *Monsieur* your brother—"

"He's not my brother," she corrected. "We're cousins. That's why we've called on Dr. Trowbridge."

De Grandin tweaked the already needle-sharp points of his small blond mustache. "*Pardonnez-moi?*" he begged. "I have resided in your country but a little time; perhaps I do not understand the language fluently. It is because you and *Monsieur* are cousins that you come to see the doctor? Me, I am dull and stupid like a pig; I fear I do not comprehend."

Dennis Tantavul replied: "It's not because of the relationship, Doctor— not entirely, at any rate, but—"

He turned to me: "You were at my father's bedside when he died; you remember what he said about marrying Arabella?"

I nodded.

"There was something—some ghastly, hidden threat concealed in his warning, Doctor. It seemed as if he jeered at me—dared me to marry her, yet—"

"Was there some provision in his will?" I asked.

"Yes, sir," the young man answered. "Here it is." From his pocket he produced a folded parchment, opened it and indicated a paragraph:

To my son Dennis Tantavul I give, devise and bequeath all my property of every kind and sort, real, personal and mixed, of which I may die seized and possessed, or to which I may be entitled, in the event of his marrying Arabella Tantavul, but should he not marry the said Arabella Tantavul, then it is my will that he receive only one half of my estate, and that the residue thereof go to the said Arabella Tantavul, who has made her home with me since childhood and occupied the relationship of daughter to me.

"H'm," I returned the document, "this looks as if he really wanted you to marry your cousin, even though—"

"And see here, sir," Dennis interrupted, "here's an envelope we found in Father's papers."

336

Sealed with red wax, the packet of heavy, opaque parchment was addressed:

"To my children, Dennis and Arabella Tantavul, to be opened by them upon the occasion of the birth of their first child."

De Grandin's small blue eyes were snapping with the flickering light they showed when he was interested. "Monsieur Dennis," he took the thick envelope from the caller, "Dr. Trowbridge has told me something of your father's death-bed scene. There is a mystery about this business. My suggestion is you read the message now—"

"No, sir. I won't do that. My father didn't love me—sometimes I think he hated me—but I never disobeyed a wish that he expressed, and I don't feel at liberty to do so now. It would be like breaking faith with the dead. But"—he smiled a trifle shame-facedly—"Father's law-yer Mr. Bainbridge is out of town on business, and it will be his duty to probate the will. In the meantime I'd feel better if the will and this envelope were in other hands than mine. So we came to Dr. Trowbridge to ask him to take charge of them till Mr. Bainbridge gets back, mean-while—"

"Yes, Monsieur, meanwhile?" de Grandin prompted as the young man paused.

"You know human nature, Doctor," Dennis turned to me; "no one can see farther into hidden meanings than the man who sees humanity with its mask off, the way a doctor does. D'ye think Father might have been delirious when he warned me not to marry Arabella, or—" His voice trailed off, but his troubled eyes were eloquent.

"H'm," I shifted uncomfortably in my chair, "I can't see any reason for hesitating, Dennis. That bequest of all your father's property in the event you marry Arabella seems to indicate his true feelings." I tried to make my words convincing, but the memory of old Tantavul's dying words dinned in my ears. There had been something gloating in his voice as he told the picture that his son and niece would marry.

De Grandin caught the hint of hesitation in my tone. "*Monsieur,*" he asked Dennis, "will not you tell us of the antecedents of your father's warning? Dr. Trowbridge is perhaps too near to see the situation clearly. Me, I have no knowledge of your father or your family. You and

Mademoiselle are strangely like. The will describes her as having lived with you since childhood. Will you kindly tell us how it came about?"

The Tantavuls were, as he said, strangely similar. Anyone might easily have taken them for twins. Like as two plaster portraits from the same mold were their small straight noses, sensitive mouths, curling pale-gold hair.

Now, once more hand in hand, they sat before us on the sofa, and as Dennis spoke I saw the frightened, haunted look creep back into their eyes.

"Do you remember us as children, Doctor?" he asked me.

"Yes, it must have been some twenty years ago they called me out to see you youngsters. You'd just moved into the old Stephens house, and there was a deal of gossip about the strange gentleman from the West with his two small children and Chinese cook, who greeted all the neighbors' overtures with churlish rebuffs and never spoke to anyone."

"What did you think of us, sir?"

"H'm; I thought you and your sister—as I thought her then—had as fine a case of measles as I'd ever seen."

"How old were we then, do you remember?"

"Oh, you were something like three; the little girl was half your age, I'd guess."

"Do you recall the next time you saw us?"

"Yes, you were somewhat older then; eight or ten, I'd say. That time it was the mumps. You were queer, quiet little shavers. I remember asking if you thought you'd like a pickle, and you said, 'No, thank you, sir, it hurts.'"

"It did, too, sir. Every day Father made us eat one; stood over us with a whip till we'd chewed the last morsel."

"*What?*"

The young folks nodded solemnly as Dennis answered, "Yes, sir; every day. He said he wanted to check up on the progress we were making."

For a moment he was silent, then: "Dr. Trowbridge, if anyone treated you with studied cruelty all your life—if you'd never had a kind word or gracious act from that person in all your memory, then suddenly that person offered you a favour—made it possible for you to gratify your dearest wish, and threatened to penalize you if you failed to do so, wouldn't you

338

be suspicious? Wouldn't you suspect some sort of dreadful practical joke?"

"I don't think I quite understand."

"Then listen: In all my life I can't remember ever having seen my father smile, not really smile with friendliness, humour or affection, I mean. My life—and Arabella's, too—was one long persecution at his hands. I was two years or so old when we came to Harrisonville, I believe, but I still have vague recollections of our Western home, of a house set high on a hill overlooking the ocean, and a wall with climbing vines and purple flowers on it, and a pretty lady who would take me in her arms and cuddle me against her breast and feed me ice cream from a spoon, sometimes. I have a sort of recollection of a little baby sister in that house, too, but these things are so far back in babyhood that possibly they were no more than childish fancies which I built up for myself and which I loved so dearly and so secretly they finally came to have a kind of reality for me.

"My real memories, the things I can recall with certainty, begin with a hurried train trip through hot, dry, uncomfortable country with my father and a strangely silent Chinese servant and a little girl they told me was my cousin Arabella.

"Father treated me and Arabella with impartial harshness. We were beaten for the slightest fault, and we had faults a-plenty. If we sat quietly we were accused of sulking and asked why we didn't go and play. If we played and shouted we were whipped for being noisy little brats.

"As we weren't allowed to associate with any of the neighbors' children we made up our own games. I'd be Geraint and Arabella would be Enid of the dove-white feet, or perhaps I'd be King Arthur in the Castle Perilous, and she'd be the kind Lady of the Lake who gave him back his magic sword. And though we never mentioned it, both of us knew that whatever the adventure was, the false knight or giant I contended with was really my father. But when actual trouble came I wasn't an heroic figure.

"I must have been twelve or thirteen when I had my last thrashing. A little brook ran through the lower part of our land, and the former owners had widened it into a lily-pond. The flowers had died out years before, but the outlines of the pool remained, and it was our favourite summer play place. We taught ourselves to swim—not very well, of course, but well enough—and as we had no bathing suits we used to go in in our underwear. When we'd finished swimming we'd lie in the sun until our underthings were dry, then slip into our outer clothing. One afternoon as we were splashing in the water, happy as a pair of baby otters, and nearer to shouting with laughter then we'd ever been before, I think, my father suddenly appeared on the bank.

"'Come out o' there!' he shouted to me, and there was a kind of sharp, dry hardness in his voice I'd never heard before. 'So this is how you spend your time?' he asked as I climbed up the bank. 'In spite of all I've done to keep you decent, you do a thing like this!'

"'Why, Father, we were only swimming—' I began, but he struck me on the mouth.

"'Shut up, you little rake!' he roared. 'I'll teach you!' He cut a willow switch and thrust my head between his knees; then while he held me tight as in a vice he flogged me with the willow till the blood came through my skin and stained my soaking cotton shorts. Then he kicked me back into the pool as a heartless master might a beaten dog.

"As I said, I wasn't an heroic figure. It was Arabella who came to my rescue. She helped me up the slippery bank and took me in her arms. 'Poor Dennie,' she said. 'Poor, poor Dennie. It was my fault, Dennie, dear, for letting you take me into the water!' Then she kissed me—the first time anyone had kissed me since the pretty lady of my half-remembered dreams. 'We'll be married on the very day that Uncle Warburg dies,' she promised, 'and I'll be so sweet and good to you, and you'll love me so dearly that we'll both forget these dreadful days.'

"We thought my father'd gone, but he must have stayed to see what we would say, for as Arabella finished he stepped from behind a rhododendron bush, and for the first time I heard him laugh. 'You'll be married, will you?' he asked. 'That would be a good joke—the best one of all. All right, go ahead—see what it gets you.'

"That was the last time he ever actually struck me, but from that time on he seemed to go out of his way to invent mental tortures for us. We weren't allowed to go to school, but he had a tutor, a little rat-faced man named Ericson, come in to give us lessons, and in the evening he'd take the book and make us stand before him and recite. If either of us failed a

problem in arithmetic or couldn't conjugate a French or Latin verb he'd
wither us with sarcasm, and always as a finish to his diatribe he'd jeer at us
about our wish to be married, and threaten us with something dreadful if
we ever did it.

"So, Dr. Trowbridge, you see why I'm suspicious. It seems almost as if
this provision in the will is part of some horrible practical joke my father
prepared deliberately—as if he's waiting to laugh at us from the grave."

"I can understand your feelings, boy," I answered, "but—"

"'But' be damned and roasted on the hottest griddle in hell's kitchen!"
Jules de Grandin interrupted. "The wicked dead one's funeral is at two
tomorrow afternoon, *n'est-ce-pas?*

"*Très bien.* At eight tomorrow evening—or earlier, if it will be convenient—you shall be married. I shall esteem it a favour if you permit that I
be best man; Dr. Trowbridge will give the bride away, and we shall have
a merry time, by blue! You shall go upon a gorgeous honeymoon and
learn how sweet the joys of love can be—sweeter for having been so long
denied! And in the meantime we shall keep the papers safely till your lawyer returns.

"You fear the so unpleasant jest? *Mais non,* I think the jest is on the
other foot, my friends, and the laugh on the other face!"

WARBURG TANTAVUL WAS NEITHER WIDELY KNOWN NOR POPULAR,
but the solitude in which he had lived had invested him with mystery; now
the bars of reticence were down and the walls of isolation broken, upward
of a hundred neighbors, mostly women, gathered in the Martin funeral
chapel as the services began. The afternoon sun beat softly through the
stained-glass windows and glinted on the polished mahogany of the casket. Here and there it touched upon bright spots of color that marked a
woman's hat or a man's tie. The solemn hush was broken by occasional
whispers: "What'd he die of? Did he leave much? Were the two young
folks his only heirs?"

Then the burial office: "Lord, Thou hast been our refuge from one
generation to another . . . for a thousand years in Thy sight are but as yesterday . . . Oh teach us to number our days that we may apply our hearts
unto wisdom . . ."

As the final Amen sounded one of Mr. Martin's frock-coated young men glided forward, paused beside the casket, and made the stereotyped announcement: "Those who wish to say good-bye to Mr. Tantavul may do so at this time."

The grisly rite of passing by the bier dragged on. I would have left the place; I had no wish to look upon the man's dead face and folded hands; but de Grandin took me firmly by the elbow, held me till the final curiosity-impelled female had filed past the body, then steered me quickly toward the casket.

He paused a moment at the bier, and it seemed to me there was a hint of irony in the smile that touched the corners of his mouth as he leant forward. "*Eh bien*, my old one; we know a secret, thou and I, *n'est-ce-pas?*" he asked the silent form before us.

I swallowed back an exclamation of dismay. Perhaps it was a trick of the uncertain light, perhaps one of those ghastly, inexplicable things which every doctor and embalmer meets with sometimes in his practice—the effect of desiccation from formaldehyde, the pressure of some tissue gas within the body, or something of the sort—at any rate, as Jules de Grandin spoke the corpse's upper lids drew back the fraction of an inch, revealing slits of yellow eye which seemed to glare at us with mingled hate and fury.

"Good heavens; come away!" I begged. "It seemed as if he looked at us, de Grandin!"

"*Et puis*—and if he did? I damn think I can trade him look for look, my friend. He was clever, that one, I admit it; but do not be mistaken, Jules de Grandin is nobody's imbecile."

The wedding took place in the rectory of St. Chrysostom's. Robed in stole and surplice, Dr. Bentley glanced benignly from Dennis to Arabella, then to de Grandin and me as he began: "Dearly beloved, we are gathered together here in the sight of God and in the face of this company to join together this man and this woman in holy matrimony. . . ." His round and ruddy face grew slightly stern as he admonished, "If any man can show just cause why they should not lawfully be joined together, let him now speak or else hereafter for ever hold his peace."

He paused the customary short, dramatic moment, and I thought I saw a hard, grim look spread on de Grandin's face. Very faint and far off seeming, so faint that we could scarcely hear it, but gaining steadily in strength, there came a high, thin, screaming sound. Curiously, it seemed to me to resemble the long-drawn, wailing shriek of a freight train's whistle heard miles away upon a still and sultry summer night, weird, wavering and ghastly. Now it seemed to grow in shrillness, though its volume was no greater.

I saw a look of haunted fright leap into Arabella's eyes, saw Dennis' pale face go paler as the strident whistle sounded shriller and more shrill; then, as it seemed I could endure the stabbing of that needle-sound no longer, it ceased abruptly, giving way to blessed, comforting silence. But through the silence came a burst of chuckling laughter, half breathless, half hysterical, wholly devilish: *Huh—hu-u-uh—hu-u-u-uh!* the final syllable drawn out until it seemed almost a groan.

"The wind, *Monsieur le Curé*; it was nothing but the wind," de Grandin told the clergyman sharply. "Proceed to marry them, if you will be so kind."

"Wind?" Dr. Bentley echoed. "I could have sworn I heard somebody laugh, but—"

"It is the wind, *Monsieur*; it plays strange tricks at times," the little Frenchman insisted, his small blue eyes as hard as frozen iron. "Proceed, if you will be so kind. We wait on you."

"Forasmuch as Dennis and Arabella have consented to be joined together in holy wedlock . . . I pronounce them man and wife," concluded Dr. Bentley, and de Grandin, ever gallant, kissed the bride upon the lips, and before we could restrain him, planted kisses on both Dennis' cheeks.

"*Cordieu*, I thought that we might have the trouble, for a time," he told me as we left the rectory.

"What *was* that awful shrieking noise we heard?" I asked.

"It was the wind, my friend," he answered in a hard, flat, toneless voice. "The ten times damned, but wholly ineffectual wind."

"So, THEN, LITTLE SINNER, WEEP AND WAIL FOR THE BURDEN OF mortality you have assumed. Weep, wail, cry and breathe, my small and wrinkled one! Ha, you will not? *Pardieu*, I say you shall!"

Gently, but smartly, he spanked the small red infant's small red posterior with the end of a towel wrung out in hot water, and as the smacking impact sounded the tiny toothless mouth opened and a thin, high, piping squall of protest sounded. "Ah, that is better, *mon petit ami,*" he chuckled. "One cannot learn too soon that one must do as one is told, not as one wishes, in this world which you have just entered. Look to him, *Mademoiselle,*" he passed the wriggling, bawling morsel of humanity to the nurse and turned to me as I bent over the table where Arabella lay. "How does the little mother, Friend Trowbridge?" he asked.

"U'm'mp," I answered noncommittally. "Bear a hand, here, will you? The perineum's pretty badly torn—have to do a quick repair job . . ."

"But in the morning she will have forgotten all the pain," laughed de Grandin as Arabella, swathed in blankets, was trundled from the delivery room. "She will gaze upon the little monkey-thing which I just caused to breathe the breath of life and vow it is the loveliest of all God's lovely creatures. She will hold it at her tender breast and smile on it, she will—*Sacré nom d'un rat vert,* what is that?"

From the nursery where, ensconced in wire trays, a score of newborn fragments of humanity slept or squalled, there came a sudden frightened scream—a woman's cry of terror.

We raced along the corridor, reached the glass-walled room and thrust the door back, taking care to open it no wider than was necessary, lest a draft disturb the carefully conditioned air of the place.

Backed against the farther wall, her face gone grey with fright, the nurse in charge was staring at the skylight with terror-widened eyes, and even as we entered she opened her lips to emit another scream.

"Desist, *ma bonne,* you are disturbing your small charges!" de Grandin seized the horrified girl's shoulder and administered a shake. Then: "What is it, *Mademoiselle?*" he whispered. "Do not be afraid to speak; we shall respect your confidence—but speak softly."

"It—it was up there!" she pointed with a shaking finger toward the black square of the skylight. "They'd just brought Baby Tantavul in, and I had laid him in his crib when I thought I heard somebody laughing. Oh"—she shuddered at the recollection—"it was awful! Not really a laugh, but something more like a long-drawn-out hysterical groan. Did you ever hear a child tickled to exhaustion—you know how he moans and gasps for breath, and laughs, all at once? I think the fiends in hell must laugh like that!"

"Yes, yes, we understand," de Grandin nodded, "but tell us what occurred next."

"I looked around the nursery, but I was all alone here with the babies. Then it came again, louder, this time, and seemingly right above me. I looked up at the skylight, and—there it was!

"It was a face, sir—just a face, with no body to it, and it seemed to float above the glass, then dip down to it, like a child's balloon drifting in the wind, and it looked right past me, down at Baby Tantavul, and laughed again."

"A face, you say, *Mademoiselle*—"

"Yes, sir, yes! The most awful face I've ever seen. It was thin and wrinkled—all shrivelled like a monkey—and as it looked at Baby Tantavul its eyes stretched open till their whites glared all around the irises, and the mouth opened, not widely, but as if it were chewing something it relished—and it gave that dreadful, cackling, jubilating laugh again. That's it! I couldn't think before, but it seemed as if that bodiless head were laughing with a sort of evil triumph, Dr. de Grandin!"

"H'm," he tweaked his tightly waxed mustache, "I should not wonder if it did, Mademoiselle," To me he whispered, "Stay with her, if you will, my friend, I'll see the supervisor and have her send another nurse to keep her company. I shall request a special watch for the small Tantavul. At present I do not think the danger is great, but—mice do not play where cats are wakeful."

"Isn't he just lovely?" Arabella looked up from the small bald head that rested on her breast, and ecstasy was in her eyes. "I don't believe I ever saw so beautiful a baby!"

"*Tiens*, Madame, his voice is excellent, at any rate," de Grandin answered with a grin, "and from what one may observe his appetite is excellent, at well."

Arabella smiled and patted the small creature's back. "You know, I never had a doll in my life," she confided. "Now I've got this dear little mite, and I'm going to be so happy with him. Oh, I wish Uncle Warburg were alive. I know this darling baby would soften even his hard heart.

"But I mustn't say such things about him, must I? He really wanted me to marry Dennis, didn't he? His will proved that. You think he wanted us to marry, Doctor?"

"I am persuaded that he did, Madame. Your marriage was his dearest wish, his fondest hope," the Frenchman answered solemnly.

"I felt that way, too. He was harsh and cruel to us when we were growing up, and kept his stony-hearted attitude to the end, but underneath it all there must have been some hidden stratum of kindness, some lingering affection for Dennis and me, or he'd never have put that clause in his will—"

"Nor have left this memorandum for you," de Grandin interrupted, drawing from an inner pocket the parchment envelope Dennis had entrusted to him the day before his father's funeral.

She started back as if he menaced her with a live scorpion, and instinctively her arms closed protectively around the baby at her bosom. "The—that—letter?" she faltered, her breath coming in short, smothered gasps. "I'd forgotten all about it. Oh, Dr. de Grandin, burn it. Don't let me see what's in it. I'm afraid!"

It was a bright May morning, without sufficient breeze to stir the leaflets on the maple trees outside the window, but as de Grandin held the letter out I thought I heard a sudden sweep of wind around the angle of the hospital, not loud, but shrewd and keen, like wind among the graveyard evergreens in autumn, and, curiously, there seemed a note of soft malicious laughter mingled with it.

The little Frenchman heard it, too, and for an instant he looked toward the window, and I thought I saw the flicker of an ugly sneer take form beneath the waxed ends of his mustache.

"Open it, *Madame*," he bade. "It is for you and Monsieur Dennis, and the little *Monsieur Bébé* here."

"I—I daren't—"

"*Tenez*, then Jules de Grandin does!" with his penknife he slit the heavy envelope, pressed suddenly against its ends so that its sides bulged, and dumped its contents on the counterpane. Ten fifty-dollar bills dropped on the coverlet. And nothing else.

346

"Five hundred dollars!" Arabella gasped. "Why—"

"A birthday gift for *petit Monsieur Bébé*, one surmises," laughed de Grandin. "*Eh bien*, the old one had a sense of humour underneath his ugly outward shell, it seems. He kept you on the tenterhooks lest the message in this envelope contained dire things, while all the time it was a present of congratulation."

"But such a gift from Uncle Warburg—I can't understand it!"

"Perhaps that is as well, too, *Madame*. Be happy in the gift and give your ancient uncle credit for at least one act of kindness. *Au 'voir.*"

"Hanged if I can understand it, either," I confessed as we left the hospital. "If that old curmudgeon had left a message berating them for fools for having offspring, or even a new will that disinherited them both, it would have been in character, but such a gift—well, I'm surprised."

Amazingly, he halted in midstep and laughed until the tears rolled down his face. "*You* are surprised!" he told me when he managed to regain his breath, "*Cordieu*, my friend, I do not drink that you are half as much surprised as Monsieur Warburg Tantavul!"

Dennis Tantavul regarded me with misery-haunted eyes. "I just can't understand it," he admitted. "It's all so sudden, so utterly—"

"*Pardonnez-moi*," de Grandin interrupted from the door of the consulting room, "I could not help but hear your voice, and if it is not an intrusion—"

"Not at all, sir," the young man answered. "I'd like the benefit of your advice. It's Arabella, and I'm terribly afraid she's—"

"*Non*, do not try it, *mon ami*," de Grandin warned. "Do you give us the symptoms, let us make the diagnosis. He who acts as his own doctor has a fool for a patient, you know."

"Well, then, here are the facts: This morning Arabella woke me up, crying as if her heart would break. I asked her what the trouble was, and she looked at me as if I were a stranger—no, not exactly that, rather as if I were some dreadful thing she'd suddenly found at her side. Her eyes were positively round with horror, and when I tried to take her in my arms to comfort her she shrank away as if I were infected with the plague.

"'Oh, Dennie, don't!' she begged and positively cringed away from me. Then she sprang out of bed and drew her kimono around her as if she were ashamed to have me see her in her pyjamas, and ran out of the room.

"Presently I heard her crying in the nursery, and when I followed her in there—" He paused and tears came to his eyes. "She was standing by the crib where little Dennis lay, and in her hand she held a long sharp steel letter-opener. 'Poor little mite, poor little flower of unpardonable sin,' she said. 'We've got to go, Baby darling; you to limbo, I to hell—oh, God wouldn't, *couldn't* be so cruel as to damn you for our sin!—but we'll all three suffer torment endlessly, because we didn't know!'

"She raised the knife to plunge it in the little fellow's heart, and he stretched out his hands and laughed and cooed as the sunlight shone on the steel. I was on her in an instant, wrenching the knife from her with one hand and holding her against me with the other, but she fought me off.

"'Don't touch me, Dennie, please, *please* don't,' she begged. I know it's mortal sin, but I love you so, my dear, that I just can't resist you if I let you put your arms about me.'

"I tried to kiss her, but she hid her face against my shoulder and moaned as if in pain when she felt my lips against her neck. Then she went limp in my arms, and I carried her, unconscious but still moaning piteously, into her sitting room and laid her on the couch. I left Sarah the nurse-maid with her, with strict orders not to let her leave the room. Can't you come over right away?"

De Grandin's cigarette had burned down till it threatened his mustache, and in his little round blue eyes there was a look of murderous rage. "*Bête!*" he murmured savagely. "*Sale chameau*, species of a stinking goat! This is his doing, undoubtedly. Come, my friends, let us rush, hasten, fly. I would talk with Madame Arabella."

"NAW, SUH, SHE'S DONE GONE," THE PORTLY COLORED NURSEMAID told us when we asked for Arabella. "Th' baby started squealin' sumpin awful right after Mistu Dennis lef', an' Ah knowed it wuz time fo' his breakfas', so Mis' Arabella wuz layin' nice an' still on the' sofa, an' Ah says ter her, Ah says, 'Yuh lay still dere, honey, whilst Ah goes an' sees after yo' baby;' so Ah goes ter th' nursery, an' fixes him all up, an' carries him back ter th' settin'-room where Mis' Arabella wuz, an' she ain't there no more. Naw, suh."

"I thought I told you—" Dennis began furiously, but de Grandin laid a hand upon his arm.

"Do not upbraid her, *mon ami*, she did wisely, though she knew it not; she was with the small one all the while, so no harm came to him. Was it not better so, after what you witnessed in the morning?"

"Ye-es," the other grudgingly admitted, "I suppose so. But Arabella—"

"Let us see if we can find a trace of her," the Frenchman interrupted. "Look carefully, do you miss any of her clothing?"

Dennis looked about the pretty chintz-hung room. "Yes," he decided as he finished his inspection, "her dress was on that lounge and her shoes and stockings on the floor beneath it. They're all gone."

"So," de Grandin nodded. "Distracted as she seemed, it is unlikely she would have stopped to dress had she not planned on going out. Friend Trowbridge, will you kindly call police headquarters and inform them of the situation? Ask to have all exits to the city watched."

As I picked up the telephone he and Dennis started on a room-by-room inspection of the house.

"Find anything?" I asked as I hung up the 'phone after talking with the missing persons bureau.

"*Corbleu*, but I should damn say yes!" de Grandin answered as I joined them in the upstairs living room. "Look yonder, if you please, my friend."

The room was obviously the intimate apartment of the house. Electric lamps under painted shades were placed beside deep leather-covered easy chairs, ivory-enamelled bookshelves lined the walls to a height of four feet or so, upon their tops was a litter of gay, unconsidered trifles—cinnabar cigarette boxes, bits of hammered brass. Old china, blue and red and purple, glowed mellowly from open spaces on the shelves, its colors catching up and accenting the muted blues and reds of antique Hamadan carpet. A Paisley shawl was draped scarfwise across the baby grand piano in one corner.

Directly opposite the door a carven crucifix was standing on the bookcase top. It was an exquisite bit of Italian work, the cross of ebony, the corpus of old ivory, and so perfectly executed that though it was a scant six inches high, one could note the tense, tortured muscles of the pendent body, the straining throat which overfilled with groans of agony, the brow all knotted and bedewed with the cold sweat of torment. Upon the statue's thorn-crowned head, where it made a bright iridescent halo, was a band of gem-encrusted platinum, a woman's diamond-studded wedding ring.

"*Hélas*, it is love's crucifixion!" whispered Jules de Grandin.

THREE MONTHS WENT BY, AND THOUGH THE SEARCH KEPT UP UNRE-mittingly, no trace of Arabella could be found. Dennis Tantavul installed a fulltime highly trained and recommended nurse in his desolate house, and spent his time haunting police stations and newspaper offices. He aged a decade in the ninety days since Arabella left; his shoulders stooped, his footsteps lagged, and a look of constant misery lay in his eyes. He was a prematurely old and broken man.

"It's the most uncanny thing I ever saw," I told de Grandin as we walked through West Forty-Second Street toward the West Shore Ferry. We had gone over to New York for some surgical supplies, and I do not drive my car in the metropolis. Truck drivers there are far too careless and repair bills for wrecked mudguards far too high. "How a full-grown woman would evaporate this way is something I can't understand. Of course, she may have done away with herself, dropped off a ferry, or—"

"S-s-st," his sibilated admonition cut me short. "That woman there, my friend, observe her, if you please." He nodded toward a female figure twenty feet or so ahead of us.

I looked, and wondered at his sudden interest at the draggled hussy. She was dressed in tawdry finery much the worse for wear. The sleazy silken skirt was much too tight, the cheap fur jaquette far too short and snug, and the high heels of her satin shoes were shockingly run over. Makeup was fairly plastered on her cheeks and lips and eyes, and short black hair bristled untidily beneath the brim of her abbreviated hat. Written unmistakably upon her was the nature of her calling, the oldest and least honorable profession known to womanhood.

"Well," I answered tartly, "what possible interest can you have in a—"

"Do not walk so fast," he whispered as his fingers closed upon my arm, "and do not raise your voice. I would that we should follow her, but I do not wish that she should know."

The neighborhood was far from savory, and I felt uncomfortably conspicuous as we turned from Forty-Second Street into Eleventh Avenue in the wake of the young strumpet, followed her provocatively swaying hips down two malodorous blocks, finally pausing as she slipped furtively into the doorway of a filthy, unkempt "rooming house."

We trailed her through a dimly lighted barren hall and up a flight of shadowy stairs, then up two further flights until we reached a sort of oblong foyer bounded on one end by the stair-well, on the farther extremity by a barred and very dirty window, and on each side by sagging, paint-blistered doors. On each of these was pinned a card, handwritten with the many flourishes dear to the chirography of the professional card-writer who still does business in the poorer quarters of our great cities. The air was heavy with the odor of cheap whisky, bacon rind and fried onions.

We made a hasty circuit of the hill, studying the cardboard labels. On the farthest door the notice read *Miss Sieglinde.*

"*Mon Dieu,*" he exclaimed as he read it, "*c'est le mot propre!*"

"Eh?" I returned.

"Sieglinde, do not you recall her?"

"No-o, can't say I do. The only Sieglinde I remember is the character in Wagner's *Die Walkure* who unwittingly became her brother's paramour and bore him a son—"

"*Précisément.* Let us enter, if you please." Without pausing to knock he turned the handle of the door and stepped into the squalid room.

The woman sat upon the unkempt bed, her hat pushed back from her brow. In one hand she held a cracked teacup, with the other she poised a whisky bottle over it. She had kicked her scuffed and broken shoes off; we saw that she was stockingless, and her bare feet were dark with long-accumulated dirt and black-nailed as a miner's hands. "Get out!" she ordered thickly. "Get out o' here, I ain't receivin'—" a gasp broke her utterance, and she turned her head away quickly. Then: "Get out o' here, you lousy bums!" she screamed. "Who d'ye think you are, breakin' into a lady's room like this? Get out, or—"

De Grandin eyed her steadily, and as her strident command wavered: "Madame Arabella, we have come to take you home," he announced softly.

"Good God, man, you're crazy" I exclaimed. "Arabella? This—"

"Precisely, my old one; this is Madame Arabella Tantavul whom we have sought these many months in vain." Crossing the room in two quick strides he seized the cringing woman by the shoulders and turned her face up to the light. I looked, and felt a sudden swift attack of nausea.

He was right. Thin to emaciation, her face already lined with the deep-bitten scars of evil living, the woman on the bed was Arabella Tantavul, though the shocking change wrought in her features and the black dye in her hair had disguised her so effectively that I should not have known her.

"We have come to take you home, *ma pauvre*," he repeated. "Your husband—"

"My husband!" her reply was half a scream. "Dear God, as if I had a husband—"

"And the little one who needs you," he continued. "You cannot leave them thus, Madame."

"I can't? Ah, that's where you're wrong, Doctor. I can never see my baby again, in this world or the next. Please go away and forget you've see me, or I shall have to drown myself—I've tried it twice already, but the first time I was rescued, and the second time my courage failed. But if you try to take me back, or if you tell Dennis you saw me—"

"Tell me, Madame," he broke in, "was not your flight caused by a visitation from the dead?"

Her faded brown eyes—eyes that had been such a startling contrast to her pale-gold hair—widened. "How did you know?" she whispered.

"*Tiens*, one may make surmises. Will not you tell us just what happened? I think there is a way out of your difficulties."

"No, no, there isn't; there can't be!" Her head drooped listlessly. "He planned his work too well; all that's left for me is death—and damnation afterward."

"But if there were a way—if I could show it to you?"

"Can you repeal the laws of God?"

"I am a very clever person, *Madame*. Perhaps I can accomplish an evasion, if not an absolute repeal. Now tell us, how and when did *Monsieur* your late but not at all lamented uncle come to you?"

"The night before—before I went away. I woke about midnight, thinking I heard a cry from Dennie's nursery. When I reached the room where he was sleeping I saw my uncle's face glaring at me through the window. It seemed to be illuminated by a sort of inward hellish light, for it stood out against the darkness like a jack-o'-lantern, and it smiled an awful smile at me. 'Arabella,' it said, and I could see its dun dead lips writhe back as if the teeth were burning-hot, 'I've come to tell you that your marriage is a mockery and a lie. The man you married is your brother, and the child you bore is doubly illegitimate. You can't continue living with them, Arabella. That would be an even greater sin. You must leave them right away, or'—Once more his lips crept back until his teeth were bare—'or I shall come to visit you each night, and when the baby has grown old enough to understand I'll tell him who his parents really are. Take your choice, my daughter. Leave them and let me go back to the grave, or stay and see me every night and know that I will tell your son when he is old enough to understand. If I do it he will loathe and hate you; curse the day you bore him.'

"'And you'll promise never to come near Dennis or the baby if I go?' I asked.

"He promised, and I staggered back to bed, where I fell fainting.

"Next morning when I wakened I was sure it had been a bad dream, but when I looked at Dennis and my own reflection in the glass I knew it was no dream, but a dreadful visitation from the dead.

"Then I went mad. I tried to kill my baby, and when Dennis stopped me I watched my chance to run away, came over to New York and took to this." She looked significantly around the miserable room. "I knew they'd never look for Arabella Tantavul among the city's whores; I was safer from pursuit right here than if I'd been in Europe or China."

"But, *Madame*," de Grandin's voice was jubilant with shocked reproof, "that which you saw was nothing but a dream; a most unpleasant dream, I grant, but still a dream. Look in my eyes, if you please!"

She raised her eyes to his, and I saw his pupils widen as a cat's do in the dark, saw a line of white outline the cornea, and, responsive to his piercing gaze, beheld her brown eyes set in a fixed stare, first as if in fright, then with a glaze almost like that of death.

"Attend me, Madame Arabella," he commanded softly. "You are tired— *grand Dieu*, how tired you are! You have suffered greatly, but you are about

353

to rest. Your memory of that night is gone; so is all memory of the things which have transpired since. You will move and eat and sleep as you are bidden, but of what takes place around you till I bid you wake you will retain no recollection. Do you hear me, Madame Arabella?"

"I hear," she answered softly in a small tired voice.

"*Très bon.* Lie down, my little poor one. Lie down to rest and dreams of love. Sleep, rest, dream and forget.

"Will you be good enough to 'phone to Dr. Wyckoff?" he asked me. "We shall place her in his sanitarium, wash this *sacré* dye from her hair and nurse her back to health; then when all is ready we can bear her home and have her take up life and love where she left off. No one shall be the wiser. This chapter of her life is closed and sealed for ever.

"Each day I'll call upon her and renew hypnotic treatments that she may simulate the mild but curable mental case which we shall tell the good Wyckoff she is. When finally I release her from hypnosis her mind will be entirely cleared of that bad dream that nearly wrecked her happiness."

Arabella Tantavul lay on the sofa in her charming boudoir, an orchid negligee about her slender shoulders, an eiderdown rug tucked round her feet and knees. Her wedding ring was once more on her finger. Pale with a pallor not to be disguised by the most skillfully applied cosmetics, and with deep violet crescents underneath her amber eyes, she lay back listlessly, drinking in the cheerful warmth that emanated from the fire of apple-logs that snapped and crackled on the hearth. Two months of rest at Dr. Wyckoff's sanitarium had cleansed the marks of dissipation from her face, and the ministrations of beauticians had restored the pale-gold luster to her hair, but the listlessness that followed her complete breakdown was still upon her like the weakness from a fever.

"I can't remember anything about my illness, Dr. Trowbridge," she told me with a weary little smile, "but vaguely I connect it with some dreadful dream I had. And"—she wrinkled her smooth forehead in an effort at remembering—"I think I had a rather dreadful dream last night, but—"

"Ah-*ha*?" de Grandin leant abruptly forward in his chair. "What was it that you dreamed, Madame?"

"I—don't—know," she answered slowly. "Odd, isn't it, how you can remember that a dream was so unpleasant, yet not recall its details? Somehow, I connect it with Uncle Warburg; but—"

"*Parbleu*, do you say so? Has he returned? *Ah hah*, he makes me to be so mad, that one!"

"It is time we went, my friend," de Grandin told me as the tall clock in the hall beat out its tenth deliberate stroke; "we have important duties to perform."

"For goodness' sake," I protested, "at this hour o' night?"

"Precisely. At Monsieur Tantavul's I shall expect a visitor tonight, and—we must be ready for him.

"Is Madame Arabella sleeping?" he asked Dennis as he answered our ring at the door.

"Like a baby," answered the young husband. "I've been sitting by her all evening, and I don't believe she even turned in bed."

"And you did keep the window closed, as I requested?"

"Yes, sir; closed and latched."

"*Bien*. Await us here, *mon brave*; we shall rejoin you presently."

He led the way to Arabella's bedroom, removed the wrappings from a bulky parcel he had lugged from our house, and displayed the object thus disclosed with an air of inordinate pride. "Behold him," he commanded gleefully. "Is he not magnificent?"

"Why—what the devil?—it's nothing but an ordinary window screen," I answered.

"A window screen, I grant, my friend; but not an ordinary one. Can not you see it is of copper?"

"Well—"

"*Parbleu*, but I should say it is well," he grinned. "Observe him, how he works."

From his kit bag he produced a roll of insulated wire, an electrical transformer, and some tools. Working quickly he passe-partouted the screen's wooden frame with electrician's tape, then plugged a wire in a nearby lamp socket, connected it with the transformer, and from the latter led a double strand of cotton-wrapped wire to the screen. This he clipped firmly to the copper meshes and led a third strand to the metal grille of the heat register. Last of all he filled a bulb-syringe with water and sprayed the screen, repeating the performance till it sparkled like a cobweb in the morning sun. "And now, *Monsieur le Revenant*," he chuckled as he finished, "I damn think all is ready for your warm reception!"

For something like an hour we waited, then he tiptoed to the bed and bent above Arabella.

"Madame!"

The girl stirred slightly, murmuring some half-audible response, and:

"In half an hour you will rise," he told her. "You will put your robe on and stand by the window, but on no account will you go near it or lay hands on it. Should anyone address you from outside you will reply, but you will not remember what you say or what is said to you."

He motioned me to follow, and we left the room, taking station in the hallway just outside.

HOW LONG WE WAITED I HAVE NO ACCURATE IDEA. PERHAPS IT WAS an hour, perhaps less; at any rate the silent vigil seemed unending, and I raised my hand to stifle back a yawn when:

"Yes, Uncle Warburg, I can hear you," we heard Arabella saying softly in the room beyond the door.

We tiptoed to the entry: Arabella stood before the window, and from beyond it glared the face of Warburg Tantavul.

It was dead, there was no doubt about that. In sunken cheek and pinched-in nose and yellowish-grey skin there showed the evidence of death and early putrefaction, but dead through it was, it was also animated with a dreadful sort of life. The eyes were glaring horribly, the lips were red as though they had been painted with fresh blood.

"You hear me, do you?" it demanded. "Then listen, girl; you broke your bargain with me, now I'm come to keep my threat: every time you kiss your husband"—a shriek of bitter laughter cut his words, and his staring eyes half closed with hellish merriment—"or the child you love so well, my shadow will be on you. You've kept me out thus far, but some night I'll get in, and—"

The lean dead jaw dropped, then snapped up as if lifted by sheer will-power, and the whole expression of the corpse-face changed. Surprise, incredulous delight, anticipation as before a feast were pictured on it. "Why"—its cachinnating laughter sent a chill up my spine—"why your window's open! You've changed the screen and I can enter!"

Slowly, like a child's balloon stirred by a vagrant wind, the awful thing moved closer to the window. Closer to the screen it came, and Arabella gave ground before it and put up her hands to shield her eyes from the sight of its hellish grin of triumph.

"*Sapristi*," swore de Grandin softly. "Come on, my old and evil one, come but a little nearer—"

The dead thing floated nearer. Now its mocking mouth and shriveled, pointed nose were almost pressed against the copper meshes of the screen; now they began to filter through the meshes like a wisp of fog—

There was a blinding flash of blue-white flame, the sputtering gush of fusing metal, a wild, despairing shriek that ended ere it fairly started in a sob of mortal torment, and the sharp and acrid odor of burned flesh!

"Arabella—darling—is she all right?" Dennis Tantavul came charging up the stairs. "I thought I heard a scream—"

"You did, my friend," de Grandin answered, "but I do not think that you will hear its repetition unless you are unfortunate enough to go to hell when you have died."

"What was it?"

"*Eh bien*, one who thought himself a clever jester pressed his jest too far. Meantime, look to *Madame* your wife. See how peacefully she lies upon her bed. Her time for evil dreams is past. Be kind to her, *mon jeune*. Do not forget, a woman loves to have a lover, even though he is her husband." He bent and kissed the sleeping girl upon the brow. "*Au 'voir*, my little lovely one," he murmured. Then, to me:

"Come, Trowbridge, my good friend. Our work is finished here. Let us leave them to their happiness."

AN HOUR LATER IN THE STUDY HE FACED ME ACROSS THE FIRE. "Perhaps you'll deign to tell me what it's all about now?" I asked sarcastically.

"Perhaps I shall," he answered with a grin. "You will recall that this annoying Monsieur Who Was Dead Yet Not Dead, appeared and grinned most horrifyingly through windows several times? Always from the outside, please remember. At the hospital, where he nearly caused the *garde-malade* to have a fit, he laughed and mouthed at her through the glass skylight. When he first appeared and threatened Madame Arabella he spoke to her through the window—"

"But her window was open," I protested.

"Yes, but screened," he answered with a smile. "Screened with iron wire, if you please."

"What difference did that make? Tonight I saw him almost force his features through—"

"A copper screen," he supplied. "Tonight the screen was copper; me, I saw to that."

Then, seeing my bewilderment: "Iron is the most earthy of all metals," he explained. "It and its derivative, steel, are so instinct with the earth's essence that creatures of the spirit cannot stand its nearness. The legends tell us that when Solomon's Temple was constructed no tool of iron was employed, because even the friendly *jinn* whose help he had enlisted could not perform their tasks in close proximity to iron. The witch can be detected by the pricking of an iron pin—never by a pin of brass.

"Very well. When first I thought about the evil dead one's reappearances I noted that each time he stared outside the window. Glass, apparently, he could not pass—and glass contains a modicum of iron. Iron window-wire stopped him. 'He are not a true ghost, then,' I inform me. 'They are things of spirit only, they are thoughts made manifest. This one is a thing of hate, but also of some physical material as well; he is composed in part of emanations from the body which lies putrefying in the grave. *Voilà*, if he have physical properties he can be destroyed by physical means.'

"And so I set my trap. I procured a screen of copper through which he could effect an entrance, but I charged it with electricity. I increased the potential of the current with a step-up transformer to make assurance doubly sure, and then I waited for him like the spider for the fly, waited for him to come through that charged screen and electrocute himself. Yes, certainly."

"But is he really destroyed?" I asked dubiously.

"As the candle-flame when one has blown it out. He was—how do you say it?—short-circuited. No malefactor in the chair of execution ever died more thoroughly than that one, I assure you."

"It seems queer, though, that he should come back from the grave to haunt those poor kids and break up their marriage when he really wanted it," I murmured wonderingly.

"Wanted it? Yes, as the trapper wants the bird to step within his snare."

"But he gave them such a handsome present when little Dennis was born—"

"*La, la,* my good, kind, trusting friend, you are *naïf.* The money I gave Madame Arabella was my own. I put it in that envelope."

"Then what was the real message?"

"It was a dreadful thing, my friend; a dreadful, wicked thing. The night that Monsieur Dennis left that package with me I determined that the old one meant to do him in, so I steamed the cover open and read what lay within. It made plain the things which Dennis thought that he remembered.

"Long, long ago Monsieur Tantavul lived in San Francisco. His wife was twenty years his junior, and a pretty, joyous thing she was. She bore him two fine children, a boy and girl, and on them she bestowed the love which he could not appreciate. His surliness, his evil temper, his constant fault-finding drove her to distraction, and finally she sued for divorce.

"But he forestalled her. He spirited the children away, then told his wife the plan of his revenge. He would take them to some far off place and bring them up believing they were cousins. Then when they had attained full growth he would induce them to marry and keep the secret of their relationship until they had a child, then break the dreadful truth to them. Thereafter they would live on, bound together by their fear of censure, or perhaps of criminal prosecution, but their consciences would cause them endless torment, and the very love they had for each other would be like fetters forged of white-hot steel, holding them in odious bondage from which there was no escape. The sight of their children would be a reproach to them, the mere thought of love's sweet communion would cause revulsion to the point of nausea.

"When he had told her this his wife went mad. He thrust her into an asylum and left her there to die while he came with his babies to New Jersey, where he reared them together, and by guile and craftiness nurtured their love, knowing that when finally they married he would have his so vile revenge."

"But, great heavens, man, they're brother and sister!" I exclaimed in horror.

"Perfectly," he answered coolly. "They are also man and woman, husband and wife, and father and mother."

"But—but—" I stammered, utterly at loss for words.

"But me no buts, good friend. I know what you would say. Their child? *Ah bah*, did not the kings of ancient times repeatedly take their own sisters to wife, and were not their offspring sound and healthy? But certainly. Did not both Darwin and Wallace fail to find foundation for the doctrine that cross-breeding between healthy people with clean blood is productive of inferior progeny? Look at little Monsieur Dennis. Were you not blinded by your silly, unrealistic training and tradition—did you not know his parents' near relationship—you would not hesitate to pronounce him an unusually fine, healthy child.

"Besides," he added earnestly, "they love each other, not as brother and sister, but as man and woman. He is her happiness, she is his, and little Monsieur Dennis is the happiness of both. Why destroy this joy—*le bon Dieu* knows they earned it by a joyless childhood—when I can preserve it for them by simply keeping silent?"

THE SOLDIER

A. M. BURRAGE

Today, Alfred McLelland Burrage (1889–1956) is remembered solely for his ghost stories, which included some of the best of his day. But he was so prolific that at the time he was just as well remembered for his many lighthearted school stories, much in the vein of Frank Richards, and his historical adventures. Many of his best ghost stories were collected as Some Ghost Stories *(1927) and* Someone in the Room *(1931), the latter under the byline Ex-Private X, an alias he had created for his book of wartime reminiscences* War is War *(1930). Burrage was so prolific that many more ghost stories appeared in magazines that were collected posthumously, including his series about ghost hunter Francis Chard. Chard wasn't Burrage's first such attempt. He had written two stories featuring the rather athletic Derek Scarpe for* The Novel Magazine *in 1920, but the series ended abruptly, perhaps through editorial stricture or because Burrage changed his mind about the character. When he returned to the genre his new detective, Francis Chard, is in the more traditional role with his consulting room and a chronicler in the form of Mr. Torrance. There were ten stories featuring Chard, an unusual number when most magazines liked to run series in sets of six, to fit in with a six-monthly bound volume. This suggests that Burrage had written twelve, but the first two featured Scarpe and then he revised everything and changed the character to Chard. Though why it took him seven years to complete the series, which was serialized in* The Blue Magazine *in 1927, is beyond me.*

Burrage came from a writing family. Both his father and uncle were prolific writers of stories for boys, and young Alfred soon followed in their footsteps selling his first stories when he was fifteen. His writing was so prolific that one barely noticed the gap in his output during the war. He was enlisted in the Artists Rifles in early 1917 and fought at Passchendaele in October 1917, being finally invalided out with trench foot in April 1918. The following story with its wartime connections is especially pertinent.

WHEN MR. LIONEL DANSON RETIRED FROM HIS ACTIVITIES IN THE City, he bought the attractive little property called Vailings, which is situated on the south side of Minthaven. Minthaven stands on the Hampshire coast and looks across at the Needles, over the western entrance to the Solent. Mr. Danson liked ships, and he was gratified by the spectacle of giant liners on their way to and from Southampton. These were visible from any of the upper windows on the south side of the house, and in order to have a more perfect view Mr. Danson purchased a powerful telescope.

The house called Vailings was a converted farmhouse, with some seven acres of land attached to it. It stood beside the road leading straight down to the sea, and the first of the few buildings between Mr. Danson's residence and the shingle beach was his own gardener's cottage, which stood about a hundred yards up the road and at the end of his own garden.

Mr. Danson kept two indoor servants, and he also required a gardener whose wife could do some of the family washing and assist with some of the rough housework. A suitable couple named Wratham was discovered in Lymington, and they were promptly engaged and installed in the cottage.

The Wrathams were not Hampshire people. Indeed, they seemed to have been in most parts of the country since the war, but despite the number of their situations their references were all excellent. Mrs. Wratham was white and neurotic and not very strong, but otherwise they were a perfect couple for Mr. Danson's needs.

Mr. Danson had been comfortably settled in his new home some three months, and was preparing for bed one night, when he heard loud blasts from a siren. Looking out of his window he beheld the dark shape, gemmed with a thousand lights, of a great liner, homeward bound, gliding up the Solent. It happened to be a perfect moonlight night, so Mr. Danson reached immediately for his telescope.

It was a large glass and clumsy to handle, and Mr. Danson had not yet acquired skill in focussing an object quickly. Thus the road in front of the gardener's cottage was brought, it seemed, within a yard of his eyes, so that he could have counted every pebble. And then, as he shifted the focus, he saw something which caused him to forget all about the liner.

He kept vigil for part of the next three nights, and what he saw at close quarters and with his naked eyes sent him to town to see Francis Chard. I was with Chard at the time and heard his story.

Lionel Danson was a short, stoutish man in the fifties and belonged to the happy type, which normally lives well and worries about nothing. He gave me the impression of being a good fellow, and at ordinary times, I daresay he would have been the best of company. But just now he was pale and worried, for sufficiently good reasons. Let me tell in his own words what he saw through the telescope.

"I wasn't astonished, for the first moment or two, when I saw that the man was a soldier. Two or three families in the village have sons in the Army who come home on furlough. But I certainly wondered why he was wearing a shrapnel helmet and what he could want with the Wrathams. Then I must have given the screw some slight adjustment, and every ghastly detail of him blazed upon my eyes. Remember it was bright moonlight, and the telescope seemed to bring him within a yard of me. I saw a small roadside weed at his feet shivering in the night air."

Danson paused. It was as if he could not bring himself to come straight to the gist of what he had to tell us.

"The gardener's cottage," he continued, "stands flush with the road. There is no garden in front and no path. As the road leads straight to the sea, it carries very little traffic, and I suppose a path would be superfluous. Well, he—it was standing before the door of the cottage and seemed to be knocking at it."

He broke off abruptly, and Chard said, "Perhaps you had better have a whiskey and soda?"

Danson smiled weakly.

"Thanks. Perhaps I had, if you don't mind. You'll think I'm an idiot, I know, but you'll remember that I saw him afterwards as close as I am to you."

He drank the contents of the tumbler, which Chard presently brought him, at a single gulp. Then he resumed.

"He was a big fellow. I couldn't guess his age, because the face I saw in profile was the grey face of a corpse. His left side was turned to me, and he knocked on the door with his right hand. He could not have knocked with the left because he had none. The sleeve hung down, ragged and empty, and I saw a slow, steady drip of blood.

"His stained and faded khaki tunic was slightly powdered with some-thing that looked like snow, and blackened with something that looked like soot. He was wearing leather equipment, but he was not in full kit. His bayonet scabbard was empty, and his haversack, instead of hang-ing over it, was on his back in place of a pack, with something rolled up underneath it."

Chard nodded. "That would be a ground-sheet," he said. "He was in what we used to call 'battle order.'"

"I can remember all these details perfectly," Danson continued, "because his appearance was such a shock to me that a complete picture of him immediately impressed itself on my mind."

"The more details the better," said Chard. "You couldn't by any chance see his numerals? I mean, what regiment did he belong to?"

"I don't know. But on his shoulder was a narrow strip of faded yellow ribbon, and underneath it, on the top of his sleeve, was a little red square, but inverted so that its angles pointed up and down and left and right. There was no mud on his boots and putties, but they looked wet. He had no rifle with him.

"The telescope shook so in my hands that I kept missing him, but I must have watched him off and on for several minutes. Not once did he move from his position, but stood there staring at an upper window and beating upon the door with his one fist. And suddenly he went—I don't know where. Just for a fraction of a second my unsteadiness of hand caused me to miss him with the telescope, and when I focussed it once more on the spot he was gone. There was only the empty road, and the same roadside weeds fluttering in the breeze.

"Well, Mr. Chard, I went to bed feeling like nothing else on earth, and when I woke up in broad sunlight I tried to persuade myself that I'd dreamed or imagined the whole beastly business. But I knew I hadn't. I knew I had seen something which is commonly called a ghost, and I knew that it must have been the ghost of a soldier killed in the late war. I said nothing to my wife or to the Wrathams, but I started making inquiries in the village. Jokingly asked if there were a local ghost, you know, but nobody had heard of one. And then, beginning elsewhere, I asked who had been living in my cottage during the war. That was easily discovered. The couple are still in the village. They have three grown-up daughters, all married, but they never had a son; nor do they seem to have lost anyone very near and dear to them.

"The only thing to do, to satisfy myself—although I hated the idea— was to sit up and see if It came again. To cut my story as short as possible, It missed two nights. Then on the third night I focussed It once more in exactly the same spot, beating upon the door as before.

"I was ready and fully dressed, so I crept downstairs and out, and up the road. It was still there, facing the door, with Its back to the road. The blows on the door made only a faint muffled throbbing, which perhaps explained why the Wrathams did not hear and come down, to be confronted by the awful Thing which wanted to enter. I passed behind It with my heart thumping like an engine, went on up the road, and waited until I felt steadier. Then I turned and forced myself to go back, and for the first time I saw It from the other side.

"Mr. Chard, I went right up to him and asked him what he wanted. Yes, I managed to do that. But the side on which I approached him was worse than the other. The breast of his tunic was blackened all over, and there was a great ragged hole in it. He took no notice of me. He did not even turn to look at me. But in that indescribable moment I felt myself fainting and reeling forward against that terrible Presence. I must have clutched at It to save myself, but I don't know if I touched anything. When I came to, I found myself lying face downwards on the road, and mercifully, alone.

"So now you will have guessed the cause of my visit. From what I have heard you would seem to be the only man able and willing to help me. I want to find rest for that poor soul who gave his body for his country, and I want to rid the neighbourhood of his terrifying presence. I don't know whether to tell the Wrathams or not. I would risk their thinking me a lunatic if it would do any good to tell them. The question is, whether it would be kinder to let them know and keep them in a state of apprehension or let them suddenly discover the horror for themselves." Chard considered, and glanced at me.

"That," he said, "is a point which we can decide later."

Danson's pale face brightened a little.

"You mean," he cried eagerly, "that you will come down and help me."

"Certainly," Chard replied. "We both will. Today if you like.

And so it befell that we accompanied Danson back to Hampshire, but before we started Chard and I had a private talk.

"Here's a very curious case," Chard commented, "pre-supposing that our friend Danson isn't a liar or a lunatic. Here's a soldier, evidently killed in the late war, haunting the outside of a cottage with which he apparently had no connection in life. What do you make of him so far, Torrance?"

"He was evidently killed by a shell," I said, "and probably his rifle was blown out of his hands at the same time. The black stuff on him must have been explosive, but I can't account for the white stuff unless it were snow."

"But what do you make of that yellow strip on his shoulder and the red patch on top of his sleeve?"

"I'm coming to that," I answered, "and it's rather a coincidence that I should know. I believe the yellow slip indicates that he belonged to the Fourth—shires, who were in the 190th Brigade attached to the Naval Division. In that case the red patch would mean that he was in 'A' Company. I happen to know, because my brother was a second loot in that very company, and was wearing the same strips and patches when I ran across him near Bapaume. Perhaps, if I write, he'll be able to help us.

"Perhaps he will," Chard agreed, "when we get a little more data. Did he ever do any fighting in the snow, do you know?"

"Almost certain, I should think. There was plenty of snow about during both the winters he was out there. I'm glad I remembered his yellow strips and red patches. It's about the first time I've been able to give you any material help, Chard."

We met Danson at Waterloo in the afternoon and caught a good train to Brockenhurst, where his car was garaged. He drove us the ten miles over a corner of the New Forest, through the western outskirts of Lymington, and down into Minthaven, which is at the head of a spear of dry land striking through marshes to the sea.

It was not a typical old-world seaside village. There was little to see, and nothing to interest the archaeologist: no crazy, dilapidated cottages leaning over cobbled streets in an odour of fish, tar and hemp. The place was open and scattered and wind-swept, and most of the buildings which took the eye were comparatively modern, but it had a charm of its own.

Mrs. Danson received us delightfully. The reason for our visit had been kept from her, and she took us to be friends of her husband and connected in some vague way with that mysterious thing called business. Danson showed us over the house and pointed out Mrs. Wratham, who was helping in the kitchen. The house being old—the oldest in Minthaven—was sufficient excuse for our being shown into every room from attic to cellar.

We both glanced at her curiously. She was a woman in the early thirties, but her hair was already streaked with grey. She looked wan and worried, and moved about with an air of lassitude. She gave me the impression of being literally tired of life.

Danson took us to the window of his room from which he had first seen the apparition. The road ran by on our right on the flank of Danson's long garden, with a low hedge between. Beyond the hedge stood the Wrathams' cottage, and Danson let us see, by lending us the telescope, how plainly he must have seen that which stood outside the door.

While Chard was looking through the telescope, the door of the cottage actually opened, and a short, thick-set man of about forty, emerged.

"That's Wratham," said Danson, and Chard involuntarily craned a little forward.

The man did not look in the direction of the house, but turned and slouched away in the direction of the sea. Chard laid aside the glass.

"Where's he off to?" my friend inquired. "I'd like to have a word with him."

"Well, he knocked off work about an hour ago, and I suppose by this time he's had his tea, and is off to drink a pint of beer at the *Cannon*."'

"That, I suppose, is the village pub," said Chard. "There's only the one road, so we can't miss it. Mind if we go down and have a word with him?"

"Just as you like," Danson replied, good-humouredly; and Chard and I got our hats and sallied forth.

The Cannon Inn was about a quarter of a mile distant and within two hundred yards of the sea. We walked into the sand-strewn tap-room, where half-a-dozen working men were gathered around the shove-ha'penny board in the window. Wratham was easily identified. He stood aloft at a corner of the counter, with a pint glass of brown ale half empty at his elbow. He looked surly and moody, his eyes were red-rimmed and there was a droop to his mouth. Chard ordered drinks for everybody in the room.

The group around the shove-ha'penny board split up as the men came shyly up to the counter to take the hastily filled glasses. Chard selected a youngish fair-haired, good-looking fellow and tapped him on the chest.

"Hullo!" he exclaimed. "Weren't you with me in the Fourth—shires?"

The other grinned and shook his head.

"No, zur. I was in the Artillery."

"Well, then, you've got a double, or, rather, you had one. I thought for a moment I'd seen a ghost. Anybody here believe in ghosts?"

He looked around the room and laughed, and everybody laughed too except Wratham. He glowered, finished his beer, wiped his mouth on the back of his hand, and stared defiantly at Chard.

"Lot o' rot!" he grunted, and slouched out.

The other men were quick to apologise for his manners.

"He don't belong here, sir, and the quicker he be gone the better." Chard laughed it off, and I could see that something had given him perfect satisfaction.

On the way back he said to me, "The Wrathams *know*. I'm convinced of that. And the mere fact that they know and haven't said a word is enough for me. I think one short talk with that woman will clear up everything. But we may as well see the apparition if we can—to satisfy ourselves, you know."

We could not use the window of Danson's room that night without arousing the curiosity of his wife, who slept next door; but overhead was an untenanted attic, and we kept watch at the window there with Danson's telescope.

It was a long vigil. Not until nearly half-past two did Chard's pose suddenly become rigid, and I heard him draw a quick, harsh breath as if he had been touched by sudden cold. He remained quite still for nearly a minute; then, without a word, he passed the glass to me, and I focussed the road just in front of the Wratham's cottage door.

I need not describe what I saw. That has been done already in Danson's words, and I have nothing to add. I had seen sights like that on the battlefield, but never broken men standing upright as this apparition of a broken man was standing. I did not look at it very long.

"You're not going—up the road, are you?" I asked falteringly, of Chard.

"I don't see the need," Chard replied, with a catch in his voice.

Neither did I.

On the following morning, soon after Wratham had started work in Danson's garden, Chard and I walked up to the cottage and knocked. Mrs. Wratham opened the door to us.

"We want to speak to you, Mrs. Wratham," Chard said solemnly.

The little white-faced woman stared at us in mingled curiosity and alarm. But she asked us in, and we followed her into the little kitchen where clothes were airing in front of the range.

"Mrs. Wratham," said Chard very quietly, "who is the soldier who comes and knocks upon your door—the poor, dead, mangled soldier?"

For answer she uttered a faint scream and clapped her hands to her eyes. In a moment I saw the tears running down under her palms.

"Don't be afraid," said Chard gently, "it would be better for you to tell us." She calmed herself and faced us half defiantly.

"He is a ghost," she said. "There are such things as ghosts, you know."

"I know. I know. But tell us who he was."

"He was my first husband," she answered, drying her eyes and beginning to talk in a dreary monotone. "So he's found us out and followed us here? I knew he would. He's followed us everywhere. Isn't there any peace for the sinful—even in this world?

369

"His name was Martin, and he was in the—shires. I married him when he was home on leave. I was only a girl then. And he went back to the trenches and left me, and I was lonely. It seemed to me when he was gone that I hadn't loved him like I thought I had. And then Wratham came along.

"Wratham was a cattle man on a farm, so they didn't make him go and fight. He spent his nights in my cottage, and nobody knew. I meant to marry him if anything happened to Tom. There'd been heavy fighting all round Cambrai" (she pronounced it Cambria), "where Tom was, but he seemed to have come through it safe.

"And then one night at the end of 1917—it was the night before New Year's Eve—Wratham woke me up and said as there was somebody knocking at the door. A quiet, muffled sound it was. And we was frightened that he'd come home on leave, so it was me that had to go down. And it was Tom Martin sure enough, but not as I'd ever seen him before, all bloody and grimed with his eyes full of sorrow and anger. And I knew 'twas his spirit and that he'd just been killed, and I gave one loud cry and fainted.

"Since then he's never let us alone for long, although we've moved here, there, and everywhere. Wratham's clever at lots of things, and he can get work anywhere. But as soon as we're settled in a place Tom Martin finds us out and comes knocking at our door of a night, and we have to move on somewhere else. We've had no peace for eight years, and the terror of it is wearing me to skin and bone. Once we got a clergyman to come and pray, but it didn't do no good. The only way for us is to end it all, and I think it will come to that at last."

And, rather to my surprise, Chard had no comfort to offer her.

"I thought from the beginning," he said to me as we walked back, "that the Wrathams might be responsible for the phenomena. You see, nothing had been seen until they took over the cottage. And when I saw them I knew that they knew, and I wondered why they hadn't told. The fact that nobody in the village had belonged to the—er—the dead man's regiment made me quite certain. There's only one thing for friend Danson to do, and that is to get rid of the Wrathams."

"Poor devils!" I exclaimed. "Can't anything be done for them?"

Chard shrugged his shoulders.

"I don't know what," he said. "This isn't a case of a haunted house—it's a case of a haunted couple. It might be dangerous to try to interfere. We've got to pay for our sins—in some way or another, you know."

I shuddered. A few minutes since it had been a warm, sunny morning, but now the wind seemed very cold.

A week later I had an answer to the letter which I presently addressed to my brother. Here is an extract:

Yes, I remember Tom Martin very well, probably because he was always panicking for leave because he suspected that his wife wasn't being faithful to him. Of course, we couldn't even send the application up to Brigade. There was too much of that sort of thing, and besides the man seemed to have no real grounds for his suspicion.

I shan't forget the morning when he was killed. It was on December the thirtieth, and there'd been snow on the ground for weeks. Everything had been suspiciously quiet for a long time, and on that morning Jerry came over in the snow, camouflaged in white smocks, and pinched part of our front line on Welsh Ridge without a shot being fired. We were in support at the time and the first we knew of it was the barrage he put over to try to stop us from counter-attacking. Of course, we had to go up and dig him out, and the communication trench (called Central Avenue) was one of the warmest places through which I ever passed. That was where Martin was killed. A whizz-bang dropped on top of the traverse right in front of him, and the ground being iron-hard, he hadn't a chance. I remember writing a letter of condolence to his wife, and wondering all the while if there was anything in the poor chap's suspicions.

"That," said Chard grimly, "is a matter on which you can assuage his curiosity—at your own discretion."

THE HORROR OF
THE HEIGHT

SYDNEY HORLER

Sydney Harry Horler (1888–1954) was the son of a varnish maker in Leyton, Essex. The family moved back to his father's native Somerset where, after his education, and a brief spell as a teacher, young Horler became a journalist on local papers before moving first to Manchester and then London, where he worked for the Daily Mail. *He also wrote propaganda for Air Intelligence during the First World War at which time he also turned to fiction. Initially he wrote mostly stories featuring football heroes but after the war, when sales of crime novels mushroomed, he switched to crime fiction and became extremely popular. His crime books, which began with* The Mystery of No. 1 *in 1925, the first of his Paul Vivanti series, were imitative of Edgar Wallace and Sapper, but were even more sensationalistic and lacked any depth. Amongst his best known novels were the series featuring Tiger Standish of British Intelligence which began with* Tiger Standish *in 1932 and ran for eleven books. At the time he was reckoned amongst Britain's bestselling crime writers, but his works have long fallen out of favour, partly because of their superficiality, but also their political incorrectness and formulaic plots. Yet, despite that, from time to time he brought more definition to his work and that is the case with his stories featuring Sebastian Quin. Not all are supernatural, but in the following, sometimes reprinted as "Black Magic," Quin displays his enthusiasm of "the Bizarre," as his chronicler Martin Huish remarks. Quin later returned in the novels* The Evil Messenger *(1938) and* Fear Walked Behind *(1942).*

"MY FRIEND AND ASSISTANT, MR. MARTIN HUISH," ANNOUNCED Sebastian Quin.

I acknowledged the introduction by bowing to the girl who sat in the client's chair in Quin's consulting-room. She was about twenty-four, I judged, tastefully dressed and normally very pretty. I say normally, because Violet Loring's face was now tortured by a look of restrained horror, which went straight to my heart.

"Miss Loring has come to us in great—very great—trouble," explained Quin. "She was about to tell me her story when you came in."

He looked encouragingly at the girl, whose hands were locked. Quite obviously, she had to brace herself before she could start on her narrative.

"What I am going to tell you, Mr. Quin, may sound so fantastic, so utterly preposterous, that you will have difficulty, perhaps, in believing I am sane." She stopped, unable for a minute to go on.

"I may say I have listened to many strange statements in my time, Miss Loring; and my experience of life is that the fantastic is usually the likeliest thing to happen—given certain conditions."

The tone was grave but encouraging. Sebastian Quin, his thin, almost cadaverous, face thrust forward, was an impressive figure in that moment. His critics, whose scoffings were in every case occasioned by bitter jealousy, might say that he looked more like a jockey than a crime investigator, but the visitor evidently derived satisfaction from his manner.

"I live at Trevelyn, in Cornwall," she continued, gaining courage. "As you know, it is a popular seaside resort in the summer, but in the winter it is very lonely and desolate. Yet my father and I have been happy—he with his books and I with my sport and out-of-doors life-until the last few months. All this trouble has happened since"—she shuddered—"that man came!"

"What man?" inquired Quin.

"The man Memory—Rathin Memory, he calls himself."

"A singular name," commented Quin. "And what—?"

"He's horrible, dreadful," cried the visitor. "Mr. Quin, help me to save my father from that devil's power!"

Violet Loring's face had become convulsed. She was struggling for breath.

Sebastian Quin made me a sign, and I brought the brandy.

After a while the visitor became more controlled.

"I must tell you everything now," she said, "and I promise I shall not be so foolish again." Her hands locked tightly, she went on with her story.

"It was in late September last that this man, Rathin Memory,-arrived in Trevelyn. He took the house called "The Height," on Pentire, which is a rocky headland jutting into the sea on the north side of the town. This house had been unoccupied for so long that the place was in a dreadful state of neglect. The iron entrance-gates were rusty and almost hidden by the weeds and coarse grass which had been allowed to grow.

"I should explain that this house, "The Height," has an evil reputation—the local story is that a dreadful murder and suicide took place there many years ago, that the bodies of the wretched people mysteriously disappeared in the night, and that the place—which is very old—is haunted. And it was to this house that the man who, for some mysterious reason, has constituted himself my enemy, came." The visitor's body was shaken by a fresh shudder before she continued:

"You can imagine, perhaps, what an interest was taken in the new resident. Everybody in Trevelyn knows everybody else, the town being so small, and the fact that Rathin Memory had taken a house which was generally believed to be haunted and which had never been let even in the summer months, had increased the natural curiosity about the man."

Quin nodded.

"Will you describe him, Miss Loring?"

Again the visitor shuddered. But the hesitation was only momentary.

"Please do not think it is my shattered nerves which make me describe him as a man one doesn't like to look at," she replied. "His age is something between forty and fifty, I should say; he is very hairy—lets his hair grow and has a beard—and has remarkable eyes. Even when he has passed me in the street in broad daylight his eyes have filled me with fear. And I am not an imaginative person usually."

"A highly curious individual, I should imagine. But please go on, Miss Loring. Is anything known of the man—where he came from, for instance?"

"Nothing very much. The local newspaper tried to interview him, but all he would say was that he had been a traveller all over the world, that he had lately arrived from Tibet, and that he wished to be undisturbed. He lives quite alone in that huge house, with only a foreign manservant."

"He has done no entertaining, then?"

"None. As a matter of fact, there isn't a soul in Trevelyn who would venture into "The Height." And the man himself—as I know to my cost— is mysterious, devilish. He has a power over people, as I shall convince you, I believe, Mr. Quin."

Quin almost imperceptibly stiffened in his chair.

"I shall do everything I can to help you, Miss Loring, but I must have your complete story."

"You shall—whatever it costs me to tell it. Perhaps you will be able to realize my position better if I say now that this—this monster is in love with me! And I am already engaged to be married," she went on before either Sebastian Quin or I could interject a comment.

"It was about a month ago that I first met Memory alone," Miss Loring explained. "I was walking on Pentire when I heard a footstep behind me. Looking around, I saw that the mystery-man—as Memory is called at Trevelyn—was close upon me. Although it was early in the afternoon and quite light, I felt myself suddenly trembling. That may seem a very weak and cowardly confession to make, but I cannot hope to convey the devilish atmosphere with which the man seems to be surrounded! I only know that it was very real to me when he looked at me with those awful staring eyes of his.

"I merely nodded when he raised his hat and went to pass on. But he placed himself in my way.

"'You are Miss Loring, are you not?' he asked, and I said 'Yes!'

"'I should like you to be friends with me,'" he went on. 'I am a very lonely man. I do not want many friends, but I should like to know you.'

"You can imagine, Mr. Quin, what my feelings were when I heard those words. For a moment I could not find my voice. But then, realizing my position, I replied: 'I am afraid that is impossible. I do not know you, and I do not want to know you. Consequently, any question of friendship between us is absurd.'

"Once again I made to move on, but he would not let me pass.

"'That which I desire I always obtain,' he said in a voice that filled me with fresh fear. 'I have asked for your friendship and I shall have it. There is no one strong enough to prevent me.'

"At that I became indignant.

"'My father will prevent it, for one,' I said.

"'Your father!' He laughed contemptuously. 'I tell you that no one is strong enough to prevent me from enjoying your friendship now that I wish it. You will see!'

"If he had not turned away then, I believe I should have struck him, for my rage had overcome my fear. The idea of this creature daring to dictate to me, presuming to force himself upon me, was so overwhelming that I scarcely knew what I was doing.

"I went straight back and told my father. Dad is usually a quiet man, whose only wish is to be left in peace to enjoy his beloved books, but when he heard my story he went straight away to consult his solicitor. Mr. Denning wrote a letter to Memory, warning him that his attentions were unwelcome to me, that I was already engaged to be married, and that any repetition of his conduct that afternoon would be communicated without delay to the local police. The local police," repeated the visitor in a hopeless voice. "Little did I realize at the time how helpless any police could be in dealing with a monster like Memory!"

Her strange words filled me with a sense of foreboding. I glanced at Quin and saw that his eyes were unnaturally bright. Evidently this case was interesting him intensely.

Before she continued, Miss Loring took another sip of brandy.

"The following night the first terrible thing happened," she resumed. "My father had gone to bed early, but I had been sitting with my—the man to whom I am engaged, Mr. Harry Sinclair. Suddenly I heard a cry. I rushed upstairs, Harry by my side. I found my father—" Sobs now choked her so that she could not continue.

"If you are too distressed, Miss Loring—"

"No! No! I must tell it and get it over. I was saying that I found my father-*paralysed*! He could speak, but that was all. He said he had cried out because he felt a strange numbness creeping over him, robbing him of all strength and power.

"No"—answering my look; "my father had not been stricken with any stealthy disease; neither had he had a stroke. The local doctor was puzzled and sent for a specialist from Plymouth. The latter in turn wired for a big London man—Sir Timothy Brash—"

"I know him quite well," commented Quin. "He is a member of the same club as I. A thoroughly good man; about as good as any in the world, I should say. What did Sir Timothy say, Miss Loring?"

The girl's body was shaken by one of those convulsive shudders which were so distressing to see.

"It was Sir Timothy who referred me to you, Mr. Quin. After examining poor Daddy, he said that it was a case outside of medical science, because, as far as he could determine, there was no physical cause for father's condition. Although not a robust man—but then Daddy had never been that—he said my father was wonderfully healthy and well preserved for his age. When I first heard him mention your name I thought you were still another doctor—"

"Naturally," was the grave comment.

"And, to be frank, Mr. Quin, while of course I was anxious to do any-thing—*anything*—which could make Daddy better, I was so disappointed that I did not act at once upon his advice. You are not a doctor, Mr. Quin?"

"No—only of the mind," replied my friend. "I can tell you why Sir Timothy Brash mentioned my name to you, Miss Loring. He considered that your father's illness was due to another agency rather than disease."

"What agency, Mr. Quin?"

"That I cannot say with certainty until I reach the spot. Huish, look up the next train to Trevelyn. We shall return with Miss Loring. There is not a moment to lose!"

I consulted the Bradshaw and glanced at my watch. "There is a train from Paddington in an hour's time."

"We will catch it," said Quin decisively.

In the train Miss Loring told the rest of her amazing story. The malig-nant influence which was at work in her life had manifested itself in another direction besides rendering her father a helpless cripple. Harry Sinclair, her devoted lover, the man to whom she was engaged, had suddenly seemed to become bereft of his senses, to lose his reason.

"Not that he has become actually mad," explained the girl, "but he regards me now more or less as a stranger, and he spends all his time mooning about on the sands. His manner has become so peculiar that he is the talk of the town, and people are saying that—that he ought to be taken away. Mr. Quin'—stretching out a beautiful hand in anguished appeal—"do you think you will be able to help me?"

"I shall do all I can," was the grave response. "I promise you not to leave Trevelyn until the mystery is solved in any case."

"What is your view, Quin?"

He turned on me impatiently.

"I have no view at present," he replied. "There may be a filmy thought at the back of my mind, but it is far too early to speak about that yet. All I can say now, Huish, is that we are faced with a problem that has so many terrors attached that we simply must not fail! Even the thought of failure is so ghastly as to terrify me!"

I knew better than to provoke him into further speech at that moment, although God knows how anxious I was. The story which had brought us post-haste from London to this dreary Cornish coast town, would have seemed incredible had I not been mixed up sufficiently in Sebastian Quin's affairs to know from experience that, to quote the words he had himself said to the victim of this diabolical plot, "the fantastic is usually the likeliest thing to happen—given certain conditions."

I looked at the man who had solved more mysteries than any other person living. He was so deep in thought over his pipe that there was a deep furrow in his forehead.

Sebastian Quin was an enthusiast of the bizarre. He was as unlike the ordinary crime investigator as the real detective is unlike the fiction variety. Possessed of comfortable means, he devoted his life to the study of crime in its more exotic and weird manifestations. He was a repository of so much varied knowledge that I often marvelled how and by what means he could have accumulated so many facts, knowing that he was still under forty. Quin had learned Chinese well enough to pass for a native within a month, and could speak altogether eighteen languages. That in itself gives proof of his mental powers.

He was far more than a mere detective of crime: he was a dissector, an analyst, an anatomist of the mind of the criminal. He was never satisfied with merely stopping a crime; he delved beneath and learned what had prompted the outrage. Altogether an amazing person, and my friendship with him was the greatest honour that I—or any other man—could have experienced. It pleased Quin to let me accompany him on certain of his investigations. The part I played was always an exceedingly humble one—I was merely a super on the stage; but Quin, like many other great men, had his moments of pardonable vanity, and he liked to have someone near him to whom he could explain and expound after a "case" had come to a satisfactory conclusion.

We had decided upon *The Grand*, because it was the hotel nearest to "The Height"—that mysterious house in which Rathin Memory lived; and, late as it was after we had seen Violet Loring safely to her own door, Quin and I had walked the half-mile of desolate cliff-land, which separated the Grand Hotel from "The Height."

I shall never forget that walk. The wind had sprung up and was howling like the spirits of tortured fiends; every now and then the thundering of giant waters sounded, and we were drenched with spray as we walked along the zigzag path that ran between the golf course and the towering range of cliffs.

"This should be the place," Quin remarked, flashing the small electric torch he carried.

We climbed the mighty headland which Violet Loring had called Pentire, and a laborious business it was. A strange and erratic mind it must have been that conceived the idea of building a house on the top of that cliff which jutted straight out into the Atlantic Ocean. Like the nest of some gigantic eagle "The Height" looked as we stood before the iron gates which were rusty with disuse and almost hidden—as Violet Loring had said—by rank weeds and grasses as tall as a man's body.

The place was a monstrous blot of gloom. Not a light showed. There was no sign of any human habitation, and yet—I told myself it was fancy

379

brought on by the story which had brought us to this spot at eleven o'clock of a winter's night—something seemed to grip me by the throat as I stood staring there in the darkness.

"Quin!" I called, and then was ashamed of myself.

My companion came up and looked at me fixedly.

"What is it?" he demanded.

I tried to laugh, but succeeded only in making a dismal croak.

"I—I can't explain it, Quin," I stammered, "but just then—when I called, I mean—something devilish seemed to be trying to choke the life out of me! It had me by the throat. I was afraid for myself and for you too—that was why I called. Don't laugh at me!" I went on angrily. "The sensation was real enough—too real for my liking."

Quin switched off his torch.

"I am not going to laugh," he replied seriously. "I had exactly the same feeling myself—and you would not call me an unduly imaginative man, Huish?"

"I should not!" I said emphatically.

Quin was silent as we walked away.

The whole affair was steeped in mystery—evil mystery. On the morning following our arrival we saw David Loring, the girl's father. He was a pitiable object. Apart from the fact that he could speak, he was a complete paralytic. But his mind was clear enough.

"I am under the spell of some devilish influence," he told Quin. "That may seem an incomprehensible thing to you—and, on the other hand, you may accept the statement because I understand you have had many strange experiences yourself, Mr. Quin. Dr. Logan will tell you the exact words that Sir Timothy Brash, the great consultant, said when he examined me."

Sebastian Quin, nodding gravely, took the grey-haired local practitioner on one side.

"From a medical point of view," said Dr. Logan, "Mr. Loring ought to be as well as you or I. He has been overhauled inside and out; all sorts of tests were made by Sir Timothy Brash, who said at the end: 'Well, the whole thing is incomprehensible from a medical point of view.' Poor Mr.

Loring himself talks a lot about some malign influence, but, of course, all that is nonsense. This is not the Middle Ages."

"It may or it may not be nonsense," replied Sebastian Quin.

A short time after this we met Harry Sinclair, Violet Loring's fiancé, as he was about to enter the house. He proved to be a good-looking, manly young fellow—at least, I should perhaps say he would no doubt have given that impression in ordinary circumstances.

Now he did not appear to be in possession of all his faculties. His mind was wandering, and he was so careless in his attire that I noticed a flash of pain come into Violet Loring's face.

As for Sinclair, he stared blankly at her and glared around at the rest of us.

"Harry, this is Mr. Sebastian Quin, from London," the girl announced.

Again she received a disconcerting, blank stare.

"Who are you? Why do you keep on speaking to me? Leave me alone!" the man said fretfully, and then a look of loathsome cunning transfigured his face as he added: "But I know who you are! You're David Loring's daughter. You're a bad lot, and I don't want anything to do with you! It's your father I want—I'm very fond of your father!" He chuckled obscenely.

A sob sounded behind me.

"You can see for yourselves," said Violet Loring, her distress racking her, "that this is not my Harry. This is some monster he has been changed into!"

While I tried to comfort her, Sebastian Quin had stepped between Sinclair and the door of the Lorings' house.

"I shouldn't go in now," he said quietly to the stricken man.

The wave of madness which made Sinclair's eyes glare and his whole body stiffen died down as suddenly as it was born when he looked into Quin's face. With a snarl like that of an angry dog, he turned away without saying another word.

For the rest of that day Quin kept a close watch on the Lorings' home, and, noticing how tense and strung-up he was, I ventured to ask him the reason.

"You may know tonight," was the only reply he would give me.

"Ah!" cried Sebastian Quin softly, yet with intense satisfaction. "There it is!"

He pointed upward. The left wing of "The Height" took the form of a short, squat tower, and it was from a window in this tower that a light—the first sign of human life or activity in the place that we had yet observed—now glowed like a star in a dark sky.

"Our vigil is ended," said Quin. "What we have to do now is to ascertain what is going on in that room with the light. The question is whether we shall achieve that purpose by entering the house, or whether we can sufficiently satisfy our curiosity by climbing up this incline, which is on a level with the window, and looking through by lying on our stomachs. I propose the latter method, for it will be quicker, and I feel pretty certain that time is valuable. Now for the climb. Be careful you don't fall!"

We were already standing beneath the shadow of the house of mystery. My heart beat at twice its normal rate when I contemplated the task which Quin had set us.

The progress of that hazardous climb, one false step in which would have meant not only the ruination of our plans, but inevitable death, is a memory upon which I never afterwards liked to look back. It seemed to last an eternity, but eventually I found myself lying side by side with Quin upon the small plateau, and looking into the room the light from which had attracted us from the ground. There were some curtains to the window, but the man inside had evidently felt so secure in his own mind about not being overseen, that he had not troubled to draw them.

"Stay perfectly still, and do not do anything until I give you the word, *whatever you may see!*" whispered my companion, stressing the last few words in a way that sent a cold chill down my spine.

Every separate nerve in my body seemed to be twitching as I saw a man enter the room. By the description which Violet Loring had given us, I recognized him at once as Rathin Memory.

She had not exaggerated the dread with which this man would have inspired in the ordinary clean-living, clean-thinking, normal person. The man, even from a distance, seemed to be surrounded by an aura of evil.

"Watch!" came the tense whisper from Quin.

Memory was carrying a bundle when he entered the room, which as far as I could see was quite bare of furniture. Placing the bundle on the floor, he first took out five brass lamps of a peculiar design. Then followed

382

a stoppered vessel. After that the man produced a white cock, alive—for it struggled—but with its feet and beak tied in some fashion that I could not ascertain because I was too far away. Then followed a knife, the blade of which gleamed in the light.

"What—?" I whispered, but Quin ordered me to be quiet.

I followed the subsequent actions of the man in the lighted room with breathless attention, for I realized that I was the witness of something which was full of significance—otherwise why should Sebastian Quin have been so absorbed?

I saw Rathin Memory measure out a space. Having counted off a number of feet—how many I could not reckon—he drew a circle of chalk. Then, taking the bottle, he pulled out the stopper and walked around inside the circle, sprinkling the chalk line with the liquid the bottle contained. At each step he stopped and made a peculiar gesture.

"The second sign of the unholy celebration," I heard Quin mutter.

The complete circle having been sprinkled, the man drew a five-pointed star with the chalk. Then, lighting the five small lamps which he had brought, he placed one at each of the five points. He seemed to be muttering some ritual as he did so, for I could see his lips move.

Placing himself in the centre of the pentacle, he commenced what must have been a chant, for his lips moved again and his hands swept upward and outward. Presently the uncanny thing which I had been expecting ever since I had first looked into the room happened—for from each of the five lamps guarding the points of the pentacle there suddenly sprang a reddish tongue of flame. These met and formed a solid barrier of fire around the man in the centre.

At this point Memory thrust out his hand and seized the white cock. Holding the knife aloft, as though first consecrating it to its task, he decapitated the bird with a single stroke, and I saw the blood splash on the floor inside the circle.

"Now that the blood is warm—" I heard Sebastian Quin mutter, but I was too fascinated by the horrible ritual I was witnessing to turn to him.

I saw the unholy celebrant lift up his hands as though saying a prayer. As he did so, the wall of flame with which he had been surrounded died down. Five tongues of flame issued out of the solid fire and returned to the lamps, which burned at the five points of the pentacle. The light of the lamps now burned low, flickered just as though assailed by a gale of wind. They were trembling as though some unseen force were trying to put them out.

"My God!" breathed Quin. "The real thing—the real thing!"

Again I was too absorbed to take any notice of my companion.

Spellbound I saw—or fancied I saw—a grey cloud beat about the figure of the man in the circle of the pentacle. I saw Rathin Memory's lips move again.

"Quickly!" A grip of steel was on my arm, and a voice that brooked no denial sounded in my ear. "Huish, get back to the Lorings' house at once! Murder may be done there at any moment! Go at once—I must stay here. Go, man!"

So strong was his control over me at that moment that I did not hesitate. I moved like a man in a dream, for the dreadful images I had seen were vivid in my mind—but I must have been quick, for within a surprisingly short space of time I found myself in the garden and climbing over the high wall that separated it from the cliff-land.

Once on the other side, I took to my heels like a man pursued by fiends. But I was not frightened. My one idea was to get to the Lorings' house cottage as quickly as possible.

Though it was long past midnight when I arrived there, I hammered at the door loudly enough to wake the dead.

But I was in the house long before the door could be opened. Going around to the side, I saw a ladder placed against a bedroom window. In a flash the realization came to me that this led to David Loring's room.

Rushing up the ladder, I flung myself through the window—just in time to prevent a man from plunging a knife into the breast of the sleeping paralytic.

"Sinclair!" I cried. "What the devil are you doing here?"

I had hold of his wrist, and the knife clattered to the floor. And although he struggled like the madman he was, I was desperate myself, and ruthless. Getting clear, I swung a rig t to the jaw that carried every ounce in my body, and he crumpled helpless across the bed of the man he had intended to murder.

"What's the matter? Why—I can move! I'm better! I'm well!"

This night of strangeness was to hold another mystery. Imagine my amazement when David Loring, a hopeless paralytic the short time I had known him, jumped out of bed and came across to me.

I'm well! I'm cured!" he cried, tears running down his cheeks.

The next moment Violet Loring rushed into the room.

"Daddy!"

She had been in his arms for several seconds before she seemed to realize that anyone else was in the room.

Then—

"Mr. Huish! . . . *Harry!*" she cried.

As she spoke his name her lover sat up and rubbed his eyes.

"Vi! I've had such a horrible dream! What am I doing here?" he said.

It was not until Sebastian Quin and I were ensconced cosily before our sitting-room fire at the *Grand Hotel* that I regained my normality. The mysteries I had seen following so quickly one upon the other that night had been too much for me to grasp.

"For Heaven's sake, Quin, explain matters—everything!" I snapped. This was 1930, and I was tired of trying to probe things to which there appeared to be no earthly explanation. Paralysed men suddenly jumping out of bed . . . madmen becoming sane through a blow on the jaw . . . tongues of flame . . . slaughtered cocks . . .

"I have already told you that Rathin Memory is dead," said Quin. "Exactly how he died is too horrible to relate, but, briefly, the evil forces which he conjured up by means of the black magic you saw tonight, and which he had used to work evil upon two other men—to paralyse David Loring and to make Harry Sinclair mad—destroyed him. Once I had wrecked the five guarding lamps of the pentacle, which I did with my revolver shortly after you had left, he was no longer safe. And the spell which he had caused to be cast upon Loring and Sinclair was broken. The devils which he could control as long as those lamps served as protection seized him. I heard one short, strangled scream of dreadful horror, and I knew it was over."

While I stared at him in speechless amazement, Quin continued: "If you told the ordinary person that Black Magic was practised in England today, you would be thought a lunatic; but the fact is true, as you have yourself had the proof, Huish. I had my suspicions that this man Rathin Memory was an adept in the unholy art when I first heard Miss Loring's story, but it was too early for me to give any opinion on the matter until I had myself seen him at the actual practice."

"But that grey shape, Quin?"

"Was one or more spirits of evil—devils, if you care for the usual superstitious term. It is too technical a matter for me to explain now at length, but there is no doubt that the rites of Black Magic have been carefully preserved and handed down. The Egyptians unquestionably had the power to raise evil spirits and use them for purposes of personal vengeance. And have you not read how Madame de Montespan consulted a witch and took part in a Black Mass with the notorious Abbe Guibourg, so that she might win back the love of Louis the Fourteenth of France? Indeed, there is evidence enough!

"In Tibet today spirit-raising is practised in its most elaborate and secret forms. That was what first gave me the idea that this man Memory was an adept—the news that he had recently returned from that land of weird and uncanny mystery. And now"—yawning—"I'm off to bed."

I too went to bed—but I could not sleep.

MYSTERY OF INIQUITY

L. ADAMS BECK

The writer known as L. Adams Beck was born Elizabeth Louisa Moresby (1860–1931), daughter of the naval commander John Moresby who undertook extensive surveying and exploration in the waters north of Australia and founded the town, Port Moresby in New Guinea, which bears his name. She was born in Queenstown, Ireland, where the family lived for many years but preferred to be known as English rather than Irish. She married Edward Hodgkinson, a naval commander, in 1881 and lived for a while in London and Sussex. She had one son. Her husband died in 1910 and soon after she married solicitor Ralph Adams Beck. Their wedding ceremony was in India and the two travelled extensively—they were in the Far East at the outbreak of the First World War. After the War they settled in Canada. It was only now, under the Beck name, that she started writing—the L. being kept ambiguously brief because although it was formally Louisa, she always liked to be called Lily. She also wrote as E. Barrington and Louis Moresby. She and her husband separated in 1921, and he returned to England, but she remained in Victoria, British Columbia, hosting regular salons and promoting vegetarianism and an interest in Buddhism and Eastern studies. She was on a trip to Japan in February 1931 when she died suddenly.

She was remarkably prolific in her last ten years producing twenty-six books. Those as E. Barrington were mostly historical romances, whilst she reserved L. Moresby for nonfiction. L. Adams Beck covered her occult works and fiction, which included the novels The Treasure of Ho *(1923),* The Way of Stars *(1925), and* The House of Fulfillment *(1927). There were also two story collections,* The Ninth Vibration *(1922) and* The Openers of the Gate *(1930), and it is the latter which includes her stories featuring the exploits of Dr. James Livingstone. Like Dion Fortune's John Taverner, Livingstone is a specialist in nervous disorders and some of the stories are only borderline supernatural—indeed Livingstone only takes part in a few, and elsewhere the stories are told to him. But "Mystery of Iniquity" shows the depth of Livingstone's knowledge and challenges him to cope with a troubled girl in Switzerland.*

THERE IS A VILLAGE IN SWITZERLAND, HIGH UPLIFTED AMONG THE mountains beside a little lake of gentian blue. Nothing could be lonelier, nothing more detached from the lower world, nothing lovelier. It is still approached by the old-fashioned diligence, toiling up mountain ways whose scanty population would not reward any higher enterprise in approach. The tourist does not know its name and from me never shall. Therefore I shall call it Geierstein after Sir Walter Scott's famous novel, and there leave it.

But I was free of the place. And when I took my yearly holiday, I took it always at Geierstein, partly because I loved the place for its beauty and quiet, partly because I had valued friends there—Pastor Biedermann and his wife. He was a Cambridge man like myself, though a Swiss, and our friendship grew in value to us both with the years.

It followed that when I arrived at Geierstein, regularly every fourth of August, I boarded with them and fell immediately into their life and that of the village as to the manner born.

Their house alone would have won the day—a chalet, long and low, with balconies up and down stairs where you could smoke and read or work or stare at the Jungfrau and her giant companions swimming in blue air or the splendors of sunset and dawn. It was a generously gabled house with running bands of decoration, which somehow expressed the simple and pious hope of the pastor's ancestors who had built it in the year 1740. Across the front in fine old German lettering ran the verse designed to express the spirit of the house and hope of the builders:

Wer Gott vertraut,
Hat wohl gebaut.
(Who trusts in God has built well.)

They had built well. Years of sunshine, rain, snow, and storm had beaten in vain at the high pointed windows, the generously sheltering eaves, the dove-cote chimneys. Warmth and strength were still the guardians of the house when the cold wrath of the mountains broke in fury down the valley and over the lake.

Peace was the atmosphere of the house; sunny golden peace in summer, warm fire-lit peace in winter. It began with the garden, Biedermann's own special charge, crammed with bushes of lovely old-fashioned roses brimming with perfume. I felt that the very dew on their petals must be attar of roses, their true spiritual essence. There was a rainbow of crowded asters. Round them crowded tawny wallflowers, lavender bushes, campanulas—God knows what. The perfume rose divinely to my balcony where I often slept in the open and woke to the dew-drenched glory of the garden with earliest dawn's call to my plunge and swim in the lake.

Biedermann was an unusual fellow, deeply religious in stanch Lutheran fashion, but with affections and consciousness wide enough to float his bark to heavens never conceived in the Lutheran limits. His wife was a household sweetness. Her low voice singing old ballads or hymns as she went about her work will always be a background in my thoughts to the strange events we were to share.

It began as simply as any household happening. It was the day after my arrival and we were sitting at supper. We had reached the stage of wild strawberries and whipped cream, when Biedermann said carelessly:

"Since you were last here, doctor, I have let the old Parson-House again."

He preferred living in his own house, and it was an understanding that he should keep up the Parson-House and make a little profit by letting it to eke out a tiny income.

"And who now?" I asked.

"An English lady and her daughter, and I'm really glad to have you near to discuss them. They're getting on my conscience."

That meant on his compassion—a raft capable of supporting all the shipwrecked of the universe. Mrs. Biedermann sighed.

"The mother's a beautiful person but hard—hard as your toast this evening. Toni! were you dreaming when you made it?" she said laughing to the little flaxen-haired maid.

"The daughter is beautiful too," said Biedermann, "but in a most peculiar way that I can't describe. I should very much like your opinion."

"But why are they here?"

"I don't know. She's very reserved. Only said her daughter had been ill and was ordered quiet and mountain air. She took the house for a year and came in April."

"Then they mean to be here in the winter?"

That was unusual. I had never seen it except for a week, but I knew what the terror and beauty of the falling snow, the raving winds would be. After October Geierstein was as cut off as a planet on the outermost orbit of the system. Everyone drew into their own concerns and family life—and what on earth would an English lady and her daughter do then? People who know the great hotels and winter sports have little notion of such a place as Geierstein when the Snow Queen sits enthroned in the valleys of the Bernese Oberland.

"And what's their name?"

"Saumarez. The daughter's name is Joyselle. They come from London and—"

"What?" I said. "Why, I knew a Dr. Saumarez, a most extraordinary—"

"Her husband was a doctor. He died some time ago."

Now it became interesting. Saumarez was a hard-bitten fellow with keen watchful eyes and set lips through which no secret would ever slip that he meant to hide. We had been medical students together and even then he was like that—ready to join in anything going but always outside it, a looker-on in spite of himself, a man no one honestly cared for. I had heard he became a clever aurist and had a house near me in London but at the other end of the street—a world away as London goes. Dead? I did not know that either, but these strangers became faintly interesting to me because of their association with Saumarez.

Biedermann said slowly:

"I should like you to meet them. I have an idea—Should you not say, Hilde, that there's some hidden trouble?"

She answered:

"Certainly. Frau Saumarez speaks from the lips outward. What is in her heart she never tells. More strawberries, Herr Doktor?"

As she spoke a girl passed along the road, going slowly towards the old Parson-House. She had no hat and was the slim short-skirted slip of a thing one sees in every street. What was her own was the distinction with which she carried a clipped satin-smooth head set on a long throat. It was too far for me to see her features, but the figure defined against a sunset sky had the confident beauty of a young birch tree alone in a clearing of the woods. A Dryad—a tree spirit, blown for a moment across human vision.

"That's the girl!" said Biedermann.

Next day, on our way to see a case in which he wanted my advice he introduced me to Mrs. Saumarez as she stood by her garden gate, with the village milkwoman milking a cow into a pail at her feet. She bowed with the usual smile when I was presented but, directly I suggested a possible acquaintance, froze. Her face stiffened and she was on guard instantly. The very tone in which she met and dismissed the subject disclosed some wound, which I knew she would have held back with tooth and claw if possible.

"My husband died two years ago. Have you noticed how beautiful the Caroline Testout roses are this year, Herr Biedermann?"

That was all. We talked a few minutes and said good-by and began our tramp up the steep little mountain road. Suddenly she called after him, and I went slowly on, piecing her together.

A locked face. Cold only (to use a contradiction) because there were volcanic elements at work under it which must be kept in check as granite hides boiling lava. Her few words were the puff of steam revealing the fire-heart within. She was handsome and had a kind of chilly dignity—a woman of whom I should have guessed that the Saumarez I knew would be the very last man she would admit to her intimacies. Well—marriage need not mean intimacy beyond what a man may have with the chance choice of a night!

Presently Biedermann came up behind me.

"She wanted to say a curious thing," he said meditatively. "Now what could she mean? It was—'Please ask Dr. Livingstone if he sees my daughter not to mention her father to her.' I'm afraid we were right. There's something painful behind it."

That was plain. We said no more on that hand but climbed on and up to the little woodland cottage set in stark and steadfast pines and staring out through low-browed windows at the giant crests of the Oberland, surging like a wave petrified in eternal defeat in some wild war on the heavens.

I saw the case he wished me to see there—a girl of about nineteen, named Lili Schneiderling, suffering from obscure nervous trouble. I diagnosed and advised and was leading the way out of the room when she called me back, speaking hurriedly and low in German-Swiss. Biedermann turned in astonishment to hear:

"I want to tell you—I want to say—how can I get well if—" She gasped and paused, putting up a hand to hide her eyes.

"If what?" I asked encouragingly, bending over her.

"If the English fräulein comes at night. Tell her not to—promise me. It should not be allowed. It should be stopped."

She panted as if the effort of getting the thing off her mind were greater than she could endure. I looked at the mother, a comely blonde Swiss with troubled eyes, who stood on the other side of the bed.

"What does she mean?"

"Indeed, sir, I can't tell. She has said it more than once. The young English fräulein passes the window on her way up to the waterfall in the woods, but she never comes in."

"A lie!" said the girl harshly. "She came in the day after they went to the old Parson-House."

The mother smiled patiently. "Why, yes, Lili! But that was only to ask her way. She never came again."

"She never needed to. She had spied out what she wanted to know. Well, all I say is—if you want me to get well tell her not to come here. *I* don't want her, the dear God knows!" She turned and caught my hand in a hot painful grip: "Will you tell her? You're English too?"

I promised—and Biedermann and I went off together.

"Is there any madness in the family?" I asked when we had set our faces upward once more.

"None. The parents are as ordinary as can be, and she's an only child now. For what it's worth, my opinion is that Lili is jealous of the other girl's health and strength. She goes out in all weathers, night and day. A week ago in a storm—I give you my word I thought she would be blown over the edge of the cliff road before my eyes. I saw the wind lift her. Actually, for a second! Right off the ground. She flung out her arms and laughed.

"A great storm goes to the head like drink sometimes, but I think she must have given a hop, skip, and jump to help it! I expect Lili has had a jealous dream. Half the antipathies of the world center there, and the dreamers forget the cause when they wake."

We went off on dreams then, I telling him all the newest notions and guesses on that most mysterious subject, and gradually as we talked we climbed up to a ragged track on the way to the waterfall. I must describe the place for my experience turns on it.

We were now four miles from Geierstein. The frightfully steep narrow little road had come with us as far as the shoulder of a crag and there deserted us, turning abruptly to the left on its winding way upward to another village two miles farther in the mountains and known as Donnerstein; a few chalets collected in the cup of a mountain valley, hugely uplifted as was Geierstein in the arms of a mountain only lesser than the Jungfrau and her mighty companions. Here we turned up the steep track. Half a mile of it led us to a great wood of pines, somber and sighing even in the hot sunshine of the late afternoon. The far distant murmur of water came on a waft of wind as we entered where a thick carpet of golden pine-needles dumbed the sound of our feet.

Otherwise, what a silence! Not a bird sang, not a cricket trilled. We were in a great cathedral of Nature's making, too high, too vast, for human worship. One could imagine the cold spirits of the mountains—no, that kind of thing has been said often enough. It means nothing except to those who have seen. Biedermann spoke low. The place enforced quiet.

"Now for a surprise. We're lucky, for the wind is the right way. You see that crag in front? You hear the silence? Now prepare to be deafened. It's fuller than ever this year."

A crag plumed with firs blocked the way perhaps two hundred yards in front with a steep fall downward. We climbed round it cautiously, for it was a place for a slip and a nasty accident and the difficulty absorbed me. In the next moment my ears were filled with the thundering roar of a terrible dance of water over maddening rocks, plunging for life, for safety, for escape from hell, as it were, down an awful precipice to the unseen lake, in a world too far below to be its own. Never before had I seen it like this.

Vain to speak. Thunder and spray and foam filled the world, deafened, half blinded me. This was the Geierstein Fall. I stood staring at it in silence, and suddenly I saw a sight entirely new to me.

About a hundred feet below at the left side jutted out into the water a jut of the forest darkened with pines. The extraordinary thing was that I could not remember having seen this promontory before. It was as strange to me as the rest was familiar and I stared in astonishment. At first I thought it was an optical illusion caused by the shimmer and slide and spray of the water. It appeared to change and flicker. I rubbed my eyes. I would have called Biedermann's attention to it with words, but the noise was thunderous. I pointed and he laughed and nodded. Finally he put his mouth to my ear and shouted:

"There's a little hut about a quarter of an hour on where I go and read a psalm or two with an old cowherd. Will you wait or come?"

I shouted, "Wait," and he went off, climbing with hands as well as feet round the bluff. I was glad to be alone in the wild and terrible place and stood looking at the water, meditating on the unfamiliarity of the promontory.

I could imagine how a weak brain might feel the fascination of the long pale green slide of water glittering in sunlight, and dream of plunging with it down through airy space in quest of life—more life—to be sought through that marvelous smooth motion. The names of more than one of my patients flashed through my mind whom I would not willingly have trusted for a moment to stand by the ever and never changing phenomenon.

I looked downward to where the strange promontory with its trees shimmered and danced through spray. It was like a mirage I had once seen in Egypt, quivering at first then settling down into what seemed to be reality. Suddenly something slipped through the gloom of trees. What in the

name of God!—a woman—a girl, mother-naked. It—she appeared to lay
a hand on the rough bark of one of the pine trees, and she stood staring
at the plunge. I saw her clear as ivory on ebony. The trees still shimmered
through driving spray. Presently she left them and advanced out on the jut
as if to meet the full rush of water, going confidently. My first thought was
the medical one—Was I going to see a case of suicide before my eyes and
do nothing?

I put my hands to my mouth and shouted, yelled—I don't know
what—that she might know she was watched, guarded. My puny voice
shattered in the enormous vibrations about me and was tossed to bits. She
stood bending forward unconscious of my presence. Suddenly she looked
up, laughing and waving her hand. I turned, more by instinct than reason,
and began to make my way back round the great bluff of cliff that we had
circled to reach the waterfall. In the hurry I slipped, fell, picked myself up
again and scrambled on with the blind conviction that I should find some
way to the rescue in the wood beyond.

Presently I regained the breathless quiet of the trees where we had first
entered and began casting about for a trail to the lower level. My brain
was clearer now that the all-stunning noise had ceased, and I hunted
with purpose and direction. It must be a madwoman, but life is life in
the maddest brain, and life attempts its salvation. I found what I thought
was a foot-track going directly downward and began the descent, using
my alpenstock for the pine-needles made it slippery as glass. Cursing my
delays I slipped and fell and struggled down and down to a point where
the trees ceased and bare rock began.

A shout above. A great cry. Biedermann's voice.

"Come back. BACK! Have you gone mad? No way there—Come *back*.
Back this minute!"

It broke some tension in my brain. I drove the alpenstock deep into the
earth and yelled. "A woman down there. Must get on. Wait!"

He was not far above me as distance goes, and I saw some shock strike
him right in the center. He shot out an arm, waving frantically. I remember the thought struck me that the quiet, self-contained Biedermann had
gone right off his head.

"Come back, I tell you. Danger! Come!"

It caught me. He knew some better way. I dragged at the alpenstock and scrambled up, reaching the boles of the pines ascending like a stairway, gained his level and leaned against one of them, gasping with the effort. I could not speak for a moment.

"In the name of God"—his voice had the solemnity of an invocation—"where were you going? What did you see?"

"A naked woman—down there!" I got out in a series of gasps. "I saw her from above. I thought—suicide. I was going down."

He said low as if to himself: "Thank God I came in time!"

Then after a moment:

"Rest—get steadied, and we'll make for home. There's nothing you can do. Nothing!"

I yielded in deep perplexity—I had had a shock far deeper than anything my scramble up and down could account for. Something that struck me deep in the heart of my consciousness, and that by no means the consciousness of the average man, for mine had been trained beyond the common by experience and discipline. I noted how if my eye turned for a moment to the downward way, Biedermann's grip tightened on his stick. I had the feeling that he would have attacked me sooner than see me attempt it. Once or twice he looked up apprehensively as the shadows darkened. It was not sunset, but the sun had dropped below a tremendous peak and the chill of nearing night was perceptible.

Presently I got up. "Ready now. Let's go. Queer experience!"

He led the way along the track I have already mentioned and said not a word until we had reached the road running upward to Donnerstein and downward to Geierstein, then halted a second, and we both looked back to the wood—black in advancing shadows.

"I want you to make me a promise," he said.

I laughed uneasily. "No blank checks for me! Give me the reason and I'll give you the promise—if they click."

He said, "That's reasonable," and was silent again, leading the way.

At that moment I heard a light step on the road above us as if of some woman coming down from Donnerstein. I turned instinctively to look. Nothing there. Let me say that during the whole time of our descent that step went with us until a point which I shall mark. I did not like it. I did not know at the time whether Biedermann was conscious of it or no, and hesitated unaccountably in asking.

"You heard something?" he asked.

"Nothing of consequence. What were you going to tell me?"

"First tell me what woman you saw? And where?"

I described the lower pinewood. The trees falling back from the mighty rush of the waterfall. He turned his head over his shoulder and looked at me fixedly. Then the naked girl:

"And the queer thing is I never noticed that promontory before. I made a scramble for it. I was as sure as I walk here that she was going to fling herself straight in. I'd been thinking it was the very spot for a crack-brained man or woman. However, if she's done it, she's in the lake by this time and has got through the Great Experience. Now for your story, Biedermann."

He looked unlike himself—a queer constrained look—and what gave the lie to my assumption of ease was that those footsteps kept us steady company a few yards behind on my left. I could not rid myself of the notion that someone who wanted to hear was keeping up with us and might draw nearer.

"I hate the subject but I see I must speak. First, there's no such jut into the fall as you speak of. Cragsmen who have climbed down beyond where you attempted to go describe a huge and terrible crevice—a crack or fault in the mountain that goes down to—heaven knows what. Just beyond where you were is a smooth face of rock; a slip—and you'd have glissaded down and nothing could have saved you."

There was that in his face which made it impossible to doubt he was in earnest. I said what naturally occurred to me:

"Then how did she get down—why did I see it? There's another way?"

"I tell you there's no such place. That phantom you saw doesn't exist."

I halted for an incredulous second. The footsteps halted too.

"But I tell you I *saw* it. I would have said it only for the infernal row of the water. There was a dazzle of spray on the jut, but I saw it. Let's go back and—"

He dragged me by the arm. "Come on. I never dreamed you'd see it."

"Hasn't anyone else?"

"Yes, two men and—"

"And you say it isn't there. It's some change in the rocks." But for the echoing footsteps I could have laughed aloud. If either of the two of us was going dotty it was not I.

"If you *will* have it!" he said, and halted. Then went on quickly: "A young fellow, Lili Schneiderling's brother, Arnold Schneiderling, saw it. His companion didn't. Then he lost it. The wooded plane was gone. He saw it no more than his friend. There's a sheer plunge there, straight as the side of a funicular. Two days after, Arnold and another man were going along the track you and I took. Suddenly he left the other and clambered like mad down the way you went, shouting. A yell and Untermeyer going down after him as far as he dared saw a frightful crevice and saved himself just in time. Arnold was never heard of again."

I reflected. "I should like to cross-examine Untermeyer."

"I've done it," Biedermann said. I noticed that his step and therefore mine had fallen into the rhythm of the footsteps behind. Was it conscious or unconscious?

"Helfman saw it next. The carpenter's son. There were three young men there at the time. The others saw nothing. He saw the wooded promontory and the naked girl. He said she looked up and laughed and waved. They had to rope him to prevent him going down. They thought he was mad and so got him home. Two days after, he was seen going up into the wood, running. He was never seen from that day to this."

I reflected. I could have done it more clearly but for the echoing footsteps. Then I said:

"The thing is perfectly clear. It's a mirage from the spray and whirl of the water. I can hardly believe the promontory isn't there, but, granting that, the woman is not difficult to account for. The dazzle and flash and smooth plunge of the water act as an intoxicant. It would affect some brains and not others. But I'm surprised it should affect me. I'm as hard as nails."

"That's a legitimate explanation," said Biedermann, "but it scarcely covers all the facts. That girl you saw on the way up—Lili Schneiderling— has never been to the waterfall, but nevertheless she gets curious attacks of—shall I call it trance?—what I described to you—in which she speaks of the woman."

"How could you expect otherwise when all the village is chattering?" I asked. "When did these things happen?"

"Within the last four months."

We walked some way in silence.

"Is there an old story about the place?"

"Yes. Four hundred years ago—you remember the little old castle on the lake?—the Baron von Falkenwald fell in love with a girl of foreign blood. Nothing is known of her but that she jilted him cruelly and he leaped into the waterfall, the first, as far as we know, of a long series of suicides there. A woman is said to have been seen with him, pointing with glee to the water."

Again I reflected. "Is that story known in the village?"

"No. I discovered it by accident when I was searching the archives at Einsiedeln in connection with a property claim. As pastor I judged it right to keep it to myself. The place has a bad enough reputation. After the happenings this year the more superstitious folk talk of a water-spirit; the wiser, of mirage, as you did."

"And you yourself?"

"I have had some reason to think there is more than meets the eye in life. I suspend judgment."

We walked a little way in silence. Suddenly I said: "Can you hear light footsteps following us?"

We stopped to listen. The footsteps also stopped instantly, and he shook his head. We went on. They did the same. I had a horrid notion that something unseen and evil was overshadowing all our talk. I should rather say I knew this, and with anger that it or they should attempt to frighten me like a beginner.

"I hear nothing," said Biedermann, striding on.

The rest of our walk was nearly silent. But as we reached Geierstein and were passing the garden gate of the old Parson-House the footsteps suddenly stopped. Immediately, Biedermann spoke:

"I have given you reasons. Now for the promise. Will you promise me never to go up alone into the Falkenwald?"

"Don't ask it. Can't you see that all this has made me doubly eager to get to the bottom of the thing? Remember my profession. If there's danger, surely it's my duty to investigate it. In your calling and mine can we show the white flag in any risks, bodily or psychic?" He agreed seriously. We went on and nothing was said in my hearing to Frau Biedermann of what had happened.

Next morning a note was brought to me from Mrs. Saumarez. It had the same effect upon me as her appearance. That of dull, secret persistence. I am sensitive to atmospheres and even those given off by letters and personal objects.

Dear Dr. Livingstone:
I should be glad to consult you on a private matter of importance. It is desirable that no one should know a consultation has taken place and I shall be in my garden at 5 P.M. today and if you could pass as it were accidentally the meeting need not seem to be arranged. I shall be obliged if you will not mention the matter. Your friendship with my husband will excuse this unusual request. No answer is needed.

Sincerely yours,
Annette Saumarez

Friendship! I thought that assumption cool after my slight admission and her grudging reply. I knew she must have been put to it before she would use that plea. My impulse was to send a polite refusal, but a doctor cannot estimate needs nor decline a duty. I sent no answer and at five o'clock was walking up the mountain road feeling strange premonitions. Sorceries were closing about me and I could not tell whence. I neared her garden.

A profusion of roses—a hard-faced woman among them in a wide-brimmed hat. The milkwoman of the village stopped to see. She would be able to report that Mrs. Saumarez looked up quite casually, went quite casually to the garden gate and made a polite remark to which I replied politely. That I then strolled in and she pointed out one or two garden triumphs. Now in a position to satisfy the unslaked hunger of Geierstein for events, the milkwoman went slowly on, and instantly (we were invisible from the house windows) Mrs. Saumarez turned to me and the mask dropped.

I saw straight black brows drawn across a forehead where the sharp downward line dividing them spoke to experience of angry temper. Hard glittering eyes in a handsome tight-lipped face. Such gentleness as one might expect from a steel trap waiting to snap on an unwary animal wandering nearer and nearer. She spoke abruptly:

"I want to consult you about my daughter. I have heard in London that you make a specialty of nervous troubles, and I believe she is in a serious state. Will you keep the matter utterly private?"

I thought the tone offensive and replied coolly:

"Your husband was a doctor. You should know the medical rule of secrecy. But if you prefer to take her elsewhere—"

"I don't prefer. You must excuse me if anxiety makes me abrupt. If— oh, if I could make you understand!"

"Is the patient ready for a visit?"

"The patient? My God! She's not to know I have seen you. She's away up the mountain. That was my chance."

"Then may I beg particulars?"

She did the most unexpected thing—laid her hand for a pleading second on my coat-sleeve. The action revised my whole conception of her and rebuked me as I have been rebuked a hundred times before for the cruelty of rash judgment. Now I saw that what I had thought temper was the iron strain of self-control imposed on wincing nature too weak for it. The hardness was the despairing clutch on strength out of reach. The face was a mask of endurance that must ask no sympathy in its griefs. A most miserable woman stood before me. I said instantly and with acute shame:

"I beg your pardon. I misunderstood. Shall we sit down?"

"Thank you. Not here!" she said hurriedly. "You see she would come in this way. We'll sit at the back in the arbor."

A tiny green bower with a rustic table. She looked nervously round for listeners and plunged straight into an extraordinary revelation.

"Dr. Livingstone, did you ever think my husband mad?"

No question could have caught me more unprepared. I stared in astonishment, and answered with some constraint:

"I knew him so little, that really—"

She flashed in before I finished.

"Not in the ordinary way. Listen! He was crazy over psychological experiments. He dissected the mind as coldly as doctors dissect bodies. He believed people could be used as slaves if you find the right strings to pull. He was a bad man. Did you know that?"

Now I began to remember dimly that I had heard some doctor speak of him as a man who was making daring experiments in what my students persist in calling "psykes" when any mental and nervous states are under discussion. He laughed about it, called him an empiric, a charlatan, and so forth. I imagined he had not achieved the success of renown or wealth, but really the whole thing interested me so little that in the press of my own work it went clean out of my head and never recurred.

"Hypnotism and so forth?" I asked.

"Partly, but much more. He believed people could be taught to project their thought-forms visibly as they do now by chance through death-bed apparitions and in other ways. He thought telepathy could be brought under scientific law and could always be accompanied with visible presence."

"Possibly it can," I said, beginning to be deeply interested.

"Yes—but for what ends? He thought the way in was by the influence of certain drugs. He called it 'The Drug Revelation' and terrible people came to the house and terrible experiments were made. A woman and a man went mad under them and there was more than I ever knew. He used the brain until it broke. There's one drug that makes all the powers flare up for a long time and then drop, as it seems, forever into idiocy. I know its name but even to you I won't breathe it. A fearful thing. I have come into the room again and again and found him stupefied, and when he woke he would pour out horrors that turned my soul to fear incarnate. Can such things be true?"

I would not discuss it with her though I held a strong opinion of my own. But here the case was clear. A bad man drawing into his own evil vortex all the evil influences to which he had thrown wide the door—I knew the way he had trodden, the point marked "Danger," where disregarding every instinct and warning he had plunged to ruin and not alone—a blind guide of the blind. I said briefly:

"Pray go on. I shall be better able to judge when the whole story is before me."

She sighed patiently.

"This went on for two years and then came a change. He called me into his room one night and before I had time to speak or see caught me and pressed a sponge over my mouth and nostrils and held me down. I saw nothing, felt nothing but green meadows and immeasurable rest—green pastures, a Shepherd leading his sheep. I wished never to wake again to the unspeakable weariness of life. But I woke lying on my bed exhausted and he cursed me and told me I was no good—no good. He must find a better."

"You had safeguards," I said with profound pity, "spiritual safeguards he could not break down. You need have no fear."

"Fear? I had nothing else. After that, he never drugged me again, but going about the house I would see strange faces, figures horrible and despairing. Thought-forms, he said, but horribly lifelike. They could speak and move but they were spectral—not human. Light did not frighten them. They went and came as they would or he bid them. Did I see them or did I not?"

She was an image of entreaty with shaking hands held out. No words can tell my pity. A good woman in the den of the only devils that exist—if the word exist may be used to express the inexpressible. But I concentrated in listening. This related itself to certain studies of my own with a very different aim and object. She sighed again when I made no answer and went on.

"My mother was dying and I was called to her. I left my daughter Joyselle in charge of an excellent old French governess, Mademoiselle Payot and an old servant, Margaret. Joyselle was then thirteen, unusually young for her age—her chief interest in life a lovely little West Highland terrier whom she loved almost as tenderly as she did me. A beautiful generous child. It was a sharp pull to leave her, but my mother was dying of cancer and it was no house for a girl. I had been away for two months receiving nothing but good news when a letter came from Mademoiselle Payot."

She drew it from her bag and laid it before me. It was in French.

Dear Madam:

Circumstances which I very deeply regret oblige me to leave my position without delay. I will not refer to them further than by saying that Dr. Saumarez's manner leaves me no alternative. I should not go in this way but that I know your confidence in Margaret and my own experience confirms it. But I think you should return as soon as possible.

There was more, relating to arrangements which I need not quote. She put it away and went on, the nerves in her face and eyelids twitching nervously. She was a patient too, if she had known it!

"I was in Carlisle and my mother clung to me. What could I do? Joyselle's letters were those of a child. Margaret wrote seldom and without detail. 'Missy was well. The house was all right,' and so forth. I wrote repeatedly to my husband. He always answered that Joyselle was in the best of health, all was well, and Mademoiselle Payot had left because her temper became unbearable. She had frightened Joyselle terribly more than once and she herself had grown alarmed at her own want of control. Several times he wrote like this. Four times he came up for a week-end and quite reassured me."

There was a pause. In far distance were the crystal peaks of the Wetterhorn and Schreckhorn, awful in beauty. All round us, roses, roses in the sweet old-fashioned garden, bees making a low drowsy bourdon in the air. Peace everywhere—but on a cracking surface disclosing rifts of horror beneath.

"My mother died and I came back. I had been away three months. At once I saw the change in Joyselle. She had been fresh and sweet as a bunch of pinks, innocent and trustful as a baby. *Now* her eyes held the knowledge of evil. They were quick, glancing—proud, concealing. She met me with a kind of hardy assurance. I should have hated it in any girl. It terrified me in my own. She might have been a woman of equal age, polite enough but holding me off with her reserves. Her dog Darroch was dead, she said carelessly, making nothing of a thing which would have rent her heart when I left. I had a feeling that love also was dead between us. She looked the picture of health, her lips crimson, her eyes sparkling as if with some inward satisfaction I could not fathom. She was then just fourteen."

"Did you make any effort to fathom it?" I asked.

"Every effort. No use. I questioned Margaret. She answered doggedly. 'Missy is well. Anyone can see that,' and so forth. Then I began to watch—to spy. A mother must! She cared for no associates—no society. She was happiest in her own room—a large one on the third floor, and there she had the most extraordinary collection of books on the brain and mind. Horrible for a girl of her age, but her father would not let me interfere—All spiritual things were dead in her, but her brain-power was wonderful. It was as if"—she hesitated for a while—"as if it were breaking loose like fire. She said she was writing a story. I couldn't keep up with her intellect. It was beyond me and she despised me."

Her voice trembled. We were drawing near the heart of horror.

"One night my husband and I had been to the play—Macbeth. It was near twelve when we got back, and the street was empty with a full moon glaring down it. I looked up at the house and saw something white fluttering down from Joyselle's balcony. You will think me mad when I say I thought for one wild minute that it was she herself coming down hand under hand on a rope. I caught my husband's arm and pointed up, shaking from head to foot. He stood, his eyes fixed and I heard him muttering to himself 'Clever girl!—well done!' and madnesses like that. I got out my latch-key and flew upstairs. Her door was locked. I rattled and banged and at last she seemed to wake and came to me. I shall never forget her face. The stiff smile, the sly anger in her eyes. Doctor, she looked a criminal! Yet what could it mean? She was there in her room—had been asleep. I saw the dent in her pillow."

"You mean," I said, "that her father had taught her his tricks? She could project herself."

"Yes—yes!" she said eagerly. "I watched. He had taught her to drug herself. He used to watch while she disengaged herself as he called it. I have seen it happen—she would fall into a drugged sleep and then leave the drugged body like a butterfly off a flower and flit about the house or out and away. I never saw where. She did awful things."

She stopped, shuddering with memory. To be honest I was by no means certain at the moment that her brain was not touched and a great part of her story hallucination. For though I knew the thing could be, on a very different plane, its perversion and openness were out of all my experience. If it were true the girl must be watched and rescued somehow or frightful dangers lay ahead. But how? I kept my most guarded professional manner and it steadied her a little.

"It's almost impossible to suppose a father would subject his daughter to the risks of drug-taking. Had he been attached to her?"

"Never. He hated her for not being a boy. But don't you *see*? He never thought all this wicked. He thought it power, riches, everything the world has to give. The magnificence of brain-power. There were rich women and men who simply poured out gold in return for what they called his magic. And remember I had failed as a subject and he wanted one to show off his power on. He said she was wonderful—People were beginning to talk of her when he died—"

She gasped and moistened her dry lips with her tongue as if to enable herself to speak.

"This went on for some years. I lost all hold of her and was afraid to complain to anyone. She was too strong for me. There was nothing she could not do. He died two years ago when she was sixteen."

"Had she access to the drug after that?"

"I don't know. But it grew worse. She began to talk quite openly about her experiences, and they were like his—ghastly and terrible beyond words. The vilest."

I said thoughtfully: "The brain had probably become diseased under the drug-taking."

"I don't think that!" she said eagerly. "She had a strong brain always and even her father did not dominate her. She hated him. But he opened a door and let her in to all the horrors of the ages. A kind of form of him haunts her, and she would drive it away but cannot. I have seen it in the room staring at her as if he had slipped behind and she was the teacher now. But I tell you—and it's true, believe me if you will, that the *will* in her, the desires in her, can slip out of her body in her own shape and do what she chooses while she lies drugged on her bed. She is off and away all night and often in the day."

I said slowly: "The saints and divinities have had that gift and we call it miracle."

She said: "Ah yes—yes!" with a smile sadder than any tears. "If her power could be turned into the spiritual channel! But that could never be; with her the brain is everything. And what terrifies me is that I see her body being drawn into it too. The flesh longs to share in the mental creations. And that means—open ruin. She's shaved it more than once."

There was a long silence. Then she half rose.

"Will you come up and see her?"

"But you said she was up in the mountains!"

"So she is. Do you think I don't know the stories of the waterfall? I'm coming to that. But her body is asleep upstairs. Come up."

Can I express the feelings with which I followed her upstairs into the quaint low-browed room looking out upon the guarding Alps? The scent of the garden made it sweet as a bower of roses. The curtains were white, the bed draped with white—a girl lay on the square white pillows as in the chalice of a lily. I stood beside her, lost in thoughts for which I can find no name.

She was a slim maid of eighteen, white as pearl, no tinge of color in her cheeks, lips ardently crimson as hibiscus blossom. She had that look of decadent divinity which appears to be the last word in fashionable and intellectual beauty. One might picture her as the evil goddess Ashtoreth of the Zidonians, stiff in a golden shrine glittering with encrusted jewels, the winged doors half open that her rigidly outspread hands might rain abominations on her worshipers. The shut eyelids and black lashes sealed on the marble cheek gave her the air of stiff hieratic mystery seated above all human law, unmatchable in evil.

"You could touch her and she would not wake," whispered the trembling woman beside me. "It's a trance. Not sleep."

I stooped again and close to the delicate nostrils where the faint breath fluttered. Yes—there was the smell of a drug which I dare not name. And very soon she would need no outer help of that sort but could set herself free, unaided, to roam the world, a danger more dreadful than a wandering tiger to every human being who crossed her path. The case was plain to me now. I followed her mother down into the garden.

There in haste as the sun neared the mountains she repeated to me the stories of the young men which I had heard from Biedermann.

"There's no kind of magic of all the ages she doesn't know!" she ended. "Look!" she picked up a book and showed it to me.

That too I knew. It has been the source of deadly dreams to the world for millenniums—"The Book of the Lady of the Great Land." It opened at the Invocation of the Maskim—the seven evil spirits before whom Assyrian men and women trembled in the guardian shadow of their winged bulls known as the Kirubu—later to become our cherubim and be hymned in Christian churches that little guessed their origin. Into what deadly perfumed evil, long hidden, mummied in nard and cassia, bandaged and bound and hidden in temple vaults and bricked tombs, and now awaking insolently in the sunshine of a later day, had I stumbled?

The invocation stood out in black capitals before my eyes:

THE MASKIM, THE EVIL ONES, THEY ARE SEVEN. THEY ARE SEVEN. SEVEN THEY ARE! TO OUR WILL WE MAY BIND AND HOLD THEM, FOR IN THE CLAY OF MAN IS KNEADED THE BLOOD OF GOD!

The beauty of the last phrase caught me. The perverted truth that might yet save the miserable girl. Seven Evil Ones—and I remembered how in the Christian Scripture seven devils were cast out of the Magdalen leaving her snow-white and virgin-pure.

We went slowly through the garden and stood for a moment each thinking our own very different thoughts. Then Mrs. Saumarez said hurriedly—the old look of panic upon her face:

"You must go. She'll be waking. But come again when I send for you and tell me what to do."

I went off, carrying the book with me unconsciously, and a little way up the steep mountain road, looking out over the blue lake as from the ramparts of a great castle. I could not go straight back to the Biedermanns' quiet circle after that experience. I must have time to assemble my thoughts and fit them to a line of action opening before me.

The hell that Mrs. Saumarez must have lived through! And I could predict with certainty that the time would come when she would either be drawn herself into the orbit of the evil or go raving mad. Those who meddle with the perversions of the mental processes little know the ghastliness that lies in wait for them at a certain turn of the road. They will learn when they near it how frightfully the surface of power and pleasure cracks, disclosing beneath it illimitable woe. For if within us is the Kingdom of Heaven (and that is God's truth) within us also is the Kingdom of Hell. Not indeed that which frightened our parents in grim sermons and mechanically repeated prayers but that which set our ancestors half mad with tales of witchcraft and dreadful rites where the polarities of good and evil meet—the deathly clay of man mingled with the blood of outraged divinity—to use the parable in the book in my hand. I opened it again.

"My Father," it cried a page farther on, "the disease of the thought has issued from the abyss! How shall the man find healing?"

How? For man too is a creator, and if in his thoughts he creates forms of terror and wickedness they will surround him living and clear, walking in sun or moonlight, visible to those who have eyes to see—his own self-chosen companions dooming him to the Pit in this life and a terrible future in others.

I reached a height where the road turned and stood meditating these things in their innermost. My work had been directed in part by a great psychologist from whom I had heard true tales which exceeded in deeps and heights of mental process the heavens and hells of our early imaginings. He had his own methods of healing for some such cases, but all differed, all needed different handling. Could I dare to thrust my hands into the delicate machinery of a brain working on lines I knew, strong with its own evilly trained power?

As I stood considering this problem I heard steps approaching the corner behind me—a woman coming down from Donnerstein; I thought no more of it than that.

But they rounded the corner. They were close on me, invisibly—and then I knew. They stopped beside me. Unseen eyes surveyed me sharpened by evil to wicked, almost spiritual power of perception. I felt the cold vibration play over me like a wind of frost. It held me for a moment—perhaps longer—and then the steps went slowly down the road. It was as though a spirit had lifted up the curtain of the dark, held me with glittering eyes for a moment, dropped it and gone on its way.

I stood to watch the dying glory of the afterglow flush the sky, dye world and heaven into a divine rose, then slowly furl its petals and abandon the world to night and the creatures who walk in dark places. I went stiffly down the hill to the Biedermanns' home, looking up as I entered to the old legend carved along the front:

Wer Gott vertraut,
Hat wohl gebaut.

Yes, that is true. Man holds the talisman of safety in his own divinity—the blood of God is kneaded into the clay of man. He need not drop it unless he will. That house will stand.

The question in my mind was—should I consult Biedermann? I did not forget the doctor's obligation of secrecy, but none the less the woman had demanded help, and if I could reinforce my own powers the obligation lay on me to do it. But I would approach the subject cautiously and so make my decision. I have indicated already that he was a man of much spiritual power; of deep piety; and, though my own inspirations do not lie along the Lutheran path, power is power, meet it where you will, and all the streams have their source in the skies.

Frau Biedermann went up early to bed, with a headache. We lit our pipes and sat in the great shadowed balcony beneath the eaves where the mountains stood bathed in moonlight, gemmed with stars, their own glory of eternal strength submerged in a greater. I led the talk with care to the point I chose, so that my question was natural when I asked it:

"Biedermann, do you believe in what is called possession?"

He turned mild blue eyes of astonishment upon me. "Naturally. Is it not in the Bible?"

"It certainly is, and yet modern science might have other explanations to offer. Would you accept the theory that a man could be so saturated with evil that his will could obey none but the evil presences formed by his own thoughts and that objective devils of his own creation dwelt in him and used his body and brain as their vehicle?"

He reflected a moment. "I think I could admit that explanation. Mind you, I believe in a real Power of Evil—call it the Devil for short—who has his own realm of power and acts in it."

"That I cannot admit," I answered. "The universe is one, with no duality, and man and nature are alike divine, but I know that man has the power to create frightful thought forms which dominate himself and may dominate other natures weak or wicked. It is a horrible stage of evolution but the seed of good—of power is in that also. The man who can create horror will turn his creative power to good and glory one of these days when he stops at another station on the long railroad of life. Am I a heretic?"

I quoted from the Gospel: "If Satan cast out Satan he is divided against himself; how shall then his kingdom stand?"

"That is true and interesting," he said eagerly. "You mean if a man can be stimulated to—as it were—rend his own flesh apart, endure the agony and fight the fight, he is sure of deliverance and the evil things may be cast out forever? I think that may be called Gospel teaching."

"If Gospel means 'good news' I think so too. I name these things differently—but I think we can shout across the road to each other. Have you seen such cases?"

He laid down his pipe and told me a dreadful story and another. Men of his profession, like my own, see the dark places that the hurrying world skirts or forgets. The second one bore most singularly on the secret my own mind was guarding and related to the young man Arnold Schneiderling of whom he had told me on the way from the waterfall. In the speech of the world the lad would be called a degenerate. Deep had called to deep with a vengeance when the English girl came his way. This threw a more focused light upon my problem.

It was late when we parted and Biedermann made a curious remark as we went upstairs.

"One should never allow oneself to be deceived by facts. They are the veil of reality."

Did I not say all the faiths coalesce at a point? I had heard that doctrine elsewhere than in a Lutheran Parson-House and had known its truth.

Facts gave way rather rudely that night—or was it the other way over? I went to sleep with the book on the table beside me and the moon looking in at the windows making two white pools of light on the black floor—a haven of peace.

As if a blow had struck me awake, I sat up in my bed to face a horror. Groveling on the floor, crawling along it, passing in and out from gloom to gloom I saw the naked body of a woman. More snake than woman she propelled herself, lying flat with oaring hands and elbows. Humanity was obliterated in the attitude. It survived only in the head, horribly lifted, with the short hair running in a sparkling crest over the ridge of the skull. Her eyes fixed on mine without any intellect were patches of darkness in a white face above stretched lips. She wallowed in and out of light and gloom. I knew my own repulsive thought-form of the girl in the old Parson-House and with a swift spiritual gesture destroyed it. The room was empty in a second, flooded with pure moonlight. To see her thus was no way to help her. As I sat thinking I heard swift steps outside and sprang to the window to see the figure of a girl in white running fleetly up the mountain road, looking behind her now and then as she ran. She vanished round a corner.

A moment and after her came a young man running desperately as if for his life. I could hear his gasping breath as he passed the balcony. It told of a pumping heart and bursting veins, but still he ran as if the devil were after him instead of before him. They were out of sight—a parable of many things; when I turned again there was nothing but silence, and the peace of sacred centuries filled the little house.

Next day Biedermann brought in the news that young Franz Rieder, son of the postmaster, had disappeared. He was known to have been heavily in debt and to have been led into dissipations at the market town of Hegenburg twenty miles distant and was only at home to demand money from his father. The supposition was that he might have done a bolt towards the frontier, but the village was alive with fear and conjecture, for this was the third disappearance in four months.

I thought it right to mention to Biedermann that I had seen a young man running up the mountain road, and ten minutes later a search party which I joined was formed, and we started for the Falkenwald, the men looking doubtfully at one another in fear and dreadful expectation. As we made the first turn we met the English girl coming down, walking lightly and gaily. She carried a long-stemmed white rose with dewy leaves in her hand and held it against her red lips to inhale the perfume. Biedermann lifted his hat and she smiled to him as she passed. I noticed two of the men whispering together and looking at her. They did not smile.

For the first time I had seen her eyes—they swept me in passing. Dark, extremely long and narrow. One could almost have said in the old Indian phrase that they touched her hair, and this gave her an oblique glance extraordinarily unusual and attractive. But I was conscious of a tingling along my hands and arms as she passed, and the Shakespearean line crossed my memory:

> *By the pricking of my thumbs,*
> *Something wicked this way comes.*

I turned to look after her in a minute and saw her standing looking fixedly after me. She went on at once.

Reaching the Falkenwald we divided and searched. I had the curiosity to climb round to the place of my last visit to the waterfall—where it made its mighty plunge from the heights. I stood there looking down for the promontory where I had seen the naked girl. Biedermann was right. It did not exist. Nothing interrupted or diverted the smooth and awful shoot of pale green water shot with flying foam, leaping to destruction leagues below. It had been mirage painted on my eyes as I saw her there. But how?

I rejoined the men. Roped, two had clambered down beyond the point I had reached on that eventful day. On the edge of the crevasse they found a shoe, a bloody handkerchief, and recognized them. What more? Columns of print could not have better told the end. But why? That question remained unanswered.

Biedermann, lost in thought, made but one remark as we reached Geierstein and separated—he to go to the boy's mother, I, to the balcony.

"The mystery of evil is at work here. We must not rest until we confront it with the Cross."

My own thought, but in other words. After sitting awhile on the balcony and strengthening my resolution, I got my hat, put her book under my arm, and set off to the old Parson-House. It was noon and hard sunlight dwarfed my shadow on the white road. I opened the garden gate and went in.

Between two linden trees an orange-colored hammock was slung and in it lay the girl reading. She turned, hearing steps, and threw her legs over the side and sat facing me.

"My mother is out!" she said, without a pretense of ordinary civility. Her manner was insolent and haughty as if something about me angered her. I was equally unconventional. Beauty blazed at me from the long narrow eyes and red lips, but I knew her and she knew it.

"I must have a few words with you," I said and pulled a garden chair under the tree to face her.

"I refuse!" She sprang to her feet. I shook my head smiling.

"You accept, for, if not, a few days will see the village break loose upon you, and if they tore you to tatters or dragged you to the asylum—and it's a toss-up which—I for one would not blame them."

Silence and the light breeze fluttering the leaves. Her fierce pride did not falter. She sat down again and stared at me.

"Are you mad? What have I to do with the village? I live my life—I go nowhere but to—"

I interrupted. "The mountain road. The Falkenwald! Did you guess where we were going this morning when you met us? Did you see me when I looked down from the shoot of the waterfall the other day? You looked up. You waved."

She laughed a little. "You're as mad as a hatter! It takes roped men, they tell me, to get down the side of the fall."

"It would take more than roped men to get where you stood, for in the world about us that place has no existence. Drop fencing! Come to reality. I tell you you are in danger."

She looked at me sidelong and warily, measuring her own weapons against mine. I read her thoughts as she set her mouth so that the lips trembled piteously, like those of a child who entreats for forgiveness in all innocence. But no obedient tears obeyed the summons to her eyes. It is an old superstition that witches cannot shed tears; which is as it may be. The pose of the young and terrified girl did not deceive me for one moment. She was folding and sheathing flamboyant power—"As though a rose should shut and be a bud again."

"How am I to help it if men go wild for me?" she asked meekly. "It happens to other girls and nobody blames them. You're a man. You should understand. Is it likely I'd have anything to do with these village louts? Not I. I despise them. We simply came here to have a little peace. When young Lethington shot himself—"

She halted in a breath at the look on my face. She had made a slip and knew it. I remembered the shouting newspaper headings, the evil room where drugged men lay and dreamed their hashish dreams. Much more also, not uncommon in the great cities. No wonder they were in hiding. She saw it all in my face and flung out into her true self again, defiant, hard as steel. I considered her a moment in silence; we were face to face now, preliminaries past.

"You never had a chance," I said. "Your father opened the wrong door for you when he might have opened the right one."

"He told me there was no other. But this is power. I've had a good time if I've had no more. I live on the desire of men. They go mad for me when I look at them. Hardly one—Where's the harm? I'm not bad-looking, am I?"

More than beautiful, my brain answered. A charm perilous and deadly. A bitter wine to drink. A honeyed sweetness, poison in the throat. The secrets of wicked forgotten worships were in those long agate eyes fringed with midnight. She represented what men will always find worth pursuit when the worst they can do has been done and unslaked longing seeks for more—yet more. But though my brain acknowledged her my heart was silent, my flesh revolted against her.

"It's no use with you," she said savagely. "Well, then—what do you want me to do? Hands up for me this time! I never spared anyone. I can't expect you to spare me. Give me back my book!"

She snatched at it from under my arm.

"What's *your* amulet?" she added. "You can't destroy my witchcraft with crosses and black cats. You know better."

"I want to ask you a question," I said slowly. "Is there never a moment when you remember yourself before your father took you in hand and wish yourself—well—what you were then—or like other girls whom men love?"

"That's a queer question!" she said with a smile in her long eyes. "No, never! I suppose I used to sometimes, for it's rather frightening at first when you see what you want to see and do glide out of you and take shape and force others to see it. I used to faint and cry, but he kept me up to it. I was a triumph of 'psykes' he said. No, I never want to go back. But I have to lie low when the papers get hold of me and sometimes I get most awfully tired and drowsy. Then I have to draw strength from other people. Not the good old blood-sucking vampire! You get into their vibration. You know."

A thought struck me. "That's what you're doing to Lili Schneiderling."

She nodded, laughing. "But I must have more. I have to be asleep nearly all day. See, I've no color. Wait till you see me with a faint, faint color like the last of the Alpenglow. I'm six times as good-looking then. I'm seedy now."

I ignored that and returned to my question. "If you could be set free would you prefer to remain what you are?"

"Infinitely. Don't let's talk nonsense. Can't you go away? I want to sleep and there's nothing to be done."

"There's a good deal to be done. Your mother consulted me—"

Her eyes narrowed. Her lips drew apart dangerously. "I'll make her pay for that!" she said under her breath.

I shook my head and answered coolly: "I think not. Mr. Biedermann and I will remove your mother today and leave you alone in the house."

"But I think not!" Her teeth showed like a cat's with retracted lips tightened above them. "She knows and you know that I can come through walls and windows while I'm asleep in my bed. There's no part of the world where you could hide her from me, because she'd call me herself. I've mastered her. She'd have to build me if I couldn't build myself."

She sat up facing me proudly.

"Death?" I suggested.

"There's no such thing! Don't try to frighten me with fairy tales. My father lives in this house as much as we do. Look up. You'll see him at the window."

I looked up involuntarily.

The detestable face of Saumarez was looking down upon his daughter and me. As I looked it was gone, but I had seen it. What a thought to have moving all but incarnate about one!

"Did you think I don't know that?" I asked coolly. "But did your father tell you of hell after death?"

"Fire and brimstone?" She laughed aloud. "No, he knew better."

"Did he tell you that men make their own hells and need no other devils and that it goes on and on? That what you most hate will be your surrounding—bodily, mental——for what will seem to you forever and ever, though it will be only a moment of eternity?"

She looked up sharply. "That's queer! I dream that sometimes."

"You will dream it for a considerable time," I said, "There's no evading that law. That marigold could sooner come up an oak than you not reap what you sow. Now, what will you do?"

"Sorry you don't like me as I am!" She laughed ironically. "You should have known me as a nice little girl in pigtails adoring my dog—" She paused and added in a different tone, "I'd like him back," and then sank into silence for a moment. Presently she lifted her head fiercely.

"What else am I to do? Even if I didn't like it—and I do—there's no turning back. You know enough to know that. When you can do as you like and herd men like sheep and dip your hands in their pockets you don't go back to the maundering jealousies and helplessness of the average woman."

"There's no turning back. True. You have learned one secret of power. You can't unlearn it, but you can go past it and on. You must decide now. This place is finding you out; and if they lynched you who could be surprised? Such things have happened and will again. You're nearing it."

Her eyes dilated on me with terror. This kind fears death very exceedingly, knowing enough to know certain things. But this kind also does not own it. She shot a look of hatred at me.

"I'm always being hunted from pillar to post. I might do better in Asia. They understand better there. But go on. You've got me—in a way."

"Naturally. You don't want your brain—your instrument of power— broken and scattered. But it's coming. One way or another it comes to women like you. You're the curse of great cities—you and your like. You drench your victims with the false occult—the intellectual, and of the spiritual you know nothing. You trade on vices and fears. You waken the devils in your victims' hearts with your obscene magic that you may wring gold and power from them and trample them into the mud. And then one day—these women and men like you—they make some fatal slip, and the law gets them and holds them up in public for the devils they are, and the prison doors shut on them."

I could only appeal to her fears, but every word I said was God's truth. The world knows too well the trader on hidden evil cults and influences. That would be her escape when the pulse of beauty flagged in her and life ran low.

She looked up and said violently: "What could I do?"

"You could throw away your drug. You could come to London and be my patient."

"Oh—I see. Money!" she said impudently. "Well, I could be a profitable patient! I have lots of money. Good for you, but I don't see what you have to bribe *me* with. You don't know these things. And I shall get more power as I get experience. I made you see my father now. I got your brain, though I couldn't get more. But I may later."

She laughed dangerously. I also, but to another tune. The scene had its humor—the rival magicians before Pharaoh, let us say! I told her in a few words that I was ahead of her there. That where she could make thought-forms to play upon the vilest strings of human nature I could command spiritual resources that were powerful to create and restore. Her instrument was the brain swayed by the primitive consciousness of forbidden things; mine was the spiritual and evolutionary consciousness of the universe mighty to unfold and develop the divine in man.

"Match yourself against me and try!" I said. "Try, though I acknowledge myself a beginner in a school that takes ages to perfect its pupils."

"It all sounds mighty dull!" she said and yawned. "Haven't we gassed long enough?"

I was silent a moment, considering, for an inspiration had shot through me—an answering flash, as I thought, to the indent I had made for a sword in the struggle. But could I speak to a debased creature like this of the most sacred experience of my life, founded on a lower consciousness and rising to infinity from the story of two dogs to the heaven-height of the woman I loved?

What is one's own but to be shared with the needy?

I told her the story in simple terms. At first she sat, marble hard, presently the sullen obstinacy of her face stirred, became more human, finally she listened intently. I ended.

"I like that," she said. "I can swear that's true. I love animals, but I can't get it in on them, have no pull on them. I can't even ride—Horses go mad if I try to touch them. They don't register me a bit, and I wish they did. Look now at that beast"—She pointed to a fox-terrier belonging to the next house down the road—"I've given him bones, biscuits. He'll not touch them. It's queer, for I want to make friends."

"Try," I said. I wanted to see, but I could have told her what would happen. Animals, especially dogs, have a very highly developed instinct against spiritual evil. That has been a common experience in all countries and times. It is not for nothing they lead a dog at the head of a Parsee funeral procession. I gave her a biscuit. I had always a supply for dog friends. He growled low and deep, disclosing shining teeth. The hackles along his back rose stealthily as he edged towards me for shelter. She flung it at him, and he leaped at her furiously. I dragged him back by the collar and he looked up in amazement that I should avert righteous judgment, then, sheltered beneath my knees, watched her steadily.

I said: "They know. They see."

She said scornfully: "Devils?"

"What else was or is meant by them? But to return: I believe you can be cured. Will you put yourself in my hands? Will you try it for a year? I know you're no coward, so I tell you frankly you'll go through hell while you're learning my way and discarding your own. But if you're game I'll stand by you shoulder to shoulder."

"There's nothing I care for except what I am, and there are things one can never drag out of one. You're talking putrid nonsense. There's nothing I want but what I have—I am power."

"Power!" I said ironically. "And afraid of being driven out of a Swiss village! Afraid of death! Afraid of life! Power! Come and get your eyes opened and you may talk of power then!"

"Never. You drive me mad; you frighten me. Go!"

"Wait," I said. "I give you a few minutes to decide. You're on an awful road. You think you're safe because you keep your body out of it as far as you can. Fool! What strength has the body against the brain? And yours will weaken daily. You'll be dragged in. My consulting rooms are full of people like you, damned on earth whatever they may be hereafter. In a year or less you'll be open to man's justice, and when he gets you he does not spare you. You'll rot in a prison or asylum for the snake of the great cities that you are!"

"Never. Never. Go away," she said, and made as if to thrust me from her.

As the words left her lips two things happened. A man looked over the fence near us, glaring at her and muttering to himself. He shook his fist at her with a curse and went on, turning and cursing as he went. It was the father of Franz Rieder. And her mother broke from behind the roses and sobbing wildly fell upon her knees before her, clasping her about the body with arms of desperate love.

"For God's sake—for God's sake!" she cried, and could say no more. The girl was pale and shuddering with a fixed face above her. I cannot word that scene nor say how long it lasted. That is beyond me. I will only say that at the end she rose and stood looking at me, mocking, insolent, defiant, yet with a look like a shadowy rainbow in black skies.

"Well—perhaps it'll be a wow. There may be some fun. I'll give you six months and if you fail—"

Her mother had crept into the house weeping terribly. The dog sat and looked at us both bewildered.

"You promise?"

"I promise."

"Then go into the house and pack. We'll start for London tomorrow."

She went without a look behind her. There was stuff in the devil that might yet make her a flame of pure fire. After deep consideration I told the story to Biedermann, asked his prayers for the fight and received his promise. Why? Because every prayer of true faith and belief, let it come whence it will, is a draft on the power of the universe which will be honored.

I took them to London, settled the mother in rooms at Henford, the northern suburb, and put the girl Joyselle in the house of a doctor friend, a remarkable psychologist, who took in only one mental case at a time and had a house and garden perfectly adapted to his work. I gave him the fullest details, and she had not spared me on the way over, so that I knew of what I spoke. The arrangement was that I should visit her three times a week and oftener if necessary.

I shall never forget the flash of fury in her eyes when she found that another beside myself was to be concerned in her cure. She defied us both openly. If Eliot had not been seasoned and armed she would have got him under her influence before my eyes. As it was he watched her with coolest professional interest. The nurse was a stolid, unimaginative woman from whom she could have no hopes and who frankly regarded her as a lunatic. Her fury was terrible when she saw herself what she called trapped—but I rejoiced to see that its very violence exhausted the powers of evil concentration on which she worked. She was draining her own reserves with every shriek and struggle. If Eliot and I had ever disbelieved the stories of demoniacal possession (with a difference) we should have been converts now. There were times when a devil and no woman struggled, swore, yelled obscenities and blasphemies, on the ground before us. I have seen Eliot wipe his forehead, pale as ash, and say:

"Done in! The asylum is the only place for her."

And yet the brain was perfectly sound all the time.

But there was another side. When I told her she must either be searched for the drug or put upon her honor that she had none, she gave her word—and cheated. We knew it next day. After I had ordered the nurse to search her I turned on her and said the one word, "Coward!"

In a moment her face and neck were flooded with the crimson of deadly shame, as if the vessel of her heart were shattered by the insult—the only one that could touch the savagery in her, nurtured on the brutal lusts and greeds of modern life. A slur on her personal hardihood—her only ethic! She could not stand that. She made a dart for the window and would have flung herself out, but I was there before her. I had got the key to her cipher and used it.

She stared at me as I left, a dumb fury with loathing eyes.

I concentrated on her that night with all the power of all my knowledge and training, knowing that Biedermann would be at the same work in his own way where the stars stand sentinel on the high mountains. We had a fixed time together. Later I telephoned to Eliot. She was asleep, exhausted by her devilries.

It is impossible that I should give all the details of that long struggle with misdirected power and the degrading influences of modern brutality.

Men of my profession *know*; others must take it on trust. Satan was casting out Satan with a vengeance and rending himself in the process. It was ten to one whether she could live through it.

Eliot dealt with her on material lines and the influence of a fine personality. I, on the psychic. I brought to bear upon her the oldest system of psychology known and focused its withering light on her aberration, and at first with no result whatever. She grew more hardened. She defied us, tried to bribe the servants, made cunning efforts at escape. I began to think we must give her the status of a certified lunatic, for the position was fast becoming untenable, and yet Eliot and I agreed that with her brainpower cool as ice it might be difficult to carry that matter through.

"She's so poisoned in every fiber that I see uncommonly little hope," Eliot said one day. "There are moments when I wish she could be reduced to imbecility and built up from the beginning if it were possible. Is there any hell hot enough for the devil who brought her to this!"

I agreed, but added:

"Look at the force in her! She's a perfect wellspring of misdirected psychic power. A cataract that destroys but may yet make light and warmth for the world. Don't despair. It's the fight of our lives, old man. Don't crab it."

He was stanch as steel. Besides he had moments of real pity and liking for her misspent courage. So one may sympathize with a rat showing its teeth in a corner in the last despairing struggle against death.

She would talk with me when I came—and that was a useful influence. I harped upon the note of courage and that always whipped her failing strength. She would not be beaten if she loathed the victory. But I began to realize the possibility of her death in the trenches. She looked a dying woman.

One day a very unexpected aid reached us. There was a high wall round the garden, unclimbable (for Eliot occasionally had certified lunatics), and a well-guarded lodge at the only entrance; therefore I cannot tell how this thing happened. As she and the nurse walked along the shady south walk at the end of the garden they saw a dog lying dead, as they thought, on the grass border. The head had been brutally clubbed, so far as we could judge. A West Highland terrier. The nurse said she fell on her knees beside it in a paroxysm not of pity but rage, threatening the brutes in language that made the woman's blood run cold. Finally she looked up.

"You damned fool, go and get stuff to wash him. No, I'll carry him in. Tell Eliot to come."

"Can't leave you!" the nurse retorted, with not unreasonable anger.

"I'm coming. Get on."

She lifted the dog in her arms with his blood dropping over her dress and carried him into the surgery. No animal had ever come near her since she went down to hell, nor would this have done so had he been conscious. She held him with fierce tenderness while Eliot removed a fragment of bone pressing on the brain and dressed and bandaged the little head. He was quick to see the points of the situation and, while he washed his hands afterwards, said artfully:

"Nurse is too busy to look after him. We'll send him to the Vet to take his chance."

I had better not record her words. She would nurse him herself. After a show of resistance, it was granted. We had gained a powerful ally.

Again I must condense. I believe that but for that living interest she would never have fought through the agony of disusing the drug. Eliot and I appreciated this and left neither that nor any other way of help untried, but it was agony under which I say deliberately I think she would have died but that she was fighting for the dog's life. I gave that up more than once; she never.

He was lying in a box one day when I came in and she had just dripped some milk and brandy through his teeth. Kneeling beside him she looked up quickly, and the picture impressed itself on my mind.

The dog breathed. That was about all, and you could not say much more for her. She was deadly ill. Her eyes burned with a waning fire in the long hollow eye-caverns into which they had sunk. All beauty was gone. The face was more like a death's head than a living one, every bone jutting through sickly skin drawn taut over it. Her body was shrunk to such emaciation and weakness that she lay on her bed all day. What wonder? She was fighting on, but against what odds! Nightly she walked through the hells of insomnia, daily through the hells of tortured nerves. Food and drink were like ashes in her mouth. I will not swear that she always kept her promise to withhold her evil powers of concentration, but on the whole she held them down. A strange and terrible sight.

Only one energy survived beside the fighting instinct—her passionate care for the dog. She called him Darroch after the dog she had had as a child and once gave a hint that she believed he had come back to her. A piteous thing to see, and yet her one hope. She would crawl to tend him. No one else must touch him, and though she cried out for the drug while Eliot allowed the graduated doses, the moment he told her that stage was past she never asked for it again. I have seen the blood run down her chin from the teeth-marks on her lip, but she endured savagely. I could respect the strength in her, if no more. There was always that background to the horrors and degradations through which she dragged herself and us, and of those I dare not speak out of my own profession.

Now as she crouched by the dog he stirred and moaned. He laid a paw unconsciously on her hand as she stroked his little breast. She bent over him and I could not see her face. I said:

"He'll live. You've saved his life."

She said, so low that I could scarcely hear: "Must he have died? Did I save him?"

"Certainly. You saved him."

Silence. I saw a dreadful trembling begin in the poor bony hands and arms. It flowed like water up her body, up into the rope-like throat muscles. It reached the quivering nerves of her face, and shook her fiercely like a storm from head to foot. She collapsed into a heap on the floor, sobbing wildly. Dry rending sobs at first. Then merciful tears to relieve the frightful tension. They poured down her face; she was too weak to raise a hand to dry them, but it was to my thought as if the granite of her heart had softened and was pouring away in rivers of living water. We laid her on the sofa, her heart's action so feeble that if it had given up the struggle I could not have wondered.

"Perhaps so best!" Eliot said, looking down upon her as she lay, tears still pouring like thunder-rain down the jutting bones of her face. Yet even then, when the dog stirred and uttered a cry to his only friend, in a moment she was dragging herself across the floor to the rescue, half sitting, half crawling with her hands. It reminded me of my horrible vision of her crawling along the pools of moonlight in my room at Geierstein. Like; but the width of heaven and hell was between the two. We did not stop her. She reached him, tended him, and then fainted. We thought she was gone.

I draw near the end. A strong soul greatly sinning is easier to redeem than a weak one when a certain stage is past. We passed it that day. Darroch recovered first and was power and strength, for he loved her—her first revelation of selfless Love, the Great Seducer whose flute all must follow when they hear its heart-piercing music. He would not leave her, so it became worth the up-hill climb to strength that she might hope one day to take him into the garden. But it needed all our pull—including the dog's—to get her through, and I would not have had her die then. She was not fit to face that problem before she had mastered this.

Then came the moment when by two minutes at a time I began to reverse her father's evil lessons and teach her the true approach to power. I dared not neglect it. She knew too much to be left with any weapons lying about which she had not been trained to handle. No dangerous vacuum must be there. Power she would have; then she must have the best.

I have never seen so apt a pupil. That was natural. I had only to reverse her learning, and the Way began to open. It interested her profoundly; in her clear, merciless mind the majesty of unalterable law presented itself as awe-striking and utterly desirable. She had the mathematical instinct and I put the right books into her hands, which connect it, for those who can see, with the ancient science now building up all her waste places. She leaped at that learning. The marshaled beauty of order presented itself to her. But, no—it would need a book to record the stages of evolution which she passed through, pressing steadily onward to her goal. She was fighting on my side now. Satan had cast out Satan, and how could his power stand?

I came one day to find her sitting in the garden with Darroch, now as healthy a little fellow as you would wish to see, at her feet. Her extraordinary education along psychic lines made communion between them possible in a way I have never seen before, but into that I have no space to enter. She lifted him and he lay in her lap while we talked.

"Tell me this," she said slowly. "Should I remember the things I did? For I can't. They're all blurring—they'll go. What about remorse? Is it another angle of my callousness?"

"Not it. It's a sign that the strength in you looks to the future. Why look back? You have tremendous reserves of power. You'll do great things yet. I back you against the world."

She smiled faintly, then:

"Do you remember the Maskim—the seven Assyrian devils? I'm like the Magdalen that had seven devils cast out of her. Mine are getting as unreal to me as dreams. Did hers, I wonder? I'd like to ask her. What happened to mine?"

"You know best. You cast them out yourself."

"No, not I. Love," she answered quickly. "Love's the conqueror whether you get it in a Christ or a little dog. I never knew such a thing existed, and now—I see nothing else. Who can stand against it? It sweeps you away like that great green glide of the waterfall at Geierstein. Nothing has a chance against it. It broke me."

At the beginning of the talk I should have dreaded that memory. Now we were swept on together. There was nothing to fear. She stroked the dog's coat gently while she spoke, and the movement of her hand was not more tranquil than her face and voice.

"I remember it all so well. No animal would ever look at me. It's strange, but I always wanted them to like me. I think now that was the only instinct that kept me human, though I could have tortured them one and all because they hated me. Not that I did. I was not devil enough for that. There are other things I shan't remember until I can laugh at their folly, and then perhaps they'll have gone right out of my head."

Her strength and curative power were astounding. I had seen what the world might call a miracle wrought under my eyes. To what shall we put a limit?

"And don't I know what I owe you? That's one of the things I'll work for—to be *your* victory. But I owe more to this than even to you. You are Wisdom. *This* is Love."

She lifted the little dog, looking into his eyes and he into hers, and added slowly:

"For in the clay of man is kneaded the blood of God."

Is it worthwhile to give any outer details of her triumph? Scarcely. The world knows her name but only a tithe of her greatness. The story can be told thus far, but like all true stories the best is hidden and there are no words for it.

THE THOUGHT-MONSTER

AMELIA REYNOLDS LONG

Amelia Reynolds Long (1903–1978) was one of a handful of women writers who contributed material to the early science fiction magazines as well as being a regular contributor to Weird Tales. *Her first appearance was with "The Twin Soul" in 1928, but her best known story is the following, which was her second sale, and appeared in the March 1930* Weird Tales. *It features an occult detective, Dr. Cummings. It is surprising that she did not use him again in other stories, especially when she moved on, more profitably, to crime and detective fiction in the 1930s, writing more than thirty books. "The Thought-Monster" was made into the horror film* Fiend Without a Face *in 1957 but the plot diverges considerably from the story. Long persevered as a writer and poet into the 1950s, and she also wrote radio scripts. She eventually ceased writing and became a museum curator. Despite many good stories and books, this is the one story for which she is remembered, although you only need one to make you immortal.*

THE FIRST OF THE SERIES OF OUTRAGES WAS THE CASE OF WELTON Grimm. Grimm was a retired farmer with a little place about three miles from town, who apparently had not an enemy in the world; yet one morning he was discovered dead in a patch of woods near his home with a look of horror on his face that made the flesh creep on those who found him. There were no marks of violence upon the body; only that expression of horrified revulsion at unspeakable things. Two doctors, a coroner, and a jury puzzled over it, and at last gave out the statement that he had been the victim of a heart attack—which nobody believed.

For a while the case was discussed, as all such things are in small towns. Then, just as it was about to drop into oblivion, the second blow fell: another man, a stranger this time, was found dead under identical circumstances in the same spot. Before the town could digest this, two half-grown boys were added to the list of victims, and the very next night a woman was found dead under similar conditions about a mile distant.

The police scoured the countryside for the culprit—for it was now admitted that the deaths were the result of foul play—but to no avail. They could find nothing: there seemed to be nothing to find. But when again the Terror struck, this time claiming for its victim the mayor himself, the townspeople decided that something drastic, must be done at once; and they sent to New York for a detective.

He came—a keen-witted, intelligent man named Gibson, with a long list of brilliant exploits behind him. After going over the case with the chief of police, he pointed out a fact that was so obvious it was a wonder we had not seen it ourselves.

"Those people have died of fright," he said. "There is someone, probably an escaped lunatic, hiding in the woods who is so hideous that the very sight of him frightens the beholder to death. Since all the deaths occurred within a mile of each other, you will find him hiding somewhere within that comparatively small area."

"But we searched the woods," objected the chief. "We searched them thoroughly. There wasn't the sign of a thing."

"Did you ever search at night!" asked Gibson.

"Well, no," the chief admitted.

"Whatever your Terror is," went on the detective, "he is too clever to come out in daylight. But at night he is sure of himself; so that is when we must lie in wait for him."

Everyone saw the sense of this plan, but few were willing to try it. At last, however, Gibson collected some half-dozen men, and they stationed themselves, armed to the teeth, throughout the patch of woods to wait for the thing. They had a series of prearranged whistle signals by which they could communicate with one another should occasion arise.

The night passed quietly; but in the morning it was found that the outrages had taken a new turn: Gibson had completely disappeared! The woods were searched for him and a pond was drained for his body, but without result. Then, about a week later, he wandered into town—a mouthing, gibbering idiot!

The morale of the people began to break under this new horror. And to add to their consternation, the grave of the mayor was opened the night before Gibson's return, and his body dragged half out of the coffin. A great mass meeting, for the purpose of taking counsel against the Terror, was now called. The hall was jammed to capacity, for all came who could come.

One of the town councilmen was addressing the assembly. He was in the most earnest part of his address when suddenly he stopped. No one had been conscious of any of the doors opening, yet we all knew that another presence had entered the room! There was an apprehensive shuffling of feet and craning of necks as uneasiness among the crowd grew. The speaker took a sip of water and tried to go on, but without success. And then it was as if a thin veil began to form between us and the electric chandelier overhead.

With that, hysteria broke loose. There was a stampede for the exits, in which three people were trampled to death. Later, the body of the speaker was found upon the platform. The face was twisted into a mask of overwhelming horror.

The people were stunned. They crept into their churches to pray. And, as if in answer to their prayers, came Michael Cummings, psychic investigator.

Cummings first presented himself before the town council. "I have been reading about your trouble down here," he said, "and I would like to try my hand at solving the mystery."

He was welcomed with open arms. He did not consider the possibility of an escaped lunatic in the neighborhood, as Gibson had done. "No madman could be responsible for all this," he said when someone mentioned the subject. "It takes more than the sight of a poor, deranged mind to kill a strong man. I believe that there is a supernatural force at work; possibly one of the little-understood elementals that are sometimes aroused or liberated by a disturbance of the laws of nature. I shall go out to the woods around dusk this evening and look the ground over."

"But, man," gasped the town treasurer, "that's suicide! No man comes out of there alive who enters after nightfall."

"There is little danger until after night has actually fallen," smiled Cummings. "Besides, even should I meet the Terror, I am armed against it in a way that none of the others were."

He went, but learned nothing. The next morning a farmer, who lived about half a mile away, was found dead in his barn.

That afternoon Cummings called upon Dr. Bradley, who was the coroner. "I am going to make a strange request, Doctor," he began. "I am going to ask that you permit me to photograph the eyes of this poor man."

The doctor, greatly mystified, gave his consent.

"In a case of violent death," Cummings explained as he set up his apparatus, "an image of the last thing seen is usually photographed upon the retina of the eye. I want to see whether a carefully developed enlargement won't show us that image."

At Bradley's interested request, he promised to let him know the results of the experiment. Two or three hours later, therefore he returned to the doctor's office.

"I have drawn a blank," he confessed. "The eye shows absolutely nothing."

"Your theory didn't work, then?" asked Bradley sympathetically.

"No," Cummings answered. "And yet I don't see how it could have failed in a case of this kind. There is one alternative: perhaps there was nothing for the dying man to see." "But," objected the doctor, "I thought it was what he saw that killed him."

"Fear," said Cummings, "can enter a man's soul through other senses than sight. Anyway, I shall work on that hypothesis for a while and see where it leads me." Abruptly he changed the subject. "Who lives in that rambling old place half a mile out from town?" he asked.

"A scientist named Walgate," answered the doctor. "I'll admit," he went on quickly, "that the location of his house and his being something of a recluse make it look as if he might be concerned with the mystery, but we have proof that he isn't. For one thing, he was here in town in the company of the most reputable people the nights that the first three outrages took place."

"Could he have any sort of creature concealed about the place on which he might be experimenting?" asked Cummings.

"No," answered Bradley. "He isn't that kind of a scientist. Psychology in its most abstract form is his line. In fact, I was around to see him myself, thinking he might possibly have something like that."

"I wonder," said Cummings, "if you would mind going again."

The next day they called upon Dr. Walgate. They found a courteous, scholarly man plainly as much concerned over the mysterious deaths as they were.

"Doctor," asked Cummings presently, "have you ever considered the possibility of the Terror's being nothing physical at all, but a kind of psychical entity?"

The doctor shot him a keen, swift glance. "Yes," he said. "I have considered that."

"And you have come to the 'conclusion—?"

"It is difficult to come to a conclusion in matters like this unless one has some definite point to start from."

To Bradley's surprise, Cummings did not follow up this very evident lead, but soon brought the visit to a close. "Why didn't you press the psychical entity opening?" he asked a little reproachfully as they walked back to town. "It was plain that Walgate either suspects or knows something in that direction."

"Suspects, may even know, but can not prove," corrected Cummings. "But he is the type of man who will not speak until he can prove. Meanwhile to attempt to force his confidence would defeat our own purpose."

At Cummings' suggestion, the people in the outlying districts kept violet-shaded lights burning outside their houses after nightfall.

"The thing which we are fighting," he said, "is supernatural, and our best weapon against it is the violet ray, which is highly inimical, and sometimes even fatal, to it."

"Look here," said Bradley, "aren't you introducing a little too much legerdemain into this? I can accept a primitive natural force run amuck, but when you begin to fight it with colored lights, I grow skeptical. Is this an attempt to give the people a mental sedative?"

Cummings only smiled, and the people went on burning their lights. The outrages ceased.

"It looks as if you had razed the ghost after all," admitted Bradley when a month had passed unmarred by any fresh tragedy.

But Cummings shook his head. "No," he said, "I have only staved trim off temporarily. As soon as we should cease to use the lights, he would return. More, he may even grow strong enough to resist them. I think that in a day or two I shall visit Walgate. Perhaps I can induce him to talk."

But that time never came. That night a car drove into town with a dead man in the driver's seat, his hands gripped to the wheel in convulsions. In the tonneau sat two more corpses whose faces, like that of the driver, were contorted with stark terror. Only the ruler-like straightness of the road and the viselike grip of those dead hands upon the wheel had kept the ear from overturning. It was like a challenge from the Terror to the town.

For the first time, Cummings was discouraged. "We can protect ourselves," he said, "but we can not protect those who come here from the outside. Something must be done at once, and yet there is nothing that can be done. The situation is even more appalling than the tragedies themselves."

And then, in the gray of early morning something *was* done.

Cummings and Bradley were sitting in the doctor's office when the telephone rang. Bradley answered it.

"Is that Dr. Bradley?" The voice at the other end was hoarse and strained. "This is Dr. Walgate. I want you and Mr. Cummings to come up to my house in half an hour. Walk straight in without ringing and go into the living-room. There you will find a manuscript lying on the table. I want you to read it. But do not come until half an hour from now."

"But why—what—?" stuttered Bradley in his excitement.

"Do as I tell you," interrupted Walgate's voice. "That is all." A metallic click told that he had hung up.

"What do you make of it?" asked Bradley when he had repeated the message to Cummings. "Is it a trap?"

432

"No, it is not, " answered Cummings promptly, "it is not a trap. Walgate is no fool, and he accordingly will not take us for any. We had better do as he tells us."

"Including waiting the specified half-hour before going out!"

"Yes. We don't know what he intends to do. An attempt to improve upon his directions might ruin his plans."

Watches in hand, they sat counting off the minutes. At last Cummings rose. "We can start now," he said. "Come."

They drove out to Walgate's house and entered as he had directed. Bradley noticed that in the near-by woods no birds sang, and that in the house itself an unearthly stillness brooded. He experienced an unnerving intuition of new horrors about to be laid bare.

They proceeded into the living-room, and Cummings pressed the electric light button, for the daylight was still dim and uncertain. Placed conspicuously on the table was a small bundle of manuscript.

"We may as well read these now," said Bradley. "There's no use stopping to look for Walgate; he undoubtedly used that half-hour to make his getaway."

Cummings picked up the manuscript and began to glance through it. "It seems to be part of a diary," he said. "It is made up of entries beginning about a year ago.

It looks—" He broke off to read several sentences under his breath. "I think I had better read this aloud from the beginning," he said.

He began to read:

"*Aug. 4.* Have been studying the material existence of thought. A fascinating subject. If thoughts have material existence, why could not the thought essence be concentrated to— Off on that wild theory again! I am too old for this nonsense.

"*Aug. 7.* I wonder if many of the so-called psychic phenomena, such as table-tipping and the like, are not in some way connected with the materiality of thought. I am tempted to try a few simple experiments.

"*Aug. 11.* I have been wasting time on these silly experiments. I must return to my respectable psychological studies.

"*Aug 13.* Success! Today I moved a small object by the power of thought

433

alone! Since this can be done, what will not be possible once the power is properly developed?

"*Aug. 25.* I have complete mental control! And now my old theory returns. Shall I consider it seriously? It seems too silly even to write down here and yet—

"*Aug. 27.* I shall do it! I shall create a mental being by the concentrated power of pure thought! I am making arrangements with an architect to build my house a room lined with lead, since lead is least conductive to thought waves, and so will not permit the precious thought essence to escape.

"*Sept. 16.* The room is finished. I have been spending five hours a day in it, concentrating upon my thought-creature.

"*Oct.* 18. Today I thought I detected a kind of gathering tension in the atmosphere, but probably it was my imagination. It is too early to look for results.

"*Nov. 24.* The strain of my experiment is beginning to take my strength.

"*Dec. 12.* I fainted today in the lead room.

"*Dec. 29.* Have been forced to give up my experiment temporarily be cause of my health. Have locked the lead room in order that the thought essence may be preserved until I can return to complete my work.

"*Jan. 5.* Am recovering rapidly.

"*Jan. 18.* All my work has gone for nothing, and through the carelessness of a servant! Mrs. Jensen, in a fervor of house-cleaning, unlocked and left open the door of the lead room! If I am to go on with my experiment, I must begin again at the beginning, for all the precious thought-essence has escaped. And just when success was so near! I have discharged Mrs. Jensen. I shall keep no more servants.

"*May 1.* We have had a sad accident here. Welton Grimm, a neighbor of mine, was found dead this morning on the road which runs by the patch of woods between his farm and my house. A pity. Grimm was barely past the prime of life. Dr. Bradley says it was heart failure.

"*May 15.* A strange coincidence; a stranger who was stopping in town was found dead in almost the same place that they found poor Grimm. Oddly enough, the cause of death was the same, too. Some of our more superstitious citizens are alarmed.

"*May 17.* Something is wrong here. Two boys, who, fired by the talk of their elders, had gone exploring after dark in the region where the deaths occurred, were found dead there early this morning. Someone is responsible for these tragedies; coincidence does not go so far.

"*May 18.* Another! A woman this time. On the face of each of the victims is a look of acutest terror. What can it mean?

"*May 20.* Had a most peculiar experience today. I was sitting in my study at dusk. Suddenly I felt that I was not alone; that there was another intelligence in the room with me. I looked up. There was no one there. I switched on the lights, and the illusion vanished. Am I becoming the victim of nerves?

"*May 25.* Another victim; this time our mayor. What is this Terror that is stalking among us? The people have sent to New York for a detective.

"*June 1.* I am being haunted. Three times this week I have felt distinctly that someone was following me, but when I turned to look, there was no one. Dr. Bradley called. Discussed series of tragedies.

"*June 2.* I am not alone in the house. Something is living here with me. I enter a room and know that it has just been occupied by another; I go down a dark hall, and feel something lurking in the shadows. Yet I search and find nothing. Only brilliant lights can hold the thing at bay.

"*June 3.* Gibson, the New York detective, has disappeared. Is he, too, a victim of the Terror?

"A thought has come to me: Is there any connection between the Terror and the Thing that occupies my house with me?

"*June 5.* I have solved the mystery of the Terror, and the solution is more awful than was the mystery itself. I had gone into the lead room for some books that were stored there. Presently I became aware that something was in the room with me. This time I did not look up, but stood perfectly still, waiting and listening. And then the air was filled with something that had being, yet was not made of matter. Great, waving tentacles were groping for my mind, trying to suck it into themselves! With a scream, I rushed from the room. The experiment which I began last fall had succeeded without my knowing it, and I have let a thought-monster loose upon the community!

"*June 7.* Even a thought-monster can not live without food. On what does this demon subsist? Can it be that—

"*June 9.* Last night I committed an atrocious crime against society, but it had to be. I entered the cemetery and opened the grave of the mayor. One glance at his blackening face showed me that he had died an imbecile. My suspicions were right; the thought-monster is a mental vampire, feeding upon the minds of its victims!

"*June 10.* Gibson has returned, but his mind is gone. The intelligence that was James Gibson has been swallowed up in the maw of my detestable invention! I am responsible for his state and for the deaths of those other poor wretches; but what can I do? If I tell the people the nature of this force that is terrorizing the community, they will not believe me. What ordinary man could accept a creature created entirely of thought!

"*June 12.* The Thing is growing bolder. Last night it entered the town hall, where nearly a thousand people were assembled and caused a panic. Three people were killed, not including one of our councilman, who fell a victim to the Thing. I am four more times a murderer! Can not heaven show me a way to put an end to this?

"*June 14.* Michael Cummings, a psychical investigator, is here to run down the Terror. Will he succeed? I doubt it.

"*June 16.* Another man has died.

"*June 18.* Cummings and Dr. Bradley were here today. Do they suspect me of being concerned with this series of deaths? They are right; and yet how far from the truth! No human mind could ever conceive the awfulness of that. I was tempted to tell Cummings my whole story, but held back. What proof could I offer him? How convince him that I was not mad? Even the relief of confession is denied me, for I would not be believed.

"*June 30.* Cummings is checkmating the Terror by means of the violet ray. Cummings' work is only temporary, but it has given me an idea. The violet ray, sufficiently intensified can destroy a psychic force. I shall have the lead room fitted with violet lights; then lure the Thing there and destroy it.

"*July 3.* Have begun work wiring the lead room. I must do the work myself, since I dare not bring an electrician here for fear of the Terror. So far it has not tried to attack me.

"*July 10.* I have completed my task. But the Thing suspects something and will not go near the room. I can feel its tentacles groping for my mind, trying to read my thoughts. I think it would attack me if it dared, but for some reason it fears me; perhaps because I am its creator.

"*July 22.* The Thing is becoming desperate through lack of food. I can feel that it is planning some bold move. Is it marking me for its next victim?

"*July 24.* This is the last entry I shall ever make in this diary, and it is addressed to you, Dr. Bradley and Mr. Cummings. Tonight I was in town when the death-car arrived. I knew then that the thought-monster must be destroyed at once.

"Nature always meets a vital emergency, and so she met this one. As I looked upon those four poor beings whose minds had gone to feed the thing I had created and whose lives had flickered out in the horror of what was happening to them, I saw clearly the one way to stop the havoc for which I was responsible.

"When I telephoned you, I bade you wait half an hour before coming here in order that I might arrive ahead of you and put the first part of my plan into execution; for I feared that should I take you into my confidence beforehand, one of you, through distorted humanitarian motives, might attempt to stop my going through with my design.

"This, then, is my plan. I shall go into the lead room with all mental guards down. The Thing has been particularly inimical to me lately and, finding me in that state, will follow me in. Then I will close the door on both of us. I do not think that the Thing will suspect; a hungry beast is seldom wary of traps. When the door is safely closed, I will turn on the violet lamps. By the time you arrive and reach the end of these papers, those lamps will have done the work for which they were designed.

"You will find the lead room at the end of the hall on the first floor. Open the door carefully (it is not locked) and, if you receive the faintest intimation of an Intelligence beyond, slam it shut again and wait for the lights to complete their task. Mr. Cummings had better attend to this. If you receive no such intimation, you will know that the monster is dead and that the curse so unintentionally laid upon you all is lifted forever. In your charity, do what to you seems best with the other thing you will find there; the thing that will have been

"Julian Walgate."

As Cummings read the last sentence, Bradley made a dash for the door.

"Not so fast," Cummings called after him. "Where are you going?"

"Going!" Bradley paused momentarily in the hall. "To that lead room, of course. The man is killing himself! Don't you see it?"

Deliberately Cummings placed the diary on the table. "If any harm was to come to Walgate," he said, "the damage is already done. If not, a few minutes more in there can do him no harm, while our too hurried and careless entry may undo the work for which he was ready to pay the highest price in man's power."

He passed the doctor and led the way down the hall, stopping before the last door. Slowly he turned the knob and pushed the door open a few inches. A bar of vivid purple light fell across his face.

"Is it all right?" Bradley whispered, close behind him.

"I think so." Cummings opened the door a bit further. In the room beyond was an atmosphere of snapped tension; of climax that had passed.

They stepped across the threshold. And then they became aware that the room still held a living occupant. From the far corner, his clothing wrinkled and torn, his hair and trim Vandyke beard in disarray, there shambled toward them a helpless, mindless idiot!

THE SHUT ROOM

HENRY S. WHITEHEAD

Henry St. Clair Whitehead (1882–1932) was a deacon in the Episcopal Church and from 1921–1929 was archdeacon of the Virgin Islands in the Caribbean. He served there during the winter of each year, returning to the United States during the summers, when he did much of his writing. Most of his adventure stories and weird tales are set in the Caribbean and several show a serious understanding of voodoo or obeah. The majority of his stories appeared in Weird Tales *where he became one of the most popular writers. Several stories featured Gerald Canevin, who first appeared in "The Projection of Armand DuBois" (1926). Canevin mostly listens to stories by others or is a witness to events. Rarely does he actually investigate a mystery directly, though there are a few such cases when he does, like "The Black Beast" (1931). There are two stories, though, set in London and which feature Canevin alongside Lord Carruth, and Carruth is the genuine article. In both the following story and "The Napier Limousine" (1933) Canevin and Carruth join forces to solve bizarre events.*

IT WAS SUNDAY MORNING AND I WAS COMING OUT OF ALL SAINTS' Church, Margaret Street, along with the other members of the hushed and reverent congregation, when, near the entrance doors, a hand fell lightly on my shoulder. Turning, I perceived that it was the Earl of Carruth. I nodded, without speaking, for there is that in the atmosphere of this great church, especially after one of its magnificent services and heart-searching sermons, which precludes anything like the hum of conversation which one meets with in many places of worship.

In these worldly and "scientific" days it is unusual to meet with a person of Lord Carruth's intellectual and scientific attainments, who troubles very much about religion. As for me, Gerald Canevin, I have always been a church-going fellow.

Carruth accompanied me in silence through the entrance doors and out into Margaret Street. Then, linking his arm in mine, he guided me, still in silence, to where his Rolls-Royce car stood at the kerbstone.

"Have you any luncheon engagement, Mr. Canevin?" he enquired, when we were just beside the car, the footman holding the door open.

"None whatever," I replied.

"Then do me the pleasure of lunching with me," invited Carruth.

"I was planning on driving from church to your rooms," he explained, as soon as we were seated and the car whirling us noiselessly towards his town house in Mayfair. "A rather extraordinary matter has come up, and Sir John has asked me to look into it. Should you care to hear about it?"

"Delighted," I acquiesced, and settled myself to listen.

To my surprise, Lord Carruth began reciting a portion of the Nicene Creed, to which, sung very beautifully by All Saints' choir, we had recently been listening.

"Maker of Heaven and earth," quoted Carruth, musingly, "and of all things visible and *invisible*." I started forward in my seat. He had given a peculiar emphasis to the last word, "invisible."

"A fact," I ejaculated, "constantly forgotten by the critics of religion! The Church has always recognised the existence of the invisible creation."

"Right, Mr. Canevin. And—this invisible creation; it doesn't mean merely angels!"

"No one who has lived in the West Indies can doubt that," I replied.

"Nor in India," countered Carruth. "The fact—that the Creed attributes to God the authorship of an invisible creation—is an interesting commentary on the much-quoted remark of Hamlet to Horatio: 'There are more things in Heaven and earth, Horatio, than are dreamed of in your philosophy.' Apparently, Horatio's philosophy, like that of the present day, took little account of the spiritual side of affairs; left out God *and what He had made.* Perhaps Horatio had recited the Creed a thousand times, and never realised what that clause implies!"

"I have thought of it often, myself," said I. "And now—I am all curiosity—what, please, is the application?"

"It is an occurrence in one of the old coaching inns," began Carruth, "on the Brighton Road; a very curious matter. It appears that the proprietor—a gentleman, by the way, Mr. William Snow, purchased the inn for an investment just after the Armistice—has been having a rather unpleasant time of it. It has to do with his shoes!"

"Shoes?" I inquired; "shoes!" It seemed an abrupt transition from the Nicene Creed to shoes!

"Yes," replied Carruth, "and not only shoes but all sorts of leather affairs. In fact, the last and chief difficulty was about the disappearance of a commercial traveller's leather sample-case. But I perceive we are arriving home. We can continue the account at luncheon."

During lunch he gave me a rather full account, with details, of what had happened at The Coach and Horses Inn on the Brighton Road, an account which I will briefly summarise as follows:

Snow, the proprietor, had bought the old inn partly for business reasons, partly for sentimental. It had been a portion, up to about a century before, of his family's landed property. He had repaired and enlarged it, modernised it in some ways, and in general restored a much run-down institution, making The Coach and Horses into a paying investment. He had retained, so far as possible, the antique architectural features of the old coaching inn, and before very long had built up a motor clientele of large proportions by sound and careful management.

Everything, in fact, had prospered with the gentleman-innkeeper's affairs until there began, some four months back, a series of unaccountable disappearances. The objects which had, as it were, vanished into thin air, were all—and this seemed to me the most curious and bizarre feature of Carruth's recital—leather articles. Pair after pair of shoes or boots, left outside bedroom doors at night, would be gone the next morning. Naturally the "boots" was suspected of theft. But the "boots" had been able to prove his innocence easily enough. He was, it seemed, a rather intelligent broken-down jockey, of keen wit. He had assured Mr. Snow of his surprise as well as of his innocence, and suggested that he take a week's holiday to visit his aged mother in Kent and that a substitute "boots," chosen by the proprietor, should take his place. Snow had acquiesced, and the disappearance of guests' footwear had continued, to the consternation of the substitute, a total stranger, obtained from a London agency.

That exonerated Billings, the jockey, who came back to his duties at the end of his holiday with his character as an honest servant intact. Moreover, the disappearances had not been confined to boots and shoes. Pocket hooks, leather luggage, bags, cigarette cases—all sorts of leather articles went the way of the earlier boots and shoes, and besides the expense and annoyance of replacing these, Mr. Snow began to be seriously concerned about the reputation of his house. An inn in which one's leather belongings are known to be unsafe would not be a very strong financial asset. The matter had come to a head through the disappearance of a commercial traveller's sample-case, as noted by Carruth in his first brief account of this mystery. The main difficulty in this affair was that the traveller had been a salesman of jewellery, and Snow had been confronted with a bill for several hundred pounds, which he had felt constrained to pay. After that he had laid the mysterious matter before Sir John Scott, head of Scotland Yard, and Scott had called in Carruth because he recognised in Snow's story certain elements which caused him to believe this was no case for mere criminal investigation.

After lunch Carruth ordered the car again, and, after stopping at my rooms for some additional clothing and other necessities for an overnight visit, we started along the Brighton Road for the scene of the difficulty.

We arrived about four that Sunday afternoon, and immediately went into conference with the proprietor.

Mr. William Snow was a youngish, middle-aged gentleman, very well dressed, and obviously a person of intelligence and natural attainments. He gave us all the information possible, repeating, with many details, the matters which I have already summarised, while we listened in silence. When he had finished:

"I should like to ask some questions," said Carruth.

"I am prepared to answer anything you wish to enquire about," Mr. Snow assured us.

"Well, then, about the sentimental element in your purchase of the inn, Mr. Snow—tell us, if you please, what you may know of the more ancient history of this old hostelry. I have no doubt there is history connected with it, situated where it is. Undoubtedly, in the coaching days of the Four Georges, it must have been the scene of many notable gatherings."

"You are right, Lord Carruth. As you know, it was a portion of the property of my family. All the old registers are intact and are at your disposal. It is an inn of very ancient foundation. It was, indeed, old in those days of the Four Georges, to whom you refer. The records go back well into the sixteenth century, in fact; and there was an inn here even before registers were kept. They are of comparatively modern origin, you know. Your ancient landlord kept, I imagine, only his 'reckoning'; he was not concerned with records; even licences are comparatively modern, you know."

The registers were produced, a set of bulky, dry-smelling, calf-bound volumes. There were eight of them. Carruth and I looked at each other with a mutual shrug.

"I suggest," said I, after a slight pause, "that perhaps you, Mr. Snow, may already be familiar with the contents of these. I should imagine it might require a week or two of pretty steady application even to go through them cursorily."

Mr. William Snow smiled. "I was about to offer to mention the high points," said he. "I have made a careful study of these old volumes, and I can undoubtedly save you both a great deal of reading. The difficulty is what shall I tell you? If only I knew what to put my finger upon but I do not, you see!"

"Perhaps we can manage that," threw in Carruth, "but first, may we not have Billings in and question him?"

The former jockey, now the boots at The Coach and Horses, was summoned and proved to be a wizened, copper-faced individual, with a keen eye and a deferential manner. Carruth invited him to a seat and he sat, gingerly, on the very edge of a chair while we talked with him. I will make no attempt to reproduce his accent, which is quite beyond me. His account was somewhat as follows, omitting the questions asked him both by Carruth and myself.

"At first it was only boots and shoes. Then other things began to go. The things always disappeared at night. Nothing ever disappeared before midnight, because I've sat up and watched many's the time. Yes, we tried everything: watching, even tying up leather things, traps! Yes, sir—steel traps, baited with a boot! Twice we did that. Both times the boot was gone in the morning, the trap not even sprung. No, sir—no one possibly among the servants. Yet, an 'inside' job; it couldn't have been otherwise. From all over the house, yes. My old riding-boots—two pairs—gone completely; not a trace; right out of my room. That was when I was down in Kent as Mr. Snow's told you, gentlemen. The man who took my place slept in my room, left the door open one night—boots gone in the morning, right under his nose.

"Seen anything? Well, sir, in a manner, yes—in a manner, no! To be precise, no. I can't say that I ever saw anything, that is, anybody; no, nor any apparatus as you might say, in a manner of speaking—no hooks no strings, nothing used to take hold of the things—but—" Here Billings hesitated, glanced at his employer, looked down at his feet, and his coppery face turned a shade redder.

"Gentlemen," said he, as though coming to a resolution, "I can only tell you the God's truth about it. You may think me barmy—shouldn't blame you, if you did! But—I'm as much interested in this 'ere thing as Mr. Snow 'imself, barrin' that I 'aven't had to pay the score—make up the value of the things, I mean, as 'e 'as. I'll tell you'so 'elp me Gawd, gentlemen, it's a fact—I *'ave* seen something, absurd as it'll seem to you. I've seen—"

Billings hesitated once more, dropped his eyes, looked distressed, glanced at all of us in the most shamefaced, deprecating manner imaginable, twiddled his hands together, looked, in short, as though he were about to own up to it that he was, after all, responsible for the mysterious disappearances; then finally said:

"I've seen things disappear—through the air! Now—it's hout! But it's a fact, gentlemen all—so 'elp me, it's the truth. Through the air, just as if someone were carrying them away—someone invisible I mean, in a manner of speaking—bloomin' pair of boots, swingin' along through the bloomin' air—enough to make a man say 'is prayers, for a fact!"

It took considerable assuring on the part of Carruth and myself to convince the man Billings that neither of us regarded him as demented, or, as he pithily expressed it, "barmy." We assured him, while our host sat looking at his servant with a slightly puzzled frown, that, on the contrary, we believed him implicitly, and furthermore that we regarded his statement as distinctly helpful. Mr. Snow, obviously convinced that something in his diminutive servitor's mental works was unhinged, almost demurred to our request that we go, forthwith, and examine the place in the hotel where Billings alleged his marvil to have occurred.

We were conducted up two flights of winding steps to the storey which had, in the inn's older days, plainly been an attic. There, Billings indicated, was the scene of the disappearance of the "bloomin' boot, swingin' along—unaccompanied—through the bloomin' air."

It was a sunny corridor, lighted by the spring sunlight through several quaint, old-fashioned, mullioned windows. Billings showed us where he had sat, on a stool in the corridor, watching; indicated the location of the boots, outside a doorway of one of the less expensive guest-rooms; traced for us the route taken by the disappearing boots.

This route led us around a corner of the corridor, a corner which, the honest "boots" assured us, he had been "too frightened" to negotiate on the dark night of the alleged marvel.

But we went around it, and there, in a small, right-angled hallway, it became at once apparent to us that the boots on that occasion must have gone through one of two doorways, opposite each other at either side, or else vanished into thin air.

Mr. Snow, in answer to our remarks on this subject, threw open the door at the right. It led into a small but sunny and very comfortable-looking bed-chamber, shining with honest cleanliness and decorated tastefully with chintz curtains and valances, and containing several articles of pleasant, antique furniture. This room, as the repository of air-travelling boots, seemed unpromising. We looked in silence.

"And what is on the other side of this short corridor?" I enquired.

"The 'shut room,'" replied Mr. William Snow.

Carruth and I looked at each other.

"Explain, please," said Carruth.

"It is merely a room which has been kept shut, except for an occasional cleaning," replied our host, readily, "for more than a century. There was, as a matter of fact, a murder committed in it in the year 1818, and it was, thereafter, disused. When I purchased the inn, I kept it shut, partly, I daresay, for sentimental reasons; partly, perhaps, because it seemed to me a kind of asset for an ancient hostelry. It has been known as 'the shut room' for more than a hundred years. There was, otherwise, no reason why I should not have put the room in use. I am not in the least superstitious."

"When was the room last opened?" I enquired.

"It was cleaned about ten days ago, I believe," answered Mr. Snow.

"May we examine it?" asked Carruth.

"Certainly," agreed Snow, and forthwith sent Billings after the key.

"And may we hear the story—if you know the details—of the murder to which you referred?" Carruth asked.

"Certainly," said Snow, again. "But it is a long and rather complicated story. Perhaps it would do better during dinner."

In this decision we acquiesced, and, Billings returning with the key, Snow unlocked the door and we looked into "the shut room." It was quite empty, and the blinds were drawn down over the two windows. Carruth raised these, letting in a flood of sunlight. The room was utterly characterless to all appearance, but I confess to a certain "sensitivity" in such matters—I "felt" something like a faint, ominous chill. It was not, as the word I have used suggests, anything like physical cold. It was, so to express it, mentally cold. I despair of expressing what I mean more clearly. We looked over the entire room, an easy task as there was absolutely nothing to attract the eye. Both windows were in the wall at our right hand as we entered, and, save for the entrance door through which we had just come, the other three walls were quite blank.

Carruth stepped halfway out through the doorway and looked at the width of the wall in which the door was set. It was, perhaps, ten inches thick. He came back into the room, measured with his glance the distance from window-wall to the blank wall opposite the windows, again stepped outside, into the passageway this time, and along it until he came to the place where the short passage turned into the longer corridor from which we had entered it. He turned to his right this time, I following him curiously, that is, in the direction opposite that from which we had walked along the corridor, and tapped lightly on the wall there.

"About the same thickness, what?" he enquired of Snow.

"I believe so," came the answer. "We can easily measure it."

"No, it will not be necessary, I think. We know that it is approximately the same." Carruth ceased speaking and we followed him back into the room once more. He walked straight across it, rapped on the wall opposite the doorway.

"And how thick is this wall?" he enquired.

"It is impossible to say," replied Snow, looking slightly mystified. "You see, there are no rooms on that side, only the outer wall, and no window through which we could easily estimate the thickness. I suppose it is the same as the others, about ten inches I'd imagine."

Carruth nodded and led the way out into the hallway once more. Snow looked enquiringly at Carruth, then at me.

"It may as well be locked up again," offered Carruth, "but—I'd be grateful if you'd allow me to keep the key until tomorrow."

Snow handed him the key without comment, but a slight look of puzzlement was on his face as he did so. Carruth offered no comment, and I thought it wise to defer the question which was on my lips until later when we were alone. We started down the long corridor towards the staircase, Billings touching his forehead and stepping on ahead of us and disappearing rapidly down the stairs, doubtless to his interrupted duties in the scullery.

"It is time to think of which rooms you would prefer," suggested our pleasant-voiced host as we neared the stairs. "Suppose I show you some which are not occupied, and you may, of course, choose what suit you best."

"On this floor, if you please," said Carruth, positively.

"As you wish, of course," agreed Snow, "but the better rooms are on the floor below. Would you not, perhaps, prefer—"

"Thank you, no," answered Carruth. "We shall prefer to be up here if we may, and-—if convenient—a large room with two beds."

"That can be managed very easily," agreed Snow. He stepped back a few paces along the corridor and opened a door. A handsome, large room, very comfortably and well furnished, came to our view. Its excellence spoke well for the management of The Coach and Horses. The "better' rooms must indeed be palatial if this were a fair sample of those somewhat less desirable.

"This will answer admirably," said Carruth, directing an eyebrow at me. I nodded hastily. I was eager to acquiesce in anything he might have in mind.

"Then we shall call it settled," remarked Snow. "I shall have your things brought up at once. Perhaps you would like to remain here now?"

"Thank you," said Carruth. "What time do we dine?"

"At seven, if you please, or later if you prefer. I am having a private room for the three of us."

"That will answer splendidly," agreed Carruth, and I added a word of agreement. Mr. Snow hurried off to attend to the sending up of our small luggage, and Carruth drew me at once into the room.

"I am a little more than anxious," he began, "to hear that tale of the murder. It is an extraordinary step forward—do you not agree with me?—that Billings' account of the disappearing boots—'through the air'—should fit so neatly and unexpectedly into their going around the corner of the corridor where 'the shut room' is. It sets us forward, I imagine. What is your impression, Mr. Canevin?"

"I agree with you heartily," said I. "The only point on which I am not clear is the matter of the thickness of the walls. Is there anything in that?"

"If you will allow me, I'll defer that explanation until we have had the account of the murder at dinner," said Carruth, and, our things arriving at that moment, we set about preparing for dinner.

Dinner, in a small and beautifully furnished private room, did more, if anything more were needed, to convince me that Mr. William Snow's reputation as a successful modern innkeeper had been well earned. It was a thoroughly delightful meal in all respects, but that, in a general way, is really all that I remember about it because my attention was wholly occupied in taking in every detail of the strange story which our host unfolded to us beginning with the fish course—I think it was a fried sole—and which ended only when we were sipping the best coffee I had tasted since my arrival in England from our United States.

"In the year 1818," said Mr. Snow, "near the end of the long reign of King George III—the king, you will remember, Mr. Canevin, who gave you Americans your Fourth of July—this house was kept by one James Titmarsh. Titmarsh was a very old man. It was his boast that he had taken over the landlordship in the year that His Most Gracious Majesty, George III, had come to the throne, and that he would last as long as the king reigned! That was in the year 1760, and George III had been reigning for fifty-eight years. Old Titmarsh, you see, must have been somewhere in the neighbourhood of eighty, himself.

"Titmarsh was something of a 'character.' For some years the actual management of the inn had devolved upon his nephew, Oliver Titmarsh, who was middle-aged, and none too respectable, though apparently, an able taverner. Old Titmarsh, if tradition is to be believed, had many a row with his deputy, but, being himself childless, he was more or less dependent upon Oliver, who consorted with low company for choice, and did not bear the best of reputations in the community. Old Titmarsh's chief bugbear, in connection with Oliver, was the latter's friendship with Simon Forrester. Forrester lacked only a bard to be immortal. But—there was no Cowper to his John Gilpin, so to speak. No writer of the period, nor, indeed, since, has chosen to set forth Forrester's exploits. Nevertheless, these were highly notable. Forrester was the very king-pin of the highwaymen, operating with extraordinary success and daring along the much-travelled Brighton Road.

"Probably Old Titmarsh was philosopher enough to ignore his nephew's associations and acts so long as he attended to the business of the inn. The difficulty, in connection with Forrester, was that Forrester, an extraordinarily bold fellow, whose long immunity from the gallows had caused him to believe himself possessed of a kind of charmed life, constantly resorted to The Coach and Horses, which, partly because of its convenient location, and partly because of its good cheer, he made his house-of-call.

"During the evening of the first of June, in the year 1818, a Royal Courier paused at The Coach and Horses for some refreshment and a fresh mount. This gentleman carried one of the old king's peremptory messages to the Prince of Wales, then sojourning at Brighton, and who, under his sobriquet of 'First Gentleman of Europe,' was addicted to a life which sadly irked his royal parent at Whitehall. It was an open secret that only Prince George's importance to the realm as heir apparent to the throne prevented some very drastic action being taken against him for his innumerable follies and extravagances, on the part of king and parliament. This you will recall, was two years before the old king died and 'The First Gentleman' came to the throne as George IV.

"The Royal Messenger, Sir William Greaves, arriving about nine in the evening after a hard ride, went into the coffee-room, to save the time which the engagement and preparation of a private room would involve, and when he paid his score, he showed a purse full of broad gold pieces. He did not know that Simon Forrester, sitting behind him over a great mug of mulled port, took careful note of this unconscious display of wealth in ready money. Sir William delayed no longer than necessary to eat a chop and drink a pot of 'Six Ale.' Then, his spurs clanking, he took his departure.

"He was barely out of the room before Forrester, his wits, perhaps, affected by the potations which he had been imbibing, called for his own mount, Black Bess, and rose, slightly stumbling to his feet, to speed the pot-boy on his way to the stables.

"'Ye'll not be harrying a Royal Messenger a-gad's sake, Simon,' protested his companion, who was no less a person that Oliver Titmarsh, seizing his crony by his ruffled sleeve of laced satin.

"'Unhand me!' thundered Forrester; then, boastfully, 'There's no power in England'll stay Sim Forrester when he chooses to take the road!'

"Somewhat unsteadily he strode to the door and roared his commands to the stable-boy who was not leading Black Bess rapidly enough to suit his drunken humour. Once in the saddle, the fumes of the wine he had drunk seemed to evaporate. Without a word Simon Forrester set out, sitting his good mare like a statue, in the wake of Sir William Greaves towards Brighton.

"The coffee-room—as Oliver Titmarsh turned back into it from the doorway whither he had accompanied Forrester—seethed into an uproar. Freed from the dominating presence of the truculent ruffian who would as soon slit a man's throat as look him in the eye along the sights of his horse-pistol from behind the black mask, the numerous guests, silent before, had found their tongues. Oliver Titmarsh sought to drown out their clamour of protest, but before lie could succeed, Old Titmarsh, attracted by the unwonted noise, had hobbled down the short flight of steps from his private cubby-hole and entered the room.

"It required only a moment despite Oliver's now frantic efforts to stem the tide of comment, before the old man had grasped the purport of what was toward. Oliver secured comparative silence, then urged his aged uncle to retire. The old man did so, muttering helplessly, internally cursing his age and feebleness which made it out of the question for him to regulate this scandal which had originated in his inn. A King's Messenger, then as now, was sacred in the eyes of all decent citizens. A King's Messenger—to be called on to 'stand and deliver' by the villainous Forrester! It was too much. Muttering and grumbling the old man left the room, but, instead of going back to his easy-chair and his pipe and glass, he stepped out through the kitchens, and, without so much as a lantern to light his path, groped his way to the stables.

"A few minutes later the sound of horse's hoofs in the cobbled stable-yard brought a pause in the clamour which had once more broken out and now raged in the coffee-room. Listening, those in the coffee-room heard the animal trot out through the gate, and the diminishing sound of its galloping as it took the road towards Brighton. Oliver Titmarsh rushed to the door, but the horse and its rider were already out of sight. Then he ran up to his ancient uncle's room, only to find the crafty old man apparently dozing in his chair. He hastened to the stables. One of the grooms was gone, and the best saddle-horse. From the others, duly warned by Old Titmarsh, he could elicit nothing. He returned to the coffee-room in a towering rage and forthwith cleared it, driving his guests out before him in a protesting herd.

"Then he sat down, alone, a fresh bottle before him, to await developments."

"It was more than an hour later when he heard the distant beat of a galloping horse's hoofs through the quiet June night, and a few minutes later Simon Forrester rode into the stable-yard and cried out for an hostler for his Bess.

451

"He strode into the coffee-room a minute later, a smirk of satisfaction on his ugly, scarred face. Seeing his crony, Oliver, alone, he drew up a chair opposite him, removed his coat, hung it over the back of his chair, and placed over its back where the coat hung, the elaborate leather harness consisting of crossed straps and holsters which he always wore. From the holsters protruded the grips of 'Jem and Jack,' as Forrester had humorously named his twin horse-pistols, huge weapons, splendidly kept, each of which threw an ounce ball. Then, drawing back the chair, he sprawled in it at his ease, fixing on Oliver Titmarsh an evil grin and bellowing loudly for wine.

"'For,' he protested, 'my throat is full of the dust of the road, Oliver, and, lad, there's enough to settle the score, never doubt me!' and out upon the table he cast the bulging purse which Sir William Greaves had momentarily displayed when he paid his score an hour and a half back.

"Oliver Titmarsh, horrified at this evidence that his crony had actually dared to molest a King's Messenger, glanced hastily and fearfully about him, but the room, empty and silent save for their own presence, held no prying inimical informer. He began to urge upon Forrester the desirability of retiring. It was approaching eleven o'clock, and while the coffee-room was, fortunately, empty, no one knew who might enter from the road or come down from one of the guest-rooms at any moment. He shoved the bulging purse, heavy with its broad gold pieces, across the table to his crony, beseeching him to pocket it, but Forrester, drunk with the pride of his exploit, which was unique among the depredations of the road's gentry, boasted loudly and tossed off glass after glass of the heavy port wine a trembling pot-boy had fetched him.

"Then Oliver's entreaties were supplemented from an unexpected source. Old Titmarsh, entering through a door in the rear wall of the coffee-room, came silently and leaned over the back of the ruffian's chair and added a persuasive voice to his nephew's entreaties.

"'Best go up to bed, now, Simon, my lad,' croaked the old man, wheedlingly, patting the bulky shoulders of the hulking ruffian with his palsied old hands.

"Forrester, surprised, turned his head and goggled at the greybeard. Then with a great laugh, and tossing off a final bumper, he rose unsteadily to his feet and thrust his arms into the sleeves of the fine coat which old Titmarsh, having detached from the back of the chair, held out to him.

"'I'll go, I'll go, old Gaffer,' he kept repeating as he struggled into his coat, with mock jocularity, 'seeing you're so careful of me! Gad's hooks! I might as well. There be no more purses to rook this night, it seems!'

"And with this, pocketing the purse and taking over his arm the pistol-harness which the old man thrust at him, the villain lumbered up the stairs to his accustomed room.

"'Do thou go after him, Oliver,' urged the old man. 'I'll bide here and lock the doors. There'll likely be no further custom this night.'

"Oliver Titmarsh, sobered, perhaps, by his fears, followed Forrester up the stairs, and the old man, crouched in one of the chairs, waited and listened, his ancient ears cocked against a certain sound he was expecting to hear.

"It came within a quarter of an hour—the distant beat of the hoofs of horses, many horses. It was, indeed, as though a considerable company approached The Coach and Horses along the Brighton Road. Old Titmarsh smiled to himself and crept towards the inn doorway. He laboriously opened the great oaken door and peered into the night. The sound of many hoofbeats was now clearer, plainer.

"Then, abruptly, the hoofbeats died on the calm June air. Old Titmarsh, somewhat puzzled, listened, tremblingly. Then he smiled in his beard once more. Strategy, this! Someone with a head on his shoulders was in command of that troop! They had stopped, at some distance, lest the hoofbeats should alarm their quarry.

"A few minutes later the old man heard the muffled sound of careful footfalls, and, within another minute, a King's Officer in his red coat had crept up beside him.

"'He's within,' whispered Old Titmarsh, 'and well gone by now in his damned drunkard's slumber. Summon the troopers, sir. I'll lead ye to where the villain sleeps. He hath the purse of His Majesty's Messenger upon him. What need ye of better evidence?'

"'Nay,' replied the train-band captain in a similar whisper, "that evidence, even, is not required. We have but now taken up the dead body of Sir William Greaves beside the highroad, an ounce ball through his honest heart. 'Tis a case, this, of drawing and quartering, Titmarsh; thanks to your good offices in sending your boy for me.'

"The troopers gradually assembled. When eight had arrived, the captain, preceded by Old Titmarsh and followed in turn by his trusty eight, mounted the steps to where Forrester slept. It was, as you have guessed, the empty room you examined this afternoon, 'the shut room' of this house.

"At the foot of the upper stairs the captain addressed his men in a whisper: 'A desperate man, this, lads. 'Ware bullets! Yet—he must needs be taken alive, for the assizes, and much credit to them that take him. He hath been a pest on the road as well ye know these many years agone. Upon him, then, ere he rises from his drunken sleep! He hath partaken heavily. Pounce upon him ere he rises.'

"A mutter of acquiescence came from the troopers. They tightened their belts and stepped alertly, silently, after their leader, preceded by their ancient guide carrying a pair of candles.

"Arrived at the door of the room the captain disposed his men and crying out 'in the King's name!' four of these stout fellows threw themselves against the door. It gave at once under that massed impact, and the men rushed into the room, dimly lighted by Old Titmarsh's candles.

"Forrester, his eyes blinking evilly in the candle-light, was halfway out of bed when they got into the room. He slept, he was accustomed to boast, 'with one eye open, drunk or sober!' Throwing off the cover-lid, the highwayman leaped for the chair over the back of which hung his fine laced coat, the holsters uppermost. He plunged his hands into the holsters and stood, for an instant, the very picture of baffled amazement.

"The holsters were empty!

"Then, as four stalwart troopers flung themselves upon him to bear him to the floor, there was heard Old Titmarsh's harsh, senile cackle:

"''Twas I that robbed ye, ye villain—took your pretty boys, your "Jem" and your "Jack" out of the holsters whiles ye were strugglin' into your fine coat! Ye'll not abide in a decent house beyond this night, I'm thinking; and 'twas the old man who did for ye, murdering wretch that ye are!'

"A terrific struggle ensued. With or without his 'Pretty Boys' Simon Forrester was a thoroughly tough customer, versed in every sleight of hand-to-hand fighting. He bit and kicked; he elbowed and gouged. He succeeded in hurling one of the troopers bodily against the blank wall, and the man sank there and lay still, a motionless heap. After a terrific struggle with the other three who had cast themselves upon him, the remaining troopers and their captain standing aside because there was not room to get at him in the melee, he succeeded in getting the forefinger of one of the troopers, who had reached for a face-hold upon him, between his teeth and bit through it at the joint.

"Frantic with rage and pain this trooper, disengaging himself, and before he could be stopped, seized a heavy oaken bench and, swinging it through the air, brought it down on Simon Forrester's skull. No human bones, even Forrester's, could sustain that murderous assault. The tough wood crunched through his skull, and thereafter he lay quiet. Simon Forrester would never be drawn and quartered, nor even hanged. Simon Forrester, ignobly, as he had lived, was dead; and it remained for the troopers only to carry out the body and for their captain to indict his report.

"Thereafter, the room was stripped and closed by Old Titmarsh himself, who lived on for two more years, making good his frequent boast that his reign over The Coach and Horses would equal that of King George III over his realm. Th old king died in 1820, and Old Titmarsh did not long survive him. Oliver, now a changed man, because of this occurrence, succeeded to the lease of the inn, and during his landlordship the room remained closed. It has been closed, out of use, ever since."

Mr. Snow brought his story, and his truly excellent dinner, to a close simultaneously. It was I who broke the little silence which followed his concluding words.

"I congratulate you, sir, upon the excellence of your narrative gift. I hope that if I come to record this affair, as I have already done with respect to certain odd happenings which have come under my view, I shall be able, as nearly as possible, to reproduce your words." I bowed to our host over my coffee cup.

"Excellent, excellent, indeed!" added Carruth, nodding and smiling pleasantly in Mr. Snow's direction. "And now—for the questions, if you don't mind. There are several which have occurred to me; doubtless also to Mr. Canevin."

Snow acquiesced affably. "Anything you care to ask, of course."

"Well, then," it was Carruth, to whom I had indicated precedence in the questioning, "tell us, if you please, Mr. Snow—you seem to have every particular at your very fingers' ends—the purse with the gold? That, I suppose, was confiscated by the train-band captain and eventually found its way back to Sir William Greaves' heirs. That is the high probability, but—do you happen to know as a matter of fact?"

"The purse went back to Lady Greaves."

"Ah! and Forrester's effects—I understand he used the room from time to time. Did he have anything, any personal property in it? If so, what became of it?"

"It was destroyed, burned. No one claimed his effects. Perhaps he had no relatives. Possibly no one dared to come forward. Everything in his possession was stolen, or, what is the same, the fruit of his thefts."

"And—the pistols, 'Jem and Jack'? Those names rather intrigued me! What disposition was made of them, if you happen to know? Old Titmarsh had them, of course, concealed somewhere; probably in that 'cubby-hole' of his which you mentioned."

"Ala," said Mr. Snow, rising, "there I can really give you some evidence. The pistols are in my office—in the Chubbs' safe, along with the holster-apparatus, the harness which Forrester wore under his laced coat. I will bring them in."

"Have you the connection, Mr. Canevin?" Lord Carruth enquired of me as soon as Snow had left the dining room.

"Yes," said I, "the connection is clear enough; clear as a pikestaff, to use one of your time-honoured British expressions, although I confess never to have seen a pikestaff in my life! But—apart from the fact that the holsters are made of leather; the well-known background of the unfulfilled desire persisting after death; and the obvious connection between the point of disappearance of those 'walking boots' of Billings', with 'the shut room,' I must confess myself at a loss. The veriest tyro at this sort of thing would connect those points, I imagine. There it is, laid out for us, directly before our mental eyes, so to speak. But—what I fail to understand is not so much who takes them—that by a long stretch of the imagination might very well be the persistent 'shade,' 'Ka,' 'projected embodiment' of Simon

Forrester. No—what gets me is—*where does the carrier of boots and satchels and jewellers' sample-cases put them?* That room is utterly, absolutely, physically empty, and boots and shoes are material affairs, Lord Carruth."

Carruth nodded gravely. "You have put your finger on the main difficulty, Mr. Canevin. I am not at all sure that I can explain it, or even that we shall be able to solve the mystery after all. My experience in India does not help. But—there is one very vague case, right here in England, which may be a parallel one. I suspect, not to put too fine a point upon the matter, that the abstracted things may very well be behind that rear-most wall, the wall opposite the doorway in 'the shut room.'"

"But," I interjected, "that is impossible, is it not? The wall is material—brick and stone and plaster. It is not subject to the strange laws of personality. How?"

The return of the gentleman-landlord of The Coach and Horses at this moment put an end to our conversation, but not to my wonder. I imagined that the "case" alluded to by my companion would be that of the tortured "ghost" of the jester which, with a revenge-motive, haunted a room in an ancient house and even managed to equip the room itself with some of its revengeful properties or motives. The case had been recorded by Mr. Hodgson, and later Carruth told me that this was the one he had in mind. This, it seemed to me, was a very different matter. However Mr. Snow laid the elaborate and beautifully made "harness" of leather straps out on the table beside the after-dinner coffee service. The grips of "Jem and Jack" peeped out of their holsters. The device was not unlike those used by our own American desperadoes, men like the famous Earp brothers and "Doc" Holliday whose "six-guns" were carried handily in slung holsters in front of the body. We examined these antique weapons, murderous-looking pistols of the "bulldog" type, built for business, and Carruth ascertained that neither "Jem" nor "Jack" was loaded.

"Is there anyone on that top floor?" enquired Carruth.

"No one save yourselves, excepting some of the servants, who are in the other end of the house," returned Snow.

"I am going to request you to let us take these pistols and the 'harness' with us upstairs when we retire," said Carruth, and again the obliging Snow agreed. "Everything I have is at your disposal, gentlemen," said he, "in the hope that you will be able to end this annoyance for me. It is too early in the season at present for the inn to have many guests. Do precisely as you wish, in all ways."

Shortly after nine o'clock, we took leave of our pleasant host, and, carrying the "harness" and pistols divided between us, we mounted to our commodious bedchamber. A second bed had been moved into it, and the fire in the grate took off the slight chill of the spring evening. We began our preparations by carrying the high-powered electric torches we had obtained from Snow along the corridor and around the corner to "the shut room." We unlocked the door and ascertained that the two torches would be quite sufficient to work by. Then we closed but did not lock the door and returned to our room.

Between us, we moved a solidly built oak table to a point diagonally across the corridor from our open bedroom door, and on this we placed the "harness" and pistols. Then, well provided with smoke-materials, we sat down to wait, seated in such positions that both of us could command the view of our trap. It was during the conversation which followed that Carruth informed me that the case to which he had alluded was the one recorded by the occult writer, Hodgson. It was familiar to both of us. I will not cite it. It may be read by anybody who has the curiosity to examine it in the collection entitled *Carnacki the Ghost-Finder* by William Hope Hodgson. In that account it is the floor of the "haunted" room which became adapted to the revenge-motive of the persistent "shade" of the malignant court jester, tortured to death many years before his "manifestation" by his fiendish lord and master.

We realised that, according to the man Billings' testimony, we need not be on the alert before midnight. Carruth therefore read from a small book which he had brought with him, and I busied myself in making the careful notes which I have consulted in recording Mr. Snow's narrative of Simon Forrester, while that narrative was fresh in my memory. It was a quarter before midnight when I had finished. I took a turn about the room to refresh my somewhat cramped muscles and returned to my comfortable chair.

Midnight struck from the French clock on our mantelpiece, and Carruth and I both, at that signal, began to give our entire attention to the articles on the table in the hallway out there.

It occurred to me that this joint watching, as intently as the circumstances seemed to warrant to both of us, might prove very wearing, and I suggested that we watch alternately, for about fifteen minutes each. We did so, I taking the first turn. Nothing occurred—not a sound, not the smallest indication that there might be anything untoward going on out there in the corridor.

At twelve-fifteen, Carruth began to watch the table, and it was, I should imagine, about five minutes later that his hand fell lightly on my arm, pressing it and arousing me to the keenest attention. I looked intently at the things on the table. The "harness" was moving towards the left-hand edge of the table. We could both hear, now, the slight scraping sound made by the leather weighted by the twin pistols, and, even as we looked, the whole apparatus lifted itself—or so it appeared to us—from the supporting table and began, as it were, to float through the air a distance of about four feet from the ground towards the turn which led to "the shut room."

We rose, simultaneously, for we had planned carefully on what we were to do, and followed. We were in time to see the articles "float" around the corner, and, increasing our pace—for we had been puzzled about how anything material, like the boots, could get through the locked door—watched, in the rather dim light of that short hallway, what would happen.

What happened was that the "harness" and pistols reached the door, and then the door opened. They went through, and the door shut behind them precisely as though someone, invisible to us, were carrying them. We heard distinctly the slight sound which a gently closed door makes as it came to, and there we were, standing outside in the hallway looking at each other. It is one thing to figure out, beforehand, the science of occult occurrences, even upon the basis of such experience as Carruth and I both possessed. It is, distinctly, another, to face the direct operation of something motivated by the Powers beyond the ordinary ken of humanity. I confess to certain "cold chills," and Carruth's face was very pale.

We switched on our electric torches as we had arranged to do, and Carruth, with a firm hand which I admired if I did not, precisely, envy, reached out and turned the knob of the door. We walked into "the shut room"....

Not all our joint experience had prepared us for what we saw. I could not forbear clutching Carruth's free arm, the one not engaged with the torch, as he stood beside me. And I testify that his arm was as still and firm as a rock. It steadied me to realise such fortitude, for the sight which was before us was enough to unnerve the most hardened investigator of the unearthly.

Directly in front of us, but facing the blank wall at the far end of the room, stood a half-materialised man. The gleam of my torch threw a faint shadow on the wall in front of him, the rays passing through him as though he were not there, and yet with a certain dimming. The shadow visibly increased in the few brief instants of our utter silence, and then we observed that the figure was struggling with something. Mechanically we concentrated both electric rays on the figure and then we saw clearly. A bulky man, with a bull-neck and close-cropped, iron-grey hair, wearing a fine satin coat and what were called, in their day, "small cloths," or tight-fitting knee-trousers with silk stockings and heavy, buckled shoes, was raising and fitting about his waist, over the coat, the "harness" with the pistols.

Abruptly, the materialisation appearing to be now complete, he turned upon us, with an audible snarl and baleful, glaring little eyes like a pig's, deep set in a hideous, scarred face, and then he spoke—he spoke, and he had been dead for more than a century!

"Ah-h-h-h!" he snarled, evilly, "ye would come in upon me, eh, my fine gents—into this my chamber, eh! I'll teach ye manners . . ." and he ended this diatribe with a flood of the foulest language imaginable, stepping, with little, almost mincing, down-toed steps towards us all the time he poured out his filthy curses and revilings. I was completely at a loss what to do. I realised—these ideas went through my mind with the rapidity of thought—that the pistols were unloaded. I told myself that this was some weird hallucination—that the shade of no dead-and-gone desperado could harm us. Yet—it was a truly terrifying experience, be the man shade or true flesh and blood.

Then Carruth spoke to him, in quiet, persuasive tones.

"But—you have your pistols now, Simon Forrester. It was we who put them where you could find them, your pretty boys, 'Jem and Jack.' That was what you were trying to find, was it not? And now—you have them. There is nothing further for you to do—you have them, they are just under your hands where you can get at them whenever you wish."

At this the spectre, or materialisation of Simon Forrester, blinked at us, a cunning light in his evil little eyes, and dropped his hand with which he had but now been gesticulating violently on the grips of the pistols. He grinned, evilly, and spat in a strange fashion, over his shoulder.

"Aye," said he, more modestly now, "ay—I have 'em—Jemmy and Jack, my trusties, my pretty boys." He fondled the butts with his huge hands, hands that could have strangled an ox, and spat over his shoulder.

"There is no necessity for you to remain, then, is there?" said Carruth softly, persuasively.

The simulacrum of Simon Forrester frowned, looked a bit puzzled, then nodded its head several times.

"You can rest now—now that you have Jem and Jack," suggested Carruth, almost in a whisper, and as he spoke, Forrester turned away and stepped over to the blank wall at the far side of the room, opposite the doorway, and I could hear Carruth draw in his breath softly and feel the iron grip of his fingers on my arm. "Watch!" he whispered in my ear; "watch now."

The solid wall seemed to wave and buckle before Forrester, almost as though it were not a wall but a sheet of white cloth, held and waved by hands as cloth is waved in a theatre to simulate waves. More and more cloth-like the wall became, and, as we gazed at this strange sight, the simulacrum of Simon Forrester seemed to become less opaque, to melt and blend in with the waving wall, which gradually ceased to move, and then he was gone and the wall was as it had been before....

On Monday morning, at Carruth's urgent solicitation, Snow assembled a force of labourers, and we watched while they broke down the wall of "the shut room" opposite the doorway. At last, as Carruth had expected, a pick went through, and, the interested workmen, labouring with a will, broke through into a small, narrow, cell-like room the plaster of which indicated that it had been walled up perhaps two centuries before, or even earlier—a "priest's hole" in all probability, of the early post-reformation period near the end of the sixteenth century.

Carruth stopped the work as soon as it was plain what was there and turned out the workmen, who went protestingly. Then, with only our host working beside us, and the door of the room locked on the inside, we continued the job. At last the aperture was large enough, and Carruth went through. We heard an exclamation from him, and then he began to hand out articles through the rough hole in the masonry—leather articles— boots innumerable, ladies' reticules, hand-luggage, the missing jeweller's sample case with its contents intact—innumerable other articles, and, last of all, the "harness" with the pistols in the holsters.

Carruth explained the "jester case" to Snow, who shook his head over it. "It's quite beyond me, Lord Carruth," said he, "but, as you say this annoyance is at an end, I am quite satisfied; and—I'll take your advice and make sure by pulling down the whole room, breaking out the corridor walls, and joining it to the room across the way. I confess I can not make head or tail of your explanation—the unfulfilled wish, the 'sympathetic pervasion' of the room, as you call it, the 'materialisation,' and the strange fact that this business began only a short time ago. But—I'll do exactly what you have recommended, about the room, that is. The restoration of the jeweller's case will undoubtedly make it possible for me to get back the sum I paid Messrs Hopkins and Barth of Liverpool when it disappeared in my house. Can you give any explanation of why the 'shade' of Forrester remained quiet for a century and more and only started up the other day, so to speak?"

"It is because the power to materialise came very slowly," answered Carruth, "coupled as it undoubtedly was with the gradual breaking down of the room's material resistance. It is very difficult to realise the extraordinary force of an unfulfilled wish on the part of a forceful, brutal, wholly selfish personality like Forrester's. It is, really, what we must call spiritual power, even though the 'spirituality' was the reverse of what we commonly understand by that term. The wish and the force of Forrester's persistent desire, through the century, have been working steadily, and, as you have told us, the room has been out of use for more than a century. There were no common, everyday affairs to counteract that malign influence—no 'interruptions,' if I make myself clear."

"Thank you," said Mr. Snow. "I do not clearly understand. These matters are outside my province. But—I am exceedingly grateful—to you both." Our host bowed courteously. "Anything that I can possibly do, in return—"

"There is nothing—nothing whatever," said Carruth quietly; "but, Mr. Snow, there is another problem on your hands which perhaps you will have some difficulty in solving, and concerning which, to our regret"—he looked gravely at me—"I fear neither Mr. Canevin with his experience, nor I with mine, will be able to assist you."

"And what, pray, is that?" asked Mr. Snow, turning slightly pale. He would, I perceive, be very well satisfied to have his problems behind him.

"The problem is," said Carruth, even more gravely I imagined, "it is— what disposal are you to make of fifty-eight pairs of assorted boots and shoes!"

And Snow's relieved laughter was the last of the impressions which I took with me as we road back to London in Carruth's car, of The Coach and Horses Inn on the Brighton Road.

DR. MUNCING, EXORCIST
GORDON MACCREAGH

Gordon MacCreagh (1885–1953) was a real-life adventurer and explorer as well as a prolific writer of adventure fiction. Details about his life vary according to different sources, including his own accounts, but it seems he was born and educated in Scotland, coming to the United States where his father came to study the Native Americans. He purportedly studied at Heidelberg University where he had a sabre duel with a fellow student and was sure he'd killed him. He hadn't, but MacCreagh fled to India and ended up collecting butterflies and insects for a museum, and then animals for a circus, extending his operations to Africa. He eventually returned to the United States in 1911 where he began writing, his primary market being the leading pulp Adventure. *In 1921 he joined the Mulford Expedition on its biological explorations of the Amazon Basin. Although it did not fulfil its primary purpose, it did return with over two thousand specimens of plant and insect life, identifying many new species. MacCreagh wrote about his experiences in* White Waters and Black *(1923). In 1927* Adventure *magazine financed an expedition by MacCreagh and his wife to Abyssinia (now Ethiopia) in the hope of finding the Ark of the Covenant. His experiences were written up for* Adventure *and expanded in the book* The Last of Free Africa *(1928). During the Second World War he went to Africa as a translator and interpreter and was shot down, but survived.*

Although all of this gave him plenty of material for his stories and lectures, it provided little for his rare forays into weird fiction, though there is some evidence that he learned many native suspicions and remedies. He wrote just two stories featuring Dr. Muncing, the sequel being "The Case of the Sinister Shape" (1932) before the magazine, Strange Tales, ceased. It is possible, but unlikely, that a third story, "The Hand of Saint Ury" was revised to remove Dr. Muncing and sold to Weird Tales in 1951 at the end of MacCreagh's career.

THE BRASS PLATE ON THE GATE POST OF THE TRIM WHITE WICKET said only:

DR. MUNCING, EXORCIST.

Aside from that, the house was just the same as all the others in that street—semi-detached, whitewashed, respectable. A few more brass plates announced other sober citizens with their sprinkling of doctors of medicine and one of divinity. But "Dr. Muncing, Exorcist": that was suggestive of something quite different and strange.

The man who gazed reflectively out of the window at the driving rain, was, like his brass sign, vaguely suggestive, too, of something strange; of having the capacity to do something that the other sober citizens, doctors and lawyers, did not do.

He was of a little more than middle height, broad, with strong, capable-looking hands; his face was square cut, finely criss-crossed with weatherbeaten lines, tanned from much travel in far-away lands; a strong nose hung over a thin, wide mouth that closed with an extraordinary determination.

The face of a normal man of strong character. It was the eyes that conveyed that vague impression of something unusual. Deep set, they were, of an indeterminate colour, hidden beneath a frown of reflective brows; brooding eyes, suggestive of a knowledge of things that other sober citizens did not know.

The other man who stared out of the other window was younger, bigger in every way; an immense young fellow who carried in his big shoulders and clean complexion every mark of having devoted more of his college years to study of football rather than of medicine. This one grunted an ejaculation.

"I'll bet a dollar this is a patient for you."

Dr. Muncing came over to the other window. "I don't bet dollars with Dr. James Terry. Gambling seems to have been one of the few things you did really well at Johns College. The fellow does look plentifully frightened, at that."

The man in question was hurrying down the street, looking anxiously at the house numbers; bent over, huddled in a raincoat, he read the numbers furtively, as though reluctant to turn his head out of the protection of his up-turned collar. He uttered a glad cry as he saw the plate of Dr. Muncing, Exorcist, and, letting the gate slam, he stumbled up the path to the door.

Dr. Muncing met the man personally, led him to a comfortable chair, mixed a stimulant for him, offered him a cigarette. Calm, methodical, matter-of-fact, this was his "bedside manner" with such cases. Forcefully he compelled the impression that, whatever might be the trouble, it was nothing that could not be cured. He stood waiting for an explanation. The man stammered an incoherent jumble of nothings.

"I—Doctor, I don't know how—I can't tell you what it is, but the Reverend Mr. Hendryx sent me to you. Yet I don't know what to tell you; there's nothing to describe."

"Well," said the doctor judicially, "that is already interesting. If there's nothing and if the Reverend Mr. Hendryx feels that he can't pray it away, we probably have something that we can get hold of."

His manner was dominant and cheerful, he radiated confidence. His bulky young assistant had been chosen for just that purpose also, to assist in putting over the impression of power, of force to deal with queer and horrible things that could not be sanely described.

The man began to respond to that atmosphere. He got a grip on himself and began to speak more coherently.

"Doctor, I don't know what to tell you. There have been no—spooks, or anything of that sort. We've seen nothing; heard nothing. It's only a feeling. I—you'll laugh at me, Doctor, but—it's just a something in the dark that brings a feeling of awful fear; and I know that it will catch me. Last night—my God, last night it almost touched me."

"I never laugh," said Dr. Muncing seriously, "until I have laid my ghost. For some ghosts are horribly real. Tell me something about yourself, your family, your home and so on. And as to your fears, whatever they are, please don't try to conceal them from me."

A baffled expression came over the man's face. "There's nothing to tell, Doctor; nothing that's different to anybody else. I don't know what could bring this frightful thing about us. I—my name is Jarrett—I sell real estate up in the Catskills. I have a little place a hundred feet off the paved state road, two miles from the village. There's nothing old or dilapidated about the house; there's modern plumbing, electric lights, and so on. No old graveyards anywhere in the neighbourhood. Not a single thing to bring this horror; and yet—I tell you, Doctor, there's something frightful in the dark that we can feel."

"Hm-m!" The doctor pursed his lips and walked a short beat, his hands deep in his pockets. "A new house; no old associations. Begins to sound like an elemental, only how would such a thing have gotten loose? Or it might be a malignant geoplasm, but—Tell me about your family, Mr. Jarrett."

"There's only four of us, Doctor. There's my wife's brother, who's an invalid; and . . ."

"Ah-h!" A quick breath came from the doctor. "So there's a sick man, yes? What is his trouble?"

"His lungs are affected. He was advised to come to us for the mountain air; and he was getting very much better; but recently he's very much worse again. We've been thinking that perhaps this constant terror has been too much for him."

"Hm-m, yes, indeed." The doctor strode his quick beat back and forth; his indeterminate eyes were distinctly steel grey just now. "Yes, yes, the terror, and the sick man who grows worse. Quite so. Who else, Mr. Jarrett? What else have you that might attract a visophaging entity?"

"A viso-what? Good God, Doctor, we haven't anything to attract anything. Besides my wife's brother there's only my son, ten years of age, and my wife. She gets it worse than any of us; she says she has even seen—but I think there's a lot of blarney in all that." The man contrived a sick smile. "You know how women are, Doctor; she says she has seen shapes—formless things in the dark. She likes to think she is psychic, and she is always seeing things that nobody else knows anything about."

"Oh, good Lord!" Dr. Muncing groaned and his face was serious. "Verily do fools rush in. All the requirements for piercing the veil. Heavens, what idiots people can be."

Suddenly he shot an accusing finger at Mr. Jarrett. "I suppose she makes you sit round table with her, and all that sort of stuff."

"Yes, Doctor, she does. Raps and spelt-out messages, and so on."

"Good Lord!" The doctor walked angrily back and forth. "Fools by the silly thousand play with this kind of fire, and this time these poor simpletons have broken in on something."

He whirled on the frightened realtor with accusing finger, laying down the law.

"Mr. Jarrett, your foolish wife doesn't know what she has done. I myself don't know what she has turned loose or what this thing might develop into. We may be able to stop it. It may escape and grow into a world menace. I tell you we humans don't begin to know what forces exist on the other side of that thin dividing line that we don't begin to understand. The only thing to do now is to come with you immediately to your home; and we must try and find out what this thing is that has broken through and whether we can stop it."

The Jarrett house turned out exactly as described. Modern and commonplace in every way; situated in an acre of garden and shrubbery on a sunlit slope of the Catskill Mountains. The other houses of the straggly little village were much the same, quiet residences of normal people who preferred to retire a little beyond the noise and activity of the summer resort of Pine Bend about two miles down the state road.

The Jarrett family fitted exactly into their locale. Well meaning, hospitable rural non-entities. The lady who was psychic was over-plump and short of breath at that elevation; the son, a gangling schoolboy, evinced the shy aloofness of a country youth before strangers; the sick man, thin and drawn, with an irritable cough, showed the unnatural flush of colour on his cheeks that marked his disease.

It required very much less than Dr. Muncing's keenness to see that all of these people were in a condition of nervous tension that in itself was proof of something that had made quite an extraordinary effect on their unimaginative minds.

Dilated eyes, tremulous limbs, backward looks; all these things showed that something had brought this unfortunate family to the verge of a panic that reached the very limits of their control.

The doctor was an adept at dispelling that sort of jumpiness. Such a mental condition was the worst possible for combating "influences," whatever they might be. He acknowledged his introductions with easy confidence, and then he held up his hand.

"No, no, nix on that. Give me a chance to breathe. D'you want to ruin my appetite with horrors? Let's eat first and then you can spread yourselves out on the story. No ghost likes a full stomach."

He was purposely slangy. The immediate effect was that his hosts experienced a measure of relief. The man radiated such an impression of knowledge, of confidence, of power.

The meal, however, was at best a lugubrious one. Conversation had to be forced to dwell on ordinary subjects. The wife evinced a painful disinclination to go into the kitchen. "Our cook left us two days ago," she explained. The boy was silent and frightened. The sick man said little, and coughed a dry, petulant bark at intervals.

The doctor, engrossed in his plate, chattered gaily about nothing; but all the time he was watching the invalid like a hawk. James Terry did his best to distract attention from the expert's scrutiny of everybody and everything in the room. By the time the meal was over the doctor had formed his opinion about the various characteristics and idiosyncrasies of his hosts, and he dominated the company with his expansive cheerfulness.

"Well, now, let's get one of those satisfying smokes in the jimmy pipe, and you can tell me all about it. You"—selecting the lady—"you tell me. I'm sure you'll give the best account."

The lady, flustered and frightened, was able to add very little to what her husband had already described. There was nothing to add. A baffling nothingness enshrouded the whole situation; but it was a nothingness that was full of an unnameable fear—a feeling of terror enhanced by the "shapes" of the wife's psychic imaginings. A nameless nothing to be combated.

The doctor shrugged with impatience. He had met with just such conditions before: the inability of people to describe their ghostly happenings with coherence. He decided on a bold experiment.

"My dear lady," he said, devoting his attention to the psychic one, "it is difficult to exorcise a mere feeling until we know something about the cause of it. Now I'll tell you what we ought to do. When you sit at your table for your little séances you get raps and so on, don't you? And you spell out messages from your 'spirit friends,' isn't it? And you'd like to go into a trance and let your 'guides' control you; only you are a little nervous about it; and all that kind of stuff, no?"

"Why, yes, Doctor, that is just about what happens, but how should you know all that?"

"Hm," grunted the doctor dryly. "You are not alone in your foolishness, my dear lady; there are many thousands in the United States who take similar chances. They look upon psychic exploration as a parlour game. But now what I want to suggest is, let's have one of your little séances now. And you will go into a trance this time and perhaps you—I mean your guides—will tell us something. In the trance condition, which after all is a form of hypnosis—though we do not know whether the state is auto-induced or whether it is due to the suggestion of an outside influence—in this hypnotic condition the subconscious reflexes are sensitive to influences that the more material conscious mind cannot receive."

Mrs. Jarrett's plump hand fluttered to her breast. This was so sudden; and she had really been a little bit afraid of her séances since this terror came into the house. But the doctor was already arranging the little round table and the chairs.

Without looking round, he said, "You need not be at all nervous this time. And I want your brother particularly to stay in the room, though not necessarily at the table. Jimmy, you sit aside and steno whatever comes through, will you." And in a quiet aside to his friend, he added, "Sit near the switch, and if I holler, throw on the lights instantly and see that the sick man gets a stimulant. I may be busy."

Under the doctor's experienced direction everything was soon ready. Just the four sat at the table, the Jarrett family and the doctor. The sick brother sat tucked in an armchair by the window and Jimmy Terry near the light switch at the door.

Once more the doctor cautioned the brawny Terry, "Watch this carefully, Jimmy. I'm putting the sick man's life into your hands. If you feel anything, if you sense anything, if you think anything near him, snap on the lights. Don't ask anything. Act. Ready? All right then, black out."

With the click of the switch the room was in darkness through which came only the petulant cough of the sick man. As the eyes accustomed themselves to the gloom there was sufficient glow from the moonlight outside to distinguish the dim outlines of figures.

"This is what you usually do, isn't it?" asked the doctor. "Hands on the table and little fingers touching?" And without waiting for the reply of which he seemed to be so sure, he continued, "All the usual stuff, I see. But now, Mrs. Jarrett, I'm going to lay my hands over yours and you will go into a trance. So. Quiet and easy now. Let yourself go."

In a surprisingly short space of time the table shivered with that peculiar inward tremor so familiar to all dabblers in the psychic. Shortly thereafter it heaved slowly up and descended with a vast deliberation. There was a moment's stillness fraught with effort; then a rhythmic tap-tap-tap of one leg.

"Now," said the doctor authoritatively, "you will go into a trance, Mrs. Jarrett. Softly, easily. Let go. You're going into a trance. Going . . . going . . ." His voice was soothingly commanding.

Mrs. Jarrett moaned, her limbs jerked, she stretched as if in pain; then with a sigh she became inert.

"Watch out, Jimmy," the doctor warned in a low voice. Then to the woman: "Speak. Where are you? What do you see?"

The plump, limp bulk moaned again. The lips moved; inarticulate sounds proceeded from them, the fragments of unformed words; then a quivering sigh and silence. The doctor took occasion to lean first to one side and then to the other to listen to the breathing of Mr. Jarrett and the boy. Both were a little faster than normal; under the circumstances, not strange. With startling suddenness words cut the dark, clear and strong.

"I am in a place full of mist, I don't know where. Grey mist." A laboured silence. Then: "I am at the edge of something; something deep, dark." A pause. "Before me is a curtain, dim and misty—no—it seems—I think—no, it is the mist that is the curtain. There are dim things moving beyond the curtain."

"Ha!" An exclamation of satisfaction from the doctor.

"I can't make them out. They are not animals; not people. They are dark things. Just—shapes."

"Good God, that's what she said before!" The awed gasp was Mr. Jarrett's.

The sick man coughed gratingly.

"The shapes move, they twine and roll and swell up. They bulge up against the curtain as if to push through. It is dark; too dark on that side to see. I am afraid if one might push through . . ."

Suddenly the boy whimpered, "I don't like this. It's cold, an' I'm scared."

The doctor could hear the hard breathing of Mr. Jarrett on his left as the table trembled under his sudden shiver. The doctor himself experienced an enveloping depression, an almost physical crawling of the cold hairs up and down his spine. The sick man went into a spasm of violent coughing.

Suddenly the voice screamed, "One of the shapes is almost—my God, it is through! It's on this side. I can see—oh God, save me."

"Lights, Jimmy!" snapped the doctor. "Look to the sick man."

The swift flood of illumination showed Mr. Jarrett grey and beaded with perspiration; the boy in wild-eyed terror; Terry, too, big-eyed, and nervously alert. All of them had felt a sudden stifling weight of a clutching fear that seemed to hang like a destroying wave about to break.

The sick man was in paroxysm of coughing from which he passed into a swoon of exhaustion. Only the woman had remained blissfully unconscious. The voice that had spoken out of her left her untroubled. In heavy peacefulness she slumped in her trance condition.

The doctor leaped round the table to her and placed his hands over her forehead in protection from he did not know exactly what. A chill still pervaded the room; a physical sense of cold and lifting of hair. Some enormous material menace had almost been able to swoop upon a victim. Slowly, with the flashing on of the lights, the horror faded.

The doctor bent over the unconscious lady. Smoothly he began to stroke her face, away from the centre towards her temples. As he stroked he talked, softly, reassuringly.

Presently the woman shuddered, heaved ponderously. Her eyes opened blankly, without comprehension. Wonder dawned in them at the confusion.

"I must have been asleep," she murmured; and she was able to smile sheepishly. "Tell me, did I—did my guides speak?"

That foolish, innocent question, coming from the only one in the room who knew nothing of what had happened, served to dissipate fear more than all the doctor's reassurances. The others began to take hold of themselves. The doctor was able to turn his attention to the sick man.

"How is his pulse, Jimmy? Hm-m, weak, but still going. He's just exhausted. That thing drew an awful lot of strength out of him. It nearly slipped one over on me; I didn't think it was through into this side yet."

To his hosts he said with impressive gravity, "It is necessary to tell you that we are faced with a situation that is more dangerous than I had thought. There is in this thing a distinct physical danger; it has gone beyond imagination and beyond 'sensing' things. We are up against a malignant entity that is capable of human contacts. We must get the patient up to bed and then I shall try to explain what this danger is."

He took the limp form in his arms with hardly an effort and signified to Mrs. Jarrett to lead the way. To all appearances it was no more than an unusually vigorous physician putting a patient to bed. But the doctor made one or two quite extraordinary innovations.

"Fresh air to the contrary," he said grimly. "Windows must remain shut and bolted. Let me see: iron catches are good. And, Johnny, you just run down to the kitchen and bring me up a fire iron—a poker, tongs, anything. A stove lid lifter will do."

The boy clung to the close edges of the group. The doctor nodded with understanding.

"Mr. Jarrett, will you go? We mustn't leave our patient until we have him properly protected."

In a few moments Mr. Jarrett returned with a plain iron kitchen poker. That was just the thing, the doctor said. He placed it on the floor close along the door jamb. He herded the others out and, coming last himself, shut the door, pausing just a moment to note that the lock was of iron, after which he followed the wondering family down to the living-room. They sat expectant, uneasy.

"Now," the doctor began, as though delivering a lecture. "I want you all to listen carefully, because—I must tell you this, much as I dislike to frighten you—this thing has gone so far that a single mis-step may mean a death."

He held up his hand. "No, don't interrupt. I'm going to try to make clear what is difficult enough anyhow; and you must all try to understand it because an error now—even a little foolishness, a moment of forgetfulness—can open the way for a tragedy; because—now let me impress you with this—the thing that you have felt is a palpable force. I can tell you what it is, but I cannot tell you how it came to break into this side. This malignant force is"—he paused to weigh his words—"an elemental. I do not know how the thing was released. Maybe you had nothing to do with it. But you, madam"—to the trembling Mrs. Jarrett—"you caused it by playing with this séance business, about the dangers of which you know nothing. Nor have you taken the trouble even to read up on the subject. You have opened the way to attract this thing to your house; you and the unfortunate, innocent sick man upstairs. You've actually invited it to live among you."

The faces of the audience expressed only fear of the unknown; fear and a blank lack of understanding. The doctor controlled his impatience and continued his lecture.

"I can't go into the complete theory of occultism here and now; but this much you must understand," he said, pounding his fist on his knee for emphasis; "It is an indubitable fact, known throughout the ages of human existence, and re-established by modern research, that there exist certain vast discarnate forces alongside of us and all around us. These forces function according to certain controlling laws, just as we do. They probably know as little about our laws as we do about theirs.

"There are many kinds of these forces. Forces of a high intelligence, far superior to ours; forces of possibly less intelligence; benevolent forces; malignant ones. They are all loosely generalized as spirits: elementals, subliminals, earthbounds, and so on.

"These forces are separated from us, prevented from contact, by— what shall I say? I dislike the word, evil, or curtain; or, as the Bible puts it, the great gulf. They mean nothing. The best simile is perhaps in the modern invention of the radio.

"A certain set of wavelengths, ethereal vibrations, can impinge themselves upon a corresponding instrument attuned to those vibrations. A slight variation in wavelength, and the receiving instrument is a blank; totally unaffected, though it knows that vibrations of tremendous power exist all around it. It must tune in to become receptive to another set of vibrations.

"In something after this manner these discarnate so-called spirit forces are prevented from impinging themselves upon our consciousness. Sometimes we humans, for reasons of which we are very often unaware, do something, create a condition, which tunes us in with the vibration of a certain group of discarnate forces. Then we become conscious; we establish contact; we, in common parlance, see a ghost."

The lecturer paused. Vague understanding was apparent on the faces of his fascinated audience.

"Good! Now then—I mentioned elementals. Elementals comprise one of these groups of discarnate forces; possibly the lowest of the group and the least intelligent. They have not evolved to human, or even animal form. They are just—shapes."

"Oh, my God!" the shuddering moan came from Mrs. Jarrett, "the shapes that I have sensed!"

"Exactly. You have sensed such a shape. Why have you sensed it? Because somehow, somewhere, something has happened that has enabled one of these elemental entities to tune in on the vibrations of our human wavelength, to break through the veil. What was the cause or how, we have no means of knowing. What we do know about elementals, as has been fully recognized by occultists of the past ages and has been pooh-poohed only by modern materialism, is that they are, to begin with, malignant; that is, hostile to human life. Then again—now mark this well—they can manifest themselves materially to humans only by drawing the necessary force from a human source, preferably from some human in a state of low resistance; from—a sick man."

"Oh, my—my brother?" Mrs. Jarrett gasped her realization.

The doctor nodded slowly. "Yes, his condition of low resistance and your thoughtless reaching for a contact in your séances have invited this malignant entity to this house. That is why the sick man has taken this sudden turn for the worse. The elemental is sapping his vitality in order to manifest itself materially. So far you have only felt its malevolent presence. Should it succeed in drawing to itself sufficient force it might be capable of enormous and destructive power. No, no, don't scream now; that doesn't help. You must all get a grip on yourselves so as calmly to take the proper defensive precautions.

"Fortunately we know an antidote; or let me say rather, a deterrent. Like most occult lore, this deterrent has been known and used by all peoples even up to this age of modern scepticism. Savage people throughout the world use it; oriental peoples with a sensitivity keener than our own use it; modern white people use it, though unconsciously. The literature of magic is full of it.

"It is nothing more or less than iron. Cold iron. The iron nose-ring or toe-ring of the savage; the mantra loha of the Hindus; the lucky horseshoe of your rural neighbours today. These things are not ornaments; they are amulets.

"We do not know why cold iron should act as a deterrent to certain kinds of hostile forces—call them spirits, if you like. But it is a fact known of old that a powerful antipathy exists between cold iron and certain of the lower orders of inhuman entities: doppelgangers, churels, incubi, wood runners, leperlings, and so on, and including all forms of elementals.

"So powerful is this antipathy that these hostile entities cannot approach a person or pass a passage so guarded. There are other forms of deterrents against some of the other discarnate entities: pentagons, Druid circles, etc., and even the holy water of the Church. Don't ask me why or how—perhaps it has something to do with molecular vibrations. Let us be glad, for the present, that we know of this deterrent. And let each of you go to bed now with a poker or a stove lid or whatever you fancy as an amulet, which I assure you will be ample to protect a normal healthy person who does not contrive to establish some special line of contact which may counteract the deterrent. In the case of the sick man I have taken the extra precaution of guarding even the door.

"Now the rest of you go to bed and stay in your rooms. If you're nervous, you may sleep all in one room. Dr. Terry and I will sit up and prowl around a bit. If you hear a noise it will be us doing night watchman. You can sleep in perfect security, unless you commit some piece of astounding foolishness which will open an unguarded avenue of contact. And one more thing: warn your brother, even if he should feel well enough, not in any circumstances to leave his room. Good night; and sleep well—if you can."

Hesitant and unwilling the family went upstairs; huddled together, fearful of every new sound, every old shadow, not knowing, how this horror that had come into the house might manifest itself; hating to go, but worn out by fatigue engendered of extreme terror.

"I'll bet they sleep all in one room like sardines," commented the doctor.

Terry caught the note of anxiety and asked, "Was that all the straight dope? I mean about elementals and so on? And iron? Sounds kind of foolish."

The doctor's face was sober, the irises of his indeterminate eyes so pale that they were almost invisible in the artificial light.

"You never listened to a less foolish thing, my boy. It sounds so to you only because you have been bred in the school of modern materialism. What? Is it reasonable to maintain that we have during the last thin fringe of years on humanity's history obliterated what has been known to humanity ever since the first anthropoid hid his head under his hairy arms in terror? We have but pushed these things a little farther away; we have become less sensitive than our forefathers. And, having become less sensitive, we naturally do not inadvertently tune in on any other set of vibrations; and so we proclaim loudly that no such things exist. But we are beginning to learn again; and if you have followed the trend you will surely have noticed that many of our leading men of science, of thought, of letters, have admitted their belief in things which science and religion have tried to deny."

Terry was impressed with the truth of his friend's statement. The possibilities thus opened up made him uneasy.

"Well, er-er, this—this elemental thing," he said uneasily, "can it do anything?"

"It can do"—the indeterminate eyes were far-away pinpoints—"it can do anything, everything. Having once broken into our sphere, our plane, our wavelength—call it what you will—its malignant potentiality is measured only by the amount of force it can draw from its human source of supply. And remember—here is the danger of these things—the measure is not on a par ratio. It doesn't mean that such a malignant entity, drawing a few ounces of energy from a sick man, can exert only those few ounces. In some manner which we do not understand, all the discarnate intelligences know how to step-up an almost infinitesimal amount of human energy to many hundreds percent of power; as for instance the 'spirits' that move heavy tables, perform levitation and so on. A malignant spirit can use that power as a deadly, destructive force."

"But, good Lord," burst out Terry, "Why should the thing be malignant? Why, if it has broken through, got into tune with human vibrations, why should it want to destroy humans who have never done it any harm?"

The doctor did not reply at once. He was listening, alert and taut.

"Do these people keep a dog, do you know, Jimmy? Would that be it snuffling outside the door?"

But the noise, if there had been any, had ceased. The silence was sepulchral. The doctor relaxed and took up the last question.

"Why should it want to destroy life? That's something of a poser. I might say, how do I know? But I have a theory. Remember I said that elementals belonged to one of the least intelligent groups of discarnate entities. Now, the lower one goes in the scale of human intelligence, the more prevalent does one find the superstition that by killing one's enemy one acquires the good qualities of that enemy, his strength or his valour or his speed or something. In the lowest scale we find cannibalism, which is, as so many leading ethnologists have demonstrated, not a taste for human flesh, but a ceremony, a ritual whereby the eater absorbs the strength of the victim. And I suppose you know, incidentally, that militant modern atheists maintain that the holy communion is no other than a symbol of that very prevalent idea. An unintelligent elemental, then . . ."

The doctor suddenly gripped his friend's arm. A creak had sounded on the stairs. In the tense silence both men fancied they could detect a soft, sliding scuffle in that direction. With uncontrollable horror Terry's heart came up to his throat. In one panther bound the doctor reached the door and tore it open. Then he swore in baffled irritation.

Through the open door Terry could hear distinctly scurrying steps on the first landing. In sudden surge of horror at being left alone he leaped from his chair to follow his friend, and bumped into him at the door.

Dr. Muncing, cursing his luck in a most plebian manner, noted his expression and became immediately the scientist again.

"What's this, what's this? This won't do. Scare leaves you vulnerable. Now let me psychoanalyze you and eliminate that. Sit down and get this; it's quite simple and quite necessary before we start out chasing this thing. You feel afraid for two reasons. The first is psychological. Our forebears knew that certain aspects of the supernatural were genuinely fearsome. Unable to differentiate the superstition grew amongst the laity that all aspects were to be feared, just as most people fear all snakes, though only six per cent of them are poisonous. You have inherited both fear and superstition. Secondly, in this particular case, you sense the hostility of this thing and its potential power for destruction. Therefore, you are afraid."

Under the doctor's cold logic, his friend was able to regain at least a grip on his emotions. With a smile he said, "That's pretty thin comfort when even you admit its power for destruction."

"*Potential*, I said. Don't forget, potential," urged the doctor. "Its power is capable of becoming enormous. Up to the present it has not been able to absorb very much energy. It evaded us just now instead of attacking us, and we have shut off its source of supply. Remember, too, its manifestation of itself must be physical. It may claw your hair in the dark; perhaps push you over the banisters if it gets a chance; but it can't sear your brain and blast your soul. It has drawn to itself sufficient physical energy to make itself heard; that means to be felt, and possibly to be seen. It has materialized; it cannot suddenly fade through walls and doors."

"To be seen?" said Terry in awe-struck tones. "Good gosh, what does a tangible hate look like?"

The doctor nodded. "Well put, Jimmy; very well expressed. A tangible hate is just what this thing is. And since it is inherently a formless entity, a shape in the dark, manifesting itself by drawing upon human energy, it will probably look like some gross distortion of human form. Just malignant eyes, maybe, or clutching hands; or perhaps something more complete. Its object will be to skulk about the house seeking for an opening to absorb more energy to itself. Ours must be to rout it out."

Mentally Terry was convinced. He could not fail to be, after that lucid exposition of exactly what they were up against. But physically the fine hair still rose on his spine. Shapeless things that could hate and could lurk in dark corners to trip one up on the stairs were sufficient reason for the very acme of human fear. However, he stood up. "I'm with you," he said shortly. "Go ahead."

The doctor held out his hand. "Stout fellow. I knew you would, of course; and I brought this along for you as being quite the best weapon for this sort of a job. A blackjack in hand is a strong psychological bracer, and it has the virtue of being iron."

Terry took the weighty little thing with a feeling of vast security, which was instantly dispelled by the doctor's next words.

"I suppose," said Terry. "That on account of the iron the thing can't approach one."

"Don't fool yourself," said the other. "Iron is a deterrent. Not an absolute talisman in every case. We are going after this thing; we are *inviting* contact. Just as a savage dog may attack a man who is going after it with a club, so our desperate elemental, if it sees a chance, may—well, I don't know what it can do yet. Stick close, that's all."

Together the two men went up the stairs and stood in the upper hall. Four bedrooms and a bathroom opened off this. Two of the rooms they knew to be occupied. The other doors stood similarly closed.

"We've got to try the rooms," the doctor whispered. "It probably can, if necessary, open an unlocked door, though I doubt whether it would turn an iron key."

Firmly, without hesitation, he opened one of the doors and stepped into the room. The doctor switched on the light. Nothing was to be seen, nothing heard, nothing felt.

"We'd sense it if it were here," said the doctor as coolly as though hunting for nothing more tangible than an odour of escaping gas. "It must be in the other empty room. Come on."

He threw the door of that room wide open and stood, shoulder-to-shoulder with Terry, on the threshold. But there was nothing; no sound; no sensation.

"Queer," muttered the doctor. "It came up the stairs. It would hardly go into the bathroom, with an iron tub in it—though God knows, maybe cast iron molecules don't repel like hand-wrought metal."

The bathroom drew blank. The two men looked at each other, and now Terry was able to grin. This matter of hunting for a presence that evaded them was not nearly so fearsome as his imagination had conjured up. The doctor's eyes narrowed to slits as he stood in thought.

"Another example," he murmured, "of the many truths in the Bible about the occult. Face the devil and he will fly from you, eh? I wonder where the devil this devil can be?"

As though in immediate answer came the rasping sounds of a dry grating cough.

Instinctively both men's heads flew round to face the sick man's door. But that remained undisturbed; the patient seemed to be sleeping soundly. Suddenly the doctor gripped his friend's arm and pointed—up to the ceiling.

"From the attic. See that trapdoor. It has taken on the cough with the vital energy it has been drawing from the sick man. I guess there'll be no lights up there. I'll go and get my flashlight. You stay here and guard the stairs. Then you can give me a boost up."

The doctor was becoming more incredible every minute.

"You mean to say you propose to stick your head up through there?"

The doctor nodded soberly; his eyes were now black beads.

"It's quite necessary. You see, we've got to chase this thing out of the house while it is still weak, and then protect all entrances. Then, if it cannot quickly establish a contact with some other sick and non-resistant source of energy, it must go back to where it came from. Without a constant replenishment of human energy it can't keep up the human vibrations. That's the importance of shutting it out while it is still too weak to break through anybody else's resistance somewhere else. It's quite simple, isn't it? You sit tight and play cat over the mouse hole. I'll be right up again."

Cat-like himself, the doctor ran down the steps. Terry felt chilled despite the fact that the hall was well lighted and he was armed. But that black square up there—if any cover belonged over it, it had been removed. The hole gaped dark, forbidding; and somewhere beyond it in the misty gloom a formless thing coughed consumptively. Terry, gazing at the hole in fascinated terror, imagined for himself a sudden framing of baleful eyes, a reaching down of a long taloned claw.

It grew to a horror, staring at that black opening, as into an evil world beyond. The effort of concentration became intolerable. Terry felt that he could not for the life of him hold his stare; he had to relieve himself of that tension or he would scream. He felt that cry welling up in his throat and the chill rising of hair on his scalp. He let his eyes drop and took a long breath to recover the control that was slipping from him.

There came a sharp click from the direction of the electric switch, and the hall was in sudden blackness.

Terry stood frozen, the cry choked in his throat. He could not tell how long he remained transfixed. An age passed in motionless fear of he did not know what. What had turned off the lights?

In the blackness a board creaked with awful deliberation. Terry could not tell where. His faculties refused to register. Only his wretched imagination—or was it his imagination?—conjured up a shadow, darker than the dark, poised on one grotesque foot like some monstrous misshapen carrion bird, watching him with a fell intentness. His pulse hammered at his temples for what seemed an eternity of horror. He computed time later by the fact that his eyes were becoming accustomed to the dim glow that came from the light downstairs.

Another board creaked, and now Terry felt his knees growing limp. But that was the doctor's firm step on the lower stairs. Terry's knees stiffened and he began to be able to breathe once more.

The shadow seemed to know that Dr. Muncing was returning, too. Terry was aware of a rush, of a dimly monstrous density of blackness that launched itself at him. He was hurled numbingly against the wall by a muffling air-cushion sort of impact. Helplessly dazed, smothered, he did not know how to resist, to defend himself. He was lost. And then the glutinous pressure recoiled, foiled. He could almost hear the baffled hate that withdrew from him and hurtled down the stairs.

His senses registered the fact that without his own volition he shouted, "Look out!" and that there was a commotion somewhere below. He heard a stamping of feet and a surge of wind as though a window had been blasted open; and the next thing was the doctor's inquiry, "Are you hurt?" and the beam of a flashlight racing up the steps.

He was not hurt; miraculously, it seemed to him, for the annihilating malevolence of that formless creature had appeared to be a vast force. But the doctor dressed him down severely.

"You lost your nerve, in spite of all that I explained to you. You let it influence your mind to fear and so played right into its hands. You laid yourself open to attack as smoothly as though you were Mrs. Jarrett herself. But out of that very evil we can draw the good of exemplary proof.

"You were helpless; paralyzed. And yet the thing drew off. Why? Because you had your iron blackjack in your hand. If it had known you had that defence it would never have attacked you, or it would have influenced you to put the iron down first. Knowing now that you have it, it will not, in its present condition of weakness, attack you again. So stick that in your hat and don't get panicky again. But we've got to keep after it. If we can keep it out of the house; if we can continue so to guard the sick man that the thing cannot draw any further energy from him its power to manifest itself must dwindle. We shall starve it out. And the more we can starve it, the less power will it have to break through the resistance of a new victim."

"Come on, then," said Terry.

"Good man," approved the doctor. "Come ahead. It went through the living-room window; that was the only one open. But, why, I ask myself. Why did it go out? That was just what we wanted it to do. I wonder whether it is up to some devilish trick. The thing can think with a certain animal cunning. We must shut and lock the living-room window and go out at the door. What trick has that thing in store, I wonder? What damnable trick?"

"How are we going to find an abstract hate in this maze of shadows?" Terry wanted to know.

"It is more than abstract," said the doctor seriously. "Having broken into our plane of existence, this thing has achieved, as you have already felt, a certain state of semi-materialization. A ponderable substance has formed round the nucleus of malignant intelligence. As long as it can draw upon human energy from its victim, that material substance will remain. In moving from place to place, it must make a certain amount of noise.

And, drawing its physical energy from this particular sick man, it must cough as he does. In a good light, even in this bright moonlight, it will be, to a certain extent, visible."

But no rustlings and scurryings fled before their flashlights amongst the ornamental evergreens; no furtive shadow flitted across moonlight patches; no sense of hate hung in the darkest corners.

"I hope to God it didn't give us the slip and sneak in again before we got the entries fixed. But no, I'm sure it wasn't in the house. I wish I could guess what tricks it's up to." The doctor was more worried than he cared to let his friend see. He was convinced that leaving the house had been a deliberate move on the thing's part and he wished that he might fathom whatever cunning purpose lay back of that move.

All of a sudden the sound of footsteps impinged upon their ears; faint shuffling. Both men tensed to listen, and they could hear the steps coming nearer. The doctor shook his head.

"It's just some countryman trudging home along the road. If he sees us with flashlights at this hour he'll raise a howl of burglars, no doubt."

The footsteps approached ploddingly behind the fence, one of those nine-foot high ornamental screens made of split chestnut saplings that are so prevalent around country houses. Presently the dark figure of the man—Terry was quite relieved to see that it was a man—passed before the open gate, and the footsteps trudged on behind the tall barrier.

Fifty feet, a hundred feet; the crunch of heavy nailed boots was growing fainter. Then something rustled amongst the bushes. Terry caught at the doctor's sleeve. "There! My God! There again!"

A crouching something ran with incredible speed along this side of the fence after the unsuspecting footsteps of the other. In the patches of moonlight between black shadows it was easily distinguishable. It came abreast with the retreating footsteps and suddenly it jumped. Without preparation or take-off, apparently without effort, the swiftly scuttling thing shot itself into the air.

Both men saw a ragged-edged form, as that of an incredibly tall and thin man with an abnormally tiny head, clear the nine-foot fence with bony knees drawn high and attenuated ape arms flung wide; an opium eater's nightmare silhouetted against the dim sky. And then it was gone.

In the instant that they stood rooted to the spot, a shriek of inarticulate terror rose from the road. There was a spurt of flying gravel, a mad plunging of racing footsteps, more shrieks, the last rising to the high-pitched falsetto of the acme of fear. Then a lurching fall and an awful silence.

"Good God!" The doctor was racing for the gate, Terry after him. A hundred feet down the road a dark mass huddled on the ground; there was not a sign of anything else. The misshapen shadow had vanished. The man on the ground rolled limp, giving vent to great gulping moans. The doctor lifted his shoulders against his own knee.

"Keep a look-out, Jimmy," he warned. His deft hands were exploring for a hurt or wound, while his rapid fire of comments gave voice to his findings. "What damned luck! Still, I don't see what it could have done to a sturdy lout like this. How could we have guarded against this sort of a mischance? Though it just couldn't have crashed into this fellow's vitality so suddenly; there doesn't seem to be anything wrong, anyhow. I guess he's more scared than hurt."

The moaning hulk of a man squirmed and opened his eyes. Feeling himself in the grip of hands, he let out another fearful yell and struggled in a frenzy to escape.

"Easy, brother, easy," the doctor said soothingly. "You're all right. Get a hold of yourself."

The man shuddered convulsively. Words babbled from his sagging lips. "It-it-its ha-hand! Oh, G—God—over my face. A h-hand like an eel—a dead ee-eel. Ee-ee!"

He went off into a high-pitched hysteria again.

There was a sound of windows opening up at the house and a confused murmur of anxious voices; then a hail.

"What is it? Who's there? What's the matter?"

"Lord help the fools!" The doctor dropped the man cold in the road and sprang across to the other side from where he could look over the high fence and see the square of patches of light from the windows high up on their little hill.

"Back!" he screamed. "Get back! For God's sake, shut those windows!" He waved his hands and jumped down in an agony of apprehension. "What?" The fatuous query floated down to him. "What's that you say?"

Another square of light suddenly sprang out of the looming mass, from the sick man's room. Laboriously the window went up, and the sick man leaned out.

"What?" he asked, and he coughed out into the night.

"God Almighty! Come on, Jimmy! Leave that fool; he's only scared." The doctor shouted and dashed off on the long sprint back to the gate and up the sloping shrubbery to the house that he had thought to leave so well guarded.

"That's its trick," he panted as he ran. "That's why it came out. Please Providence we won't come too late. But it's got the start on us, and it can move ten times as fast."

Together they burst through the front door, slammed it after them, and thundered up the stairs. The white, owlish faces of the Jarrett family gleamed palely at them from their door. The doctor cursed them for fools as he dashed past. He tore at the knob of the sick-room door.

The door did not budge.

Frantically he wrestled with it. It held desperately solid.

"Bolted from the inside!" The doctor screamed. "The fool must have done it himself. Open up in there. Quick! Open for your life."

The door remained cold and dead. Only from inside the room came the familiar hacking cough. It came in a choking fit. And then Terry's blood ebbed in a chill wave right down to his feet.

For *there were two coughs*. A ghastly chorus of rasping and retching in a hell's paroxysm.

The doctor ran back the length of the hall. Pushing off from the further wall, he dashed across and crashed his big shoulders against the door. Like petty nails the bolt screws flew and he staggered in, clutching the sagging door for support.

The room was in heavy darkness. The doctor clawed wildly along the wall for the unfamiliar light switch. Terry, at his heels, felt the wave of malevolence that met them.

The sudden light revealed to their blinking eyes the sick man, limp, inert, lying where he had been hurled, half in and half out of the bed, twisted in a horrible paroxysm.

The window was open, as the wretched dupe had left it when he poked his foolish head out into the night to inquire about all the hubbub outside.

Above the corner of the sill, hanging outside, was a horror that drew both men up short. An abnormally long angle of raggy elbow supported a smudgy, formless, yellow face of incredible evil that grinned malignant triumph out of an absurdly infantile head.

The face dropped out of sight. Only hate, like a tangible thing, pervaded the room. From twenty feet below came back to the trembling men a grating, "Och-och-och, ha-ha-ha-heh-heh-heck, och—och." It retreated down the shrubbery.

Dr. Muncing stood a long minute in choked silence. Then bitterly he swore. Slowly, with incisive grimness he said, "Man's ingenuity can guard against everything except the sheer dumb stupidity of man."

It was morning. Dr. Muncing was taking his leave. He was leaving behind him a few last words of advice. They were not gentle.

"I shall say no more about the criminal stupidity of opening your windows after my warning to you; perhaps the thing was able to influence all of you. Your brother, madam, has paid the price. Through your fault and his, there is now loose, somewhere in our world, an elemental entity, malignant and having sufficient human energy to continue. Where or how, I cannot say. It may turn up in the next town, it may do so in China; or something may happen to dissipate it.

"As far as you are concerned it is through. It has tapped this source of energy and has gone on. It will not come back, unless you, madam, go out of your way deliberately to attract it by fooling with these silly séances before you have learned a lot more about them than you know now."

Mrs. Jarrett was penitent and very wholesomely frightened, besides. She would never play with fire again, she vowed; she would have nothing at all to do with it ever again; she would be glad if the doctor would take away her ouija board and her planchette and all her notebooks; everything. She was afraid of them; she felt that some horrible influence still attached to them.

"Notebooks?" The doctor was interested. "You mean you took notes of the babble that came through? Let me see. Hm-m, the usual stuff; projected reversal of your own conceptions of the hereafter and how happy all your relatives are there. Ha, what's this? Numbers, numbers— twelve, twenty-four, eight—all the bad combinations of numbers. What perversity made you think only of bad numbers? Hello, hello, what—From where did you get this recurring ten, five, eight, one, fourteen? A whole page of it. And here again. And here; eighteen, one, ten? Pages and pages—and a lot of worse ones here? How did this come?"

Mrs. Jarrett was tearful and appeared somewhat hesitant.

"They just came through like that, Doctor. They kept on coming. We just wrote them down."

The doctor was very serious. A thin whistle formed in his pursed lips. His eyes were dark pools of wonder.

"There are more things in heaven and earth—" He muttered. Then shaking off the awe that had come over him, he turned to Mrs. Jarrett.

"My dear lady," he said. "I apologize about those open windows. This thing was able to project its influence from even the other side of the veil. *It made you invite it.* Don't ask me to explain these mysteries. But listen to what you have been playing with." The doctor paused to let his words soak in.

"These numbers, translated into their respective letters, are the beginning of an ancient Hindu Yogi spell to invoke a devil. Merciful heaven, how many things we don't understand. So that's how it came through. And there is no Yogi spell to send it back. We shall probably meet again, that thing and I."

THE CASE OF THE
HAUNTED CATHEDRAL

MARGERY LAWRENCE

Margery Lawrence (1889–1969) had long been fascinated by the super-natural and later in life became a spiritualist, writing about all forms of psychic experiences in Ferry Over Jordan *(1944). Her father, a solic-itor, had funded her first publication in 1913, a book of poems,* Songs of Childhood, *and after the war she turned to writing fiction, initially short stories, several of which appeared in* The Tatler *and were collected in* Nights of the Round Table *(1926). She had early success with her romance novel* Red Heels *(1925) and thereafter she felt obliged to pro-duce similar works to sustain an income, although this was alleviated in 1927 when she married Arthur Towle, manager of the St. Pancras Railway Hotel, and controller of all the hotels on the London, Midland, Scottish Railway. This allowed her more freedom, along with the success of her novel* Madonna of the Seven Moons *(1935), about a woman with a dual per-sonality, which was later filmed. She produced two further books of weird tales,* The Terraces of Night *(1932) and* The Floating Café *(1936). After completing a long novel of reincarnation,* The Bridge of Wonder *(1939) and her book on spiritualism, Margery returned to short fiction. She had always liked the John Silence stories by Algernon Blackwood and created her own specialist in the supernatural, Miles Pennoyer, whose cases are recorded by Jerome Latimer. The first book of seven stories,* Number

Seven, Queer Street was published in 1945, but it was years before she completed the second volume of longer stories, Master of Shadows *in 1959. August Derleth published one final story, "The Case of the Double Husband" in 1971, making twelve stories in total.*

"YES," SAID PENNOYER, "IT'S A GLORIOUS PIECE OF WORK, AS YOU say. Small, perhaps, as cathedrals go—probably one of the smallest cathedrals in the world, but a beautiful piece of modern architecture. A sad thing that it was its architect's swan-song."

"What do you mean?" I asked.

"Didn't you know that the man who designed it—Gregg Hart—died six months after it was finished?" said Pennoyer.

He glanced oddly at me and I pricked up my ears, for that sidelong glance generally meant that a story lay somewhere hidden behind the apparent casual speech.

He paused a moment and then added softly, "He committed suicide—was found dead on the altar steps. Didn't you know?"

I shook my head.

"No. It probably happened while I was abroad somewhere—you know how much I miss, wandering about as I do. And besides," sheer honesty forced me to add, "frankly, I'm not much of a religionist, you know, and I don't suppose the death of anybody in a cathedral—even the architect of it—would make any particular impression on me."

"Probably not," said Pennoyer as he turned the leaves of the handsome folder of photographs of Nant Valley Cathedral that I had brought back with me after my recent visit. "But you *are* interested in the odd and the uncanny, and there were stories . . . look!" He stabbed a place on one of the photographs with the point of a pencil. "That's where the body was found. Lying sprawling halfway up the steps, as though he'd tried to reach the altar and failed." He paused and then went on reflectively, "No wonder—and yet he found forgiveness in the end, poor chap, after all."

"After all what?" I said determinedly, pulling my chair to the fire and taking out my tobacco-pouch and pipe. "You settle down and tell me the story that's behind all this, Pen! I know the signs by now."

Pennoyer laughed.

"It's a long one," he said. "But interesting . . . yes, very interesting. I'll get you a whisky and soda, then, and let you hear it. Odd that by sheer chance, out of interest in modern architecture, you should have gone to see this place—the setting for one of the strangest and most pathetic haunting cases in all my experience. Here you are—help yourself. I never know the right proportion of that poison of yours. Well . . .

"It was about a year after the death of Gregg Hart that I was called in to consultation by the Church Authorities—the Dean and Chapter of Nant Cathedral. I found them in a considerable state of agitation, I may say, and I was soon aware that there had been much arguing and counter-arguing as to whether I should be called in or not. But the matter was getting out of their hands.

"It had all begun, I gathered, even before Hart's death—stories, rumours, whispers of odd happenings, nothing very tangible, but still they were there. And since his death they had grown and spread so rapidly that they were beginning to have a very bad effect not only on the various church officials, from Canons, major and minor, down to choristers, vergers, lay-clerks, bell-ringers, and so on, but even with many of the congregation. Indeed, matters had become so serious that attendances were falling off, and the Dean and Chapter was getting deeply concerned! So at last a special meeting was summoned at which the situation could be discussed and, it was hoped, cleared up to everybody's satisfaction.

"But unfortunately the meeting did no such thing, as it was found that the opinions of the five worthy clergymen—who, with the Dean as head, formed the meeting—themselves were far from uniform. Canon Hotchkiss frankly scoffed and declared that there was 'nothing in it,' and that the only attitude was to pooh-pooh everything and carry on as though nothing had happened, hoping that the various rumours would, if persistently ignored, die out in time. Canon Maple was frankly puzzled and apprehensive and admitted that he did not know what to think. Canon Whippet supported him, declaring that the stories were being deliberately spread by the Church's enemies, and advised police action, while Canon Fraser doggedly maintained, in the teeth of his brother Canon, Hotchkiss, that 'there were more things in heaven and earth, etc.' Moreover, he daringly decided that he had himself heard and seen certain matters in the Cathedral that he could by no means dismiss as pure imag-ination—at which Canons Hotchkiss and Whippet plunged into action and the meeting became something resembling a general wrangle! So the Dean dismissed it, realizing that united action of any kind was, in the face of such varied feeling, for the moment, impossible.

"So the matter had been allowed to drift on and on, and the rumours grew and flourished, until at last things came to a head when a visiting Bishop, conducting the Communion Service, cried out and fainted as he was holding the Chalice to the lips of a communicant and had to be hastily carried out to the vestry while another priest took his place. The Bishop took some time to recover, and when he did, the first thing he did was to declare that there was an Evil Force abroad in the Cathedral, and that it had tried to prevent the communicant—an elderly woman, a decent, pious body well known to the Dean—from touching the Cup. Questioned further by the perturbed clergy, the Bishop declared that he was holding the Cup out to the communicant when (to use his own words) 'another face—a *man's* face—seemed to slide over hers, to come down like a mask as it were, as though to try and prevent her lips reach-ing the rim of the Cup—or to get its own there first! And at the same moment I felt a cold hand on my wrist and a voice seemed to whisper, 'No, *no!*'

"The alarm and consternation amongst the clergy at the incident was great, as you may imagine, and the matter was hastily hushed up, and a story concocted to the effect that the Bishop had had a heart-attack. But it was quite impossible to prevent the rumour spreading that *something* had been heard—or seen—by the Bishop, which naturally lent evidence to the stories of other things that had been heard or seen by less important people; and attendances at the services fell off to such a degree that in sheer desperation the Dean called another meeting, and it was decided to try exorcism. But this failed, the hauntings persisted, and at last the Dean—much against the advice of several of his brother-priests, who saw in me a sort of necromancer having dealings with devils, various and assorted—wrote me a note inviting me to come and see him."

"How did he come to know about you?" I demanded.

Pennoyer crinkled up his eyes at me and laughed.

"That, as Kipling says, is another story," he said. "As a matter of fact I dealt with a rather nasty obsession case in which his niece was mixed up. I'll tell you about that another time if you like. But apparently the Dean was sufficiently impressed with that business to risk sending for me—and of course I went down to Nant at once, and found a charming, rather fussy, anxious little man, with a face like an elderly Donatello cherub and white hair growing in a sort of tonsure round a pink bald pate, waiting to greet me in the drawing-room of a pretty house in the Close. Where's that brochure of yours? I think there's a picture of the Close that shows his house."

He flipped over a page or two of the booklet and showed me a charming photograph of a row of pleasantly designed houses, each set back in a neat garden, that clustered round the Cathedral—which stood magnificently alone upon a great stretch of green sward—like a group of guards standing in a square round the throne of a King. He pointed to one of the houses and continued.

"The Dean was a bit shy at first and rang for tea while he talked trivialities. And then a dear little silver-haired sister came in, as round and pink and cherubic as he was. They reminded me irresistibly of a pair of elderly whats-their-names . . . that outmoded celluloid doll that used to be popular with children? Thing with an inane baby face and a blue bow on its tummy."

"I know! Kewpies!" I said with a chuckle. "Go on, I can just see them."

"Well," said Pennoyer, "they gave me a sumptuous tea—home-made scones and jam sandwiches, and chocolate cake in such quantities that I no longer wondered where the dear little man had got the pot-belly that bulged out his cassock like a small football! They were charming; the little old lady twittered at me and pressed cake on me, and at the end of tea we had grown more at ease with one another, so that when the tea and Miss Conover took themselves off together, I sat back in the comfortable leather-covered chair and said to the Dean, 'Now, sir, what's the trouble?' And he told me the whole story quite simply."

"You mean the beginning of the story," I quibbled. "Obviously if he had told you the whole story he would not have needed to ask your advice."

"I hate obvious and rather ham-handed jokes," said Pennoyer severely. "And anyway if ordinary people could solve psychic problems, where would a psychic doctor like your venerable friend get a living? Anyway, he started by giving me a surprise—because he told me that the Cathedral was haunted by *two* ghosts. One had been seen—or heard—*before* the death of poor Gregg. And Gregg Hart was—or so it was presumed—the second."

I opened my eyes.

"*Two* ghosts?" I said. "I thought the haunting must be Hart, of course, when you told me he'd committed suicide in the Cathedral itself. But *two*? What could have happened to produce two ghosts in a completely new building? If it had been a hoary old pile . . ."

"I know," said Pennoyer, "but you do sometimes get haunting in a new house, you know—generally a ghost that belongs to an old house that has been pulled down to make way for the new! I remember once in a brand-new ultra-modern steel-and-glass bungalow built by a rich young man on the Sussex Downs—Still, that's not the yarn I'm telling. But apart from that, a double haunting sounded interesting, so I asked the Dean to go into details.

"He told me that rumours that the Cathedral was haunted were pretty widely spread several months before Hart's death. Precisely when they started he did not know, but certainly he became aware of them about three or four months before the building was finally completed. The story was that it was a *child-ghost*—sometimes seen, or more often, footsteps pattering, the flutter of a frock, a childish voice singing or whispering, that sort of thing—even some of the workmen engaged on the building swore they had seen something. And in connection with this, the Dean said, an odd incident occurred.

"Gregg Hart was fulminating to him, as he so often did, about the slackness of some of the men, about their readiness to knock off early, even before the dusk drew in, and jokingly the Dean said perhaps they were anxious to leave before dark for fear they might see the ghost of the child that there was so much talk about . . . and this remark had the most alarming effect. Hart went absolutely green, and almost collapsed! Frightened the Dean to death—though Hart recovered in a minute or two and passed it off—but it was obvious, said the Dean, that Hart himself had seen or heard *something*, or why should he look so scared and sick? Later on, of course, I had another theory, but for the moment I accepted the Dean's, and he went on. Apparently it was about a month after that conversation that the Cathedral was finished and consecrated, and three days after the consecration Hart was found dead in the nave of the Cathedral—and *then* the double haunting started!

"I began to be distinctly interested and asked for more details. How many people had seen the two ghosts together—when and how, for how long a time—and the Dean answered me with a tense frown on his chubby face, obviously trying to be as exact as possible. Reports varied, it seems—probably with the varying psychic perception of the seers. Some people apparently saw only the child . . . a faint, shadowy sort of shape flitting round the High Altar or running across the chancel; others said they had seen a man only, an outline, tall and dark; a *very* few said they saw the two together; while many people complained of a feeling in the Cathedral of intense unhappiness, of strain and distress—one described it as 'a sort of spiritual tumult indescribably painful and bewildering.' And of course there was the usual lot who didn't actually see or hear anything concrete, but who merely sensed an 'atmosphere' about the Cathedral—especially towards evening—that made them feel uneasy. Oh, it was a nice haunting case. Very thorough and complete . . ."

"How did Hart come to die there . . . on the steps of the altar?" I said. "Singularly dramatic! Was it an accident?"

Pennoyer glanced at me.

"It wasn't," he said briefly. "He committed suicide. Took poison . . ."

I felt a faint thrill of horror and pity combined. To commit suicide on the steps of the altar of the great Church that was the crown of one's life-work, the very peak and summit of one's ambition! For a man to do this must surely mean reaching a pitch of despair the very thought of which chills one's blood. . . .

"Again, for the sake of the Cathedral, this was hushed up, and the doctor gave a verdict of death by heart-failure," said Pennoyer. "Luckily one of the vergers coming in early in the morning found the body, locked up the Cathedral, and ran to fetch the Dean. The Dean's brother—who's a doctor—was staying with him then, and they went over together. Dr. Conover knew what a dreadful business it would be for the new Cathedral to start its ministries, as it were, by having to wipe out the stain of a sui-cide's blood, so heart-failure it was, officially, and all was well. I don't think anything queer was suspected by the world outside the Close, nor even inside, until the double haunting started. . . ."

"But what on earth?" I began incredulously. "What reason . . ."

"You'll know, all in good time," said Pennoyer. "Well, I wormed all I could out of the Dean about Hart. I was specially anxious to know the reason for his suicide . . . but this last nobody seemed to know. Hart had lived in Nant—more or less, at least—for the last three or four years of the building of his masterpiece. He rented a small house in the village, and the old woman who owned the house 'did' for him—and as far as anybody knew, there was no reason why he should have thrown away his life so pitifully. He was still only fifty-six or so, had a fine name, the building of the Cathedral had set the coping-stone on an already notable career, he had plenty of money, more commissions than he could deal with . . . he was unmarried, and had no particular troubles as far as the outside world could discover.

"But I gather he was a terribly difficult man to deal with—as many geni-uses are, of course—and during the last two years he had become more and more difficult. In fact, the Dean told me that his old landlady, Mrs. Griffiths, often declared that if it hadn't been for her being so deaf that she didn't hear his swearing and cursing when he was in one of his rages, she would never have stayed with him so long. I gather he used to write down his orders and she carried them out, and so life remained peaceful for her, at all events . . . if a man has to start expressing his anger by means of writing, it flickers out!

"I understand, from what the Dean said, that though Hart must always have been a moody, awkward-tempered cuss, he grew much worse during the last year of the Cathedral's building, as various hitches occurred from time to time in the delivery or the execution of the work that used to infuriate him to almost madness . . . and there were times, the Dean said, especially towards the end, when he feared seriously for his reason. The last few months must really have been hell-and-blazes for all concerned, as between the stories of the child-ghost putting the men off their work and Gregg Hart going apparently bit by bit off his head—well, life was simply awful, and my poor little Dean was driven almost hysterical at times."

"Well," I said, "frenzied rages, however unpleasant they may be for a man's friends and acquaintances, don't necessarily mean lunacy, or even weakening of the brain!"

"I know," said Pennoyer. But, apart from what Hart *said,* he really did, it seems, start behaving more than a little oddly towards the end. It appears that he was naturally a rather solitary, surly sort of bloke; hated society, made very few friends, refused all the local ladies' invitations, though they tried hard to lionize him, till they found it wasn't any use. He used to go up to his London studio pretty often, and now and then he'd bring back a brother-architect or artist to have a look at the Cathedral—but mostly he kept very much to himself in Nant. Used to spend hours by himself in the Cathedral after the workmen had gone, walking about and studying it, and thinking out endless new details . . . the place was his mania, he'd lived and dreamt and planned and hoped for it for years, and his real absorption in and love for his work was one of the things that made the Dean and others forgive him a good many *bêtises.*

"But towards the end he changed very much—he seemed to avoid the Cathedral after dark, and wouldn't go there alone even during the day if he could help it. And another thing was odd! From being a teetotaller—or very nearly—he took to drinking in a big way. And from being a moody, solitary sort of a chap, never going out and snubbing any overtures of friendship, he suddenly took to accepting any invitation that was thrown at him, and clinging so persistently to anybody who would tolerate him as to become something of a nuisance. Didn't seem to want to be alone—ever—especially at night! Of course, not only this caused a lot of talk, but his changed attitude towards the Cathedral, his reluctance to go into it except during the daytime hours, or when there were others about, revived the rumour that he had seen the child himself—but when this was hinted to him jokingly at some party or other, he first went white and then flew into such a violent rage that it was never mentioned afterwards. Of course, it may have been true and he *had* seen the child, but didn't want to admit it. The very violence of his reaction to the suggestion rather seems to suggest that . . . ."

"When did the Dean see him last?" I asked.

"About three days before he died," said Pennoyer. "It was at the consecration—a great occasion, of course, with all the County there, and the choir-stalls packed with clergy from all over the diocese, and a garden-party with champagne and strawberries at the Dean's afterwards, and I don't know what-all! Apparently Hart had been very white and *distrait* all day, and during the consecration ceremony he gave a queer kind of cry and collapsed in a heap in his pew. He was taken out and looked after at once, and though of course it *might* have been that he had merely been overcome with quite natural emotion at seeing his greatest achievement completed at last, still some people whispered and looked at each other queerly, because as he was coming round apparently he raved and wept and talked hysterically about some child or other . . . but there was nothing definite to be made out of what he said. Of course, he may not have been talking about the ghost-child at all, but about a perfectly ordinary child—but the obvious conclusion was drawn once more. And when he became conscious, he looked, I'm told, truly ghastly, with his eyes sunk in his head and his face lined like an old man's. After that his fear of being alone amounted to a mania! He hung round people till he became a perfect plague, and actually tried to persuade the Dean to let him come and live with him as a P.G.; but apart from the fact that poor Hart's temper made him anything but a pleasant housemate, the Conover *ménage* had no room for a third person—and a few days after that Hart was found dead in the Cathedral on the steps of the altar. And it was after this that the double haunting began, and the Cathedral of Nant Valley began to be deserted by its worshippers and dreaded by its servants, until the afternoon came when I sat in that pleasant little drawing-room with Dean Conover, eating hot scones at a Chippendale table, and promised him I would do my best to lift the cloud that was impeding the work of his beloved Church!"

Pennoyer sat back, took a sip of orange juice, and continued.

"Obviously the first thing to do was to examine the ground for myself, and I requested permission to spend the night in the Cathedral, which I got without difficulty. It was not without a certain amount of trepidation that I nodded goodnight to the elderly verger who led me to a pew facing the High Altar, tucked me round with a rug—I had come provided with a warm coat, a rug, a flask of coffee, and sandwiches, as it was not my first experience by a good many of the dank chilliness of these vigils!— and I heard his footsteps going slowly away down the long echoing nave towards the door. The faint click of a distant latch told of his departure, and I sat back staring up at the magnificent arched chancel before me.

"The moon was high, and I could see sufficiently well to appreciate the austere beauty of the place.

"The scent of the incense from the evening service that had taken place before still lingered faintly in the air, and mingled with the strong sweet odour of the Madonna lilies that shone like white stars in the gloom from the tall brass vases on the altar, whose green velvet frontal, embroidered from end to end with embossed gold and silver thread, gleamed richly at the head of the flight of seven shallow steps of black and white marble that led up to it. I stared at those steps, seeing in my mind's eye the sprawled body of the dead man as it had lain along them when they found it—and my eye travelled from the steps to the gilded altar-rail of the Sanctuary, up to the altar and the gorgeous reredos behind it, all goldwork, mosaic, and carving, with the great golden Crucifix in the centre, and up again, higher still, to the six tall narrow windows that rose above it, their shape echoing the six tall narrow candles that flickered on the altar between the lilies. Windows that repeated in their lustrous stained-glass panels set with jewels, the myriad colours of the reredos.

"High above the chancel swung the seven lamps, like seven glowing ruby eyes eternally on duty, guarding the shrine . . . . I blinked at them and shivered, yawning and wondering whether it was imagination, or was I really feeling oddly shivery, with that queer inner chill that means something 'otherworldly' coming near? A chill utterly different from the mere gooseflesh brought about by normal cold . . . .

"I glanced at my watch. It was just on twelve o'clock, and though my experience has taught me that ghostly happenings do not by any means necessarily *only* take place at midnight, yet that witching hour is still the time when the veil between the Two Worlds wears thinnest, and queer things are most likely to happen.

"There was no sound—the utter silence of a great structure like that, in the dead of night, has to be felt to be believed. There is no real silence out of doors, no matter how dark the night. In the city there is the occasional hoot of a taxi, the measured tread of a policeman, voices, and laughter as a stray group of partygoers hurries home, the rumble of a distant electric train or an early market-cart, the squall of a lovesick pussy-cat abroad on the tiles—and in the country the cheep of sleepy birds, the stealthy rustle of a prowling night-hunter in the undergrowth, an owl's hoot, the sigh of wind in the branches, the bark of a watchdog, a thousand other sounds. But there, within this immense pile of masonry, soaring skywards God knows how many feet above my head, there was a silence that could be felt, almost handled, and accustomed as I was to eerie atmospheres, I had to gather all my strength of mind and courage to meet it without a qualm!

"I sat there watching the altar, wondering whether amongst the shadows that I thought I saw moving aimlessly about before it there loomed already the dim shape of a man—or a child?—and warning myself to keep my imagination quiescent, to free myself merely to observe, not to invent. I had been told that the Cathedral had been haunted by a child and a man, and that knowledge might impel me, if I were not wary, to construct those actual shapes out of the vague movement of shadows, out of the effect of the moonlight that fell, blurred and strangely coloured by the many-hued glass through which it filtered, in long narrow panels along the marble floors of sanctuary, of chancel, and of nave . . . .

"But even as I told myself this, I was conscious of a growing tension in the atmosphere about me, of a sense of palpitating emotion rising and growing stronger and more painful every moment, that beat about my spirit as the waves beat about the foot of a rock, disturbing it, threatening, almost, to overwhelm it! Holding my inner senses steady, I tried to analyse the rising tide, to sort out its component parts, knowing that if I could only do this I might find some clue that would lead me towards the inner heart of this mystery.

"I was conscious, first of all, of a queer sense of bewilderment—of frustration and suspicion—and then suddenly fear seized me, an almost panic terror! But it was not *my own* fear that I felt. I was sensing the fear that had been felt by someone else—that somewhere was *still* being felt! I felt that fear reach out and touch me, and the first vibration mingled with it, that strange wild sense of bewildered frustration—but now it was rising rapidly to anger mingled with hate, both fierce and turbulent, yet, I felt, directed not so much at any thing or person in particular, as against all things and all men alike. I got a sense of blind, thwarted rage akin to the lunatic fury of a madman who, driven by forces beyond his comprehension or control, turns and rends whatever comes nearest to his hand, blind to all but the furious need to assuage by action, the more violent the better, the fever that is riding him! All about me these furious vibrations raged and swirled, strong as a palpable tide almost, bewildering and distressing to such a degree that confusedly I thought that with my actual ears I heard sounds of weeping, of curses and cries of rage and anger, the gnashing of teeth and thin wails of mortal fear. . . . I had to hold tightly to my sense of balance, and my heart swelled with pity for whoever it was, how many or how few I had no idea, that was sending forth these waves of such desperate suffering!

"I stared steadfastly up at the altar, which, as far as I could make out, seemed to be the focus from which these vibrations swept outwards into the main body of the great pile, and, holding tightly to the carved wooden arm of my pew, and mentally concentrating upon the great golden Cross above the altar, tried to keep my head above the waters of the wild tide of emotions that whirled and strove about me, and then suddenly—I saw it! A tall, dark shape that stood halfway up the altar steps. A figure very faint and indistinct—but clearly the figure of a man.

"I had never met Gregg Hart, and in any case the shape was too shadowy for any features, etc., to be seen in detail—and moreover, as he stood looking up at the altar, his back was towards me and I could not see his face. But it was a man tall and lean and rather stooping, as they had described Hart, wearing lightish trousers and a loose dun-coloured coat—and the Dean had told me that Hart's working attire was invariably light grey flannel trousers and a brown tweed jacket. He was standing halfway up the shallow flight of steps below the altar, staring up at it, as though waiting or watching for someone. He stood perfectly still, and all the time that maelstrom of tangled emotions surged about me, anger and fear and bewilderment, blind fury, and mortal anguish. And now I perceived that a fresh element had entered into that dreadful tide that beat about me! The sense of guilt. Somewhere, someone was either suffering or had suffered—I was too confused and shaken to be able to distinguish which—some overwhelming sense of shame, of horror, of self-loathing so immense as to be truly dreadful! Someone, grovelling, abject, wept in agonized guiltiness, without hope of forgiveness or of pity. . . .

"And then suddenly I saw that at one corner of the altar there was another figure—the figure of a child! She stood, or rather crouched, against the dull green-and-gold shimmer of the altar-frontal, watching the tall shadow of the man standing below her at the further side of the altar steps—and even as I followed her I saw that he was not there any longer! As though the appearance of the child had meant his banishment, he had vanished like a blown-out candle-flame, and only that shrinking little shape was left, cowering there in the dusk.

"I leant forward eagerly, straining my eyes to see through the gloom, and as I moved she moved also, creeping cautiously along the front of the altar as though only now, after the disappearance of the man, did she dare to make a movement. She stood for a moment or so before the altar, finger-ing the embroidery and the lace, reaching up to try and touch the flowers or the tall brass candlesticks, and staring vaguely up at the great golden Crucifix that shone high in the centre of the altar against the reredos. Now I could see her more clearly, thanks not only to the moon that, coming out of the clouds, threw a stronger light through the tall windows, but to a faintly shining quality that seemed to outline the forlorn little figure as though a luminous pencil had drawn her upon the dusk. It was a poor little scarecrow of a child—a girl of about seven or eight years old. A little girl dressed in a ragged red frock—the colour showed in the gloom like a dark red rose against the altar-frontal—with wild dark tangled hair, hatless and barefoot. I could see no detail again, no distinguishing feature—the shape looked like just another of the poor, poverty-stricken little slum or gipsy children that, alas! were all too common in the mining districts that lie close to the fringe of the Nant Valley. . . .

"For a few moments she lingered near the altar, then turned, and coming to the top of the altar steps, seemed to pause a moment—then came warily down, and turning sharply to the right, darted across the shadow-striped floor of the chancel and disappeared through the choir-stalls in the direction of the vestry. I waited several minutes, but she did not appear again, and I was conscious now that the tide of strange and exhausting emotions that had been endeavouring, it seemed, to engulf me, was slowly withdrawing itself, retreating once more to whatever place had sent it forth.

"This, then, was the sense of 'something dreadful' which many people experienced, even though they had not seen either of the ghosts. 'Spiritual tumult and suffering'—the Dean was right. I had—as I had hoped—seen and felt it all, and I blamed nobody for avoiding the Cathedral! I waited until that shattering flood of vibrations had completely faded away and then got up, shivering with cold, damp with the sweat of emotion and excitement, and feeling as limp as a rag, realizing that my ordeal was over—for one night at least. And what had I learned?

"It was in a rather sober mood that I left the Cathedral, now dark and still, untenanted and undisturbed, and made my way across the smooth stretch of turf to the Dean's house in the Close, where I was staying—he had said, and I agreed with him, that it would cause less comment and keep my real errand private if I merely came to stay with him as a friend. I tumbled thankfully into bed—though it was not yet one o'clock I was tired to death from the intense psychic strain of my experience—and slept soundly until eight o'clock, when I bathed and dressed and went down to breakfast with the Dean, who was waiting on tenterhooks of interest to hear my report. Miss Conover always breakfasted in her own room, so we were alone, and I plunged at once into my adventures of the night.

"He sighed faintly as I finished, and nodded.

"'Yes—yes. It happens just so. Sometimes the child is seen—sometimes the man; sometimes it is only that dreadful atmosphere that is felt, and people are terrified and won't come into the place again.' He sighed. 'I can't say I blame them! I have felt it myself—though I have seen nothing. But the *feeling* is awful—that dreadful mingling of rage and fear, of shame, of agony of mind. . . .' He shivered and stopped. 'What *is* your opinion, Dr. Pennoyer? Or haven't you had time to form one?'

"I haven't—yet," I replied. "I think I have seen the haunting—or rather hauntings—complete, so to speak, because that is the work I've been trained to do. To see the whole where less highly-trained sensitives only see, as you say, in scraps. But precisely what these two poor souls have to do with each other—if anything!—I don't know yet. Nor do I know the meaning of that whirlpool of terrible emotions that comes with them—whether that again belongs to those two, or does it perhaps mean a third and quite separate sort of haunting? Though I feel the three belong together in some way. As regards the more mature elements in the vibration wave, I think most of them emanate from the man. Somehow, some of them . . ." I hesitated . . . "the overwhelming feeling of shame, for instance, and the sense of violent anger and desire to destroy . . . these seem to me too mature, if you know what I mean, for a child. The child-element comes through, I fancy, on the *fear*-vibration . . . but what had she to fear, and what has that to do with the man, if anything?'

"'If it was an older building' said the Dean, 'I would have thought one or other of the hauntings dated back to ancient times. But that can't be. The Cathedral has only been finished and open for worship six months.'

"It hasn't been built on the site of an older church by any chance, has it?" I said. "Because in that case it might have 'inherited' a ghost from the earlier building."

"The Dean shook his head.

"'No,' he said decidedly. 'It was built on virgin ground—the land was part of a park owned by Sir William Nant, who gave it over to the Church as a thanksgiving for the recovery of his only son from a long illness.'

"There was evidently no solution there, and I brooded over the problem all day, but without much success. I examined the altar and all about it as a matter of routine, but without finding anything whatever out of the ordinary; so I decided to go once more to the Cathedral that night to see if anything more enlightening took place.

"The night was darkish, and it was only occasionally that a chance shaft of moonlight managed to pierce the high windows and help the dim red glow of the high-hung Sanctuary lamps . . . but it all happened again, just as before. Again the tide of warring emotions rose about me, shaking and horrifying me with sheer pity and terror both and longing to help—and as the tide rose to its climax, came the man standing on the altar steps, and then the child.

"I sat through the same painful experience, and all happened as before until the little figure of the child came down the steps and darted away

into the dusk through the choir-stalls—and on her disappearance immediately the atmosphere lightened, the sense of oppression vanished, and
within a few moments I could sit back, breathe, and wipe my sweating
brow and wonder how much more of this I must endure before beginning to find some solution of the problem. If I could find out where the
child disappeared to it might help. So shaking off my rug, I followed in the
direction where the figure of the child seemed to have gone, and found
myself in the Dean's vestry, from which an outer door, now locked, led
out upon the green platform of turf that surrounded the Cathedral. The
vestry was open and empty but for various surplices hanging ghost-like
from their hooks, and as I peered from the little window I saw, with the
aid of the moon, that had for a moment floated clear of the clouds, that the
smooth green turf lay quiet, untroubled by a shadowy little figure flitting
across it. The child had disappeared again, leaving no trace, and again, disappointed, I returned to the Dean's house and to bed.

"Well, for about a week, night after night, I kept this tedious vigil, without any sort of result, except considerable exhaustion on my part, and I
was really beginning to wonder whether I might have to write this case off
as one of my failures—which I should have very much disliked doing!—
when by sheer chance one night I forgot the latchkey with which the Dean
had provided me so that I could let myself in on my return without waking
the household.

"I had been through the selfsame experience that night as all the other
nights—the two figures, the awful sense of despair, of fury, or mortal fear,
and it had ended as it always did, with the disappearance of the child's
figure into the shadow-filled choir-stalls—and again I had followed her
and tried to see where she went, but without success. Either I was never
quick enough to catch her leaving the Church, or else she simply did not
exist—or appear, however one might describe it—anywhere except in the
Church itself. If this were true, indeed, as far as I saw, I stood little chance
of solving the problem!

"The grim and pitiful scene looked like going on indefinitely, like some
ill-omened film shown every night in the heart of the new Cathedral
to anyone who dared to watch, and I was definitely feeling rather cast
down about it as I left the Cathedral and crossed the close-cut grass and

approached the Dean's house—and finding I had left the latchkey in my bedroom, cursed my folly roundly! It was barely one o'clock in the morning. I was tired and depressed, and the prospect of either having to walk about all night, sleep in the Cathedral, or else rouse the little man's household to let me in, did not please me at all.

"I tried the front door, but it was securely locked, of course. I went round the neat little garden to the back door, to find that also locked, and there remained only one hope—the Dean's study at the back of the house. If he had forgotten to shut and latch the window, as in his absent-minded way he might have done, I *might* succeed in getting in that way. I thought I spied a faint light between the folds of the halfdrawn curtains and wondered whether he might possibly be sitting up reading late, as occasionally, defying the disapproval of his sister, he did.

"I stepped as lightly as I could between the plants below the window and peered in—and got the shock of my life. The thick velvet curtains hung well apart, and I could see most of the room—and the light within came from no earthly lamp or candle! It came from the shape of a child that stood in a far corner of the room, beside a large closed desk. Yes, it was *the* child—my little ghost!

"Here, seen at closer quarters, she was more distinct, and indeed the faint light that seemed to hang about her shone out in the darkness of the room as though she was surrounded with a queer kind of phosphorescence. Yes, there she was, that red-frocked, ragged little shadow with bare feet and tangled dark hair falling shaggily over its eyes, like that of a little wild thing of the woods rather than a child of human parentage. For a moment I stood transfixed, staring, as she stood by the desk, stroking its surface, passing her hand over it with that absorbed attention, almost wondering, that a child gives to something that holds some peculiar interest for it . . . then in the blink of an eye she was gone, and with my heart thumping with excitement I managed to push the window open (which was, as I had hoped, ajar), and scrambling into the room, went to examine the desk where she had been standing.

"I was disappointed at first. It was a handsome but perfectly ordinary modern rolltop desk, with nothing notable about it in any way. If it had been an antique piece, I felt it would have held out more promise. . . . But anyway, this was getting somewhere at least outside the Cathedral, and directly after breakfast that morning I tackled the Dean.

"He was most excited at my tale, and when I told him where the child had been standing, his cherubic pinkness deepened almost to crimson in his excitement.

"'My dear sir—my *dear* sir! But that is a desk that I bought at the sale of poor Gregg Hart's belongings! It belonged to him!'

"I bounded out of my chair.

"That was Gregg Hart's? My God, then we've found out at least something. There *is* a connection between him and the child, though what, it remains to be seen . . . at least we've solved that much. They are not two independent hauntings, but one—connected by some link that we've still got to find. Perhaps that link is hidden in that desk. . . .'

"By this time we were both out of the breakfast-room and in the study, and the Dean was fumbling with the key of the desk. It was, he explained, not used very much as a rule. He had bought it for the use of his sister, to keep her account and housekeeping books in, the notes and records of her various activities connected with the Church, the Dorcas Society, Mothers' Meetings, Y.W.C.A., Girl Guides, and all the rest—but the little lady had been disappointed in it. It was too large and masculine in type for her taste—more suitable for her brother's study, she had acidly declared, than for her pretty drawing-room! So it had remained in a corner of the Dean's own study, though, devoted to his own desk, he did not use it—he had, indeed, intended to sell it again and buy his sister another desk that would tune in more effectively with the Chippendale furniture that was her passion. Meanwhile she was using the pigeon-holes at the top to store a few odd papers in, but the drawers were all empty, as far as he knew. . . .

"Without waiting for Miss Conover's permission—another sin for which I fear the little Dean subsequently got into trouble!—we turned out the desk thoroughly, finding, as the Dean had predicted, that all the drawers were empty, though the pigeon-holes were fairly full of odd papers, bills, recipes, lists, letters, account-books, notes, brown-paper and string, a varied collection of small boxes, labels, and similar small things. We sorted all these out with meticulous care, but found nothing at all relevant to the matter we had in hand. We pulled out the drawers and looked behind them, but even when the whole thing stood gaping, empty, I still had the feeling that there *was* something there to be found, if only we could find it . . . and sure enough, there was!

"I have made something of a study of secret drawers and the like, as you know. Many of these modern desks have a secret drawer somewhere, and this one had—cleverly concealed behind the pigeonholes that filled in the back of the desk. I fumbled about for a while, but at last I found the tiny catch for which I was looking—four pigeon-holes came forward in a solid block. I lifted them out, and behind them was a tiny door! It was locked, but I easily forced the lock with the tiny pocket-jemmy that I always carry—which made the Dean's eyes bulge somewhat!—and a crumpled litter of papers tumbled out, and with them a little red-leath-er-covered pocket book.

"As I pounced on it the Dean gave an exclamation.

"'A diary . . . Gregg Hart's! I've often seen him use it.' A faint qualm seized him. 'A dead man's secrets . . . my dear sir, do you think we ought . . . ?'

"'I don't know what *you* feel you ought to do,' I said with firmness, 'but *I've* been called in to get rid of this haunting that is ruining your lovely Cathedral, my dear Dean! And with your leave—or without it—I intend to leave no stone unturned until I do. This diary—all these papers—may be of untold value. I am going to my room now to study them from beginning to end.'

"I spent an absorbing two hours. The loose papers were of no value, though I examined them with care; there were drafts of letters—mostly of a rather acrimonious sort, showing that the rumours anent poor Hart's bad temper had by no means been exaggerated!—bills, notes, a few odd sketches, and so on. But the diary. . . . As I read it I shuddered, and yet all the time I felt, beside my horror, that sense of overwhelming pity rising within me again. . . .

"The diary started about a year before the finishing of the Cathedral—started, it seemed, almost at random. Something like this.

"'. . . a positive hoodoo on this building! Another man ill—this means those murals held up again, for God knows how long. *Why* must it be my key-men who always fall ill?'

"A few days later . . .

"'Driving me mad, these continual hitches. The very weather against us. Would have thought that spire proof against any storm . . . and now they say there must have been some weakness in the construction, to bring it down! I lost my temper . . . said what I suppose I ought not. Do they think me an amateur not to know how to choose sound stuff, or how to construct. Stupid . . . but one's tempted to wonder if there isn't something in the old idea that the Devil hates the building of a church and tries his best to stop it. . . . Something positively uncanny about these continual hindrances . . .'

"Later again it went on:

"'Yes, it *would* happen to me! The only earthquake for fifty years—and only a tiny one, they say, but enough to crack my marble flooring . . . simply isn't natural for these misfortunes to come one after another. And yet I swear I *will* finish it, my *magnum opus,* the loveliest thing I ever built! These things are maddening . . . can't sleep, can't eat, and my nerves are getting frightful. . . .'

"I read on slowly and carefully, page after page, seeing with a mixture of pity and fear the man's storm-torn mind as the feeling gradually grew upon him that there was something uncanny, inimical, fighting against the completion of the glorious creation upon which he had set his heart. . . .

"The luncheon bell rang before I had got more than halfway through the diary, and slipping the book into my pocket I went down to join the Dean and his sister.

"The little lady had already got over her annoyance at our ruthless rifling of her papers, and smiled upon me as she doled out plentiful portions of roast duck and green peas, with apple-charlotte to follow.

"Over coffee with the Dean in his study afterwards, I told him something of what I had already found in the diary. The Dean's face lengthened with pity.

"'Poor fellow!' he muttered. 'Poor fellow! Oh, yes, I know that towards the end, in spite of all that I could say, I fear he really began to believe that something that was not of our world was deliberately thwarting him—holding the work up, trying to prevent its completion.'

"'Was there *really* an undue amount of difficulty in getting the Cathedral finished?' I asked.

"The Dean wrinkled his brows.

"'Well' he said, 'there *were* a great many hindrances, I'll admit, of one sort and another, especially during the last year, when that diary was written—though I think to Hart, with his excitable, hysterical temperament, they loomed larger and more sinister than they would have done to a more steadily balanced man. After all, there are hitches, delays, disasters in the building of any place, great or small! There was a strike amongst the masons at one time, and then I remember two Italian expert workmen engaged on the mosaics behind the altar fell ill and were in hospital for several weeks so that work was held up, as nobody could touch that sort of work. Then the first spire blew down in a storm, and then a transport ship bringing a cargo of special Sicilian marble sank—and again, there was an epidemic of influenza that kept three-quarters of his men away for weeks. And, of course, towards the end, men began dropping off because of this story about the ghost-child that appeared directly it grew dark. . . . Oh, I can't remember everything in detail, but really, one could scarcely blame the man for getting almost crazy with worry and anxiety as to whether he would *ever* get the thing really finished. But to blame it on deliberate action by the Devil . . . well!' The Dean laughed deprecatingly as he stirred his coffee. 'Of course, that was frankly childish, as I told him . . . and he didn't like that at all, poor man; he lost his temper and said most regrettable things. In these days one doesn't accept the medieval Devil, horns and hoofs and tail, who deliberately sets out to prevent the building of a church.'

"I suppressed the answer I had in mind to make—that if the Dean had had the personal experiences of Evil that I had had, he might not talk quite so confidently!

"'Quite,' I said. 'But don't you see that that idea, in the mind of a man already anxious, worried, highly strung—on the verge, if you like, of losing his balance—that idea might well become in time a positive obsession? In a word, even if untrue, it might well in time become a very dreadful truth—*to him*? And the less people believed him, the more he would feel it incumbent upon him, the only person who *really* knew the truth, to cope with it and vanquish it himself, at no matter what cost...'

"The Dean looked at me attentively.

"'I don't quite know what you're leading up to,' he began ... but I interrupted as I rose from my chair.

"'I don't either,' I said, slapping my pocket. 'But I've an uneasy suspicion that I shan't voice until I've read the rest of this. I hope it isn't true, this suspicion. But I've an unpleasant feeling that it *is*....'

"That unpleasant feeling was justified! I spent the afternoon reading the rest of the diary, and then, feeling unwontedly sober, sent a message by one of the maids to ask whether the Dean would see me after tea, alone, in his study. I had a request to make. When I put it he stared at me in silence for a moment, and when he spoke his voice was incredulous.

"'Impossible, my dear sir! It's *impossible*. Both what you say—and the request you make!' His scared blue eyes were on mine as he repeated, 'Impossible!' and I shrugged my shoulders.

"Well, there it is. I've solved your problem—or rather, I've got to the root of the problem and put you in the way of solving it. I can't solve it myself. Only an ordained priest can do that. If you don't take my advice, frankly, I see nothing for Nant Cathedral but to endure these hauntings indefinitely.'

He stared at me afresh.

"You think—*that*? Oh, but no! It would be awful ... we have lost already more than half our workers, to say nothing of our congregations. People are getting terrified ....' He wrung his hands. 'Of what use is a church where none come to worship?'

"'Precisely!' I said. 'And it is because I think you are a man really strong enough to work with me in the releasing of this lovely place from the curse that has come to rest upon it that I have asked you—what I have.'

"I stared at him straight in the eyes as he murmured something distractedly about the Bishop and twisted his fat little hands together again—but I sensed a yielding in his attitude and went on more emphatically.

"'Come, come, sir—what, after all, do I ask you to do? Help me to release a suffering soul—to lift the shadow away from this holy place.

Surely doing that is God's work, even if I ask you to do it in a rather unconventional way?'

"He looked at me shrewdly and intently with his candid blue eyes—and after a pause suddenly drew a long breath and nodded his head.

"'I'll do it.' he said firmly. 'Whether it would please my superiors I really don't know, and frankly, I'm not going to ask! I believe you are a good and spiritual man, Mr. Pennoyer, though your way upwards is far from being mine. But since God looks behind the action for the motive—and I believe your motive pure, and am humbly sure that mine is—I shall follow your lead in this, and trust that God in His infinite mercy will guide us both aright."'

Pennoyer paused and poured himself out another glass of orange juice. He smiled at my absorbed face—absorbed is the word, for I had clean forgotten my pipe, which lay half burnt out in the ashtray—and I protested.

"Go on, man—you haven't told me the rest of the diary yet."

"That will come out in due course," said Pennoyer sententiously. "Let me tell my story in my own way—if I told you what was in the diary now it would anticipate my climax, and that would be bad storytelling! Well, thirty-six hours later we set out. I would have gone the very next night, but the Dean insisted on preparing himself by keeping vigil with prayer and fasting for the whole of the night beforehand, and I am the last person to quarrel with anybody else's system of putting themselves *en rapport* with the Unseen. So the night after that, at a quarter to twelve, we set out for the Cathedral.

"There was a lovely gibbous moon watching us as we crossed the Close, and it was as bright, almost, as day. The Dean kept glancing nervously from side to side, and I felt rather like a conspirator, and certainly we looked the part, me in my black cloak and my old sombrero, and the Dean in his cassock! If any of the Dean's parishioners had been abroad that night, they would have stared to see their reverend preceptor out at such a time, for the good folk of Nant went early to bed. But luckily there was no sign of anybody save a stray cat as we crossed the moonlit space of ground and gained the side entrance to the Cathedral. I remember thinking, as we walked towards it, how like a snowclad thing it looked, with the moonlight sharply white on spire and turrets, arch and gable, and the inky shadows lying in between—then we were inside the vestry and the Dean began with trembling fingers to don surplice and stole in preparation for his part in the drama we were about to play together.

"I suppose that is rather an irreverent phrase to use but it was true. I had coached the little man carefully in his role; I knew that only he could play it. For all my knowledge and training, there are things only an ordained priest could do, and I was a layman; and when at last the little man stood ready, wearing his snowy surplice above his long black cassock, the rich Roman-purple of the stole cutting a stripe of lively colour down each side of the surplice, and the black biretta crowning his thick white hair, he attained suddenly a presence so impressive and dignified that I thought how true was the old saying that the apparel makes the man . . . yet there was more to my little priest than mere brave attire. I came close to him and took his hands in mine. They were cold and rather shaky, but his blue eyes met mine courageously as I spoke.

"'Sir, I hope you don't think I don't appreciate this that you have undertaken to do—I honour and admire you for it more than I can say! I've only got one thing to ask you—whatever you may see or hear tonight, *don't give way!* Go through with the rite to the end. You say you have only occasionally heard or felt . . . something. But tonight, because I am here—and I shall be concentrating all my psychic strength on you, to help you to do what only a fully ordained priest *can* do—you may also, for the moment, see what *I* see! If—then—you give way, through fear or shock, as your Bishop did, then all this effort that we are putting forward will be wasted, and this thing that we are trying to cure may even be intensified. These two souls so pitifully earthbound may be bound here for ever. . . .'

"He nodded.

"'I understand—and as far as it lies in the power of a weak man to undertake to follow through a thing to the end, Mr. Pennoyer, I give you that undertaking, for the sake of the good we are both trying to do. And may God prosper us!'

"'Amen to that,' I said. 'Now, are you ready? It is close on midnight. Give me time to get into my place—and then come.'

"Drawing a long breath, he nodded again—and I left him and hastily took up my accustomed place in the body of the Cathedral.

"My heart was beating with excitement as I settled back against the hard wooden back of the pew and fixed my eyes upon the scene now so familiar—the seven marble steps up to the altar with its clustered lilies and shining brasses; the giant golden Crucifix in the centre, the gorgeous reredos and the painted windows behind, and against them, like ser-pents' eyes, the seven crimson-lighted lamps hanging motionless in the incense-heavy air. As I watched I saw the little figure of the priest emerge slowly from the side approach to the altar, and kneeling before it, bow low in prayer . . . and even as I watched it, I was conscious of that familiar tensity swelling in the atmosphere about me, flaming upwards, like a fire just lighted, as though the appearance of that little figure possessed a sig-nificance far deeper than I had realized . . . and suddenly they were there! That now-familiar vibration all about me told me so even before I saw them, or rather him. For, as always, the man appeared before the child.

"He stood, as usual, halfway up the steps before the altar—staring up at it, and his back was towards me, so I could not see his face as he watched with a queer kind of hungry intensity the figure of the Dean, now risen from his knees, moving quietly about the altar preparing for what he had to do—and from where I sat I sensed that intensity with a sharpness almost painful. I knew how a prisoner, held fast behind bars, might watch someone who, outside that prison, showed him the key. . . .

"The Dean turned, and I heard his sharp-drawn breath and knew that he saw even as I saw. More clearly indeed, since he saw the man's face, and for a moment I caught my own breath, wondering what effect the sight was going to have on him . . . but I need not have feared. There was sterling stuff in the little priest, and after a moment I heard his voice, quavering at first, but gathering strength as he spoke, ringing out in the silence.

"'Walter Gregg Hart, is it you that I see standing there?'

"The figure bent its head in assent, and I felt that wild and bitter tide of emotion well about me like a swelling tide—shame, anguish, and, above all, bitter, bitter repentance surged about me, and above it the Dean's voice rose again.

"'Is that which I fear true—that you have stained your hands, your hands that built this holy place, with blood?'

"Again the shadowy figure bent its head, and the utter wretchedness of its pose brought stinging tears to my eye. I wiped them hastily away as the priest went on.

"'Do you haunt this place because of your sorrow for that most dreadful sin, and do you with your whole heart and being repent?'

"For the third time the figure nodded—and the Dean drew a deep breath and went on.

"'Then, Walter Gregg Hart, I call upon the spirit of the child who died at your hands, and who also haunts this place because of the fear and suffering you caused her, to come now, and grant you her forgiveness, if she will, in the Name of the Child who died for her and for you and for all sinners!'

"I sat sharply upright in my place—for even as he spoke, there she stood, close to his side! One small hand, it seemed, catching the fringe of his purple stole, shrinking against him as for protection, her eyes fixed on that dark, despairing figure that stood with hanging head halfway up the steps below the altar—unable to approach nearer the holy place.

"That faint phosphorescent light still shone about her, and seemed, as she stood close to the Dean, to be brighter than usual—or else my sight was momentarily sharpened, for I saw a pinched little face with wide, scared dark eyes under the tangle of shaggy hair. Eyes that started at the figure of the man, and stared and stared . . . when suddenly he fell upon his knees and stretched out both arms to her in a gesture most piteous to see, a gesture of agonized supplication, a gesture that was at once a prayer and an appeal. As though in accord with this action, the tensity of the atmosphere pulsating about me deepened and strengthened until I shook all over with the mighty force of the vibrations, clinging to my balance and sanity with an effort that cost me almost more strength than I could summon up . . . and then even as I caught my breath and brushed the perspiration out of my eyes, I saw the miracle happen! The thin little hand of the child reached up and touched the hand of the Dean! And—all honour to my little priest, though, he told me afterwards, it came as a terrific shock, that sudden chill touch like an icy wind, and he scarcely blamed his Bishop for fainting!—when he looked down and saw what stood at his side his pity and his longing to help rose stronger than his fear. For she

515

was smiling up at him shyly, faintly, and as he looked down she pointed first to the kneeling shape that had once been a man, and then to the Cross above the altar.

"'Walter Gregg Hart,' said the Dean—and his voice quavered like a leaf in a wind, and I did not wonder. I, too, was almost at the end of my tether, for the whirlpool of emotion that had shaken me each night in this place had been nothing to the terrific intensity of that which I was passing through tonight. 'Be thankful in your soul, and bow yourself with gratitude! The child you murdered grants you her forgiveness—and on your sincere repentance I herewith grant you the pardon of the Church. Down on your knees, and greet it humbly!'

"The little man seemed somehow to grow immense, the whole Cathedral shook and throbbed about me like the beating of a great heart, and my dazed eyes seemed to see the childish shadow that still stood shyly clinging to the Dean's side shine out suddenly into a blinding Glory above a dark shape bowed in humility—and high above the uproar and tumult in my ears I heard the great words of the Exorcism ring out.

"'. . . *Our Lord Jesus Christ, who hath left power to His Church to absolve all sinners who truly repent and believe in Him, of His great mercy forgive thee thine offences! And by His authority committed to me, I absolve thee from all thy sins. In the Name of the Father, and of the Son and of the Holy Ghost! Amen.'*

"There was a mighty flash like a blaze of summer lightning as the Dean made the Sign of the Cross, and as he made it I saw that which is so rarely seen by man—the Sign itself remaining, hanging in the air, as it were, in pure white brilliance, for the space of a breath! Then as it vanished the whole world seemed to shake and split into a thousand pieces that went spinning round my head to the accompaniment of a terrific roaring like that of some colossal waterfall, and the last thing I knew before I lost consciousness was that above all the tumult I seemed to hear a distant sound, faint but glorious, of singing, high and triumphant, as though in welcome. And a childish voice was leading it. As I sank away into the darkness the words 'there is more rejoicing over one sinner that repenteth' flashed across my mind. . . .

"After a long time, it seemed, I came back into myself, and I found I was huddled in a heap in the corner of my pew, and that the Dean was kneeling in prayer before the altar. When I went up to him, he rose, trembling, and all but collapsed in my arms. Poor brave little man—he had done wonders! But he was so nervously shattered that he was almost weeping, and I had great difficulty in getting him home at last, he was so shaky at the knees—and then I was obliged to sit beside him for quite an hour before I could get him off to sleep. He had been amazingly plucky, carried things through, as I had begged him, to their ultimate end, and freed not only those two poor earthbound souls, but his beloved Cathedral, from bondage. So it was well worth it—for since then the two figures, with the dreadful atmosphere of suffering they brought with them, have never been seen again."

There was a long pause. I was more moved than I dared to admit. "That," I said at last, "is a thundering good story! But I want to know various other things. Obviously Hart murdered the child—but why and how and when?"

"As regards the *how*, I can't tell you," said Pennoyer. "But after the Exorcism was over, the Dean got permission to take up one of the flagstones at the corner of the altar—where she always appeared first—and found what I told him he would find. The remains of a child. A little girl, dressed in a ragged scarlet frock. She was buried reverently in a corner of Nant churchyard—and it is obvious that Hart, driven mad by the constant hindrances and hitches to the building of the Cathedral, conceived the awful idea that only a human sacrifice would appease whatever Force he imagined was opposing him, and murdered her, poor little soul. I suppose he lured her into coming there one night by a promise of sweets or money, killed her somehow—strangulation, I imagine—and buried her there. Brrh! It's an ugly story. Only hinted at in the diary—but I pieced it together."

"But *why?*" I persisted. "What was the idea?"

"Oh," said Pennoyer, "It's an old superstition, you know, that a living thing *must* be buried under any building as a sort of sacrifice to the gods of the earth. You often find bones ... animal generally, but sometimes human ... under the centre-posts or hearthstones of old buildings. And the practice is by no means entirely dead even today—it still exists in certain parts of the world."

"I suppose," I said, "Hart's obsession that he was being deliberately hindered by the Devil worked on the man to such an extent that he lost his mental balance."

Pennoyer nodded.

"That's right," he said. "He was always a man of very violent temper, and the set-backs consequent upon the building of the Cathedral fairly drove him mad with rage. You see, the whole of that tragic story expressed in emotions was still living and vital in that infernal symphony of vibrations that came with them—I picked up the 'echoes' of those earlier moods of his, as well as the later. I think this child was probably a 'stray' belonging to some gipsies who used to wander through here occasionally—she looked a gipsy type, blackhaired and lean and ragged. There you have the element of fear and shrinking—the child's part in that awful symphony—and the later reaction also of poor Hart, when he realized what he had done ... shame and horror, guilt and a desperate anguish of repentance! Obviously he committed suicide because of what he had done. I should not be surprised if he himself saw the child—there are one or two cryptic remarks that read as though he did, in the latter part of the diary. But equally obviously, once out of the body, with his mind no longer clouded by semi-madness, he realized to the full his awful sin, and could not leave this place until he had received forgiveness both from the child he had murdered and from the Church he had defiled."

"What about the phosphorescent effect that you got with the child?" I said. "And why didn't you get it with the man as well?"

Pennoyer laughed.

"There are questions that even a fairly experienced psychic such as myself can't answer with *absolute* assurance," he said. "But I imagine that the real answer would have something to do with the child's essential innocence that expressed itself thus—as opposed to the man's older, more darkened spirit. I believe poor Hart had led a pretty ragged sort of moral life, while she had died—been killed—while her aura was still pure, untouched. At least, that is the only answer I can give you."

I was silent for a moment.

"There's another thing too," I said at last. "Now at the end, when the Dean gave the absolution, apparently it was *you* who passed out in a faint, while he didn't. You said that when you came to he was kneeling in prayer at the altar. He was shaken, but that was all . . . and you had collapsed! With your experience and powers that surprised me. I should have thought you were the tougher of the two."

"My dear Jerry," said Pennoyer with a wry smile. "There are limits to the physical strength and endurance of the most highly trained practitioner of any art! And don't you realize that sitting there in the Church, apparently taking no active part in the whole affair, I had actually been providing, so to speak, the blood—the psychic force and the strength—needed by the little Dean to get through the whole thing? He was amazingly plucky—and if he had not been so brave he would have failed. But sitting there quietly in the body of the Church, out of the limelight, so to speak, *I* was providing the main strength on which he was depending. And further, I saw what he didn't at the finish—I saw the *proof* that Hart was pardoned. I saw the visible Cross of Light Itself, hanging in the air—and that is an experience that will temporarily knock out most psychics. The intense power, the almost terrible purity of it . . . well, there you have your explanation."

He rose as a signal that the evening was over, and reluctantly I rose too, and shook out my unsmoked pipe.

"Pen," I said, "you are a queer chap—and a rather wonderful one." Pennoyer shook his head.

I'm only using gifts that all of us possess in a greater or lesser degree," he said. "And believe me, often it is a curse to possess 'em in a really highly trained and developed form! Many is the night's sleep I've lost not only in going through these experiences, but in thinking of them afterwards. . . . Psychic work takes it out of you to a terrific extent, and however well you may train your courage, there are sights and sounds that shake it to the core and leave you as weak and shaky as a kitten. He laughed. "Never mind! It's all in the day's work—and I wouldn't be doing anything else for anything in the world! Bless you—goodnight."

THE SHONOKINS

MANLY WADE WELLMAN

Just when you thought that nothing new could be added to the occult detective format, along came Manly Wade Wellman (1903–1986). Wellman had, in fact, been around for a good few years, selling his first story to Weird Tales *in 1927, but had concentrated on science fiction and other genres during the 1930s before returning to his love of the weird. Wellman had been born in Portuguese West Africa (now Angola), where his parents had been medical missionaries, and though they returned to the United States when he was six, he still had memories of listening to the folktales of the locals, of shape changers and shamans. Living first in Kansas, where Manly desired to be a cowboy, but later moving to North Carolina, he became fascinated by the folklore of the Appalachian mountain men. Wellman first created the occult specialist Judge Pursuivant in "The Hairy Ones Shall Dance" (1938), and the Judge took centre stage in three more stories but then took on the role almost as a godfather or mentor to the other occulteers that Wellman created: John Thunstone, John the Balladeer and Lee Cobbett. Pursuivant even gives Thunstone his silver sword-cane. It is perhaps in the John the Balladeer stories where the lode of Appalachian folklore proves most fertile, but Wellman used this as seasoning in many of his stories. With Thunstone he created the shonokins, a race of human-like creatures who had dominated America before the arrival of humans and who seek to reassert themselves. The following is the first story where we meet them head on.*

Thunstone is not unlike Wellman himself—large, bluff, strong, and determined. The first Thunstone adventure, "The Third Cry to Legba," appeared in Weird Tales *in 1943, and at that time Wellman wrote fifteen stories, but returned to him thirty years later with further stories and two novels,* What Dreams May Come *(1983) and* The School of Darkness *(1985). The other Thunstone stories were collected in* The Third Cry to Legba *in 2000.*

LESS THAN FIVE PERSONS HAVE EVER SEEN JOHN THUNSTONE frankly, visibly terrified, and less than two have lived through subsequent events to tell about it. Fear he knows and understands, for it is his chief study; but he cannot afford it very often as a personal emotion.

And so he only smiled a little that afternoon in Central Park, and the hand at which Sabine Loel, the medium, clutched was as steady as the statue of Robert Burns under which she had asked him to meet her. A few snowflakes spun around them, settling on their dark coats. "I say that you are in more than mortal danger," she repeated breathily. "I would not have dared recall myself to your attention for anything less important."

"I believe that," smiled Thunstone, remembering when last they met, and how he had demonstrated to her complete satisfaction the foolish danger of calling up evil spirits without being ready to deal with them. Not one ounce of his big powerful body seemed tense. His square face was pale only by contrast to his black eyes and black mustache. Not even his restraint seemed overdone.

"Whatever you think of my character, you know that I'm sensitive to spirit messages," she went on. "This one came without my trying for it. Even the spirit control that gave it was in horror. The Shonokins are after you." "I might have known that," he told her. "After all, I acted with what they might consider officious enmity. I stopped them, I hope, from a preliminary move back toward the world power they say they held before human history began. A Shonokin died, not by my hand but by my arrangement, and his body was buried at a place where I want them never to come—living

Shonokins, it seems, avoid only dead Shonokins. Their very nature forces them to strike back at me. But thank you for the warning."

"You think," ventured Sabine Loel, "that I want to be your friend?" "You do, though your purpose is probably selfish. Thank you again.

Now, I never had any malice toward you—so, for your own safety, won't you go away and stay away? Avoid any further complication in—in what's to happen between me and the Shonokins." "What precautions—" she began to ask.

"Precautions against the Shonokins," explained Thunstone patiently, "are not like precautions against anything else in this world or out of it. Let them be my problem. Good-by."

Going, she looked back once. Her face was whiter than the increasing snowflakes. Thunstone filled his pipe with tobacco into which were mixed one or two rank but significant herbs. Long Spear, the Indian medicine man, had told him how much such things did to fight ill magic.

Thunstone was living just then in a very comfortable, very ordinary hotel north of Times Square. He entered the lobby confidently enough, and rode up in the elevator without seeming to be apprehensive. But he paused in the corridor outside his own door as cautiously as though about to assail an enemy stronghold.

He bent close to the panels without touching them. Earlier in the day he had closed and locked that door from outside, and had dripped sealing wax in three places at juncture of door and jamb, stamping the wax with the crusader's ring he habitually wore. The wax looked undisturbed, its impress of the cross of Saint John staring up at him.

With a knife-point he pried the blobs away. They had not been tampered with in the least. Inserting his key in the lock, he let himself in and switched on the lights in the curtained sitting room.

At once he started back against the inner side of the door, setting himself for action. His first thought was that two men were there, one prone and one standing tensely poised. But, a hair-shaving of time later, he saw that these were dummies.

The reclining dummy was made of one of Thunstone's suits and a pillow from the bed in the next room. It lay on its back, cloth-stuffed arms and legs outflung. A tightly looped necktie made one end of the pillow into a headlike lump, and on this had been smudged a face, crudely but recognizably that of John Thunstone. Ink from the stand on the desk had been used to indicate wide, stupid eyes, a slack mouth under a lifelike mustache—the expression of one stricken instantly dead. The other figure stood with one slippered foot on the neck of the Thunstone effigy. It was smaller, perhaps a shade under the size of an average man. Sheets and towels and blankets, cunningly twisted, rolled and wadded together, made it a thing of genuinely artistic proportion and attitude. A sheet was draped loosely over it like a toga, and one corner of this veiled the place where a face would be.

"Substitution magic?" said Thunstone under his breath. "This is something that's going to happen to me . . . " He turned toward the desk. "What's that?"

On the desk seemed to crouch a little pixy figure. Made from a handkerchief, like a clever little impromptu toy to amuse a child, it looked as though it pored over an open book, the Gideon Bible that is an item in every hotel room. Stepping that way, very careful not to touch anything, Thunstone bent to look.

The book was open to the Prophet Joel, second chapter. Thunstone's eye caught a verse in the middle of the page, the ninth verse:

They leap upon the city; they run upon the wall; they climb up into the houses; they enter in at the windows like a thief.

Thunstone has read many books, and the Bible is one of them. He knew the rest of the frightening second chapter of Joel, which opens by foretelling the coming of terrible and ungainsayable people, before which no normal creature could stand. "They enter in at the windows like a thief," he repeated, and inspected his own windows, in the sitting room and the adjoining bedroom. All were closed, and the latches still bore blobs of wax with his seal.

These phenomena had taken place, it remained to be understood, without the agency of any normal entry by normal beings. Movement and operation by forces at a distance—telekinesis was the word for it, fondly used by Charles Richet of France, and tossed about entertainingly by the Forteans and other amateur mystics. Thoughts crossed Thunstone's mind, of broken dishes placed in locked chests by Oriental fakirs and taken out mended; of Harry Houdini's escapes and shackle-sheddings, which many persons insisted were by supernatural power; of how the living body of Caspar Hauser had so suddenly flicked into existence, and of how the living body of Ambrose Bierce had so suddenly flicked out. There were a variety of other riddles, which many commentators purported to explain by the overworked extra-dimensional theory. Somebody or something, it remained, had fashioned a likeness of his own downfall in his own sitting room, without getting in. Again approaching the desk without touching the Bible or the little figure crouched beside it, Thunstone drew out a drawer and produced a sheaf of papers.

The top sheet was a second or third carbon of his own typescript. Other copies of this sheet were sealed in various envelopes with equally interest- ing documents, placed here and there in the custody of trusted allies, each envelope inscribed To be opened only in the event of my death— John Thunstone. The knowledge that such collections existed was a prime motive of some of Thunstone's worst enemies to keep him alive and well. There was Sabine Loel's warning, for instance . . . Sitting down well away from the grotesque tableau, Thunstone glanced over his own grouping of known and suggested facts about the Shonokins.

Those facts were not many. The Shonokins were, or said they were, a people who had been fortuitously displaced as rulers of America by the ancestors of the red Indians. A legend which they themselves insisted upon was that ordinary human evolution was one thing and Shonokin evolution another. They hinted here and there at tokens of long-vanished culture and power, and at a day soon to come when their birthright would return to them. To Thunstone's carbon were appended the copy of a brief article on the "Shonokin superstition" from *The Encyclopaedia of American Folkways*; a letter from a distinguished but opinionated professor of anthropology who dismissed the Shonokins as an aboriginal myth less well founded than Hiawatha or the Wendigo; and Thunstone's own brief account of how someone calling himself a Shonokin had made strange demands on the Conley family on a Southern farm, and of what had befallen that same self-styled Shonokin.

Finishing the study of his own notes, Thunstone again regarded the grouped dummies, which he had thus far forborne to touch.

The standing figure, with its foot on the neck of the Thunstone likeness, had hands that thrust out from under its robe. They had been made of a pair of Thunstone's own gloves, and on closer scrutiny proved to be strangely prepared. The forefinger and middle finger of each had been tucked in at the tip, so that the third fingers extended longest. The only Shonokin that Thunstone had ever met had displayed third fingers of that same unnatural proportion. Thunstone nodded to himself, agreeing that this was plainly the effigy of a Shonokin. He turned his mind to the problem of why the images had been thus designed and posed.

A simple warning to him? He did not think so. The Shonokins, whatever they really were and wanted, would not deal in warnings—not with him at least. Was the group of figures then an actual weapon, like the puppets which wizards pierce with pins to torture their victims? But Thunstone told himself that he had never felt better in his life. What remained? What reaction, for instance, was expected of him?

He mentally put another person in his place, a man of average mind, reaction and behavior. What would such a person do? Tear up the dummies, of course, with righteous indignation—starting with that simulation of the Shonokin with a conquering foot on its victim's neck. Thunstone allowed himself the luxury of a smile.

"Not me," he muttered.

Yet again he went to the desk, and returned the paper to the drawer. He opened another drawer. Catching hold of the Bible, he used it to thrust the little handkerchief-doll into the drawer, closed and locked it in. Then, and not until then, he approached the two full-sized figures. They were arranged on a rug. For all its crumpled-fabric composition, the simulated Shonokin seemed to stand there very solidly. John Thunstone knelt, gingerly took hold of the arm of his own image, and with the utmost deliberation and care eased it toward him, from under the foot of its oppressor. When he had dragged it clear of the rug, he took hold of the edge of the rug itself and drew it smoothly across the floor. The Shonokin shape rode upright upon it. He brought it to the door of the empty sitting room closet, opened the door, and painstakingly edged the thing, rug and all, inside.

This done, he closed and locked the door. From the bedroom he brought sticks of sealing wax, which he always kept in quantity for unorthodox uses. After some minutes, he had sealed every crack and aperture of the closet door, making it airtight. He marked the wax here and there with the Saint John's cross of his ring. Finally returning to his own likeness, he lifted it confidently and propped it upright in a chair, and sat down across from it. He winked at the rough mockery of his own face, which did not seem so blank and miserable now. Indeed, it might be said to wink back at him; or perhaps the fabric of the pillowslip was folded across one of the smudgy eyes.

A little quiver ran through the room, as though a heavy truck had trundled by somewhere near. But no truck would be operating in the sealed closet.

Thunstone lighted his pipe again, gazing into the gray clouds of smoke he produced. What he may have seen there caused him to retain his smile. He sat as relaxed and motionless as a big, serene cat for minutes that threatened to become hours, until at last his telephone rang.

"Hello," he said into the instrument. "This is John Thunstone." "You danger yourself," a voice told him, a voice accented in a fashion that he could not identify with any foreign language group in all his experience. "And you are kind to warn me," replied Thunstone with the warmest air of cordiality. "Are you going to offer me advice, too?"

"My advice is to be wise and modest. Do not try to pen up a power greater than hurricanes."

"And my advice," returned Thunstone, "is not to underestimate the wit or determination of your adversary. Good day."

He hung up the receiver, reached for the Bible, and turned from the Prophet Joel to the Gospel of Saint John. Its first chapter, specified by the old anti-diabolists as a direct indictment of evil magic's weakness, gave him comfort, though he was reading it for perhaps the four hundredth time. The telephone rang again, and again he lifted it.

"I deplore your bad judgment in challenging us," said the same voice that had spoken before. "You are given one more chance."

"That's a lie," said Thunstone. "You wouldn't give me a chance under any circumstances. I won't play into your hands." He paused. "Rather unusual hands you have, don't you? Those long third fingers—"

This time it was his caller who hung up suddenly. Musing, Thunstone selected from his shelf of books a leather-bound volume entitled These Are Our Ancestors. He leafed through it, found the place he wanted, and began to read:

Stone-age Europe was spacious, rich and uncrowded, but it could ac- knowl-edge only one race of rulers.

Homo Neanderthalensis—the Neanderthal Man—must have grown up there from the dim beginning, was supreme and plentiful as the last gla-ciers receded. His bones have been found from Germany to Gibraltar, and his camps and flints and fire-ashes. We construct his living image, stooped and burly, with a great protruding muzzle and beetling brows. Perhaps he was excessively hairy—not a man as we know men, but not a brute, either. Fire was his, and the science of flint-chipping. He buried his dead, which shows he believed in an after-life, probable in a deity. He could think, per- haps he could speak. He could fight, too.

When our true forefathers, the first Homo Sapiens, invaded through the eastern mountain passes or out of the great valley now drowned by the Mediterranean, there was battle. Those invaders were in body and spirit like us, their children. They could not parley with the abhorrent foe they found. There could be no rules of warfare, no truces or treaties, no mercy to the vanquished. Such a conflict could die only when the last adversary died.

This dawn-triumph of our ancestors was the greatest, because the most fundamental, in the history of humanity. No champion of mankind ever bore a greater responsibility to the future than that first tall hunter who crossed, all aware, the borders of Neanderthal country.

The book sagged in Thunstone's hands. His eyes seemed to pierce the mists of time. He saw, more plainly than in an ordinary dream, a landscape of meadow and knoll and thicket, with wooded heights on the horizon. Through the bright morning jogged a confident figure, half-clad in fur, with his long black hair bound in a snakeskin fillet, a stone axe at his girdle and a bone-tipped javelin in one big hand. If the frill of beard had been shaved from his jaw, he might have been taken for John Thunstone.

He was trailing something—the deer he had waylaid and speared earlier in the day. There it was up ahead, fallen and quiet and dead. The hunter's wise eyes narrowed. Something dark and shaggy crouched beyond it, seeming to drag or worry at the carcass. A bear? The javelin lifted in the big tanned fist, the bearded mouth shouted a challenge.

At that the shaggy thing rose on two legs to face him, and it was not a bear.

Thunstone's eloquent fancy had identified the hunter with himself. It was as if he personally faced that rival for the dead prey, at less than easy javelin-casting distance. It stood shorter than he but broader, its shoulders and chest and limbs thatched with hair. Its eyes met his without faltering, deep bright eyes that glared from a broad shallow face like the face of a shaggy lizard. Its ears pricked like a wolf's, it slowly raised immense hands, and the third fingers of those hands were longer than the other fingers.

Thunstone rose from his chair. The fancied landscape of long ago faded from his mind's eye, and he was back in his hotel sitting room. But the hairy thing with the strange hands was there, too, and it was moving slowly forward.

Thunstone's immediate thought was that he had expected something like this. The Neanderthal man, says H. G. Wells, was undoubtedly the origin of so many unchancy tales of ogres, trolls, mantacors and similar monsters. Small wonder that such a forbidding creature had impressed itself on the night memories of a race . . . It was not coming toward him, but past him, toward the sealed door. Its strange-fingered hands pawed at the sealed cracks.

Thunstone's pipe was still in his hand. It had not gone out. He carried it to his mouth, drew strongly to make the fire glow, and walked across the carpet to the very side of the hairy thing. When he had come within inches, he blew a thick cloud of the herb-laden smoke into the ungainly face.

Even as it lurched around to glare, it was dissolving like one scene in a motion picture melting into another. It vanished as the smoke-cloud vanished. The telephone was ringing yet a third time.

Patiently he answered it.

"You are now aware," he was told by the same accented voice, "that even your own thoughts may turn to fight you."

"Any man may dismiss his own thoughts," replied Thunstone at once. "I have a special hell to which I send thoughts that annoy me. Can you afford to go on blundering? Why do you not call on me in person? My door is unlocked."

"So is mine," replied the other coldly. "On the floor below yours. Room 712. Come down if you dare."

"I dare, and do defy you for a villain," quoted Thunstone from Shakespeare, who also made a study of supernormal phenomena. Hanging up, he took from his smoking stand a glass ash tray. In this he painstakingly built a gratelike contrivance from paper clips, and upon the little grate kindled a fire of wooden match sticks. When it blazed up, he fed upon it some crumbs of his blended tobacco and herbs, and when these caught fire he poured on a full handful of the pungent mixture. It took the flame bravely. He carried it across the room, setting it in front of the sealed closet. The smoke curled up as from an incense burner, shrouding the entire wall from any magical intruder. Thunstone nodded approval to himself, went out, down one flight of stairs, and knocked on the door marked 712.

The door opened a crack, showing a slice of sallow brown face. A deep black eye peered at Thunstone, and then the door opened. A hand with a too-long third finger waved as if inviting him in. He crossed the threshold. The room was dim, with curtains drawn and a single crudely molded candle burning on a center table. Three Shonokins were there—one motionless under a quilt on the bed, one at the door, the third sunk in the armchair. They might have been triplets, all slender and sharp-faced, with abundant shocks of black hair. They all wore neat suits of gray, with white shirts and black ties, but to Thunstone it seemed that they were as strange to such clothing as if they had come from a far land or a far century. The door closed behind him. "Well?" he said.

The Shonokin by the door and the Shonokin in the chair gazed at him with malignant eyes of purest, brightest black. Their hands stirred, rather nervously. Their fingernails appeared to be sharp, perhaps artificially cut to ugly points. The Shonokin on the bed neither moved not stared. Toward him Thunstone made a gesture.

"I guessed more correctly about you than you about me," he said. "Your languid friend yonder—would it be tactless, perhaps to suggest that he lies there without any soul in him? Or that his soul is upstairs, animating a certain rude image which I have sealed carefully away?"

"We," said the seated Shonokin, "have never been prepared to admit the existence of souls."

"Tag it by whatever name you like," nodded Thunstone, "this specimen on the bed seems to be without it, and worse for being without it. Suppose we establish a point from which to go on with our discussion. You were able to fabricate, in my room, a sort of insulting tableau. I, for my part, was to enter, be surprised and angry, and attempt to tear it to pieces. Doing that, I would release upon myself—what?"

"You do not know," said the standing Shonokin tensely. It was his voice, Thunstone recognized, that had given the various telephone messages.

"Oh, it might have been any one of several things that hostile and angry spirits can accomplish," went on Thunstone with an air of carelessness. "I might have become sick, say; or have gone mindless; or the cloth, as I loosened it, might have smothered me strangely, and so on. Strange you went in for such elaborate and sinister attacks, when a knife in the back might have done as well. You intend to kill me, don't you?"

He looked at one of his interrogators, then the other, then once more at the figure on the bed. That Shonokin's face looked as pale as paper under its swarthiness. The lips seemed to quiver, as if trying feebly to gulp air.

"I think that it has been well established," Thunstone resumed, "that when a body sends forth the power that animates it, for good or for evil, it will die unless that power soon returns. But this doesn't touch on why you dared me to come down here. Did you dream that I wouldn't call your bluff. For it was a bluff, wasn't it?"

The eyes of the two conscious Shonokins were like octopus eyes, he decided. The Shonokins themselves might be compared to the octopus people, whose natural home was deep in ocean caves, from which specimens ventured on rare occasions to the surface when man could see and divide his emotions between wonder and horror . . .

"Thank you for giving us another thought to turn against you," said the Shonokin in the chair.

The dark room swam, swam literally, for to Thunstone it was as though warm rippling waters had come from somewhere to close over his head.

Through the semi-transparency writhed lean dark streamers, like a nest of serpents, their tips questing toward him. At the ends furthest from him they joined against a massive oval bladder, set with two eyes like ugly jewels. An octopus—and a big one. Its eight arms, lined with red-mouthed suckers, were reaching for Thunstone.

By instinct, he lifted his hands as though in defense. His right hand held his pipe, and its bowl emitted a twirl of smoke. Smoke under water!—But this was not water, it was only the sensation of water, conjured out of his chance thought by Shonokin magic. As the wriggling, twisting tentacles began to close around him, Thunstone put his pipe to his lips and blew out a cloud of smoke.

The room cleared. It was as it had been. Thunstone tapped ashes from his pipe, and filled and lighted it as before.

"You see," said the seated Shonokin, "that any fancy coming into your mind may blossom into nightmare. Is it a pleasant future to foresee, John Thunstone? You had better go up and open that sealed door."

Thunstone's great head shook, and he smiled under his mustache. "Just now," he said, "I am thinking of someone very like you, who died and was buried at the Conley farm. Why not make him appear out of my meditations?"

"Silence!" snarled the Shonokin who had opened the door. His hand lifted, as if to menace Thunstone with its sharp nails. "You do not know what you are talking about."

"But I do," Thunstone assured him gently. "Living Shonokins fear only dead Shonokins."

"Shonokins do not die," gulped the one in the dark.

"You have tried to convince yourselves of that by avoiding all corpses of your kind," Thunstone said, "yet now you are in dread of this dying companion of yours. His life is imprisoned upstairs. Without it he strangles and perishes. I learn more and more about your foolish Shonokin ways."

"You learn about us?" snapped the standing one. "We are ancient and great. We had power and wisdom when your fathers were still wildbrutes. When you understand that—"

"Ancient?" broke in Thunstone. "Yes, you must be. Only an unthinkably old race could have such deep-seated folly and narrowness and weakness.

Do you really think that you can swarm out again from wherever you have cowered for ages, to overthrow mankind? Human beings at least dare look at their own dead, and to move over those dead to win fights. You vain and blind Shonokins are like a flock of raiding crows, to be frightened away by hanging up a few carcasses of your own kind—"

"I have it!" cried the Shonokin who had stood by the door.

Weasel-swift and weasel-silent, he had leaped at Thunstone, snatched the pipe, and leaped away again. A wisp of the smoke rose to his pinched nostrils, and he dropped the pipe with a strange exclamation that might have been a Shonokin oath.

"Without that evil-smelling talisman," said the seated one, "I leave you to your latest fancy—raiding crows."

The room was swarming full of them, black and shining and clat- ter-voiced. A whir of many wings, a cawing chorus of gaping bills, churned around Thunstone, fanned the air of the room. Then, of a sudden, they were swarming—where?

"Now do you believe that your kind can die?" said Thunstone bleakly, his voice rising above the commotion. "The crows believe it. For they attack the dead, not the living."

The crows, or the vision of them, indeed thronged over and upon the bed, settling into a black, struggling mass that hid the form that lay there. "I thought on purpose of carrion-birds," said Thunstone. "Your power

to turn thoughts into nightmares has rebounded."

He spoke to the backs of the two living Shonokins. They were running. He wondered later if they opened the door or, by some power of their own, drifted through it. He followed them as far as the hall, in time to see them plunging down the stairway.

Stepping back into the room, he retrieved his pipe and drew upon it. At the first puff of smoke the crows were gone, leaving him alone with the silent figure on the bed.

Now he made sure, touching the chill wrist and twitching up a flaccid eyelid, that the Shonokin was dead. He made a tour of the room, in which there seemed to be no luggage—only a strange scroll of some material like pale suede, covered with characters Thunstone could not identify, but he pocketed it for more leisurely study. Out into the hall he strolled, smoking thoughtfully. He was beginning to like that herb mixture, or perhaps he was merely grateful to it.

Back in his own quarters, he opened the sealed closet door without hesitation. On the floor lay a crumpled heap of sheets, garments and other odds and ends, as if something had worn them and had shaken them off. Thunstone carried them into his bedroom, then dismantled the image of himself. He telephoned for a chambermaid to make the bed and a tailor to press the suit.

At length he departed to find a favorite restaurant. He ordered a big dinner, and ate every crumb with an excellent appetite.

When he returned to the hotel late that evening, the manager told him of the sudden death, apparently from heart disease, of a foreign-seeming man in Room 712. The man had had friends, said the manager, but they could not be found. He was about to call the morgue.

"Don't," said Thunstone. "I met him. I'll arrange funeral details and burial."

For a Shonokin corpse, buried in the little private cemetery on the farm he had inherited, would make that refuge safe from at least one type of intruder.

The manager, who knew better than to be surprised at Thunstone's impulses, only asked, "Will you notify his relatives?"

"None of his relatives will care to come to the funeral," Thunstone assured the manager, "or anywhere near his grave."

LUCIUS LEFFING IN

THE DEAD OF WINTER APPARITION

JOSEPH PAYNE BRENNAN

Joseph Payne Brennan (1918–1990) was one of the last great writers to appear in Weird Tales *before it ceased publication in 1954 (though it has since been revived many times). A native of Connecticut, but of Irish descent, Brennan seemed a writer of the old school, but always keen to experiment with new ideas. A poet by inclination, he worked for forty years as an acquisitions assistant at the Sterling Memorial Library at Yale University, so was steeped in memorabilia, academia, and ancient studies. Rather uncharacteristically his first dozen or so story sales were westerns, and his first story in* Weird Tales, *"The Green Parrot" (July 1952), was rather mild, but his next appearance was with an instant classic, "Slime" (March 1953) followed by the highly atmospheric "On the Elevator" (July 1953). When* Weird Tales *ceased, Brennan started his own little magazine,* Macabre, *in 1957 as some small replacement, and it was here, in 1962, that the first story featuring Lucius Leffing appeared, "The Haunted Housewife." Leffing was a far cry from John Thunstone or Jules de Grandin. He was a throwback to the early days, and although he lived in Connecticut, he evinced the Victorian era and had more in common with Sherlock Holmes. In many ways, the appearance of Lucius Leffing brought the occult detective full circle as he feels more at home with Martin Hesselius and Flaxman Low than with the modern sword wielders. The Leffing stories have been*

collected in The Casebook of Lucius Leffing *(1973),* The Chronicles of
Lucius Leffing *(1977),* The Adventures of Lucius Leffing *(1990) and
one novel,* Act of Providence *(1979). Not all the stories are supernatural,
but neither Brennan (who narrates the stories as Leffing's colleague) nor
Leffing shirk the sinister, or the horrors of the day, as the following story
shows.*

AS I REVIEW NOTES CONCERNED WITH THE CASES OF MY FRIEND,
Lucius Leffing, psychic investigator and private detective, I find it difficult to decide which episodes may entail the most reader interest. A case
which intrigues one reader leaves another indifferent. The best I can do,
therefore, is to rely on my own far from infallible judgement and hope for
the best. Although for various reasons Leffing refused many cases, it will
never be possible for me to record all of his exploits. My time and energies
have become far too limited.

One case, however, which has haunted me down the years, I find outlined under the title *The Dead of Winter Apparition.*

The business began in rather routine fashion. One winter evening,
over a decade ago, Leffing telephoned to tell me that he expected two prospective clients, a husband and wife, to visit him the next day. He knew
little about the case and was by no means sure he would accept it, but he
cordially invited me to be "on hand," as he put it, in the event he followed
through on the investigation.

Late on the following afternoon he cheerfully welcomed me into his
little Victorian-furnished house at 7 Autumn Street. Only a few minutes
elapsed before the door chimes sounded and I was introduced to a Mr.
and Mrs. Paul Pasquette.

Pasquette was a somewhat undersized, stocky individual with black
hair and eyes. The suggestion of a scowl appeared to be permanently
etched into his forehead lines. He possessed a ready smile however,
which quickly transformed his features. The scowl vanished; his dark eyes
seemed alight with good humor.

His wife, Viola, frail and blonde, was taller than he by a good two
inches. Had it not been for sunken cheeks and frown lines of worry, she
might have been decidedly attractive—even striking in appearance.

Both the Pasquettes were obviously laboring under some kind of nervous strain. They appeared apprehensive, subdued and ill at ease.

Paul Pasquette began speaking with hesitation and reluctance.

"Maybe you'll think we're both crazy, Mr. Leffing, but this thing has gone on too long and we can't take it much more. We went through it last winter and we hoped that was the end of it, but now it's started again—" He broke off as if groping for words.

Leffing tried to reassure him. "Believe me, Mr. Pasquette, I am firmly convinced that both you and your charming wife are totally sane, normal individuals. Please start at the beginning, take your time and explain matters as best you can."

Pasquette resumed. "It commenced, I suppose, two years ago this past summer when we bought a tiny house up in the township of Comptonvale— that's in Tolland County, far northwest corner. We were tired of apartment living; we like the country and I don't mind driving to work.

"The house was very small—only two undersized rooms and a kind of kitchenette—but it still seemed a bargain at the price. A little land went with it—enough for a garden and a yard. We were short of ready cash after buying the place, but we fixed it up a bit and settled in. Everything went fine through the rest of that summer and into the fall. We didn't notice a thing wrong until the weather began to get real cold. That was late October—up there anyway. It's often twenty degrees colder in Comptonvale than it is here in New Haven on the coast."

Leffing nodded. "I have experienced a few winters in northern Connecticut! Nothing like Maine, but severe enough for me!"

Pasquette's scowl deepened as he groped for words. "It's hard to explain just how it started. First, we both got, well, edgy, jumpy. We didn't sleep good. Finally we both admitted that we were often having bad dreams— nightmares. Most of the time we couldn't remember the dreams in any detail. We just had a sense of something getting into the house, hating us, threatening us somehow—something filled with spite, a desire for revenge—I don't know what for!

"The colder it got the worse it got—our dreams, I mean. And then—I realize it sounds loony, Mr. Leffing—but the first time it snowed, it got worse than ever. It became so we dreaded snow. We could hardly sleep at all. The whole house seemed filled with hate. We'd lay awake by the hour, while the hate seemed to come at us in waves. We could feel it some during the day, but it was always a hundred times worse at night. And we couldn't *see* anything or *hear* anything. It was just this feeling of evil—sort of—what's the word?—enveloping us."

Pasquette paused, took out a handkerchief and dabbed his forehead.

"It went on that way all winter. About the time we felt we couldn't stand another night in that house, the weather turned warm and we began to sleep better. The dreams faded away, not overnight, but in a week or two. By the time summer came, everything seemed normal. We both decided that maybe the stress of moving, of money problems and other pressures, had jangled our nerves so that we had begun to imagine things. Although we had talked of selling the house, we decided to stay."

He glanced at his wife. "But as the summer wore away and the first leaves began turning I know we both began to get worried again. We had a wonderful October that year. The weather stayed warm during the day and there was only a light frost once or twice. I guess it's what they call Indian summer. Anyway it lasted right into November and we began to hope that our nightmares were behind us."

He shook his head. "We were living in a fool's paradise. About mid-November the weather turned bitterly cold; the very next day it started to snow. It was like some kind of signal. That first night we both had horrible dreams. The old feeling of hate and evil surrounded us again—stronger than before.

"We'd wake up from nightmares—but the nightmares didn't end even after we got awake. Hatred seemed to be eating its way into the house—into us! It was as if we were losing our minds. There weren't any neighbors for miles; everybody up there liked us. We never saw anyone lurking around. The only wild animals of any size were deer and maybe a few bobcats.

"We began trying to doze during the early evening and stay awake later to see if we could glimpse anything. But, while the hate feeling grew worse, we still couldn't see anything—"

"Until," his wife broke in, "the awful blizzard!"

He sighed. "By evening, we could feel it coming. It got so cold we couldn't keep warm even in that tiny house. Our wood stove stayed red-hot but still the cold got in. We looked out and saw the snow piling up, driven by a blizzard wind. We went to bed finally, almost in desperation. And that night we saw—something."

Leffing's eyebrows arched. "Indeed!"

Pasquette frowned. "We were lying in bed, wide awake, with only the glow from the stove for light, when this—aura—of hate began to encircle us. It was worse than we ever remembered it. It was like some kind of pressure all around us. It built up—intensified—for what seemed hours. And all the time the blizzard got worse. The snow never let up and the wind howled and moaned around the house like some kind if living thing."

He paused. "I don't know just what time it was, but I'm sure it was well after midnight when we both noticed a kind of dim yellowish light becoming visible at one end of the house—not the bedroom but the adjacent living room. It looked like mist rising up off the flow. It swirled into a vague shape and swayed there, an inch or two above the floor. We were too petrified to speak at the time, but we both admitted later that the waves of hate and evil which we felt definitely came from this yellowish shape."

Leffing's eyes were alert with interest. "Can you describe this shape in any detail at all, Pasquette?"

Our client reluctantly shook his head. "It was too—amorphous. It seemed about four feet high and once—just for seconds—I thought I saw something like a face—all twisted up with rage. The thing seemed to keep flowing back into itself and swirling around. I don't know how long it remained; it seemed like hours, but I imagine it was only a few minutes. In spite of our terror, both of us finally fell back on our pillows and—well, passed out—something between a faint and a sleep! That—thing—just kind of sapped our energies. I think we passed out from exhaustion as well as fright. When we came to, a grey dawn was filtering in. The blizzard was still raging. The snow and wind didn't stop until late that afternoon."

"I think you have described the incident very well," Leffing commented. "Do you have anything to add to it, Mrs. Pasquette?" he inquired, turning to our client's wife.

She hesitated. "I think not. My husband has told you all that I recall. I might add this: that misty, horrible thing reminded me—momentarily at least—of some type of evil, yellowish dwarf. Like my husband, I had the passing impression that just briefly the semblance of a face took shape within that swirling smoke—or whatever it was. The—face—wasn't at all clear but"—she shuddered—"it was hideous and filled with malice."

"Have there been similar incidents since the one you just described?" Leffing asked.

Pasquette resumed his role as spokesman. "Similar to some degree, but none as bad as that night. You see, we haven't as yet had another blizzard up there. Heavy snows a number of times, but nothing like a real blizzard."

Leffing put the tips of his long fingers together. "The—manifestation—always reappears when the area experiences a strong snowfall?"

Pasquette scrubbed his chin. "Well—yes. To some degree. It's almost like a—what would you say?—mathematical equation. The greater—and more prolonged—the snowstorm—the stronger the manifestation. Even without any snow of course, we still have terrible dreams and that feeling of—pulsating hatred—never leaves the house entirely until the winter is over."

Leffing leaned back in his favorite Morris chair and remained silent for some moments.

At length he sat forward. "I will accept the case. It has features which, if not unique, are at least intriguing!"

Pasquette sighed with satisfaction but in a moment his scowl returned and he cleared his throat. "About your fee, Mr. Leffing. We—"

Leffing cut him off with a wave of his hand' "Do not concern yourself about it, Mr. Pasquette. My fees are always flexible."

I groaned inwardly. I knew that Leffing would sometimes accept a case for almost nothing, if it interested him sufficiently. His indifference toward money provided me with good story material but frequently left him hovering on the brink of actual hardship.

Before the Pasquettes left, Leffing elicited some further information: the name of the former owner, the agency which had handled the house sale and so forth. None of these facts appeared to offer any solid leads and I said as much.

Leffing glanced at me quizzically. "You should know my methods by now, Brennan! Every avenue must be explored, no matter how unpromising it may appear."

All the real estate agency could do was provide us with the name and address of the former owner, Mr. Charles Verton of Fairfield, Conn. The house had not been on their list until Verton decided to sell and turned the matter over to them. They knew nothing concerning prior owners.

After some difficulties, Leffing reached Verton by telephone and arranged for a visit.

One wintry evening we drove down to Fairfield; Verton lived in the select Black Rock residential area of the town, in a substantial frame house which appeared to have been newly renovated.

"A far cry," Leffing commented as we rang the bell, "from the Pasquettes' little home up in Comptonvale!"

Verton, a tall, muscular-looking man of middle age, with close-cropped grey hair and alert eyes, received us politely but without enthusiasm.

He revealed that he had bought the Pasquette house from the town of Comptonvale about three years before selling it. He described it as a "bloody mess." He had spent the purchase price several times over, he added, in order to make the place habitable. He mentioned that he had never intended to make the little structure a permanent home. He went up to Comptonvale on weekends during the summer and in the fall and he used the small house as a sort of hunting lodge. He was ordinarily accompanied by four or five friends on his hunting expeditions. He admitted that the quarters were cramped, revealing that several of his friends began calling the house "the sardine shack."

He had never met the Pasquettes until the agency arranged for the closing. He appeared honestly mystified by the difficulties the new owners were experiencing.

After a reflective minute, he shrugged. "All I can say is that the place *was* infernally hard to heat in the autumn. And usually we didn't sleep too well. But I put that down to the fact that there were so many of us crowded together in there—not really room enough for the whole gang to stretch out comfortably."

As we drove back toward New Haven, Leffing glanced up at the wintry night sky. "I fear, Brennan, I shall have to spend some time in Comptonvale. Verton's sparse information does not move us ahead very far. You will be able to accompany me?"

I nodded vigorously. "Tomorrow if you like."

"Make it the following day. I'll telephone Pasquette tomorrow and ask him to arrange accommodations for us somewhere in Comptonvale."

We started out for Comptonvale two days later under blue skies. The weather was moderate for mid-December.

As we drove north however, the blue skies became overcast and a sharp wind arose.

We arrived in Comptonvale in time for lunch at the town's only inn, The Crestfield Arms, where Pasquette had already reserved rooms for us. The Crestfield Arms was an old clapboarded sprawling sort of building with creaky floor boards and drafty halls. Central heating had been installed, but I became convinced that at least half the heat slipped away through the ancient building's countless crevices.

After lunch we drove out to see the Pasquettes. Their tiny house was several miles from the center of town.

They welcomed us warmly. It was evident that the cloudy skies and rising wind were already beginning to make them nervous.

The Pasquette house was indeed undersized but neat as the proverbial pin. The pot-bellied stove threw out a generous amount of heat.

After a somewhat cursory—or so it seemed to me—inspection of the premises, Leffing sat down in the living-room.

Pasquette shook his head in frustration. "Now that you're here, everything seems fine. Wouldn't you know!"

"There have been no new—manifestations?" Leffing asked.

"Not since we got back. Just the bad dreams—and no worse than usual."

"A storm appears to be slowly building up," Leffing observed. "Suppose we make arrangements now to exchange lodgings some time before it starts to snow!"

The Pasquettes eagerly acceded to the suggestion. It was agreed that as soon as it was obvious that a storm was about to begin, the Pasquettes would take over our rooms at The Crestfield Arms and we in turn would move into their little house.

We drove back to the inn, spent the rest of the afternoon prowling about the town and returned for dinner. There were only a few people in the dining room, and we secured a table near the large open fireplace. The meal was served in a leisurely informal manner; the food was plain but carefully prepared and substantial.

As we sipped a liqueur after dinner, Leffing nodded toward the fireplace. "At the rate those sparks are rushing up the chimney, a storm is settling in."

He was right. The next morning we awoke to white skies and an icy wind. By lunch time a few flakes were beginning to sift against the windows.

When we drove out to the Pasquettes at midafternoon, the flakes were falling more thickly—not large feathery flakes, but small hard ones that clicked audibly against the car windows.

The Pasquettes were packed and ready to leave when we arrived. They appeared both hopeful and apprehensive.

Mrs. Pasquette, in particular, seemed worried. "If anything happened to you, we could never forgive ourselves," she told Leffing.

He touched her shoulder reassuringly. "Have no fears, Mrs. Pasquette! We are merely about our business. I feel confident we can cope with whatever arises!"

Everything had been made ready for us. There was fresh bed linen, ample provisions, plenty of firewood stacked up, and the telephone was in perfect working order—at least at the moment.

After watching our clients drive off through the snow, we sat down near the stove. "The place seems normal enough," I commented. "It will be a bit—embarrassing—if nothing whatever occurs!"

"If nothing whatever occurs," Leffing pointed out, "that in itself will provide a clue."

"I'm afraid I don't follow you, Leffing."

"It will indicate," he continued, "that the manifestation, or whatever you choose to call it, has some personal relationship with the Pasquettes."

I remained skeptical. "If there *is* any manifestation."

"Well, we shall see. I scarcely think, however, that our clients would fabricate the entire series of events. I cannot see what earthly—or unearthly—purpose such a fraud would serve."

After a light supper, we sat in the living-room and talked in desultory fashion. Snow continued to fall steadily; a frigid wind blew against the house.

As we sat on, a subtle feeling of uneasiness began to imbue me. I experienced a vague but mounting sense of apprehension. I felt as if the atmosphere in that small house was beginning to create a kind of pressure, almost imperceptible at first, but soon unmistakable in its intensity.

I glanced across at Leffing, who sat silent and motionless.

I shifted restlessly in my chair. "I think it's—beginning."

Unmistakably," he replied quietly. "I suggest we move into the bed-room, as the Pasquettes would probably do."

After turning out the living-room lights we retreated into the bedroom. Leffing sat on one side of bed; I on the other. The pot-bellied stove in the living-room emitted an eerie red glow.

We sat without speaking while snow clicked against the window panes. Freezing blasts of wind buffeted the house at intervals.

The sense of pressure grew stronger. At length I began to feel acutely uncomfortable. An atmosphere of sustained hostility entered the house. In my own mind I identified this hostility with the increasing severity of the storm which raged outside, but I knew this was not actually the case. The storm merely set the stage, as it were. The hostility had its origin in some other phenomenon.

As we sat on, the aura of animosity closed in upon us like something palpable. Although the house became colder and colder, I could feel per-spiration on my forehead. The pressure strengthened until it appeared to wash over us in waves of pure hatred—a hatred which seemed weirdly impersonal, mindless, almost infantile—and yet deadly.

Loosening my shirt collar, I looked over at Leffing. I was about to speak when I saw that he was staring intently at a particular spot in the living room.

Following the direction of his gaze, I at first saw nothing. But as I contin-ued to watch, a faint yellowish glow became visible. It had the semblance of a dim reflection which arose from the floor itself. For a few minutes it was no larger than the flame of a candle, but by no means as concentrated. Although it remained dim and diffused, it slowly grew in size. At length it seemed to swirl up from the floor like an eddy of yellow smoke lifted by the wind. Maintaining an erratic but still discernible circular motion, it gradually grew in stature and sharpened in outline until it bore a repellent resemblance to some kind of amorphous but active and living entity. And there was no doubt in my own mind that the pulsations of rage and hatred which now seemed to fairly pound at us, originated in this hideous yellow shape which had slowly materialized.

As we continued to stare at it, transfixed, the manifestation's circular motion slowly continued until the thing finally stood a good four feet in height.

Wind-driven snow hammered at the house; a fearful chill settled into the very marrow of my aching bones. Strangely enough, I felt that this indescribable cold emanated from the unearthly thing before us and not from the storm outside.

Leffing made no comment, nor did he move in his chair, but I knew that he was appraising our unwelcome "guest" with an all-observant intensity of which I was incapable.

As we watched on, the swirling shape moved more slowly, and as its motion lessened, it coalesced until there gradually grew visible the monstrous caricature of something which might once have been human—a ghastly, hunched, spindly limbed thing with the mockery of a face which expressed such hatred, rage, and suffering as I never hope to witness again.

Even Leffing gasped with horror as that frightful countenance momentarily consolidated to mirror the churning hell within.

Shifting, slowly circling, blurring at intervals, it swayed there before us, an apparition escaped from hell, the full force of its hatred and fury now focussed directly upon us.

For a few heart-stopping seconds, I felt that I might faint and that as I lay helpless the raging yellow shape would be upon me.

Just as I grew convinced that I was incapable of enduring the malignant thing's pulsations for one minute longer, its outline and features began to blur more frequently. Its hideous face dissolved back into a sort of greasy yellow smoke; its sticklike limbs disappeared and very gradually it diminished in height until at length it literally ebbed away into the floor.

I lay back in my chair, trembling with a cold which was not physical in origin. I felt weak and exhausted, as if every last trace of energy had been wrung out of me, nerve by nerve and fibre by fibre. I believe that if the house had caught fire, I could not have moved to save myself.

Long minutes passed before Leffing spoke. "I believe we have seen the last of it for this night. The thing has succeeded in sapping our strength to an alarming degree. I suggest we attempt to get some sleep."

Neither of us cared to lie down on the bed. We lay back in our chairs and tried to sleep. I dozed at intervals, tormented by tenuous but terrifying nightmares.

The dirge of the wind never ended; all night long drifts of snow grew deeper around the house.

Dawn was grey and grudging but we welcomed it. We awoke in a house which had grown frigid and this time there was an obvious physical cause: the fire in the pot-bellied stove had nearly gone out.

Nursing the embers carefully, we soon had the stove glowing again. A few minutes later we sat down to a breakfast of bacon, eggs, toast, and coffee. I felt that I might survive after all.

"What do you make of it?" I asked as we sipped our second cup of coffee.

Leffing looked out at the blowing snow. "The house has obviously become the focus point for an entity of peculiar but dangerous malignancy. At this phase I have no idea of its origin or intent. I believe, however, that, consciously or otherwise, it does possess vampiric tendencies—not in the traditional sense, but in the sense that it tends to draw into itself the vital nervous energies of others. This probably sustains and strengthens it. Small wonder the Pasquettes look so peaked and worn!"

A few minutes later the Pasquettes telephoned and were relieved to learn that we had survived the night with nothing more than jangled nerves and depleted energies. Leffing arranged to meet them at the inn as soon as the town plow had cleared the roads.

Appearing about mid-morning, the road crew not only plowed the main highway but cleared a path right to the Pasquettes' door. We drove off without difficulty. It was still snowing, but the biting wind had finally subsided into occasional gusts.

In our rooms at The Crestfield Arms, Leffing described the events of the night to the Pasquettes in matter-of-fact fashion.

"I strongly urge you," he told the harassed couple, "to remain here at the inn until I have cleared up this diabolical business."

The Pasquettes wearily agreed. After lunch they drove off to get some clothes and gear from their house. They had already engaged a room at the inn.

We had dinner with them that evening. Leffing steered the conversation into casual channels until after the meal. Inevitably at that point, we returned to the topic which had brought us together in the first place.

The Pasquettes could add very little to what they had previously told us. The encounter which Leffing and I had experienced paralleled in large measure previous experiences of their own.

At one point Leffing asked Pasquette if he had ever inspected the cellar.

Pasquette shook his head. "There is no cellar."

Although he seemed surprised and somewhat disconcerted, Leffing made no comment.

A few minutes later, we retired to our respective rooms.

"Where to now?" I asked, settling into an armchair.

Leffing paced the floor restlessly. "Tomorrow morning I intend to look into the town clerk's files. There is a possibility that I may unearth some pertinent fact concerning that house."

By the time I awoke the next morning, Leffing had already left. In spite of feeling like a slacker, I enjoyed a late and leisurely breakfast.

My friend returned in time for lunch. "Any luck?" I inquired as we sat down.

He frowned. "Possibly. I discovered that the Pasquettes' house was originally a small school, owned and operated by the town. It stood abandoned for many years. I presume that is why Mr. Verton of Fairfield described it as 'a bloody mess.' He took it over from the town, you will recall, and spent a good sum on restoration. I am not sure, however, that this brings us any closer to the explanation we seek. I fear further digging is on the agenda."

"If there is anything I can do—"

"All you can do at this time is stand by. In fact I am not sure of my own next move."

He spent most of the afternoon sprawled in an armchair in our rooms, while I read. By evening he appeared to have arrived at some kind of tentative decision.

"You have a lead?" I asked.

"I have at present no more than a theory," he replied.

"I expect to spend tomorrow morning at town hall again. It may turn out to be a complete waste of time, but I cannot afford to leave any possibility unexplored."

He would say no more and I knew better than to press him.

Early the next afternoon when he returned to our rooms at the inn, he appeared moderately hopeful but by no means ebullient.

"I may have a promising lead," he told me. "I unearthed the names of various local women who taught at the Pasquette house when it was used as a school many years ago. Most of these women are dead, but the town clerk, who is steeped in local history, has informed me that the last woman to teach at the little school, a Miss Maud Rasters, is still alive, though in extremely poor health. She is in her nineties now and is confined to a convalescent home in Windover."

"You believe she may provide a clue which will explain the manifestation?"

Leffing sat down and stretched out his long legs. "She may, Brennan, she may. We can no more than try."

The next morning we set out for Windover, a small town located about thirty miles from Comptonvale. The roads had been well cleared and we had no trouble in finding the Windover Rest Home.

The one-story, white-painted brick building was set back some distance from the road in the exact center of a large tract now covered with wind-driven snow drifts. A few evergreens, all but buried in snow, clustered around the structure.

After introducing ourselves to the receptionist, we warmed our heels in the waiting-room for about twenty minutes. At length the head nurse, a Miss Vanning, brisk and efficient-looking in a gleaming white uniform, swept in and asked why we wished to see Miss Rasters.

"It is a rather complicated business, Miss Vanning," Leffing explained, "but I can assure you that the happiness and perhaps even sanity of two people may depend upon it."

Miss Vanning looked skeptical. After some hesitation, she replied. "Well, you may see Miss Rasters, but only briefly, and you must promise not to agitate her. Her condition is very nearly critical."

Leffing bowed. "We shall take no more time than is absolutely essential, Miss Vanning. And we shall do our best not to disturb the lady."

After leading us through a maze of corridors, Miss Vanning instructed us to wait outside a small room. She closed the door and went inside. After about five minutes, she reappeared and nodded for us to enter.

Miss Maud Rasters lay propped up in bed near the center of the compact room. Age and prolonged illness had reduced her to little more than a living skeleton. I doubt if she weighed ninety pounds. Her skin was blotched and yellow-looking. She lay back with her mouth open and gazed in our direction with filmy eyes which appeared to focus somewhere on the wall behind us.

After introductions, which Miss Rasters acknowledged with a vague nod, Leffing moved up closer to the bedside.

"Miss Rasters, I have learned that you were the last teacher at the little country schoolhouse at Comptonvale. Records indicate you taught there over ten years. After you left, that school was abandoned by the town. I understand that a new, larger school was built closer to the center of town. Is that information correct?"

At Leffing's words, the old woman stiffened to a kind of wary attention. Her clouded eyes sought my friend's face.

She closed and opened her mouth several times before replying. "That—is right. I taught there—last. Yes."

Leffing then went on to explain in detail the nature of the problem with which we were confronted. As he spoke, Miss Rasters shifted restlessly in bed. At length her growing excitement and agitation became obvious.

Miss Vanning stepped forward and felt her pulse. She frowned. "Gentlemen, I must ask you to leave. I cannot permit Miss Rasters to be disturbed any longer."

After a moment's hesitation, Leffing shrugged resignedly and started to turn away.

But Miss Rasters' yellow claw of a hand fluttered out and plucked at his coat.

Shaking her head, she spoke directly to Miss Vanning. "No. Let him stay. I can explain everything. I have been—tormented—too long." Tears came to her filmy old eyes and ran down her face.

Miss Vanning was obviously unhappy, but after a brief minute or so of indecision, she sighed and lifted a bottle from a small medicine table which stood next to the bed.

"All right, Miss Rasters. But first take two of these." She shook two tablets from the bottle.

Miss Rasters swallowed the tablets with some water and returned her attention to Leffing.

As she began her story, Miss Vanning hovered by the door with an air of uncertainty. It was apparent to me that she didn't want to leave her patient, but at the same time didn't want to intrude on any private matters.

Miss Rasters quickly resolved the dilemma. She beckoned for Miss Vanning to return to her bedside. "Please stay here. I want a witness I know."

Thus reassured, Miss Vanning stood by the bed while the old woman unfolded her story.

"I can't remember dates," she began, "but I can never forget what happened at Comptonvale, at that little schoolhouse. I'd taught there a year or so, and everything went well, when Martin Keeler started school. His parents were awfully poor and either he'd been born somewhat deformed or had grown so due to malnutrition. His shoulders stuck up higher than they should have and his arms and legs were like sticks. But he had a keen mind and he was perpetually in some kind of mischief. He seemed— imbued—with a kind of feverish nervous energy which never ran out. From the very beginning he caused trouble. He kept that little school in a constant uproar. The other children found him amusing and often abetted his mischief."

Shaking her head, she sighed and sipped a glass of water which Miss Vanning extended.

(I might as well say here that Miss Rasters' story was broken by many such interruptions. To include them all would serve no sensible purpose.)

"I put up with little Martin as well as I could," she went on, "but he taxed my patience sorely. He did not respond to either punishment or—well, cajolery. I made him stand in the corner; I whipped him; I scolded him incessantly. I had long talks with his parents. They were sympathetic, but if they took any measures, those measures were ineffectual. For a time I tried giving Martin special privileges, but he simply took mischievous advantage of them. Absolutely nothing had any effect on him. He was a born imp and an imp he remained—to the end."

Miss Rasters lay back in bed, not so much as if she were resting but more as if she were arranging her thoughts and words in coherent order. At length she continued.

"One bitter winter's day he became completely incorrigible. Hour after hour he kept the other children in a state of absolute turmoil. A storm was obviously approaching and a kind of electric tension seemed to fill the air. I tried to be—tolerant—and blame the unending uproar on the gathering storm, but toward the end of the school day, I simply—well—lost control. I gave little Martin Keeler the worst whipping he'd ever had. The room quieted down after that but, even then, Martin refused to cooperate. Although he stopped interrupting me; as he had been for most of the day, he sat scowling and refused to pay any attention to his lessons.

"For some reason this infuriated me more than his noisy outbursts had. Shortly before classes were to end, I told him that he would have to remain after the other children were dismissed. By this time the storm had started. The wind rose and snow began blowing past the windows."

She shook her head sadly. "I don't know what got into me. I should have known better. But foolish as it may sound now, I felt that my trouble with Martin had developed into a contest of wills—and I had to win, if I was to go on teaching in that school.

"Martin expected he'd get another whipping, worse than before, and I could see him steeling himself for it. But that wasn't what I had in mind.

"Although the children were unaware of its existence, underneath the school there was an unused dirt cellar. The only entrance or exit to it was a small trap door which was located under a carpet directly beneath my

desk. I had discovered the trap door by accident one day when I was cleaning the carpet after school hours. Lifting the trap, I saw a rickety wooden
ladder leading down to little more than a scooped-out pit. There was
nothing in it that I could see. I decided then that its existence had better
be kept secret from the children. Would to God I had never discovered it!

"I decided that terrible day that I would give Martin the fright of his
life—perhaps, I reasoned, it would bring him to heel.

"When we were alone together in the room, I pulled aside the carpet
and opened the trap door. By this time the wind was howling outside
and the snow was falling thickly, but I ignored it. Beckoning Martin up
to the desk, I showed him the dark pit and ordered him down that brittle
wooden ladder. I told him he was going to stay down there—with the
door closed—until he was ready to fall on his knees, apologize for his past
conduct, and promise never to cause trouble again.

"He went down the ladder with a great deal of hesitation but without
a word of protest. I slammed the trap, put the carpet back over it and sat
there at my desk.

"I fully expected that within a very few minutes I would hear the little
imp's cry of surrender. But, although the cellar was pitch dark and freezing
cold, not a sound came out of it.

"The longer I sat at my desk, the angrier I got. I was furious that my
scheme was—obviously—not working. I had been sure that it would. I
waited a half hour—an hour—and still there was no call from below.

"All this time the storm was building up. The wind moaned dismally
over the growing drifts of snow. Gentlemen, at that point, the devil
himself must have entered into me. I decided to steal quietly out of the
schoolhouse and leave Martin in the cellar."

At the expressions of shock and disbelief which must have passed over
our faces, Miss Rasters held up her hand.

"I know it sounds horrible now but—I try to tell myself anyway—it
wasn't as bad as it appears. I fully expected that as the cold grew really
unbearable, Martin would climb back up the ladder, lift the trap door and
make his way home." Tears trickled down her sunken cheeks. "Almighty
God knows that I didn't intend what happened."

After regaining some measure of composure, she continued. "As I trudged home through the snow, I was still so angry that I scarcely noticed the severity of the storm. As things turned out, it was a real blizzard—one of the worst we'd had in years. Long before morning the roads were impassible. Huge drifts came halfway to the eaves.

"The next morning I felt guilty about what I'd done. For all his nervous energy, little Martin was really quite frail. I assumed he had had a struggle fighting his way home through the storm.

"But he never reached home. About noon the next day, after the plows had been out and the storm had begun to diminish in intensity, Sirus Borton, one of the town selectmen, stopped at my house. Of course there was no school that day. Sirus told me that Martin Keeler was missing. He hadn't showed up at home and his folks feared he had been lost and overcome in the storm. The other children had already told their parents that I had kept him after school. Sirus wanted to know how long I had detained him."

Miss Rasters paused and took a labored breath. "Since that hour I have lived in Hell. I have been haunted and tormented all my life. But let me go on.

"Instead of telling the truth, as of course I should have done, I lied glibly. I knew what was at stake. I assured Borton that I had kept Martin only a few minutes and that, in fact, I had walked part of the way home with him. When I left him, I said, he was less than a half mile from home.

"Borton believed my lies and many of the townspeople did also. Martin was such an unpredictable, devil-may-care little rascal, his next move could never be safely assumed to be the sane and obvious one. It would be just like him, many agreed, to wait until I was out of sight along the road and then go dashing off into the woods. It would not be beyond him to stay out deliberately in order to get me into trouble with the town authorities.

"From that day on the town was divided. A majority felt sympathy for me, but a minority sided against me—and never forgave.

"Quite naturally I assumed that Martin had waited too long in the school cellar and had then been trapped in the storm. Search parties started out as soon as the snow stopped.

"Since many children lived on back roads which had not yet been plowed, school was called off for the remainder of that week. The morning after the blizzard, however, I bundled up and made my way to the schoolhouse. I don't know what prompted me. Perhaps it was some kind of intuitive warning. But I remember thinking that Martin might have left the trap door open and that if this were discovered, I would be in deeper trouble."

Trembling, she reached for the water, swallowed and set down the glass. "It was far worse trouble than I could ever have anticipated. When I first entered the school, I sighed with relief. All seemed in order. Even the carpet which covered the trap door was set back neatly in place. Too neatly, knowing Martin. As I looked at it, a strange foreboding overcame me. I twitched it aside and raised the trap.

"Enough light filtered down so that I could see what had happened. The rickety wooden ladder had collapsed. Little Martin lay motionless on the dirt floor.

"Although I was overwhelmed with horror and shock, I went to work like a person possessed. I clung to the faint hope that a spark of life remained in the boy. Fighting my way through the drifts to a small supply shed in the rear of the school, I finally located a rope. I knew that there was no ladder on the premises. After dropping a shovel into that freezing pit, I tied the rope to a leg of my desk, dropped the line through the open trap and slid down. I saw at once that there was no hope. Little Martin had frozen to death. The sequence of events was obvious. As the cold became unbearable, he had finally started up the ladder. When he was only partway up, the rotten wood had given way. The ladder had collapsed, hurling him to the hard floor of the cellar. One of his legs was grotesquely twisted; I assumed he had broken it in the fall. In spite of that, he had apparently fought to get out. His hands were nothing but raw bloody stumps of flesh. In his frenzy of fear and pain, he must have torn at the walls of the cellar, hoping perhaps to tunnel his way out. It was impossible of course. At last he had mercifully frozen to death. He had not died peacefully however. Even in the dim light I could see his face frozen into a frightful mask of suffering and rage. I am sure he died hating and cursing me."

Following a long pause, during which Miss Vanning gave the old woman more tablets, Miss Rasters resumed.

"Most of the cellar floor was frozen hard, but there was one small area, directly beneath the pot-bellied stove on the floor above, where the frozen ground consisted only of a crust an inch or two deep. In that spot I managed to dig a shallow grave. I dragged the body of Martin into it and covered it as well as I could. I threw the shovel up through the open trap door and then—with the strength of desperation, I suppose—I managed to climb back up the rope. I returned it to the shed, closed the trap, covered it with the carpet and made my way home. If I was seen at the school, nobody attached any importance to it. I told several neighbors later that I had gone back to get a file of test papers for correcting.

"I taught in that school for three more years, haunted and tormented every minute of the time. Often I imagined I could hear Martin down there in the cellar, screaming and cursing at me. I remember looking up on occasions to see if the other children had heard anything.

"I felt as if Martin were down there alive, hating me, plotting revenge, scheming to get even somehow. I never dared stay in the school alone after classes were dismissed. I took all my papers home. Ten minutes after the last pupil had left for the day, I was out of there myself. It was horrible.

"During the winter months, tension built up in me until I often thought I would go mad. Sometimes I felt that I already had. When a storm was approaching, in the dead of winter, it seemed that pulsations of hate pounded up at me out of that ghastly little pit. More than once I felt impelled to blurt out the whole story to the children and let the chips fall where they would.

"It was only by a supreme effort of will that I managed to keep my self-control. Of course my health deteriorated. At last I managed to transfer to another town—yet I was still haunted by the memory of what I had done. My punishment has never ended—but it will end shortly, gentlemen, and I am not sorry. I have been tortured so long that I no longer fear death—nor what may come after."

She lay back, exhausted and overcome. Her filmy eyes closed; she breathed laboriously through her mouth.

Scurrying into action, Miss Vanning injected medication into the frail body of the woman and quickly ushered us from the room.

As we drove to Comptonvale through the desolate winter landscape, Leffing gazed moodily at the snow-covered tamaracks which bordered the highway.

"I trust you see the picture clearly enough, Brennan. The spirit, psychic residue—call it what you will—of Martin Keeler, earth-bound by hatred, plus the physical and mental anguish which marked his tragic death, clung to that schoolhouse cellar grave. To such a surviving remnant, time has no meaning, no reality, as we know it. Decades may be no more than minutes. Over the years, moreover, his unforgiving spirit has reinforced itself, as it were, with the vital energies of those who remained in that schoolhouse. In the beginning the force of hate and vengeance was quite naturally focussed on Miss Rasters. But even with her departure, the haunting did not cease. The Pasquettes, although innocent of any involvement, have been partially drained of psychic strength by the unrelenting and vindictive attacks of this fearful residual survivor. Its power has grown until it now—as we know—has sufficient force to project itself in visible form. It has become, down the years, a vampiric projection of evil, bearing, perhaps, little actual resemblance to the original spirit of Martin Keeler. I might almost say that its hatred survives through force of habit, bizarre as that may sound."

"How can we be rid of it then?" I asked.

"There may be one solution," Leffing replied. "With the removal of the remains of Martin Keeler from that cellar pit, the thing may dissipate—abruptly or gradually. It is impossible to predict."

I frowned. "One prosaic but vital problem puzzles me. Pasquette told you that the house had no cellar!"

Leffing nodded. "A good point. But I have little doubt that the original cellar pit was filled, either by the town, or by Mr. Verton of Fairfield, after he bought the school."

A subsequent investigation disclosed that the town itself had filled the cellar hole before putting up the structure for sale. The town clerk told us that the dirt walls were caving in and that town officials, not wishing to spend any more than was necessary on the building, had simply packed gravel into the pit and sealed up the trap door.

The Pasquettes listened to our recital of Miss Rasters' confession with a mixture of horror, relief—and foreboding. They welcomed any solution to their problem, but Pasquette admitted frankly that he simply did not have sufficient money to move the house and dig out the old cellar hole.

Subsequently, town officials of Comptonvale held a private meeting, with Leffing in attendance, and agreed to shoulder expenses. The tiny house was moved aside with surprising ease and the old cellar pit was cleared of fill. In the dirt floor, exactly where Miss Rasters had indicated, the poor, twisted skeleton of Martin Keeler was found. Although no surviving relatives could be located, the remains were given Christian burial in the Comptonvale Congregational churchyard.

Long before her confession became public knowledge, poor old Miss Rasters had passed away.

After their house was returned to its original site, the Pasquettes moved back in, albeit with many misgivings. From that day on, however, the haunting ceased. The Pasquettes lived without fear and slept without nightmares.

I like to think that Leffing brought lasting peace not only to them and to a tormented old woman who must have paid many times over for a foolish and tragic act—but also to the spirit of a poor doomed child who had died after fearful suffering—filled with unforgiving fury and hatred, and a desire for vengeance so intense that it survived and transcended his own pitiful death.

MONSIEUR DELACROIX IN

THE GARDEN OF PARIS
ERIC WILLIAMS

Eric C. Williams (1918–2010) is rather the forgotten man of British sci-
ence fiction. Although he was there in the early days of fandom and the
original Science Fiction Association just before the outbreak of World
War Two, mingling with the likes of Arthur C. Clarke and John Beynon
Harris (he had yet to become John Wyndham), and placing a few stories
in the fan magazines, he remained behind the scenes and made little mark
on the field until almost thirty years later. Then, after years working in
various establishments, including as a bookdealer, and spending his days
and nights building telescopes, he suddenly started to be published pro-
fessionally in John Carnell's anthology series New Writings in SF *and*
elsewhere. Amongst these anthologies was Weird Shadows from Beyond,
which included the following story, the first outing for Monsieur Delacroix,
a man who is called in by the UNO when something odd crops up. He was
in some ways the first investigator of the "X-Files," but in Paris. Williams
wrote several other stories featuring Delacroix, but they remained unpub-
lished until his final years when they were run in Philip Harbottle's Fantasy
Annual *series and companion volumes. Yet this first story remains the*
most dramatic.

THE MESSENGER DISTRIBUTING MAIL TO THE VARIOUS MINISTERIAL
offices occupying the top floor of the Palais de Chaillot, Paris, reached
into the bag hanging from his shoulder and extracted one last bundle. It

was a thick packet of odd-shaped and coloured envelopes, all torn open, in varying degrees of impatience, and all with two words scrawled across each "Delacroix-Chaillot." The Messenger gave his habitual groan of disgust and plodded to the end of the corridor where he ascended a short flight of stone steps that let out of one wall and led to a redwood door upon a small landing. A card tacked to the door announced "Monsieur Delacroix UNO." The Messenger opened the door and said in an irritated voice, "Good morning, Mademoiselle Lamaroux, early as usual." The office was small, its ceiling low, its two windows made to look small by virtue of the overhanging eaves just above them, and the whole effect of cramp exaggerated by two large, old-fashioned desks and equally as dated filing cabinets that occupied all but various narrow lanes on the floor.

Mademoiselle took the preferred bundle with the barest of smiles. She did not deign to answer the implied criticism which had been put in one form or another almost daily for the past ten years. How could she explain that she came early through love for her boss. She had loved him for twenty years, but ten years ago being by chance early in the office, she had arranged all the letters in alphabetic order of sender's name and this had pleased him very much. Since then, she had done him this ridiculous service each morning at the cost of twenty minutes of her own time per day. She knew that now if she omitted to do this gratuitous act he would be most ill pleased and think her remiss. Not that her love could ever be assuaged or even revealed since Monsieur Delacroix was a most respectable man and had been married fifteen years. But the habit of love died hard in her breast and every day she allowed Monsieur Delacroix to be a king in his office, speaking only when she sensed he required talk, making his coffee, cleaning his desk, not moving while he thought, and being altogether an inferior being.

Monsieur Delacroix held a peculiar position in UNO. To his office were sent each day all those letters which UNO, by virtue of its idealistic nature, attracts from thousands of idealists who insist they have a scheme or information that must be acted upon for the good of Mankind. These writers are a persistent race and pester the various offices of UNO year in and year out with their letters. Mixed with these ravings, and often indistinguishable to the unpractised eye, is the occasional far-fetched but pregnant scheme and the anonymous warning with real information. Paris set Monsieur Delacroix up in a remote office, out of reach of the more insistent evangelists and appointed him to answer the cranks and sift out the gold from the brass. He did this job thoroughly and better than most. His mind was so uncomplicated and literal in its appraisal of things that he had much in common with the people who wrote the letters he was given to answer, and was thus able to sense unbridled sincerity when he read it and to discard it. Whenever, on the other hand, he encountered the flavour of sincerity plus knowledge, he investigated.

This morning, after the unvarying succession of actions and words that accompanied his entry and passage across the office each day, he picked up the pile of letters, placed them in the middle of the blotting-pad before him, saying, without really listening for an answer, "Anything interesting, Mademoiselle?" He was already intent upon opening the first letter which was written by a M. Abime, he read: "Once again I have to report that I heard a scream from the grounds of the Jardin des Plantes. This was at 3.0 during the morning of September 6th. On looking from my window I saw, as on other occasions, lights shining through the trees of the grounds. I am convinced that we have here in the heart of Paris a cell of the sinister 'Union d'execution' set up by Moscow and of which I have sent you many details. I pray you to hasten to eradicate this nauseatious limb of . . ."

Monsieur Delacroix did not read on: his inner ear had caught something. Across the top of the letter was written "Please answer. This character has written us and the police 50 odd letters over the past 5 years. There is nothing in it. Put him off. Vesta extension 7211."

Monsieur Delacroix picked up the phone and asked for Monsieur Vesta's number.

"Hallo!" said a high-pitched, genial voice.

Monsieur Delacroix introduced himself, "I would like to see some of those other letters," he said "and if you have it, the report of the investigation. I don't feel I can answer properly without a bit more background."

"Certainly, certainly. I have a complete file here, police correspondence and everything. I'll send it along. Only for heaven's sake, get him off my neck. I'll be getting nightmares if I read many more of these things about screams in the night!"

Two days later Monsieur Delacroix felt himself in a position to write to Monsieur Abime. Vesta had not exaggerated; there *were* fifty letters in the file, plus correspondence between UNO and the police requesting investigation of the matter and a long report adding up to very little except that these letters always came at or near full moon, and as no murders were actually committed in the grounds of the Jardin des Plantes, it could only be assumed that Monsieur Abime was affected by the full moon.

Monsieur Delacroix dictated a polite letter expressing interest and suggesting that both he and Monsieur Abime should keep vigil together at the next full moon in eight days time in the hope of hearing screams issuing from the Jardin des Plantes. His suggestion was accepted by return of post.

In the intervening weekend, Monsieur Delacroix took his family to the Jardin des Plantes to get a clear picture in his mind of the layout of this park cum zoo cum botanical school cum museum. He himself had not been to the Jardin since his teens, when he remembered taking a young lady to see the monkeys, but his children knew the place well and unerringly led their parents to the most sensational of the animals, and then at their father's request, to the labyrinth adjacent to Rue Geoffroy St. Hilaire where Monsieur Abime had his flat.

They climbed the spiral track around the tree-covered hillock that comprised the labyrinth, but were unable to reach the derelict gazebo on the crest as the path had been railed off by the authorities. Monsieur Delacroix stood for some moments at this highest permissible point surveying the probable scene of Monsieur Abime's reported screams. The place was quite wild and tangled in shrubbery. The paths were edged with high iron-rod fences that precluded any possibility of sightseers leaving the path, although Monsieur Delacroix could see no reason to protect what seemed such a dreary, untidy wilderness. Below, through the trees, he could see the Administration Buildings on the left and the hothouses on the right. Beyond the Administration Buildings would be the zoo, and beyond the hothouses the formal beds of the botanical gardens; fifty or so metres behind him was the wall of the Jardin with the noise of occasional traffic echoing from the tall, concrete-fronted buildings overlooking the Jardin from the other side of the street. This corner of the Jardin seemed old and forgotten and drear as if the vitality of the soil had been used up.

"I feel cold," complained Madame Delacroix. "I don't like this place. What are you up to, standing there like Napoleon watching Moscow?"

Monsieur Delacroix in no way resembled Napoleon at Moscow except perhaps that he, too, was suddenly cold. He took Madame Delacroix's arm and briskly walked her down to the sunlight at the foot of the mound.

"I shall be watching the hill from across the road next Wednesday night," he told her. "I wished to see it at close hand before then. I must say I'm disappointed in the place."

Madame Delacroix gave her husband a penetrating look, but simply said: "You will be careful, dear!"

To which Monsieur Delacroix replied, "Let's go in the cactus house; I'm chilled. It's as cold as a morgue under those trees."

Being early September, it was quite dark when Monsieur Delacroix rang the bell which announced him to Monsieur Abime's apartment. There was a long pause, and then the tall wooden door opened and a shadowy figure in the dim-lit vestibule asked Monsieur Delacroix to enter.

"We have no concierge," apologised Monsieur Abime, leading the way into an elevator just large enough to accommodate them both. "My place is on the top floor." The elevator rose with obvious effort to the fourth floor. Monsieur Abime had left the door of his apartment open and showed Monsieur Delacroix directly into the well-lit lounge.

"This building is very quiet," observed Monsieur Delacroix. "I presume they were offices we passed on the lower floors." He studied Monsieur Abime for signs of full moon madness as he said this, but there was nothing peculiar about Monsieur Abime's visage except its pallor. His eyes were gentle, there were no tics about his mouth.

"Yes," confirmed Monsieur Abime. "It is very quiet. At two or three in the morning you can hear every bit of chatter from the zoo. I believe I am the only resident in the whole street."

"No," said Monsieur Delacroix, "there *are* other residents, but as it happens none of them sleep overlooking the Jardin. The point was checked by the police."

"Let me show you my bedroom," said Monsieur Abime, rising. "You will be able to see the view I have."

He opened a door leading to another room which was lined with books, even between the two tall windows overlooking the street. There was a bed and a table, but no wardrobe.

Monsieur Delacroix saw all this in the light from the inner room, then Monsieur Abime shut the door and there was darkness except from the pale light of the street lights forty feet below.

Monsieur Abime threw open one set of the door-like windows. There was a narrow balcony outside. It seemed to Monsieur Delacroix as he carefully leaned out of the window, that the leaves of the trees in the Jardin were a mere arm's length away.

"The moon will not be full until about 1.0 a.m.," said Monsieur Abime. "Until then, I think I had better tell you all I know about the Union d'execution."

"Where is the nearest entrance to the Jardin," asked Monsieur Delacroix, deliberately ignoring Monsieur Abime's suggestion.

Monsieur Abime pointed a little way to the left. "Just there on the corner of Rue Cuvier. There's another about a hundred metres down Rue Cuvier."

"And to the right?"

"Oh, right up at the far end of the Zoological Museum where this street joins Rue Buffon. I have a large-scale map next door which shows all the entrances to the Jardin."

The two men retired to the lounge where, with the map open on the table and a glass of brandy each, they speculated upon the probable source of the light Monsieur Abime claimed to have seen whenever there were screams from the Jardin. In this way Monsieur Delacroix prevented Monsieur Abime from airing his particular obsession for some time, and finally, there was only time for a brief outline before it was necessary for the silent vigil to begin.

They returned to the dark bedroom, carrying chairs, and sat at the open windows.

An occasional car hurtled down the street below, but as 1.0 a.m. came and went, all noise of human life died out leaving only faint, sporadic, noises from the zoo. Monsieur Abime sat motionless at his window. Monsieur Delacroix dozed and woke and dozed and woke in the warm air, his eyes fixed on the dark trees on the other side of the street. The sky seemed pale-blue with the light of the moon now standing vertically above, but below the trees was intense black.

Suddenly Delacroix realised that he was looking at several spots of yellow light through the trees and that Abime was gesticulating violently at him. Immediately Monsieur Delacroix shook off sleep and concentrated his attention. The light seemed to float indeterminately in a line somewhere in the direction of the cactus house, but it was impossible to know whether it was a moving light or the effect of swaying boughs in front of a stationary light.

Suddenly a most appalling shriek tore Monsieur Delacroix's nerves to cringing pieces. It exploded like a magnesium flare of sound on the silent night. Delacroix involuntarily turned away in horror. Almost immediately the shriek became muffled and then ceased.

Monsieur Abime was on his feet in triumph.

"There!" he called. "That's it! You heard that."

"Quick," said Delacroix, "let us get down to Rue Cuvier; we may see someone come from the Jardin."

The elevator descended quicker than it ascended, but it still seemed funereal to Delacroix. He burst from the building and ran down the street towards the junction with Rue Cuvier. Abime hurried behind. As they came to the junction a small car drew away from the front of the entrance heading their way accelerating fast. Monsieur Delacroix teetered on the kerb between heroic excitement and caution, and in a second the car had roared past and away.

"Don't worry," said Monsieur Abime, "I got his number."

They returned to the flat and as a good, public servant Monsieur Delacroix forthwith reported the scream over the telephone to the police. He was told by a voice already committed to disbelief that the matter would be investigated.

"You did not say anything about the car?" commented Monsieur Abime, his pale face just the faintest bit flushed with excitement.

"They will not find a corpse, will they?" explained Monsieur Delacroix. "It would be infringing on a citizen's privacy to give his name uselessly to the police."

Monsieur Abime nodded silently and remained watching Monsieur Delacroix.

"It will take no more than an hour for me to secure the car-owner's name tomorrow," said Monsieur Delacroix, thinking as he stood. "It is quite certain that he or she is connected in some way with the scream— and I am sure that people do not scream like that unless they are being killed in some horrible way. The police have failed to find any sign of violence before, therefore this person is very cunning and we shall have to be equally as cunning to catch him. We must secrete ourselves in the grounds at the next full moon and watch. Are you willing to do this?"

Monsieur Abime paled again.

"You don't realise how ferocious the Union d'execution is!" he appealed.

Monsieur Delacroix compressed his lips in exasperation.

"You may be assured, Monsieur Abime," he said, "that there is no cell of the Union d'execution in Paris. This has been checked and checked again by our police and Interpol. There is nothing. Your fears in this respect are groundless. Whatever it is we are dealing with here, it is not political assassination. Please use your head. The regularity of these—whatever they are—indicates only mania. We shall be perfectly safe if we stay together and hidden."

Monsieur Abime was unconvinced, but resigned to the fact of his own involvement. Monsieur Delacroix departed at 3.0 a.m. with a promise of rendezvous in a lunar month's time.

The car, a little corrugated iron, hunchbacked Simca, was owned by Monsieur Philippe Medan, of Rue Lecourbe. Mademoiselle Lamouraux, who was good at this sort of thing, soon ascertained that he was a bachelor, aged thirty-seven, living with his mother, that he had played a gallant part in the Paris uprising of 1944, had trained in Botany—without notable results—and was now employed at the Jardin des Plantes specializing in cactus plants. He had written a few papers for scientific journals and one

small book for the amateur on cactus growing. From the telephone oper-
ator in the Jardine des Plants Administration building, Mademoiselle,
playing the part of a young woman interested in Monsieur Philippe, learnt
that he was a solitary kind of fellow who did a lot of voluntary overtime at
the Jardin; that he had no lady friends, that he was known in the Jardin as
"Sandy," and that he had a little office of his own just near the back door
of the building.

With this smattering of knowledge Monsieur Delacroix passed an
afternoon in the Jardin, and by casual gossip with various persons working
among the flower-beds, he was able to get the "cactus authority" pointed
out to him without the necessity of addressing him personally. Medan was
a swarthy-faced block of a man, probably with Corsican blood, deliberate
in his walk like some tired peasant, and with a ridged brow that gave him
a brooding look. He looked more like fifty than thirty-seven, there was
no animation in his step. Life seemed to have beaten him. "Nevertheless,"
thought Monsieur Delacroix, "judging by those shoulders you're as solid
and strong as an ox."

Medan entered the tropical house with his private key and a few minutes later Monsieur Delacroix saw him through the glass erecting a ladder
to examine the summit of a tall palm. "I wonder what you're up to?"
mused Monsieur Delacroix as he walked away. "Do you climb the trees
and scream at the full moon? You look like an ape." Monsieur Delacroix
stopped in his tracks. The possible connection with animals had not
occurred to him before. Could it be that murder was committed and then
the body thrown to the lions so that no remains were found? It certainly
seemed a possible explanation of the one mysterious thing about this
business—where did the bodies go if there had been fifty murders? Of
course—meat for the animals! By dawn, all evidence chewed and licked
up, clean as a whistle!

Monsieur Delacroix returned to his office a little aghast at his explanation, but triumphant.

Full moon in October fell on the 1st of the month. September had continued mild until two days previous, and then had ensued a steady, strong
wind from the north pushing all summer air out of the streets. The sun

fought through on both days about midday, but soon retired exhausted. The citizens of Paris now hurled their cars along the cobbled boulevards with a different kind of abandon, with a hurrying grimness as if they felt the breath of winter close behind. Mademoiselle Lamouraux appeared in the office garbed in a thick woollen two-piece suit and numerous accessory garments to ensure protection from the blasts.

Madame Delacroix categorically forbade her husband to spend the night in the Jardin des Plantes (not that she knew the true reason for his proposed vigil) "at your time of life—you must be mad!"

"My dear, I shall be wrapped up warm and we shall be in a sheltered place. After all, it will not be all night."

"Paul, you are not to go!"

Monsieur Delacroix expressed the overpowering flux of UNO affairs by a shrug.

"I must. But I shall be careful," he said miserably.

As he crouched with Monsieur Abime in the lee of the brick wall at the rear of the hothouses, Monsieur Delacroix knew his wife to be correct in calling him mad. It was as black and as cold as Space beneath the trees, and his knees and shoulders ached with what felt like deposits of ice crystals. Monsieur Abime groaned softly every now and again and prayed for a cigarette. From their "hide" they could observe the path that passed between the Australian and Cactus houses and forked left to the labyrinth and right to the Administrative building. The nearest loop of the path circling the hillock was a mere five or six yards away, and in the light of the full moon filtering through the trees from high above Monsieur Delacroix was sure they would be able to definitely identify any person climbing the labyrinth.

"It's midnight," breathed Monsieur Abime.

Monsieur Delacroix nodded wearily, then clutched his companion's arm. In the distance was the faint crunching and squeaking of a wheelbarrow being wheeled over the stony paths. Someone was coming from the gate by the Conciergeries on Rue Cuvier. The noise became more distinct and presently they could hear a peculiar mumble of conversation accompanying the harsh cracking of grit. The wheelbarrow was pushed to the foot of the path ascending into the labyrinth and here the pusher rested.

In the quiet Monsieur Delacroix felt sure the mumbler said, "Tort your helm," but the voice was so quiet and slurred that he could not believe his ears.

Monsieur Abime breathed into Delacroix's ear, "That's a drunk talking to himself!"

"Or a maniac!" answered Monsieur Delacroix in similar fashion.

The squeaks began again. The two watchers fixed their eyes upon the dappled path and presently a black shape moved in the blackness and became a forward-leaning figure pushing a wheelbarrow in which lay the ragdoll limp shape of another man. As the pair passed the "hide," the limp shape raised its head and began cursing in a nonsensical way, only to collapse back almost immediately. The pair passed onwards into the shadows.

"Did you see his face?" asked Delacroix softly.

"No, it was in shadow."

The noise of the barrow stopped, and there was the distant noise of a key rattling on iron as a keyhole was searched for.

"He's going through the gate at the top," said Monsieur Abime. "Shall I go after him?"

"Wait," commanded Monsieur Delacroix.

After a few indistinct noises, they heard the barrow returning, the slam of the gate, and then a helter-skelter skidding as the pusher rushed back along his tracks. He was past Monsieur Delacroix and Abime before they could see his face.

"I'm going up to see what he's done to that drunk," said Monsieur Abime. "You stay here, I won't be a minute."

At that precise moment a ghastly scream from above seemed to clamp a ring round their hearts. It finished on one last uprising yell of horror. Monsieur Abime was the first to recover. He athletically clambered over the iron railings on to the path and disappeared towards the summit. Monsieur Delacroix also negotiated the railings but clumsily and stood trembling on the path. Suddenly he was aware that the lights of the Cactus House had been switched on. This was no strange, floating light. He could see the tracery of iron struts forming the skeleton of the greenhouse silhouetted against the lights inside. The murderer was performing his customary ritual. Where was Abime?

There came a second scream, more shattering than the first, since it began with the call "help' but gargled into a shriek of incoherent horror and pain.

Monsieur Delacroix hurled himself up the path towards the gazebo on the summit. As he ran up to the gate near the summit, he heard a tremendous thrashing going on among the shrubbery surrounding the gazebo. The spiral nature of the path still made it necessary for him to make another half turn of the hill before coming to the level top upon which the gazebo stood, and it was this which saved Monsieur Delacroix's life. Panting around this stretch of weed-grown path, with the terrifying vegetable noise going on only a yard to his right, fear had time to give him caution. He stopped and peered into the dappled light around the gazebo. He saw the half-severed body of Monsieur Abime hanging in the myriad toothed jaws of a gigantic snake. The tube of the snake's body was already distended where it had begun to ingest Monsieur Abime, and it convulsed with the prodigious effort of crushing the bones in his limbs.

Monsieur Delacroix nearly fainted. He reeled back into the bushes, then sick and panic-stricken rushed down the spiral path to the lighted beacon of the Cactus House. Blindly he dragged open the heavy, iron-framed door of the greenhouse, and fell into the heat and light. Philippe Medan was on his knees before one of the tree-like cacti. "Help!" rattled Monsieur Delacroix staggering: "In the labyrinth. Oh God! Monster."

Philippe Medan stood up, his face twisted with emotion. He had some kind of short gardening tool in his hand. With this he struck Monsieur Delacroix across the head. "Fool!" he shouted. He struck Monsieur Delacroix again and again with his full bull-like strength. Too late Monsieur Delacroix realised his folly. He collapsed unconscious upon the concrete floor.

When consciousness had pushed its way up to the surface through layers of pain and sickness, Monsieur Delacroix found himself propped against one of the walls of the greenhouse with his ankles tied together and his arms tied behind his back. Medan was busy at the base of the cactus tree, working with the flitting notions of a barber around a rich client. He had a pad on which he wrote figures after consulting certain spots on the trunk of the cactus, and he also had a syringe which he plunged in the plant to draw off liquid. Between these motions, he circled the trunk fingering the scale-like spines and exhibiting nervous anticipation, as if he expected some miraculous metamorphosis to take place at any moment. Suddenly he stood back, almost falling over Monsieur Delacroix's legs.

"Ah!" he exclaimed. He stretched his arms up towards the crest of the cactus like a pagan priest welcoming the sun. Monsieur Delacroix was amazed to see the triangular scales forming the bark near the summit of the cactus trunk, lifting and falling back as if puffs of air agitated them from within. This motion quickly spread down the trunk until the twenty-foot column was covered with rhythmic pulses of movement.

"This time!" appealed Medan to the quivering plant. He clenched his fists and visibly willed the plant to do something. Suddenly there was a noise like tearing cloth and the dirty green of the bark parted at the summit and from the yard-long split welled out a most stupendous blossom of tightly packed petals. Simultaneously Monsieur Delacroix breathed in such a powerful perfume that his eyes closed in a paroxysm of delight. The flower burst open in a stunning flamboyance of red and yellow, rustling like a silken umbrella being opened.

Medan fell to his knees at Delacroix's side.

"What do you think of my lovely?" he breathed.

"It's incredible!" answered Delacroix sincerely.

"Worth killing for," amplified Medan with enthusiasm.

Delacroix remained silent, not knowing what to answer.

The flower gave out dense waves of perfume so disturbing to the senses, that Monsieur Delacroix felt the onset of that fever-like disorientation that comes with drugging.

"She must feed," shouted Medan, "so I kill for her." Without looking at Monsieur Delacroix, Medan went on, "You know what she is? She's a survivor from the Miocene. I reared her myself from a seed." He laughed. "That's *one* thing we have to thank the war for—dropping a block-buster so that it blew the insides out of a hill in which a seed had been imprisoned for 40,000,000 years. I found her sprouting there on the side of the crater—near the corpse of a cow." He laughed uproariously.

"I recognised a stranger and I potted her. Even then her root was a size. It took me five years to realise that she was unique on this Earth. I went back and investigated the place where I had found Selina." Medan checked momentarily at the realisation that he had revealed his secret name for the plant. "There was a railway tunnel through the hill, and this bomb had pierced the covering of rock and exploded in the tunnel, literally blowing out the heart of the hill—it was all pure Miocene stuff. That and the resemblance to some fossil pieces that can be found in most museums convinced me. She was a pre-historic fern." Medan closed his eyes and breathed deeply of the scent which filled the greenhouse. He smiled evilly with his eyes still closed.

"She likes blood," he said. "I found that out one day when I was repotting her. She has a tubular root that is mobile along its length and toothed all the way along inside—like a barracuda's mouth, and as I lifted her out of the old pot, the root came free and took the end off my finger. She loved it! She grew six inches over night. After that I got the idea, and fed her mice and things of that size. There was no holding her. It became impossible to keep her potted in my apartment, so I moved her into here—surreptitiously, you understand, and by the time she was a big girl, people thought she had been here all the time."

Medan laughed convulsively at that. Tears ran down his face.

"Of course, she tried to have her root free for hunting in the greenhouse, but I had to discourage that. I kept burying the root until she was forced to burrow under the walls and outside. I lost her for several years after that—the root, I mean—until one night she caught a tramp who had gone into the gazebo for a sleep. I was washing her down at the time and I heard the screaming, then she seemed to come alive under my hands. I realised the connection at once and before the noise had stopped I found out where her root was. The meal transfigured her. She bloomed like you see her. For the first time in her life she bloomed. What an amazing sight! What an incredible phenomenon! Flower for two to three hours, and then an explosion of seed. I collected every one of those seeds—and on every subsequent occasion on which I have been able to make her bloom. Millions of seeds I have. Sacks of them. Every one potentially a beauty like my Selina. Soon I shall embark on my pilgrimage of planting them all over Europe. The Miocene shall be born again!"

Monsieur Delacroix who had been listening to Medan and watching the plant in a semi-coma, was suddenly speared through by the realisation that Medan could not tell him all this and allow him to live.

Medan seemed to be recalled from his dream too. He turned his head and looked at Monsieur Delacroix. "She has never had *three* bodies in one night," he whispered. "I wonder what she will do."

"No!" croaked Monsieur Delacroix.

Medan fetched the wheelbarrow, and despite his wriggling, bundled Monsieur Delacroix into it. He stuffed a handkerchief into Monsieur Delacroix's mouth and secured the plug with some scrim.

"We must hurry," he told Monsieur Delacroix. "Once the flower drops she will not feed until another full Moon."

Monsieur Delacroix was too horror-struck to reflect on the humour of Medan's use of the word "we." Come what may, he was going to the most ghastly death conceivable. There was no hope of help—Abime no more now than fertiliser for the plant, as was the hapless drunk before him. Only his wife knew of his intention to watch in the labyrinth—and she would be now deeply asleep. Tears sprang to Monsieur Delacroix's eyes as he said good-bye to his wife. Medan wheeled him through the gate left open in Delacroix's frantic escape. They began the last dozen or so yards of ascent. The moonlight was still as strong in the open and the shadows as black beneath the bushes. Monsieur Delacroix became almost demented in his writhings as they came to the end of the path at the edge of the small clearing around the gazebo. If he had not been gagged he would have shrieked his fear of that terrible mouth lurking somewhere in the bushes, but all that came from him were vague mumbles.

"Selina!" called Medan coaxingly. He stamped on the grass. "She can't hear, you understand," he explained to Delacroix. "She is sensitive to vibrations in the ground. Selina! Selina!"

There was a rustle in the bracken to one side of the gazebo, and then with a rush the great mouth reared up into the moonlight weaving from side to side like some stupendous cobra. "Ah!" shouted Medan in adoration, and pushed the wheelbarrow nearer. The blind mouth swished over Delacroix missing his recumbent body by a few inches. He had a momentary look right down that fibrous tube and saw the glint of hundreds of spines moving with a wavelike motion into the blackness.

The tube was growing longer with every second, smoothly expanding from the hole under the gazebo. It waved high into the air right above the two men seeming to yearn at the bright moon overhead. Medan stamped his foot again. The mouth seemed to look downwards. Its ghastly, thorn-lined maw gaped wider and then it dived down, mouth fully extended and swallowed Medan completely. Delacroix, rigid with terror, was knocked from the wheelbarrow by the convulsions of the plant. He rolled into the bushes near the entrance to the path and watched in horror the bulge of Medan pass downwards into the earth. The mouth lay prone on the ground in satiation, and then slowly contracted back into its burrow.

Delacroix writhed to his knees and with the strength of panic, gained his bound feet, and hopped from the clearing. He moved in huge staggering hops round the spiral to the gate, then fell on the wider public path and rolled. His senses became blurred and eventually left him. He lay senseless, bound hand and foot half way to the foot of the mound.

Just after dawn, one of the gardeners passing near the labyrinth on his way to look at the Tropical House furnace, heard Monsieur Delacroix groan. Monsieur Delacroix was very feeble with cold and cramp and not very intelligible. The gardener spread his thick coat over Delacroix, then went off to phone the police and ambulance. The gardener returned with a bottle of brandy and a pair of secateurs. He cut the innumerable strands of string that bound Monsieur Delacroix's wrists and ankles, then helped him to sit up and drink from the bottle. Both the restored circulation and the brandy were agony and Monsieur Delacroix fainted again.

An hour later, in a private room in a nearby hospital he was able to tell his story to a policeman. The man had him repeat the story, asking only short questions from time to time. He then went off and to Monsieur Delacroix's consternation Madame Delacroix was then admitted. The ensuing scene was astonishing for the mixture of tenderness and temper. Monsieur Delacroix was forced to admit his own imbecility in undertaking to sit up all night in the Jardin at this time in the year. At length he was asked to tell what had happened. Madame Delacroix looked at him with increasing bewilderment. "Are you joking, Paul?" she interrupted. "No, my dear," he replied, "what I tell you is true." Madame Delacroix burst out crying. "Oh, my poor Paul!" she sobbed. The nurse came in and administered a potent sleeping draught, then led Madame away. As he slipped into sleep, Monsieur Delacroix realised with dismay that neither his wife or the policeman had believed him.

There was another visit the next day from a more superior police officer, accompanied by a doctor, who sat listening intently to everything that passed Monsieur Delacroix's lips but only made comment with his eyes. Monsieur Delacroix found himself watching the doctor when making his replies and endeavouring to make his story less spectacular, but there is little that can be done to make a man-eating plant appear mundane.

The police officer stood up and retrieved has cap from the bedside table.

"It is an astonishing story, Monsieur," he said. "The only part we have been able to confirm so far is that Philippe Medan has not been seen since the evening on which you claim the events took place, although his car has been found in Rue Cuvier outside the Jardin. Also, we have not been able to find Monsieur Abime, but he appears to have been a man of somewhat peculiar ways and may have taken it into his mind to go off. Never fear, Monsieur, we shall investigate every aspect of your account until we arrive at the truth."

Monsieur Delacroix was rather put out by this ambiguous statement.

"Have you found no blood by the gazebo!" he exclaimed despairingly.

"No, Monsieur," replied the officer briskly. "Now, please excuse us. We shall return again."

The ensuing week was the most depressing Monsieur Delacroix remembered spending. He was most courteously imprisoned in the hospital, despite all his vehement assurances that he was well. They were, apparently, afraid of "shock." The doctor lectured Monsieur Delacroix on the mysterious unpredictability and dreadfulness of "shock." "At your age, you are more prone to after effects than at any age," he affirmed. "It would be—we shall not say suicidal, but most certainly extremely dangerous—for you to resume your normal life until the body has had a chance to adjust."

"Is it shock or mania you are afraid of," asked Monsieur Delacroix with a bitterness that was most unusual for him. "Never have I heard of a physically well man being detained in hospital at government expense just in case he should experience a reaction. If I had been assaulted by a thief instead of a mad botanist I have no doubt but that I should have been released the first day. You believe I am mad and that I have made away with two men."

The doctor moved to the door.

"The police are checking your story for truth. I am only interested in you as a medical patient, and I know you are unwell. Please try to rest. Good day."

"Unwell," the euphemism did not deceive Monsieur Delacroix.

He questioned Madame Delacroix closely about her conversation with the police and with the Matron of the ward. He persisted in an attempt to make her admit that she herself thought him mad, until she exhausted the number of ways of saying "no" and cut short her visit in exasperation.

Monsieur Delacroix spent one day laying on his back in silent despair, examining all the signs of madness within his mind. He spoke to no one and drank only one cup of coffee the whole day.

Eventually the police officer reappeared, accompanied once more by the doctor. The door was fastened behind them. The officer would not sit down and stood stiffly beside the bed with his light-grey eyes pinning Monsieur Delacroix to the pillow.

"We have completed our investigations," he announced. "We have found the bodies of Monsieur Abime and Medan."

From the corner of his eyes Monsieur Delacroix could see the face of the doctor fixed rigid like a staring under-coloured tailor's dummy. His heart seemed to turn over. He knew that the bodies had been found in circumstances that incriminated him. His mind suffered a sudden confusion of thoughts that centred upon the certainty that, after all, he *was* mad, and the whole terrible night was an illusion thrown up by his guilty mind to drown out the actual crime. What had he done!

"Are you all right, Monsieur?" queried the doctor in concern. He took Monsieur Delacroix's wrist.

The police officer remained silent, keeping his unwavering eyes on Monsieur Delacroix while the doctor counted out the pulse.

"A drink of water," said the doctor, and helped Monsieur Delacroix to take it.

"Go on," croaked Monsieur Delacroix.

"It took time because we had to obtain permission from the directorate of the Jardin for our every move," said the officer. "But we dug up the gazebo. We found the tube. I was there when we found it. Monsieur, you must have had a terrifying experience."

"Oh!" said Monsieur Delacroix, closing his eyes. His relief was so intense that tears ran from beneath his lids.

"Fortunately, the thing was inert and did not attack us. We obtained permission and dug up the cactus described by yourself. The remains of both men were found in a sac at the base of the plant. It is thought that some chemical that Medan kept about himself as a protection from the plant poisoned it. The plant was already beginning to decay when we dug it up."

"Oh!" sighed Monsieur Delacroix. He looked at the police officer through the distorting lenses of his tears. "That was a terrible experience for you."

"One gets used to such things," said the officer grimly.

"So I'm not mad," murmured Monsieur Delacroix. "Am I free?"

"Of course, Monsieur!" answered the officer. "You have not been a prisoner. Of course you are free."

Monsieur Delacroix looked at the doctor, who shrugged as he stood up. "I think you may go."

The two men left. The nurse opened the door and ushered in Monsieur Delacroix's full family. The youngest child bore a giant bouquet of flowers.

Monsieur Delacroix shrieked and fell back on to the bed. The doctor re-entered almost immediately.

"That's better," he observed with satisfaction as he stooped over the trembling Delacroix. "Didn't I tell you about the dangers of shock."

ST. MICHAEL & ALL ANGELS

MARK VALENTINE

Mark Valentine (b. 1959) is one of the new breed of devotees of the occult detective. He is a connoisseur of books and a dedicated researcher into all matters weird and fantastic, being editor of the journal Wormwood *and having written several books such as the studies* Arthur Machen *(1995) and* Time, a Falconer *(2010) about the diplomat and fantasist "Sarban." His love of books is evident in the volume* Haunted by Books *(2015). Much of his own fiction is collected in volumes issued by specialist publishers so are increasingly rare, such as* In Violet Veils *(1999) and* The Nightfarers *(2009), but more accessible are* Selected Stories *(2012) and* Seventeen Stories *(2013). He has edited several anthologies including one of occult detectives,* The Black Veil and Other Tales *(2008). He has written two separate series featuring occult detectives. The earliest was Ralph Tyler which have been collected in the volume* Herald of the Hidden *(2013), who features in the following story. Tyler is not like other such sleuths. He has no special esoteric knowledge or private means. As the author himself says, "Ralph Tyler was an attempt to have a scruffier, less reliable occult detective than the classic figures. Like me, he was untidy, vegetarian, leftish, and smoked foul cigarettes. Unlike me, he was also adventurous." His other detective, in stories written with John Howard, is* The Connoisseur, *the complete opposite to Tyler, being an aesthete brimming with arcane knowledge. His stories have been assembled in* The Collected Connoisseur *(2010).*

I PEERED WISTFULLY INTO THE MURKY DUSK OF AN OCTOBER evening from a window of number 14, Bellchamber Tower. I knew from his preoccupied air that my friend Ralph Tyler had become absorbed in a certain slender pamphlet.

I had found him studying it when I called: aside from brief greetings and an assurance that he would "be with me in a minute" we had exchanged hardly any conversation.

At length he sighed, put down this intriguing literature, stretched, then adopted the slumped, lazy position in his threadbare armchair which usually betokened a reflective mood, or the prelude to some thinking aloud. In accompanying Ralph Tyler during his researches into strange and disturbing matters I cannot pretend to have very often contributed much by way of practical insight or specialised knowledge, but I believe that he was often glad of the presence of someone to whom he could expound his theories, or put forward several possibilities. This process seemed to enhance the ready intuition which was his most notable faculty.

"It is like this," he began, suddenly, and without any other preamble, almost as if resuming an interrupted conversation. "St. Michael and All Angels, near Enderby, is a redundant church, obtained by a trust last year, who have taken on the task of preservation. It stands on the edge of parkland belonging to the local Hall, though of course it was previously used by both the family and the village. Enderby is much depopulated and the retention of the church was no longer a viable proposition; demolition was even a possibility, but the exertions of certain local figures sufficed to raise enough funds to prevent this. St. Michael and All Angels is therefore administered by its own charitable trust, but kept freely open to visitors who naturally are encouraged to donate towards expenses. I believe the sale of guidebooks . . ."—Ralph indicated the booklet he had been reading—"and postcards and so on also helps in this way."

I nodded, murmured my interest, and waited for Ralph to resume his narrative. He lit a cigarette, whose fumes stole insidiously through the air with a bizarre reek, before continuing.

"I became interested in all this because of a brief note in *The County*—" (This was a weekly newspaper covering mostly village affairs in the south and west of our shire). "... It said that vandals have been hindering restoration work on St. Michael's. They supposedly climb up the scaffolding against the tower and then throw large blocks of masonry down."

"Pretty dangerous," I commented.

"For the vandals, yes. Very hazardous. Clambering up apparatus about sixty feet high, balancing along an unsafe roof and hoisting off heavy chunks without toppling over? Hardly likely, I thought."

I began to appreciate my friend's point. Whilst someone out for a "lark" might well want a certain element of risk involved, this escapade seemed to stack the odds rather too highly.

"With little else to do, I decided to take a look out there. You know I'm always keen to delve into anything curious of this kind. Often there is the most prosaic and uninspiring explanation, but then again, once in a while. ... Anyway, I found that the church is quite notable in its way. For one thing, it is built in the form of an *equal-armed* cross, not the conventional elongated crucifix. But it also has an interesting past. I'll come to that in a minute.

"When I arrived at Enderby, I was straightaway doubtful about the vandal accusation. The place is so remote: even allowing for the possibility of drunken hooligans on a rural joyride, it was scarcely the most likely area for such exploits as the paper described. Daubing graffiti, smashing windows, trampling over graveyards, that goes on from time to time, due to sporadic outbursts, but not this. My examination of the outside of the church confirmed my suspicion. The possibility of footholds is slim, beyond trained workers: and although the stolid bulk of the tower could be tackled by use of scaffolding, it would require an astonishing attainment of dexterity and coolness.

"On the path which encircles the church could be seen several large lumps of stone amid debris which made it plain they had hit the ground with considerable force. I gave them a pretty thorough examination. Yes, I'm sorry, I even applied the old magnifying glass to a few."

Ralph grinned rather sheepishly at this commonplace contrivance of detection.

"Then I decided I might like a brief tour inside, but not surprisingly the door was locked. A note pinned to the porch board advised that keys were available from the custodian at a nearby address. I strolled over and obtained these, and naturally did not miss the chance to cast a few pertinent questions. The opportunity arose when the old chap urged me to 'Please be sure to lock up after, what with the trouble they'd had lately.'"

"I wonder he let you in," I interposed drily.

"I was looking quite respectable I assure you," returned Ralph with mock dignity.

I snorted.

"I told him I'd read about the vandal problem," continued Ralph, unperturbed by my jibe. "And asked whether they'd caught anybody yet. He ventured the opinion that the (ahem) so-and-sos had got clean away. No, he could not say what they looked like, no-one had actually seen the culprits, despite their decidedly prominent position high on the church roof. Perhaps it was after all accidental damage, I suggested. Certainly not—the contractors for the restoration were adamant that there was outside interference.

"I murmured in sympathy, then made my way back to St. Michael's. Inside, I picked up the booklet which describes its history and architecture. I already knew some of this, having consulted some background material before setting out on my excursion. The church was founded about 1140 by the Fitzgilbert brothers, Guy and Peter, barons of this domain. They had conducted an irregular war against each other in those troubled times of King Stephen, skirmishes over lands or possessions, but these culminated in a feud so bloody and stained with such atrocities that the intercession of neighbouring magnates, prelates, and even the King himself was necessary. The enforced truce was to be commemorated and sustained by the building of this church as a united enterprise between the brothers. It is presumed the design of the equal-armed cross symbolised the absolute parity between them, and such careful balance is evident elsewhere in the fabric of the church. The eastern arm contains the altar; the western the tower; the southern the entrance porch; and the northern, the Fitzgilbert family crypt.

"The endowment of the church did not succeed in tempering the enmity between the brothers, but it taught them to lace their hatred with religious zeal. As well as proclaiming each other traitor, outlaw, and usurper, charges of heathenism and witchcraft were levelled. This picturesque era was brought to an end when, before work on the church had even finished, Peter Fitzgilbert died suddenly, how and why not being known, and his brother Guy was left in sole possession of all he surveyed. His dynasty retained this state of affairs until it succumbed during the Wars of the Roses.

"As to the interior of the church itself, it was fairly unexceptional, rather colder than some I have visited, due to disuse no doubt, and missing the minor trappings which go to make up what you might call a working church. It gives the impression of being an empty, forlorn shell. The crypt of the Fitzgilberts is railed off, and, as the booklet reminds people, not accessible to visitors. After a few cursory glances around, I placed some coins in the collection box and left, carefully locking the low arched door behind me.

"When I returned the keys, I asked the custodian if I might obtain permission to go into the Fitzgilbert crypt. I said (which was by now quite true) that I was very interested in the church and wished to research it further. He gave me the address of the Trust's secretary and recommended I put my request in writing. I have done so. I also mentioned in my letter that I was disturbed to read of the vandalism, and should they require any help and support in this matter I would be glad to oblige. I hope I expressed this in such a way that it might sound like common concern for such an antiquity, yet with rather more significant interest between the lines."

"Very deft," I complimented, ironically. "Any response?"

"This." My friend produced from within the guidebook by his side a letter on headed blue notepaper:

From R.W. Alwyn, M.A., F.R.S.A., Hon. Secretary.
St. Michael's (Enderby) Trust.
Dear Mr. Tyler,
Thank you for your letter of third inst.
I confirm that access to the Fitzgilbert crypt at St. Michael's will be permitted on the date you propose. I shall myself be present to accompany your inspection.

I am grateful for your concern regarding certain unfortunate incidents at the church recently. Perhaps we may discuss this matter further when we meet.

Yours faithfully etc. etc.

"Hmm, impressive, if cautious," I conceded. "When are we going?"

"On Saturday. I chose a day when you could come along. There may be nothing to all this, but on the other hand . . ."

"Might I be correct in believing that you are refraining from telling me all you know?" I suggested, gauging a certain intonation in Ralph's voice.

"You might," he replied non-committally.

As arranged, we both caught one of only four buses per day serving the district around Enderby, alighted at the little wooden shelter, and made our way to the church. It lay at the foot of a rise in the ground, a green knoll, in the far corner of Enderby Hall's parkland. Bleak, nearly leafless trees clung grimly to the sward, some brackish and neglected ornamental ponds shuddered with a dark rippling sheen nearby, and the footpath was slimy underfoot. We passed through the gate of corroded iron palings, into a churchyard in which lilted that mouldering odour, a mingling of damp evergreens and rank decay, so often to be found in such sites. At the porch we were met by a dignified but slightly distant gentleman of between fifty and sixty, whose greying hair receded from the forehead but clustered in unorthodox and mildly eccentric locks about the nape. Ronald Alwyn introduced himself, eyed us with polite but keen detachment, and ushered us into the gloomy interior of the church. We exchanged casual, general conversation about the purpose of our visit, as he unlocked the tall barred railings guarding the Fitzgilbert crypt, and gestured for us to follow down shallow, worn stone steps.

Electric light had been installed via one acorn-shaped lamp in a nook of the low ceiling, and this cast a brightness over the hushed, slumbering cell in which were interred the remains of a dynasty five hundred years old. I felt no particular distress about the confined presence of mortality, indeed I was reminded of a museum atmosphere, with its dusty exhibits estranged from any semblance to real flesh-and-blood people of times long ago. Ralph seemed absorbed in a close scrutiny of a number of fragmentary tomb slabs, and there was an expectant silence as Ronald Alwyn waited for him to finish. For my part, I merely stared vaguely about the crypt, feeling rather uncertain of my role here.

After a while, my friend got up from his crouched position near a particular monument, nodded affably to our guide and led the way back up the steps. The gate was locked again behind us.

"Thank you for allowing me this opportunity, it is very co-operative of you," Ralph commented, as we emerged. Then he turned directly to the particular cause of our call.

"Mr. Alwyn, I don't want to sound unnecessarily mysterious, but am I not correct in saying there is rather more to the vandalism on the church roof than has been made public?"

The Hon. Secretary cleared his throat. This bald assertion seemed to disconcert him a little.

"Not at all," was his first wary response. "Why do you say that?"

"I am sorry," returned Ralph, "I may sound like an outsider interfering. I realise the Trust must be careful to preserve the sanctity of the church and is anxious not to compromise its own credibility. But I do not believe vandals have been anywhere near this church in the manner which has been suggested. This means either that your contractors are less than competent and have caused the damage themselves, or . . ." Ralph paused significantly. "Or is there another explanation?"

Ronald Alwin sat down rather heavily on an ancient, polished pew. He seemed suddenly wearied.

"I am not at liberty to discuss this matter," he began, unconvincingly.

"Then I shall take my case to the newspaper. I must tell you that my own researches point in a rather alarming direction. I am sure it will prove extremely lurid attraction for a populist editor," was Ralph's somewhat callous response.

The ageing scholar sighed again.

"You are most persistent," he objected in exasperation.

There was a dull silence. Then:

"Both of your alternatives might well apply. Our dilemma is this. The contractors whom we, the trustees, engaged to carry out the meticulous restoration work, have been most disappointing. They have progressed very slowly, with almost constant interruptions, and a negligence I regard as next to culpable. That is bad enough. But the excuses they give are equally disturbing from a company of supposedly professional reputation. They allege their work is being hindered all the while, and that some of their employees have refused to work on the site, because of . . . hummm, certain reasons.

"At first we thought they were merely fabricating or exaggerating, to disguise their own faulty and plodding workmanship. Relations became very strained, and we took legal advice as to the possibility of dispensing with their services. At this point, their director insisted upon me speaking personally to some of his employees. What they told me, in no uncertain terms, has left me in something of a quandary. I do not know if I am misled most infamously, or if . . ."

He broke off, as if in an agony of indecision.

"Mr. Alwyn," interjected Ralph, "I know you have been involved with this church and the village for a while now. You are also an authority on our regional history. So tell me if you know of a legend relating to the Fitzgilberts."

"There are many. Historical events often become intertwined with folk tales and romantic fiction. . . ."

"I am thinking of one in particular. It endured in progressively corrupted forms from the very earliest times until last century, although today it may only be encountered in obscure antiquarian papers. It has a particular relevance in view of our present dilemma."

The academic looked at my friend incredulously.

"It is preposterous," he murmured, dismissively.

Ralph lit a pungent cigarette, a tactless irreverence I thought, though it clearly did not occur to him, for he was immersed in a line of thought I could not follow.

He continued abruptly, "I am not an expert. You are. Please confirm for me a number of points.

"Not long after its foundation, the dedication of this church was changed, wasn't it? It had been to Saints Cosmas and Damian. Presumably they were appropriate at the time. . . ."

"They were brothers with a reputation for skilful and pious healing," asserted Ronald Alwyn, stirred by this diversion to the historical origin of the church.

"Quite. And then this was altered to St. Michael and All Angels. Would it be fair to surmise that this occurred when Guy Fitzgilbert took complete domination, and the original dedication was somewhat . . . inconvenient?"

"Yes, that is what is usually believed."

"We saw Guy Fitzgilbert's tomb chest in the crypt. The stone carving is very worn and blurred, but I believe it originally depicted Michael slaying a fearsome dragon."

"Yes, it is a scene from the *Book of Revelation*. The dragon represents Satan."

"And that symbol occurs everywhere in the crypt."

"That is natural. It represents the church's patron saint. It became, too, something of a heraldic device for the line."

"Guy Fitzgilbert's line," emphasised Ralph. "Where is Peter Fitzgilbert's grave?"

"No-one knows," replied Alwyn. "Presumably his brother forbade his burial within the crypt, so he was interred elsewhere, possibly in an unmarked cist somewhere on his own estate."

Ralph mused for a few moments, still drawing at his cigarette.

"I have a further question. To your knowledge, has the church been restored at any time before?"

"It would seem not. That is why it so badly needs repair. There was, I believe, an attempt to carry out major work last century, but it was never carried through. Perhaps the expense . . ." Mr. Alwyn's conjectures faded as he was struck by a new thought.

There was a quite lengthy pause. In the stagnant air I felt a sudden sense of unease.

Ralph spoke quietly.

"I think by now you know the nature of my interest in this church. I am in complete earnest. I can tell you what the contractor's workmen said to you, and furthermore I will show you why, in your position, I would believe them."

Ronald Alwyn said nothing. He bore an expression of tired resignation.

"Amongst other talk about the general atmosphere up on the roof, the high incidence of accidents and suchlike, you were told that they have caught glimpses of a huge winged creature, like a giant bat or vastly abnormal crow, I should think. It has disturbed them before: but just recently it soared out of the tower and alarmed them quite drastically, probably around dusk. They said they had never encountered such a beast before and it quite unnerved them; and that it must be removed or confined before work can continue, because its sudden appearance again could undoubtedly cause a workman to lose his balance and either fall or do irreparable damage. They put all this to you as cautiously as they could; but plain beneath their practical observations was a hint of deeper dread and aversion."

Mr. Alwyn nodded very slowly.

"That is why there was no work going on when I looked around here a few days ago: and why there has been none since?"

He nodded again, weakly.

"If you are ready, I would like you to look outside," proposed Ralph, and he pulled open the heavy arched door, causing a sudden rush of sunlight that made me blink. Ronald Alwyn and I followed as he ambled along the churchyard path to one of the chunks of dislodged masonry. He crouched down beside this, turned it slightly to one side and held it steady for our inspection. Visible despite the battered surface caused by impact were eight deep grooves gouged into the mellow stone, in two sets of four. The lack of weathering or grime suggested that these marks were recent. They were such that only a hard, sharp tool could be responsible, or . . .

"I believe these to be claw marks," said Ralph, calmly, "And I have examined some of the smaller shrapnel that has exploded on the ground after being pushed from the roof. Similar markings may be discerned."

Ronald Alwyn looked rather pale and uncertain.

"But what you are saying is . . ." he objected.

"That this church either harbours some zoological freak or another kind of monstrosity, yes," interrupted Ralph.

He stood up and pointed at the desolate trees, stark against the cold sky.

"Look: stout and strong limbs have been torn or broken from those trees. There has been no storm. What was responsible? No-one's been doing any lopping have they?"

It was evident from Mr. Alwyn's reaction, his gaze becoming more agitated, that no such arboriculture had been undertaken.

"I must have time to think about this. I really do not know what to think. Perhaps . . . yes, I will see the Rector, Eric Hollis. He is a Vice-President of the Trust."

"It would be a good idea. I am only too happy to come along. Or meet him later, as you choose. I will be around the village, and waiting until six o'clock. Please meet me before then."

"Yes, do leave this with me, Mr. Tyler. I will take urgent steps, and see what can be done."

We strolled away across the grounds along the thin damp footpath, and back to the village. It was a quarter to one, time enough to partake of a pint or two, and maybe obtain a snack. We found The Plough in Enderby to be a decent inn with a vacant corner table, and after a welcome draught of bitter, I burst into the fray.

"Come on then, what do you think? What's the legend about the Fitzgilberts?" I demanded to know.

"You heard what I said," objected Ralph.

"Yes, but you didn't say everything. I felt I was getting half the story," I protested.

Ralph lowered his voice.

"In straightforward terms it is this. We don't know how the elder Fitzgilbert, Peter, met his death, but we can pretty well guess it was at the instigation of his brother. Now the old tales allege that in the course of their feuding, both of them were guilty of great infamies, and not above invoking forbidden powers. There used to be a whole ballad cycle about the hideous crimes they committed, but now only fragments are preserved. One of the most enduring but obscure episodes has the dead Peter Fitzgilbert returning in the form of a banshee-dragon creature which is eventually slain by a champion owing allegiance to Guy. This is undoubtedly a very coloured version of some original myth, since it has taken over certain characteristics from the renowned St. George tale. We do not therefore know whether the rededication of the church to St. Michael was a cause or a result of the myth."

I was beginning to feel a little uneasy at the direction this conversation was taking.

"You surely don't think that this giant bat . . ." I rather gulped out, as a certain process of thought presented itself to me.

"I'm only following the facts," insisted Ralph. "From the beginning, having excluded vandals, I was presented with a feat of great balance and agility. Then I observed the markings on the debris and the snapped branches. I was already aware of the traditions surrounding the church, but detailed research confirmed my suspicions in a very singular way. The disruption is caused by a winged beast, the same seen by the workmen. What remains to be seen is whether it will appear again, and if it will respond to a certain course of action."

"Why has it emerged now?" I wondered bitterly. "Because of the disturbance caused by the restoration work?"

"Partly that, I would say. But also, don't forget, the church has been redundant for more than a year."

"So?"

"No services. No prayers. Little use. And if I suspect correctly, one ceremony in particular was neglected."

"Was it the custom," enquired Ralph of the Reverend Hollis, when we had gathered at the custodian's cottage in response to a message from Ronald Alwyn, "to hold a special service on or near the 29th September every year?"

"Why, yes, of course. That is St. Michael's feast day, and it is only natural that a church dedicated to the saint should commemorate the fact."

"What form did the service take?"

"It was fairly unexceptional. I would lead the congregation in a general procession around the church, blessing its physical structure. There would follow a sermon always upon the theme of St. Michael, a special prayer and a reading."

"So the service was not necessarily of local origin?"

"Mmmm, it follows certain common formalities, true, yet there were characteristics I believe to be unique."

"Such as?" prompted Ralph.

"The most notable was the reading. It was not from a book of the Bible, but from an apocryphal text. You will perhaps know, Mr. Tyler, that such works are often far from orthodox. Though they originate at about the same time as the books of our Bible, they were excluded because in some way they were not satisfactory. Some, however, are of greater value than others. They vary from the preposterous to the intriguing. I . . ."

"Could you tell me a little more about this particular reading?" interrupted Ralph, adroitly avoiding further exposition about the nature of apocryphal gospels.

"It was from the *Testament of Abraham*. That is a work attributed to the second century, I may tell you. There is a passage which describes St. Michael rescuing souls even from the depths of Hell. It is very powerful. An incumbent of the nineteenth century has written it out in a very elegant style, and it was my practice to read from that."

"And for how long has this custom continued?"

"It is hard to say."

"Did it originate with the Victorian incumbent you mentioned?"

"Oh, most certainly not. Amongst the parish records there used to be his journals, covering about nine years. He speculates at intervals about the origin of the unusual reading, but so far as is known it has always been a feature of the St. Michael's Day service."

"And there was no service this year?"

"No. The church is redundant."

Ralph turned to Mr. Alwyn, who had been listening intently, like myself, to this dialogue.

"And when did the workmen begin to feel uneasy? When did they first catch sight of the . . . *giant bat*?"

The secretary of the Trust answered as if reluctantly.

"Earlier this month."

"So. No service, complete with its unusual elements, is held on the 29th September, though this has been the custom since time immemorial. A few days later, in October, the disturbances begin. There is clearly a connection."

My friend was spelling out his suspicions in an attempt to win over the Reverend Hollis, who had earlier voiced misgivings. He repeated them now, politely, carefully.

"I am familiar with the incidents at St. Michael's, Ralph," he began. "And, like yourself, find the explanations so far to be unsatisfying. But you have impressed our Secretary here with a very bizarre theory. We must not allow our concern at these misfortunes to get out of hand. Although the church is no longer in my direct care, I naturally take a great deal of interest in its continued wellbeing. What you are propounding will attract a notoriety that is far from desirable."

Ralph scowled and slid further into his armchair.

"I do not believe you fully appreciate your position," he responded coldly. "There will be no work upon the church until this matter is resolved. It will not go away. So far as my past experiences suggest, it is usual for the image, or creature, however you wish to regard it, to gather in strength and purpose by every day and night it is left beyond control. Eventually, its instincts will be concentrated to a supreme degree, which it will be too late to halt. At the moment it appears falteringly, at intervals, venturing little beyond the church. But for how long?"

Eric Hollis stared at Ralph gravely.

"What is your solution?" he asked, cautiously.

"We have to be there when it next appears," my friend replied. "That means a round-the-clock watch, though I do not think we will have long to wait. And we must be prepared to act."

There was silence. I was conscious of the unnaturally loud ticking of a wooden-cased clock on the sideboard of the custodian's parlour, as if in emphasis at Ralph's words.

"Alright," at length accepted Revd Hollis, sighing. "I'll go along with your plan, with the absolute condition that, whatever transpires, our explanation to the general public shall deal solely with plain and rational matters. I will let you try out your theory because otherwise whatever else I do will involve publicity—whether changing contractors, calling in the police or experts, or consulting other clergymen."

I grimaced. Ralph shrugged.

"There is little interest in this matter outside of Enderby," he replied, "aside from a few idle lines in the local paper. And the contractors need only be assured that the problem has been dealt with. When it is appropriate to do so, I will let the facts be known. But not for a number of years."

That evening witnessed certainly the most unusual service that had been held in the church of St. Michael at Enderby. It contained the form and ritual of the St. Michael's Day commemoration, surely the first time this had been held nearly a month late. The congregation was small, even by modern standards, numbering only four, and that including the vicar. The doors were locked against the remote possibility of other worshippers. And one of those present paid little heed at all to the proceedings, but roved restlessly around the aisles and corridors of the church.

It was at Ralph's suggestion that this curious re-enactment of the old service was undertaken. He was convinced that it must play a crucial part in recent events, its absence a kind of catalyst to the sombre happenings since. So, the Revd Hollis led us through the blessing of the walls and structure of the church, in a solemn if uneasy procession, and then spoke with commendable conviction of the legend of St. Michael, to his audience of two, Ralph being preoccupied. Sitting on the narrow pew, my mind too was, as it is said, "elsewhere." A tingling, dry-mouthed nervousness had been with me since we had enclosed ourselves within the dim, cold, hollow expanse of this disused church. Always in the past, when I had accompanied Ralph Tyler on his researches into the stranger, darker incidents of provincial existence, there was an element of doubt. The Herefordshire case, for instance, might have been an unfortunate accident only, events at Hubgrove could admit of a psychological explanation: the still unsolved quarry burial case was replete with uncertainties. But this was altogether different, for my implicit faith in my friend's judgement led me to anticipate some distinctly real encounter with a force outside of rational experience.

I heard and registered mechanically, without paying any extra attention, that Eric Hollis had begun to read from a sacred text. His quiet, soft tones were echoed in hushed whispers by the ancient place. The wan yellow electric light we had sparingly employed at the altar end of the church left much of the rest in a grey shadowed twilight. I let my glance stray around the stone walls, stained glass, marble tablets, cold tiled floor. I peered upwards to the low vaultings, and hesitated.

There was a blurring up there. I sensed it was wrong. It was like a gathering of dark dust, so that the dimness was deeper than it was below or beyond. I stared harder. I clambered to my feet, and clung to the back of the pew, steadying myself as I gazed, neck craned. The vicar's voice halted abruptly as he noticed this disturbance. Ronald Alwyn followed my stare. Ralph swivelled around from the depths of the church and marched hurriedly towards us.

Seeping as if from all the walls and perimeters of the church, great rays of black motes funnelled into the focal cloud that hovered in the upper air near the roof. It seemed to gather into itself deep, floating shadows wrenched from the very stones. None of us uttered a word. The concentration of the dark form became more intense, it took an opaque, almost tangible appearance, and began to boil and squirm as if in some struggle of frantic proportions. With a sickening, rattling squeal this process became complete, and a tangible body emerged, a winged beast, perhaps five feet in length, with shining flesh and dark limbs. Shrieking in high pitched sobs, it flapped heavily, clumsily above us, then swooped unerringly at our petrified forms. Jerked out of inaction, we sprawled onto the floor. Sweeping past our heads, the creature emitted another wail and plunged down the stairwell of the Fitzgilbert crypt.

Still prone on the slabs on the floor, I raised my head reluctantly, fighting to suppress a swarming hysteria. Ralph and Eric Hollis were already on their feet, faces grim and fixed. Ronald Alwyn was staring as if in a state of daze. Slowly, we moved towards each other, and Ralph steadily led us to the open gates of the crypt. It occurred to me only afterwards that at this point I had not the merest idea of what we were to do. Some physical attack upon the beast was out of the question, for its agility was far beyond ours, and in any case had we not seen it resolve from the very atmosphere? Blindly, hesitatingly we descended the steps. The welcome wave of electric light that burst out at the flick of the switch at the foot of the stairs nonetheless callously revealed a hideous scene. I remember croaking an oath of disgust. The dark winged creature was squatting upon the tomb chest of Guy Fitzgilbert, talons gripping, clawing frenziedly at the ancient stone lid. This was in itself a repulsive sight, but it was the sudden lurch of the neck, bringing the beast's visage to glare awfully at our own which brought me close to extreme nausea: it was a human face, or nearly; that of one terribly scorched, crusted with ash and dead black skin, a mask of deformed, torn flesh.

Eric Hollis began praying loudly, firmly, in a bold chant of words I do not now recall. The creature spat, gibbered, lunged menacingly. I huddled against the wall, prepared to bolt. It became increasingly evident that the rector's solemn invocations were only holding the apparition, keeping it at bay, but scarcely testing its defences. At any hesitation or sign of tiring, it would be upon us again, and we should have unleashed upon the outside world a being we were powerless to control. I saw it open out its wings and sway forward. In the close-confined, poorly lit cell the span of its wings blotted out much of our illumination. It reared above us. The vicar's prayers became more rapid, imploring: we backed off. Plainly, the crisis had come and we must withdraw, get out as best we might.

Ralph motioned Eric Hollis to stop, stepped forward and shouted a single phrase, in an unfamiliar tongue, faltering slightly in the middle but finishing with a roar of command. At the same time, he drew back his right arm as if in the act of throwing something, and ended by pointing with outstretched hand at the creature. He did this again and again, each time with the strange, miming action, and gradually, as if truly struck, it shrank back, until with a howl it fell in a contorted mass upon the floor. Flames burst all around it, leaping from the stale, crumbling atmosphere in a blaze of brilliant, cruel glory. I saw the creature's head jarred agape in a paroxysm of pain and fear, baleful black eyes gleaming in shocked frustration, limbs pinned irrevocably back by the sudden furnace. I remember clearly the comforting crackling of the tongues of fire, a golden screen obliterating what should have never been. Then, Ralph's urgent, hoarse whisper to the Reverend Hollis, "Now! The reading!" and, above the flames, the clergyman's calm, clear voice, telling from the *Testament of Abraham*, how the angel Michael rescued souls from the depths of hell.

Ashes tumbled slowly, softly in suspenseful air, for a few moments a translucent silence fell, the fire faded swiftly, and all was still. I groaned, and subsided onto the narrow, stone steps.

It was a while after this experience that I felt reassured enough to seek from Ralph a few further details about the manifestation at St. Michael & All Angels, Enderby. Our meetings and conversation since had been rather painstakingly light and casual, as we avoided by mutual understanding discussing so intense an ordeal. But at length, I wished to know what it was he had used to finally suppress the being.

"Around Guy Fitzgilbert's tomb," he replied cheerfully, "is inscribed a motto that has more or less escaped the attention of historians and so on. Those who have noticed it have been unable to decipher its full wording, since much is worn away, and it seems anyway to have been concealed within the sculpted beading which is also around the base of the chest. When I examined the crypt, the significance of the many St. Michael symbols was soon evident, and so I surmised the motto might have relevance too. At any rate, I copied the fragments that could be discerned. Whether what I recited made any sense I honestly couldn't say. I don't know Latin. But in any case, I feel it was the sound as much as anything else, for it is clearly a very ancient protection."

"And—what we saw?" I enquired, tentatively. "Any theories?"

"Well, speculation. I would propose that Peter Fitzgilbert was burned to death by his brother, either as part of warfare or in an execution. That would account for the legends that one or other, or both, were involved in witchcraft or sorcery. Now, as to why a lingering being, still steeped in hatred, should lie within the church, I wonder whether the supporters of Peter did not perform a final, macabre trick, and arrange to have their lord's ashes mixed into the mortar and stones of the unfinished church? Then, the manifestations began and it was necessary to rededicate it to a powerful protector, St. Michael, slayer of evil winged creatures. The yearly ritual especially helped to hold back the beast. But nothing could cleanse or purify the site, for it was built by hatred, and in a certain sense, even with hatred.

"So that, properly understood, what we saw was a concentration of all *both* brothers ever wrought in the name and form of evil. It was released almost by accident, because the traditional ceremony was missed, and the sanctity of the church was eroded by disuse and the interference of the restoration work.

"It would be my contention that Guy Fitzgilbert, obsessed both by the fate and spectre of his brother, and the destiny of his own soul, arranged the ritualistic reading from an apocryphal text which seemed to promise redemption even from the depths of damnation. It was our privilege . . ."

here Ralph grinned wryly, "to witness the working of a minor miracle. By intervention through us, not only was the creature finally released from its earthly state of captivity in a despicable form, but, we may hope, restored to a better world."

"You surely don't believe . . ." I began, but Ralph interrupted.

"No, I don't. But it's difficult to account for what we saw in any other way."

JEREMIAH

JESSICA AMANDA SALMONSON

Jessica Amanda Salmonson (b. 1950) has written ghost stories, dark fantasy, folk tales and heroic fantasy. Her early work included the trilogy about the twelfth-century female samurai warrior, Tomoe Gozen, which began with Tomoe Gozen *(1981). She also won the World Fantasy Award for her anthology of heroic fantasy stories featuring strong women warriors,* Amazons! *(1979). She has also undertaken considerable research discovering lost and forgotten stories by both leading writers and those deserving of more attention, such as Julian Hawthorne in* The Rose of Death *(1997), Olivia Howard Dunbar in* The Shell of Sense *(1997), Sarah Orne Jewett with* Lady Ferry and Other Uncanny People *(1998) and Jerome K. Jerome with* City of the Sea *(2008). Her own output of short stories is extensive with a number collected in* The Deep Museum *(2003). Her psychic detective, Penelope Pettiweather, lives in Seattle and explores the environment for any weird events and then writes about them to her friends in England. The first three stories appeared in a small-press booklet,* Harmless Ghosts *in 1990, and these and others have long been hard to find until all were reissued in* The Complete Weird Epistles of Penelope Pettiweather, Ghost Hunter *(2016). It brings our journey through the archives of the fighters of fear to a conclusion.*

"Je suis dégoûté de tout."
—René Crevel, 1935

My dear Jane,

I'm glad you received that copy of *Satan's Circus* by Lady Eleanor Smith. One frets about the overseas mail. You'll note that while the spine says the publisher is "Doran," the title page says "Bobbs Merrill," yet both purport to be the first edition. I'm told that Doran had a habit, in those days, of purchasing unbound sheets of other publishers' overruns and reissuing them under their own imprint. So you see, it isn't really the first edition except on the inside! I was also delighted by your perceptive comments on the outstanding story "Wittington's Cat." The compiler of *Giddy's Ghost Story Guide* completely misunderstood that one, didn't he?

Thank you for that perfect copy of *Stone-ground Ghost Stories*. I could never have afforded it over here. You'd pale at the American prices for old British books! The stories struck me as quaintly amusing rather than horrific, but there is a lot more to them than meets the eye, though once more the compiler of *Giddy's* failed to see much in them. There's so much to the central protagonist's character that could be further explored if some talented and enterprising fellow ever wished to add new episodes about the haunted vicar and his parish.

But, enough of mere fictional ghosts. I was chilled to the bone by your recent experience with those two paintings you were restoring. If you wrote that one up as a "fictional" adventure you could certainly sell it to one of the fantasy magazines. They needn't know it actually happened. But what a shame the paintings had ultimately to be covered up. Not that I blame you; still, I'd like to have seen the one of Death on my next trip abroad, and that won't be possible now that it's safely "preserved" under whitewash.

Did my colleague Mrs. Byrne-Hurliphant bother you *that* much on her English journey? She can be a pest, certainly. Please forgive my giving her your address. Now, at least, you'll know exactly what I'm on about!

Yes, yes, I did promise to tell you what happened over Christmas if you'd tell me that horrid adventure with the paintings "Gravedigger" and "Death." Well, a bargain is a bargain, so now I suppose I must. It's much more terrible than any of the little accounts I've sent to Cyril for his antiquarian journal. So brace yourself, and remember—you asked.

It was three weeks to Christmas. I planned holidays alone. All my friends would be off to other states to visit kin. And while Christmas is no big thing to me—growing up with both East European Jews and Southeast Asian Buddhists in one's motley family helps to weaken the impact of Christian holidays—it can yet be gloomy and sad when one's options are unexpectedly restricted. I can't count a couple of pre-Christmas parties I would probably attend. The fact that people are so fantastically tedious makes the *doing* something as depressing than the *not*, so you can see I was just in no mood for anything.

I'd finished some early grocery shopping and was coming up the backstairs out of a bleak afternoon rain, two bags squashed in my arms, when I heard the phone ringing. You just know when you hurry, things take longer. I dropped the keys. Then I tried the wrong key. Then I tried the right key upside down. By the time I'd tossed the torn bags and their content across the kitchen table and grabbed the receiver, all I heard was a faint "click." Surprising how discouraging that click can be at times.

But before I'd put all the groceries away and pulled together the majority of the bulk beans I'd scattered, the phone rang again.

It was the feeblest voice I had ever heard.

"Miss Pettiweather?"

"Absolutely," I replied, affecting the prim and the resolute.

"I beg your pardon?" said the faint, elderly voice of a woman who must have been a hundred and fifty-eight if her age matched such a sad, rasping, tired timbre.

"Yes, this is Miss Pettiweather," I said, donning a more conservative aspect.

"I read your article in the Seattle *Times*," said the cracked old voice. "The one about the haunted houses."

I winced. It hadn't been an article but an interview. And while the reporter tried her best to be straight-faced about it, it was so garbled and misquoted that even I had to wonder if the interviewee weren't a lunatic.

"Did you?" I said affably.

The feeble voice said, "If it happens to me again, I don't think I can make it."

It seemed she was on the verge of tears.

"What's happened?" I asked, worried that some wretched woman was truly in need of my special talents, but so old it would be difficult for her to communicate her problem. "Who am I speaking to?"

"Gretta Adamson," she said. "My heart isn't as good as it was. If he does it again, I'll die. I tried to tell the doctor but he said not to excite myself. He doesn't believe me. Do you believe me, Miss Pettiweather? Won't anyone believe me?"

"Oh I can believe just about anything; but I don't know anything about it as yet, Miss—Misses?"

"I'm widowed."

"Mrs. Adamson. You haven't told me . . ."

"It's Jeremiah," she said. "He comes back."

"Is it bad?" I asked. That was the simplest way I could put the question. And she answered even more simply.

"It's terrible."

Then very quietly, very sadly, she added: "Every Christmas. But . . . but . . ." She broke down at that point and could barely finish: "He isn't the same."

She lived alone in a small, run-down house in a run-down part of the city. The house hadn't been repainted in a full generation, for even curls and flakes had long since come loose and disappeared, so that the whole grey structure looked as though it had never been painted at all. Most of the windows were cracked; some of the cracks were taped; and a few small panes had been replaced with wood or plastic.

The lawn was a miniature meadow for inner city field mice. A wooden fence set her small property apart from the surrounding houses and cheap low-rise apartment buildings. The fence was falling down in places. The front gate was held closed with a length of rope, which had been woven about in a curious manner, as though the inhabitant beyond had a secret method no one else could duplicate, thereby making it possible to tell whenever someone had tinkered with it. I retied the gate in a much simpler manner, then strode a broken stone walkway between the two halves of her little meadow of frozen, brittle grass.

When Mrs. Adamson opened the door, her white, creased face looked up at me from so far down, it made me feel like I was a giant. In her gaze was a world of pitiful hope, worry, and despair. Her head was cocked completely on its side, resting on a shoulder in a spectacularly unnatural posture.

"I'm Miss Pettiweather," I said, hoping my ordinary demeanor and harmless, frumpy middle-agedness would be enough to reassure her. In such a neighborhood, it was no wonder she was leery of opening her own front door.

She was badly hunchbacked and the spinal deterioration caused her obvious pain. The smell of medicine assured me she had a doctor's care at least. Her neck was so badly twisted that her left ear was pressed against her shoulder and she could by no method straighten her head. But it was a kind soul inside that ruined body, and they were kind eyes that glared up at me.

I followed her into the dimly lit, grubby interior. Her shuffling gait was slow and awkward, as it was difficult to walk with such a horribly calcium-leached spinal column. For her own part, she seemed to count herself lucky to be able to walk, and bore up boldly.

She was eighty-five.

"Jeremiah died when I was seventy," she said in her familiar cracked voice. I sat with her at her kitchen table. "Fifteen years ago, Christmas eve, in Swedish Hospital."

"What did he die of?" I asked, moving my rickety chair closer to Mrs. Adamson, to better hear her thin, distant voice.

"He was old," she said.

"Yes, I know, but, well, it will help me to know more. Was he in his right mind? I'm sorry to be so blunt about it, Mrs. Adamson, but it's only a few days to Christmas. I assure you I *can* help, but I'll need as much information beforehand as you can give me. Was he able to think clearly until close to the end?"

"Lord, no," she said, her sideways head staring with the brightest, sharpest, bluest eyes. "He had Alzheimer's."

I sighed. I would have to grill her a bit more, to find out what Mr. Adamson' final days were like. But I could already guess, and later, after an interview at Swedish Hospital, I would be certain. The raving last moments, the delusions—in this case, the delusion that he had gotten into such a state because his wife had poisoned him. It was often the case with the more malignant spirits that they died in abject confusion, anger, and horror, hence they could not go on to a better existence elsewhere.

The tea kettle whistled and though I insisted I could make it myself, Mrs. Adamson obviously wished to entertain me. She got up, for all the agony of motion, and toddled weirdly round the vile kitchen. A moldy pork chop sat in hard grease in a rusty pan on the stove. A garbage bag was filled with tuna fish and Chef Boyardee spaghetti cans. Something totally beyond recognition reposed on a plate upon the counter, and, though it was days old, whatever it was appeared to have been nibbled on that very morning, whether by Mrs. Adamson or some rat I didn't want to speculate.

In some ways she was sharp as could be. In others, she was indubitably senile. I kept her company the long afternoon. She rambled on about all kinds of things, mostly pretty dull, but was so terribly lonesome I couldn't allow myself to leave. Fifteen years a widow! And all those years, she had spent Christmasses alone in that crumbling house—every year awaiting . . . Jeremiah. The toughness of someone that frail is really surprising, though such stoicism had left its mark.

She was cheered no end that I promised to spend Christmas Eve with her. I think her relief wasn't entirely because I convinced her I could lay Jeremiah to rest. Fifteen years is a lot of Christmasses spent alone. Such loneliness is hard to bare, even had there not been the terror of a ghost. So it seemed as though Mrs. Adamson was more interested in our Christmas Eve together than in the laying of a ghost. Indeed, she took for granted I could save her from the long-endured horror, and was more worried about the months or years she might have yet to live by whatever means available.

Later that evening, at home in my own warm bed, I was filled with sorrow to think of her. I fought back my tears as I pondered that wreck of a body, the years of desperation, the terrible thing she faced year in and year out, darkening her whole life. What will *our* last years be like, Jane? Who will come to visit us? Who will keep us company when we've lost even the skill to write our letters?

I was so involved with the pitifulness of her material situation, I was not preparing myself sufficiently for my encounter with Jeremiah. What could be worse than a sick old age, separated from the rest of the world? Well, Jane, something *can* be worse, as you and I have learned and relearned in our explorations. But I wasn't thinking so on the day I met old Gretta Adamson.

Her odd, sad sort of strength was the other thing that left me unprepared, and the simple way she took for granted that I would put an end to the horrors. She had looked so frail, and had endured so long, how could I have expected her particular demon to be a bad one? I wasn't ready, that's all, though I did do my research, and never imagined there were surprises waiting.

I visited Mrs. Adamson on two other occasions before the holiday in question, and reassured her about my research at the hospital where her husband died. She hadn't known the worst of his last hours, as she had been ill herself, and unable to be constantly at his side. The day he died, she had been with him only a short time in the morning, thus was spared the worst of his venomous accusations, hallucinations, and the screaming hatred that preluded his death-rattle.

I had talked to a head-nurse, who had been a night nurse at the beginning of her career fifteen years before; she gave me a vivid, startling account of Jeremiah Adamson's raging thirst for revenge against a wife he imagined to be his murderess. I certainly wasn't going to fill in Mrs. Adamson at this late date, and was therefore careful to avoid telling her too much of what I had discovered.

That that head-nurse remembered so much should have been a warning to me, as death is too common in hospitals for a nurse to recall one old man in detail. But I chalked it up to her youthfulness at the time—we all remember our first encounters with grotesque tragedy—and Jeremiah *had* been memorably inventive in his repellent promises, given his otherwise impaired faculties.

So I had learned all too well Jeremiah's state of mind in his last moments of senile dementia. Mrs. Adamson was able to tell me a bit more, and remembered other things piece by piece whenever I probed as gently as the situation allowed. But I couldn't delve far at a time, for some of it was too much for her to bear recalling, and much else, I presumed, was genuinely lost to her own age-related difficulties with memory.

"I would like to see Jeremiah's personal papers, whatever you may have," I asked a couple of days before Christmas Eve. Mrs. Adamson was aghast, for she herself had never interfered with his privacy, had never sorted through his personal letters and what-nots in the fifteen years since his death. This should have been another clue informing me that Jeremiah's tyranny began well before senility set in. But I continued to be blind. I thought only to convince Mrs. Adamson of what was essential.

"You see," I explained, "I have to find out more about him. You mustn't think of it as really being Jeremiah. It's only a shadow of him, and a shadow of his darkest mood at that. The afterlife mentality is very simple compared to life. It fixes on a few things. In his private papers, there may be some clue to the thing that he most feared, or most wanted, and whatever it is can become a tool to erase his lingering shade."

"He wouldn't like us to know those things about him," Mrs. Adamson insisted, protecting her husband with a peculiar devotion, and looking at me sadly with those sharp blue eyes in her sideways expression.

"Do you know the meaning of an exorcism, Mrs. Adamson?" She wasn't Catholic and wouldn't know much, but of course everyone knows a little. "There are many ways to lay a ghost, but exorcism is the cruelest. It is a real fight. It's a terrible thing for the exorcist and for the ghost. But there are other means. Sometimes you can reason with them, but it is like reasoning with a child, and you have to be careful. But think a minute, Mrs. Adamson, about the classic type of exorcism you may have heard about, with holy water and the cross of Jesus. To tell the truth, such a procedure is worthless unless the individual had some personal belief in these things while living. The cross of Jesus is a powerful amulet against the ghost of a Catholic. But if he wasn't mindful of holy things in life, then his ghost won't care about them either.

"But other things can become equally significant. Once I got rid of a ghost by showing it a rare postage stamp it had never been able to get when living. A pretty rotten spirit it was, too, but gentle as a lamb when it saw that postage stamp. And the ghost never showed up again.

"Only by careful research can I find out what that special item might be. The more personal the papers, Mrs. Adamson, the better it will be."

She sat like a collapsed rag doll in a big overstuffed chair, pondering all that I had told her, her bright eyes expressing what a dreadful decision I was forcing her to make. At length I helped her stand, reassuring her the whole while, and she led me to a musty closet in which we were able to dig out two shoeboxes held together with rubber-bands so old they had melted into the cardboard of the boxes.

Inside these shoeboxes were faded photographs and mementoes and yellowed letters and a lock of baby's hair in a red envelope labeled "Jeremiah."

"I recollect that," said Mrs. Adamson. "Jeremiah showed it to me. He had a lot of hair when he was a baby. Lost it all."

And her dry, horrible old voice managed a sweet laugh as she fumbled the envelope open and gazed at the little curl of hair tied with a piece of thread.

She told me, as best she could, who were the people in the family photos.

She became very silent on discovering, for the first time in her whole long life, that Jeremiah had once been unfaithful, the evidence being a love-letter written by her rival several years *after* Jeremiah married Gretta.

I patted her liver-spotted hand and assured her, "It is sometimes just this sort of thing that brings them back. He may have wanted to spare you knowing."

But that kind of haunting was rarely menacing, so I kept sorting through the two boxes. Jeremiah kept no diaries—it is usually women who do that, and they're the most easily laid as a result—and it didn't seem there were going to be many clues to the sort of thing it would take to lay Jeremiah come Christmas Eve.

In the bottom of the second box I found an old black and white photograph of the handsome young man and the strikingly good looking woman I'd learned were Gretta and Jeremiah when they were courting. What a smile he had! He wore a soldier's bloomers. Her hair was short and little curls hung out from under a flowered hat. Very modern, both of them, in their day. As I looked at this photograph a long time, the bent old woman beside me leaned to one side to see what I had, and she went misty-eyed at once.

In the photo, Gretta was holding a round Japanese fan. The camera had focused well enough that I could make out a floral design painted upon it.

"Jeremiah gave me that fan," she said. "I still have it."

And she rose painfully from the chair beside me and tottered back into her bedroom. She returned with the antique fan, dusty and faded from having been displayed in countless ways over countless years. To see that crooked old lady holding that fan, and to see the young beauty holding it in the photo in my hands, well, I cannot tell you how I felt. And she was so moony and oddly happy in her expression, I was once again convinced Jeremiah's ghost couldn't be all that bad, or she wouldn't still think of him tenderly.

"It was the day we were engaged, that picture was taken. He'd been to fight in Asia and for all we knew might fight somewhere else soon, and die. He gave me this fan and I've always kept it."

"It's our Cross of Jesus," I said, somehow overawed by the loving emanations from the woman as she held that fan.

"Do you think so?" she asked.

"Jeremiah died with the delusion that you wanted to hurt him, Gretta." I told her this as unhurtingly as possible.

"That fan will remind him that such a delusion couldn't have been true."

I'd been doing this sort of thing a long time, Jane. I really thought I had it worked out.

On Christmas Eve I came early and brought a chicken casserole and a small gift. Gretta was overwhelmed and wept for joy. And we did not mention Jeremiah during our humble repast, for it would have put a pall upon our cross-generational friendship and Gretta's first holiday with anyone in many a long year.

She tittered pleasantly and made her usual horrible tea in dirty cups. The Christmas spirit was so much upon me that I actually drank the terrible stuff without worrying if her tea were infested with beetles. She opened the smartly wrapped present—nothing special, just an old Chinese snuff bottle that I'd had for years and been quite fond of. It had roses carved on two sides and it had seemed appropriate because we'd talked about roses a few days before.

Then to my surprise, Gretta came up with a box as well—wrapped in some quaint, faded, crinkled paper recycled from two decades before, and crookedly taped all over with yellowing, gooey, transparent tape.

In the box was a tiny ceramic doll that must have been fifty or sixty years old if it was a day, and far more valuable than the bottle I'd wrapped for Gretta. I raved about the beauty of the tiny doll, coddled it tenderly, and really didn't have to put on an act, I was honestly overwhelmed.

"It was my grandmother's," said Gretta, at which my jaw dropped open, realizing my guess of "fifty or sixty years" was off by a full century.

"You shouldn't part with it!" I exclaimed. "It must be terribly valuable."

"I won't need it any longer, Penelope. In fact, I haven't needed it for years. I almost couldn't find it for you. So, you be pleased to take it and don't go thinking it's too much."

Our eyes held one another a long while. How ashamed I was of what I thought of that neck-bent, hunchbacked woman when first I laid eyes on her. Not that I ever thought ill. But it wasn't her humanity that struck me at the start. The things I had first noticed were her crippled pitifulness, her loneliness, her wretched old age, and the decades of accumulating dirt and clutter that surrounded her fading existence. Somewhere down the list of first impressions, I must have noted her own unique individuality, but it hadn't been the first thing.

And now, despite that she looked at me with her head fused to one side, with her face turned upward from her permanently crooked posture, I could see, how clearly I could see, that *this* was indeed the young beauty of that old photograph.

We sang carols out of tune and reminisced about our childhood winters; we laughed and we bawled and had a grand day together. She remembered her youth with far greater clarity than she could recall her widowed years. Then long about nine-thirty, she was terribly worn out.

Though she ordinarily didn't require a lot of sleep, this had been quite an exciting day. I could see she could barely keep her eyes open.

"Gretta," I said, "we've got to put you to bed. No, don't argue. If you're thinking of waiting up for Jeremiah, there's no need. I've got your fan right here, and with it I will lay him flat; you won't even have to be disturbed. When you wake up in the morning, I'll be there on your sofa, and we'll celebrate a peaceful Christmas day."

It was a half-hour more before I actually got her to bed, somewhat after ten. Though she insisted she would be wide awake if I needed her at midnight, she was snoring in homely fashion even before I closed her bedroom door.

I walked down the hall, passed the kitchen, and entered the dining room. I surveyed the room and began quietly to push Gretta's furniture against one wall. She had told me in one of our earlier interviews that Jeremiah would first appear at the living room window and make his way to the kitchen and thence to her bedroom. I went into the living room to move that furniture out of the way also. Such precautions were probably excessive, but I didn't want to stumble into anything if for some unforeseen reason I had to move quickly.

It was still some while to midnight, so I turned on Gretta's radio very quietly and listened to a program on change-ringing. The day had been tiring for me as well. Like Gretta, I thought I would be wide awake until midnight. But the next thing I knew, the radio station was signing off the air, and I was startled awake by a change in the house's atmosphere.

I was not immediately alert. The realization that it was suddenly midnight, coupled with a vague movement beyond the front room window, caused me to stand abruptly from where I'd set napping. The sudden movement made my head swim. A black cloud swirled around me. The brittle old paper fan had fallen from my lap onto the floor. I bent to pick it up and nearly lost consciousness. I was forcing my mind to be more fully awake, slowly realizing my dizziness wasn't the natural cause of standing too quickly, but was imposed upon me by something *other*.

As I picked up the fan and moved toward the window, I was brought up short by Jeremiah's sudden appearance there. His black gums were bared, revealing a lack of teeth and reminding me of a lampray. His eyes were fogged white, as though he were able to see only what he imagined and not what was. It was a very complete materialization and he might easily have been taken for a mad peeping tom. He raised both his hands, which were bony claws, and shoved them writhing toward the glass. I expected it to shatter, but instead, the specter vanished.

By the increasing chill, I knew he was in the house.

I hurried toward the kitchen, recovering my senses more than not, holding the paper fan before me. I was shaking frightfully, beginning to comprehend the depth of his malignancy.

There he was, in the kitchen, bent down, scrabbling wildly but noiselessly at the door under the sink. The cupboard opened under his insistence, and he tried to grasp a little faded blue carton, but his clawed hands only passed through it.

Then he stiffened and slowly stood, his back to me. He sensed my presence, and his very awareness gave me shivers. His shoulders stiffened and he began slowly to turn about. I took a strong posture and held the paper fan in front of me, so that it would be the first thing he saw.

He turned and, for a moment, was no longer a spidery old man. He was a young soldier, and he looked at me with sharp but unseeing eyes. I can only describe it thus, because, although his gaze fell directly on me and was no longer clouded white, he seemed to see something infinitely more pleasing to him than I could have been. I supposed he thought I was Gretta, and he was imposing upon my form his memory of her when she was as young as he himself now appeared to be.

He came forward with such a look of love and devotion that in spite of my persisting alarm, and due I'm sure to some occult influence rather than my own nature, I was momentarily terribly aroused. He reached outward to clasp his youthful hands at the sides of my shoulders. I held my ground, certain that my humane exorcism was having its intended effect.

When his ghostly fingers touched me, I felt a warming vibration, as though my whole upper body were encased in fine electrical wire, the voltage slowly increasing. The fan began to shine so brightly that I felt I risked blindness if I failed to close my eyes, but close them I could not.

Before my gaze, the young Jeremiah's angelic face grew sinister by rapid degrees. Simultaneously, the electricity that held me in anguished thrall became more painful. His perfect smile became twisted; his white teeth yellowed and grew long as his gums receded; and then there was only that toothless maw yelling at me without making a sound, dreadful threats I blessedly could not hear. The young soldier had withered and wizened; it was evil rather than years that aged him; and the claws that gripped my shoulders drew blood.

When he let go of me, the light of the fan went out, and I collapsed upon the floor, half sitting against the door jamb. Jeremiah loomed over me with menace, yet my rattled thoughts were pondering in a distant, withdrawn place. I wondered idly if the electrical shock had stopped my heart. I was dimly aware that my lips were wet with froth and drool, and for a moment I was concerned mainly with the nuisance of being unable to move my arm to wipe my mouth.

If these sorts of things were the usual result of my investigations, I should not be so in love with haunted places. I have occasionally felt real danger, but this was the first time I had been so insufficiently prepared that physical harm became inevitable.

His blackening claw grasped me anew and he dragged me across the kitchen floor. His other hand wound into my hair as he pushed my face under the sink, so that I saw before my eyes a thirty or forty year old package of poison—a brand from the days when it was still possible to purchase strychnine to kill rats or even wolves—a damp-stained blue package with skull and crossbones printed in black.

And I realized at that moment what it had to have been that I had overlooked: the critical information without which I was helpless before so malignant a spirit. *Gretta had indeed poisoned her husband,* out of love I do not doubt, and to end his awful suffering. It explained why, on that Christmas Eve fifteen years before, she had spent only a few minutes with him. There would have been no reason for the physicians to suspect such a thing; but Jeremiah had known, though he lacked the capacity to understand it as an act of mercy.

And now my face was shoved hard against the open package of poisonous salts. I clamped my eyes and mouth shut. Jeremiah's ghost was trying to kill me, and at that moment I felt he had a good chance at success.

Then a sad, raspy voice came from the kitchen doorway, saying, "Let her go, Jeremiah. It's me you want."

The calm resignation in her voice was heartbreaking.

The black claws let go of my arm and hair. I pushed myself away from under the sink. I was still smarting from the shock of Jeremiah's first touch. I could barely see, and when I tried to focus, it looked to me as though a young woman was moving toward me in a dressing gown. She reached across my shoulder and removed the strychnine from under the sink. A sweet, youthful voice said, "I guess I should have told you all of it, Penelope, but I thought you could stop him from coming without knowing everything. I'm sorry. Now it's left to me to finish, and there's only one thing that will give my poor Jeremiah peace."

"No, Gretta, no," I said, struggling to rise, reaching outward and trying to grab the package from her hand. But I fell back all but senseless, still gripped by the paralysis of the electric shock. I watched as from a dream as Gretta moved about the kitchen, heating water on the stove, calmly making herself a cup of tea, and heaping into it a spoon of strychnine as though it were sugar.

Standing beside her the whole while was the young soldier. She talked to him in loving terms, and addressed me from time to time as well. She thanked me for a lovely Christmas Eve while I strove uselessly to break the paralysis, tears streaming down my eyes.

Then Gretta and her soldier left the kitchen. I heard her footsteps, inexplicably spritely, echoing down the hall. I heard her shut her bedroom door.

And that, Jane, is the gist of a sad adventure. It was over. Oh, I had to suffer interviews with police and coroner. But it didn't take long, because, unfortunately, suicide is the commonest thing among the elderly. I was not pressed to tell the whole story, which they certainly would not have believed. As to myself, I suffered no ill after effects of the spiritual electrocution, which was, after all, less dangerous than actual electricity. In fact, if you will believe it, the next day I felt partially rejuvenated, and seem since that night to have gotten over my mild arthritis.

And now you may open the gift box I sent along, and which said on it not to open until after you read my letter. As you will see, it is Gretta's paper fan. I bought it at the estate sale, together with a few other small mementos of a brief friendship.

You will observe that the fan, for all its simplicity, is of the finest craftsmanship, completely hand-made in a manner not seen in over half a century. When I first saw it, it was faded, dusty, and tattered to thinness as though occasionally sampled by moths. And the fan I've sent you *is* the same one, miraculously restored, as though cut and pasted recently, the classic floral design as bright as though painted yesterday.

I take this surprising restoration as evidence that Gretta is forgiven by Jeremiah and that they are now happily reunited—out there in the "somewhere" we're all destined one day and eternally to know.

COPYRIGHT ACKNOWLEDGMENTS
AND STORY SOURCES

"The Stranger" by Claude & Alice Askew, first published in *The Weekly Tale-Teller*, 11 July 1914 and collected in *Aylmer Vance: Ghost Seer* (Canada: Ash-Tree Press, 1998).

"Mystery of Iniquity" by L. Adams Beck, first published in *The Openers of the Gate* (New York: Cosmopolitan Book Corporation, 1930).

"The Dead of Winter Apparition" © 1975 by Joseph Payne Brennan. First published in *Alfred Hitchcock's Mystery Magazine*, February 1975, and collected in *Chronicles of Lucius Leffing* (West Kingston: Donald M. Grant, 1977). Reprinted by permission of the agent for the estate.

"The Soldier" © 1927 by A. M. Burrage. First published in *The Blue Magazine*, September 1927, and collected in *The Occult Files of Francis Chard* (Canada: Ash-Tree Press, 1996). Reprinted by permission of the Author's Estate.

"Samaris" by Robert W. Chambers, first published in *Saturday Evening Post*, 5 May 1906, and in *The Idler*, January 1907, and incorporated in *The Tracer of Lost Persons* (New York: Appleton, 1906).

"The Villa on the Borderive Road" by Rose Champion de Crespigny, first published in *The Premier Magazine*, 24 October 1919, and collected in *Norton Vyse: Psychic* (Canada: Ash-Tree Press, 1999).

"The Seven Fires" by Philippa Forest, first published in *Pearson's Magazine*, March 1920.

"The Subletting of the Mansion" by Dion Fortune, first published in *The Royal Magazine*, December 1922, and collected in *The Secrets of Dr. Taverner* (London: Noel Douglas, 1926).

"The Story of Yand Manor House" by E. & H. Heron, first published in *Pearson's Magazine*, June 1898, and collected in *Ghosts, Being the Experiences of Flaxman Low* (London: Pearson, 1899).

"The Whistling Room" by William Hope Hodgson, first published in *The Idler*, March 1910, and collected in *Carnacki the Ghost-Finder* (London: Eveleigh Nash, 1913).

"The Horror of the Height" by Sydney Horler, first published in *Mystery Stories*, April 1928. Unable to trace author's estate.

"The Sanatorium" © 1919 by F. Tennyson Jesse, first published in *The Premier Magazine*, June 1919, and collected in *The Adventures of Solange Fontaine* (London: Thomas Carnacki, 1995). Reprinted by arrangement with the Royal Society for the Prevention of Cruelty to Animals.

"The Haunted Child" by Arabella Kenealy, first published in *The Ludgate*, June 1896, and collected in *Belinda's Beaux and Other Stories* (London: Bliss, Sands, 1897) as "An Expiation."

"The Swaying Vision" by Jessie Douglas Kerruish, first published in *The Weekly Tale-Teller*, 16 January 1915.

"The Case of the Haunted Cathedral" © 1945 by Margery Lawrence, first published in *Number 7, Queer Street* (London: Robert Hale, 1945). Reprinted by permission of David Higham Associates, Ltd., on behalf of the author's estate.

"Green Tea" by Joseph Sheridan Le Fanu, first published in *All the Year Round*, 23 October–13 November 1869, and collected in *In a Glass Darkly* (London: Richard Bentley, 1872).

"The Thought-Monster" by Amelia Reynolds Long first published in *Weird Tales*, March 1930. No record of copyright renewal.

"Dr. Muncing, Exorcist" by Gordon MacCreagh first published in *Strange Tales*, September 1931. No record of copyright renewal.

ABOUT THE EDITOR

MIKE ASHLEY is the award-winning author and editor of more than one hundred books, and is one of the foremost historians of popular fiction. His books include *Adventures in The Strand: Arthur Conan Doyle and the Strand Magazine, Out of This World: Science Fiction But Not as You Know It,* and the biography of Algernon Blackwood, *Starlight Man.*